THERE IS NO PARTING

Maris grinned audaciously, delighted with herself, and to her immense surprise, so did he.

'So, the kitten has claws, has she?' Callum put both hands on his hips, low down, lounging gracefully, his weight on one leg. The sun burnished his hair to a deep chestnut and his eyes narrowed against its rays, the vivid blue-green of them glinting, softly now, like sapphires lit by candle flame. She was entranced and could barely speak, since this was the first time he had smiled at her, but drawing from somewhere a composure she was far from feeling, she did.

'It's a fair offer, Callum.' Oh Lord, oh dear Lord, she had said his name, her heart beating fast as she did so. Callum . . . Callum. She loved him so much that she was dazed by it, by its intensity.

Also by Audrey Howard,

The Mallow Years
Shining Threads
A Day Will Come
All the Dear Faces

About the author

AUDREY HOWARD was born in Liverpool in 1929 and it is
from that once great seaport that many of the ideas for her
books come. Before she began to write she had a variety of
jobs, among them hairdresser, model, shop assistant,
cleaner and civil servant. In 1981, out of work and living in
Australia, she wrote the first of her ten published novels.
She was fifty-two. Her fourth novel, *The Juniper Bush*,
won the Boots Romantic Novel of the Year Award in 1988.
She now lives in her childhood home, St Anne's on Sea,
Lancashire.

There is No Parting

Audrey Howard

CORONET BOOKS
Hodder and Stoughton

Copyright © Audrey Howard 1993

First published in Great Britain in 1993 by
Hodder and Stoughton Ltd

First published in paperback in 1994
by Hodder and Stoughton
a division of Hodder Headline PLC

A Coronet Paperback

10 9 8 7 6 5 4 3 2 1

ISBN 0-340-59422-5

Printed and bound in Great Britain by
Cox and Wyman Ltd, Reading, Berks.

Photoset by Rowland Phototypesetting Ltd,
Bury St Edmunds, Suffolk.

Hodder and Stoughton Ltd
A Division of Hodder Headline PLC
338 Euston Road
London NW1 3BH

For Russell.
11 November 1956–16 February 1961

'So long as there is love there is no parting.'
Song

The O'Shaughnessy Family

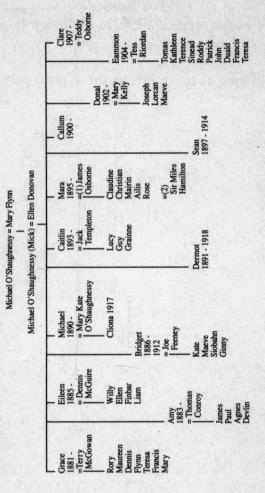

The Hemingway/Osborne Family

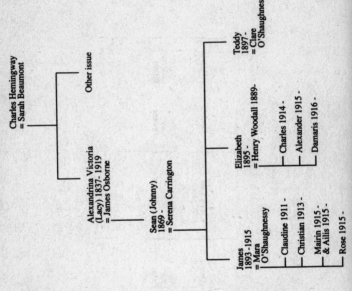

Charles Hemingway = Sarah Beaumont

- Other issue
- Alexandrina Victoria (Lacy) 1837- 1919 = James Osborne
  - Sean (Johnny) 1869 - = Serena Carrington
    - James 1893 -1915 = Mara O'Shaughnessy
      - Claudine 1911 -
      - Christian 1913 -
      - Máirín 1915 - & Áilis 1915 -
      - Rose 1915 -
    - Elizabeth 1895 - = Henry Woodall 1889-
      - Charles 1914 -
      - Alexander 1915 -
      - Damaris 1916 -
    - Teddy 1897 - = Clare O'Shaughnessy

1

The man leaned his back against the waist-high ship's rail, his elbows resting on its well-polished wood, his left leg bent at the knee, his foot on the bottom rail. He was completely at his ease, unaware of his fellow travellers, his eyes narrowing slightly against the glare of the sun on the water as he stared off somewhere into the far distance of the estuary beyond the single ship's funnel. The expression on his face was pensive, his eyes somewhat unfocused, though it appeared the thoughts in which he was absorbed did not displease him, for his mouth curled into a fleeting smile.

It was a strong face, clean-shaven and dark-complexioned, slashed by swooping black eyebrows. The chin was thrusting and inclined to arrogance, warning those who might care to dispute it that he was a man well-used to giving orders and to having them instantly obeyed. The mouth was firm, even hard, with deep clefts on either side, but it had a lift at each corner which spoke of sensuality and a certain whimsical humour. A slightly decadent face, one of the women who had loved him had called it, lived in, a face that had seen life but which did not take what it saw too seriously. Not a classically handsome face but one which was immediately attractive to the opposite sex. He was tall, lean, with strong-muscled shoulders which strained at the seams of his well-cut jacket, and his hair was a deep brown, crisply curling, smoothly brushed, lit by the afternoon sun with streaks of rich chestnut.

But it was his eyes which were his most remarkable feature. In the midst of so much masculine darkness they were a beautiful and vivid colour somewhere between blue and green and yet of neither. Turquoise perhaps, or aquamarine, the colour of the Mediterranean seas across which he had often sailed, clear and deep and framed with exceedingly long lashes. The skin around them was lightly scored by lines which might have been formed by laughter or perhaps from focusing into sunlight more powerful than any to be found on the waters of the River Mersey.

He turned then, looking back across the shining estuary to the landing stage at Woodside which served Birkenhead and from where the ferry had just come. He crossed his forearms on the ship's rail, again resting his left foot on the lower rung and again the cloth of his jacket stretched dangerously tight across his broad back. He was dressed in a tweed sports jacket of impeccable cut in a mixture of brown and beige wool with well-pressed grey flannel trousers. His shirt was cream and he had a long four-in-hand tie knotted beneath its collar in a narrow, quiet stripe of brown and cream. Like many men of his day he was hatless. His masculinity was absolute, and not a few young ladies glanced in his direction as they were jostled past him on the crowded upper deck of the ferry boat. He had noticed them, of course, since he was a man who had an eye for a pretty woman, but he had done no more than give one or two of the more attractive an appreciative glance from beneath his dark lashes, since his sophisticated taste ran to a more mature, more exotic kind of woman than these who travelled from Woodside to the Pier Head landing stage across the river.

Callum O'Shaughnessy was thirty-four years old and

long past the age when the virginal innocence these demure young shop girls and secretaries seemed to offer had any attraction for him. Gone were the days when, as a young soldier in the war which had been over these sixteen years, he had been thrilled to the core of his boyish male longings when Kathleen Donavan, who had lived next door in Edge Lane, had allowed him a clumsy feel of her ripe young breasts in the shadow of the privy at the back of their adjoining gardens. Seventeen he had been and on his first seventy-two-hour pass before he sailed for France, big and uncertain in his new, ill-fitting uniform but proud as a dog with two tails to be wearing it alongside his brothers, Michael, Dermot and Sean, two of whom had not come back from the 'front'. Sean had been killed in the first months of the war at Ypres, and it was this which had determined the then fourteen-year-old Callum to offer his youthful sacrifice in the service of his country. Dermot, the clever one of the family, had been shot by a stray sniper's bullet as the bugles had announced the very armistice which was to end it all. It had ended it for Dermot all right and for millions of others who had answered the call to do battle in what was to be named by many the 'great' war, though what had been great about it those who had fought in it would never comprehend. He and Sean, Michael and Dermot, along with the multitude who had been intent on 'getting in on it' before it finished, had found not greatness but blood and filth, death and mutilation, blindness and gassing and emasculation, rats and lice and gangrene, trench foot and lung rot, bitter disillusionment, grief and anger and the sure belief that they had given their lives and their manhood, their young, unscarred bodies, for something none of them

3

would ever understand. Naïve they had been when they went, innocent and trusting and bursting with patriotism as they presented themselves for the wholesale slaughter which had devastated not only his family but almost every family in the land.

Callum tipped back his head and his eyes narrowed even further as they pierced the achingly blue sky above the ship's two dipping pole masts. The lamps at their top, unlit now, bobbed in unison as the boat ploughed through the slight swell. On the drifting breeze a dozen seagulls hung motionless, keeping pace with the vessel though their wings, wide and graceful, did not appear to move. The sun, sinking now towards the west, touched their white underfeathers to a pale gold in sharp contrast to the grey plumage on their backs and to their black heads and tail feathers. They shrieked raucously and continuously, the noise they made mingling with all the other familiar sounds of the river: the peremptory toot of the tug boats as they went fussily about their business of guiding in the big passenger liners; the booming call of a great, four-funnelled 'Cunarder' – as it was still called, though it was now part of the newly merged 'Cunard-White Star Line' – bearing slowly to its moorings after its race across the Atlantic. A ship's bell clattered, and pleasant on the ear was the cheerful whistle of the men who would lower the ferry's wide gangway on its arrival at the landing stage. Sounds Callum had grown up with as he lived beside the river which had given life and sustenance to generations of his family.

Michael O'Shaughnessy, his grandfather, had been manager of one of the 'Hemingway Shipping Lines' warehouses at the back of Princes Dock in the days of the American civil war, and his own dead father, the

4

Holy Mother give him eternal peace, had taken up the very same post towards the end of the last century. Two of his brothers, Eammon and Donal, worked there, one on the docks unloading the cargoes which came from every corner of the globe and the other, Donal – the second 'clever' one – in the offices, well on his way, it was reported, to being the third generation of O'Shaughnessys to become warehouse manager. Both married, the spalpeens, with a tribe of growing children apiece, each and every one the joy and pride of their grandmother's – Callum's own mother's – heart. Callum had nieces and nephews galore for he was one of eighteen children, thirteen of whom had lived to reproduce themselves, except himself, at least as far as he knew! Many of his brothers' and sisters' offspring were connected in their employment with one or other of the Hemingway and Osborne business concerns, and he was himself a master on a Hemingway merchant vessel. A vast empire it was, or had been before the war and the depression which had come after it.

One of his nephews, Christian Osborne, whose mother was Callum's sister, Mara, was now the owner of the Osborne estate. The Osborne family who, through past marriages, owned most of the Hemingway holdings, had lost sons, one dead – Christian's father – and one dreadfully wounded in the war. The Osborne daughter, Elizabeth, married now to Sir Harry Woodall who himself had lost two brothers at the Battle of the Somme, had been the support and mainstay of her crippled brother Teddy, until he married. He was confined to a wheelchair and always would be, and how were her ladyship and himself to hold it all together until the growing son of the next generation, her grandson, Christian, could take it from them, Callum's

5

mother often asked sadly, shaking her head, for she had an inordinate fondness for Lady Woodall, who was her own daughter's sister-in-law. Sweet Jesus, the convoluted connections of his own family with that of the Osbornes and the Osbornes with Woodalls never ceased to bemuse him, and he was glad he was well out of it in his own chosen profession and way of life.

The ferry boat was crowded, not with those who commuted daily from Liverpool to Birkenhead but with hundreds of men and women and their children who had gone over the water to see the excitement when their Majesties, King George and Queen Mary, emerged from the brand-new splendour of the Mersey Tunnel which had opened on this very day. It ran an incredible two and a half miles beneath the river, had cost nearly eight million pounds to build, and had been under construction since 1925, when Princess Mary, Viscountess Lascelles, daughter of their Majesties, had inaugurated the sinking of the first shaft on December 16th. A wonder it was, a marvel of technical skill and ingenuity, and the people of Liverpool whose city it was, whose river it was, whose *tunnel* it was, had come to take a proprietary interest in its beginnings. Shoulder to shoulder they were along the ship's rails, crowding the upper and lower decks and jammed like sardines in the two saloons. There were children, tired and grizzling, clinging to their mothers' skirts and begging to go home. Fathers at the end of their tether, swearing under their breath that it was the last bloody time and wishing they were among their wiser cronies belly up to the bar, where they should have been in the first place on this day of public holiday. Sorry they were that they had suggested the bloody outing, petulant and aggrieved that what they had thought of as a treat had

6

ended in this ungrateful turmoil. The trams would be packed, their jaded expressions said, just like the boat, and God alone knew when they would sup that first pint.

'Stop that bloody whinin', will yer,' Callum heard one hiss malevolently, tried beyond endurance by the close proximity of his own children, longing to give his scarlet-faced son a thick ear if he could only get at him in the crush. They were working-class families, most of them, with the breadwinner lucky enough to be in employment in these depressing times. They were told by those who knew about such things that the worst was behind them, that they were better off than they had ever been. Mr Chamberlain informed them all that the country had finished the story of *Bleak House* and could now sit down to enjoy the first chapter of *Great Expectations*, which did not mean much to them since most of those unemployed had never read a book of Charles Dickens, nor would want to if they could. The *Liverpool Echo* was more to their liking. The sports page! And what if the Chancellor of the Exchequer *had* reduced the standard rate of income tax to 4s 6d in the pound, it meant very little to those who had no income to start with! Those who were without jobs – numbering almost thirty percent of the population in some parts of the country, the highest figures in Durham, South Wales and here in Lancashire – had to conform to the hated 'means test' to claim their 'benefits', could barely manage to feed and clothe their children, and were penalised if they were of a thrifty nature and had saved a few bob against such a rainy day as this. How were they to manage on these same 'benefits', an ironic description if ever there was one of what they received? The unemployed could certainly not take their family on jaunts such as this across the river, and it was they who formed the bulk of the massed crowds who had stood to watch their King and Queen at the new tunnel's mouth on the Liverpool side.

The ferry boat *Bidston* was brand-new and very fast, still with the sharp redolence of freshly applied paint about her. She had a smooth, barnacle-free black hull with white ship's rails and struts. Her one red funnel carried the ship's colours, and on the masthead was a symbol of a ball which meant she sailed for Birkenhead and belonged to Birkenhead Corporation. Her bow was sharp and proud and her stern wide and rounded, and along her top deck were wooden slatted seats, all filled to capacity with those who had been first up the wide, bouncing gangway at the start of the journey. A wild race in which many were in great danger of being trampled underfoot or flung into the murky waters of the river by the press of people. There were lifebelts, of course, fastened along the outside of the rails at intervals, and a lifeboat slung on davits at the stern, ready to rescue any soul unlucky enough to be immersed in the river's floating, heaving filth. Ships' garbage was tipped willy-nilly over ships' sides by careless galley boys, quite without concern for the pollution it caused. The waters were wide, weren't they? rising and falling thirty feet twice a day and what the gulls didn't get would be swept down the estuary and out to the seas which were deep, endless and all-consuming.

Two children squeezed past him, laughing and excited, two children better dressed than the rest, and behind them was a red-faced papa, evidently enjoying their game as much as they. Callum smiled as he remembered the Sundays, after Mass, naturally, when he and Sean and Donal, before the birth of Eammon who was the youngest of his brothers, had played such a game of hide-and-seek with their own father. A ride down Dale Street to the Pier Head on the tramcar from Edge Lane, the top deck, of course, and outside at the front where they could hear the clash and clatter of the tramcar's overhead arm as it raced along the wire, and the ding of the conductor's bell when the vehicle stopped and started. It had been grand standing in front of the Daddy's legs, protected by the wire mesh put up to stop small boys like himself from falling over the rails on to the track, but it had been even grander to finish up on the deck of the ferry boat. Full it would be, going over, but coming back, after disgorging all its 'sands'-destined travellers at New Brighton, he and Daddy, Sean and Donal had the ferry to themselves. They had run up and down the stairways, in and out of the empty saloons with the Daddy hot on their heels in the most wonderful games, before going home to the superb Sunday dinner the Mammy would have ready for them.

It was the commotion made by the group of young people which brought Callum back from the past into the present. He had begun to contemplate the antici-pated pleasure of the evening to come which he had arranged to spend with a certain lady of his acquaint-ance, seeing in his mind's eye the intimate dining room of the Adelphi Hotel which, since it had been rebuilt in 1914, was considered to be quite unsurpassed any-where in the world, even Paris. He had booked a secluded table for two, with flowers and champagne, naturally. There would be the expensive aroma of French perfume and cigars, subdued lighting, the laugh-ter of pretty women, the small quartet playing all the very latest romantic tunes from the pen of Irving Berlin,

9

and all to create the sophisticated, languorous progression towards the mutual satisfaction he and the lady would find in the small but comfortable house he rented in the semi-rural district of West Derby. He would not take his motor car, a wicked little MG sports model in a beautiful racing green. It was somewhat unsuitable for transporting the opposite sex since it was a small two-seater with barely any shelter from the weather, and though it certainly attracted the ladies, being as masculine and well turned-out as he himself was, to ride in it was a purely male enjoyment. The ladies, he had soon discovered, did not care to have their hair blown about, nor to suffer the rain-showers which frequently assaulted them through the flimsy side-shields which took the place of windows. And though seduction had not been unknown amongst the gearbox and brake pedals – in fact sometimes it added a certain piquancy – this one would continue in the deep and comfortable confines of the taxi-cab behind the panelled glass of the discreet driver, and would not end until the early summer dawn slipped over the Pennine hills to the east of the city and the sun touched the deep velvet curtains at his bedroom window.

They would sleep then, his companion and himself, until they were both refreshed, and perhaps begin again if it was agreeable to them both; and if not they would arise and dress smilingly, well pleased with each other, and say goodbye in the knowledge that when they both were ready for it, *if* they both were ready for it, and there was no certainty that either would be, they might repeat the whole delightful procedure in the future. It was a highly civilised way of life which he prized. There would be no talk of love or commitment. No sighs or languishing looks, just the sheer physical pleasure they

10

both enjoyed with one another but could find, really, with any other normal, red-blooded member of the opposite sex.

'Really, Christian, you can be such an ass at times,' a drawling male voice said derisively, and at the sound of the name Callum's head turned sharply towards the bows and his eyebrows swooped in a fierce frown. Christian! There were not many of that name in this era of Georges and Alfreds, Edwards and Henrys, Alberts and Arthurs, made popular by the Royal family. Still, *this* Christian had been one of those, for was not the royal Prince of Wales, who would one day be Edward VIII, called Edward Albert *Christian* George Andrew Patrick David, and had not Callum's headstrong and fanciful sister, who was this young man's mother, decided that what was good enough for a prince of the realm was good enough for Mara Osborne?

The young man who had spoken did so in the long-vowelled accent of the privileged classes, which was as out of place here amongst the thick adenoidal tones of the Liverpool working man as that of a skylark's song in the company of cawing crows.

'Just because your mother was Irish and came from Irish stock . . .' the voice continued, but Christian Osborne interrupted it.

'*Is* Irish, dammit, and watch what you say about my mother's people, Alex Woodall.'

'Very well, *is* Irish, and I mean no disrespect to her or her family, but do you have to act as though you were born in a sod cottage on the banks of the Shannon? We are not all as intrigued by the Irish question as you seem to think we are, and to listen to you drivelling on and on about matters which are of interest to no one

11

but the Irish themselves is becoming extremely tedious. As *you* are with your bogus Irish patriotism. You'll be wearing a green suit next or a shamrock in your cap to display your affinity with the "owd" country and adopting that charming Irish brogue of your mother's. Sure an' lovely it is too, begorra, but you *are* English, my lad, and . . .'

'No, I am not. This is not my country. I've the Irish bred in the bones of me . . .'

The first young man hooted with laughter. 'Come now, Christian, you really are . . . well, whimsical, talking in that quaint Irish fashion. You'll be claiming that you're related to Brian Boru in your next breath. Your grandfather, or was it your great-grandfather, came over here with all the other . . .'

'Don't you dare mock my forebears. They came from Ireland to escape the oppression of the bloody English landowners . . .'

'And did very well out of it from all accounts, some of them, men like your grandfather . . .'

'. . . they had to leave their homes in their tens of thousands in the 1840s because of men like your father . . .'

'What's *my* father got to do with it?' The speaker was highly amused, looking round at the others in the group as though to ask could they really believe such nonsense, because he couldn't! 'As far as I know he's never been to Ireland in his life and certainly . . .'

'He's a landowner, that's what, and an oppressor . . .'

'And *yours* wasn't, and your grandfather Osborne? As you are yourself. Don't forget your name is Osborne and not O'Shaughnessy and you are owner of Beech-wood and all the land . . .'

'I don't want it. None of it.'

'Rubbish! Just wait until the time comes . . .'

'I tell you I don't want it.'

'Now listen to me, you two, don't you think this argument has gone far enough?' a third male voice snapped irritably. 'Besides which, it's extremely boring since we've heard it all before, hundreds of times.'

'The divil take it . . .'

'There you go again, you idiot, pretending to be some barefoot Irish boyo . . .'

'Watch what you're saying, Alex, or I swear I'll . . .'

'Yes, *Paddy*, you swear you'll what?' This was the third young man speaking again, but instantly, just as though he must do battle with anyone who put in a word, whether that word was in his defence or not, the man called Alex Woodall turned on him, his expression one of truculence.

'You stay out of this, Charlie. This is between me and Christian.'

'Don't fight with me, brother. I was only agreeing with you, for God's sake.'

'I don't need you to agree with me, *brother*, and I can fight my own battles as well you know.'

'Jesus, don't we all?'

'Oh for pity's sake, don't you two start,' a female voice pleaded. 'We've had a lovely day out and it would have remained like that if Christian, or *Paddy* as he begs us to call him, hadn't started drivelling on about Home Rule and the Irish Free State and the tariff which has been slapped on imports from Ireland, whatever *that* means . . .'

'I only happened to mention the Land Purchase Acts. De Valera says that the English stole the land from the Irish in the first place so why should we buy back our own land, that's all I'm saying, which seems perfectly reasonable to me.'

'*Your land!* That's rich! You already *own* your land, or will do one day when . . .'

'*That's it! That is it!* I've had enough of your bloody English pig-headedness, and if you mean to continue to insult my ancestry then I suggest we settle it in the only way possible. Take off that fancy jacket, Alex Woodall, and . . .'

'Christian, that's enough,' one of the two young ladies in the group admonished, 'Alex means no harm. You know he only does this to make you blow up, which you always oblige him by doing. Put your jacket back on, you fool, and you, Alex, wipe that snarl off your face. If you're not fighting Christian then you're after Charlie, and I won't have this wrangling in public especially on a day such as this. Your mother would be mortified.'

'Never mind my mother, and if you continue to grin like that, Charlie Woodall, I'll take you on as well.'

There was a swirl of movement, a circling of the group as the hot-headed argument threatened to blow up into a full fist-fight. The three young men revolved round one another, snarling like dogs in an alley. The two young women stepped hastily between them, in danger themselves of a box on the jaw. There was a great deal of jostling in which one young lady almost lost her fetching hat, then, as she began to laugh, for really, wasn't the whole thing too ridiculous for words, the tension eased. Callum heard her laughter rise above the hubbub of the fascinated crowd, who were highly entertained by the goings-on of the young gentry. A laugh that was joyous, young and rich, and even in the midst of his own growing exasperation he felt it tug at

14

the corners of his mouth, making him want to laugh too. He had heard the expression an 'infectious' laugh and this girl had one, just as though nothing had ever come to trouble her young life. The world in which she lived was a glorious place, it seemed to say, giving her cause for joy, and she saw no reason to restrain it.

Her companions began to laugh too, unable to resist the sheer merriment, even the three young men who had been about to clench their fists in one another's faces. Onlookers who had stood about, stepped back, disappointed, for they had been ready to enjoy a 'spat' between members of the upper class who, even when pressed, were normally disciplined to show self-control, particularly in front of the lower orders, themselves in fact.

Callum relaxed, preparing to move away towards the wide gates which would open on to the gangway when it was lowered, for the ferry boat was nearing the landing stage at the Pier Head. It appeared there would be no need of a confrontation, thank God, no need for him to intervene in what could have been a nasty incident, or at least an embarrassing one. His sister's children, for that was who they were, Rose and Christian Osborne, were smiling in that – whatever Alex Woodall might say – merry Irish way which they had inherited from the O'Shaughnessy side of their heritage, and Alex Woodall himself had courteously taken the second young lady's arm, protective as he had been taught to be by his Nanny in his nursery days. Alex's brother, Charles Woodall, Callum presumed, followed behind, cool, unhurried now, the perfect English gentleman as he lit a cigarette, flicking the match over the ship's rail.

The group moved towards Callum, cutting a swathe through the wilting masses which made way for them as though they were royalty. Even in this enlightened and democratic age when all men – and some women too – had the vote and were – supposedly – equal in the sight of God and each other, it was still an instinct bred in them since the days of feudalism and hard to shake off, to move aside for their so-called 'betters'.

They were handsome, all five of them, with that polish and grace which their upbringing, their education and generations of authority had given them. Young lords and ladies with an air of knowing exactly who they were and how they were to conduct themselves in any circumstance. Unaware of anyone but themselves and their own enjoyment. Not unkind or ill-mannered to those who were, quite naturally, beneath them, but showing indifference and a careless disregard for the lower classes. They had been brought up not to notice that class from which their servants came, which they had in plenty. They were finished, rounded, balanced, despite their youth, and their fellow travellers instinctively recognised it.

The two young ladies were dressed in the very latest fashion: two-piece suits, the skirts mid-calf, the jackets short and boxy, one in a pale shade of cream and coffee, the other in cornflower blue, linen with matching silk blouses beneath. Each wore a tiny pill-box hat perched over one eye and high-heeled, open-cut shoes of lizard skin with art silk, flesh-coloured stockings. Each carried a small, flat 'pochette'. They walked with long, graceful strides, elegant, confident, seemingly unaware of their own splendour. The men were dressed exactly as Callum was. Tweed sports jackets, grey flannels, bare headed, lounging and indolent. It seemed the flare-up between them was forgotten.

They were about to pass by and Callum was about to let them when the young man who had insisted so loudly on his own 'Irishness' caught his eye and, recognising him, stopped immediately. He grinned in obvious pleasure, holding out his hand enthusiastically.

'Uncle Callum.' His voice was clear-cut and of that upper-class quality which allowed him to be heard no matter what the circumstances, with no trace of the lilting Irish brogue he had so recently claimed as his heritage. The rest of the group stopped also and turned as he spoke.

'Christian,' Callum answered politely with a nod of his head, then reluctantly took the proffered hand.

'When did you get back, sir? Grandmother made no mention of it when we last spoke. We thought you were still at sea.'

'I was until yesterday, lad. We made better time than expected and docked last night. I shall be over to see my mother tomorrow when I've taken care of one or two business matters which need my attention, tell her. That's if you should see her.'

'Oh, I don't think I will, sir. We're all off to a party tonight at a friend's home . . . the Winters, do you know them . . . no . . . well, they have a place over Croxteth way. It's Freddie Winters' birthday and we've all been invited. Rosie and I and . . .'

'Rosie . . .' This time Callum O'Shaughnessy's smile was one of genuine pleasure as the lovely young girl, his niece and the one in blue, stepped forward, inclined to shyness since they scarcely knew this dashing and exceedingly attractive uncle of theirs who had spent most of their young lives, and his, at sea. 'Will you give me a kiss then?' he teased, holding out both hands.

'Uncle Callum.'

'It's been a long time, darlin'. You still had your hair in a plait down your back and now look at you, a young lady grown and as beautiful as the day.'

They exchanged a hurried kiss, conscious not only of the amused stares of the other members of the group but of the open-mouthed interest of the crowd which milled about them.

'Well, I don't know about that, Uncle Callum, but I *am* nineteen now and Christian and I have often talked of you and wondered where you had sailed to.'

'And Claudine and the twins? And your mother, of course. Are they well? The last time I heard from Mara she was in New York.'

'Yes, she travels with her . . . she travels quite a bit.'

'So you have been staying with Lady Woodall at Woodall Park?'

'Yes, whilst mother and her . . . whilst mother is away.'

'And what puts you on the ferry boat today of all days? I should have thought you would have been at the royal opening of the Mersey Tunnel.'

'Oh we are, Uncle Callum, but we are to cycle through afterwards to see what is happening in Birkenhead, at least Alex and Charlie and I are. We want to be among the first to go through after the official opening. Our cycles are on the lower deck.'

'Well done.'

'Oh yes, sir, it will be very fine. Did you mean to see it?'

'No, I have some business to attend to.'

Dear God, but this bloody politeness and family camaraderie was hard when it took place under the fascinated gaze of those around them. It was this which had caused his reluctance to be noticed by his sister

18

Mara's children. Tomorrow, when he meant to drive over to the Mammy's, he would have taken pleasure in renewing their acquaintance. He hardly knew them really. They had been small children when he came back from France in 1919, living for the most part with their aunt, Lady Elizabeth Woodall at Woodall Park, since their mother, widowed in the war and remarried to some high and mighty mucky-muck baron or other was always off with her husband, in London, or jaunting about the renewed splendour of the capitals of Europe. Her children, five in all, had been virtually brought up by Lady Woodall and her husband, Sir Harry, along with their own children.

Turning to look at them he found himself staring directly into the deepest, most intense pair of brown eyes he had ever encountered, even among the races of Africa where such a colour was common. Soft and glowing and surrounded by long fine brown lashes, narrowing against the sunlight – or was it to get a more focused look at himself? Eyes which did not look away as they met his. A clear, steady gaze, and in them he saw the interest to which he, as a man, was no stranger. Beneath her perky hat her hair was a short crop of fair curls exposing the slender white vulnerability of her neck.

'I'm Maris Woodall,' she said, though he had not asked, with no hint of the reserve his niece had shown, holding out a firm, sun-tanned hand. 'And these are my brothers, Alex and Charlie. We've heard a great deal about you, Mr O'Shaughnessy, haven't we, boys, so at last we can say we have met the brave sea captain who single-handedly feeds the great port of Liverpool and without whom those who live here would undoubtedly starve.'

'Oh yes, sir, Mrs O'Shaughnessy talks of nothing else when we visit her. Her son the sea captain . . .'

'You visit my mother often, do you, lad?'

'Well, now and again, sir, when Rosie asks us.'

'Is that so?' Callum could feel the irritation well up in him as Alex Woodall smiled mockingly at him. It seemed this young fighting cock was ready to take issue with any man's son on almost every topic under the sun, whether it be the accent he used, the matter of his politics or even the subject of a man's employment. A youth, no more, who could take offence at the slant of a man's jaw, and if none was meant he would prick and prod until he *did* offend. For a moment, before the irritation took hold, he had a strange feeling of déjà vu as though somewhere, in some other place, he had met this aggressive young pup, but that couldn't be for the lad was no more than twenty and he himself had been away from home, on and off, these past fifteen years.

'Yes indeed, sir, and to hear Mrs O'Shaughnessy speak one would think you were the great adventurers Marco Polo and Sir Walter Raleigh all rolled into one.' Alex relented then as though he was suddenly aware that he had been impertinent. 'But then she is your mother and all mothers think their sons to be perfect. I know mine does.' He smiled then with immense charm, a smile again so familiar Callum felt a distinct thump in his rib-cage where his heart was, but still he could not place it. Alex Woodall was dark, with an unruly mop of thick curls. His eyes were a clear hazel somewhere between brown and green, and though he was tall he still had a certain gangling awkwardness about him, slender and boyish.

'When did you get home, sir?' the third young man asked politely, the absolute exemplification of the well-bred, privileged son of the class which had produced him. He was as unlike his brother as two people could be, fair, as his sister was, with the same deep brown eyes, tall, handsome, courteous to an older man with none of Alex's impudent and mocking charm.

But it was his own nephew who dominated the group, though how long that state of affairs would last Callum would not care to hazard a guess, eyeing the restless vigour of Alex Woodall and the haughty arrogance of his brother Charles, the heir to the baronetcy and the estate of Woodall Park. Christian was the eldest, of course, which would have given him an advantage during their shared childhood, and the biggest. He was broad-shouldered, deep-chested, as all the O'Shaugh-nessy men were, with the fierce scowling brow and quick-tempered look about him which he had not inherited from his father's side of the family. Ready to take up his Irish heritage, or so he said, and to hell with the Osbornes and the inheritance which would one day be his. Obsessed with the Irish side of his nature which battled with the gentler-bred quality his father had bestowed on him. Nevertheless, he owned the Osborne estates and would one day be expected to take them up, to cherish and safeguard what generations of Osbornes and Hemingways had built and would pass on to him.

It would make for interesting observation, Callum O'Shaughnessy thought, as he watched his nephew and the young Woodalls push their bicycles towards the gangway as it crashed down on to the landing stage at the Pier Head. Interesting, but carrying with it the explosive danger of hidden dynamite. They were scarcely out of boyhood, Christian Osborne, Alex Woodall and his brother Charlie, but if Callum was any

21

judge of character, and life at sea had taught him to be that, there would be a rivalry between these three which, if not controlled by some force, perhaps in one of *them*, could lead to something he did not care to dwell on.

2

'Will I take me brolly, d'you think, Gracie?' Ellen cast
an anxious glance from her kitchen window towards
the wide stretch of sky which could be seen above the
high roof-top of the house whose garden backed on to
hers. It was achingly blue, the deep and tender blue
which only comes for a short time in the northern counties of England during the summer. 'Sure an' it looks
as though it might rain,' she continued shamelessly,
'an' I don't want to get me new hat wet. Seven and
sixpence it cost me an' at that price it's to last 'til me
dyin' day, so it has. D'you like it, pet? You've not said,'
moving to the mirror above the scullery sink where
once her dead husband had washed himself for supper.
She preened into its discoloured surface, adjusting the
hat to a more becoming angle then turned back to her
daughter. 'Nut brown, the colour is, or so the wee girl
in the shop says. Is it? I says, sure an' it just looks an
ordinary brown to me but no, 'tis nut brown, she says
an' grand it'll look with me beige frock, or so *she* said,
the two shades complementing one another, whatever
that might mean, an' why folk can't speak plain English
is beyond me, really it is. Now what about me brolly?
See, Cliona, run up to Grandma's bedroom an' fetch
me brolly out of me wardrobe. Better to be sure than
sorry, I always say, an' after that thunderstorm last
night it could be unsettled the day.'

'Mammy, your hat looks grand, grand so it does, *an'*
your frock, but will you look at the sunshine. 'Tis fit to

crack the flags so you'll not be wantin' your brolly. An' if we don't get a move on we'll not get a place to see the King and Queen. The ceremony'll be over, so it will. In fact, if we don't go now they'll have got through the tunnel an' out the other side before we even leave the house. Now, where's the camp stools, oh, there they are, good lad, Joseph, an' will you carry out that basket, Tomas?'

Ellen watched her two grandsons for a moment as they carted the enormous picnic basket and two camp stools through the kitchen doorway and into the passage which led to the front door of the house, pushing and shoving one another with what seemed to be their usual method of getting from one place to the next. Her face was puckered in a worried frown, and she bit her lip as though some enormous decision on which the fate of the world rested must soon be made.

'Wisht, Gracie, will I just make a few extra sandwiches? Them lads've big appetites an' I don't want them to go hungry . . .'

'Mammy, there's enough to feed us, their Majesties an' most of the bloody crowd . . .'

'Now, Eileen, I'll have no swearin' in my house.'

'Sorry, Mammy, but if we don't get a move on it'll all be over.'

'Matty, see . . .' to the old woman who pottered at the hearth, '. . . put the kettle on an' I'll just make up another flask of tea.'

'*Mammy*, will you give over! There's a dozen flasks in the back of Michael's car an' Cliona's brought over cake an' scones an' biscuits an' what with the pies me an' Amy made sure an' we could be there a week an' not go hungry.'

'Oh I know, darlin', but there's a lot of us an' . . .'

'Jesus, Joseph an' Mary, you can say that again.'

'Now then, Amy, I'll not have . . .'

'I know Mammy, I know, but at the last count there were twenty-one of us to go in three cars. Michael says he can manage one in the front with you and five in the back if they promise to behave themselves. Donal's got his two an' Mary, so he can squeeze in another couple an' Cliona's got one of her Daddy's big motors from the garage an' will take me an' Amy an' Eileen with a bairn on each lap. Oh, an' Matty, of course. Begod, the rest'll have to take the tram an' if they don't look lively they'll have to walk because the trams'll be full, so they will.'

'Bejasus, I can't think straight with all this racket goin' on an' me not wantin' to spoil me new hat if it rains. I'd best take me brolly, don't you think, pet? Look at them clouds comin' over . . .' which was true this time as the sun disappeared for a brief moment.

'Run an' fetch Grandma's brolly, Cliona, for Heaven's sake, or we'll not be gettin' a minute's peace . . .'

'Begorra, Amy O'Shaughnessy, I'll not be spoken about as though I had one foot in me grave.'

'Sorry, Mammy, but what with this lot . . .'

Ellen O'Shaughnessy relented at once. 'I know, pet, enough to try the patience of a saint, so they are. See, let me give you a hand with that baby, Tess, whilst you see to John. Sure an' he smells like a skunk, so he does. Hand Tess a clean nappy, Eammon. There's some I aired only this mornin' on the . . .'

The tumult was overwhelming and above the noise of what seemed to be at least a hundred excited children screaming that if they didn't get a move on, sure an' it would all be over, the anxious voice of Ellen

O'Shaughnessy, mother, grandmother and great-grandmother to the lot of them begged anyone who would listen to her to tell her that it was not going to rain. Not that she cared, mind. It was only once that you got a chance to witness the grandest sight a body could hope to see *and* to get a glimpse of the King and Queen of England who were to be part of it, but just the same she'd not want to spoil her lovely new hat for the want of a brolly.

The kitchen where the worst of the commotion was exploding in typical Irish, O'Shaughnessy fashion moved like a disturbed ants' nest. Grace, Amy and Eileen, Ellen's three eldest daughters, were flushed and slightly dishevelled. Their neatly ordered hair which all three had had 'permanent-waved' for the occasion, at the exorbitant cost of nineteen and sixpence, was showing signs of wear, beginning to lose the symmetrically placed 'finger waves' in which the hairdresser had arranged it. All three had new frocks, what were known as 'washing frocks' and therefore more durable, in rayon with an inverted pleat at the front of the calf-length skirt, and a yoked bodice. One had chosen brown, the second navy blue, and the third, Eileen, youngest of the three at the age of forty-nine, a rather daring apple green. Each frock had cost five and six-pence at Owen Owen's. They would wear hats, of course, for no decent woman went out without a hat. The same style again for all three of them, 'tyrolese' with a dashing feather and worn over one eye.

Gracie was a widow. Terry McGowan had died, like so many others, in the 'great' war, as had her eldest son, Rory, but her five remaining children and her numerous grandchildren were all there squabbling over who should sit in the front with Uncle Michael in his roomy

Lanchester 40. The motor car was fourteen years old and nothing but a heap of scrap when he bought it in 1920, almost totally wrecked by some wild sprig of the gentry to whom it had belonged, but handsome now that Michael had restored it to its original glory.

Uncle Michael, Ellen's eldest boy, had survived the war though his young wife had not. The Spanish influenza, as it had been called, was arguably the greatest killer after the carnage of the war, and it had carried her off in two days, leaving her husband with a baby daughter, Cliona, to bring up alone. Ellen had begged him to live at home with her and old Mick, who had been alive then, but he had gently refused, saying he must make a new life for himself and his child. He had rented a house in West Derby and engaged a clean-living war widow of over forty to 'do' for him, and each day before Cliona started school at the age of five years he would take her over to be looked after by Ellen whilst he worked in the small but increasingly successful garage he had started with his war gratuity. A chauffeur he had been before the war, knowing all there was to know about what went on under the bonnet of a motor car, and that knowledge had been put to good use in the burgeoning motor trade which had come after the war. There was a growing number of men, not only the wealthy but working men, who owned small motor cars, as they had become mass-produced and therefore cheaper, and Michael O'Shaughnessy was the man to 'keep them on the road', which is what it said on the sign over the wide doors of his garage. He was a hand-some man of forty-four with an air of quiet sadness about him, which was not surprising with his young wife dead at the age of twenty, but though his mother had thrown every good Catholic girl she knew across his

27

path he had never remarried, to her eternal sorrow.

Amy and Tommy Conroy, with their four, the youngest born in 1919, nine months to the day after Tommy got home from the trenches, and Eileen and Denny Maguire, with their Willy and Ellen – after her grandmother – and Finbar, and Liam and about them their clutch of grandchildren who numbered a round dozen. Bridget, Ellen's fourth daughter, had died in childbirth over twenty years ago and her husband, Joe, had remarried, with Ellen's daughter hardly cold in her grave, or so Ellen said bitterly. He had moved away from Liverpool taking Ellen's grandchildren with him. Sad it was, she often said to Matty, her old kitchenmaid, as they sipped a companionable cup of tea before the fire they had shared for nearly forty years, when a grandmother was denied a sight of her own flesh and blood, the divil take Joe Feeney, a good-for-nothing limb of hell if ever there was one.

Donal, Ellen's next-to-last son, and his wife Mary, were with two of their three. The third, Maeve, was among the thousand Liverpool elementary schoolchildren who had been chosen to be part of the ceremony. A signal honour for Maeve, though Ellen was of the opinion that the boot was on the other foot, for was not Maeve one of the brightest, prettiest little girls at the Convent of Our Lady of Perpetual Sorrow!

Eammon, the last boy in Ellen's family, lounged against the chimney corner, nursing his fourth child, with his Tess, like a beached whale in old Mick's chair, huge in pregnancy for the ninth time in nine years, and as Ellen said, again to Matty and in private, though she was a firm believer in accepting what the good God gave in the way of children, their Eammon should show a bit of restraint, so he should, and keep his

28

pants buttoned to give his poor Tess a rest, God love her. Still, she didn't seem to mind, reminding Ellen of herself at the same age with the wee 'uns milling about her skirts like chicks about a mother hen, the babies John and Duald, sixteen and six months respectively both whining to get at her continuously full breasts!

'Will I set off then, Gracie?' a voice from the front door shouted, and instantly all the children except the very youngest began to screech and run in the direction from where the voice had come, begging Uncle Michael to take them with him, devastated that they might be the last to go, or worse not go at all. The pitch of excitement rose until the whole house was bursting with the intoxication of it all, and Eammon's Sinead, a child of five, was sick all over her father's best suit.

'Jesus, Joseph and Mary, will you take the child from me, Tess,' he yelled, dabbing frantically at the good black stuff of his Sunday go-to-Mass best, and his mother, just for good measure, cuffed his ear as she took the little girl on her knee, for big as he was he'd no need to take that tone, not in Ellen O'Shaughnessy's kitchen, the spalpeen.

'For the sake of sweet Mary, let's get goin',' Donal roared. 'If one of you'll just tell me who I'm to take then I'll be off, so I will. It's like a bloody madhouse in here . . .'

'Donal . . . !'

'Sorry, Mammy.'

'An' why haven't they gone for the tram yet? Have you seen the queue outside the tram depot? 'Tis a mile long already, so it is, an' not seven-thirty yet.'

'They're comin' now, Donal,' his wife shrilled. 'Devlin, Joseph and Lorcan'll look after Tomas,

29

Kathleen and Terence, won't you, lads? Now you know where we'll be, don't you?'

'Yes, Aunty Mary.'

'Have you got your fare safe?'

The big boys sighed. 'Yes, Aunty Mary.'

'Well, off you go then an' watch out for the little ones an' sure if you get there first save us a place.' Expecting six assorted children to 'save a place' for the rest of the enormous family did not strike her as at all illogical.

'I wish our Christian and Rosie and the twins could have been here, so I do,' Ellen said fretfully, nursing Sinead whilst Matty sponged down her son's suit. The faint smell of vomit soon became overlaid with that of the pine disinfectant Matty had dabbed on her cloth. 'They should be here with their family, so they should.'

'They said they were bicycling through, Grandma.' Cliona's voice came from the passage where, a child on one hip and another holding her hand she was shepherding the flock she was to carry to the appointed spot. A good driver was Cliona, even if she was only seventeen years of age. Taught by her Daddy who was the best, of course, and adept at the wheel of the bright blue Vauxhall, again of the early twenties and restored to its former splendour by Michael O'Shaughnessy. They were showpieces, Michael said, the two beautiful cars on which he had spent all his spare time in the past ten years, instead of the woman he should have had, in his mother's opinion. An advertisement for his own work in his garage and workshop, and though he had been offered double what they were worth, even at today's prices, he would not part with them.

'*Bicycling through!*' Ellen shrieked. 'May the Saints

30

preserve us! How can they do that with their Majesties and the royal cortege . . . ?'

''Tis afterwards, Grandma. I heard Christian say they were to follow . . .'

'That boy! He'll be the death of the lot of us yet. Just like his mother, so he is, contrary and stubborn as a mule, may the Holy Virgin guard him.'

'Threepence to go through on a pedal cycle an' then they all mean to come back on the ferry.'

'The Woodalls too?'

'I believe so.'

'Jesus and all His angels! Well, come on then the lot of you. The whole thing'll be over if we don't get going,' just as though she had had nothing to do with the hold-up. 'See, Liam, run up an' get Grandma's brolly from the wardrobe, there's a good wee boy. It's hanging on the hook behind the door.'

It was a sunny day, and warm, though a few high clouds made those ladies who wore their best hats, recently purchased for the occasion, look anxiously skywards. The crowds had been gathering since before dawn and even now at just gone eight o'clock there was scarcely a place to be found in the vicinity of St John's Gardens, St John's Lane and William Brown Street. It reminded Ellen of the first Remembrance Day, she remarked somewhat tearfully, for who would ever forget that sad day in 1919 when she and Mick and thousands of other mothers and fathers, wives and sweethearts had stood in silence for two minutes to remember all the lovely boys, two of Ellen's among them, who had not come back. As if they would ever be forgotten! The area around Kingsway had been black with people then, as it was now, but now they were laughing and exchanging banter with one another in the true spirit and tradition of the Liverpudlian. She sat on her camp stool among them, carefully protected by her three large sons and her equally large grandsons, admiring the dais where the royal couple would perform the ceremony. In front of her was the tunnel mouth, the great Mersey Tunnel which was to carry thousands upon thousands of people in their motor cars and hackney vehicles, on their motor cycles and pedal cycles and even in their hearses, so she had been told, to the other side of the water, though why they should want to go was a mystery to her. Why was it that in the last twenty years all that folk wanted to do was move from one place to another, and when they got there desired nothing more than to come back again? What was wrong with stopping where God had put you in the first place? Mind, she had heard that goods vehicles, which up until now had been forced to take the long and winding route up one side of the estuary and down the other, could now go *under* the river to achieve the same destination, which would save time and money and, so Michael had explained to her and it made sense, bring down the price of the goods carried, so that couldn't be a bad thing, could it?

'Aren't the golden pylons lovely, Grandma?' Cliona murmured in her ear, 'and all the flags.'

'They are so, darlin', but sure there's nothing to beat those children,' and it was indeed a striking and original spectacle. Over a thousand of the city's schoolchildren, dressed in frocks and hats of many different colours, carefully grouped to form a 'floral' display, covering in tiers the whole of the wide steps of the Liverpool Museum.

'Did you see our Maeve, so? Knocks spots off the rest of them,' Ellen said proudly, for despite her age her eyes were sharp, and of them all it had been she who had spotted her granddaughter in her buttercup yellow frock and hat.

The rest of her words were drowned out as with a crash which sent the pigeons into the air in a grey and fluttering cloud, the band of the Liverpool City Police struck up 'Land of Hope and Glory'. All those who had been seated, on camp stools or rugs or old newspapers, scrambled to their feet, and from over 100,000 voices the great old song roared forth, and from many eyes tears fell, for the words held a meaning and reverence to these intensely patriotic men and women of Liverpool. It was an impressive few minutes, made the more so by the momentary deep silence which followed as the last notes faded away.

The crowd began to murmur then, and handkerchiefs were put away, and in the distance could be heard a swelling roar, like breakers rolling on to a beach. Those about the O'Shaughnessys stood on tiptoe, and people in vantage points at windows along the route which their Majesties would take craned their necks. All eyes were focused on the corner of London Road from which the Royal procession would come.

'Shall I be liftin' you up, Mammy?' Michael shouted, for you had to shout to be heard above the roar of the crowd, the blue-green eyes in his face which all of Ellen's children had inherited, sparkling with mischief. 'Will I sit you on me shoulder?' for everywhere were small children being picked up by their fathers, straddled like clinging monkeys about their necks and shoulders. A hundred thousand hands waved a hundred thousand flags, and when the royal motorcar appeared, the royal standard fluttering on the bonnet, the 'garden' of children came to life as the 'child-flowers' waved and cheered.

'Mother of God, I've never seen anything so grand in all me born days,' Ellen wept, overcome with the joy of it all, and in typical O'Shaughnessy fashion, not knowing whether to laugh or cry, she did a bit of both. 'Will you look at the beautiful Queen, may the Holy Mother bless an' keep her, an' did you ever see such a lovely hat?'

'Yours is just as nice, grandma,' young Kathleen said loyally.

'Wisht, child, an' a fine one you are yourself. But will you look at the lovely colour of it. Blue as Our Lady's robe. Begorra, she looks grand, an' will you look at the silver thread in her frock. See how it sparkles in the sun.'

Ellen was as satisfied with Her Majesty as if she herself had put her together that morning. She was the first Queen Ellen had ever seen. She had been in the crowd when Queen Victoria had visited Liverpool in 1886 to open the International Exhibition of Navigation and Commerce. It had poured with rain on that occasion but nothing daunted, the royal party had donned waterproofs and put up their umbrellas and were driven along the procession route in open landaus, to the enthusiastic delight of the crowd, but at such a spanking pace old Mick, young Mick as he had been then, had not had time to lift Ellen up to see them.

No, this Queen lived up to all Ellen's expectations of how a royal personage should be and she was glad she had come, she told Gracie, since she reckoned she'd not see another one in *her* day.

'Sure an' 'tis not over yet, Mammy. Her Majesty's going to inspect the Territorial Nurses. See, they're the guard of honour, an' then there's the speeches.'

He made a lovely speech, the King, really he did,

Ellen told herself, but she was getting tired now and would be glad to get back to Michael's motor car and home. A cup of tea would be nice. A real one, not that stuff that came out of the flask. It didn't taste like proper tea and besides, it didn't seem to keep hot, no matter what they said. They'd eaten every last crumb of the food, the spalpeens, and she was worried that the children might be hungry again. She'd left a good pan of vegetable soup simmering on the stove for them to come home to, besides the endless pies, ham and turkey and pork, apple, gooseberry and three dozen jam tarts and a custard or two, which would keep them going until the enormous sirloin of beef she had put in the oven just before she left home was ready. It was twelve o'clock and she had been sitting on that dratted camp stool or standing on her tiptoes for the best part of four hours now, and her back, not what it used to be, was giving her gyp.

'I am happy to declare the Mersey Tunnel open,' His Majesty was saying. 'May those who use it ever keep grateful thoughts of the many who struggled for long months against mud and darkness to bring it into being.'

Thank God, Ellen thought, clinging to Michael's strong arm, but the sight which silenced the crowd as the King pressed the switch to conclude the proceedings was magical. The towering yellow poles bearing golden banners which had been lying flat on the ground, rose in unison to an upright position about the royal dais, and the emerald green curtain draped across the tunnel entrance parted, each half fixed to a pole.

The crowd sighed in awed unison, one drawn-out breath that could be heard through the amplifiers placed at the exit to the tunnel on the other side of the

water in Birkenhead. The raising of the curtain revealed the mysterious blackness of the tunnel, and across the entrance, in red letters was the message:
MERSEYSIDE WELCOMES YOUR MAJESTIES.

The party had gone on until past midnight, for really it had been such a grand day they didn't want it to end. Once she was in her own kitchen, in the familiar and much loved surroundings where she had spent over fifty years of her life, Ellen's tiredness and backache disappeared. *She* was the queen here, imperious and as regal in her own way as Her Majesty. *This* was *her* realm, not as splendid as Queen Mary's, but she wouldn't swop it for a gold clock, for it was here she ruled her growing multitude of children, grandchildren and great-grandchildren, the uninterrupted generations she and Mick had created out of their love. There *was* love here, love and loyalty and devotion as she had seen displayed to the royal majesty today, and Ellen was the centre of it, the life force from which it had all come.

'See, eat up, Terence, or sure an' you'll never grow to be as big as your Daddy,' giving Eammon, the boy's father, a fond cuff round the ear. 'He never had to be told to clear his plate, did you, son? I can remember when he was smaller than you an' . . .'

'Aah lay off, Mammy, the boy doesn't want to know what I did as a wee 'un, do you, son?'

'Of course he does, don't you, darlin'? A real limb of the devil, so he was, him an' your Uncle Donal with Sean and Rory, may their sweet souls rest in peace . . .' crossing herself reverently as they all did, for had not her son and grandson been laid to rest in the battlefields of France. 'I can see them now, doin' handstands against the wall in the passage an' tauntin' the girls to do the same so they could see their knickers.'

'*Mammy!* We never did so.'

'Did you think I didn't see you, you eejit? Eyes in the back of me head, so I had.'

'An' still have, Mammy.'

''Tis true so you'd best behave. Now why isn't that baby in his cot, Tess O'Shaughnessy? Not twelve months old yet an' still up at nine o'clock. Mine were all tucked up at the latest by seven when they were his age.'

'Mammy, if Tess wants to nurse the child, let her. After all 'tis hers . . .'

'Don't talk back to me, Eammon O'Shaughnessy . . .' whilst the placid Tess, who cared not where the baby was for sure if she hadn't one in her arms then t'would be another, calmly lifted a glass of stout to her lips and took a deep draught. '. . . An' I shudder to think what state the poor wee chap'll be in when he's had a drink of his Mammy's milk after *that*,' Ellen concluded, indicating the stout. She circled the table like a top that cannot keep from spinning, so great was the momentum of her energy in the service of these she loved.

From the front room where no one went unless there was a family get-together the sound of someone playing the piano drifted down the hall.

'I get a kick out of you . . .' Cliona's voice warbled above the tinkling of the instrument which she herself would be playing since her father had wanted her to have all the accomplishments a young lady should, and before she had begun the second line they had all joined in. Her father, Donal and Gracie and Amy, and Amy's husband Tom, who had a drop took and was already

37

'legless' though it was barely nine o'clock. Eileen and her Dennis and the dozens of children who had somehow all crammed themselves into Ellen's parlour. Standing on one another's shoulders, Ellen didn't doubt, and soon there would be more as those who still sat round the kitchen table pushed back their chairs and eagerly headed up the hall.

'Play "You're the tops", Cliona, then we can dance.'

'Dance is it, well it'll have to be in the street,' Ellen shouted as she battled her way through the heaving throng to take her rightful place beside the piano, '. . . an' never mind that modern stuff, darlin'. Let's be hearin' "Yankee Doodle Dandy". Sure an' I love that song . . .'

'No, grandma, that's old-fashioned . . .' and Eammon's elder girl, Kathleen, and no more than eight years old, began a fair imitation of what Ellen called 'that Jazzy stuff'.

> It don't mean a thing if you ain't got swing,
> Doo-aa, doo-aa, doo-aa . . .

'*Doo-aaa* . . . Blessed Mother, what *is* the world comin' to . . .'

It took several moments for the sweet strains of the timeless melody so dear to the heart of every Irish man and woman, to lift softly to the ceiling. They were silenced for a second or two, and then they took it up. Their voices were warm and full, for it was not only the Welsh of Liverpool who could sing of their beloved homeland. Throats clogged with tears, for they were as big-hearted and sentimental about the country not one of them had ever seen as if they had just come over on the boat.

38

'"Oh Danny boy, the pipes, the pipes are calling . . ."' and even the little ones knew every word. They sang it through to the end, male and female voices blending, the sweet pipe of the younger children adding to the blessed unity of the moment.

'Wisht, that was grand, darlin',' Ellen murmured, patting Cliona's shoulder and wiping a tear from her eye for about the tenth time that day. The rest cleared their throats and blew their noses and begged Cliona to 'go on, pet, an' let's have a bit of a dance'.

'Lift the piano into the garden, Daddy, why don't we?' Lorcan begged. 'Sure an' it could stand on the path an' be as safe as houses. Me an' Joseph'll do it, won't we, Joe, then we can dance in the street like grandma says.'

'Begod, I didn't mean it, child. The neighbours . . .'

'When have the neighbours ever minded a party, Mammy? Remember the night the war ended?'

'Aach, so I do, begorra. What a night . . .' wiping another tear, for it had been joyful and sad, that night of the Armistice.

'Oh, come on, grandma, let's . . . please . . .'

'Well . . . oh, why not. Jesus, Joseph an' Mary, it's not every day we get us a new tunnel to take us to the other side of the water,' just as though Ellen O'Shaughnessy was to be one of those who made the journey each day.

The street joined in as it always did when the O'Shaughnessys had a bit of a 'do', friends and neighbours who had known them for years, particularly Ellen, who was always the first over the doorstep if there was illness or trouble. They loved a sing-song and a bit of a dance, did the O'Shaughnessys, and anyone was welcome to join in. Mrs Donavan next door, who had lost her Ernie on the same day as Sean O'Shaughnessy died, gave Cliona a break from the piano to dance with her uncles and cousins. Even the tram drivers and conductors who came into the depot opposite on their last shift found themselves with a pint in their hand or a pretty girl in their arms.

'I think I've bloody died and gone to 'eaven, Fred,' one was heard to call out to his mate.

'You'll not think tha' when you ger 'ome to your old woman, Bert.'

They'd not forget in a hurry the day the Mersey Tunnel was opened, Ellen thought as she sank to her knees in prayer beside her bed, thanking the Mother of God for such a grand day, and the new hat had been a huge success, if she did say so herself, Blessed Mother.

3

She was sitting in the chair in which his father, Mick O'Shaughnessy had always sat until his death, and Callum did not even wonder at his own lack of surprise at the sight of her. What he did feel was irritation and something else which he did not at that moment recognise. God's nightgown, there she sat, was the first thought in his mind, pleased as punch with herself over what she thought of as her own cleverness and worldly wisdom, casually lounging in his mother's kitchen, drinking tea and chatting to Rosie – who had the grace to look somewhat embarrassed – just as though it was nothing out of the ordinary for a Woodall, the daughter of a baronet, to take a cup of tea in their kitchen. Perhaps it wasn't. He knew that his mother was attached to this girl's mother because of some event in the past which he knew nothing about, but he was pretty certain that Maris Woodall did not make a practice of calling on a woman such as Ellen O'Shaughnessy, despite the somewhat tenuous ties between her family and his.

No, she was here for one reason only and that was himself. A young girl fascinated by what she saw as, perhaps, some *fun*, a daring and wicked way to fill her no doubt boring life, an association with a man a great deal older than herself, more experienced, a man of a different class from her own and therefore all the more exciting. He knew, of course, since he was no fool, that he was attractive to women. He liked women, and not just for their bodies, but this one infuriated him with her calm assumption that should she place herself within his line of vision he would be unable to resist her splendid charms. She was using his unsuspecting mother for her own purposes and he found he resented it enormously.

'God love you, darlin',' his mother shrieked as he entered the kitchen, flying like a girl into his arms, the disordered top knot of her silver white hair coming to rest just beneath his chin. She had worn her hair like that ever since he could remember, drawn up into what she considered to be a 'tidy bun' on the top of her head. Once her hair had been the colour of his own, thick and long and curling, a joy to her young husband, who had loved her from the moment he had clapped eyes on her until the day he had died in her arms. When he had married her the bun had been vigorous, as she was, springing from its ribbons in an excess of curls which he had wound round his strong fingers. Now it was finer, like spun silk, pure and silvery white, but still managing to wisp in endearing tendrils about her frail and wrinkled neck. Callum had no idea how old she was. Probably about seventy, but he had never known her to be in any way different since he had been old enough to notice. Volatile and loquacious, passionate about her family which she loved and chastised in equal measure, about her religion which was the stuff of life to her, about her home which was her world and her life's work, she lived her life by the creed which she had taken in with her mother's milk. There was good and there was evil. You loved and you cherished the first and abhorred the last, doing your best to destroy it, for if you did not it would surely destroy you. She loved her children, her grandchildren and her great-grandchildren with all of her big heart, which had room and to spare for them all and indeed for any living creature which had need of it. She could cry and laugh at the same time, work her fingers to the bone in the service of those she loved and give her last penny to those in need. Loyal, steadfast, illogical, humorous, as kind as the spring sunshine but with a tenacious idea of what was right and what was not. The Catholic faith guided her life, and she had brought her children up in it, and even if there had been one or two 'backsliders', her instinct, as a mother and as a believer in the true faith, told her they would return. There was no such thing as an *ex*-Catholic, she argued stoutly, and Callum, and Mara who had married two husbands, neither of them members of Holy Mother Church, did and said nothing to disillusion her.

'Rosie told me she'd seen you yesterday, you spalpeen, on the ferry boat from Birkenhead, an' what you were doin' on it only the Holy Mother herself knows, an' me expectin' you every minute of the live long day an' yourself not here. Business, says she, an' what business could be keepin' my boy from his Mammy, says I, an' her without a sight of him these past four months. Australia is it, where the heathens live, an' on the other side of the world altogether. Aach, you should have been here with us yesterday instead of gallivantin' about over the water, so you should. A grand day, we had, didn't we, Matty? The whole family of us an' the Queen as lovely as the Mother in Heaven. But aren't you the fine one yourself, so you are, in your lovely tweed jacket . . .' clasping her arms about her son and sniffing deeply the masculine smell of him, '. . . but you're here now, thanks be to the Blessed Virgin for Her goodness an' here's meself without a decent bit of food to put in your mouth an' you with an appetite like a young bull . . .'

'Mammy, Mammy, will you let up now so that I can get a good look at you, so. Bejasus, but you get prettier every time I come home, never mind the old Queen, an' if you're after telling me to stop me blarney when did an Irishman ever do that? Jaysus, it's bloody good to see you . . .'

'Callum, you know I'll have no swearin' in this house.'

'Sorry, Ma, but's true. You never change, thanks be to God,' lifting her from her feet and holding her tightly to him.

'Put me down, pet, an' Matty can be makin' us a cup of tea.'

'Matty! Good God, is she still here . . . ?' turning to the old woman who hovered in the doorway to the scullery. Tall and thin where Ellen was small and plump, the servant's hair was smooth and grey, almost painted on her narrow skull, tight and shiny. She wore a grey dress and a snowy white apron and in her pallid face were two eyes which glowed lovingly, for this family was *her* family, all she had ever known, and this was the return of one of *her* children. She had helped to bring them up, each and every one, and they were *her* life as they were her mistress's.

'By all that's holy, I thought you'd be in your grave by now, so I did,' he joked, '. . . but here you are, alive an' kicking an' ready to give me what for . . .'

'I did it when you were a lad an' there's nothing to stop me doing it now, Callum O'Shaughnessy.'

'I don't doubt it, you foolish old woman.'

'Now then, we'll be havin' none of that,' bobbing her head as though in reproval, but Callum would have none of that either and he swept her, unresisting, into his warm embrace. She had been kitchen-maid and companion to his mother for what seemed a lifetime, which it was, since she had been at number eleven Edge Lane since before he was born. She allowed his hug for a moment then she pushed him away. 'Well, I've no time to stand here messing about, young Callum, not with company . . .' indicating with a nod of her severe head the two young women who sat before the glowing fire, lit even on this warm July day. 'I'll be putting the kettle on and them scones we made this mornin' will need to be buttered, Mrs O'Shaughnessy, an' perhaps a bite of that walnut cake, for the lad'll need something inside him after that long journey.'

'I've not done the trip from Australia in one day, Matty.'

'That's as may be. A growin' lad . . .'

'Now then, Matty,' his mother intervened somewhat sharply, not best pleased at having her son's attention taken from her within five minutes of his return. 'Wet the tea, there's a good girl . . .' this to a woman who was older than herself, 'an' pull the fire together.'

'Never mind the owd fire, Mammy. Let me get a good look at you, so.'

It was always the same, he thought wryly. The moment he had his foot in the door he reverted to the way all his family spoke, the lilting Irish brogue he himself had not realised was so strong in him until he went to France and mixed with young men from many walks of life. Even at the Marine Training School in Liverpool there had been tongues from many parts of the country, some as strong as his own but others clear, well enunciated and accentless. He had, years ago, without really thinking about it, begun to eradicate

45

most of the brogue which sang on his family's lips like that of a nightingale, but it returned as soon as he was amongst them again.

'Aah, never mind me, darlin', 'tis yourself we want to look at, don't we, girls? Thank God and the Blessed Virgin for your safe journey home . . .' sketching a hasty cross as her son settled himself at her table, and all the time Maris Woodall watched Callum O'Shaughnessy with the wide-eyed fascinated attention of an innocent, untouched girl for an older and presumably experienced man. She had heard a great deal about him, of course, from his mother when she and Rosie called, which was quite often whatever Callum may have privately thought; from her Aunt Mara and from Rosie herself, who, though she scarcely knew him, repeated word for word what her grandmother told her about the wonderful progress made by her Uncle Callum from his humble beginnings as an apprentice on a cargo vessel and who, when he had completed his time, would have a junior officer berth. He had served his four years' apprenticeship to gain practical experience before sitting his entrance examination for the Marine School of Training, which catered for merchant navy officers who wished to acquire their 'tickets'. He had learned the hard way 'before the mast' during his four years, gaining knowledge of 'boxing the compass', stabilisation procedures, rope-splicing and many other duties expected of an experienced seaman. He had studied ships' articles and mathematical theory, picking the brains of helpful deck officers on how to determine a ship's position, how to plot a course, and many intricate details of navigational procedure. He had passed the navigational examination at the top of his class, gaining his 'master's ticket', and in the next six years

46

had moved steadily up the ladder of progress until at the age of thirty he had become master of his own ship. A cargo ship of the Hemingway Line which was called, after a long line of others, by the name of SS *Alexandrina Rose*.

The 'old man', as he was called in the tradition of cargo ships' crews, had to be intelligent, with practical common sense, ready to listen to all options from his officers, but capable of forming an independent assessment of any given situation. He had to be fair but hard, dependable, a man in whom his crew could feel confidence, but it was none of these things which Maris saw on that day in July when she first was in his company, nor on the following day in his mother's kitchen.

It had taken all her powers of persuasion to get her cousin Rose to come with her to visit old Mrs O'Shaughnessy.

'We can take Charlie's motor, Rosie. I'll drive. Charlie won't mind. I heard him tell father he was going up to the grouse moor to see how the game was for next month's shoot. You know how they are about it, worried to death in case there shouldn't be enough birds for every gentleman to kill.'

'Never mind that, Maris. What I'd like to know is why this sudden desire to go and see my grandmother. We were only there last Tuesday.'

Rose Osborne narrowed her vivid, emerald-green eyes, those which seemed to come out in various members of the Osborne family every generation or so. No one knew from where, only that her grandfather Osborne had been known to have them, then her Aunt Elizabeth, and now herself. They were surrounded by thick, soot-black lashes, and set in a creamy-skinned face that was broad of brow and pointed of chin. She had straight and heavy silken hair with the colour and gleam of a blackbird's wing in it, and a tall, full-breasted figure which came from neither her own mother, nor, it was said, from her father's side of the family since *his* grandmother had been tiny and silver-haired. Rose was a young woman of striking beauty, the perfect foil to her dainty blonde cousin, the one who was at this moment doing her best to persuade her to let her have her own way, not an unusual circumstance as Rosie Osborne knew very well. Maris was like that. Sweet and amenable, smiling and demure, but underneath as strong as steel. She knew that men could not resist her since she seemed fragile and mysterious, which she was not; cool and serene, which was also far from the truth. It was when you looked into her deep brown eyes that the truth of her nature was revealed. There was passion there, wilfulness and tenacity, and the certainty that she had only to exert all three and there would not be a person alive, male or female, who could resist her. She had known nothing but loving kindness, even indulgence, from her parents, being the only girl. She was her father's pride and joy, and all her life had managed, by one means or another, to have and do everything and anything she had ever wished for.

'Come on, Rosie, be a sport. Let's motor over to Edge Lane and take tea with your grandmama and . . .'

'. . . and perhaps renew our acquaintance with my handsome uncle who you know full well will be there since you heard him tell us yesterday that he would.'

'Rosie! How could you? I have absolutely no interest in your uncle . . .' Maris smiled wickedly, '. . . but you must admit he *is* rather splendid with those broad shoulders and those absolutely devastating blue eyes, or were they green?'

48

'God knows,' Rose answered sourly, '. . . and they are nothing at all to do with you, Maris Woodall, whatever their colour. He's far too old for you *and* too much for you to handle. He's no Freddie Winters. He'd eat you for breakfast . . .'

'How delightful.'

'. . . and then look round for the next course.'

'What a way you have with words, Rosie dear, though I must admit they are very apt. So will you come?'

The two girls were lying on a rug beside the lake at the back of Woodall Park, home of the Woodall family for past generations. The house was constructed of stone, as were so many old houses in Lancashire, and its peace and dignity had withstood the long passage of time, mellowing into a beauty that was eternal. It was set in vast acres of deer park, serene and untouched, though the three farms which had once surrounded it had long been sold. There were trees about the house, set in broad stretches of lawned gardens, the beds at this time of the year massed in glory with the flowers of summer. Generations ago arbours had been erected and now they were overgrown with creepers, vines and an explosion of climbing roses which badly needed pruning, the scent of which drifted down to the edge of the lake where the cousins sprawled. They had ordered iced lemonade which a trim maid had brought out to them on a splendid silver tray, coming across the wide terrace at the back of the house, down the crumbling stone steps and past the old sundial on which a previous Woodall had inscribed the initials JW and the date 1648. Gardeners were hard to come by, since the war had decimated a generation of men, but the fountains and rose gardens, the ponds and rockeries, the garden maze and the wild and tangled stand of trees beyond the lake, though not as perfect as the pre-war army of gardeners and under-gardeners and labouring lads had kept them, were still in some sort of control, kept that way by one old man and a couple of village lads.

Maris watched Callum O'Shaughnessy now, hardly speaking, taking no more than a morsel of scone and a sip of tea lest she miss a word or an expression on his mobile face as he described to his mother and Rose and the awe-struck Matty, the wonders of the countries he had visited on his trip to Australia. He had taken a cargo of coal, returning with one of wool, he said, not even looking at her which, if she had had more experience of men, would have told her of his exact interest. Gibraltar, Malta, Suez, Aden, Singapore, names which conjured up exotic sounds and smells, deep blue nights and hot golden days, amber-skinned people with slanting eyes and fragile limbs. Then on to the magnificent harbour of Sydney with its newly built bridge, and the wild country behind it where the black man lived.

'Are they cannibals?' his mother breathed fearfully, crossing herself again, for her boy went into such dangers, and how could she bear it if she lost another of her precious sons? Two in the trenches in France, may they rest in eternal peace, and now this one gallivanting about the oceans of the world as though it was no more than crossing the waters of the River Mersey.

'No, Mammy, but they are a strange wild people. They live, many of them, as they have done for tens of thousands of years, painted and uncivilised even in this modern day . . .'

'God help us.'

'But I met none in the streets of Sydney.'

'God be praised.'

'And you, Miss Woodall,' he said, turning suddenly, politely, to Maris. 'What do you do with your time?' the words and the way he said them implying quite plainly that whatever it was it could have no meaning nor worth in the real world where men – and women – must earn their living. He seemed not to consider that his own niece, who sat on the other side of the table, led exactly the same life. The life women of their class had led for generations, whatever that might be, for he certainly had no interest in it.

'Why . . . I ride to hounds in season, and . . . well . . . I like to . . .' turning brightly to Rose, '. . . what *do* we do, Rosie? We are playing tennis with friends tomorrow, aren't we . . . ?'

'Yes . . .'

'. . . and . . . well, we go shopping and make calls, as we are doing today on Mrs O'Shaughnessy and . . . what else, Rosie?'

'I help Uncle Teddy with the accounts . . .'

'Of course you do, and I accompany mother to the shipping office when she has a meeting . . . shareholders, you know the sort of thing.'

'I'm afraid I don't, Miss Woodall.'

'Well, I act as chaperone, if you like, when father cannot manage it . . .' which was quite often, Callum had heard, for Sir Harry Woodall had been badly gassed in the trenches, his lungs damaged, and it was a wonder he had lasted as long as he had. Only the patient and devoted care of his wife kept him alive, or so it was said. What with a crippled brother and a frail and vulnerable husband, the remarkable Lady Elizabeth Woodall, and she *was* remarkable, Callum had been told, had had a hard row to hoe.

'There is the season . . .' her foolish daughter was saying, 'London, you know, which has just finished, and I have been to school in Switzerland until quite recently. So there you are, Captain O'Shaughnessy,' Maris smiled, brilliantly, triumphantly, '. . . we are enormously busy, are we not, Rosie?'

'How very fascinating.' Callum wondered why he was going to the trouble of goading this quite innocent and harmless girl. Why was it her delicate loveliness, her bright, strong spirit which would not be cast down, the deep brown glow of admiration in her eyes, should irritate him so? She had come here today with the sole purpose of showing herself off to him and why not, if that was what amused her? And why not take her up on what could obviously be his if he cared to reach out and claim it? She was certainly pretty enough, and could be made very versatile in the erotic arts if he was prepared to go to the trouble of teaching her. Then he caught himself up short, chiding himself for his callous disregard for a young girl's feelings. She thought herself to be so polished, indeed he had thought so himself at their first encounter yesterday, as she moved towards him through the throng on the ferry boat. And her laugh! Despite himself he remembered the joy of it, the way it had curled up the corners of his own mouth, creating a bubble of laughter within himself which had been hard to resist.

But then she had been amongst her peers, her own kind, and the working men and women who travelled on the boat had meant nothing to her. Now, in the presence of the unknown, a mature male, not the callow young men to whom she was accustomed, but a man older and therefore delightfully dangerous, or so she would think, she was out of her depth.

He took pity on her, the brilliant dazzle of his extra-ordinary eyes softening, as though he addressed a child.

'You are indeed a busy young woman, Miss Woodall,' he began, ready to turn back to his mother who once again was showing signs of restlessness at having to share her son's time, even with the daughter of her dear friend, Lady Woodall, but Maris was no fool, young as she was.

'Don't patronise me, Captain O'Shaughnessy. What I do might not seem of much importance to you, indeed it may sound utterly trivial, but I would like you to know that I do my best to . . . to . . . well, to make something . . . to do a worthwhile . . . if I could I would . . .' I would do as *you* do, Callum O'Shaugh-nessy, she was saying, if I were not a child of my environment. I would be an aviator, a politician, a great explorer, she was telling him, telling them all, but most of all, telling herself. A product of her upbringing, of the class in which daughters did not 'go out' to work, she filled her days with all the trivia her mother, her grandmother and presumably all the women of her family had done, waiting for her destiny, which was to get married herself and bear children, whose daughters would do the same.

Except, of course, the great-grandmother she had shared with Rosie, the legendary Lacy Hemingway who had lived to be over ninety and who had started the shipping line for which Callum O'Shaughnessy's ante-cedents had laboured and which now employed him and two of his brothers, not to mention a couple of nephews and a niece or two.

'I beg your pardon, Miss Woodall,' he said sooth-ingly, 'I did not mean to belittle . . .'

'Yes, you did, Captain O'Shaughnessy. You

intended to do just that. To let me see that you despise what I am and what I do, which isn't much, I suppose, but . . .'

'Indeed it has nothing at all to do with me, Miss Woodall, and I would not presume to criticise your way of life.'

'Perhaps not with words, but the tone of your voice said it all. To you I am nothing but a . . .'

Ellen O'Shaughnessy, Matty and Rose looked from one set face to the other and then at each other, visibly startled and not a little bewildered at this sudden sparking of tension between the light-hearted, good-humoured and delightful Maris Woodall, whom everybody knew for the most amiable of young women, providing she was not crossed, and the son of the house who surely should not have cared in the slightest what their visitor did, or thought. He would not say so, naturally, nor even show it, not to a guest of his mother's, but the sparks were flying in the most curious way and what were they to make of it?

'Wisht, what on earth's got into you, Callum O'Shaughnessy, to say that Maris does nothing all the live long day . . .'

'That's not what I said, Mammy, or at least if I did I did not mean to. I was only asking . . .'

Godammit, the blasted girl had him arguing with his own mother now and him not in the house five minutes. She really was the most damnable nuisance, and if she wasn't a guest in Mammy's house he'd have told her so.

'Yes, son?'

But before Callum could answer Maris stood up abruptly, herself bewildered at the strength of her own feelings, whatever they were, not at all sure what she

54

was going to do at this precise moment, only aware that she needed quite desperately to get away from the sudden wash of hurt that had attacked her. She had felt a terrifyingly strong sense of attraction to Callum O'Shaughnessy yesterday, right from the moment when he turned his clear, far-seeing eyes in her direction, but he had merely looked at her, taken her hand, and then turned away. She had been quite devastated by her sense of . . . of loss, and amazed by his obvious indifference, for she was Maris Woodall, eighteen years old and very pretty. So what had she done to *him* to make him so rude to *her*?

She was quite beside herself as she looked around the warm and spacious kitchen in which for nearly seventy-five years the O'Shaughnessys had laughed and wept, rejoiced and mourned, loved and quarrelled. Ellen had come here as a bride. She had borne eighteen children within these walls, and had reared thirteen of them in the warm benevolence of the house which could be felt as soon as you entered the front door. It lapped about you as lovingly as the warmth from the black-leaded hot plate over the fire and the shining oven beside it. It was reflected in the polished brass fender and rose in praise of Ellen's loving spirit from her red, stone-flagged floor. The gleaming rows of copper pans, from the tiniest milk pan to the heavy preserving pan, were like the smiling faces of good friends; the preserve jars, flat-lidded, salt-glazed stoneware which contained Ellen's jams and apple rings, plums and chutneys, were a wash of warm colours from pale primrose to chocolate brown. The dresser groaned with crockery, amongst which the Coronation mug commemorating the crowning of their Majesties took pride of place. There were soup dishes, gravy boats, vegetable tureens which

seemed to be filled to their brims with the shining kindliness which overflowed in this kitchen, in this house.

And the smells which delighted the senses. Freshly
ironed petticoats 'airing' on the pulley high in the ceiling above the fire. The heavy cast-iron stock pot,
replenished with meat and vegetables daily in the
certainty that one, or even half a dozen members
of her family might drop in, which they invariably
did; the scones, the bread, the biscuits which were
baked almost by the hour, for Ellen would never let
it be said – except by herself – indeed would have
been bitterly shamed to find that she hadn't a bite to
eat in the house!

Maris had seen it all a hundred times or more when
she and Rosie had visited Rosie's grandmother. They
were almost the same age, Rosie being the elder by no
more than a month or two. They were friends as well
as cousins, the more reserved and sensible Rosie a
restraining influence on the impetuous and often vulnerable Maris. They both had strength of character
which would mature as they became older. They often
quarrelled but they were as devoted as sisters, or true
friends. Maris had grown up accepting her Aunt Mara's
humble origins and the family from which she came,
treating it and being treated *by* it without question as
part of it, along with her brother Alex. Strangely,
Charles had never concerned himself with his cousins'
Irish family, finding company among his own class more
to his liking, but Maris and Alex were looked on affectionately by Ellen O'Shaughnessy. She had an especially soft spot for Alex who, or so she said, could have
been taken for Irish himself, the divil in him and the
charm of him reminding her of her own dead Sean,
God rest his sweet soul.

Callum O'Shaughnessy stood up as the girl he had just humiliated for some unaccountable reason turned wildly about her as if searching for escape, though from what none of the others could even guess.

'I must go now, Mrs O'Shaughnessy, if you will excuse me,' she babbled, turning towards the kitchen door, thankfully it seemed to Rosie, who had, perhaps of them all, guessed at what was in her cousin's mind.

'Faith, child, you've been here no more than a minute or two, so you have, an' Matty was just about to make another pot of tea, weren't you, Matty?'

'No . . . really, it is most kind of you,' mouthing the words which she had been taught in the nursery, and Callum continued to stand, polite as any gentleman who must not remain seated whilst there was a lady on her feet. There was a certain air about him of boredom, and impatience for her to be gone. She was no more than a silly young girl, his attitude seemed to say to her, and her usual bouncing confidence drained dismally from her.

'I'll come with you.' Rosie reached Maris in one graceful stride, her tall figure standing protectively over the smaller one of her cousin. 'It's time I was going myself. I promised Aunt Clare I would help Uncle Teddy about the kennel. He wants to see the hound puppies he's bred for the hunt. He and Aunt Clare are driving over to see Aunt Caitlin and Uncle Jack in Yorkshire at the weekend.'

'Are they so? Well, tell them to give every last one of them children a kiss from me, the darlins. And to ask Caitlin when she's comin' to see her old Mammy.'

'I will, grandmother. I promise.'

'. . . and before our Clare goes tell her to drive over here an' pick up some of me scones an' p'raps me an'

Matty'll make an apple cake, oh, an' those children love their grandma's gingerbread biscuits so we'll knock up a few whilst the oven's hot.'

'I will, grandmother, though I'm not sure Aunt Clare can get over here before . . .'

'Never mind then, Callum can take them over, can't you, pet?'

'Well . . .'

'Of course you can. Now then, Matty, hand me that bakin' bowl an' give the fire a stir . . .'

'They're not going until Saturday, grandmother,' Rosie protested weakly, knowing exactly how much notice Ellen would take of her, which was none, and at the kitchen door Maris stood fumbling with her purse and her perky hat, her back to Callum O'Shaughnessy whom she loved and hated with every instinct that was in her. She did not understand him. She could not penetrate the complex masculine depths of him. She wanted to scream at him, 'look at me, *look at me*, see me not as a tiresome girl but as someone worth looking at,' but she was not quite nineteen years old. She had known only boys, not a man in full maturity, and she was frail in her ignorance. All she could do now was to run away from it, and from him.

Rosie drove Charlie's little car home. Though Sir Harry Woodall was a tolerant, even indulgent father, quite radical in his views – or rather those his wife put in his head – on the bringing up of children, he would not allow either his daughter or his niece, whilst she was in his guardianship, to have a motor car of her own. Alex had taught both Maris and Rose to drive, since he and Charlie each had a dashing sports car, and neither brother was ungenerous when it came to allowing the cousins to drive them when they could do so without the knowledge of their father. So far they had got away with it.

They drove along Edge Lane without speaking. Once, not very long ago, there had been open fields all about the O'Shaughnessy home with a park nearby and a reservoir set in pleasant countryside. Now, directly opposite the house the corporation had erected a tramway depot. Very handy for the trams to town, Ellen had said, when she and old Mick had fancied a look at the shops, or when she and Amy or her other daughters had put on their best hats and treated themselves to afternoon tea in Lewis's café. But who wanted to look at tramcars and hear their clatter as they turned round at the terminus all day long? The Botanic Gardens were still there, but not as splendid as once they had been when she and Mick and their growing family had sauntered in the gardens after Mass on a Sunday to listen to the military band.

Rosie was a good driver. She took the corner into Childwall Valley Road with a flourish, changing down and then up again as well as Charlie himself did. They were in open country now. The hedgerows were a tangle of wild flowers festooned with bryony and honeysuckle. Blackberry blossom, pink and profuse, gave promise of a heavy fruit to come. The banks on either side of Netherley Road, just before you came to Yew Tree Farm, were massed with tall purple foxgloves and the nodding heads of grasses bursting with pollen. Haymaking was in progress in the fields surrounding the farm and the farm labourers waved as the brilliant scarlet sports car roared past. The Woodalls were *their* family in these parts and Sir Harry, God bless him, was well liked. Had he not given his health, and his two brothers their lives, in the service of their country?

Rosie pulled the car to a stop beside the coppice on Water Lane. She turned off the engine, reached into her handbag and produced a battered packet of cigarettes, offering one to Maris. She took one herself, lit them both from one match and, rather inexpertly, the two girls puffed in silence for a couple of minutes. Stubbing out her cigarette on the sole of her shoe, Rosie threw the butt into the grass verge.

'He's too old for you, darling, you know that, don't you, and far too experienced,' she said at last.

'I know, but . . .'

'. . . but you like him just the same.'

'He . . . he thinks I'm nothing but a spoiled brat . . .'

'. . . which you are.'

'I know that, too, but all the same he should not have jeered at what I am. After all, you are exactly the same. But there is just something here which . . .' She struck her breast with her clenched fist, her young face unutterably sad since this was the first time she had been hurt by a man.

'What is it, Maris?'

'I don't know, Rosie. The strangest feeling inside me and one I've never had before. D'you think I could be in love?' Her voice was wistful, almost childlike.

'I don't know, darling. I don't know what being in love feels like.' Rose kept her voice quite serious.

'Neither do I, that's the trouble. I've had no experience in *anything*. It's just that your . . . your uncle . . . God, he sounds positively *ancient* . . .'

'He is.'

'Well, just the same I could go quite mad for him.'

'Freddie Winters is mad for *you*.'

'Sod Freddie Winters.'

'You did not say that at last night's party. You danced all night with him.'

There was a long, heavy silence, then, 'Callum.'

'What? What about Callum?'

'Nothing. I just wanted to say his name.'

'Well don't. Try saying Freddie instead.'

'*Freddie!* My God, *Freddie.* Hasn't *that* got a grand ring to it?' and the two young girls fell against each other laughing, the slightly hysterical laughter of which the young are capable, brought about by nothing except their own light hearted high spirits and lack of anything more worrying than the length of one's skirts or knowing the steps of the very latest dance. They laughed until they cried, but the tears which sprang to Maris Woodall's eyes were, of course, not tears of helpless laughter.

4

The expression on Maris Woodall's young face was
unsmiling and her eyes were blank and sightless as she
and her pretty sorrel waded slowly through the summer
grasses which edged a field of rippling uncut corn on
Jed Ditton's farm. 'Welshman's Farm' it was called,
presumably because, long before Farmer Ditton
became its tenant, it had once been let to a man called
Parry. It was very old, the farmhouse and the attendant
outbuildings which led off Penny Lane, built of local
blue-grey slate, a magpie architecture of roughened
rubble walls with barns and shippons attached, and
all whitewashed a hundred times or more since it was
originally built. There were wide chimneys and deep
windows, a low pitched roof and a sturdy porch from
which Farmer Ditton's wife had just waved as Maris
skirted the cluttered farmyard.

'A right fine day, Miss Maris,' she called cheerfully
before re-entering her shining kitchen to express her
belief to her eldest, a girl of fourteen who had just left
school, that the squire's daughter looked 'fair mazed
an' it were a good job that there animal of hers knew
its way home otherwise the pair of 'em could end up
in Blackpool by the look of 'er'.

She was right. Maris had not the faintest notion
where she was headed. She had saddled Pearl an hour
ago, leaping into the saddle with the graceful expertise
she and her brothers had learned as soon as they were
tall enough to get a foot in the stirrup, cantering from

the stable yard and heading across the parkland where she broke into a full gallop. She had scattered a browsing herd of fallow deer as she went like the wind towards the small stand of trees known as Fox Clump, her nose no more than an inch from the sorrel's flying mane, her own normally tumbled hair lying flat against her skull as the wind scooped it back from her brow.

With hoofs digging great clumps of earth from the grass and tossing them high into the air, the animal, guided by her rider's sure hand, skirted the woodlands. Straight across Far Paddock they went, leaping the shoulder-high fence, soaring effortlessly into the air, horse and rider locked together as one entity. Across the park in the opposite direction they thundered on until they came to Old Wood; through the ancient trees which carried the great and bounteous burden of summer leaves, shaded in a dozen colours of green from the palest willow to the darkest laurel. The sunlight glimmered, golden and dazzling on the heavily laden branches above her head, forming patterns of light and shade so that she could hardly see, so great was her speed. She galloped on, unconcerned with danger, escaping from something which she could not shake off, or was it just for the sheer thrill of it? Who could tell, only she knew, guiding the sorrel almost by instinct since she had known these woods in every season and at every hour since she was a child.

Oak, enormous and venerable. Ash, though not achieving the grandeur of oak, graceful and sturdy with its lovely foliage and pale grey bark. Beech, its great limbs spread out to form an enormous crown, its trunk like the smooth and soaring columns of a cathedral, and at their feet, hidden almost from sight among the great roots, were wood sorrel and anemone and earth

63

carpeting mosses. Fallen logs and the cut stumps of trees barred her way, but she avoided them adroitly, and in their secret nests the woodcock and pheasant bred by her grandfather for sport, multiplying and allowed to live by her father, who could not bear to shoot another living creature after the carnage of the trenches, held their breath and ducked their heads as horse and rider plunged terrifyingly on. Branches hung low, snatching at her head, but she dodged them, hardly seeing them but knowing with her country-bred senses that they were there nevertheless; steering the sorrel between rough-barked trees with no more than an inch to spare, until the trees began to thin out and suddenly she was away from them, crossing more parkland until she came to the front of the estate. Ahead was the small lodge house, empty now, where once the lodgekeeper had been in charge of the coming and going of his lordship's guests, and as it came into view Maris slowed the sorrel to a trot and then a walk.

They were both breathing hard but it seemed Maris had not shaken off the devil which had pursued her, for when she passed through the gates of her father's estate and entered Colton Lane she was set of face and pale of cheek.

She sighed deeply as she and her sorrel meandered along the empty, sun-drenched lane in the direction of Colton village. The reins were slack in her hands. She released her feet from the stirrups and let them dangle as though she was riding bareback and when she turned on to Farmer Ditton's land – which was in reality her father's land – it was in this careless posture and trance-like state that she was greeted by Mrs Ditton.

Maris had neither seen nor heard Mrs Ditton. She had, in fact, neither seen nor heard anyone since the wryly gleaming, incredibly beautiful eyes of Callum O'Shaughnessy had glanced impersonally in her direction. She had *seen* her mother and father at dinner and at breakfast, just as she had *seen* her two brothers. She had held conversations with all four, joining in the numerous discussions on the splendour of the Mersey Tunnel opening, the shining magnificence of their Majesties as they had graciously waved to the cheering crowds, and the thrill, once the Royal cortège was well under way, of following it on their bicycles through the tunnel to the Birkenhead side. She had chatted idly to her mother on the possibility of growing her short mop of unruly curls into a sleek 'page boy' bob in the style of Greta Garbo, and to her father on the possibility of owning her own little runabout one day. They had seen no difference in her, of that she was sure, though of course she was another person from the one who had taken part in the excitement, the *youthful* excitement she was inclined to think in her new-found maturity, of the outing.

She had not known Callum O'Shaughnessy then!

She sighed again, deeply troubled by the recollections of the past few days which she carried in her warmly obligated, softly pledged young heart. The one she had given without stint, completely, and, she was certain, irrevocably, to Rosie Osborne's uncle. Dear God, it sounded so *ludicrous*. Rosie, who was her own cousin, the same age as herself, but somehow, in the time it took to turn round and smile politely, for was he not a member of Rosie's family and therefore due her respect, she had loved him. She had found herself defenceless against the strange magnetism, the masculine vitality of him which she could not resist.

It had been the same at Mrs O'Shaughnessy's house.

She had shamed herself with her own flagrant and obvious fascination, staring at him, doe-like, she was sure, not able to tear her eyes away from his. The impossible turquoise of them, cold when they looked at her, chilled to the unyielding quality of sapphires, but warm as the Mediterranean seas over which he sailed when he smiled at his mother. They were fringed with dark lashes, and set in a brown and challenging face which seemed to ask her what the devil she thought she was up to, invading his mother's kitchen for her own childish indulgence, which had no effect on him. He had known, of course he had. He could not have misinterpreted her dreaming glances, her mouth which she was positive had hung open as she listened to him speak of his travels. He was a man of the world and knew at once what it meant when a female cast her glance, veiled as it might be, in his direction.

She had been ignorant of how to deal with it, that was the trouble. She had not been prepared for the fist which had struck her, right in the spot below her left breast where she supposed her heart to be, and it had left her winded and senseless. And his complete lack of interest had quite devastated her. God, it was awful, being in love, for that was what she was. A woman in love. She had imagined it so often. What it would be like. A lovely state, the loveliest state for a woman to be in, but then whenever she had thought of it, which lately had been quite often, like most women of her age she supposed, she imagined that the man on whom she was to bestow her sweet and passionate concern, would love her.

Callum O'Shaughnessy did not.

High above her head, no more than a dot in the arched blue of the sky, a lark poured out its heart in liquid song and, coming from her reverie, Maris tipped her head back to stare upwards. As she watched it dropped like a stone then rose again just before it touched the rippling corn in Farmer Ditton's field. Maris, startled at where she found herself to be, looked about her in consternation.

'How did we get here, Pearl?' she asked the sorrel, who pricked her ears at the sound of her voice. 'The last time I looked about me we were on the road to Colton.' She sighed. 'I suppose it was you who decided where we should go, since I don't seem able to think of anyone but that damned man. Lord, it clouds my mind so that I don't know whether to go left or right, or even to go at all. I'd probably still be in the middle of Fox Clump if it weren't for you.'

She stared off blindly into the distance. On one side of her the field of corn stretched out in an ordered golden symmetry, the stalks heavy with their burden, sighing and swaying as the breeze whispered through it. The land was not quite flat, rising up gradually towards a stand of oak trees, hedged, as were all the fields, with hawthorn, tangled in wild flowers. It rolled on to the empty horizon in neat squares of pale green, dark green and gold, coloured by the variety of crops the farmer grew. In one cows were grazing, all standing up and facing the same way, knee-deep in lush meadow grass and clover. To her right was a field studded with the brilliant scarlet of poppies, contrasting vividly with the thick grass, drawing the eye to one lonely elm at the top of the rise, leaning away from the prevailing wind which blew from the estuary. Dog roses, white and trailing, climbed its ancient trunk.

Maris put her feet in the stirrups and took a firmer hold of the reins. She pushed one brown hand through

67

her hair and it sprang up in silky, wind-tossed curls about her head, touched by the sun to tawny streaked silver. She put her heel to the animal's side, guiding her along the rough, weed-tangled path which ran round the perimeter of each field, skirting the bit of woodland known as George's Wood, through another patchwork quilt of green and brown and gold, wheat this time, and maize, until she came to the gate which led her back on to Penny Lane. She dismounted, fastened the gate, led Pearl through it, and after fastening the latch again, remounted.

Which way to go now, she pondered? turning her head first in the direction of Colton village and then back towards Woodall Park. If she rode on through the village she would come to Beechwood and Rosie, who had told her earlier she was to go over some accounts with Uncle Teddy, so she'd not be much company. And she was not awfully sure she *wanted* company as she allowed the sorrel to move towards the grass verge where the animal began to crop.

The reins fell free again, hanging about Pearl's neck. Sinking once more into a vast contemplation of her own predicament, not just her sudden painful feelings for Callum O'Shaughnessy but where to go now in an attempt to escape them, Maris slipped her feet from the stirrups again, lifting one booted leg and folding it across the horse's arched neck. She leaned one elbow on her knee, staring with unfocused eyes at nothing at all, the peaceful loveliness of the soft countryside all about her escaping her attention completely. She did not know *where* she wanted to go so she went nowhere, wrapped about in her own painful thoughts, and when the smart green sports car came surging round the corner from Tue Lane into Penny Lane it was on her before she could even grab the reins to guide the sorrel in towards the hedge.

The car didn't hit her or the animal but in its mad attempt not to it was forced to swerve violently, its tyres screeching on the road's surface, flinging forth a puff of smoke as the rubber burned. The driver, his face a horrid and horrified grey, swung the wheel in what, later, Maris was to acknowledge as a masterly piece of driving, and with a thump which shook the little car quite forcibly, it crashed, bonnet first, its front wheels dropping alarmingly into the ditch.

She was occupied for several heart-stopping minutes with trying to get her horse under some sort of control, and when she had, in soothing her terror with soft hands and soft words. She leaped to the ground, her hands on Pearl's nose and quivering neck, the animal and herself standing almost thigh-deep in the flower-filled ditch on the opposite side of the road to the crashed sports car.

It was the man's voice which jerked her from her frantic ministrations of the sorrel and it was as though, dwelling on him as she had done interminably for the past few days, she had conjured Callum O'Shaughnessy up with the strength and despair of her thoughts.

'What in God's name were you doing standing like that in the middle of the bloody road?' he roared. 'Are you quite mad or just completely witless? This is a public highway, not a path through the middle of your father's woodland, and strange as it may seem, vehicles *do* come along here from time to time. Were you asleep? Jesus Christ . . . Jesus Christ, didn't you hear me coming or are you deaf as well as without brains? Just look at my bloody car, and how in hell's name I managed to avoid you I'll never know.'

He advanced towards her menacingly and she flinched away from him, certain he was about to hit her. She still held the sorrel's reins and when, sensing the violence in the approaching man, the horse reared back nervously, Maris was dragged with her, going down beneath her arching neck.

'Sweet Jesus,' Callum hissed, his teeth gritted in what Maris knew was a violent rictus of rage. He was white-lipped and savage, but without any thought of danger from the horse's flailing hoofs, he pulled Maris roughly to one side, grabbed the reins from her and with little ceremony fastened them and the animal to the close-laced hedge. Taking her arm he half lifted, half dragged her from the ditch and across the narrow road, until they stood side by side on the verge across which the car was slewed. Its bonnet was sadly crumpled and the windscreen was shattered. Both front wheels were still slowly revolving.

Callum's voice shook as he spoke and though most of its cause was rage, the shock he had suffered at the sudden appearance of a horse and rider where none should be, had generated a concern for the poor wan creature beside him, which further provoked him. He still held her arm in a vice-like grip.

'Look at her. Godalmighty will you look at her, poor sod, and all because some stupid bloody woman thinks she, or her family, own not only their own bit of land but every damn acre which surrounds it. Daydreaming like some bloody schoolgirl . . . Jesus . . . I can't believe it . . .' He ran his hand distractedly through his thick hair, talking to himself rather than her, hardly aware that she was there as he agonised over his smashed and beloved car.

'I'm sorry.' Her voice, tiny and penitent, startled

70

him. He looked down at her, and as though the feel of her arm which he still held was more than he could bear, he flung it away from him quite violently and she almost fell. Her heart was still pounding in her ears with fright and shock and her whole body yearned towards him, wanting nothing more than to be drawn into his arms, her face pressed to his chest, just below his chin, against the warm brown flesh of his strong throat. She wanted to be soothed and stroked and petted and told that it was all right and there was nothing to worry herself over, as her father had always done, but Callum was looking at her as though she was some abomination which had stuck to the sole of his shoe.

'Sorry! Is that all you can say when you have just wrecked my car, not to mention almost killed the pair of us *and* the bloody horse? Godammit, have you any idea what might have happened if I'd struck it, and you . . . you crazy . . . you could do with a damned good thrashing.'

She began to cry and as though that was the last straw, he groaned and turned away.

'Jesus, Joseph and Mary, not *tears* now. Spare me those, for God's sake, and don't, I beg of you, tell me you're sorry again. Instead do something useful like running, or better yet, riding the bloody horse to the nearest farm, one with a telephone if you know of such a place and ringing my brother. My brother Michael, the one with the garage. You have heard of him, I presume?'

She admitted she had, stuttering through the violent spasm of sorrow which his words and manner wrenched in her. There was a great emptiness left inside her after this man's contemptuous dislike had struck right at the heart of her. She was hollow, not aching or hurting, but dragged down by an unutterable sadness at the realisation that in the three times they had been in one another's company she had done something which had actively displeased him. She wanted his approval, his admiration, but most of all she wanted . . . God help her . . . his love, and all she ever seemed to awaken in him was irritation and contempt, exasperation and now a rage and loathing which, really, she was not able to bear.

'Well . . . ?' he demanded to know, his black snarling anger ready to erupt, and God only knew what would happen when it did.

'I think they . . . that they have . . . a telephone at Welshman's Farm,' she hiccuped.

'And how far is that?' He held himself in check by the slenderest of threads. She stood there, slight and vulnerable, and he knew he was behaving atrociously. She was no more than a child really, in her tight-fitting riding breeches and short-sleeved silk shirt, though the lift of her round young breasts and the peaks of her tiny nipples against it told him otherwise. She was no child, though by God, she acted like one each time they met. The tears brimmed from her enormous eyes and slipped down her cheeks, great fat tears which ran with the fluency of raindrops across a window-pane. He had never seen anyone cry like that, he thought, silently and sorrowfully, as though her heart was breaking, and for a fraction of a second he felt an amazing urge to hold out his arms and tuck her inside them. To say 'there, there' as one would to a wounded child, but at that moment something cracked ominously inside his stricken motor car and he turned to it at once.

'For God's sake, go, and be quick about it. How far did you say it was?'

'No more than . . . just back up there . . .' lifting her arm vaguely in the direction of Welshman's Farm, where she knew they had a telephone, but making no attempt to get to it.

'What are you waiting for then?' roughly, running a caressing hand along the tipping side of the MG, not looking at her again as he jumped down into the ditch.

'Nothing.' She turned away, a small, dejected figure, dragging her feet as she made her way to where her horse was tethered, then, as though it had just occurred to her, and what had she got to lose anyway since he already despised her, she turned back defiantly.

'The speed limit's thirty, you know,' she said.

'What?' He looked bewildered.

'You must have been going at more than thirty miles an hour, the way you came round that corner.' There was a mutinous curl to her pink mouth.

'Bloody hell, so it's my fault now, is it?'

'I didn't say that. All I'm saying is that you were going too fast to take that corner safely so I don't see why I should take all the blame.'

'Jesus wept!' He had been about to lift the precarious bonnet of his car. He had removed his jacket and thrown it carelessly into the long grasses but now he leapt from the ditch as though he had uncovered a hornets' nest in its dry bottom. His face was livid, and Maris backed away, her boots catching in the rough verge where Pearl now cropped peacefully.

'You're an experienced motorist, is that it . . . ?'

'No, but I know the speed limit and you were above it.'

'So you said and perhaps I'll not deny it, but by God, if you don't get a move on I'll . . .'

Something in her snapped then, something small but rebellious, for though she was aware that she should not have been daydreaming – as he said – in the centre of a public highway, it was thoughts of *him*, this man, which had taken her senses and made her foolishly dazed. So, as she said, why should *she* take all the blame? And why should she simply stand here and let him *roar* at her as he was doing? For two pins she felt like telling him to get his *own* bloody car out of the ditch and even run to Welshman's Farm to get the help he needed to do it!

'Don't you threaten me, Callum O'Shaughnessy,' she said hotly. 'We have only met three times but on each occasion you have shouted at me or sneered at me and what I would like to know is why? What have I done . . . Oh, I know this is partly my fault and for that I'm truly sorry . . . but the day on the ferry and when we met at your mother's house . . . I had done nothing to oblige you to be so rude.'

He could not have been more surprised if it had been the horse which had spoken. He moved away from the car and looked down into her turbulent face, a face which was now flooded with colour beneath its slipping tears.

'I know I should not have been . . . loitering where I was,' she went on, her drowning eyes still overflowing. She had wiped her tears away with a dirty hand and there was a streak of soil on her cheek. She had some grass in her hair and her breeches were stained where she had fallen beneath the sorrel. God, what a mess she was, he thought, like some mucky kid who has been in a fight with others. Her eyes were glowing now as her own temper grew hot and her own integrity was menaced. 'But you were just as much at fault, yes you

74

were, so if I ride to the farm *and* pay for the damage done to the car, will you call it a truce?'

She was amazed, awed and strangely proud of her own daring. Five minutes ago she would not have believed herself capable of talking to this godlike being who, or so Rosie said, would eat Maris Woodall for breakfast. Now, incensed by his manner of speaking, *shouting* at her as though she was a half-witted and irresponsible child, she had dragged her courage from somewhere to answer him back.

She grinned audaciously, delighted with herself and to her immense surprise, so did he.

'So, the kitten has claws, has she?' He put both hands on his hips, low down, lounging gracefully, his weight on one leg. The sun burnished his hair to a deep chestnut and his eyes narrowed against its rays, the vivid blue-green of them glinting, softly now, like sapphires lit by candle flame. She was entranced and could barely speak, since this was the first time he had smiled at her, but drawing from somewhere a composure she was far from feeling, she did.

'It's a fair offer, Callum.' Oh Lord, oh dear Lord, she had said his name, her heart beating fast as she did so. Callum . . . Callum. She loved him so much that she was dazed by it, by its intensity, by its almost holy intensity, and she could not believe that he did not *know* it. It had exploded in her heart with the force and vividness of forked lightning, tearing through her senses, her *sense*, and she knew quite unequivocally that it would never diminish. That nothing could diminish it. Whatever *he* might do or not do, it was in her heart and her woman's body, which desired his until she drew her last breath. How did she know? That question she could not answer. Perhaps if she could the mystery of why one woman loves one man and not another would be revealed to her, and did she really care? *Now?* Callum was smiling at her . . . *smiling* . . . *interested* . . . *amused*, she could tell, and please . . . please whoever it was up there who planned and guided fate . . . don't let her spoil it. Don't let Maris Woodall say or do something which would dissipate the joyous and unique moment which had been spun between them.

'I suppose it is,' he was saying, 'but it doesn't alter the fact that my bloody car is off the road and will be for the whole time I'm in port while my brother repairs it in his workshop,' but he was still looking at her without that awful *indifference* he had shown previously. Without that rancour and irritation she had seemed to awaken in him.

'Could you not borrow one from your brother? I promise, really I do, that I will pay for any inconvenience. In fact, I would like to offer you . . . dinner at the Adelphi by way of an apology, if you have an evening to spare.'

Had she really said it? Dear Lord, had she *really* asked Callum O'Shaughnessy, the man who, an hour ago, had been as far from her as the furthest star in the night sky, with no hope that she could see, of ever reaching the splendour of him? A man who wined and dined and presumably did other more intimate things with women who were as beautiful and as worldly as himself. She, Maris Woodall, eighteen years old, fresh from school and with nothing to offer him but her fast-beating, love-filled, ecstatic heart.

He was *really* grinning now, his smile stretched across the slash of his even white teeth, his eyes lazily assessing her, and her meaning, and she held her breath, doing her best to appear unconcerned, mature, sophisticated, a woman of the world, though her legs trembled so much she thought they would buckle at the knees, and her heart thudded like the enormous drum which had headed the parade at the opening ceremony of the Mersey Tunnel.

'You've got the cheek of the devil, d'you know that? You are the cause of an accident . . . well, almost. Your carelessness has smashed up my car and inconvenienced me to the extent that I don't quite know how I shall get about Liverpool in the execution of my work and yet you have the gall to invite me out to dine just as though these . . . these catastrophes meant nothing. You've a bloody nerve, d'you know that?'

'Why?' Her impudent smile lifted the corners of her long, tender mouth, drawing his attention to its ripe, apricot fullness.

'Where I come from it's the gentleman who is supposed to invite the lady, not the other way round,' but he was intrigued and amused by her outrageous and what might be considered *wicked* behaviour, she could tell. No lady, no woman of any class, would ever be so forward as to ask a member of the opposite sex to take her out. It was just not done. She might *hint* that an invitation would not be unwelcome, offer encouragement if he should seem to need it, but at the same time it was only correct to wait, politely, for him to speak first.

'I'm treating you to dinner, not asking you to take *me* out,' she answered boldly, watching him with quivering breathlessness, terrified of his refusal as his eyes touched for an exquisite moment on her breasts. She was dishevelled and tear-stained but quite engaging in her new-found bravado, he thought, and he had a sudden fancy to see her dressed in a sleek dinner gown, perhaps of silver lamé, if she was as clever as he thought she might be with clothes. A silver lady from the top of her riotously curling head to the tips of her tiny, high-heeled feet. A dress which clung, emphasising her daintily curving figure, low-cut and daring. And it was only one night after all and if he was bored, which was quite likely, then he would make some excuse to curtail the evening and deposit her on the steps of Woodall Park before going on to more exciting pleasures.

He was not bored. In fact he felt quite sorry that he was to sail on the first tide the next morning. She amused him with her charming, light-hearted chatter and her sparkling, quite radiant joy at being in his company. She was a novelty to him. She looked absolutely superb as she moved gracefully before him across the dining room of the Adelphi Hotel. It was as though she had read his mind that afternoon. Her gown was of silver tissue, the back so deep and plunging it was virtually non-existent and he wondered at Lady Woodall for allowing so young a girl to be seen in public in it. It revealed the satin smoothness of her back almost to the cleft of her buttocks. It was cut on the cross, clinging to her body as though it had been dampened as far as her knees, where it flared out, falling in a hundred narrow pleats to the floor. The shoulder straps were made of rhinestones sewn on to narrow bands, and she had scattered them in her hair, which glimmered like a jewel when she moved her head. It had been brushed into a tumble of wild curls, slightly and deliberately dishevelled, giving her the appearance of an enchanting and naughty child. Though she wore high-heeled silver shoes she barely came up to his shoulder, and they made a striking couple as they were seated ceremoniously at the best table in the dining room. An ethereal, fairy-like figure, shimmering and drifting beside his own dark-suited, dark-visaged strength, and he found he enjoyed the small sensation they caused as every male head in the room turned to stare and every female frowned.

Her eyes were bright with mischief as the head waiter supervised the opening of the champagne, 'Veuve Cliquot' naturally, that she had ordered by telephone, becoming a warm, transparent gold when she saw the admiration she had craved, in his.

'Well, Miss Woodall,' he whispered in her ear as the cork popped, 'you don't do things by halves, do you?'

The company were positively transfixed at the end of the evening when the well-known and delectable Maris Woodall, the 'silver girl' as he had thought of her, snapped her fingers for the bill, and when the head waiter brought it to the table were even more amazed when she paid it, whilst the gentleman she was with grinned hugely round the cigar she had just lit for him.

5

'You know Maris is infatuated with my Uncle Callum, don't you?'

Alex Woodall, crouching beneath the belly of his mare, turned in amazement to his cousin, and the tall animal whose front shoe he had been examining reared back skittishly, tossing her head and rolling her eyes. The reins by which he held her slipped almost from his gloved hand and Alex straightened up, cursing under his breath. He quietened the animal, rubbing her nose and murmuring her name before giving Rosie his astonished attention.

'What the hell does that mean? Infatuated? And how do you know? Has she told you? Has she been seeing him without our knowing? Good God, we only met him the other day.'

'I know all that, Alex, and I also know it's ridiculous, but believe me she seems to find him irresistible.'

'Good God, and does he find *her* irresistible as well, because if he does I'll kick his bloody teeth in.'

'Don't be silly, but you must admit he is very good-looking.'

'I know nothing of the sort, besides which he's old enough to be her father.'

'Hardly.'

'He's well over thirty.'

Rose sighed. 'I know that too but it makes no difference. He's given her absolutely no encouragement, to answer one of your questions. In fact, he doesn't seem to like her very much. When we were at grandmother's the other day he was quite rude to her, curt and sarcastic just as though she was a foolish young girl who had disregarded some good advice he had given her. Treated her as though she was no more than a kid . . .'

'Which she is.'

'She's only a year younger than you and a few months younger than me.'

'Years don't count, Rosie mine. Sometimes I feel as old as Methuselah when father goes on about what I should do with my life.' He groaned, pressing his face against the mare's neck. 'You know how he is. Charlie will inherit Woodall Park in the good old tradition of primogeniture but there is nothing to prevent me from becoming his agent, father says, and sharing the load and the rewards, one presumes. Or why don't I take up a position in the shipping office, he asks, or if I don't fancy that he knows a chap who is big in the City and could get me in there, or in merchant banking. Jesus, the possibilities are endless for a bright fellow like me, or so he tells me, but the trouble is, none of it appeals to me. I feel positively *ancient* when I consider the future with me stuck in some godawful office.'

'You like the land. Why don't you work on the estate?'

'Because I have no intention of taking orders from Charlie, that's why.'

His face set into the familiar expression of scowling truculence Rosie knew so well. The one which appeared whenever Charlie's name was mentioned. It was not that the brothers actively disliked one another, but from the first there had been between them what seemed like an inborn desire for combat. Over nothing at all, it appeared to those about them, even from their baby days they would knock one another to the ground, pummelling and biting and scratching like two kittens caught in the same basket. Of course, Alex would do the same with Christian or Freddie Winters, or indeed any of the young gentlemen with whom he, Charlie and Christian had gone to school, appearing to take a perverse pleasure in ruffling some perfectly good-natured chap's feathers and then, when he protested, brandishing his fists and begging for a fight. 'Tommy opposite' his mother called him, for he agreed with no one, always took a contrary view to those put forward by others, and would fight to the death to defend his own position or belief, right or wrong, snarling and snapping in that dark and frowning way he had had from being a young boy. If Charlie had a toy train he valued then it would not do until Alex had it from him, discarding it immediately when it was apparent Charlie no longer cared for it. Stubborn and hot-tempered in contrast to Charlie's ice-cold hostility, to have them together in the same room was often a sore trial to those who were in their company. There was a competitiveness between them which came from no one knew where, since they had been treated as equals all their lives, even Charlie as the older son and heir, being given no more of his parents' attention than their other two children.

Alex had ridden over that morning from Woodall for no particular reason except perhaps that he was comfortable with his cousin Rose, and it felt *natural* to be in her company, more so than with anyone he knew, even his own sister or mother. Though she and Christian, and the twins, Mairin and Ailis, spent most of their time at Woodall – Claudine, the eldest, having married the previous year – when Rosie rode over to

Beechwood to visit her Aunt Clare and Uncle Teddy, Alex was always restless, roaming about the estate as though her tranquillity, which had been known to calm him when nothing else could, was sorely missed and might be found in the pheasant wood, beyond the lake in the wild tangled coppice, or drifting through the park with the deer herd which lived and multiplied there.

Rosie's Aunt Clare was Ellen O'Shaughnessy's youngest child. She was twenty-seven years old now, and ten years ago at the age of seventeen she had considerably startled not only her own family but that of the Osbornes by announcing that she and Teddy Osborne, then a man of twenty-seven, were to be married. She had been in the habit of cycling over to Beechwood almost every day, especially in the school holidays, ostensibly to visit her sister Caitlin who was at the time housekeeper and nurse to Teddy Osborne, but it was Teddy who had drawn her and whom she had come to love, and marry him she would, she announced firmly in true O'Shaughnessy fashion. Teddy Osborne had been no more than a boy himself when he had lost both his legs on the battlefield of the Somme. He had, for a while, been in danger not only of losing his legs but his mind, and the child Clare, as she was then, had, with childlike trust and complete acceptance of him as he was, started the process which was to heal his mind, if not his mutilated body.

Ellen O'Shaughnessy was overwrought when she was told of her seventeen-year-old daughter's plans, saying it had taken the heart out of her when two of her other daughters, Mara and Caitlin, had married out of the true faith and now it was to happen again, and not only that but Clare was throwing her life away on a man who was . . . well . . . no man at all, poor soul. Legless and mindless, she had heard and why was Clare to live a life of . . . well . . . celibacy when there were a dozen good Catholic boys ready and willing to marry her and give her a dozen good Catholic children? But Ellen had lost too much to risk a life of emptiness without her 'baby', which would be bound to happen since the baby in question swore she would have Teddy Osborne with or without her mother's *or* the Church's blessing. Nobody ever knew the exact state of their physical relationship and no one cared, or dared to ask, but their marriage appeared to be a successful and happy one.

Caitlin and Jack Templeton, on the death of Jack's elder brother, had moved to Yorkshire where Jack took up the inheritance his brother's death had brought him, and Clare, with Lady Elizabeth Woodall's guidance, managed Beechwood Hall whilst her young, crippled husband supervised the running of the estate from the special chair Clare had had made for him. One day Christian would run his own estate since he was the son of Teddy's older brother, and it was the boy's duty to become his uncle's support and right-hand man, but it was Rosie who drove Teddy Osborne about the estate, pushed his chair, helped him with accounts, wrote letters when he was tired, delivered messages and generally became his 'legs' whenever she could.

This afternoon she had brought him round to the kennels in the pony-drawn dog-cart which, nearly eighteen years ago, his father had designed and had made for him when the hope had still been in him that his son, young Lieutenant Osborne, might lead some semblance of a normal life. The dog-cart had never been used until the young Clare O'Shaughnessy had got him into it. It carried his chair as well as himself, and on his 'good days', once his man had lifted him into it, he would often be seen alone, slapping the reins against the pony's rump as he urged it from the steps of the house to the stables or the kennel or in the direction of the home farm to pick up the fresh dairy produce with which the farm supplied the house.

'These pups are grand, Rosie. Have you seen them?' he called now as he wheeled himself from the kennels, the man in charge of them beside him. 'Charlie will be pleased. They will make a splendid addition to the pack when they are trained.'

'Yes, they're very sweet, Uncle Teddy,' Rose answered absent-mindedly, her eyes still on Alex's scowling face.

'Sweet! Good God, isn't it just like a female to call working dogs "sweet".' Her uncle turned, expertly manoeuvring his chair and impatiently waving away the hand with which the kennelman would have helped him. The two men disappeared round the corner of the building, and Rose and Alex were alone again.

'So what about Maris and my Uncle Callum?' she said at last.

'What about them?'

'He's going to hurt her badly, Alex.'

'If he has no interest in her then I fail to see how he can. And I don't know what we could do even so,' but his face softened, for after Rosie, Maris held a warm place in his life. Unlike Charlie she did not ignite his fighting spirit and inflame his restless nature. She was his sister, aggravating and trying his patience at times, but then sisters were like that. Even so he would hate to see her hurt herself on the sharp and sometimes dangerous rocks of love. Not that he knew anything about love. He had had his first woman at the age of

85

sixteen, he and Christian and Charlie for once in full accord and even cronies on the afternoon which they had spent in the hayloft at Yew Tree Farm in the company of the cowman's daughter, who was known to be obliging in that direction. Obliging she had been, amiably removing all her clothing and standing naked in a shaft of sunlight for the three boys to admire, before lying down and passively rendering the oldest service in the world for the price of a shilling apiece.

'Where is Maris now?' he asked suspiciously, soothing the restless mare.

'She's gone with Aunt Elizabeth to the shipping office in Water Street. There is a directors' meeting or something, and then they were to have lunch at the Adelphi. I have an idea, though, that Maris, quite casually of course, will try to inveigle Aunt Elizabeth into calling on grandmother.'

'In the hope that the bold Captain will be there?'

'Exactly, though she will be disappointed, for grandmother told me he had sailed this morning.'

'He seemed a nice enough chap, I suppose.'

'Well he is, but not the man for Maris.'

'What can we do? When one is in love one is blind, or so they say.' He grinned.

'Do they, Alex?' and so did she.

'Indeed they do, cousin,' and they both began to laugh softly, intimately, one might almost have said.

'Come on, let's go for a walk,' reaching for her hand. 'I'll put Bess in the stable and we'll take ourselves off. Perhaps have a dip in the stream like we used to as children. We haven't done that for ages.'

'I haven't got my costume with me.'

'Borrow one from Aunt Clare.'

'No, I . . . no, I can't . . .' and for some reason her

heart missed a beat, which was strange since after all this was only Alex who had been part of her life for as long as she could remember. He didn't notice her slight discomfiture, or if he did it meant nothing to him. His face was smiling down into hers, for though she was tall, he was taller by half a head. He lifted her hand, holding it between both of his.

'It didn't bother us then when we forgot our costumes, Rosie. Do you remember the eight of us escaping from Nanny that very hot summer, when was it? I'd be about ten, I suppose, but Claudine must have been fourteen or so. We were all as naked as the day we were born. We boys were poleaxed because Claudine actually had breasts like a real woman and didn't mind flaunting them. She was always the exhibitionist . . .'

His voice faltered, for it suddenly occurred to him that he should not be talking like this to his girl cousin. Not about breasts as one might to another chap. The trouble was Rosie was so . . . so . . . complete. So satisfactory and *satisfying* to be with. They were alike, she and him. They *matched* somehow. They did not have to talk sometimes, and at others they rambled on about every subject under the sun, which seemed to interest them both equally, and so he sometimes forgot that one must be more circumspect with a female than one would with, say, Charlie or Christian or Freddie.

'You will know what I mean,' he finished lamely, wanting to apologise for being so crass but loth to do so, perhaps making the whole thing worse by intimating that there had been something offensive in his words.

'I remember.' Rose did not look away in that silly, giggling, embarrassed manner which many girls adopted but smiled, and her vivid green eyes, just for a fleeting second, seemed to send him some message, but before he could decipher what it might be she turned lightly on her heel and strode towards the path at the back of the stables which led to the house. 'I can't, though,' she called over her shoulder. 'I promised Aunt Clare I would help her to pack and get all Uncle Teddy's things together for tomorrow. You know what an exercise it is whenever he goes anywhere. They're off to Yorkshire for two weeks to stay with Aunt Caitlin and Uncle Jack. I thought you knew.'

'I suppose I did.' The strange moment had gone and Alex crouched down again to lift the mare's foot which she had been favouring, resuming his study of her shoe. 'Can I help in any way?' he continued half-heartedly, making no attempt to rise and follow her. His face had fallen into the scowling irritability which was becoming more pronounced each month that passed. A clenched set to the jaw and a down-drooping of the mouth which said quite clearly that he was not at peace with himself, with her, with his world.

Rose turned to wave and seeing it, she hesitated. Again her heart moved in her breast, with pity, she supposed, for really Alex seemed so unhappy at times. Such a *misfit*, if that was the word, amongst the rest of his contemporaries. She had been tempted to take him up on his invitation to go for a dip in the stream since it *was* hot, and besides, her Aunt Clare did not really need her for another half an hour or so. She had felt the need to appease him, to keep that whimsical smile of his for a little while longer, but somehow the idea of herself and Alex swimming alone, and naked, did not seem quite as *easy* as once it had been. The image of them removing their clothing and diving casually into the deep, cold waters of the stream beneath the overhanging and secluded trees at the back of Beechwood was not . . . well, she didn't even know what the word was she was searching for, she only knew her mind shied away from the picture.

'Tell you what,' she said, surprising herself as well as Alex, who stood up expectantly.

'What?' beginning to smile again.

'When we get back to Woodall I wouldn't mind a row in the dinghy. Just for half an hour. It will be cool on the lake.'

'You're on. I'll ride straight home and meet you in the boat-house.'

Alex rowed. Or at least he made a show of it, but the boat was allowed to drift more than be propelled. It moved like a silent shadow on the mirror surface of the water taking its reflection with it, the only sound on the warm, still air the musical fall of drops from the blades and the soft swish of the boat as it moved through the water. The lake narrowed dramatically almost to a point at its far end, running into what was known as Old Wood. The trees were thickly clustered together, forming a motionless green canopy above the dinghy, and it was like gliding into a dappled tunnel. Here and there the wood thinned a little, revealing patches of sunlit clearing, and Alex and Rose could see groups of deer browsing silently, exquisitely dainty, the rich red tint of their coats slashed against the green foliage of the undergrowth. The bucks were growing their new antlers and they were short, not yet the magnificent spread they would achieve. The does moved slowly, heavy with the fawns they would drop any day now. Some had already done so, but they were well hidden in the bounteous vegetation which grew deep within the wood.

Rose leaned back in the stern of the boat, her head

89

against the battered old cushions which had been tossed in as they left the boat-house. She trailed her fingers through the water, then withdrew them quickly.

'Cold, Rosie?' Alex asked, almost in a whisper, not wanting to break the enchantment.

'Mmm, icy.'

The boat touched the bank of the lake, and as it did so a small fleet of swans drifted slowly from beneath the overhang of a willow tree. They were not at all uneasy, so peacefully had Alex and Rose approached, mysteriously beautiful, slipping through what had taken on the texture of a sun-embroidered dream.

They sat for a long time, not speaking, reluctant to shatter the tranquillity and the completeness of what they had found with one another on this magical afternoon. It was as though they were the only two people in the world, for no human sound could be heard, nor human presence felt. Alex rested his forearms on the oars, turning his head slowly this way and that, studying the beauty all around him, his face for once relaxed and calm. His eyes, surrounded by the impossibly long, gold-tipped lashes over which he had been unmercifully teased since he was a child, were unfocused and soft, and he breathed slowly as though even his lungs had slackened their pace.

He sighed then, deeply.

'What . . . ?' Rose asked for she had been watching him intently from beneath her own half-lowered lids.

'I was just thinking what a lucky bastard Charlie is.'

'Yes, I know.'

'You always know what I mean, don't you, Rosie?' His voice was no more than a murmur, soft and sad.

'It . . . seems so,' for when had Rose Osborne not

been attuned to every nuance of every mood Alex Woodall fell into. There was barely eight months between them, Alex being the older, and since they were children they had somehow gravitated towards one another, often playing apart from the rest of the children. They were alike in so many ways. They both needed to be alone at times, apart or together, which was difficult when eight assorted brothers, sisters, cousins, all lived close in one nursery. The only time the two of them were parted was when Rose's mother, Alex's dashing Aunt Mara, who was married to the baronet, swept in from New York or Paris or London, from Biarritz or Monte Carlo, and gathered her children about her, carrying them off to Beechwood House for a week or two. Her extensive luggage would be crammed with presents for them all, beautifully made dolls or fire-engines, dresses for the girls – often too small – silk shirts for Christian – completely unsuitable – but before long her aristocratic husband would need to be off again, and she with him. Her children and their Nanny would be 'dropped off' like so many parcels at Woodall Park, with kisses and hugs all round and exhortations to be good girls and a good boy until 'Mama' as she liked to be called, now she was titled, came home again, 'which will not be long, my darlings', but was often three, four or even six months.

Claudine, Rose's eldest sister, was by then growing into a young lady and liked nothing better than to be with her Aunt Elizabeth, and the social position the Woodalls enjoyed. The twins had one another and Christian, well, Christian was Christian with thoughts of nothing but his O'Shaughnessy connections and how best he could become part of them, and the absence of his mother did not appear to concern him. But Rose had felt abandoned, like a small puppy with whom her mother played enthusiastically for a while and then pushed carelessly to one side when the novelty wore off. She was the youngest and had never known her father, who had died at the 'Lancashire Landing' on the shores of Gallipoli eight months before she was born. She was more in need, therefore, of her mother's presence and love than the others, and though Aunt Elizabeth was kindness itself there were *eight* of them to share it.

But there had always been Alex, and though the invisible bond which drew them together was never spoken of, indeed they were scarcely aware of it, so natural was it to them both, it was a powerful force in their existence.

'I love this place,' Alex went on, his face dreaming towards the woods, the lake at his back and the house beyond the lake hidden from him. He had been born there, had lived all his life within its protective walls and, though he would never have voiced the thought, even to himself, he would like to die there.

'I know, Alex.'

'You always know what I mean,' he said for the second time.

'Well, you have just said it, Alex . . .'

'You understand what I'm telling you, Rosie?'

'That you wish you had been born first.'

'And so you know why I can't work for Charlie.'

'It would be . . . difficult.'

'It would be impossible. And yet I am finding it very hard to bring myself to leave.'

Rosie's heart gave a great bound in her chest and this time she felt its pain. It was not pity for Alex either, but an actual pain at the thought of him leaving. She sat up slowly and in the small dinghy their faces were no more than six inches apart.

'*Leave!* You're not leaving, Alex?' There was entreaty in her voice.

He smiled, all the truculence and stubborn ill-humour transformed into a joyous charm, since this was Rosie who asked nothing of him but what he was.

'You'd miss me then, Rosie?'

'You know I would, Alex. We've been . . . well, together . . . friends for so long I would hate it if you went away. Oh, I know Maris and I are close but you and I . . .'

'Yes, Rosie, you and I . . . ?' and into his clear hazel eyes there came a strange and not at all familiar expression. One she had not seen before. The flecks of brown in their pale green depths darkened and his pupils grew enormous. He drew back a little as though to get her face into focus, as though he was too close to see her properly, then he raised his hand and tenderly placed it against her cheek.

'Rosie . . . ?' he said wonderingly, a question in his voice and in his expression. Her heart moved again in a great wallowing lurch but she could not move away, indeed she had no wish to.

'Alex . . . I . . .'

'What is it, Rosie? You can tell me. We're friends. You just said so . . .' and still his hand was at her cheek and she knew an incredible urge to turn her mouth into its hard palm. She drew back abruptly and the small boat rocked and at once the seedling of new emotion was trampled on, as she had meant it to be. She had no idea what had happened. She only knew that it was not . . . not her and Alex. For a moment they had been strangers looking at one another with strangers' eyes,

93

different, dangerous . . . *lovely*, her wilful heart whispered . . . but not her and Alex.

'Let's have a walk, shall we?' she said lightly.

'But I thought you didn't want to walk,' Alex's voice was testy again and he turned impatiently to retrieve an oar which was in danger of going into the water, '. . . and for God's sake stop moving about . . . no, don't stand up, you fool, you'll have us over . . .'

'I'm only going to step out on to the bank, Alex, and there is no need to shout. I can hear you quite plainly.'

'Dear Lord, women really are the bloody end.' Alex's face had darkened ominously and his mouth was set in a straight, grim line. 'Could you not for once make up your mind what in hell's name you *do* want . . .' which was monumentally unfair since of all the women he *did* know Rosie was the least one to shilly-shally. His own words appalled him, even as he said them. This was Rosie, his loved and loving cousin, and he was bawling at her as if she was . . . well, Christian or Charlie, who always *needed* to be bawled at.

'Sit down,' he said more gently, '. . . and let me ship the oars and then, if you have the time we'll walk back. We can leave the dinghy here and come back for it later.'

'I'm not sure that I want to now.'

'Rosie . . . come on, don't let's quarrel, not you and me . . .' His voice was pleading, and there it was again, that sudden rush of warmth towards him which had nothing at all to do with Rose and Alex. It was *them* again, the two people who had sat in the dinghy and looked at one another with completely different eyes.

Alex stood up ready to step ashore and the boat did a crazy roll to one side, nearly throwing them both out.

'Jump,' he shouted, catching her hand, beginning to

laugh, holding her steady as they flung themselves sideways among the duckweed and crowfoot which grew thickly along the side of the water. The dinghy moved jerkily away, floating out in the direction from which they had come, and one oar fell into the water. They managed to grab a handful of the reeds which grew among the duckweed, pulling themselves up on to the grassy bank beneath the trees, wet from the knees down but shrieking with laughter now, their strange quarrel forgotten. They lay on their backs, their fingers still entwined until the laughter subsided and the satisfying harmony which had existed between them returned. They were quiet then, staring up at the ceiling of motionless leaves high above their heads.

'It's been a . . . a good afternoon. We should escape more often,' which is what it seemed to Alex, an escape.

'Escape?'

'Yes, and come over here on our own.' His thumb rubbed the base of hers in a friendly way and she sighed with pleasure.

'It's certainly peaceful.'

'It is now,' and they laughed again, softly this time, 'but then you always have that effect on me, Rosie, did you know that?'

'I'm the only one who will put up with your bad temper.'

'Have I a bad temper, Rosie?' His voice was lazy.

'You know you have.'

'I suppose so. Why do you think that is when mother and father are so . . . amiable?'

'God knows, I don't.'

'Neither do I.'

There was another long and pleasant silence.

'I suppose we had better be getting back,' Rose said at last, making no attempt to rise.

'I suppose so,' and neither did Alex.

Again they did not speak for several minutes.

Then, 'I don't want to go away, Rosie, but I must. There is nothing for me here, you do see that, don't you?'

As he spoke Rose's hand jerked in his and her drowsy eyes flew wide open.

'Oh no . . . no Alex, you can't . . . you can't . . .'

'Why not, Rosie? Why do you want me to stay here?' He rolled over on to his stomach, looking down into her strained face, but before she could answer there was a crash among the undergrowth, an explosion of sound as two dogs, a golden retriever and a black labrador, flung themselves upon Alex's back. Behind them was a man on horseback whom neither Rose nor Alex had heard approach across the wood's soft-carpeted floor.

The dogs, who were only young, were ecstatic, leaping and diving over the supine couple, whom they evidently knew, and it was not until the man had called them savagely to heel that Rose and Alex managed to sit up.

'I might have known it was your bloody animals,' Alex snarled. 'Can't you keep them under control, for God's sake?'

'I might ask you the same question, Alex, only about yourself.' Charles Woodall was evidently provoked beyond reason, and for a bewildered moment neither Rose nor Alex could understand what it was that had caused it, or even what he meant. He was looking at them, or at least at Alex, as though he would like nothing better than to take the riding whip he held against his bay's neck to his brother's amazed face. His gaze was chilled, like ice on a pond, and his stiff-backed hauteur spoke of a great endeavour to hold himself in check, as was the custom of his class.

'What in hell's name are you talking about?' Alex's voice was as astonished as the expression on his face. He sat up, giving a hand to Rose, pulling her up until they stood side by side. She was flushed and lovely. There was grass in her hair and they both had a distinctly dishevelled look about them. They were barefoot, for they had removed their wet shoes and stockings, and her hand was still held closely in his.

'You know exactly what I mean. I've seen you enough times in the same pursuit of . . . what you are about now.'

Alex slowly drew up his tall frame, and the smooth brown skin of his face became dangerously suffused with blood. His eyes had narrowed in sudden under-standing and the violent intention in them was plain to see. A clear signal to his brother that he had gone too far, but at the same time, in them and in Rose's was the recognition of what Charlie, in his own rage, had revealed to them.

'You had better take that back, brother, unless you mean to insult Rosie. In which case you had best step down from that horse and we'll decide here and now exactly what you do mean.'

'Alex . . .'

'Stay out of this, Rosie . . .' but he turned to her for a moment, putting her carefully to one side and it was plain to see now in both their faces. The concern for one another, the need to protect on his part and to comfort on hers, to avert distress or hurt, to give only the sweetness of the emotion which had come on them so swiftly.

'No, Alex. Charlie meant no insult, did you, Charlie?'

'Not to you, Rosie, but I'll not have this . . . this . . .' He could evidently think of no slur scurrilous enough to describe his brother, at least not one he could voice in front of a lady. '. . . I'll not have him treating you like some parlourmaid . . .'

'He wasn't, Charlie . . .'

'Get down off that horse, Charlie.' Alex's voice was silky, but he had begun to circle the animal menacingly, half-crouched, his fists clenching and unclenching like some wrestler ready to dash in at the first opportunity and annihilate his opponent. He was quite dazed with his fury. Even Rose had ceased to exist as the need grew to drag his brother from his horse, to beat him to a bloody pulp, perhaps tear out his eyes first before grinding his sneering, well-bred face into the mud beside the lake.

'With pleasure . . .' and Charlie, who was just as incensed but who held it to him in the cold, ice-cold manner of the English upper class dealing with an insubordinate, as he had been taught at the well-known public school he had attended, prepared to step down and do exactly the same to Alex.

'NO . . . NO . . . NO . . .' Rosie's scream stilled the murmur of wildlife which abounded in the woodland. Deeper in among the trees the deer froze, not a muscle moving between them, and several grey squirrels ran for their lives up the trunk of a wide oak. A cock pheasant which had been about to cross the path which led through the undergrowth stood as if turned to stone.

The two young men, blind and deaf in their passion,

one deathly cold, the other fever-hot, had begun to circle one another. The primeval instinct in each to guard, or claim what was theirs, or what they would *have* as theirs, had carried them into a vacuum in which there was nothing but hatred. All the years they had fought and snarled and glowered at one another, each wanting what the other had, had been nothing, two ungrown cubs playing at battles. Now they were men, and though neither had known it until this very hour, they were ready to tear one another to pieces over the girl who screamed and trembled at their backs.

'Alex . . . Charlie . . . don't . . .' and not knowing what else to do as they charged at one another, their fists raised, she simply stepped between them. It was Alex's fist which blacked her eye and Charlie's which split her lip, but the fight was over before it had begun.

They both fell to their knees, appalled and begging her forgiveness as she lolled between them. They looked frantically at one another in the way they had done as boys when they had committed some dreadful crime together for which they knew they would be punished. How were they to explain it? How were they to break the news of it to their parents, smooth over mother and father's wrath, and if it had not been so horrifying, and, but for the agony of her cut mouth, Rose might have laughed out loud. They were two small boys again, almost in tears so deep was their remorse, begging her to sit up . . . no, lie down . . . hold the dampened handkerchief to her bloodied nose . . . Jesus . . . the swelling . . . what would they tell mother, her Aunt? . . . could she ever forgive them? . . . here, lean on . . . hold my hand . . . and on and on and on.

'Let me put you on Ruby and take you home. You can ride before me, if you are able. I won't let you fall.'

'It's the only way, Rosie. Let Charlie lift you up. Dear God, that eye. It's going to be every shade of the rainbow by morning . . . Christ . . .'

'There, don't cry, sweetheart, put your foot in the stirrup and let me . . . see, Alex, go round to the other side and help her . . . there's a good chap.'

'Right, Charlie, and watch that . . . be careful . . .'

'I will . . . there . . .' and only moments before they had been ready to kill one another over her, was Rose's last thought as she slipped mercifully into a state of semi-consciousness. If it had not been for Charlie's strong arms about her as they rode slowly towards Woodall, she would have fallen to the ground.

Alex ran beside them, ready to catch her if she did.

6

'And where are you off to, Maris Woodall? This is the third night in a row you have got yourself all gussied up like a dog's dinner and driven off into the night in a taxi, with that smug smile on your face, just as though you were the cat who had swallowed not only its own saucer of milk but every other moggy's in the kitchen.'

'Really, Alex! Dogs, cats? Your conversation leaves a lot to be desired. Can you not ask a simple question without peppering it with references to the animal world? I am *not* gussied up like a dog's dinner, as you so colourfully put it, nor am I smug. I am merely happy that I am to be accompanied by the most attractive, charming and . . .'

'Dear God, can we be speaking of Callum O'Shaughnessy? That paragon of excellence whose feet barely touch the ground, so miraculous and numerous are his virtues. Who is as honourable and fine as the highest in the land and yet as humble as the lowest. A saint, in fact, whom we lesser mortals would be well advised to emulate . . .'

'Oh stop it, Alex.' Maris's voice was good-natured and her smile complacent, since nothing anyone said could steal the joy, the quiet glow of rapture, which had been with her now for the past three months. Indeed, since that first night when she and Callum had dined together at the Adelphi. That magical night when it had all begun. The fairy-tale love she had dreamed of and which, though Callum had not yet said the words, would lead, she knew, to the fulfilment of every dream she had had of him since they had met. She could scarcely believe it sometimes, that he, a worldly and sophisticated man, should see qualities in her which he found admirable, and she would wake in the night, terrified that it would all stop, that he would no longer telephone her when he was in port, that he would tire of her. He enchanted her, held her captive with his aggressive masculine beauty, the vigour of his curling hair, the tall, lean strength of him, his broad, powerful shoulders under her hand when they danced, his startling eyes gleaming in sardonic amusement between heavy black lashes. His teeth were whiter, his smile more wickedly humorous than that of any man she had known, and she loved him utterly, devastatingly, waiting with fast-beating heart and breathless anticipation for the day when he would tell her he felt the same. Dare she allow herself to believe it possible? She could not judge, for her eyes were too dazzled, and yet why should he seek her out if what was in her heart was not also in his? She lived only for the days he spent in Liverpool. Evenings dining at the Adelphi or dancing to Billy Cotton's Band at the Rialto Ballroom. Or perhaps at the Grafton to the melodious rhythm of Joe Loss and his Orchestra, followed by intimate little suppers at a smart restaurant, of which Callum seemed to know more than a few. He took her to see the irrepressible Harry Roy and his show at the Empire, and The Rotunda, or the 'Roundy' as it was called locally, the best music hall in Britain, or so it was said in Liverpool, where the funniest comedians played to packed houses every night. Ted Ray, Bud Flanagan, Issy Bonn, Lucan and McShane. It was as lively outside the theatre as it was inside, with the neighbouring shops ablaze with lights until midnight and the cheerful, good-natured 'Mary-Ellens' in their shawls selling fruit and flowers from large baskets outside its doors.

They went to the races at Aintree where Maris shouted herself hoarse, urging on the lovely animal on which she had put a bet. A sleek chestnut mare named 'Love of my Life' which, of course, was why she had chosen it, and when it won, leaping over the last fence like a bird in the sky, winning her the splendid sum of three guineas, she was like a child in her dazzled excitement.

When Callum was in port they saw all the new films, going to the Trocadero in Camden Street to sit through *The Lives of a Bengal Lancer*, starring the diffident Gary Cooper, and to listen to the splendid organist Sydney Gustard at the 'Wonder Wurlitzer', which rose in a magical way from the bowels of the earth at the front of the cinema.

She was lost in the blissful and blessed state into which Callum O'Shaughnessy had cast her that first day on the ferry boat from Birkenhead to Liverpool, bewitched and quite disbelieving that this was happening to her. That this fascinating and – at the moment – good-humoured man should find her worthwhile, and when he held her hand, or kissed her lightly on the cheek when they parted she saw nothing strange in its almost avuncular chasteness. He was a gentleman treating a lady – herself – as a gentleman should, and if their 'romance' moved at a slower pace than she would have liked, was that not a sign that his respect for her would not allow him to take liberties with a girl, a woman he intended . . . surely . . . to marry?

Her parents did not like it. They had no objection

to Captain O'Shaughnessy himself, they said. He was the son of one of her mother's oldest friends, and as far as they were aware there was nothing they could call . . . well . . . disreputable about him. Indeed, he was a man to be admired in the way he had 'got on', a valued employee of the Hemingway Shipping Line, a fine master of his ship and, again as far as they knew, an honest and honourable man.

It was his age, her father said unhappily, looking into his daughter's mutinous face, and his . . . his worldly experience, which was far too much for her to handle, though he did not voice this last sentiment. A man of his own generation, it seemed to Harry Woodall, not his daughter's, but she would let no one stand in her way, declaring passionately that if her mother and father could give her no positive proof that he was a man unworthy to escort their daughter about the city when he was in port, then she would continue to see him. She was nineteen now and able to judge for herself what kind of man was suitable, if that was the word, and Callum would hardly be likely to . . . to dishonour the daughter of Sir Harry and Lady Woodall, now would he, when their families were so close in one way or another.

Sir Harry and his wife were forced to agree. They were both of a gentle and peace-loving nature, and their often self-willed and stubborn children were sometimes beyond their understanding. *They* had never been like that, they told one another, but then the world had been so different when they were young, before the war which had come to blow away the great and varied taboos which had existed. The pace of time had been slower, a different rhythm to the one the young marched to today. A dreaming era as they looked back on it, with all the time in the world to stand and enjoy the passing days, without this frantic search for enjoyment their children, especially Maris, seemed to find necessary.

She and Callum liked one another's company, Maris continued triumphantly, her pride in the fact putting roses in her cheeks and stars in the clear golden-brown depths of her eyes, and her parents, in view of who Callum O'Shaughnessy was, and since they knew of nothing dishonourable about him, could only let her have her way and pray to God that, if they did, it would fizzle out like all the rest of her 'romances'.

The Adelphi Restaurant was packed that night. Callum drew deeply on his cigar, the smoke from it drifting lazily about his smoothly brushed head, watching Maris as she ate her way through her third chocolate meringue, devouring the sweetmeat as though she had eaten nothing for days. They had dined on Italian consommé, salmon à la genevese, a speciality of the chef who worked – if such a plebeian word could be used to describe his artful genius – in the kitchen of the splendid Adelphi Hotel; galantine of poulet in aspic jelly, a dozen delicious salads, and a choice of a dozen delicious desserts to follow, of which she had chosen the chocolate meringue.

Her enjoyment of food, and the enormous amounts she could eat without putting on an ounce of surplus weight, never ceased to amaze him, though it further highlighted the difference in their ages, he was inclined to think. The young, and she was certainly youthful despite the way she dressed, could do such things, indeed *enjoyed* doing them, like children, but still it amused him to see her wade through course after course, talking, as she ate, in that ingenuously

105

engaging, one could almost call it, scatter-brained, way she had.

'For a young lady of such dainty proportions you have a remarkably robust appetite.' His eyes narrowed and one dark eyebrow rose in amusement.

'I was hungry.'

'So it would seem.'

'I've eaten nothing all day. I've been too busy.'

'Doing what?' blowing smoke into the already smoke-laden air of the restaurant.

'Getting ready for tonight.'

'All day! What in hell's name do you women do to yourselves that takes all day, for God's sake? Though I must admit to finding the end result very pleasant.'

She preened, not only at the compliment but at the word 'woman', though she was not awfully sure she cared for the way he was smiling at her as he said it. He was like that. He said the nicest things but with a certain curl to his mouth which she was not quite sure how to decipher. As if it gave him immense enjoyment to . . . to tease her, which he did quite often. Not hurtful, not malicious, but with a wicked smile, a glint in his eye which she could not interpret. He was a complex, deep-layered man who allowed no one, man or woman, to see the hidden fathoms of himself. A man who enjoyed life, the life he led which had given him so many good things, a man who was inclined to let others do as they please as long as they did not interfere with Callum O'Shaughnessy. A man who denied himself nothing he could take without hurt to others, and as he watched the lovely young girl it had pleased him for the past three months to squire about Liverpool when he was in port, he wondered for the umpteenth time why he had done it. Not for her sexual favours, that was certain, since he was not fool enough to interfere with the innocent and inexperienced body of the daughter not only of one of Liverpool's most respected gentlemen, a baronet and a hero of the Great War, but of the woman who was one of his mother's especial favourites. When he was not down at the docks or with Maris, he was often to be found in the company of the rather more mature woman he had found so agreeable for over twelve months now, married to a gentleman of wealth who, being much older than herself and no longer concerned with pleasures of the flesh, looked the other way when she was pleasuring *hers*, providing she was discreet. An attractive woman of great wit, but who asked no more of Callum than he did of her.

So why did he bother himself with Maris Woodall, he often asked himself, and the answer was still hazed in mystery. He admired her tenacity and resolve. She had the knack of making him shout with laughter at her sheer audacity, as she had on their first night out together. She was honest and kept her word, which was somewhat rare in the women he had previously known. She had paid every penny of the cost of repairing his MG, arguing hotly with him when he would have taken it upon himself, demanding that he keep *his* share of the bargain they had struck, which was to allow her to make amends in the only way she could. He had taken a fancy to her, he supposed, enjoying *her* immense enjoyment of every single moment of the hours they spent together. She was quite lovely in a delicate, spun-glass way, like a diaphanous bit of lace, dainty and fragile as gossamer with her silver-streaked tawny hair and her liquid golden eyes, the fine ivory and rose of her. Slender as a willow, a fluff of swansdown to be blown this way or that by any chance breeze, or so it seemed, but nevertheless she was strong and brave of spirit. She sometimes gave the impression that she was shy, her step light and wary, reminding him of the does he had once seen in the parkland of her home. Not cautious exactly, but with the air of one who expects great and exciting dangers ahead but is prepared just the same to meet them head-on. She had a lovely proud tilt to her head which he liked and despite the smallness of her stature, an upright carriage which spoke of her inherited pedigree. She was warm, good-humoured, and he had found her company very pleasant.

So, it had amused him to take her about with him when he was home. He could not understand his motive in doing so, but it was really time to put a stop to it before she began to expect more of him than he was prepared to give. She would be a fine woman one day when she grew up a little more, and though he had seen what was in her shining eyes and melting glances and knew what it meant, she was very young and would soon get over it. She would meet some eligible sprig of the gentry, Lord this or Sir that, marry and settle down to the life these 'good' families enjoyed. Have children and keep going the line of breeding which was so important to the likes of the Woodalls. Yes, tonight must be their last night, regretful as it was. He was to sail to Buenos Aires tomorrow, carrying a cargo of coal, which would take about a month, and bringing back one of tinned corned beef among other things. He would be away almost three months, long enough for this pretty child, who was now sipping a glass of wine with what he knew she thought to be sophisticated unconcern, to take up with some more suitable and younger man than himself.

'You're very beautiful, Maris,' he heard himself say, for so she was, and he could have bitten his tongue when the colour flowed delightfully beneath her fine white skin, and her eyes narrowed into luminous, gold-filled pools.

'So are you,' she breathed, leaning into the lamp-light. The soft folds of her gown, which was like a sheath of ivory about her, so pale it was difficult to distinguish where the fabric ended and her flesh began, fell forward as she moved, and he could see the tops of her breasts and even the upper circle of the pale, coffee-coloured aureole of her nipples. He felt an intense and devastating desire to put out an enquiring finger and draw down the silk even further to reveal those sweet little breasts completely, to contemplate at his leisure the hard pink centre of them, perhaps feel them in the palm of his hand, but leaning back, conscious of his quickening breath and the sudden discomfort of his own suddenly swollen manhood, he drew on his cigar deeply and sensuously, giving the impression he had nothing on his mind but his enjoyment of it.

'You're not supposed to say that, my pet, but I must admit I have known a woman, or even two, who have admired my . . . charms.' He grinned wickedly.

It had the desired effect, doing just what he intended in letting her know that though he was here with her tonight he was a man who had known many women in his chequered and *long* past.

'I'm sure of that but . . .'

'But what?'

She had wanted to say 'but that is over now, surely, now that you have met me and we are . . . or at least I am, so much in love I can't see beyond you', but some

109

small prick of light in his eyes, she was not exactly certain what it was, told her she must be careful. Or was it her own female instinct that knew that though it had been her audacity which had started their relationship, her audacity in asking him to dinner at the Adelphi, she could not push him along any faster than he was prepared to go? He was a man of his time and would not take kindly to her assuming *his* role, which was that of the pursuer with herself as the pursued. But she wished he would pursue her with more *ardour*. She had seen quite plainly where his eyes had gone when she leaned forward, and was experienced enough, *woman* enough, to have sensed the sudden tension in him. Freddie Winters had looked like that when she had teased him with her pert breasts, and if she could only entice Callum to put a hand on her, *anywhere*, and in private, she was sure she could persuade him to more than those virtuous kisses he sometimes bestowed on her cheek.

'But you are still a good-looking man,' she finished lamely.

'Thank you, Maris, and now, if you have finished your wine I think I had better get you home.'

'I am not a ten-year-old child, Callum.'

'I am well aware of that, Maris,' smiling round his cigar. 'You would not be here with me now if you were. I have children up to my ears every time I visit my mother at Edge Lane, and it often seems to me that my brothers, with the exception of Michael, and my three eldest sisters are intent on populating the country all on their own.'

'Don't you like children, then?'

'Do you know, I'm not awfully sure. Those I have known have been members of my own family and I

110

suppose one feels a duty to have a certain affection for them.'

'What a funny thing to say.'

'You have none in your family so you cannot know what I mean, my pet. Wait until your brothers start to sire the next generation and you are inundated with nephews and nieces before you make judgments, though I doubt they will be as prolific as mine.'

'Would you not . . . care for children of your own, Callum?'

He hesitated for a fraction of a second, sensing where this might be leading, but it was such a small hesitation she did not notice it.

'I have no idea, Maris, and honestly I'm not sure I even want to try. I am probably too old now to change my ways, and children would certainly do that.'

She was very quiet in the taxi to Woodall. He had motored over in his MG, leaving it in the drive whilst he shared a polite sherry with Elizabeth and Harry Woodall, and when Maris appeared they had driven to town in the taxi he had ordered.

He had paid the driver of the taxi, which was moving off, turning to Maris to say goodbye to her. It would be final this time, though he had no intention of telling her so, which he knew was cowardly but, he thought, easier on them both. She had moved across to his little motor car and was climbing into it, a shimmering ghostly figure in the dense and pitchy black of the autumn night.

'Just a minute, young lady,' he called, smiling, doing his best to sound elderly and far too set in his ways to take part in any shenanigans she might have in mind, but his masculine memory was suddenly plagued by the recollection of those delightful little breasts, and his feet, with a will of their own which took no account of age or the proprieties, walked him across the gravel to his car. The hood was up and he could hardly see her in the darkness.

'Come on, Maris, I really must go,' he said half-heartedly, even to his own ears.

'Just one cigarette, Callum, then I'll go in.'

'Just one, then.'

'Of course.'

He lit it for her and one for himself and they sat in a thick, tense silence whilst they smoked them.

She began to shiver. It was almost the end of October and the nights were cold with a hint of frost in them. She wore nothing but the fine, silky gown and he could not see her cold, he told himself as he put an arm about her and pulled her to him.

'You *are* cold, aren't you?' he murmured, remembering the times as a youth and a young man he had said the very same words for the sole purpose of getting his strong, warming arms about the female companion of the time.

'Yes, oh yes, Callum,' and he was not certain that the answer she gave him was in response to the question he had asked. She lifted her face, no more than a shimmer of white in the darkness, and her mouth found his waiting for it. She was really only an English schoolgirl with no more knowledge of the erotic arts than a toddling child, but she had it in her to entice and arouse him, and he knew that unless he moved away from her, now, at once, got out of the car and escorted her to the door, then he would fall into the soft pit of hot delight she seemed to be offering, *was* offering, and be suffocated by it. Suffocate! What an insane idea, but that was how he felt. She would suffocate him with her own desire and what had been light and, yes, strangely tender would change, had *already* changed since he desired her too.

Her lips opened, flower-like beneath his own, her warm, wine-scented, wine-tasting breath entering his mouth. His senses, his *sense* fled away, try as he could to keep them leashed, and his breathing quickened. Dear God . . . what was he doing . . . kissing her and loving it, loving the feel of her in his arms, knowing exactly what he wanted, what *she* wanted, and when his free hand cupped her face it was to hold it steady against his shoulder as though he was afraid she might move away.

Her body began to writhe, and he heard her moan out loud as he touched her. She clutched at him, not only with frantic hands but with all of her body, wrapping its length about him, and she moaned again, in welcome this time as his hand, at last, *at last* pushed aside the slipping folds of her bodice and took her breasts, first one and then the other, in his hard sailor's hand. They were small and sweet and high, like ripe, firm apples thrusting themselves into his palm, moving in a way which rubbed the nipples until they were hard and distended.

His man's body had wilfully taken over from his careful, sensible man's mind, and he freed her for a moment to pull the bodice of her gown down to her waist, lifting and holding her up against him while he tasted the sweet young flesh which was being offered so eagerly to him. Her dress slipped further down about her hips as her naked breasts pressed against his face, and he took her nipples between his lips, one at a time, his hands holding her beneath her armpits. He smoothed his mouth against her skin, biting and licking, down

113

from her breasts and across her flat stomach until it came to the thick golden bush of her pubic hair, which had miraculously become freed from her garments. She was astride him now, her legs parted and kneeling on either side of him, her slim buttocks pressed cruelly against the steering wheel, and his mind, which had once known exactly how to deal with such acrobatic problems, cast about feverishly on how to have her lying down, or standing up, in fact in any damned position which would allow him to take her, to pierce her body in an act of simple unrestrained passion. He must have her . . . must . . . Oh Jesus . . .

He fought it, that return to sanity which told him he was about to seriously damage not only this young girl but his own life. His maleness hated his reason, begging him to ignore it. To go ahead and take the small, bird-like frailty of her, since it was all there was of importance in the world at this precise moment. She was squirming in his grasp and he knew it was in the same pursuit as himself. The tiny part of him which was detached from the physical, the lusty, the flesh, was amazed and delighted at the strength and determination of her slender body to accommodate him and herself in the cramped space which was available to them in the small sports car, and had they been anywhere else it was certain it would have happened. Had they had an inch or two more room he would have had her, and he was to thank God, later, that it was not obtainable.

'Maris . . . Maris . . .'

'Oh Callum . . . please . . . don't stop . . . don't . . .' and her mouth sucked desperately at his as though, deep down where her female instincts were formed she knew, *knew*, that this would be her only chance. Once they had made love, 'gone the whole way' as it was coyly phrased by her girl friends, there would be no turning back. She was not deliberately trying to trap him. She loved him deeply and sincerely and with all her young heart, and she wanted him to make love to her, to give herself, *herself*; to belong to this complete and intricate man who had swept her from girl to woman.

But it was not going to happen. He was drawing away, leaving her, no longer taking part in the frantic, despairing progression of their bodies towards fulfilment, resisting her hot mouth and the loveliness of her breasts which she tried to press eagerly into his hands. He had become perfectly still. He was gentle and kind as he extricated her from the steering wheel; as he found her undergarments and shoes, handing them to her wordlessly; as he put her back into her lovely gown, kissing her lightly on the cheek and the forehead, smoothing back her hair from her fevered face.

'Maris, I'm sorry, please forgive me. It was inexcusable . . .' he even went so far as to say, as though at the offence he might have given her. 'I should not have . . . gone as far as I did. I'm sorry. It was unpardonable of me, but you are very . . . sweet. I know that is no excuse . . .'

'*Sweet* . . . Dear God in heaven!'

'Yes, darling . . .' sorry at once that he had used the endearment which had slipped out of its own accord.

'I am not your darling, am I, Callum?'

'Maris, it's time you went in now. I'm sure your parents know that the taxi came half an hour ago.'

'You didn't think of that when you had me naked across your lap just now.'

'Maris!' For some reason he was shocked. A young girl to speak like that; then his heart was strangely

115

moved, for that was all she was. A young girl who had been hurt by what she saw as his rejection of her.

'Maris, go in now, there's a good girl.' He did his best to be patient, kind. He did not want to hurt her any more than he had, but the truth was that if she didn't go soon he might be tempted to start again. He could still feel the hardness of her nipples in the palm of his hand, and his mouth remembered the taste and texture of her fine flesh. There was that certain musky smell that came from her, the smell of a woman aroused, which called to the male – *denied* – sexuality in himself, and by God, if he didn't get away soon he would not be answerable for the action his hard, eager, *man's* body might soon take. *It* took no account of the youth and innocence of the girl beside him. *It* knew exactly what it wanted to do. It was only his civilised mind which was holding him back, which was telling him that it would be monstrous to make love to this child and then walk away from her for good.

'Do you not care for me at all, then?' she asked quietly.

'Maris, you must not . . . you are a beautiful young girl and how could any man *not* be . . . moved . . . honoured even . . .'

He was babbling, he knew he was, wanting to tell her the truth, wanting not to hurt her with it. The truth which was, quite simply, that for the past three months he had amused himself with her and that he was ashamed. How could he say it? How could he strike the blow to her woman's pride and self-respect, to her youthful belief in herself and her own luminous quality, which was quite unique? How could he tell her that he did not love her and that this was the last time they would meet? How was he to end it? Dear God, how?

116

She did it for him. Without speaking, she opened the door of the car and got out, and with simple dignity which moved him in its restraint, she walked up the steps of the house and went inside.

7

The disturbance began at half-past one on a bitter cold night in January. More like November than January the day had been, Wilson the butler was heard to say to Mabel Preston, housekeeper to the Woodalls, and he had seen a few so he should know. Seventy-five if he was a day, and butler to Sir Charles Woodall who had died in 1912, and Mabel Preston had been no more than a housemaid then. Aye, a raw, dank day which wormed its way inside your very bones, into your head, so that even your teeth were on edge with it, and into your lungs so that it hurt to breathe.

Sir Harry had been bad all week. He had never left the constant warmth of the room he and Lady Woodall shared, but even so he had been cough, cough, cough every minute of the day and night, so that it sounded as though the shredded lungs he had brought back from France could barely stand another paroxysm and would tear themselves apart.

'Poor old soul,' said Elsie, the only one of the original housemaids left now at Woodall, what with the war luring all the girls in service into munition factories where they had earned double the wage, and them never coming back. In the old days Wilson, or the old housekeeper who had then served the Woodall family, would have severely rebuked such a disrespectful remark but neither Wilson nor Mrs Preston had the heart. It was true, he was a poor old soul and him such a lovely man to be suffering so.

The disturbance was at Master Alex's bedroom door, and it was his frantic mother who made it.

'Telephone for the doctor, Alex . . . tell him to hurry . . .' Wilson heard her say. Wilson had been in service when a butler *was* a butler, the sort who were never in their beds when a member of the family were out of theirs, and he felt it keenly that he was not as young as he was. Then he had always been there in case of need since it was his job to be, but his arthritis was playing him up something dreadful these days. Spirit willing, flesh weak, they said, and it was true but it was hard to change the habits of a lifetime.

'What can I do for you, m'lady?' His voice was calm and kind, and at once she turned to him as her son galloped down the stairs to the telephone. They had been saying for years that an extension should be put in Sir Harry's and his wife's room, but like so many things which seemed to have no urgency it had never been done.

'Mrs Preston . . . ?'

'I'll fetch her, m'lady . . . and perhaps some tea?'

'Thank you, Wilson. I would be grateful . . .' hurrying back to the room along the landing from where no sound of coughing came now, only the most appalling gasp and wheeze with a long painful silence between each drawing-in of breath.

Doors were opening along the wide landing. Maris and Rose appeared, then Charles, who was in a state of some confusion since he had got into his bed no more than half an hour ago and he had been in the deepest sleep. He had visited the Grafton Rooms with Freddie Winters to see the floor show, which had included the excruciatingly funny Barry Lupino, and afterwards they had danced to the music of Roy Fox

119

and his Band. He and Freddie had treated a couple of young ladies to a few 'gin and its', and the four of them had crammed themselves into Charles's dashing little Alvis sports car and roared off into the night for what they hoped would be – at least he and Freddie did – a 'bit of fun'. His head still throbbed and he thought he would never get it clear again as he ran towards the door of his parents' upstairs sitting room. Rose and Maris followed, hesitating on the threshold.

The curtains were drawn and the lamps were lit. There was a good fire burning, and Sir Harry's chair, which had been empty for a week, was pulled up before it as though at any moment he would come out of the bedroom and pick up his book, which lay upon the side table. Elizabeth Woodall could be heard speaking softly to her husband through the open doorway which led into the bedroom. Her voice was no more than a low murmur, and over it was the painful rasping sound of air struggling to penetrate the damaged lungs of Sir Harry Woodall. His son, his daughter and his niece crossed the sitting room, hovering in the doorway, and sensing them there he turned his head a little and lifted his hand, gesturing to them to come closer.

'I'm having . . . one . . . of . . . my turns . . .' he wheezed, trying to make light of it, for he had seen the distress in the eyes of all three. No more than a hoarse whisper really, coming up through layer upon layer of the pain he suffered, but even now he did his best to allay their fear. His face was the colour of clay, clammy with sweat, and about his mouth was a dangerous-looking white line. There were deep furrows slashed in his cheeks, only his eyes, as deep and warm a brown as those of his daughter, remaining of his young good looks.

'Don't talk, darling,' his wife begged him, doing her best to hide the anguish in her face and in her voice lest she alarm him, but it was hard since she could not bear to contemplate life without this beloved man. 'The doctor will be here in a moment. Alex has gone to telephone . . .'

Her younger son slipped quietly into the room as she spoke, his eyes going at once to the man in the centre of the enormous canopied bed. His father was propped into a sitting position to ease his breathing, supported by half a dozen pillows, but it seemed to be of no help. He was fighting it, fighting death which had come for him at last, just as he had fought it in the trenches when the gas drifted about him, but he was weak now, no longer the young man he had been then, and though it had waited patiently for sixteen years it seemed it had come to claim him now.

The doctor strode in and cleared the room of everyone but his patient's wife, and in the sitting room Alex and Charlie, Rose and Maris waited, not looking at one another lest they see something they did not care for, the two men moving from table to window to fireplace, fiddling with their mother's ornaments, poking the fire, twitching the curtains and staring out into the darkness as though dawn might bring about a miracle.

'Is he going to die?' Maris quavered, a child again suddenly. She was huddled on her mother's chaise-longue, and at once Rose went to her and took her in her arms. She did not speak.

Mrs Preston came in quietly and murmured something, her face drawn and sad. Beyond her on the landing Wilson hovered, and at his back was Elsie and a couple of young kitchen-maids. Cook was there at the top of the stairs, since she could remember when she

121

had made almond macaroons for Master Harry, as he had been then. In the kitchen there would be a tenant or two and old Hodge, the gardener, for word had got round that Sir Harry was badly.

The door from the bedroom opened and the doctor came out. He shut it gently behind him. He bowed his head for a moment as though he too would mourn the passing of such a fine man.

'He will not last the night, I'm sorry. His heart has been considerably weakened by the constant . . . well, you will know what I mean. I can do nothing more. He wants to see you. A minute no more, please, and only one at a time. And no tears . . .' looking sharply at Maris whose face had already begun to crumple, '. . . not for his sake, though it would distress him enormously, but for your mother's. Cry in private if you please.'

Rosie was the first to go in. She knelt by her uncle's bed. Her uncle, who was in all but blood her father. She did no more than hold his hand to her face, kissing the back of it, her expression calm but infinitely sad. Her Aunt had moved away, waiting for her children to say their farewells, before clutching the last few precious hours which were all she had left with her husband of twenty-one years. It was too soon, too soon, for he was no more than forty-five years old, Rose knew, and they should have had another twenty at least, but their life together could be counted only in hours now, perhaps even minutes.

Rose got to her feet, and leaned over the bed to kiss the cheek and then the brow of Sir Harry Woodall. She loved him, and looking into his fading eyes her expression told him so, and she was rewarded with a sudden last warming of his. She did not weep, none of them did until they withdrew from his room for the last time, leaving him and his wife to their own parting.

Maris began to lose control as Charlie, his arm about her shoulders, led her from the upstairs sitting room and along the landing towards the staircase. She had done as the doctor ordered. She had held her father's dear hand, which was by then too feeble to return her young grip. She had put her head on his frail shoulder, screaming silently at herself to hold on for a moment longer before looking up to smile at him.

'Good girl,' he had whispered, but she had not wept. She had been conscious of her mother's impatience to have her gone, and had resented it, for this was her father and she loved him. To have Alex and Charlie and Rose gone so that Elizabeth and Harry Woodall might have what was left of their time together alone.

Mrs Preston and Elsie, the kitchen-maids and the cook they served, were all weeping as the four young people moved down the stairs, and so was Wilson, for he had seen the passing now of two generations of Woodalls. Old Sir Charles, his two sons Hugh and Tim, brothers to the present baronet, and now Sir Harry.

They entered the drawing room, Alex and Charlie, Maris and Rose, where the fire had been rebuilt and Wilson had left a pot of hot coffee and a decanter of brandy, since it was evident that the latter might be needed. Indeed, the doctor was already sipping a glass as he waited for that last melancholy call which would come soon.

This was Elizabeth Woodall's room. She had made it as it was after the end of the war when the last of the maimed, the mutilated, the pain-racked young soldiers had been removed to a more permanent place.

123

Woodall Park had for two years been a military hospital, and it was in this room that the surgical patients had suffered the torments of having their ghastly wounds dressed twice a day, screaming their agony.

But there was no ghost of them here now. Only a beauty and peace as gracious as Elizabeth herself. Quiet good taste and elegance. A thickly piled carpet in a deep shade of apricot thirty feet square, and around that was a vast width of shining polished oak flooring. It was a big room with comfortable chairs and sofas in the palest of green velvet, and floor-length silk curtains in shades of cream and deep apricot. Low tables, waxed and burnished by Elsie to a high gloss, on which books and newspapers were carelessly scattered, for this was a family room where absolute tidiness was not demanded. Lamps had been lit, half a dozen of them, and the flames from the fire licked up the enormous stone chimney. A copper tub stood on the hearth filled with applewood logs, and the doctor reached out to throw a couple to the back of the fire as the family entered the room.

They were hesitant and nervous, all four of them, as though he was the host and they guests, ready to jump at the slightest unexpected movement, for they were all deep in shock. Frail as he had been, Harry Woodall had been the raft to which they had all clung at one time or another, and the realisation that he had gone, or nearly so, was more than they could take in.

'Come and sit down,' the doctor told them kindly, and when they did so he asked each one of them if they would like a sip of brandy, even the two girls. They all refused.

'Now,' he went on, 'what about Mairin and Ailis?'

since they all needed to be made to face up to their coming loss, and the only way to achieve it was to bring them to their senses with the knowledge of what there was to be done.

'What . . . ?' Alex was on the sofa with Rose, who had begun to cling to him quite desperately, and he turned in the doctor's direction.

'Your cousins, Alex.'

'Oh . . . they are with friends in . . . where is it, Rosie?'

'Cornwall.'

'Cornwall, sir.'

'I see. Well, perhaps it would be as well if a telegram was sent . . .'

'Yes . . .'

'And perhaps . . .'

Maris stood up and moved towards the window in a blind fashion, her hands out before her as though she was searching for something. They watched her for a second or two, then the doctor spoke soothingly as one might to a wayward child.

'Come and sit down, Damaris, and I'll pour you a cup of . . .'

'I DON'T WANT TO SIT DOWN OR A CUP OF COFFEE! I WANT MY FATHER!'

She began to shake then, turning in the direction of the door which Charlie had closed behind them. Her voice had risen in growing hysteria, and the tears she had forced herself to contain in her father's room, streamed across her face.

'I didn't weep, Doctor Mitchell, really I didn't. Not then, but I must see him again. I want to tell him how much I love him . . .'

'He knows, Damaris.'

125

'But I didn't tell him and now . . .'

'You cannot go back, child. Your mother needs to be with him . . .'

'But he is my father . . .'

'He is her husband. They . . . love one another and must spend what time there is left . . . alone. Can you not understand that?'

And suddenly Maris Woodall could. She had been introduced to it a mere six months ago, and though what she felt in the deeply wounded depths of her was known to no one, not even dear Rosie, she certainly knew how it felt to lose . . . yes, to lose someone, even if he had not been hers to have in the first place. Callum O'Shaughnessy's sardonically smiling face, which she had tried so desperately hard to forget since nothing could come of her . . . what was it? . . . her foolish attachment to him, printed itself for a moment against her closed, tear-washed eyelids.

She had seen him only once since their last evening together in October and it had been just the same. A formless yearning towards him, a terrible longing for something it seemed he could not give her since to him she was so obviously just another folly-struck young girl. He had been away, of course. To Canada, so his mother said, to the West Indies and on other sea trips, taking and bringing back cargoes on the *SS Alexandrina Rose*. He had been sun-tanned and handsome, filling the ballroom, the very hotel, with that abundance of masculine aggression and arrogance which fascinated her so much and which made all the other gentlemen pale shadows beside him. It had been at the Adelphi when she and Freddie Winters and another couple had gone to dance the evening away to the music of Geraldo and his Gaucho Tango Orchestra. He had been with a woman, fashionable, lovely and sophisticated, and at least ten years older than Maris. They had been laughing intimately, their hands touching lightly on the table, the promise between them very evident. He and the woman had danced together, very expertly and very close, and when he had caught sight of Maris he had nodded coolly. No more. She had wanted to get up from the table where she had been seated with Freddie and Angela and Richard and run from the ballroom. To hide and weep and nurse her aching heart, but she had laughed and talked too loudly and drunk too much and made a fool of herself, in her own eyes at least, though Freddie had said he had never seen her so . . . what was the stupid word he had used . . . oh yes, so vibrant.

The doctor was looking at her sympathetically, with compassion even. She was such a little bit of a thing, with her silvery cloud of curls in a tangle about her head and her enormous brown eyes drowned in her tears. Like all men he thought her to be frail and vulnerable and in need of protection, and her grief had made her even more defenceless. She wore a pretty housecoat affair in some flimsy material which appeared to consist of nothing but lace and satin, which drifted about her as she moved, sliding a little off one shoulder since she had put it on so hastily. Her feet were bare, small with the toenails painted a delicate shell-pink. She really was quite delightful and he almost wished, elderly as he was, that she would turn to him for comfort in place of her brother.

A frantic knocking at the door brought the rest of them to their feet and Wilson, his old face seamed and drooping with his own sorrow, burst through it, calling for the doctor in a hoarse voice.

It was barely ten minutes later when the doctor returned.

'Sir Charles, I deeply regret to inform you that your father has just passed away. I am very sorry.'

Sir Charles! It was then that they knew, that they *really knew* that the man they had all loved was no longer with them, and how were they to accept his loss and come to terms with the new baronet, at least *one* of them thought?

The ground was as hard as iron when they put Sir Harry Woodall in it. Another bitter cold day, but this time a real January day, stiff with hoar frost and white all over the churchyard and headstones and the bare, skeletal trees. Pretty really, his daughter thought, as she studied the way the frost had formed in thick ridges down one side of each tree trunk. The grasses in the fields which surrounded the church, and in the ditches and hedge-rows lining the lanes along which the mourners had come, were stiff and spiked with it, and there was a winter mist hanging about at waist-level towards the woods. A hazed orange sun hung low in the sky, which was the palest oyster pink; and the black of mourning, worn by every person for miles around in the vicinity of Woodall Park and who, or so it seemed, were all at the graveside, was stark and dramatic.

Maris stood dry-eyed beside her mother, her hand in hers, and behind them were the tall, stern sons of the dead baronet: Sir Charles Woodall, the heir, and his younger brother Alexander, pale-faced and grim-mouthed but both, as they had been taught to be, con-trolled and courteous and particularly protective of their still lovely mother. Calm they all were, in direct contrast to Ellen O'Shaughnessy, who cried as though

128

her heart would break, though she had scarcely known the dead man. It was in her nature to display her grief or her joy, and today she wept for Lady Woodall who, though she made no show of it, Ellen knew was suffering.

They were all about Ellen, the O'Shaughnessys. Her son Michael, who had lost his own wife in tragic circumstances and who, perhaps because of it, had been especially kind to Lady Woodall whom he barely knew, holding her hand and murmuring something to her which nobody could quite catch. It seemed to comfort her, Ellen thought, for she smiled briefly.

Callum was on the other side of his mother, his attendance at the committal a mark of respect for the dead man, as was the presence of several other captains who were in port, masters of Hemingway's ships, since shares in the Hemingway and Osborne concerns had come to the Woodall family through Lady Woodall, and now of course it all belonged to the new baronet. It had been no surprise to those who knew them that Serena and Sean Osborne, Johnny to his family and friends, and parents of both Elizabeth and Teddy, the only two remaining after the death of James, had left a great deal of their holdings to Elizabeth when it seemed that Teddy Osborne, uncle to the heir, would never be capable of managing his own affairs. A wealthy woman, Lady Woodall, though of course the estate of Beechwood belonged to her nephew, Christian, who, at his age, should now have settled down to managing it for himself.

Three of Ellen's daughters stood about her. Mara, Lady Hamilton as she was now, with her aristocratic husband who had both *flown* home from Paris, would you believe? Ellen certainly couldn't when she was told, but here she was and appearing to be none the worse for it, having landed only that morning at the new Liverpool Airport at Speke, officially opened two years ago. Michael had told his mother all about it at the time, and of his own visits there to see the thrilling flying exhibition which took place over the Speke farmland. He had even offered to take her to see it herself, but she had declined. Sir Alan Cobham, the great British aviator had brought what was known as a 'Giant Moth' to the city and had gone so far as to give the Lord Mayor a 'ride' in it, and after that, of course, everyone had wanted a 'go'. Ordinary men in the street, including her own son who was as enthusiastic about aeroplanes as he was about motor cars, had 'gone up', may the Holy Mother bless and keep him safe. 'Joy-riding' it was called, but for the life of her Ellen could see no joy in taking to the air like a bird, which after all had the wings to do it. No, as she told Michael at the time, the solid earth beneath her feet was good enough for her.

Mara looked as smart as paint in her Paris gown and cartwheel hat, black, naturally, and Ellen marvelled at how she had got the thing inside one of those tiny aeroplanes Ellen had seen above the rooftops of Liverpool. Mara looked no more than thirty though she was, by Ellen's standards, a middle-aged woman of almost forty. Standing slightly behind her, as was only proper to her position, were three of her four daughters, Rose, Mairin and Ailis. Claudine, the eldest, had not put in an appearance, for at six months gone in her first pregnancy it was felt she might be excused. It was well known Mara deplored the coming event since she had no wish to be a grandmother at thirty-nine, or at *any* age for that matter.

Caitlin Templeton and her husband Jack had motored over from Yorkshire with their only son, Guy, who was fourteen and the spitting image of old Mick, the pet. Clare Osborne, standing behind the wheelchair of her husband Teddy, worried to death, Ellen could see, in case he caught cold on this bitter day, fussing a little with his rug and his scarf.

Only Christian was missing, off on some serious Irish mission of his own, his family could only surmise, and strangely, his cousin Cliona, Michael's girl, and Ellen would have something to say to the pair of them when they turned up, the spalpeens. Christian she could understand since he hated the gentry, especially the English gentry, and had scarcely a good word for Sir Harry despite living in his home for the best part of his young life, but Cliona was different, and where she had got to was a mystery and a worry. Mind, Ellen had seen her and Christian in a huddle a time or two, and if he was stuffing the girl's head with the nonsense in which he believed Ellen would knock him sideways, so she would.

They were all there then, bar those mentioned, Woodalls, Osbornes, Hemingways and O'Shaughnessys, cousins and second cousins, nephews and nieces, and dozens upon dozens of people who had worked for Sir Harry, on his estate, on his farms, in the Hemingway's shipping office and on the docks unloading his ships. Servants in his home and standing among them, for Lady Woodall had insisted that there must be no class distinction at the laying to rest of her husband, were the men and women of authority and prestige of Liverpool, and even a sprinkling of nobility. Titled folk who had respected Sir Harry Woodall and rubbed shoulders now with the common men who had

131

cause to love him, for he had been that rare thing, a true and gentle man. Woodall tenants who had been pensioned off and had seen old Sir Charles to his last resting place stood in utter silence as Sir Harry, his son, was put in his.

They all motored back to Woodall, the still January air biting into the flesh of their faces as they got out of their vehicles before the broad steps of the house. There was an enormous fire burning in the wide hall and in every room in the house which had a fireplace, since many of the mourners were to stay the night. Lady Woodall and her son, Sir Charles, were at the door to greet them, taking each hand which was put out to them with perfect courtesy and control. Beyond them was Alexander and his sister Damaris, ready to be polite to those who presented themselves. There was wine and superbly prepared snacks on silver trays for the mourners to nibble on, and for an hour or so there was polite conversation, hushed and respectful.

'I'll have to be away now, Mammy,' Callum O'Shaughnessy murmured in his mother's ear. 'I've some business to see to at the shipping office, cargo manifestoes, stuff like that,' for though the Hemingway concerns had closed for the hour when Sir Harry was laid to rest, business must go on, despite the sadness of his death. 'With me being off to New York on the first tide tomorrow I have a lot to see to today. Michael will take you home, won't you, Michael?'

'I will so, lad. You get off an' we'll be seeing you later.'

'Don't wait for me, Mammy. I might not be able to get over until tomorrow but I'll drop in to say goodbye.'

'Don't worry, son. Caitlin and Jack are to come home with me so I'll be havin' a lovely wee talk with them,' for even a melancholy occasion such as this one brought its compensations in the gathering of her family around her, which was grand.

Callum began the task of looking for his overcoat, which the butler had taken from him and whisked away somewhere as he came in. He wondered where the hell he had put it, cursing at the same time since a certain lady was expecting him to call. Several doors which led off the main hall proved to be fruitless, turning out to be cupboards filled with what looked like junk to him, or small rooms which the servants appeared to use in their work. A long corridor off the wide front hall was just as unproductive, containing nothing but two sprawling dogs, a black labrador and a golden retriever, who both lifted their heads and wagged their tails amiably before resuming their doze. Had the butler put the guests' coats in a bedroom, he wondered, and where the hell was he just when he was needed, since Callum was under the impression that manservants were always on hand, quiet, efficient, unobtrusive. Not that he had any personal knowledge of them. Mind, this one . . . Wilson, he had heard her ladyship call him . . . was as old as the hills and had appeared to be particularly distressed, which he supposed was natural if he had been with the Woodalls for years as it seemed he had.

He tried the last door on the landing, and was half-way across the room before he realised that it was occupied and that the person who was sitting on the floor in the corner, her back to the wall, was Maris Woodall. She was weeping. Her knees were drawn up to her chin, her arms wrapped around them and her head was bowed in deepest desolation. As he turned away, ready to tiptoe out again, for the last thing he wanted was to

133

be a comforter to the grief-stricken daughter of the man they had just buried, a draught took the door and it banged to behind him. She lifted her head at once and despite the irritation she had caused him in the past, and his own wish to avoid it and her, a great wave of pity washed over him. She looked so forlorn, so small and helpless, a child who had suffered a great tragedy and could not find the means or strength to bear it. He had never seen such tears, even amongst his own kinswomen who could cry, or laugh, with the best of them. They burst from her eyes in a wild fountain of grief, silent and still, just a drowning of Maris Woodall's face and bright spirit in appalling pain.

'Maris . . . Dear God, I am so sorry . . . I didn't mean to intrude . . .' He didn't know what to say in the face of such agony. She sat like a statue, a hollow statue, and without thinking he moved towards her, not knowing what he was to do but aware that he couldn't just murmur a polite apology and leave.

'Will I fetch . . . your mother or . . . Rose . . .' since he knew she and his niece were close. 'Perhaps a drink . . . ?'

'I'll never see him again,' she moaned and before he knew what he was doing he sat down on the floor beside her, and realising with some strange perception that words would not comfort her, he put his arms about her shoulders and drew her to him. She sank against his chest, a small animal seeking the comfort of another, and her face continued to flow with her tears, staining his shirt front as she burrowed against him.

'I loved him so much,' he heard her mumble.

'I know you did.'

'. . . and now, I don't know what I shall do without him . . .'

134

'You will manage . . . in time, really you will,' patting her shoulder, fumbling in his pocket for his clean handkerchief which she took, then drawing her even closer to him as she soundly blew her nose. Her hair, which had remained so demurely beneath her close-fitting black hat and veil during the funeral service, was now released, and it sprang about her small head in a tumbled mass of silvery, honey-streaked curls. It was soft and sweet-smelling beneath his chin, like silk and yet wildly springing so that he felt the urge to smooth it back from her flushed, tear-stained face. The moisture which had run so freely from her eyes flowed into her hair, and wet tendrils clung to his chin. He brushed them gently aside with one finger, then lifted her chin to smile down at her. She had quietened now, but her arms still clung round him, her hands gripping each other at his back.

'Are you all right now?' He smiled as one would to a child whom one has soothed.

'Better, thanks.' Her eyes, as she looked up at him, were clear and unswollen, the lashes still dripping and heavy with her tears. She blinked slowly several times and he found himself watching them, quite fascinated by the movement. They had darkened so that they seemed almost black, and her parted lips were peach-pink, moist and swollen where she had bitten them in her paroxysm of grief.

'Thank you, Callum,' she said, and her sweet breath touched his mouth. There was no intention on his part to do more than offer comfort and on hers to thankfully receive it. She meant to stand up, smooth down her skirt, perhaps apply a little powder to her nose, thank him quietly for his kindness and proceed down the stairs to her mother's drawing room, where the mourners

135

were gathered. He would follow her politely, perhaps ask for her assistance in finding his overcoat. When it was located he would put it on, shake her hand, avoiding any personal involvement, for the circumstances of their last meeting had been . . . well, to say the least, awkward and embarrassing.

He had made no attempt to contact her during the past three months, and apart from the evening when he had dined at the Adelphi where she had been with friends, had not seen her. He admitted to a sneaking feeling of guilt, a small prickle of shame, for he had taken her up on a whim, as he would any woman to whom he was attracted, then, when their relationship had run its course as he had decided it had, he had simply stopped seeing her. He had done it a dozen times in the past with no harm to himself or his partner, but then they had all been older women who knew the way things were done.

Maris Woodall had been different. He could not say exactly that he had *worried* about it since his life at sea did not allow for dwelling on his life in port, but he had felt a certain relief when he had seen her, bright and laughing and very evidently enjoying herself with her 'top drawer' friends in the Adelphi restaurant. She had got over her infatuation as he had told himself she would, with no damage to her self-esteem or confidence, and was oblivious to anyone including himself as she hung round the neck of the gentrified sprig who accompanied her.

So now he must stand up and leave, smiling and wishing her well, telling her again how sorry he was about her father's death. Polite, friendly, regretful, sympathetic, but somehow, though he meant to be all these things and certainly meant to take his leave at the earliest possible moment, his mouth hovered above hers, tasting her warm breath. It was just as he remembered it – why was it he remembered it so clearly – he asked himself perplexedly, long and tender, the bottom lip full, the corners turned up; and with no thought for the consequences, with no thought for who they were, what had happened the last time they met and what had taken place barely an hour ago in the churchyard, he bent his head and placed his mouth on hers. He did not stop to ask himself why, and if he had he would no doubt have told himself that the gesture was merely a continuation of the condolence one would give a hurting human being. 'There, kiss it better', and the hurt would be alleviated. But Maris's arms reached about his neck, drawing him down to her, and his tight- ened, crushing her, taking her sweetness, smelling her fragrance, feeling the texture of her fine skin. His big brown hand, strong, hard-palmed, cupped her face then moved down to caress her throat, dipping into the neck of her black mourning outfit to find her breasts. The outfit was a two-piece of fine wool, long-sleeved, the blouse softly draped and fastened from neck to waist with tiny satin-covered buttons. The skirt, which had slid up her thighs, revealed the tops of her black silk stockings and two inches of satin white flesh. They drew him, those black and white thighs, and his hand moved to the flesh which was exposed by her slipping skirt and the wide-legged cami-knickers she wore. It was white and smooth beneath his brown hand until his fingers reached the dense bush of her pubic hair and they found the secret silkiness of her womanhood.

This time there was no holding back. They were oblivious to the world outside the bedroom, and after- wards, when the fever had gone, Callum was to marvel at his own disregard, not only of the decencies, the *respect* which should be shown a lady, meaning Lady Woodall, in her own home on the day of her husband's funeral, but at his own male weakness in allowing her daughter's body to captivate his. He was not a man unused to women. He had made love to one only the night before, but Maris Woodall's fine, perfectly proportioned body clouded his brain, his mind, his normally lucid good sense, and this time it swept him on towards disaster. His male eagerness to have this dainty child pinned to the floor by his own thrusting masculinity was too much for him and he could not wait, let alone stop. It was as though he was a boy again with his first woman. She was like an eel in his hands, her flesh slippery with her own sweat, vibrant, with a bursting depth of passion and fever which once again astounded him, as mad for him as he was for her. He could hardly hold her as she offered to his hands and mouth any part of her writhing body he cared to sample, and he was only too willing to oblige. She was alive and trembling, her spirit soaring, changing, frantic as he laid her roughly on her back and without ceremony pierced her at once, cruelly, and with no thought of withdrawal, the rhythmic strokes of his own pounding need too urgent, too headlong to stop.

She moaned, deep in her throat, and the colour flooded to her face, a lovely flush of rose which deepened as her pleasure grew; then in an explosion of high cries which he silenced with his mouth she came to orgasm with him.

It was several minutes before either of them moved, and then it was in the stiff and jerky manner of marionettes. She was the first to speak.

'My . . . could you pass my . . .' indicating the silken wisp of her cami-knickers which he had flung savagely to the floor in the turmoil of their passion, and which were now just beyond her reach. He passed them to her, looking away politely as she slipped them discreetly up her legs, then arranged her dishevelled clothing neatly about herself. He adjusted his own clothing, standing up and turning towards the window as he did so to stare sightlessly beyond the glass to the white-spun magic of the winter landscape.

'I don't quite know what to say.' His voice was harsh, angry, even to his own ears, *trapped*. He was himself again now and quite appalled at what had happened.

'Why should we say anything now?'

Now! He turned and she was smiling, her face soft with that look a woman achieves when she has been well loved, well satisfied, ready to purr and curl up in dreaming contemplation of what has just happened to her.

'You are not . . . offended?' *Offended!* Indeed she was not offended, just the opposite he would have said, as though today she had been given a present of priceless worth, one she had not expected but would not part with for the world. Still he stumbled on. 'I mean . . . today of all days . . . it was inexcusable of me to take advantage . . .'

'You did not take advantage of me, Callum. I was not . . . unwilling.'

She bobbed her head shyly, the smart young woman her friends knew her as, one of the 'bright young things' of Liverpool, glamorous, stylish and completely up to the minute, gone in a soft flush of something he was frightened to even name.

'But surely . . . I mean . . .' He was flustered. *Him*,

flustered at his age, but Jesus Christ, he had just taken her virginity on the floor of her bedroom whilst downstairs her family and their friends, including his own mother, were deep in mourning for her father.

So why was she not wringing her hands and weeping, and why in God's name did he not get out of here before one of her brothers, a servant, or worse still the girl's poor bereft mother walked in on them?

'I'm sorry, Maris. I really must apologise for my boorish behaviour.' God's holy nightgown, what was he babbling about? He sounded like the hero in one of those penny dreadfuls shop girls liked to read, but she was smiling at him with bloody great stars in her eyes and . . . oh Jesus . . . oh Jesus . . . surely she didn't think . . . ? Christ almighty . . . she did . . . *she did*! Because he had . . . because they had . . . she thought . . .

'Don't say you're sorry, Callum, please. I know . . . well, today of all days . . .' Her eyes filled with tears again but she dashed them away with the back of her hand. '. . . I'm not sorry so please, don't tell me you are . . .'

'Well . . .' doing his best to be polite, to be calm, to be as unconcerned as she appeared to be.

'I knew, you see.'

'Knew?'

'That it would be . . . as it was.' Another shy nod of the head. *Sweet Jesus!*

'But I think you had better go now, don't you?' There was a glint of surprising mischief in her eyes, eyes which were still drugged in the aftermath of their lovemaking. 'Perhaps it might be best if you slipped down the back stairs,' she continued, looking about her with an air of drawing him into an intimate conspiracy, a gesture which suggested there was something between them which no one else was to share.

'Will you be all right?' he murmured, only too eager to slip down the back stairs and be gone. Sod his overcoat. Sweet God, he didn't know how it had happened. Despite his own good sense and good intention last year he had fallen into the oldest trap in the world, that made by his own maleness which should have known better, *which should have bloody well known better*, the trap set by her instinctive female body which had known only too well what it was about.

Reaching up on tip-toe she kissed him softly and with infinite tenderness. 'Oh yes, I will now.'

8

Despite the thirty percent of the Liverpool adult population which was unemployed that month, the city raised £30,000 towards the King's Jubilee Fund. It was helped by the Council's donation of £10,000, no doubt of that, for they were determined that for a few days at least the depression which grew, not only in Liverpool but in many other parts of the country, should be lifted.

It was May 6th, 1935, warm and sunny, and the tramcars did brisk business with sixpenny 'all day' travel tickets, and on the one day alone a record 920,000 passengers were reported to have taken advantage of it, moving from one grand sight to another as the celebrations came alive.

The pubs were open from eleven-thirty in the morning until ten-thirty at night, which was tantamount to giving every Tom, Dick and Harry a licence to get 'legless', which excuse none of them needed in Ellen's opinion, especially not their Eileen's Denny, who required no encouragement whatsoever to fall over with a 'bevvy' in his fist.

A thousand local schoolchildren took part – not their Maeve this time, more's the pity, Ellen was heard to remark – in the city's pageant, the theme of which was 'Silver Trumpets' and was to illustrate in mime, song and dance the major events of the King's reign. Souvenir jigsaw puzzles were distributed, and there were tea parties on every street and in every school yard.

Ellen helped to make the decorations for the area of Edge Lane in which Number Eleven was situated, coloured paper, silver and gold, and the bunting, flags and balloons which were hung from lamp post to lamp post. Mountains of sandwiches she turned out of her crowded kitchen, cakes and jellies and biscuits, with Matty declaring if she saw another jam sponge she'd put her head in the gas oven, so she would, which would be hard seeing they didn't have one!

At night the bonfires were lit, manned by boy scouts, those of a conscientious nature, at Mossley Hill, Birkenhead, Formby, Wallesey and New Brighton and many other places, lighting the sky all along the coast, and the one which was built on Snaefell in the Isle of Man was so enormous its glow could be seen in Blackpool, a distance of some forty-five miles.

The parks were floodlit and so were many buildings, and Liverpool's illuminated tramcar with a dance band on its upper deck moved along the main routes of the city, followed by countless young people who neither knew nor cared that their King and Queen had reigned for twenty-five years. They were having a good time and that was all that concerned them. And if the tramcar left them behind, every window of every house was open, with a wireless set turned on, those who were fortunate enough to have one, and the strains of Henry Hall's and Jack Payne's music floated out on the night for them to dance to.

Mass unemployment had hung like a constant shadow over English life since the last decade, and not even the Silver Jubilee of King George the Fifth and Queen Mary could chase it away for long. The Unemployment Act of 1934 was meant to resolve, if not unemployment itself, at least the way the benefit was administered, or so said Neville Chamberlain, the man who had inspired it. The Unemployment Assistance Board was born, but the new national rates of benefit, far from being increased when they were introduced in January in this year of the King's Jubilee, were less than they had been, particularly in the most depressed areas. There had been public demonstrations, and with a general election expected surely it might be expedient for the governing bodies to reconsider the rates of 'assistance', as it was now to be called.

To obtain benefit under the old National Insurance scheme, which had been introduced in 1911, it had been necessary for each claimant to attend a labour exchange every day. A man with a wife and three children might then receive twenty-three shillings a week, if he was insured. Many were not, and were forced to turn to the Poor Law or to private charities. Meagre as it was, the benefit was again reduced, due to the financial crisis, and those men who received the lower amount were obliged, after six months of being unemployed, to undergo a 'means test' and to prove that they were actively seeking work, where none was available. Men from the 'dole' were allowed to enter the unemployed man's home to establish that he was not living in undue comfort, to enquire into the state of his savings and to ascertain whether any member of his family was working. After this, if he passed the test, he was allowed fifteen shillings and threepence a week.

There were hunger marches on the move again, white-faced men, thin and dressed almost in rags, bony-shouldered and stooped, tramping from the north to lay their grievances before anyone who would listen. Deeply sunk in their poverty, utterly destitute, twenty per cent of the population of the country were described as 'poor'. In Liverpool there were agencies which would provide an old pair of shoes or a bit of blanket for a child, and old soldiers might obtain a bob or two from regimental funds, but in the broken-down homes the 'poor' burnt the refuse from the street, scraps of paper, twigs, wooden crates and potato peelings, in an effort to keep warm.

'It's going to be a repeat of the famine in Ireland nearly a hundred years ago,' Christian Osborne told his cousin Cliona and the assembled company in his grandmother's warm kitchen. 'You mark my words, they'll be dying in the ditches beside the roads before long if they don't find them work, just as they did in Ireland.'

'Don't talk so daft, boy,' his Uncle Michael told him from across Ellen's groaning table, '. . . and stop filling this girl of mine's head with your blather.'

'She's Irish, isn't she, Uncle Michael, like I am and like you are and if we're not concerned, then who will be?'

'Concerned about what, for God's sake?'

'With what's going on over the water.'

'And what *is* going on over the water?'

'You call yourself an Irishman and you don't know what is happening to your own countrymen.'

'Watch your tongue with me, lad, for I'm not too old to give you a clip round the ear an' you're not too old to get it.'

'But Uncle Michael, you must know of the injustices in Ireland?'

'The injustices, as you call them, have been resolved years ago. The problems were religious and economic. Sure you're not the only one to follow the newspapers. The Roman Catholic restrictions and the exploitation

145

of the so-called peasants was ended with the Government of Ireland Act. The Catholics have been emancipated, the Protestant Church has been disestablished and the landlords have been bought out . . .'

'It's not so, Uncle Michael. The Treaty of Ireland . . .'

'Oh, don't give me that old treaty. The Dail approved it . . .'

'By sixty-four votes to fifty-seven only. De Valera resigned . . .'

'Aye, 'tis so but the British government still transferred power to them. There was a majority vote for it an' that's democratic enough for most . . .'

'That's a simple view, Uncle Michael, if you don't mind my saying so. Ulster is still part of the United Kingdom, and the authorities appointed by the bloody British government still rule from Dublin Castle. The Irish Republican brotherhood were not satisfied and you know the outcome of that. Michael Collins . . .'

'Not himself again, for God's sake.'

'He was a patriot, along with Allen and Larkin and Countess Markievicz and all the rest. The Irish Republican Army had no choice but to make war on the British when all their peaceful endeavours came to nothing and so they should . . .'

'War! Fighting their own kind.'

'Invaders they fought. The bloody British, God damn them to hell . . .'

'*That's enough!* Will the pair of you stop it this minute for I'll have none of that language in my kitchen, so I won't, an' well you both know it. Sure an' you knock me heart sideways in me with your arguing, an' today of all days. Now sit down the both of you . . .' for Christian and Michael had risen from their chairs

146

the better to bristle up to one another in one of the eternal arguments Christian always seemed to cause.

Ellen's son reluctantly returned to the chair by the fire, still called 'the Daddy's chair', where he had been nursing one of Eammon's bairns, two-year-old Duald, who had been thrust unceremoniously into his father's arms when the argument had erupted. It would not do to give Christian a 'thick ear' with an infant bawling under one arm.

'Sorry, Mammy,' he muttered, his face still hazardous as he continued to watch his nephew, who really was the very divil sometimes with his blather about the 'cause' and the Irishmen and women who had died for it. Bringing his mad ideas into his grandmother's kitchen and filling the heads of the wee 'uns with his nonsense. That's how it lived on, passed from one generation to another, and if they didn't give over it would go on for ever.

'He's right, Daddy,' a quiet voice from the back of the kitchen said, and everyone turned to stare in astonishment, and Michael's sun-browned face was quite visibly seen to blanch. 'Oh, I know you all make fun of him, so you do, and say he's a stage Irishman acting out a part he thinks is thrilling, but he believes in it and so do I.'

'Sweet Mother of heaven . . .' Ellen crossed herself hastily and prepared to leap into the middle of what was going to happen, whatever that might be, for surely something would. Of all her grandchildren and great-grandchildren, the dozens who made up her family, of them all Cliona would have been the last one she would have expected to take up the nonsense Christian spouted from morning till night. A good sensible girl, quiet and serious, but with a lovely glint of humour in

147

her which turned her gravity to merriment in a moment. Thoughtful and kind and peaceable, with none of the wildness in her of some of them. Now if it had been Joseph, Donal's lad, who at fourteen was a bit of a handful, or Devlin, who hung about with some rough lads from the Irish area of Liverpool when his mother wasn't looking, she could have believed it, but not Cliona. Not a sweet and gentle girl like Cliona.

Her father evidently felt the same, for he sat with his mouth hanging open and the most awful expression of bewilderment in his vivid blue-green eyes, which his daughter had inherited.

''Tis true, Daddy, they did no more than attack a few police stations and ambush a convoy or two and the British government sent in the "Black and Tans" . . .'

'But that was years ago, Cliona, and it was done to regain order.' Alex Woodall's voice was mild as he entered what he saw as a discussion, the revelation of Cliona's surprising support of Christian's convictions not yet plain to him. *He* was not an Irishman as the rest of them were in the room, except Maris, and though he was normally incensed by almost everything Christian Osborne did or said, just as a matter of course, hidden beneath the tablecloth his hand was in Rosie's, and her caressing thumb against his palm had a calming effect on him.

Michael O'Shaughnessy sat as though he was turned to stone, and the rest of the family watched with growing interest what they could see was going to be a real 'ding-dong'. They did love a good 'ding-dong' or indeed anything which fired the blood and quickened the breath and put a gleam of excitement in the eye. The implication of Cliona's words, like Alex's, had not yet penetrated their understanding.

'*Order?*' Cliona's voice had risen angrily. 'They terrorised the people and created more trouble than there already was, didn't they, Christian?'

'They did indeed. They were men with a liking for fighting and brutality.'

'But what of the Irish Free State that had been granted . . .'

'It was no more than a ploy . . .'

'But the Irish won their fight, so why cannot they be reconciled, instead of this hardening of the grievances between Northern Ireland and the Free State?'

'The Irish Republican Army doesn't think they won their fight.' The words, so much more menacing on the lips of a young girl, hushed every voice in the room for they had all begun to argue the merits or otherwise of the Irish 'cause'.

'I can't understand why you, as Irishmen . . .' sweeping her flashing eyes about the room to encompass every male present, '. . . can't see it. Christian and me have spoken to . . .'

Michael rose from his chair again like some wounded, baited animal poked from its lair with a stick. His face was livid and his eyes had the hardness and brilliance of sapphires in his rage. The whites were tinged with red and his teeth were revealed, just as those of a tormented animal's would be, in a vicious snarl.

'Get your coat, lady, an' we'll be leaving. Sure, I'll not sit here and listen to a daughter of mine mouthing the bloody rubbish this . . . this excuse for a man has filled your head with. God's holy nightgown, how long has this been going on? How long? An' me trusting you, teaching you to drive the bloody motor car so that you could get about. To Holy Mass, I thought, or here to your grandmother's, and all the while you've been goin' behind me back consorting with this sham Irishman and only the Holy Mother herself knows who else. And you . . .' turning violently on his nephew who sat, calm and relaxed at his grandmother's table as though they had been discussing no more than the cricket scores, '. . . if I see you near my girl again, by God, I'll wring your bloody *English* neck, so I will. You do what you want and *think* what you want but I'll have no child of mine . . .'

'Stop it, Daddy, *stop it*. Sure you can't make me think any way other than I do. The thoughts are already in my head and I can't wipe them out. I believe . . .'

'*You believe!* 'Tis not your beliefs or your thoughts that are in your head but this . . .'

'Uncle Michael, it does no good shouting at Cliona. I really cannot understand you.' Christian's voice, which remained well-bred no matter how hard he tried to ape his Irish relatives, had become impassioned in his appeal. 'Have you no notion of the . . .'

'No, an' I don't want to know. I've better things to do with my time than . . .'

'Yes, I saw you the other day with . . . a certain lady of our acquaintance, and I can quite appreciate how difficult it must be for you to see the need your own people have of you when you are so concerned with those of hers.'

There was a deathly pallid silence in Ellen's kitchen, for the words Christian Osborne had just flung at his uncle were not only offensive, but contemptuous. Those about the room seemed to draw back a little as though something unpleasant had been introduced into the homely room. Eammon hugged his little son to him and put out his hand to draw John, who was three now,

150

against his leg. His wife Tess, with the new baby who would soon be usurped by a newer, hissed sharply between her teeth. Eammon and Donal exchanged glances, ready to shuffle the dozen children, the younger ones, from what was evidently to become a battlefield into the hallway or better yet, the garden, for though there had been many a 'spat' in this kitchen, they had been nothing to this.

'Donal . . .' his wife Mary whispered, letting him know she'd not have him involved even if it *was* his brother who had just been insulted.

It was Ellen's birthday. None of them knew her age since she said that was *her* business, hers and the Lord's. They had all come, McGowans and Conroys, McGuires and O'Shaughnessys, children, grandchildren and great-grandchildren, and the party was spread from kitchen to parlour and even out into the garden, though it had turned cold after the Jubilee celebrations. Snow a week later, would you believe, in the middle of May, and dirty browned patches of it still clung beneath the bushes.

Christian and Rose, of the Osborne family, had come to bring their grandmother a birthday present and to tell her her daughter Clare would be over presently, and with them were Alex and Maris for it seemed these days that where Rose went Alex followed. Maris, who looked a little peaky, Ellen was inclined to think, had been put in the chimney corner where it was warm and where, twenty-odd years ago, her own mother had been tenderly seated as a treasured guest of Ellen O'Shaughnessy.

Michael O'Shaughnessy had fallen into a deep and painful silence and his broad shoulders sagged. For some unaccountable reason his amber skin turned a furious and what could only be described as an *embarrassed* scarlet. He looked from face to face in some confusion, the last one that of Alex Woodall, almost as though he was afraid to look him in the eye, and Alex returned his look with some sympathy. If the chap wanted a bit of comfort with some woman, the look seemed to say, what of it? He was still a youngish man, a widower for sixteen or seventeen years now, and surely no one believed that such a personable, *masculine* man would not have sought female company in all that time. It was a wonder he had not remarried, since there must be dozens of women, those who had lost their men in the trenches, who would be more than willing to take him on. Alex had always liked Michael. Somehow he could not bring himself to call him Uncle as Rosie did, but that was all right since he was not *his* uncle really, was he? A nice chap with a good brain and the initiative to use it. He had made a success of his garage despite the financial climate, and Alex was inclined to admire that in a man since he seemed unable to do it himself. And Michael O'Shaughnessy was brave too, for he'd won a medal in the war when he had saved the life of Alex's *real* uncle, Teddy. Carried him to safety and stayed with him though he had been wounded himself, Alex's mother had told him. A good fellow to have on your side, he would have said.

He allowed Michael to see the slight smile which curled his mouth, then he winked. Just a small one to let him see that Christian wasn't worth the bother of fighting. He'd done it himself more times than he could count, and would again, he was sure of it, but surely the stupid and completely irrelevant remark Christian had made was beneath Michael O'Shaughnessy's notice?

For some reason the peril dissipated, and Michael shook his head as though he was glad to be rid of it. There was still the question of Cliona to be considered, and he would deal with that soon enough. She had always been a sweet-natured girl, amenable and no trouble to him at all. It had been a daunting task to take on, the rearing of a motherless girl, but he had done it and he was proud of his bright and pretty daughter. A credit to her family and to the nuns who had the teaching of her, and he was having no bald-faced youth corrupting her with his talk of the old days, of the old Ireland and the so-called patriots who were tearing the heart out of her with their cry for Home Rule.

The boy's wink had shown him how foolish it all was.

'Get your coat, darlin',' he said to his daughter, beginning to smile, amused with himself for letting these two, who were no more than children really, with no idea of what life was all about, get his back up, ready to put the whole silly nonsense from his mind when he had given Cliona a good talking to, but Cliona's face had assumed that stubborn expression which Ellen at least was very familiar with. They all had it to some degree, her family, and her heart sank in her breast. She put a hand to it to stop its wild beating, for surely it was doing her no good, the dreadful way it felt in her chest.

'I'm sorry, Daddy, but I will not be treated like a child . . .'

'You *are* a child . . .'

'Seventeen, and I believe in the cause just as Christian does.'

'Cause! What bloody cause?'

'Jesus, Joseph and Mary, give us the strength to . . .

153

oh please, Michael, let the girl alone now. Sure an' enough's been said . . .'

'Aye, Michael, let it alone now,' Donal's reasonable voice added, but Michael O'Shaughnessy's good intentions had begun to crumble again, and every man in the room stood up, or moved away from the wall against which he had been leaning, ready to protect what was his in the way of women and children.

'We *have* a cause, Uncle Michael, and Cliona and I are part of it now. We have joined the movement and . . .'

'What!' The roar of rage set every child in the room to crying and Matty ran into the scullery like a frightened animal which has lost its senses in its terror. Ellen was white-faced and weeping, crossing herself feverishly and babbling a prayer to the Mother of God to stand against this wildness, this malevolent force which had come creeping, scarcely noticed, into her kitchen. Ten minutes ago they had been laughing as she opened her birthday presents . . . so many of them . . . so many. Familiar faces, loved faces shining with good will towards her and towards each other, brother smiling at brother, and now her son and her grandson were facing each other with their hatred and their defiance a visible thing to see. Even Cliona, her gentle granddaughter who had given her the loveliest blue shawl for her birthday, was hard-faced, hard-eyed, hard-mouthed.

'We are members of a group of Liverpool Irish patriots who are determined to fight the injustices which have been done and are still being done to our countrymen over the water. We mean to wage war against those who would . . .'

'Oh, Jesus Christ, Cliona . . . darlin' . . . don't talk like that . . . not like *him* . . .' Michael gestured in the direction of his nephew, unable to bring himself to even look at him lest he spring for his throat. His horror was so great it outweighed his rage. His face was ravaged by it, and he put out a trembling hand to his daughter. He had always been a strong man, a strong-willed man but good-humoured, with that whimsical Irish merriment which was so endearing in his race. Quick to temper and quick to be sorry about it, but this . . . *this* defeated him since it had come so quickly, so unexpectedly, and he did not know what to do about it. He needed time to think, to get his plunging, bucketing thoughts in some kind of order, to think of the best way, the *right* way to convince his daughter that what she was about to do was . . . was preposterous. A boy could be thrashed, hammered with Michael's hard fists until some sense was knocked into his thick and foolish skull, but a girl, a young woman, his *daughter*!

'Please, Daddy, I don't want to fight *you*. Try and allow me to think for myself, to have my own opinions . . .'

'They're not *your* opinions, darlin'. They're *his*,' and this time his gesture of contempt was as utterly merciless as the cold and perilous look he gave his nephew. 'He's been babbling about Ireland and the evil done there for long enough, so he has, that hasn't it turned his brain to mush, an' if he's so bloody keen on it, why in hell's name doesn't he get over there and live with those he claims to admire? Holy Mother of God, he's never even put a foot on Irish soil . . .'

'You don't have to live there to know . . .'

'*You know nothing, boy*, nothing. Nothing of life and nothing of death. And nothing of injustice, or fighting. Speak to your uncle in his wheelchair about what's fair and what isn't. Speak to your Aunt Gracie here, to

155

Lady Woodall about her husband and her two brothers and her husband's two brothers, and even your own grandmother, who lost two of her sons in a war which was far from just to those who died in it. Talk about fighting to those who were left to grieve, and see what they have to say . . .'

'Please, Daddy, don't . . . don't . . .' Cliona was crying bitterly, but she did not move towards her father. Instead she turned to Christian, who had taken the stance of a soldier against the door, a soldier who waited only for orders from some unseen commander, to be off and at the enemy. His young face was, for the first time, strong and sure in his belief, replacing that slightly hysterical need to be listened to which had always marked his features. He had suffered the jibes and jeers and amused contempt of his cousins, on both sides of the family. They had mocked him and called him a theatrical Irishman, a sham, but somehow, with the supportive approval he had unexpectedly found in Cliona, it was as though her belief in the cause and in him had hardened his resolve to the texture of steel and it could not be broken, not now. Cliona's belief had given his own credibility.

'Cliona?' His voice was quiet and questioning.

'I must go home with Daddy, Christian.'

'Of course.'

'I won't let you down.'

'I know. I'll be off then.'

'Yes, it would be best . . .' whilst the assembled company listened with rapt attention.

'Goodbye, Grandmother,' he said but there was no answer from Ellen O'Shaughnessy. Her head was bowed as nothing had bowed it in the past, for no matter what had happened in this family it had happened

156

to them all. Together. They had stood against the world together. Never divided. Even the death of her old Mick, of her daughter Bridget and her two precious sons, Sean and Dermot, had been shared, a shared devastation, but now there was a division. She could not seem to pull herself together, and what was worse, she did not even want to try. There was bitterness and hatred in her kitchen where it had never been before. Pain, hopelessness and fear, for what was to happen now to her son, her Michael who had already lost so much, for there were things in his past only he knew and *she* guessed at and she had spoken of it to no one, not even him. If he lost his baby, his girl child who he had raised so carefully and loved so tenderly; if she went off, as seemed likely; if Christian had his way and gave her life to the cause of the Irish, how would Michael put his life together again, as he had done long ago, painfully and courageously? Ellen had thought the Irish 'troubles' to be over. They all had, but men like Christian, patriots as they called themselves, would not let it end, and God only knew what it would take to make them see sense, and in the meanwhile Michael O'Shaughnessy was to have his heart broken for the second time.

There was a rustling sigh through the kitchen as Christian Osborne left it. The sound of his motor cycle rattled every window in the house, and Sinead, the little girl who had been crying the loudest, put her hands over her ears as though she could stand no more.

'Come to grandma, darlin'.' Ellen held out her arms and the child ran thankfully into them, burrowing on her grandmother's knee, her head pushed comfortingly between Ellen's sagging breasts. Instantly Ellen felt herself relax. The child calmed her, comforted her as children had always done. If there were children what else mattered? They were the future. They were hope. They were love, born of love, giving love, and that was all that mattered. And she had so many. So much love and hope for the future though her own was not for long.

She rested her cheek on the little girl's dark hair and stared into the fire. There was nothing she could do. Nothing anyone could do to stop the young from moving on. Try as you might you could not hold on to them, particularly this new generation of young men and women who were emancipated as her daughters had never been – except perhaps for Caitlin, who had done her own share of fighting in the suffragette movement – and certainly as she herself had never been. Cliona would do whatever she felt was right for her, as Caitlin had done, and if she made mistakes then Ellen would be here, at least for a while, to comfort her. To give of her bounteous, never-ending love as she had always done. To them all.

No one spoke, afraid to break the awful silence with perhaps the wrong word. Michael stood with his head bowed to his chest, and Cliona wept quietly. Rosie's hand clung to Alex's and he held it fiercely, and in the chimney corner Maris moved and cleared her throat. They all turned to look at her expectantly.

'And when is Callum to be home, Mrs O'Shaughnessy?' she asked in a bright, conversational tone.

Ellen's mouth opened and closed a time or two, and it took her a moment to gather her wits.

'Why . . . I'm not sure, child. Next week some time, he said, so he did. Canada this time . . .'

'Yes, so I believe, only I was just wondering . . . ?'

They all hung on her every word.

'Yes, pet . . . ?' and for some reason Ellen's skin prickled.

'I was wondering how many times he has been home since the day of my father's funeral?'

Ellen's face took on an expression of some surprise which turned to sudden wariness, though only the Blessed Mother might have said why.

'. . . a time or two, but why . . . ?'

'Two?'

'Aye, pet, but why would you be asking? What . . . ?'

'It is just that I am to have his child, Mrs O'Shaughnessy, and I think he should be told.' She slipped senselessly to the floor as Ellen began to moan.

9

It was probably the first time in their entire lives that her sons were in complete agreement, Elizabeth Woodall decided distractedly, the irony of what had drawn them together giving her the most urgent desire to laugh quite hysterically. She did not do so, of course, since there is certainly nothing to laugh about when you have just been told that your only daughter is almost four months pregnant and that, or so her sons said, she would be married before the month's end. They were merely waiting for the father-to-be to come home when he would then become the bridegroom.

'I will speak to Damaris first and I will speak to her alone.'

'Mother, I really think you should leave this to us, to Alex and me. The *Alexandrina Rose* will dock on Sunday, and we intend that all the arrangements should be in hand by then so that we can present them to . . . to the blackguard who . . .'

'Charlie, will you allow me to speak?'

'Mother, Charlie is right. There is really nothing to discuss. There can be no other alternative. The O'Shaughnessys agreed . . .'

'I do not care to be spoken to like that, Alex, and I do not care *what* the O'Shaughnessys agreed. I will speak to my daughter in my sitting room immediately.'

'You must not let her make excuses for him, mother. The bastard . . . I beg your pardon, but he took advantage of her when she was defenceless against him, at her very lowest ebb in her grief, and he must not be allowed to get away with it.'

'You were there, were you, Alex?'

'I beg your pardon?'

'When Callum O'Shaughnessy seduced your sister?'

'Mother!'

'Don't preach, Alex, it does not become you, and do not make judgments about something of which you know nothing. Maris has told us she loves Callum and is to have his child, and I can understand your horror and anger, but let us not have this . . . this censure, either of her or Captain O'Shaughnessy until we know the whole story.'

'Mother, I can't understand you. Are you saying it might not be *his* fault?'

'Darling, it takes two people . . .'

'But Maris is no more than a . . . than a young girl, and she has been gently reared. She would not be party to . . . to . . . not willingly . . .'

'You are saying she was raped, then, Charlie . . . ?'

'Dear God . . . no . . .'

'Then I suggest you let me speak to her as I asked. Charlie dear, I can appreciate how appalled you and Alex are. Maris is your sister and you feel that she has been taken advantage of, against her will perhaps, though that is not likely, so let us hear from her what happened . . .'

'Godammit, it is obvious what happened . . .'

'Not to me it isn't, and I wish to know, and also what she wants to do about it.'

'There is only one thing to be done about it, mother. She has no choice. She must marry this man and at the earliest possible moment. Good God . . .' Charlie's young face, so autocratic in its determination to have the 'right thing' done and the family name untarnished by the scandal which would certainly erupt, crumpled for a moment in despair. 'How many more of our family are to be linked with the damned O'Shaughnessys . . . ?'

'Steady on, Charlie,' Alex muttered, indicating the silent figure of Rose, but Charlie did not care to be steady at this dreadful moment. 'It seems no matter which way we turn there they are in their thousands, intent on becoming part of our family. First Aunt Mara when she married Uncle James, then Aunt Clare with Uncle Teddy, and now this. They will be moving into Woodall next, which brings us to the question of where Maris and . . . and . . . are to live. A Woodall cannot be expected to move into some awful semi in Prescot or Knotty Ash . . .'

'Charlie, Charlie, leave that for now. One thing at a time, so I would be glad if you will give Maris and me a chance to have a talk . . .'

'About what, mother? What on earth is there to discuss except when the wedding day is to be?'

Black and white. That was all the young knew, Elizabeth agonised. They could see no further than the tunnel through which they peered and which must be got through no matter how many alternatives there might be to navigate it. They were so . . . rigid, so certain that a wrong had been done which must be put right and the only way to do that was *their* way. There were no shades of grey, no mitigating circumstances, nothing to excuse or understand. Their sister had wandered from the narrow path the women of this family were expected to walk, and no matter what the circumstances – indeed did the circumstances concern them? – she must be led back, or forced back to her place, her proper place.

162

'Stop it, Alex. I hate to see you take this unforgiving attitude towards your sister, and please, stop thrashing about my drawing room like a caged beast. You will have that table over in a minute.'

Maris huddled herself deeper into the corner of the green velvet sofa. She knew that her cousin Rose, who was sitting on the other side of the fireplace and was one of the O'Shaughnessys, at least on her mother's side, whom Charles purported to despise so much, was trying to catch her eye. It was Rosie's face which had been the first to swim back into her dazed consciousness when she recovered from her faint. It was Rosie who had lifted her and half-carried her from the bedlam of the O'Shaughnessy kitchen to Alex's motor car, and it was Rosie, almost single-handedly, snarling it seemed to Maris like a lioness in defence of her cub, who had held them all at bay, all those excited Irish faces which had crowded about her. All talking at once while Mrs O'Shaughnessy, herself a lioness protecting the good name of *her* cub, her son Callum, shrieked that it was all a lie, that none of her sons would do such a thing, and it was coming to something when a supposedly well-bred girl like Maris Woodall had the gall, the barefaced effrontery to accuse one of them of such a mortal sin.

Alex, unable it seemed to make head nor tail of the whole sorry business, stunned to silence by his sister's revelation, and worse still, by the way she had revealed it, had jumped to Rose's barked orders, opening the front door of the house, the motor car, stuffing Maris into it between himself and Rose, starting the engine and roaring away from Mrs O'Shaughnessy's recriminations, and the grim-faced assembly of men and women and wailing children, as though the devil himself was at their heels.

Now he and Charlie were pacing her mother's elegant drawing room, as her mother had said to Alex, like two animals who find themselves unexpectedly and terrifyingly behind bars and can see no way out of it. Their voices were loud in her ears, loud and shrill, even that of her mother, who was normally so soft-spoken and calm. She wanted to wail herself, to tear at her own hair in her pain and terror, for it seemed to her she was going mad, or being pursued by a violence she could not even name. A hunted creature she felt herself to be, cowering from them all with no shelter or protection. They were all converging on her with their loud voices and angry eyes, and all she wanted was to have Callum here, just herself and Callum, and quiet, so that she could tell him what had happened to her, to them both, for it was his child as well as hers, and make arrangements for the wedding. There would be a wedding, naturally. It was unthinkable that there might not be. Callum had only to be told and everything would be as it should be. As things *were* for girls of her class. An engagement and then a wedding, and if she had known when he was in port, if she had only been able to see him, been able to talk to him on the two occasions his mother said he had been home, it would all have been arranged. She loved him so much, and what had happened on the day of her father's funeral had been the culmination, the expression of that love, the love between Callum O'Shaughnessy and Maris Woodall. If she could only have *seen* him . . . if he had only been to see *her* . . . why? . . . Oh God . . . why had he not been to see her? . . . why? . . . after what had happened . . . why? She had waited for him, hardly stirring from the house, her ear cocked for the sound of the telephone, the front door bell, Wilson's knock

at the drawing-room door to say there was a caller . . .
a telephone call . . . but it had not come. *He* had not
come, and she had carried her burden, the one that
was growing inside her and the one that weighed down
her aching heart, alone and terrified of them both. The
dreadful realisation that he did not *intend* to come,
the knowing which she had kept at bay for three long
months, swept over her, and she put her hands over
her ears as if the action would prevent her from hearing
her world break in pieces. She began to moan.

Instantly Rose was on her knees before her, her arms
out ready to take her, and gratefully she collapsed into
them.

'Maris darling, it will be all right, really it will,' Maris
heard her mother's anguished voice say. 'You will not
be forced to do anything you don't want to do. We will
speak to . . .'

'Rosie . . . please . . .' and on either side of her, her
two brothers stood, hard-eyed and suspicious.

'She can't talk now. Let her alone, Alex, and you
too, Charlie. Aunt Elizabeth, if I may . . .' Rosie was
coaxing her cousin to stand up and lean on her.

'Yes, darling, anything . . .' and Elizabeth Woodall's
harrowed face was dreadful to see. There was an
expression in her eyes, strange and deep and unread-
able, but she seemed to be suffering something which
had nothing to do with her daughter.

'Let me take her upstairs to bed.' Rosie's arms tightened about Maris, who was trembling and white-faced,
her breath hard in her chest.

'But we have decided nothing, Rosie.' Charles
pushed a distracted hand through the fair tumble of his
hair, then shoved both hands deep in his trouser
pockets and turned impatiently away, longing to be

done with the whole sorry business, but knowing he could not. He was Sir Charles Woodall, and his sister had got herself 'into trouble' as they said, and the sordidness of it was almost too much for his fastidious nature to contemplate. Of course girls *did* get themselves into trouble but they were shop girls, factory girls, servants, and certainly not the daughter or sister, to a baronet. Really, it was too bad of Maris to have allowed it, and with one of the O'Shaughnessys as well. A man old enough to be her father, experienced and therefore all the more reprehensible. Still, it would all be resolved as soon as the bastard put a foot on the dock next Sunday. He and Alex would see to that.

Rosie and her mother bathed her themselves, murmuring comforting sounds, none of them particularly intelligible. They wrapped her in an enormous white fleecy towel, standing her before her bedroom fire, which had been hurriedly lit, and rubbed the curly mass of her streaked silver hair until it was dry. They put her in a clean nightdress and tucked her into her lavender-scented bed, hugged her and kissed her and promised her the worries would all go away and that they would be here whilst she slept.

'Why did he not come, mother?' she asked as she drifted off to sleep, looking scarcely more than a child in her ruffled lawn nightgown, though the evidence of her pregnancy could be seen in the fullness of her breasts and the roundness of her stomach as she had stood naked before them. Only slight, and had they not known of it it is doubtful they would have noticed, but there nevertheless.

'I don't know, darling, I don't know,' her mother whispered into her hair.

*   *   *

If he was surprised to see the Woodall brothers coming up the gangway of his ship as he stood on his deck to receive them, Callum O'Shaughnessy's face made no show of it.

The One O'Clock Gun at Morpeth Dock had just been fired, as it was every day at the same time. When the second mate knocked on his cabin door to say he had visitors on the dock, and was he to let them up, Callum had checked the time against his own watch.

A commotion from the next dock lifted into the warm, Sunday morning air as the livestock which came from Canada and Ireland was unloaded. A hoarse voice shouted, and cattle were lowing anxiously as they were driven on to the dock. The drovers would herd them through the streets of the city, which were quiet on a Sunday, 'helped' by crowds of excited children, along Leeds Street, Alexander Pope Street, Richmond Row and on to the abattoir. Famous was Liverpool's 'cattle trail', and it was not unusual for a careless householder who forgot to close his front door to find a cow in his kitchen. Callum could remember how as children he and Sean and Michael used to escape after Mass to join the trail, to their mother's annoyance, and even follow the cows to the slaughter-house to wait for them to be killed. It was possible when the gruesome job was done to obtain a bladder which made a great football.

He had brought the SS *Alexandrina Rose* through the swing bridge entrance to the Canning Dock early that morning, helped by the tugs *Langton* and *Victoria*, and she was neatly berthed ready for the unloading of her cargo. Next to her was the Canadian Pacific liner, the SS *Duchess of York*, and at the dock entrance waiting her turn for the tugs, was the TSS *Vandyck*, a cruise vessel launched only three years ago and said to be

167

unbelievable in her luxury. She was the first ship to have a shop on board, the goods for sale in it supplied by Lewis's, one of Liverpool's foremost stores, which was a subject of much interest, especially to the wealthy ladies who sailed in her.

A three-masted sailing ship was being guided towards her berth further along the dock, and busying themselves like black-garbed 'nannies' with a collection of straying children were cock-tugs and tenders and gig-boats, luggage boats, river hoppers and barges, all lending credence to the belief that the Liverpool docks and the busy highway of the river which led to them were the most active in the world.

The track of the electric overhead railway hung elevated above the warehouse roofs, winding its way along the dock estate from Gladstone Dock, above Hornby Dock, Alexandra Dock, Langton, Brocklebank and Canada Dock, bending towards the river where it met Regent Road in Bootle, then on to Liverpool and beyond to Dingle. It was like some giant spider's tracery hanging in mid-air, with the constant clack of its traffic's wheels on the rails reminding those beneath that time was of the essence here and it would not do to stand and stare. You could see thirteen of Liverpool's finest docks and the wonders of the giant ocean liners from the splendid viewpoint of one of its trains for as little as ninepence, but it also served the docks in a more utilitarian manner as it carried people and goods from and to the ships which would journey the world's seas. There were stations all along its length of thirteen miles, where it picked up and put down thousands of travellers a day. Because of the shelter it gave it was nicknamed 'The Docker's Umbrella'!

At regular intervals along the flat roof of each warehouse, cranes were hung, dipping and bobbing in their task of loading and unloading freight. A dock AEC lorry loaded with tea chests was parked in a 'dockie's' way, and the driver was fiercely rounded upon and treated to a mouthful of ill-mannered 'scouse' as he desperately swung the starting handle in an attempt to get his vehicle's engine started. A dock 'bobby' in his navy uniform and summer lightweight helmet, all silver buttons and braid and whistles on a chain, sauntered over with the clear intention of giving someone a piece of his mind, but the engine fired and calm was regained. Men shouted and whistled, hammers clanged and the noise and confusion seemed to have no sense or order, but Callum knew from his fifteen years' experience of docks and ships and the sea that, despite it all, each ship was divested of or filled with its freight with the fastest possible speed, since the dockers worked on a bonus system. The old floating crane moored in the river and known as the 'Mammoth' was the one the men would fight to get hired on, since the tonnage it could lift ensured a grand bonus.

Accommodation on freight carriers in the British merchant navy was basic, but the skipper was entitled to his own bathroom adjacent to his cabin. Not that the bath in it, or in any of the other crew bathrooms, was ever used for bathing, for the simple reason that not enough fresh water was carried for such refinements. The deck hands, firemen and apprentices used a bucket. The mates' and engineers', 'sparks', the stewards' and cooks' cabins were all fitted with a washbasin, but as there was no drainage other than a bucket under the plug-hole this was viewed with some scorn, since the bucket must then be emptied anyway! Captain O'Shaughnessy was no different from the rest of his

169

officers, and all that morning his thoughts had dwelt longingly on the white enamelled bath in the modern bathroom of his house in West Derby. The question of a lavatory was not such a problem as his cabin bathroom had an up-to-date flush system using salt water, but a hot bath, a really piping *hot* bath, large soft towels and perhaps, afterwards, or even *during*, the attentions of the lady he had arranged to meet the moment he got into port. As he watched the Woodalls climb the gangway it seemed likely that it might be some time before he enjoyed either, and he supposed even then, as his impassive face turned politely to Sir Charles Woodall and his brother Alex, he knew what it was they had come about.

'Sir Charles,' he said, 'this is indeed an unexpected honour.' His expression was mocking as his despairing heart slid uneasily into the depths of his chest. '. . . And your brother. How kind of you to meet my . . .'

'There is no need of pleasantries, or sarcasm, O'Shaughnessy,' Sir Charles snapped, and his brown eyes were like cold pebbles in his flushed face. The weather had turned warm again, and some deep emotion in him had put a slight sheen of sweat on his skin.

'Well then, perhaps we had better . . .'

Alex Woodall shoved his brother to one side, and in his face was the violent rage this man's attitude had brought boiling to the surface. Not only had he made love to a sexually innocent girl, Alex's sister, impregnating her, but he had sailed away on his next voyage without even the pretence of concern that he might have left her with the terrible results of their encounter. Alex knew he had probably left port within a day or two of his father's funeral, but it appeared he had been in Liverpool twice in the time between, and he had not once approached Maris, for any reason. He had treated her as though she was some waterfront whore who could presumably take care of herself, and if she couldn't, what was it to Callum O'Shaughnessy? And now, in the face of his obvious depravity, he was smiling and affable just as though Alex and Charlie were come on a social visit. A tour round his ship perhaps, and then a drink in his cabin to end a pleasant hour or two.

'You bastard . . .' he roared, so that even the bobby turned sharply and put a hand to his truncheon.

'Alex . . . not here . . . not where everyone . . .' but Alex was deaf to Charlie's plea for control. He wanted nothing more than to get his hands round Callum O'Shaughnessy's throat and squeeze it until those brilliantly turquoise eyes of his popped out on to his cheeks. He sprang at him, his face a livid scarlet, his eyes on fire with his contempt and savagery, but the bit of deck where Callum had stood was suddenly empty, and from behind him strong arms held his cruelly, and a snarling voice in his ear called him 'boy' and told him to step lively down to his cabin where they would continue their discussion in private.

'Don't you agree, lad, that whatever you have to say should be said where other ears cannot hear you? It must be important to bring you and your brother . . . that's right, down these steps and to the left . . .' and Alex was frogmarched, to the amusement of the watching deck-hands, down to the Captain's cabin by the 'old man' himself. He was thrust inside, and when he turned, Callum held up his hands, palm outwards, his eyes watchful, the expression on his face saying it would be very foolish to try that again. He had knocked about the world's ports for a great many years, and the first thing a seaman learned was how to take care of himself.

And yet, though neither of the two young men could see it, there was pity in him and understanding, for would he not be the same, react in the same way if . . . well, whatever it was they had come for . . . had happened in his family?

'You bastard . . . you . . .'

'Yes, lad, I get the picture. I take it you don't care for me and that you have come here to tell me why. Now why don't you sit down and we'll have a . . .'

'My brother and I have not come to drink with you, Captain, if that was what you had in mind. In fact it is as much as we can manage to remain in the same room with a man of your degeneracy. If indeed you can even be called a man . . .'

'Be careful, Sir Charles, whatever I am to be accused of and whatever I may, or may not have done, I will be insulted by no man.'

Charles Woodall took not the slightest notice of the interruption. He had the chilled hauteur and control his ancestry had bred in him. He was speaking to a man of the working class, a man who, a few years ago, would have touched the peak of his cap, or even removed it when addressed by a gentleman such as himself. He was also a man who could seriously damage the good name of Charles's family, and he would not contaminate himself by touching him, as Alex had tried to do. A gentleman did not engage in fisticuffs with a man of the lower orders. His hatred and contempt was no less than Alex's, nor his pity for his sister, though he did condemn her lack of control. But he was here to right the situation and though it went against everything he had been brought up to believe to give her to this . . . this man who was not a gentleman, it must be done.

Maris must be married. It was too late to find another husband for her, even one willing to take her on as she was, so it must be this one.

'It seems my sister is in what I believe is called "an interesting condition" and that you are the man who caused her to be . . . in it . . .'

'Jesus Christ, Charlie, how can you be so bloody calm and so bloody *prissy* about it? You sound like some old maid who can't say the right words in case they taint her tongue. My sister is to have a child, Callum O'Shaughnessy, and it seems you're the sod who gave it to her and so, a week on Saturday, you and she are walking up the aisle together, is that clear? Because if it isn't, perhaps this will make it plain to you. She is to be a respectably married woman and if she is not you will no longer be master of a Hemingway ship.'

There was a silence so deep and dreadful all three men felt as though they were drowning in it. Though Charlie and Alex hated the man who had, in the parlance, 'done down' their sister, as men themselves, brothers under the skin so to speak, they could not help but feel a certain kinship with Callum O'Shaughnessy's predicament, and had it not been their sister they would have been commiserating with him on his ill-luck. What man, if he were honest, wouldn't? Hadn't every man at some time or other known the subconscious fear – afterwards, of course, since in the heat of the moment a man thought of nothing but *now* – that he might be caught. Trapped. That the sperm he sent so ecstatically, so triumphantly on its journey, might find a cosy nest and do untold damage to his life. That the girl might 'fall', and come after him demanding that he make an honest woman of her. And now, caught in that trap was Callum O'Shaughnessy, and all for a few moments of lust which he had been unable to resist.

'An honourable man can do no less, Captain, don't you agree?' Sir Charles kept his voice cool and his anger on a tight rein. 'And my sister is a fit wife for any man . . .'

'Jesus, Charlie, there's no need to paint a pleasing picture of Maris, just as though we were trying to persuade . . .'

Again, Charles ignored the interruption.

'. . . so I am sure you will have no objection to marrying her. What man would, an honourable man, that is. You heard what my brother said . . .'

'Yes, I heard and I don't think, gentlemen, that I care to be blackmailed.'

'And we don't give a damn what you care for, Captain.' Alex's voice was as tense as his brother's was steady. 'We have made arrangements for a special licence and the preacher is willing and able to perform the ceremony on that day. The church at Colton, ironically, where we buried my father. Your family have been invited since we want as little gossip as possible, and their presence will still any rumour that things are not quite . . . in order. I believe your mother and older brother are to attend . . .'

'*My mother* . . . you bastards, you conniving little bastards, you've been to *my mother* with this. Christ almighty, I'll . . .'

'You will do nothing, I think, Captain O'Shaughnessy,' and the two young men stood shoulder to shoulder, their expressions identical, hard, determined: the expressions of men who will have their way.

'Will I not? You expect me to turn up at Colton Church a week on Saturday in my best suit, and tamely marry your sister as though I was some bloody puppet whose strings the Woodalls pull? That by running to my mother and brother with this . . . tale, the pair of you can . . . two bloody little whippersnappers . . .'

'It was not we who told your mother, Captain, it was Maris herself. It must have caused quite a stir. Jubilee Day it was, when I believe every last one of your family was present . . .'

'Sweet Christ . . .'

'. . . really, as you say, but if it gets out it will make it very awkward for you in Liverpool, not only in the shipping world but in the bosom of your own family. To take advantage of a young and innocent girl . . .'

'Get off my ship.'

'Is that your answer?' Alex Woodall swayed on the balls of his feet as though he really could not keep himself from launching his violence against Callum O'Shaughnessy a moment longer. His mouth was so tightly clenched he could barely speak. His contemptuous loathing was an almost visible presence in the cabin, surprising even his brother, who knew him for a hot-head and a fighter.

'It is to you, and if you don't get the hell off my ship I'll have you both thrown off.' Callum's mouth was as grim as Alex's. A pulse ticked dangerously fast in his jaw and the air about him was top-heavy with peril.

'We would like a proper answer, Captain. Yes or no? It seems you are not denying the accusation.'

Callum turned away so that the two younger men could not see the expression on his face. Of course he was not denying the accusation, nor was he denying the fact that for these past months Maris Woodall had been in his thoughts more than he cared to acknowledge. He was no debaucher who would use a young girl and walk

175

away without a backward glance, as these brothers of hers seemed to think, but he had decided it would be best to lie low and see what the day brought. To wait and see if there were to be any repercussions from that one delightful episode. If not, then he had had a lucky escape and he would breathe a sigh of relief and learn a lesson from it. He had been surprisingly enchanted with Maris Woodall and her body's response to his own, and had she been older, more experienced in the ways of men, with that sophistication which recognises the needs of the flesh without the turmoil and complication of the heart, he might have resumed and explored their relationship further. But she was a girl, a girl of the age which believed in love, and would have expected, needed, more from him than he was prepared to give. In his life he only had room for women who understood the rules of the games he played. Married women if possible who could demand nothing of him. He had slipped, once. He had allowed himself to be 'seduced', if that was the word, by a sweet young girl, and now she had him, as they said, by the balls.

He let his eyes wander about the cabin which had been his home, his *true* home, for so many years. He loved the sea. He loved the life he led. He had worked hard for it, and was he to see it torn away from him because of one small mistake? Was he to have his ship, this world of his taken from him because for one moment he had let down his guard in his compassion for a young girl's grief and had been led, as they *both* had, into the sweet pleasures of the flesh? Of course he might find another ship, another berth, another company willing to have him skipper for them, but once the word got out that he had been fired from a Hemingway vessel the choice, if he had one, would be very limited.

He studied, almost clinically, the simple beauty of the mahogany panelling which lined the walls of this 'home' of his. He had had shelves let into the wood in which his favourite books were placed. Rider Haggard, Conrad, Tolstoy and Jack London. Two prints hung above his bed, a Monet and a Gauguin. There was on the floor, instead of the usual coconut matting, a lovely Chinese rug in shades of lime green and royal blue, fringed in cream. A fixed wall mirror edged in brass and a brass paraffin wall lamp had been burnished until they winked in the shaft of sunlight which pierced one of the port-holes. He had not really known until this moment, when it seemed it might all be lost to him, how much it meant to him. He did not love Maris Woodall, and he knew they would say he had married her to keep all this, his ship, the world of the sea which was all he knew, but he admitted to himself that that was only half the truth. He heard that infectious laugh of hers, the one which had made him smile on that first day and her face swam into his vision. It was framed in one of the port-holes, small and sad and defenceless as it had been on the day of her father's funeral. A pixie face, with a halo of silvered curls in which there was a warm tangle of gold. An impudent face, laughing and free of care, as it had been when they first met. A defiant face with perhaps a hint in it of the strength which could be in her if she was allowed to grow.

But that was really not what mattered. She did not matter and nor did he, but the child she carried was undoubtedly his and could he abandon his own child and still live with himself? An O'Shaughnessy?

177

He sighed sadly, deeply, his strong face strangely gentle, then he turned abruptly.

'Tell your sister I will call on her this afternoon.' His voice was brisk. He might have been making arrangements to visit his banker or accountant, since he had both. Callum O'Shaughnessy had been careful with his money and it was in the power of a sea captain or indeed any officer who had cash to spare, to make a little extra buying goods in a foreign port, goods of an exotic or rare nature, selling them for a handsome profit when he got back to England. He had investments, a number of five per cent Perpetual Preference Shares in the Overhead Electric Railway Company, and some in the New Mersey Tunnel. Money bred money, he had found, and the Woodalls would be left in no doubt that he could support a wife.

'About three if that is convenient,' he went on. 'I have the unloading of my cargo to supervise and I must call at the shipping office, the Hemingway shipping office, my employers.' His eyes gleamed with sardonic humour and one dark eyebrow arched. 'But I should be finished by three.' For a second his face became strained with some inner disquiet. 'I must visit my mother . . .' He straightened his long back then and smiled coldly, since he and his mother were none of their business. 'So, if that is all, gentlemen, I'll bid you good day. I dare say I shall not see you until my wedding day. You can find your own way out, I'm sure.'

'It seems we are to be married,' he said to her that afternoon at three, more abruptly than he meant to, and was sorry when the wary but nevertheless eager expression on her face changed to one of confusion. Dear God, this was impossible and could really not be got through, but it must. He had given his word – and his life – a bitter, resentful part of him whispered, and he could not escape it. He tried to recapture the compassion he had felt for her earlier in the day, but by all that was holy, it was hard. He had already done so much harm to this girl who, in her terrible innocence, had confused sexuality with love; but now he must try, if only for the sake of the child they had so heedlessly made, to put it, somehow, no matter how awkward it might be, to rights.

'Perhaps it will not be so bad,' he said, trying to smile, to bring a smile to her face, but she was ill at ease, unsure of herself and of him, and scared.

'I . . . did not mean to . . . well . . . my brothers were . . . you saw how they are . . .'

'Indeed I did, but . . .'

'Yes . . . ?' Eager again, longing to be friends at least.

'The child must come first.'

It was not what she wanted to hear, he could see it in her face, and he relented.

'We . . . will . . . perhaps do very well together,' not knowing what else to say, then added impulsively, '. . . Stella Maris.'

'I beg your pardon?' She leaned a little towards him, sensing a softening in him, reminding him suddenly of a young pup a shipmate of his once had. It had done wrong, some mischievous thing as puppies will, and had been reprimanded. It had sat at its master's feet, its eyes never leaving his face, straining to be noticed and forgiven, for a word of approval, a lifting of the discipline its master had imposed, and when it had come, that hand to pat its head, its joy had been unconfined. She was the same. Hesitant, hopeful, only waiting for that hand to come and stroke away the desolation the sharp word had caused.

'Stella Maris. Star of the sea. Have you not heard of it?'

'No . . . how lovely . . .' She smiled. If you will only take that first step in my direction, her expression clearly said.

'To light the way of sailors, they say.'

'And does it?'

He sighed, for how were they to get through this if not by the way it had begun? With the senses. With the body and its physical needs and awareness. With the touch of her body against his, his arms about her, their desires speaking the words he at least could not utter.

He opened his arms wide and smiled, and without hesitation, her eyes enormous with her love for him, she flew into them.

10

The bride was trembling and white-faced, plump in a pretty dress of oyster pink, with a flowered hat to match, and not the white which was customary, given away by her eldest brother, who, when he put her hand in Callum's, looked as though he would rather stick a knife in his back any day of the week. Her other brother, the dark one, had glowered at everybody, Woodall, Osborne and O'Shaughnessy, it made no difference to him, and Lady Woodall had bitten her lip and straightened her already straight back, conscious of dozens of sympathetic eyes on her as she came into the church on his arm. It was only four months since she had buried her husband here, and could she help but be saddened by the circumstances which had brought them here again today, Ellen had asked herself, feeling just as sad as she watched her son exchange his vows, Protestant vows without even the benefit of a blessing from his own Church to see them through.

It was a quiet wedding, naturally, in the circumstances, but there was a sprinkling of the gentry to the left of the church, the women with their smart hats with the brims rolled up in the front; their fashionable, glacé kid, high-heeled shoes; their silk, afternoon dresses, calf-length, with the latest 'cowl' necklines; in sharp contrast to the plain, no-nonsense hats, the plain and sensible summer shoes, the plain 'washing' frocks of rayon worn by the women on the groom's side of the family.

Critical eyes, on both sides of the aisle, watched the bride as she entered the church, her nervous state very apparent, not at all the bold and dazzling young woman to whom they were all accustomed. She spoke the words in a voice so quiet it could be heard only by those in the immediate pews. Her neck seemed to droop, and when her groom put the ring on her finger she was seen to sway a little. A lovely bride, none could deny it, but strangely frail.

A lovely bride indeed, the congregation murmured, rising to its feet as the organ swelled and the bride, as she came from the altar walked, nay, *skipped* beside her husband, her hand through his arm, triumph in her deep and glowing brown eyes. Her complexion, which had been so palely wan half an hour since, was warm and soft with the intense colour of her joy, that which she was certain she would feel every day of her new life. Smiling at everyone with the huge endearing smile of a child who has just opened a Christmas present to find it contained the very toy it had asked Father Christmas to bring.

There were kisses for everyone, from her, of course. For her mother and mother-in-law, her cousin Rose, and her new sisters-in-law who responded with true O'Shaughnessy vigour. She bubbled with it, like a bottle of champagne newly corked, flaunting her happiness, her husband and even their coming 'happy event' with a child's uninhibited glee.

Her husband was not quite so generous with *his* joy, if he could be said to have any, but she did not appear to notice. He handed her quietly into the handsome, chauffeur-driven motor car – alas, not lined with white silk as the carriage of her mother's wedding day had been – on its journey to the small gathering at Woodall where the bride and groom's health was toasted in the vintage champagne her late father had laid down years ago for this special occasion.

Ellen O'Shaughnessy was still in the shocked and sorry state of mind that had been caused by her son's precipitate marriage to Maris Woodall. Ready to burst into tears at the drop of a hat, sighing about the house like the north wind, and what Father Paul would have to say about it didn't bear thinking about, she said despondently to Matty. It was not that she had any objection to Maris Woodall, Maris O'Shaughnessy now, begod, since the child was like one of her own and had been in and out of Ellen's kitchen as often as Ellen's grandchildren ever since she was a wee thing. Whenever Rosie came, more often than not so did Maris, and of course you could not say a bad word to Ellen about her mother. A gracious and lovely lady was Elizabeth Woodall, who had known her duty and done it as ladies of her upbringing did. No, although it had been a dreadful shock, it was not the bride herself who had taken Ellen's peace of mind and played havoc with her composure, but the awful situation of having not one but *four* of her children marry out of the true faith. First there had been Mara, who had borne five children, none of whom had been brought up in the Roman Catholic Church. Then Caitlin with her three, and God alone knew what religion *they* had, if any; and although it was unlikely Clare would have children, Ellen was not sure that this was even worse. Now her Callum, one of her precious sons who, it was true, was something of a backslider, had married, not only into the gentry as her other three had done, but the *Anglican* gentry and in an Anglican church, and the possibility that the child

183

to come would be brought to Holy Mother Church was unlikely.

And the way it had come about! Callum, her boy, the fruit of her womb and, in her eyes, perfect, to do such a thing to a young girl and to do it on the day they buried the young girl's own father, or so Maris had tearfully confessed, may the Holy Mother forgive them both. It was inexcusable, and though she had not at first believed it and had even gone so far, in the privacy of her kitchen and only to Matty who did not count, to voice the fear that Maris Woodall might be carrying some other man's child, it did not, when she had recovered somewhat and could think more clearly, seem likely. Not a daughter of Elizabeth Woodall's. A 'good' girl, if Ellen was any judge. High-spirited and cheeky at times, but honest and not at all the sort of girl who would allow any liberties to be taken before her wedding night unless her affections were sincerely involved.

But it was not until her son, her Callum, had taken her aside and told her quietly that it was so, that he and Maris had . . . and that he intended to marry her which, naturally, was all he could do in the circumstances, that she had accepted it for the truth. She had attended his wedding, poor thing that it was, since she could hardly refuse when she had watched her daughter Clare marry Teddy Osborne in the very same church.

And now they were away in Scotland somewhere, her son and his new wife, staying at some lodge or other which belonged to the Woodalls; her son, she was well aware, for who knew him better than his mother, fidgeting about the place just as he did in *her* house, longing to be back on his ship with the deck beneath his feet and the wide oceans calling him on. As far as she could remember, he had never had an actual holi-

184

day in his life, for, as he said, he travelled the world for most of the year and what did he want with a trip to some sunless, rain-swept corner of the British Isles? What would he do for two weeks tramping about the Scottish moors with a woman, girl really, he barely knew? A bit of shooting, she had heard Charlie Woodall remark, but as far as she knew her son had never owned a gun in his life and wouldn't know one end from the other. Of course, the pretty little thing he had married would keep him amused at night, Ellen had thought tartly, but what about the rest of the time? What about the rest of his life? They'd gone roaring off in that green monster of his, his wife of three hours with stars in her eyes and a dashing feathered cap pinned to her flaunting curls, waving and calling to Rosie, and himself looking grim beside her as though he was off to prison instead of a fortnight's honeymoon.

The front door banged. ''Tis only me, Ma,' a voice called cheerfully, interrupting her sad musing, and instantly she brightened, for if there was anything which was guaranteed to cheer her up it was a visit from one of her family, and Michael, God love him, was especially dear to her. Her first-born son, and with him having so much sadness in his life she was always glad to hear his key in the lock. A nice chat they would have, she an' him, over a cup of tea, and perhaps, if she could persuade him and he was not dashing off to whatever Cliona had cooked for him, a bite to eat.

'Come away in, darlin', an' get to the fire. Matty, wet the tea for himself . . .'

'No, Mammy. I only came to see if Cliona was here, so I did.'

'No, pet, I've not seen her the day. She came by yesterday afternoon an' had a cup of tea with me then

185

she dashed off, you know how they are these days, saying she had so much to do she hadn't even time to have one of me scones an' them fresh baked. "Sure an' they'll only spoil," I says to her, but didn't they get eaten when that lad . . .'

She stopped speaking abruptly, and put a hand to her mouth as though she would dearly love to press back the words she had just spoken, and her eyes grew confused and sorry.

'Which lad, Mammy?' Michael smiled and Ellen looked at him guiltily, then she tossed her head, for if she could not have who she liked in her own kitchen then she might as well climb into her coffin and close the lid. This was her life here and her visitors were her life's blood, and though she was well aware since that dreadful, dreadful day of the Jubilee that Michael had not cared to be in the same house with him, let alone the same room, Christian was her grandson, flesh of her flesh, and she could not, *would* not deny him her house despite his daft ideas.

'Go on, Mammy. What were you going to say? Who was here yesterday?' Michael's voice had grown cool as though he knew perfectly well who it had been, and her old heart dropped. It was terrible when something like this happened in a family. When one member of it would have nothing to do with another, and as the thought shot its anguished bolt through her it brought back the time, over twenty years ago now, when her Mara had married James Osborne.

It had nearly put an end to Ellen. She had denied her daughter the house, stony-faced and stony-hearted, and it had taken the death of another daughter to bring them all together again. Now Ellen was more . . . what was the word . . . tolerant perhaps, her views not so

186

narrow, or was it the realisation that her own dogmatism had separated her from those she loved best? She was an old woman, and what years she had left she wanted to spend at peace with her family, and somehow she had come to believe that despite what the priests said to the contrary, the Holy Mother, whose own Son had been dear to her, knew what was in Ellen's heart and forgave her if she was sometimes lax.

''Twas just before Cliona left, pet, that he came. I know you said you wouldn't have him near her and . . . well, they were together for no more than five minutes and barely a word spoken between them. Are you well, says he. I am so, says she, so it was obvious to a man on a galloping horse they'd seen neither hide nor hair of each other, so surely . . . ?'

'Mammy, I said I'd not have him near her an' I meant it. At my house or at yours, an' if I hear again that you've let them visit you, both together, I'll not answer for the consequences.'

'*Michael!* God save us all, what are you sayin' . . . ?'

'You heard what I said, an' you heard what I said three weeks ago, an' I meant it, Mammy. He's a bad influence with his eejit ideas an' I'll not have him putting them in my daughter's head. She's at an impressionable age, there so.' His voice softened and he leaned forward to take his mother's hand. She was looking at him with an expression of such misery he felt ashamed. She was an old woman who lived for her family, and her joy was to have them about her, young and old alike. If they were happy she laughed with them, and when they wept she comforted them with her hugs and kisses and promises of a treat, with her cakes and buns and biscuits, her housewifely, motherly

187

gifts, which were all she had to offer. Herself, in fact, and it was not in her to turn one of them away, even one as incorrigible as Christian Osborne. She would continue to welcome him, kiss him and bully him, feed him and worry over him, as she did them all until her last breath. Well, that was all right just as long as the lad did not come near his Cliona. The good talking-to he had given her seemed to have done the trick. She had listened and agreed that everyone must be allowed their own opinion on matters such as politics, religion and indeed many other subjects, but one must be prepared to listen to all sides of any argument. She had listened to his, and though not saying a great deal, which was not unusual since she was what the rest of the family considered a 'deep one', she had gone about her day-to-day activities since with a quietness in her eyes and on her calm face which had reassured him. She was a sensible girl, was Cliona, they all agreed on that, and would take no harm from the brush she had had with Christian's nonsensical views.

'I'm sorry, Mammy, 'tis not your fault, so. We'll do our best to keep them apart. Take no chances but I'll not have him spouting his foolishness to me, or to Cliona if we should meet under your roof.'

Ellen beamed and kissed him, going to the front door with him to wave him off in his grand motor car, making him promise he and the girl would come for Sunday dinner, and had he heard from Callum, not that a man would be likely to write to his brother on his honeymoon, but perhaps a postcard. No, neither had she, the spalpeen, but then he'd better things to do . . . smiling . . . and weren't them begonias doin' well this year already, an' don't forget to go to Mass on Sunday an' drive carefully, darlin', smiling fondly at her son for sure wasn't he the grand fellow and so handsome despite his age.

He did not look handsome at half-past two the next morning when his frantic knock at her front door, then the sound of his key in the lock, brought herself and Matty trembling down the stairs, one behind the other in fear and trepidation.

'Jesus, Ma, I wish you'd let me put a bloody telephone in,' were his first words as he tumbled over the doorstep into the hall.

'A telephone . . . what . . . ?'

'I could have rung . . .'

'Rung? What for . . . ?' and her heart banged furiously inside her chest.

'To see if she was here.'

'Who . . . ?'

'I don't want you to be frightened, Mammy, but I've been in touch with everyone I can think of . . .'

Mother of God, she *was* frightened now for she had never seen him look so ghastly, not even when his young wife died.

'What . . . oh merciful Mother . . . what?' sketching a hasty cross on the embroidered yoke of her nightgown.

'Is Cliona here?'

'*Here* . . . ?' His fear was so contagious she felt ready to fall to her knees and beg the Holy Mother to protect them all. Cliona . . . here? Why should she be here at half-past two in the morning an' them both in their beds, her and Matty? She had told Michael only a few hours ago that Cliona had not been near since the day before, so why was he banging on her door at this ungodly hour when the child should be in her bed asleep . . . shouldn't she . . . wasn't she? . . . Jesus, Joseph and Mary . . . she must be . . .

'Oh God . . .' Michael leaned his back against her wall and hung his head, groaning deeply. His arms hung by his side, limp and useless. He wore no jacket. His shirt was crumpled, the sleeves rolled up to the elbows and his hair stood wildly on end as though he had pushed frantic fingers through it a hundred times.

'Oh God . . .' he repeated dully, ''tis that hell-spawn who's taken her. That young bastard with his high-flown beliefs, filling her head with impossible dreams, nonsense, rubbish, and she believed in it. I thought . . . hoped, she'd seen sense . . . but he must have . . .'

'Michael . . . oh please, Michael . . . sure an' I don't know what you're talkin' about. Who's got her . . . who . . . ?'

'That snivelling bastard of Mara's . . .'

'*Christian* . . .' and for a rapturous moment she felt the horror lift, for Christian was an O'Shaughnessy, despite having the name of Osborne. He was Cliona's cousin, Ellen's grandson, and if Cliona had for some reason which was as yet unclear gone somewhere with him, then she would be as right as rain. As safe as if she was with her own Daddy, since Christian would see no harm came to her. He would guard her and keep her safe until she came home to them and . . . but why? . . : what? . . . where had they gone? . . . and why? . . . at this hour . . . and slowly but surely the agony of it came back, filling her old body, her tired mind with such dread, such a dreadful *knowing*, she sagged against Matty and the two old women clung together for support. The grandfather clock, which had stood in the corner of the hall at the bottom of the stairs for as long as Ellen had been mistress of this house, as though to emphasise that time was wasting, struck the quarter hour, a quarter to three, and Michael raised his head as its musical chime penetrated his stunned senses.

'I've rung everybody, Ma . . . Elizabeth . . .'

'Elizabeth . . . ?'

'Lady Woodall . . . I never thought to ask if Christian was there . . . Clare at Beechwood, Gracie . . . all of them that I could think of, and those who've no telephone I've called on. No one's seen her, so I thought perhaps . . . I should have known, so I should, if she'd been here she'd have rung me but I had to try . . .'

He pushed himself upright, an old man suddenly who did not seem to have the strength to stand straight. His shoulders were slumped and there was a tremble in his big, broad-shouldered frame that would not let him be still.

'I'll go and see if she's taken any of her clothes, though . . . how would I know, Mammy? Sure, I don't keep track of what she buys . . . Oh Jesus . . .'

'Rosie . . . ?'

He brightened for a moment. 'Aye, Rosie. Perhaps she has heard them talk, or overheard something . . . if they were planning . . . An' sure she'd be knowin' if Cliona took anything . . . with her.'

'Michael, oh darlin' . . . will you not have a drink . . . a whiskey or . . .'

'An' the police will have to be told. I'll see that young sod in prison if it's the last bloody thing I ever do, or I'll swing for him, I swear it. Kidnapping, so it is. A girl of eighteen, under age . . .'

'Mary, Mother of God . . .' Ellen began to weep, clinging to Matty, two frail old women suddenly as they

191

crept back up the hallway towards the kitchen and the only comfort they could hope for this night.

'Will I be makin' us a cup of tay, Mrs O'Shaughnessy?'

'Aye, Matty. Darlin' . . . will you . . . ?' turning back to her son, but he was halfway through the front door, leaving it standing wide open as he ran like the wind down the long garden path, jumped into his car and roared off down Edge Lane towards, she supposed despairingly, the nearest police station.

They scoured the city that night and the next day and the next night, the O'Shaughnessys and the Woodalls, since the two brothers felt in honour bound to help in the search for Cliona. Christian was their cousin, more's the pity, Charles and Alex said, and they felt a certain responsibility for him and so naturally they must help to find O'Shaughnessy's young daughter, though *she* was not related to them except, they supposed, by marriage. Nevertheless, it was surely up to them to lend a hand.

But where to start? Michael O'Shaughnessy was well known amongst those who had motor cars in Liverpool and also as a member of the Irish Roman Catholic community, and he soon had the name, or at least the whereabouts, of the 'movement', as Christian had described the group of young, Liverpool-born Irish with whom he, and presumably Cliona, had associated. They were close-lipped and cold-eyed, the young men, asking how they could be expected to know the location of a man such as Christian Osborne? They were nothing but an Irish Catholic working men's club, they said, who met to play snooker and have a 'bevvy'. Yes, they knew of the 'troubles' in Ireland, but if Mr O'Shaughnessy cared to look about the 'club' he would find no guns here.

Mr O'Shaughnessy was in no mood to play games, he said, taking the biggest youth by his shirt front and dragging him almost off his feet until they were nose to nose.

'Has my daughter been in here, you little prick?' he hissed through clenched teeth, his face livid, his eyes wild and glaring, but the youth would not be browbeaten though he knew the older man could flatten him, as he promised to do if he did not give the right answer.

All about the tense couple, O'Shaughnessys and Woodalls muttered menacingly, circling those of the 'club' who would have intervened; Donal and Eammon, Denny McGuire who had a beer belly on him so huge it threatened to pull him on to his face, Flynn McGowan, Eileen's boy Finbar, James and Paul Conroy, and Donal's boy Joseph, who was no more than fourteen. Alex and Charlie stood by, Alex ready to swing his fists with the rest, Charlie somewhat aloof and longing quite plainly to give the louts who were squaring up to the O'Shaughnessys the length of his well-bred tongue.

' 'Tis a men's club, Mr O'Shaughnessy. No women allowed, so.'

'That's not what I heard,' his grip tightening on the youth's shirt front until he was in danger of strangling him on his own collar and tie.

'Sure an' I don't know what you heard but there's nobody here but us,' and no matter what threats were made, and there were more than a few, they would not be budged. Hard-eyed and close-mouthed, and not at all the kind of amiable Irishmen who would meet for

193

the purpose of playing games and falling down drunk.

'I'll be back.' Michael was trembling on the edge of murderous violence, and Donal and Eammon had to drag him from the man.

'Sure an' why not, sor, but they'll still not be here.'

It was the second day and still there was nothing. Cliona O'Shaughnessy and Christian Osborne had vanished as thoroughly as fog vanishes in the warmth of sunlight, and even the police, who had questioned a hundred people and watched the ferry services for thirty-six hours, had begun to say they could do no more. Of course they would continue to keep a look-out for Mr O'Shaughnessy's daughter, of course they would, but it seemed she had gone off with a relative so she could be in no danger, wasn't that so, and there was no evidence of a crime having been committed, wouldn't Mr O'Shaughnessy agree? but they would certainly keep looking, and details of the case had been sent to branches of the police force up and down the country, along with copies of the photograph Mr O'Shaughnessy had provided of his daughter.

Ellen was drinking a cup of tea. She had lost count of how many times Matty had put the kettle on in the last thirty-six hours. She had donned the first dress which came to hand when Michael had hurtled out of the house the night before last, and she was still in it. She had done no more than rinse her face and plait her hair, winding it about her head, before she and Matty had begun to throw things together ready to feed the dozens of men who had flung out of the house in search of Cliona, for they must eat. It had kept her busy, her hands performing the familiar tasks which they had performed a thousand times before. Kneading dough, rubbing fat into flour, stirring soup and broth and batter, cleaning and chopping vegetables for the stock pot, until she had enough food in the larder to feed not only the O'Shaughnessy and Woodall boys but the entire police force of Liverpool.

Very little of it had been eaten. Michael had been persuaded to go home for an hour, told to lie down and take a wee nap, which Ellen knew he would ignore, to change his shirt and have a shave and come back to Edge Lane for a meal. Perhaps there would be a letter, a telephone call, a message of some sort from somebody. Rosie had checked Cliona's wardrobe but even she had not known if anything had been taken from it, so perhaps . . . if the Blessed Virgin could find it in her heart to be merciful, Michael might even find Cliona there, though it seemed unlikely now.

He came into the house so quietly she and Matty did not hear him, and when he just appeared in her kitchen doorway she nearly dropped her cup of tea.

'Michael . . . God almighty, sure an' you gave me a start. An' will you look at you, pet. A clean shirt, I said, for no matter what . . .' She stopped speaking abruptly. She placed her cup of tea carefully on the table and stood up, her eyes never moving from her son's face. Matty, who was in the other chair, put her hand to her eyes and began to moan.

'Be quiet, Matty,' Ellen said sternly, waiting for the blow to fall, since it surely would. Michael's eyes were dead. The lovely blue-green sparkle of them had been washed away, by his tears, if Ellen was any judge, and his face was the colour of the dough she had so recently pounded and which now stood waiting its turn for the oven beneath its cloth on the table.

'Tell me, son.' She moved towards him, her arms

195

which were suddenly strong as they had always been in the service of her family, ready to take him.

He lifted a weary arm. There was a letter in his hand.

'She's gone.' His voice was as lifeless as his eyes.

'Where, darlin'?'

'Ireland.'

'Holy Mother, bless us now . . .' crossing herself as Matty did.

'Would you be lettin' me read it, Michael?'

He held it out to her, then sank into a chair by the table, and placing his folded arms next to the rising dough he bowed his head on them.

'Dear Daddy,

I tried to do what you said, to look at it from both sides but it made no sense. There's so much to be done. We want Ireland to be free and whole and that won't happen by just talking about it, Daddy. We hate oppression and we must strive to overthrow it. We have to fight, and that's what Christian and me are going to do. We have been helped to get here and we are to train . . . well, I can't tell you where. I love you, Daddy, and I'm sorry we couldn't agree. Kiss grandma for me.

Cliona.'

The man wept harshly on the woman's breast and she cradled him to her in a passion of love.

'Hush, my darling, hush. You must not weep so for I cannot bear it. It breaks my heart to see you in such despair.'

His arms, which held her to him, gripped her more tightly, and his body shook convulsively, moving hers and the bed in which they lay. Daylight showed round the edges of the drawn curtains at the window, and the sound of bird-song was clear close by. The room in which they lay was evidently part of a country inn of sorts, for the ceiling was low and heavy with oak beams, and the window behind its curtains was mullioned. The walls were plainly whitewashed. There was a porcelain jug and basin on the marble-topped oak washstand, and the bedcover, which had been pushed to the end of the bed, was quilted in cheerful squares of many colours. The old cottage-style door was bolted, and articles of clothing lay about the room. They were both naked. A handsome couple though no longer young, both dark. The woman had a wing of white in her straight, heavy hair, which was loose and tumbled on the pillow, and the man had a peppering at each temple.

'Jesus, I don't know how I would have got through this without you,' he muttered, his mouth against her distended nipple, like an infant seeking nourishment from a source which it knows will never be denied. Not the nourishment of food but that of comfort, love, understanding, hope.

'I am always here, my love, you know that. I shall always be here.'

'Promise me . . .'

'Anything.'

'When this is over and I have her back you'll marry me.'

'I will marry you, darling, but . . . not for a while.'

'Is he still standing between us then, after all these years?'

'No, it is not Harry who stood between us, you should know that, but my own fear.'

'Of me?'

'Yes, and the world. Your world. *Our* world. Harry was safety, and the girl I was then needed that.'

'And . . . no longer?'

'That world has gone, my darling, and with it so much that we thought important, but *we* survived and I think *our* time has come at last.'

'My dearest heart.' He kissed her tenderly. 'But there is one thing . . .'

'Yes, Michael?' though of course she knew what he was about to say.

'The boy. Our son. Is it not time, or will it not be time when we marry, I mean, to tell him who I am?'

There was a long, troubled silence. Elizabeth turned her head on the pillow to stare sadly towards the window and the deep peace beyond, and the man watched her.

Then, 'I will do whatever *you* want to do, Elizabeth, sure an' you know that.'

'I do know that, my love, and it breaks my heart sometimes when I look at him and know that he has been denied the great gift of having known you as his father. You are a fine man, a good man, my darling. A fine father to Cliona, and the sadness is almost more than I can bear, not only for him but for you.'

She turned back to him and tears welled to her eyes and brimmed over the corners, sliding down each temple and into her hair.

'But I cannot be sure he will . . . not be devastated by the realisation that . . . He loved Harry dearly and Harry loved him. Alex *likes* you, Michael. May we not do more harm and create a situation where we *both* lose him if we tell him that the father he deeply mourns was absolutely nothing to him, at least by blood, and that the man he thinks of as perhaps a well-liked friend is in fact his father?'

Michael laid his drawn cheek on her breast, and she

smoothed his hair with loving fingers. 'I know you have longed for years for the right to acknowledge your son,' she went on quietly, 'to have the world know that this fine young man is yours. But Alex is an innocent participant in this and is it right to . . . to strike him a blow, not for *his* sake but . . .' sadly, '. . . for ours? So that *we* may have the joy of sharing our son at last. And there is not only Alex. Damaris and Charles, Ellen . . . so many hearts would be sorely hurt.'

He was quiet for a long time.

'Michael . . . ?'

'Yes.'

'My love, I am so sorry.'

'No, you're right. It would serve no purpose. 'Tis only to satisfy my own pride, but the boy, our son, must not be hurt.'

'As you are hurting?'

'Aye, but then I have you now and will for always.' Michael raised his head and looked passionately into Elizabeth's eyes, then he smiled, though his face was still marked with his grief.

'They're still the same incredible colour they were when I first saw you. Bejasus, I looked into them and loved you. 'Twas as simple as that. You took my heart then and you still have it. Twenty-five years ago an' both of us no more than children. At least you were. Scared to death of me, so you were, looking at me with those big eyes as though you thought I was goin' to eat you up, but as haughty as a young queen despite being afraid.'

'I was fifteen.'

'Aye, so you were, an' me not much older. Sweet Christ, 'tis a long time ago and a long while to wait for a woman, my darling, but I'll not wait much longer.

There's no need now so if you won't tell the world, I will.'

'I'm not asking you to wait much longer, but for the sake of the children I must be . . . circumspect.'

'Aye, the children . . .' and the man sighed deeply, then turned his bitter gaze towards the window.

'You've heard no more?' She touched his face gently to draw him back from his brooding contemplation of what had happened, and when he turned to look at her she lifted her mouth to his before he answered, letting him know that whatever happened, whatever pain he suffered she was here, his, ready to share it with him as they had shared so much in the past.

'No.' His reply was muffled as he ran his mouth along her still clear jawline and down her arching throat to her lovely breasts. She had borne three children, one of them his, but they were still firm and high.

'Don't give up hope, my darling. You will. She will write. She loves you, as I do. Oh God, Michael, as I do.'

'I know, sweet girl, I know, but don't talk, not now . . .'

'But I can't live here alone.'

'Then might I ask what you propose to do? Go home to your mother? You knew I was a seaman when we married and a seaman's life is at sea. I shall be away no more than three weeks on my next trip . . .'

'*Three weeks!*' Maris's voice rose in a wail of horror, and Callum winced, doing his best to keep his impatience in check. Just as he had in the two weeks since the wedding. Two bloody weeks kicking his heels in some rustic backwater of Scotland where the nearest pub was five miles away if he could have gone, but it seemed his new wife did not care for them, considering them to be somewhat 'common'. She didn't want to 'share' him with anyone, she said, and could they not have a cocktail in the comfort of their own sitting room? A *cocktail*! Jesus!

They went walking – hand in hand since his wife considered it suitable for a couple on honeymoon – up on the hills, which he admitted were very lovely with the gorse bearing its summer flowers in an abundance of gold, cheek by jowl with purple bellheather spreading as far as the eye could see in the empty rolling landscape. Bracken as high as his waist, in which his tiny wife was almost lost. There were lakes, or lochs as the local people called them, like misted sheets of glass where he might fish, so he was told, or perhaps he might care for a bit of shooting. Thank you, but no, he had said coolly, since he could see no reason to kill an innocent bird, or animal, or even a fish, just to pass the time of day, which caused a few raised eyebrows.

He had made love to her every night, sometimes twice, and every morning, and on occasion in the bright light of the afternoon, which she thought quite enchanting. A couple of times in the heather as well, bringing her to soaring, singing delight, satisfying his own body at the same time, and it was only then that they met on any common ground.

Now it was over, thank Christ, and he could get back to his proper life, leave behind this farrago into which a moment's pleasure had thrust him. At least for the space of three weeks, and when the child came perhaps he could arrange to do only long sea trips, to the east or Australia or New Zealand, leaving his pretty little wife under the matriarchal wing of his mother, who would like nothing better than to see the coming child properly reared in the Catholic faith, God love her. And when Maris settled to it as settle she must, perhaps they might lead some kind of married life congenial to them both. He was certain she would get over this girlish infatuation she had formed for him, and when that happened they might even be friends. When she matured. When she grew out of this fantasy dream which she, and, he supposed, all young girls lived in. A handsome man to sweep her off her feet, marriage in a white dress, which unfortunately she had had to forgo. A house and two babies and a life that would be lived happily ever after. She would see the reality of it, and with *his* mother to guide her, *not* her own, to teach her how to be a housewife and a mother, she would settle down. They might have another child in a year or so, or even make it three, keep her busy, make some sort of fist of the terrible circumstances in which they had landed themselves. Not that *she* seemed to think that they had, clinging to him and declaring how much she loved him a dozen times a day, stars in her eyes and a flush to her soft young cheek which was quite delightful, and which he would have *found* delightful had he loved her. Perhaps with a bit of luck, though, he had ruminated in the dead of night whilst his wife slept, still clinging to him, there might be acceptance without hurting one another too badly.

They had just come through the front door of the house in Seymour Road which Callum had rented now for almost five years. A semi-detached pebble-dashed house built just after the war. There was a small front and back garden. There was a garage attached to the house since the motor car, the builder had decided, was here to stay. Two bay windows, one above the other, looked out from the 'front' room and the 'front' bedroom, with a tiny box room above the porched front door. It had electricity, of course, with a power point in each room, a modern kitchen and bathroom, but Callum had done no more than put down a square of carpet in each living room and bedroom, set a comfortable armchair and a sofa in the front room, a sideboard in which to store his crockery, and a large, comfortable bed in the front bedroom. There were no 'knick-knacks', no pictures, no wireless, since Callum was not there often enough or long enough to listen to it, and the skimpiest of curtains at each window. No lamps, nothing, in fact, to put an identity in the rooms, the identity and character of the man who lived there since he didn't, not really. It was merely a place to lay his head when he was in port, a place to eat his breakfast, preferably with some pretty but temporary young lady on the other side of the table. He had rented it so that he might escape the impossibility of living with his mother. It was as simple as that. Dearly though he loved her, he was a man with his own life to live, and his mother still thought of him, and treated him, as a boy, and could not understand even now why he needed a place of his own when he had a perfectly good bed going begging at Edge Lane. It wasn't as if he was married, she had protested, or even spent more than a night or two at a time at Seymour Road, but he had set his jaw and told her firmly that he would get married one day and this way he had a home all ready for his bride of the future.

And now she was here standing in his hall and looking like some abandoned kitten he had found in a storm and had brought home for a saucer of milk.

Whilst he and Maris had been on their honeymoon, Lady Woodall and Rosie had packed all Maris's clothes and personal possessions and had motored over with one of the gardening lads to help with the lifting. They must have made several journeys by the look of it, Callum thought grimly, as he surveyed the mound of boxes and suitcases. They had made some attempt to unpack, bewildered, he supposed, by the lack of space, putting as many of her dresses as they could into the one wardrobe, beside his own suits; but in the hall and spilling over into the 'back' room, which had in it nothing but a kitchen table and four chairs, were a dozen suitcases, two trunks, several boxes and an enormous bedding chest.

'We'd best get some order out of this lot,' he said, heaving in his own suitcase and the already bursting trunk Maris had thought necessary to take on her honeymoon. Full of lovely dresses and lacy underwear, wisps of chiffon and silk with which to enchant her new husband, walking outfits, tennis outfits and even a bloody *ballgown*, would you believe? She had put it on to allow him to admire her in it, and the only thing he could think of to do with her was to pull it down about her waist and caress her breasts until she herself stepped out of it and into their bed.

That was how it had been. Every contact leading to their bed. They had no other, no meeting of the mind or the heart, only of the flesh, and though he had found it quite delightful at the time, once it was over she bored and irritated him to the point where he found it hard not to simply pack his bag and walk out on her. Get in his car and go somewhere, *anywhere* as long as she was not there.

'Where shall we put them?' she asked now, somewhat tearfully, looking about this tiny dolls' house which she had visited only once before their marriage and which, at the time, she had thought to be 'great fun', and in which her husband had just told her she was to live completely alone while he was at sea. Naturally, she knew he *went* to sea. Well, as he had just said, sailors did, but not once in the last rapturous few weeks had she given a thought to what would happen *after* the honeymoon. She had danced through them, light as thistle-down, radiant and eager to begin this wonderful new life she and Callum were to have together. Her dream had come true. Her prince, her knight in shining armour, had come at last to rescue her from the horror and scandal of bearing her child, his child, alone and unsupported by a husband. She had no idea why he had not come before and, as yet, she had not cared to ask in case his answer should not be to her liking. He had come, that was all that mattered, and he would not have done so, she told herself, had he not cared for her. Not as she loved him, she was wise enough to realise that. He was reserved, not at all as demonstrative as she herself was, but that would change, she was certain. She would show him what a splendid wife she would make, and a loving and patient mother to his child, and they would grow together, get to know one another. The 'bed' side of their marriage was lovely. She loved it and so did he, she could tell that, inexperienced as she was, and so with this as a foundation they would build their life and their marriage until it was as splendid as that of her mother and father.

'God knows,' he answered, one hand pushing through his rough, curly hair, looking about him in despair.

'Couldn't we leave the maid to do it?' Her deep brown eyes melted in his direction, innocent and trusting, and he felt a distinct urge to hit her.

'What bloody maid?' His voice was bitingly calm.

'There is no maid?'

'Right first time.'

'But . . . how shall I manage? I have . . . well, my mother always has a maid to . . . and she helped me and Rosie, with our clothes, you know . . .'

'Well, you will have to manage your own clothes now, and the rest of the things women of my class have to do.'

He relented a little, for she was trembling on the brink of tears, small and wan and terribly helpless, fragile even, intolerably so despite her advancing pregnancy, and again he felt his frustrated impatience wash over him. Jesus Christ, was he to spend the rest of his life making amends to this child for what he had done to her in a fit of what could only be called madness?

Soothing her fears and doing his best to excuse her for what she did not know or understand.

'I'll see if my mother can get you a woman to do the heavy cleaning and a man to see to the garden.'

'Thank you, Callum.' Her head hung in pretty but helpless misery, and he forced himself to move towards her, to take her in his arms and hug her to him, to kiss the top of her rumpled curls and then her eager mouth when she turned it up to him.

'Could you not do the garden, Callum?' she asked earnestly, her eyes shining now, ready to share out the duties of man and wife, as the working classes did, or so she believed.

'I've just told you. I am to go to sea the day after tomorrow.'

'Yes, of course.'

'Tell you what, though.'

'What?' wide-eyed, eager like that puppy he had remembered on the day he had told her that they would be married. Beginning to believe, in her naïvety, that he was about to tell her that he would give it all up, get a job which would keep him at her side, and again he was to quench that light in her eyes.

'Why not ask Rosie to stay with you for a while? She would be company for you until you get used to . . . well . . . all this.' Thank God, that was the answer. His niece Rosie who was a good sensible girl and who would bring some order into the life of this child he had married. She came from humble beginnings on one side, and had the blood in her veins of her down-to-earth Irish grandmother. Surely *she* could make Maris understand, guide her in the way she must go, make her realise what her life was to be, since he was damned if he could. He could not stand the bloody *tears*, the

207

hangdog look of that bloody puppy which had just been spoken sharply to.

'She could stay until the child comes, if you like, help you to put the house in order . . .'

Instantly her face lit up, and she stepped back into the role in which she saw herself. Wife to Captain Callum O'Shaughnessy, mistress of this house, mother-to-be with a husband whose name she bore.

'Oh yes, we could make it really sweet, Rosie and I. A dear little house just like the one I had as a child. I know it's small, but there is some lovely furniture in the attic at Woodall, and there is a shop I know in Bold Street which has the most beautiful carpeting. I was in there with mother only . . .'

'Hang on a minute, Maris. There's nothing wrong with what we already have and I don't think we are reduced to needing your family's cast-offs. You will have ample housekeeping . . .'

'Oh, I know mother won't mind if I raid the attic, and I have some money of my own. I'll buy the new carpets and decent curtains. Velvet, I think in a pretty shade of . . .'

'I'm afraid not,' and again he took the lovely light from her eyes with his coldness, and again he was sorry and irritated. But she must be made to realise that *he* was the provider in his own home. He was the wage-earner and what he earned must keep them. He would have no Woodall hand-outs, of furniture from the attics or from his wife's personal income.

'Maris.' He lifted her chin, which was drooping again, and looked into her eyes. He cupped her face with his big hands and kissed her soothingly, feeling like a brute as he did so, but she must be made to understand right from the start who she now was.

'Maris, you are my wife, the wife of a working man, and in our world the man supports his wife and children. I am well able to provide for you both, even to provide the cleaning woman and the occasional gardener, but I cannot allow your family to give us . . . things. The furniture here, at the moment, is perfectly adequate.'

'But you said put the house in order,' she said, mournfully.

'I meant . . . rearrange it to suit yourself. I see we shall have to have a bigger wardrobe . . .' his expression wry, '. . . and a chest of drawers, and naturally, if Rosie comes, a single bed to put in the back bedroom. Get what you think we need and I will pay for it. And then there is the child to think of and provide for. The . . . what d'you call it . . . the layette to buy, but my mother will help you with that, I'm sure. You will be decently, comfortably provided for, but you are the wife of a working man and must live as one.'

'May I visit my mother?'

He laughed and drew her into his arms again. 'Of course you may, though I don't know how you will get there.'

'Oh, I mean to buy a small car now that . . .'

He put her from him almost savagely and walked over to the window, looking out on to the small square of garden which was bordered on three sides by a burgeoning privet hedge. It was so overgrown it exploded into the garden, barely leaving space for the weeds in the bit of lawn which grew almost to waist height. He did not see them. He was no gardener and though the front was tidy enough, being mostly crazy-paved with a straggling border of unpruned rose bushes, he could not remember ever going out into the back.

'You don't listen, do you?' he said, apparently to the glass in the window. 'I have just told you that as my wife you will be provided for, but that does not include a car.'

'I said I would buy it with my own . . .'

'No, you will not, Maris. I was not aware that you had that much money nor do I know what you will do with it. I do know that it will not be spent on anything for this house or for my child. If we are to make any sort of . . . success of our marriage, it must be in the way of my class. I am the provider, as men like me have always been, and I must be allowed to be what I have been brought up to be and which I believe is my role, and you must fit yourself into yours. There will be no prettying-up of this place into the kind of . . . of . . . well, a place for you to play at house. It is our home, yours and mine and that of our child. You will run it, as my mother runs hers, and you will have no time to be dashing about town in a motor car. And even if I allowed it, you cannot drive in your condition. The wives in families such as mine do not . . .'

'It seems to me the bloody wives in your bloody family – of which you seem so proud – do nothing but have children, scrub floors and agree with every bloody thing their lord and master tells them.'

He turned, astonished, in fact he could not have been more astonished had he put out his hand to a canary and had it taken off at the wrist by a vulture.

'You have spent the last ten minutes telling me what I may *not* do; now perhaps you will give me some inkling as to what, as your wife, I am allowed to do?'

'I have told you. Exactly what my mother does, and my sisters.'

'I see, and what is that, apart from the scrubbing and the bearing of children?'

Her small face, which had been so pale and miserable, was aflame with vivid indignation, and for some strange reason though she seemed to be about to defy him, he felt a prickle of pleasure. She was like the lively girl he had first seen on the ferry. The one who had amused him for three months, who had danced and flirted and laughed, her head tossing, her brown eyes deep and glowing and her lips pouting, ready to be kissed. Now she was showing her teeth in her sudden rage. It was as though she had come to the last inch of her restraint, that which had submerged itself in love and gratitude, for and to himself, and the true and spirited Maris Woodall – she was not an O'Shaughnessy just at this particular moment, her demeanour said – had broken free. She had been willing to do anything to please him, but she would not be changed from what she was to what he thought she should be.

She said so.

'You cannot expect me to become as the women in your family are,' she tilted her head imperiously, 'just because that is what you are accustomed to, Callum, though that was not one with whom you were dancing at the Adelphi. I have been brought up in a certain way and to believe in certain things and I cannot change overnight. In fact, I'm not sure I want to change at all. I like myself as I am.'

She dared him to argue, but it was in him to *agree* with her. He rather liked her as she was at this precise moment, too.

'We are man and wife now, but that does not mean I am a doormat,' she went on, 'and I shall do as I please.'

'Will you now?'

'Indeed I will, and if I wish to have new carpets and curtains in my home, since this *is* my home, it seems, then I shall, *and* a little runabout to take me to visit my mother and my friends. I can afford it and I can think of no reason to ask your permission on how to spend my own money. I am not accustomed to being ordered to do this and not do that . . .'

'Well, madam, you had best *get* used to it, because that is what women in . . .'

'I don't notice your mother jumping every time you or your brothers ask something of her. Just the opposite, I would say.'

'That's enough. My mother is old and . . .'

'When she was young, my age, did she do exactly what her husband told her? Did she have no thoughts in her head other than those he put there?'

'That's nothing to do with you. Besides, my mother and father had a good marriage. *She* didn't get herself . . .'

He stopped abruptly, aware that what he had been about to say would be deeply hurtful, and that should the words be uttered they could not be retrieved, but she had already heard them though they had not been spoken.

'She did not get herself pregnant, is that what you were about to say? Well, I did not do it alone, Callum. You had some part in it . . . it was . . . not all my doing,' and before his eyes she seemed to fall in on herself, to deflate like a small balloon which has been bouncing merrily along until a cruel pin is thrust into it. Her eyes filled with tears, just as a child's would, and her lips quivered.

'Please . . . oh please, don't let us quarrel,' she

212

moaned. 'I love you so much and I can't bear it when
. . . I have only you and if you are cross with me then
how will I bear it?'

He had been enjoying her. Enjoying the defiance and
the exchange of sharp words which had flashed between
them. She could not, of course, continue to be the girl
she thought herself to be. She could not dash about in
her own small car like the bright young things with
whom she was acquainted. She could not spend her
days idling round the shops, making calls and receiving
them, passing her days in the pleasant and useless ways
of the gentry. It would not do. She was his wife, like
it or not, and more importantly would be the mother of
his child; but whilst she had been bucking and plunging
against the reins which marriage, or at least marriage
to a man such as himself, would impose on her, he
had admired her spirit, the hot depth of her eyes, the
flag of scarlet indignation in her cheeks. She had been
like a small white dove on his hand for the past few
weeks and it had been stimulating to have her turn and
peck at him. Now she was the dove again, craving his
hand, his attention, needing him, demanding, and his
impatience and resentment returned.

He did his best to keep it well tamped down. He had
chosen, if that was the right word, to marry her when
he needn't. If he had wished he could have walked
away from the situation, as men can, got a berth as the
master of some tramp steamer. But he had done the
right thing, and now he must do the best with it that
he could. She was pregnant, he told himself, and must,
just now, be indulged. He would be away the day after
tomorrow and then his mother could take her over, see
that she behaved herself until the baby came, that she
behaved as his wife should, but until then he must be

213

patient. God only knew how he was to do it. Already he felt he could not wait to get away from the stifling restraint that had been put on him. Jesus . . . oh sweet Jesus . . . why had he not patted her on the head on the day of her father's funeral four months ago, clucked sympathetically as one does in these situations and simply walked away? Why . . . Oh God . . . *why* . . . *why* . . . why had he not . . . but what was the use . . . what was the bloody use?

Clamping his teeth together, and without making a sound, he held out his arms, and when she ran into them he lifted her against his chest and carried her up to bed, bringing them both a measure of peace in the only way he knew how.

The little green MG sports car turned out of Seymour Road into Thomas Lane, speeding on through the maze of streets which surrounded it, until it hit Childwall Valley Road. The noise of its engine altered as it passed under the railway bridge which carried the Cheshire Lines Railway, then became a roar again as it sped away far beyond the speed limit allowed, out into the open countryside.

There were meadows on either side of the speeding vehicle, golden with buttercups, and here and there were patches of red where the sorrel was beginning to flower. The hedges were bright with wild rose, elderberry and honeysuckle, and on the rise at the top of the fields a cutting machine was at work, the buzz of it like an insect on the warm summer air. There were cows standing up to their knees in wild clover, their heads down but lifting to watch the passage of the little green motor car, their tails moving rhythmically as the midges swarmed. Tall grasses in the ditch swayed in the breeze caused by the passage of the car, and the perfume of the wild flowers was heavy and sweet.

The sun shone on the driver's silvery blaze of hair, rippling it about her head, and she lifted one hand from the steering wheel to push it through the heavy mass of curls. Her face was set in lines of oppression which sat ill on one so young. Her eyes were shadowed, the memory of some recent pain lurking in their depths, and yet there was a defiant jut to her small chin.

The car lurched as the left front wheel hit the verge of the grass, and she hastily put her hand back on the wheel, righting the car somewhat clumsily.

'I'm out of practice,' she muttered to herself, slowing down a little. She knew she had been going far too fast, but she had wanted to escape as quickly as she could from the past hour, and the speed of the car as it fled from the scene of the misery had given that illusion. Get away from it and that horrid little house. Put as much time and space between now and that awful good-bye, and then perhaps she might begin to feel better. More . . . content, though why she should *not* feel content when she had everything she had ever wanted – except that horrid little house – she could not imagine.

The neat rectangular fields continued to speed past her, edged as they had been since the days of enclosure with thorn and elm hedgerows. She whipped smartly through the village of Colton, startling a couple of elderly gentlemen who sat outside the pub with their pints of foaming ale. Church, inn, manor house and parsonage were grouped in the usual village quartet, and in the centre was the green in which a pond was set. A line of ducks, which cut serenely through the water, scattered in confusion as the roar of the sports car disturbed their afternoon peace.

'Bloody idiot,' one old gentleman remarked, wiping the foam from his moustache with the back of his hand.

'You're right,' said the other, doing the same.

The gates to Woodall Park stood wide open. The gatehouse was deserted now and had been since its last occupant had marched cheerfully away to war and never returned. His family were dispersed, his wife remarried, and nothing but mice and house martins occupied the small building. There was no need of a gatehouse keeper now. Since her husband had come home stricken by the mustard gas he had inhaled, Lady Woodall had committed herself entirely to his care, having few callers beside the family. She and Sir Harry, unlike Lady Anne Woodall and Sir Charles Woodall who had a constant stream of visitors and guests, had no longer entertained. Once upon a time, old Tommy, as he had always been called – though he had been no more than thirty – since the prefix 'old' had been a tradition which never seemed to die, had been for ever running in and out to open and close the gates, but no one bothered now and they stood open at all times. Those old days were long gone, sadly.

Beyond the gates was the curved drive skirting the dower-house to which Lady Woodall would move when the baronet married. Passing through the stand of trees which lay beside the park and surrounded the house, there it was. The house. A proper house. Woodall Park, her home.

Wilson appeared at the front door, as he always did, as if by magic. He moved slowly and majestically down the steps to open the car door for her.

'Good afternoon, Mrs O'Shaughnessy,' he murmured, startling her considerably with the use of her married name, and if he was surprised to see her so soon after her return from honeymoon, of course he did not show it.

'Good afternoon, Wilson, but please, I am still Miss Maris,' she answered, smoothing down the folds of her cotton dress. It was in a shade of pink which had been created after the birth of the second daughter of the Duke and Duchess of York, and called, as she was, Princess Margaret Rose, and the lovely warmth of the colour suited the ivory and rose of Maris's skin and the pale silver gleam of her hair. It had become very popular to name colours after the female members of the royal family, or royal events. Marina green for the Duchess of Kent and Jubilee blue, very appropriate in this Jubilee year of 1935, were just two of them.

'Indeed you are, Mrs O'Shaughnessy,' Wilson answered, and her already heavy heart sank even further. There had been nothing more she wanted in this world than to be Mrs Callum O'Shaughnessy, but somehow she had the most dreadful feeling that in the process of becoming her she had lost her own identity. And the curious thing was, she didn't know how or why. Wilson calling her by that strange and foreign-sounding name when at this particular moment she felt she was just Maris Woodall, coming home perhaps from a day out with Angela or Rosie. Afternoon tea in Lewis's, shopping, gossiping, laughing in that careless way that had once been so natural. That was how she felt. Not Mrs Callum O'Shaughnessy, a married woman with a husband, and a child growing in her womb. He had gone, and so, momentarily, had his wife. This afternoon, she had told herself, she would be Maris Woodall. In fact, whilst her husband . . . *her husband* . . . wanting to giggle since it seemed so absurd, feeling instantly better, whilst he was away she would be Maris Woodall *all* the time and do all the things she usually did. And she positively knew she would get round him in the end. She had always got round men, from her father since she was a baby right up to Freddie Winters when she had become a young woman. Indeed, all the young men she had known had fallen in love with her, longing to do as she commanded. So could Callum deny her all the things she planned to do, and have? Her own little car for a start, in which she could get about, and in the meanwhile she would use his. The thing was doing nothing but sit in the garage attached to that horrid little house, and she was certain it would do the engine, or something, good, to be used, or at least that was what Alex always said. A car engine needed a good 'blow through' was how he put it, and so she was really doing Callum a good turn by giving one to the MG.

She smiled as she justified her own rebellious action.

'Is my mother at home, Wilson?' she called over her shoulder, as she ran lightly up the steps.

'She is, madam . . .' – Good God, *madam*! – '. . . she and Miss Rose are in the garden taking tea.'

'Tell Elsie to bring another cup, there's a good chap, Wilson, and ask Cook if she has any of her ratafia biscuits about her, will you? I'm absolutely famished.'

'Very well, Mrs O'Shaughnessy.'

She turned, and her face was set defiantly, her eyes vivid with some emotion Wilson could not interpret.

'Wilson.'

'Yes, madam?'

'I would appreciate it if you would continue to call me Miss Maris when I am at home.'

'Very well, Miss Maris.'

'Thank you, Wilson, and don't forget the ratafias.'

'No, Miss Maris.'

Wilson watched her stride through the wide hallway, her step buoyant and springing. She turned into the drawing room, and as she approached the french window which stood open on to the terrace he heard her speak out loud.

'Lord, but it's lovely to be home.'

12

'Mother wants me to help Uncle Teddy with Beech-wood until Christian gets back, which, knowing Christian, shouldn't be long. He'll soon get fed up with playing at soldiers, but he can stay away for ever as far as I'm concerned for I quite fancy myself as manager of the estate. Just the kind of work I'm sure I could take to. A big favour, mother said. I think she guesses sometimes how ready I am to move on, and this is merely a ruse to keep me here a bit longer. Uncle Teddy is getting on in years . . .'

'He's not forty yet.'

'Isn't he? God, he looks it.'

'So would you if you had no legs and had to sit in a chair all day long.'

'I'd rather be dead.' Alex shuddered dramatically and his face seemed to pale as he studied his own strong young legs which were stretched out on the grass, straight and whole, before him. The terrible prospect of them not being there was more than he could bear, and he stood up as though to reassure himself that he still could. 'I don't know how he got through it without doing away with himself. I know I would.'

'Would you?' Charlie leaned back in the deck chair, tipping the old panama hat he wore over his eyes. 'How would you do it?'

'God knows. I suppose if one has no legs it narrows it down a bit, the ways, I mean. One could hardly slip

220

down to the lake and drown oneself, nor jump off a chair with a rope about one's neck.'

'*Alex*, stop it. How could you? Poor Uncle Teddy. What a dreadful conversation. The pair of you should be ashamed of yourselves, really you should, but having said it . . . well . . . Aunt Elizabeth told me that had it not been for Aunt Clare, he might.'

'Might what?'

'Have killed himself.' Rosie's compassionate young face was quite stricken, and her two companions turned towards her. Alex sank to the rug beside her. They had spread it away from the trees beneath which Elizabeth Woodall and Ellen O'Shaughnessy sat. Between the two older women was the new bride and mother-to-be, who, it appeared, was being treated to a lecture on how to be good at both. Michael O'Shaughnessy had brought Maris and her mother-in-law over in his Lanchester, the day being fine after a spell of wet weather, saying he would pick them up at four, and tea was being served to them by Elsie and Wilson.

'Really? Good God,' for though he had just sworn that he would rather die than be as his Uncle Teddy was, Alex was quite dumbfounded to be told Uncle Teddy had felt the same. Teddy Osborne was a handsome, likeable chap, good-natured and always ready for a chin wag. One quite forgot what was missing beneath the rug which covered him from the waist down, and if you saw him bowling along in the trap, chirruping to the fat pony to 'get up there, Floss', you would never know he was not as capable of climbing out of it as anyone else.

'Mmm, Aunt Elizabeth said that Grandfather Osborne kept all the guns locked up even though they were downstairs in the gun room where Uncle Teddy couldn't reach them anyway. He just sat in his room for years, she said, doing nothing, and it was not until Aunt Clare befriended him, as a child – remember when Aunt Caitlin and Uncle Jack lived at Beechwood? – that he began to recover.'

'Good God,' Alex said again.

'So you see, though he has done so well in the last ten years or so he is not going to be able to go on for ever. That is why your mother is so worried about Christian and when he will return. He should be here. Lord, he should have taken over as soon as he left school. I've helped as much as I can but I shall be . . .'

Rosie stopped speaking suddenly, and beneath the fold of her full cotton skirt her hand gripped Alex's, hiding, as they had hidden their feelings, not from each other, but from everybody else. They hadn't really said anything to one another, not in so many words, but they had known that as soon as the right time came they would marry. They were the same, in spirit and bone and blood, cousins, sharing the same grandfather, even looking somewhat alike with their dark sweep of hair and a certain lift and turn of the head. In the tilt of their eyebrows, and the curve of their strong young mouths, but where Alex's mouth was wilful, stubborn, Rose's was tender and compassionate.

It smiled a little now, and in her eyes as she looked at him was the end of the sentence she had been about to say out loud. '. . . but I shall not be here for ever. I am a woman who will marry and bear children and the running of a great estate is not for the likes of me.'

Alex smiled back at her and for that split second they were two minds blended into one. One mind which knew exactly what was meant by the words which had not been spoken.

222

'Yes, I see what you mean,' he said.

'Well, I'm afraid I don't,' from Charlie, and Alex gave his brother a pitying look which said how could he when he was not loved by Rosie Osborne.

'It means, old boy, that someone has to look after Beechwood and all that entails until that ass Christian comes to his senses and gets himself back home. If Uncle Teddy isn't able to manage then someone has to do it. Mother can't, and you have Woodall, so it looks as if it will have to be me.'

'And you'd be prepared to take it on knowing that when our Irish cousin returns from whatever it is he thinks he's doing over there, you will simply be told to push off, probably without even a thank you, knowing Christian.'

'What else am I doing but kicking my heels and waiting for something splendid to turn up? When father was alive he was for ever trying to interest me in something or other, dreading that I might turn out to be one of those frightful chaps who live on hand outs, waiting for their allowance every month's end. Mother hasn't bothered since. She seems preoccupied with . . . well, I don't know . . . she's not with us yet, which I suppose is natural, after being so recently widowed. When she broached the subject last week I was dead against it at first, but she threw in a sweetener I couldn't resist.'

'Oh, and what was that?'

'Besides a pretty decent wage which an estate manager would naturally receive, she has promised me that little house the old lady used to live in.'

Charlie Woodall sat up straight and removed the panama hat. The sun had burned his skin to a deep golden brown and bleached his already fair hair to a pale ash blond. His teeth were incredibly white in his brown face as, for a moment only, he smiled. His smile turned quickly to a frown as the implication of his brother having his own residence suddenly occurred to him. It was plain he did not care for it. Not at all. Whilst he was hemmed in at Woodall, which, though it now belonged to him, had his mother in residence and his Osborne cousins whenever they had a fancy to stay, Alex was to play the gay young bachelor with his own place in which to do it. Mairin and Ailis were often away. They were both academically gifted so they had been allowed to go to college, learning God knows what it was young girls of today learned in the advancement of some career or other. In the holidays they went with friends, tramping about the country with rucksacks on their backs and a pair of stout boots on their feet and presumably, because there were two of them, everyone seemed to imagine it was quite all right to do so. Rosie stayed often at Beechwood, helping Uncle Teddy, and it was perhaps this, just as much as envy of Alex's coming freedom, that Charlie did not care for.

'That's a bit much, isn't it? Couldn't you stay at Beechwood? There's plenty of room.'

Alex grinned wickedly, and in his hand he felt Rosie's press warningly.

'I dare say, but how much better to have one's own place,' and his fingers caressed hers so that for some reason Charlie couldn't fathom, nor care for, he didn't know why, she blushed.

'What's going on?' he demanded truculently.

'Going on? In what way, old chap? I am to be given, if only temporarily, a job I shall enjoy. I shall be answerable to no one, once I have learned the ropes, and I am to leave home which lots of chaps do, I believe. It's high time, don't you think? I shall be

224

twenty-one soon and in the eyes of the law no longer a minor. I'm looking forward to it immensely. In fact Rosie has promised to help me fix up great-grandmother Lacy's house, and she and I are off this very minute to see what needs doing.'

'I'll come with you.'

At once Alex's smiling, pleased-with-itself face turned sour and truculent, and his brows swooped in a ferocious scowl.

'What the hell for? It's my house, or will be, and there's absolutely no reason for you to vet it.'

'I'm not coming to vet it, for God's sake. It's Sunday and I've nothing else to do. We could ride over. I'll go and tell Jackson to saddle up the horses . . .'

'You'll do nothing of the sort, brother. When you're invited to come over to *my* place then you can come, but not before.'

'*Your* place! Since when has any part of Beechwood belonged to you or mother? It belongs to the Osbornes and that's Christian.'

'Is that so? Then perhaps you had better have a word with mother, because she is under the impression that she has the right, and Uncle Teddy agrees with her, to let her son live there. And why not if I am to be working . . .'

'*You! Working!* You've done nothing but hang about the place for the past two years doing bugger all, so why should it be different when you get to Beechwood?'

'Are you calling me a layabout? A sponger? Are you saying when I get to Beechwood I shall do nothing to earn my salary . . .'

'I shouldn't be surprised. Particularly as there will be no one to supervise your movements . . .'

'You bloody little swine . . .'

225

'Now then, brother, there is no need for name calling. If you cannot stand the truth . . .' and Charlie's cool and supercilious manner, which was meant to infuriate, did.

They had both sprung to their feet, Alex in the grip of an uncontrollable rage, Charles more than willing to defend himself from it, and under the trees where the ladies sat, Maris and her mother sighed resignedly. It was to be one of Alex's and Charles's quarrels, it seemed, an occurrence to which they were well accustomed, and though Ellen had not been a spectator at many of these set-to's she was not unused to hot-headed young men snarling and bristling up to one another in her kitchen.

'Charlie, is there something wrong, dear?' his mother called, ready to stand up and move across to her sons before they knocked one another to the ground. Really, you would have expected them to have progressed beyond this sort of thing at their age, her expression quite clearly said.

'They never seem to grow up,' she apologised to her friend of long standing, Mrs O'Shaughnessy, who agreed, having several of the same kind at home. Indeed, it had now passed on to the next generation, this necessity to stick one's fist in a cousin or a brother's eye.

'Sure an' won't they both be men soon,' she answered comfortably, just as though Alex and Charlie Woodall were ten and eleven years old.

Maris yawned, rather inclined to wish they might start a fist-fight, for it would give her an excuse to get away from Mrs O'Shaughnessy's over-protective interest in her coming grandchild. Five months now and only yesterday she had felt the first fluttering movement

226

inside her, which had been somewhat frightening, and she meant to take Rosie back with her to Seymour Road now that the single bed had arrived from Lewis's. It was three weeks since Callum had sailed for Canada, and he would be home by the end of the month, but until then she would be glad of Rosie's company in that awful house where she had spent the last three weeks alone. She had, of course, gone out each day in Callum's MG and was rather proud of her own driving now. It had much improved, and she meant to show off her dashing style when she and Rosie took to the road. And also it had occurred to her that it might be a good idea if something was done about the . . . well, the mess the house was in. She hadn't really got the hang of clearing out the fireplace, or keeping up with washing the dirty dishes which seemed to pile up whenever her back was turned. And she had on her last clean pair of knickers, which meant she would have to tackle the pile of soiled clothing in the bathroom or go out and buy some new. She had managed to keep old Mrs O'Shaughnessy from the house so far, but she was fast running out of excuses.

Rosie would know what to do.

The boys had been smoothed down, Charlie had gone off in a cold rage, and Rose and Alex had strolled away in the direction of the lake, going God only knew where, giving the impression, at least to Maris, that the moment they were out of sight they would be hand in hand, when Wilson announced that Mr O'Shaughnessy was here for the ladies.

He walked across the lawn towards them, tall and smart in his grey flannels and tweed jacket, and to her surprise took her mother's hand and lifted it to his lips, bowing in the manner of a gentleman born.

'Lady Woodall,' he smiled, the nervous strain of the past few weeks and Cliona's disappearance seeping away for a moment into some other emotion.

'Mr O'Shaughnessy,' her mother answered graciously, 'will you have some tea before you go?'

'Thank you, that would be very pleasant,' and had it not been too ludicrous for words, Maris could have sworn that under the cover of moving chairs and adjusting the table-cloth, Michael O'Shaughnessy winked at Lady Woodall.

The key turned in the lock reluctantly, its screech of protest telling them that the door had not been opened for a long time.

'When did great-grandmother die?' Alex whispered, just as though the house was still peopled, if not by those living, then at least by their ghosts.

'I can't remember. During the war or perhaps just after. I know she was very ancient.'

'I can't say I remember her.'

'They say Maris looks just like her. The same colouring. There's a picture of her, so Aunt Elizabeth told me, on one of the walls.'

The dower-house stood in a shallow depression about a hundred yards inside the walls which surrounded Beechwood Hall and to the left-hand side of the curving drive. It had its own walled garden, and looked out over wildly unkempt beds of rioting perennials and uncut grass to the small lake and the beech wood from which the big house got its name. It had a long, low front rising from the flagged and terraced forecourt, square, mullioned and latticed windows, and was obviously much older than the main house. A climbing white rose had gone quite mad, covering the softly mellowed blocks of Lancashire stone of which the house was built, from the flags of the terrace to the old roof tiles.

'It's lovely,' Rose breathed raptly as they came upon it basking in the late afternoon sunshine, like a fat, contented tabby curled up on itself, needing no one at the moment but ready to give a welcome when they arrived. Three flagged steps led down from the over-grown garden to the forecourt, then two more to the low front door, and all about lay silence, no sound but that made by a skylark, invisible in the blue arch above the roof, and far off, the barking of a dog.

'It's perfect,' Alex agreed reverently, 'just what we want,' and she did not even think to question his use of the word 'we'. The door opened under his hand, and they stepped together back into the past, the great-grandchildren of the indomitable lady who had once shocked Liverpool with her 'carryings-on', and had made a fortune while she did it.

The hallway was a complete square with the staircase winding around three of its walls to a wide landing. The steps were shallow and uncarpeted, crafted from some lovely polished wood that shone with age and the feet of the many generations which had trodden them. The handrail was smooth and the newel posts were intri-cately carved, like sticks of barley sugar.

There was an arch on the back wall of the hallway, leading into what looked like a sitting room filled with a golden light, as the last of the afternoon sun streamed through a window. It was warm, and in the air was the faded scent of lavender.

'Oh, Alex . . .'

'I know . . .'

'I don't remember . . .'

'Neither do I.'

They went from room to room, each one filled with old, beautifully made furniture. Not huge and clumsy as the Victorians had loved it, but simple, elegant and yet sturdy. There was oak panelling on all the walls except the old kitchen, which was of brick and had been whitewashed, and in one bedroom where hand-painted silk in a delicate shade of apple green had faded and worn. It was still as beautiful as the skin of an old woman can be beautiful, fine and soft to the touch.

'This was hers.' Alex stood in the centre of the lovely room which retained, though he was not sure how, the feminine presence of the woman who had once slept there.

'Yes, and look at the view right across to the lake.'

'And the picture . . . it must be . . .'

Lacy Osborne. There she was above the fireplace in an exquisite white dress, gauzy and drifting, with white ribbons of apricot velvet at the waist and edging the dozens of flounces about the wide skirt. Her silver-streaked tawny hair was tumbled in charming disarray with tendrils curling about her ears and neck, and tilted dashingly over her eyes was a cream straw leghorn hat, flat and wide, with matching apricot ribbons about its crown. The woman in the picture was dainty and fragile as moonshine. Her clear, crystal grey eyes were wicked with mischievous laughter, and her fine ivory skin was flushed with rose at the cheekbones. She was enchanting and she knew it, her impish smile said so, and could anyone resist her? On her left hand was a broad wedding ring.

The young couple stood for five minutes, their senses captured by this radiant woman who was their great-grandmother, unable to tear themselves away from the fascination she seemed to emit, a charm which sprang from the frame and made them want to smile with her, to share whatever delightful secrets her smile seemed to say she concealed. An appeal that was at one and the same time womanly and yet as heart-warming and merry as a child's.

All about the room were her things, dusty and draped with cobwebs, but appearing, nevertheless, as though their owner had just stepped out of the room. The bed, a half-tester, had been stripped of its bedding and some careful housemaid had folded the white lace bedspread and placed it neatly on the bed, ready, she had supposed, to be put away. There was a slim-legged rosewood table beside the bed, on which was a pot-pourri bowl with a pierced lid to let out its aroma. Inside it were rose-petals, so old and dried they had shrivelled almost to dust, and yet there was still a memory of the perfume which must have once lingered on the air. Beside it was a scroll-patterned, engraved gilt casket with Sèvres china plaques set into the lid and sides, which, when it opened, revealed one white silk glove, its missing partner a mystery no one now would ever solve. Two china candlesticks and a pair of oval, silver-framed portraits, miniatures, one of a man, the other a small boy, and a leather-bound book with a bookmark in its pages. A book of poetry; and when Rose picked it up, with the awed reverence of someone handling a holy relic, it fell open at a poem written by Christopher Marlowe over three hundred years ago.

> 'Come live with me and be my love
> And we will all the pleasures prove,
> That valleys, groves, hills and fields
> Woods or steepy mountain yields . . .'

In bold script a hand had written at the top of the page, 'These words are echoed in my heart', and it was signed simply, 'James'.

'Her husband, our great-grandfather, James Osborne,' Alex said, and his voice trembled with emotion. He turned to Rose and placed careful hands, one on either side of her face, and with the greatest delicacy laid the deep curve of his lips against hers. They were soft, tender, with nothing of sensuality in them. A token, a pledge, as Lacy and James had pledged their love and started the dynasty which had led to these two young lovers. It was not the first time he and Rose had kissed. Gentle, friendly kisses when they met and parted. There was time for the other sort later, since they had the remainder of their lives together to enjoy them, their unspoken understanding had been, but this one had the depth and breadth and absolute commitment of Alex Woodall's true love for Rose Osborne in it, and hers for him. Her mouth moved lovingly beneath his.

'Rose . . . Rosie . . . has the time come, d'you think?' he said at last.

'Oh yes, Alex . . .' her breath mingling sweetly with his.

'Then this shall be *our* room,' he said, touching his mouth to her eyes. Putting his arms about her, he drew her to him, tucking her body neatly along the length of his. They both turned their heads in the direction of the dressing-table which stood against the deep window. There were cut-glass scent bottles on it with silver tops, a pretty lace fan, faded and yellow with age, a silver-backed hairbrush, badly tarnished.

'Nobody has been here, Alex. How strange. Everything is just as she left it. Nothing moved or cleaned or put away.'

'But who would do it, Rose? Aunt Clare is the obvious one, being known as mistress of Beechwood, but I suppose she felt it was not her place to interfere with great-grandmother Osborne's possessions. Mother is the only other Osborne, except you and your sisters, and she was concerned only with father in the latter years. It has just been . . . forgotten.'

'Left for someone who would care about it.'

'Like you and me.'

'Yes.'

'We won't change it, will we, darling?' The endearment was given and received quite naturally. 'We will keep it just as it is, as she lived in it.'

They both saw the miniature at the same time. It stood apart, alone on the dressing-table in a slender shaft of sunlight, the silver of its frame as tarnished as the hairbrush and the tops of the scent bottles. It was of a woman, a very beautiful woman, as dark and exotic as Lacy was fair and ethereal. She wore a dress of emerald green, silk it seemed to be, the bodice low-cut and tightly fitting, her shoulders and the soft curve of her breasts a startling alabaster white above it.

Her eyes were the exact colour of her gown.

Rose and Alex moved slowly across the bedroom towards it, their hands still clinging, and when they reached the dressing-table they stood very close together as though for protection.

'It's . . . it's Aunt Elizabeth,' Rose whispered, and the ghostly echoes of the past seemed to whisper from the lace drapery above the bed, drifting high to the ceiling and slipping like smoke down the silken walls.

'No.' Alex's voice could scarcely be heard, and Rose felt the hairs on her arms and at the nape of her neck, rise and prickle.

'No, Rosie, it's you,' and so it could have been.

'Who . . . who is it, d'you think?' moving even closer to Alex.

'God knows, some relative, I suppose, perhaps of the Hemingways or the Osbornes. Must be, for the likeness to you and mother is quite incredible.'

'Grandfather Osborne had the same colour of eyes, so Aunt Elizabeth told me.'

'There you are then,' and for some curious reason they both sighed deeply as though in vast relief. They turned away, still conscious, both of them, that the lovely, sad . . . yes, that was how her eyes had been . . . the sad eyes of the unknown woman seemed to watch them as they left the room.

They wandered, still hand in hand, down the three-handed stairs, pausing for a moment or two in the hushed hallway. There was a timeless feeling of continuity about the place, an essence lingering of what had gone before, and, through them, would go on into the future. They smiled at one another, then shutting the door behind them turned the enormous key in the lock.

They were seven for dinner that night. Clare had driven Teddy over in the trap along the winding and, for the most part, still quiet lanes between Beechwood Hall and Woodall Park. Through the somnolent evening sunshine which lay over Colton village, turning left at Hanging Gate into Lower Lane, then right across the level crossing of the St Helens and Runcorn Gap Railway over which, twenty-five years ago, young Michael O'Shaughnessy had once rattled on his bicycle on his way to the Woodall stables.

Charlie and Alex had lifted their Uncle Teddy in his

chair from the trap and up the steps, from where he had been wheeled to the drawing room. They would stay no longer than nine-thirty, Clare declared, since she was not at all sure she liked the idea of driving the trap back in the dark, even though she knew the lanes as well as she knew her own little herb garden. Teddy would be ready for his bed, by then, and so would she, for she led an active life in the service of her disabled husband. Her hand had hovered at his thin cheek for a moment, and they had smiled at one another, sending some private signal which was lost neither on Elizabeth nor Rose, who was herself in a state of cloud-floating, star-dazzled love. Maris had not returned to Seymour Road with Michael and Mrs O'Shaughnessy earlier in the day, having decided to stay the night at Woodall and put off for a little while longer the decision to be made about the washing of her underwear, and her own heart contracted at the obvious love which linked Clare and Teddy Osborne.

They had dressed that night, though the custom which had once been taken for granted every evening, whether guests were present or not, was no longer kept up when there was just the family. The gentlemen, even Teddy, were immaculate in black dinner-jackets, double-breasted, and black evening-dress trousers with one braided seam on the outside of each leg. They wore single-breasted black waistcoats and pristine white shirts with black bow ties.

Elizabeth herself was in black, a printed velvet, almost backless, long-skirted and slim-fitting. Her arms were bare, and around her throat she wore the Woodall diamonds, a plain choker close to her smooth, white throat, which would one day be passed on to Charlie's wife. She wore her hair in a smooth and heavy chignon with a single diamond pin like a star against its dark gloss.

Clare was in cream, a satin sheath with no sleeves, and cut like Elizabeth's, low at the back but high at the front. It had a smart diamanté collar. Rose had chosen green, a vivid emerald green in a rich lace over a crêpe de Chine foundation slip. It hugged her superb, almost junoesque figure to the knees, where it flared out round her ankles. The narrow shoulder straps were of diamanté. She looked like a mermaid, Alex had whispered in her ear as they had entered the drawing room together, and had the gown been a crinoline she might have been the mystery lady in the miniature.

But it was Maris who caused a mild sensation when she appeared, the last one to do so, in the open doorway of the drawing room, standing for a moment so that no one might miss a detail of her splendour. She had put on the cocktail pyjama suit she had bought only the day before and which cleverly hid her thickening figure, though what her mother-in-law would make of the outfit would not bear repeating, Clare Osborne was inclined to think somewhat wryly. In gold silk with very wide full trousers and a hip-length tunic worn over them. She had wound a length of golden silk about her forehead, as once they had done in the 'twenties, with a fringed end hanging to one side and over her shoulder. She looked quite stunning with her silver and tawny hair rioting above the band in a positive explosion of tumbling curls.

'Very smart, darling,' her mother murmured smoothly, wondering, one supposed, how this child of hers, since she *was* still a child, would manage one of her own.

They were each sipping a glass of sherry, even Maris,

236

despite her mother's frown. Teddy, Clare and Elizabeth were discussing the general election which had taken place in June and the possibility that with Stanley Baldwin and his National cabinet in power, there might now be some progress in alleviating the appalling state of unemployment. Charlie, Maris and Rosie were at the piano where Charlie was picking out the tune of 'Dancing cheek to cheek' whilst the girls warbled the words. Wilson hovered at the back of the room, ready to refill a glass, waiting for Cook's summons to say that dinner was ready to be served; and lounging in the window-seat, his hand on the head of the retriever at his feet, Alex stared out at the shadows which lengthened over the lawn. The low sun was a crimson ball in a sky which shaded from orange and pink to lavender where it touched the tops of the trees, and three birds flew across it, black against its vivid glow. The waters of the lake were pink and rippled with gold, swathed still in the heat-mist brought by the day, which clung about its edges.

He turned and caught Rose's eye. Smiling, he held out his hand to her, and without hesitation she moved across to him.

'Where are you off to?' Charlie called after her. 'We need you to give us the words, don't we, Maris?'

Rose put her hand in Alex's, and, aware suddenly that something momentous was about to happen though not yet sure what it was, Charlie stopped playing and swung round on the piano stool. Maris sang on for a moment or two, then finding herself alone stopped to look at her brother and cousin.

The conversation died, all heads turning to the young couple, for what reason none of them knew, though, of course, afterwards they told one another they should

237

have guessed. Alex was so obviously in a state of tension, not his usual sort where he would gladly argue that black was white, or vice versa, but one which clearly gave him a great deal of joy, and Rosie, though calmer, looked as if she might simply float into his arms and spin away to where music played which only she and Alex could hear.

'We have an announcement, Rose and I,' Alex said, putting his arm about her. Charlie stood up, with an expression of warning on his face.

'Really, old chap, I wonder what that might be?' Teddy smiled, for it seemed he was the first to guess.

'Rosie and I . . . we are engaged to be married.'

Elizabeth Woodall put a trembling hand to her mouth and her eyes widened. She put her sherry glass very gently on to the small table at her side, taking great care that it was quite safe before she let it go. Her eyes, whilst she was performing the small, unimportant task, never left her son's face.

There was a quaver in her voice when she spoke.

'To be . . . to . . .' Her face had drained of every scrap of colour, the cream of her skin becoming pallid and lifeless, and Clare and Teddy heard her moan, deep in her throat.

'Well, a pair of dark horses you both are, I must say,' Maris laughed, seeing no reason for anything but rejoicing.

Clare and Teddy exchanged glances, aware that though there *seemed* to be nothing against the match, Maris was the only member of the Woodall family, except Alex of course, who was showing any sign of pleasure in it. There was absolutely nothing to stop Alex and Rose from marrying, for though they were first cousins, the law allowed it. Rosie's father, James, had been Elizabeth's brother. There appeared to be a great deal of intermarrying, true, between the O'Shaughnessys, the Osbornes and the Woodalls, but what was wrong with that, their exchanged glances seemed to say; so why did both Elizabeth and Charlie look as though they had been stabbed in the back by someone they trusted implicitly? Elizabeth gave the impression that she had seen a ghost walk into the room, one of the worst sort, one which had her in a grip of alarming and curious horror.

But it was Charlie who drew the eyes of everyone present, even those of the happy and recently engaged couple. He simply stood up, strode across the room, yanked open the door before Wilson could get to it, and disappeared, banging it behind him with a crash which shook the frame.

13

'Maris, are you absolutely certain Uncle Callum . . .'

'I wish you wouldn't call him *Uncle* Callum, Rosie. My God, it makes me your *aunt*, do you realise that? I hadn't thought of it until now. Lord, I feel so *old* and *fat* and how I'm to get through the next few months . . .'

'That's what I mean, if you would only listen for a moment. I don't think you should be driving this car and I'm astonished that Uncle Callum . . . all right then, Callum, lets you do it. Frankly, I don't know how you manage to squeeze yourself behind the steering wheel with that . . . protuberance you have . . .'

'What a way you have with words, Rosie darling . . .'

'. . . and you are going far too fast. We don't have to drive back to Woodall today for my other suitcases, you know. I appreciate how tiny the boot of the car is, but tomorrow would do just as well.'

'I don't mind.'

'I know you don't, but aren't you tired?'

'Not a bit of it . . . well, perhaps a little.'

'Let me drive, then.'

'You can drive back but don't tell Callum; in fact, Rosie darling, I would be obliged if you wouldn't tell him about *me* driving. No one knows, you see, except you and Angela . . .'

'*Maris*, you blithering idiot. Do you mean to tell me that you have been using Callum's car for three and a half weeks without his permission? God, he'll spiflicate you. Have you any idea how much he loves this thing? And besides which, with your pregnancy surely it's a strain . . . well, on something . . .'

'Please, Rosie, we're to be sisters now as well as cousins, so won't you support me on this? I promise I won't drive again after today. Well, I shan't have to if you're to come and stay for a while. I only did it to get out of that awful house.'

'*Awful!* I thought you couldn't wait to get there, or so you kept telling me before you and Uncle . . . before you and Callum were married.'

'It was *him* I wanted, not that dreadful little box he lives in when he's home. Honestly, I had no idea it was so *small*. There's absolutely *nowhere* to put anything and things just seem to pile up, dirty dishes and clothes, and I can't find the time to see to them . . .'

'Can't find the time? What on earth do you do with yourself?'

'Well, I don't get up until about eleven . . .'

'*Eleven!*'

'. . . and then I'm dashing off to meet Angela or I come to you at Beechwood or to Woodall, and by the time I get home I'm so whacked I simply fall into bed. I *do* try, Rosie. I really mean to make it into a lovely home for Callum to come home to, but the days simply rush by and before I know it another one's gone and there's nothing been done. I wanted to buy some curtains and . . . Well, Callum said . . . we really didn't need . . . anyway, there was this electric thing. I believe Elsie uses one on the carpets at . . . home . . . Woodall but when I tried . . . at Seymour Road, I mean, the damned thing didn't seem to work. I wish he didn't go to sea, Rosie. I feel as though I barely know him and here I am, in his house all by myself. The woman next door knocked . . . it seemed very . . . quaint . . . to see if I wanted to go into her house for a cup of tea but she was so awfully . . .'

'Common?' Rosie raised a quizzical eyebrow.

'I didn't say that but . . . well, yes she was, so I said I had some washing to do and hadn't the time. Can you imagine me washing and ironing? Well no, neither can I. I'm supposed to have found a woman to "do" for me, but really, Rosie, I'm not used to that sort of thing and I haven't the foggiest where to look.'

'Well, look at the damned road for a start. You nearly had that cyclist in the ditch.'

'I know how to drive, thank you. That's one thing I *can* do, and I was nowhere near the cyclist.'

The noise made by the little sports car echoed hollowly into and out of the railway tunnel on Child-wall Valley Road, coming suddenly to the right-hand turn into Bentham Drive, which led to the complexity of streets amongst which was tucked Seymour Road. It was a sharp turn going almost back on itself, and the trouble was that you were on it before you knew it after coming out of the tunnel.

'Not so *fast*, Maris . . . for God's sake there is no need to go at such speed . . .' but it was too late, and as Maris fought for control of the steering wheel, which seemed to have got away from her clutching hand, the dashing little car did a complete about-turn, then another, clipping the trunk of a kerbside tree as it went. It lost its balance then, the two nearside wheels lifting a sickening eighteen inches off the ground and slowly, ever so slowly, it tipped on to its right side, and even more slowly, or so it seemed to Rose, she fell heavily against Maris, tiny, plump Maris, crushing her to the closed door of the vehicle.

They were not hurt. Miraculously, they were not hurt, was her first coherent thought as excited passers-by lifted her and Maris carefully on to the pavement. Motorists who had stopped, having no choice since the MG blocked the road, all talked at once, telling one another what had happened, and could you be surprised with a woman at the wheel and another beside her? Talking, most probably, the pair of them, and taking no care or notice of what was on the road, and one of them as big as a house in the family way. And a sports car as well, which looked as though it was a write-off, from the state of it lying there with its side all bashed in and one of its front wheels twenty yards down the road. There should be a law against women motorists, really there should, and perhaps the police constable who had just arrived on the scene, somewhat out of breath since he had been patrolling his beat in Broad Green Road, which was a fair step away, might put a stop to it.

Rosie put her to bed. No, she was perfectly all right, she said and no, she didn't want her mother, or Callum's mother, or the doctor, or anybody, and her small pinched face was the colour of suet and her eyes were haunted, for how was she to tell her husband of barely a month that she had wrecked his car? *Again!* That she had deliberately disobeyed him, just to show him she could, despite her appeal to Rosie not to tell him she had been driving, which made a nonsense of the whole thing. If she was to defy him and he was not aware that she was defying him, what was the point?

She began to bleed a couple of hours later, and when Rosie, frantic and terrified, rang for her Uncle Michael since he was the nearest and had a telephone, and besides which had already been contacted to deal with his brother's car, Maris was in the bitterest agony as she brought into the world not a live child but one that was dead.

He came home two days later, her husband. She clung to him, a frail, wan little girl, or so it seemed to him, nothing of her under the bedcovers of the bed she expected him to share with her.

'I'm sorry, Callum, I'm so sorry,' she said over and over again, weeping against the good blue serge of his uniform, and he was not awfully sure whether she regretted the wrecking of his motor car – for the second time, or the death of his child.

'So am I, Maris.' He voice was gentle, for though a child is wilful and disobedient, a grown man does not take it by the shoulders and shake it viciously as he felt like doing.

'It is done with now, so go to sleep and get well again. The doctor says you must rest . . .' trying to put her back among her pillows.

'I know, I know, Callum . . . I know that, but please, please say you forgive me.'

'I forgive you, Maris, really I do.'

Elizabeth Woodall hovered by the door. Behind her on the tiny landing was Michael O'Shaughnessy, who, for reasons best known to himself, perhaps because he had been the first one to see the agony of his brother's wife, or was it because of the loss of his own daughter, had barely left the house. He had sat up with Elizabeth and Rose through two long nights, with Ellen when she was brought from Edge Lane, and even on his own beside the sleeping, childlike figure of his sister-in-law, for whom it seemed he felt the greatest pity. They had all come during the past two days, giving Maris a fore-taste of what her future held as an O'Shaughnessy,

244

bringing their bunches of flowers, their grapes and their sadness. When one of their own, and she was that now, suffered, so did they all. Alex and Charlie popped their heads round the door, though not together, awkward in the presence of pain and sorrow. Gracie and Amy and Eileen came, and Clare Osborne, and even Caitlin had telephoned from Yorkshire, for had she not known herself the grief of child loss?

A boy, a perfectly formed boy he had been, and even the doctor could not say with any certainty that it was the accident which had caused it. Mrs O'Shaughnessy had not been injured in any way though she must have been thoroughly shaken, and it was a pity she had not called him in to examine her directly after the accident. Maris had looked quite bewildered, not at all sure the Mrs O'Shaughnessy he spoke of was actually *her*.

No, Mr, or was it Captain O'Shaughnessy? the good man said later, and alone, to the bereaved father, it would probably have made no difference . . . it was hard to tell . . . she was very delicately built, though her mother insisted she had a strong constitution. It couldn't be helped, and, of course, it went without saying that the sooner she became pregnant again the better it would be for her, emotionally speaking. Another child was the best cure for the . . . well, he was sure Captain O'Shaughnessy took his meaning.

He was bewildered himself by the brooding expression on Captain O'Shaughnessy's face. Yes, brooding, the doctor would have said, if anyone had cared to ask, as though he looked at some black spectre from the past, or perhaps a vision of the future which he did not care to contemplate. Eyes like iced sapphires, which was fanciful, the doctor knew, but they were indeed so cold in the warm brown of his face they seemed to pierce you to the very marrow of your bones.

She recovered quickly, and though Doctor Manley had said two weeks in bed without putting a foot to the floor, and though she had a score of willing nurses, her mother, Callum's mother, Gracie, Amy, Eileen and Rosie, to cosset and pamper her, she was up and about a week later.

'No, you must all go home,' she said cheerfully, throwing back the bedcovers and leaping from her bed, shocking Ellen to the core, since her cheerfulness in the face of what had happened to her grandson was not at all to Ellen's liking. Had she not been driving that blasted machine none of this would have happened, and if Ellen had her way, Callum would tie this little snip of a girl to the kitchen sink, the stove and the bedroom where she belonged. Another child on the way by the end of August was the answer, and the sooner he got at it the better. She'd keep an eye on her this time, by the Holy Mother she would. No more racketing around Liverpool as it appeared she had been doing for the past month, and she'd told Callum so, but he'd been quiet and uncommunicative. Ellen hadn't cared for it, since it was not like one of hers to have nothing to say. Mind, the whole sorry business had been a fiasco ever since the day he had told her he was to marry Maris Woodall. But, there you are, you made your bed so you must lie in it, and the pair of them would have to buckle down and do the best they could. But she was a wilful one, this dainty bit of lace who was her son's wife, and she was inclined to think a durable length of cotton would have suited him much better.

'Get back in that bed, girl. Sure an' you're not to get

out of it again, not at all, not while I'm here, at any rate.'

'I'm as right as rain, Mrs O'Shaughnessy, and there is no way I can lie in that bed pretending to be ill when I'm not.'

'Darling, perhaps Mrs O'Shaughnessy is right,' her mother said anxiously. 'I shall come and look after you, at least until the end of the week. I can easily drive over from Woodall each day. Or Rosie will stay a little longer, won't you, Rosie. I'm sure your poor husband . . .' smiling in the direction of the quiet man in the chair by the bedroom window, '. . . will be glad to see the back of us, but really, darling, you are not well enough to be left alone all day whilst he is down at the . . . ship and the shipping office.'

For who knew *where* Callum spent his day? her tone seemed to ask, and Rose was disposed to agree with her. It was certainly not with his wife, his wife's cousin thought to herself. Each morning he rose from the sofa in the front room where he spent the night, and after dutifully enquiring of his wife how she had spent *hers*, a polite good morning to his niece and an even more polite thanks for the breakfast she cooked him, he would bathe and shave and leave the house, catching the tram at the end of the road, since of course he had no car, and go off only God knew where. Rose could tell it upset Maris, for he was the first one she asked for each day when she woke.

'He is very angry with me,' she said dolefully on the first day he was home, 'but I will make it up to him. I shall make everything right again,' repeating the words to whoever sat beside her in the manner of a child who has transgressed but who will do better next time if only she is given the chance.

'Is that Callum?' she asked Rosie half a dozen times a day. 'I thought I heard the front door. Run down, darling, and tell him I want to see him at once. I have something I must say to him. Oh, it's . . . only Mrs O'Shaughnessy. I thought it was . . .'

'Can I hear Callum's voice, mother? Oh please, do ask him to come and kiss his wife . . . No? it's Alex . . . how lovely. Now as soon as he comes in . . .'

'Did Callum say when he would be back, Rose . . . ?'

'No, darling.'

'I hardly see him . . .'

'He is busy, I suppose, with . . .'

'With his cargo, of course . . .'

They all went at last, not at all sure she should be left alone with the silent, bleak-faced man, who, it seemed, could not get over the loss of his son and was finding it very difficult to forgive his wife for her foolhardiness, even negligence, in behaving as she had. Perhaps the doctor was right. Perhaps the child would have been stillborn in any case, but not one of them really believed it, not even Maris O'Shaughnessy's own mother, though she did her best to hide it. Callum, who had been home for two weeks now, was to sail again at the end of next week, so perhaps with a week alone together they might begin to mend the horrendous tear in the already fragile fabric of their marriage.

They faced one another across the small front room that night, two strangers, the one polite, the other desperate.

'I shall cook us a meal,' she said brightly, after spending an hour in the tiny bathroom, washing her hair then brushing it until it stood about her head in a froth of light. She put on one of her prettiest dresses, what was called a 'cinema' frock of dove-grey chiffon, fitting

closely to her once more slim figure, the hem just touching her ankle-bone, the sleeves pleated and very full.
It had cost six and a half guineas at Bon Marché, an
exorbitant price to pay but well worth every penny, she
thought, as she twirled about before the mirror which
was set in the door of the wardrobe.

'In that?' was all her husband said as she made her
announcement.

'Is it not suitable for dining?' Her face lost some of
the excited colour the prospect of an evening and then
a night alone with him had put in her cheeks. It would
be like a second honeymoon, this coming week, with
long, lazy mornings in their bed as they had in Scotland.
They could take the car . . . oh no, not the car . . .
unless they could borrow her mother's old Morris, or
one of Michael's since he had two, and go into the
country, the forest of Delamere perhaps, or up on to
the moors of the Pennines. A picnic across the water on
the Wirral Peninsula, intimate dinners at the Adelphi, a
show or two, Greta Garbo's latest film *The Painted
Veil*, or *Here is my Heart*, starring the inimitable Bing
Crosby. They would begin again. Even another child if
Callum wanted it, and this time she would be a model
wife *and* mother.

'Absolutely, but not for cooking in.'

'Why not, Callum?'

'Maris, really. Those sleeves for a start. They would
catch fire in a moment. But you must do as you think
best of course,' shaking out the newspaper he was reading, then turning the page to let her knew that as far
as he was concerned that was the end of the matter. It
was *her* decision.

'Have you . . . perhaps an apron?'

'I'm afraid I haven't an apron.'

249

'Oh dear, then I suppose I had better change.' She stood, undecided and hesitant in the doorway, looking at the newspaper behind which her husband had retreated.

'Just as you like.'

'Well then . . .' but it seemed he had contributed all that he was going to. She turned away, the picture of dejection, and though he was not actually looking at her or even at the words of the newspaper, if he was truthful, Callum felt her misery wash across the room in great waves. He sighed and lowered the newspaper.

'What are you to cook?' he enquired, keeping his voice polite.

'Well, I thought perhaps a fillet steak with some mushrooms and a salad, then a chocolate soufflé to follow. I do love chocolate soufflés, don't you?'

'Indeed I do, and fillet steak. You have the ingredients, I presume?'

Her face fell again and the increasingly familiar feeling of irritation pumped through him. Jesus, she was unbelievable. Fillet steak and chocolate soufflé, which she was going to prepare and cook in a dress which would not have looked out of place at a Court Ball. She was so bloody *naïve* and so incredibly exasperating he didn't know how he was to get through this evening, let alone the rest of his life with her. For the past two weeks he had managed to keep himself from going mad by the simple expedient of spending as little time in her company as possible. That hopeful, expectant face, those woebegone eyes pleading for something he could not give her, drove him to despair, and the only way he could escape it was to leave her, though he was aware it was not right, to the care of her mother, his mother and the rest of the assorted females who had invaded his male privacy.

Now they were alone and how was he to manage it?

'Ingredients?' she asked.

'Yes, the things that are needed to make a meal.'

'I thought . . .'

'That they were in the kitchen cupboard, and if they were, could you *make* a soufflé and grill a steak, toss a salad, fry mushrooms? Do you even know how to set a table or wash dishes . . . ?'

Jesus, he was losing his self-control. If he didn't get away from her he really didn't think he could keep his hands off her. He wanted to take her by the shoulders and snarl into that pathetic face of hers, ask her what the hell she thought she was doing in his house? Play-acting the part of his wife, all dressed up as if she was to dine with the Queen, and twittering on about soufflés and mushrooms as though he and she were an ordinary, *loving* man and wife. He wanted to be cruel to her, to hurt her, to turn her into a terrified animal with her back against the wall, but most of all he wanted her to leave his house and him and let him get back to his own life, to be himself, to resurrect Callum O'Shaughnessy who had been buried beneath the mountain of 'domesticity' which now filled his house and his life.

'I'm sorry, Callum.'

'Maris . . .' doing his best to keep his voice steady, '. . . if you tell me once more how sorry you are I swear I shall . . .' He took a deep breath and clamped his jaw tightly together.

'I'm . . .'

'Stop it.'

'Oh, Callum.' Her voice was only a thread of sound, and he bowed his head, feeling that he had just kicked

251

that puppy again. There was silence for a long time. A cold deep silence. He kept his head down, staring blank-eyed at the crumpled newspaper in his lap and when, finally, he managed to lift his head and look at her she was still standing in exactly the same spot, her arms hanging limply at her side, and her face awash with the amazing tears he had seen and marvelled at in the past. They simply ran from her eyes, big soft teardrops, one following the other, welling over her bottom lashes, held for a moment, then sliding down to her chin and on to the dove-grey chiffon of her dress.

'Oh Jesus . . . oh Jesus . . .' he groaned wretchedly. He held out his arms and she ran in to them, curling up in his lap, pushing her wet face into the hollow of his neck, sobbing uncontrollably now, but without words. His hand went to her hair, smoothing it away from her forehead, and blindly her mouth reached for his. She tasted salty as he kissed her. She was small and crumpled and fragile beneath his hands. Her neck was like silk and her breast was sweet and pointed to his touch where, miraculously, her dress had opened for him.

Sweet Christ . . . oh dear God . . . was this all there was . . . nothing else . . . nothing else but this . . . ?

She was like an excited child who, thinking she was not to go to the pantomime, suddenly finds herself in the front row of the stalls. She was enchanting, flushed and nearly naked in the wisp of filmy, transparent chiffon and lace. The dress was tied about the waist with satin ribbon, and nowhere else, or so it appeared. Her feet were bare and her hair was a cloud of silver tumbled curls in lovely disarray. He made love to her as gently as he knew how, for it was barely two weeks since the birth – and death – of their child.

'*Now* we will cook a meal,' he said heartily as she lay drowsing in his lap, smiling and replete. Putting her from him and leaping from the chair, doing his best to keep the momentum he had started with their love-making, the good-humoured cheerfulness of a husband who had also been well satisfied by his endeavours, he reached for his trousers and was startled when her voice commanded him to put them down and stand still.

'I thought you were hungry, woman. I know I am, and I mean to start your education at the stove. At least you will be able to cook an omelette when I've done, that's if we have any eggs.'

'Stand still, Callum, please.'

'Stand still, why?'

'I want to . . . to look at you. You are so beautiful.'

He was ready to smile, to make a joke out of it, but her voice was serious, and in the glow from the fire's flames, so was her face.

'I didn't know a man could be so . . . perfect.'

'*Perfect!* Maris, really.'

'It's true,' and so it was, for he had the body of an athlete: strong, supple, graceful, with long legs and a lean, flat belly. His chest was deep and his shoulders broad, but he was not heavily built. There was a balance, a symmetry, a fineness about him which was very appealing. His skin was the colour of amber, and though he was so dark and his hair so thick and curling on his head, that on his chest and running down his stomach was fine and light. His pubic hair was a dense, dark bush and from it, as her eyes ran over him, his penis grew and thickened, and it was another half-hour before they reached the kitchen.

She drifted about him like a pale butterfly, fetching him the salt, the butter, putting 'this' over there and

253

'that' in the sink, blithe as a skylark and completely confident that Captain and Mrs O'Shaughnessy were, at last, on the road to the happiness she, at least, expected to have. She set the table – 'yes, my darling, I can at least set the table' – and lit a candle she had found in the cupboard. She kissed him frequently, allowing him to untie the satin ribbon she offered to him with the perfect conviction that he would oblige. Her breasts peaked into his hands and her little white buttocks flaunted themselves for his inspection. The outline of her body shining through the drifting, misted folds of her dress was meant to tantalise him and it did, and when they sat down to the simple omelette he had cooked and the bottle of wine he had opened, she made no attempt to cover the sweet line of her white thighs nor the dark triangle of her pubic hair which was revealed as her dress fell open. He was male and could not resist her, smoothing his hand and his strong fingers across her satin flesh and up to the openly inviting core of her womanhood so that she squirmed in delight.

'Now me,' she whispered, daringly undoing the buttons on his trousers, teasing and mischievous as her fingers slipped inside.

She was lovely. She was the perfect lover, exciting and wanton, wickedly saucy, loving and impertinent and inventive, and he was dazed with her, excited by her and despairing of her, for it was only when she was like this that they found a place where they might meet as partners.

He lay in their bed after she had fallen asleep and stared into the darkness, his heart like lead in his chest. They were 'all right now' weren't they? she had murmured as she drifted towards sleep, sighing and contented.

'Shall we start another baby?' she asked ingenuously the next evening as they were about to get into bed.

His answer was cautious.

'Don't you think it would be as well if you got over this one first?' He had been very careful to ensure that she would not be pregnant when he left her on his next trip.

'But we will, won't we, Callum? We'll have lots of babies, won't we? The boys will all look like you and the girls like me.'

'I should hope so. Think of the consequences if it should be the other way around.'

'And . . . would you . . .'

'What is it?'

'Would you allow me to buy you another car?'

She knew she had gone too far by the way he stiffened, and she distinctly heard his heart, which was beneath her ear, lurch in his chest.

'That would be out of the question.' His voice was cold. 'Besides, Michael says he thinks he can do something with mine. The MG, I mean. What's the good of having a brother who has the best damned repair shop in Liverpool if he can't fix your vehicle for you when it has . . .'

'Been smashed up by your foolish wife?' She finished the sentence which he had bitten off, wracking her brains to find something which would get them back to that sweetness they had found together in the last two evenings and which she had just shattered by mentioning his car.

'Anyway, I intend to be very busy whilst you're away this time,' she babbled.

'Oh indeed, and with what?' though really did he care, his dispassionate mind asked. As long as she behaved with some propriety and did not shame the O'Shaughnessy family and himself, did he care?

'I'm going to see if I can knock some order into that garden at the back of the house. Mother says I may borrow her gardener for a few days. He can start it off and tell me what is needed in the way of plants, and . . . well, plant it out for me, and then if I could have a man in, say, once a week to keep it tidy, mow the lawn – I shall need a lawn, Callum, your mother told me, so that the perambulator . . .'

'Maris, for God's sake . . . *the perambulator* . . . !'

'For later, Callum, later when . . .'

'Of course, I'm sorry . . .'

'Now you're doing it.'

'What?'

'Saying you're sorry.'

'Go to sleep now. You must be tired.'

'I am, after all that lovely . . .'

'Yes, it was . . . lovely . . .'

He sailed a few days later. He had escaped . . . what a word, Jesus, what a word . . . whenever he could into his man's world of ships and shipping, leaving behind the dramatic upheaval of 'domesticity' she seemed intent on creating, the time-wasting outings in his brother's Lanchester, which he had borrowed. The search for and interviewing of a decent woman to clean – a Mrs Flynn supplied by his mother, since another Irish Catholic in the house with her daughter-in-law could surely do no harm? Dinners for two, candlelit, of course, which his wife thought terribly romantic, followed by the latest dance music played on the gramophone, and a stab at ballroom dancing in what Maris airily called the 'drawing room' and then, naturally, an hour of the delightful, tumbling, sense-reeling activity in their bed before she fell asleep. She never seemed to tire of it, and her energy was boundless, despite the fact that she had given birth so recently. He marvelled at her recuperative powers, whilst deciding that the frailty of the female, particularly the upper-class female, was no more than a myth.

She kissed him passionately in the hallway when he left, tearful and melancholy, telling him she would miss him terribly, and how handsome he looked in his officer's uniform, and to take care because really, she didn't know what she would do if anything awful happened to him. She stood at the gate and waved to him as he walked to the corner of Seymour Road, where he would hail a taxi, not aware that as he drew further away his step grew lighter, along with his heart.

He was free. For three bloody months he was free. He was to steam to Argentina with nothing more nerve-racking in his life than the great swelling southern oceans beneath the hull of his ship, and the sweeping arch of the southern skies dipping above her funnel. A thirty-day passage. By the end of two weeks whatever he ate would be salted, tinned or dried, and the potatoes, by the end of the voyage, would not be fit to feed the pigs. The flour would run out, it always did, and ship's bread would be non-existent, and he and his crew would be compelled to drink the everlastingly bitter lime juice to ensure the necessary intake of Vitamin C. There would be storms and the possibility of a ship's breakdown holding up his vessel, which would mean a diet of ship's biscuits, complete with weevils!

But what did it matter? What did any of it matter? He was free, and in his pocket was a letter to his wife telling her that due to a change of plan in the company's arrangements, the voyage he was to make would take

257

not the three weeks he had envisaged but three *months*.

He began to whistle cheerfully, causing a few heads to turn in his direction as he ran towards the taxi he had just hailed.

14

There was no doubt about it: the Woodall boys, as the two sons of Elizabeth Woodall were called, despite their age and the imminent marriage of one of them, had become even more hazardous in their dealings with one another, causing their poor mother considerable heartache, those who knew the family were saying. Her husband not a year in his grave, and the pair of them snarling at one another like two dogs over a bone, not exactly coming to blows, at least in public, but exchanging unpleasant, sarcastic, sometimes abusive words with one another over what seemed to the onlooker to be nothing at all.

There was the story of Sir Charles's bay, Ruby. He had found her one wet morning in the stable yard, saddled and mud-stained, her head hanging as though she had been put to fences and hedgerows which had taken all her reserve of strength. There was no one about, those who spoke of the incident said, but at that moment his brother Alex had appeared round the corner of the building from the direction of the garages. He was plastered with mud, especially down his back, and his face was not at all clean. He was whistling, and had about him an air of cheerfulness just as though he had experienced something greatly to his liking.

There was no doubt that had it been anyone but his brother, Sir Charles would have pronounced himself mystified by his animal's appearance and gone off to find the groom whose job it was to care for her.

'And where the hell have you been?' he snapped instead, or so the story goes.

His brother stopped in his tracks for a fraction of a second, evidently surprised to see Sir Charles there, then he came on, continuing to whistle until he and his brother were face to face.

'And what's it to you? Have I to acquaint you with my every move, or is this just one of your usual bouts of boorishness?'

'Where the bloody hell have you been on my bay, that's what I would like to be acquainted with, and who gave you permission to ride her?'

Alex looked surprised, turning to study the animal. All it took, and in normal circumstances *would* have taken, was a word or two: 'It wasn't me, Charlie,' but that was not the way of the Woodall boys, not any more.

He grinned, his teeth a startling white in his brown face, his eyes on fire with delight at tormenting his brother, one supposed.

'So, I've been out on your bay, brother, is that it? Not content with my own mare I've been riding Ruby to hell and back, by the look of her, is that what you're saying?'

The bandy-legged groom who had just appeared at the stable door, the one who was later to spread the story of what had happened, heard the sneer in Alex Woodall's voice, glad, it seemed to him, of any excuse to get his hands on Sir Charles.

'You bastard, and you haven't even the decency to unsaddle her and rub her down.'

'Who are you calling a bastard, brother?'

'And who are you calling *brother*, you bastard?' The words were spoken softly and with a terrible loathing,

260

and the groom, who had done nothing more than ride the bay down to Far Paddock and walk her back through the muddy fields, and was about to rub her down and return her to the stable, shouted a warning, an explanation; but it was too late, or they didn't care to hear him, which seemed more likely.

They were both down in the littered and malodorous yard, the two amiable dogs who were always about barking frantically in some confusion; down in the mud and mire and manure which still lay about the place waiting for the groom's attention. They were shouting hoarse, meaningless words at one another, rolling over and over, first one on top and then the other, aiming blows wherever they could, but finding few targets since they were evenly matched and knew one another too well. Nevertheless, blood spurted from Charles's nose and from a split in Alex's lip. Their clothing was torn, and much of the matter which had coated the cobbled yard was now plastered to the two men.

'You bloody good-for-nothing wastrel . . .'

'I'll kill you, I swear to God I'll kill you . . .'

'. . . break your bloody neck . . .'

'. . . cheating swine . . .'

It took the groom and one of the gardener's lads, who happened to be near by and came to stare at what was happening, a good five minutes to get them apart, and when they did the brothers stood, swaying, arms limp, moving from foot to foot, heads lowered, glaring with maddened eyes through the mud and horse-muck at one another, and stinking, the pair of them, of the dank and fetid odour of the stables.

'Christ, Sir Charles . . . it was me . . . 'twas me took the bloody bay. I didn't like the look of 'er so I walked 'er 'ome . . .' the groom had managed to gasp, but for

261

all the good it did he might just as well have saved his breath to cool his porridge, or so he was to report.

'You cross my path again and I warn you . . .' the baronet hissed malevolently at his brother, nothing left of the charming, well-bred milord who had absorbed the culture and customs of the English privileged classes since infancy.

'Why wait until I cross your path, Sir Charles?' his brother mocked, having ingested the same upbringing himself. 'Take me now, go on . . .' beckoning with both hands to his brother, eager to be at it again, to inflict pain or worse on the filth-spattered figure who circled him and who was scarcely recognisable as a human being, let alone a gentleman.

'Sir Charles, Master Alex . . . for God's sake . . . 'twas me . . . 'twas me . . .' and even if it had *not* been him but Master Alex who had taken the bay, was there any reason to act as these two were, the horrified expression on the groom's face asked.

It was not the first nor would it be the last incident to drive the wedge deeper and deeper between Alex and Charles Woodall, and during the winter of 1935 and the spring of 1936 it was very noticeable that whenever they were in company together they addressed not one word to each other.

'I can't imagine what ails them,' Maris wailed to Rose on the occasion of her mother's birthday and the joyful family reunion which had been planned to celebrate it. Clare was there with Teddy, as were Caitlin and Jack Templeton from Yorkshire, who, though they were not related, had been close friends of Elizabeth's since the war. Maris came, without Callum, who was at sea, and Sophie and Gilbert Lawrence came for the weekend from Chester, where Gilbert was in business. Sophie

262

was Harry Woodall's sister, a woman much the same age as Elizabeth. Alex and Rose came, of course, Rose wearing the exquisite rose cut-diamond engagement ring Alex had thought appropriate, and Charles.

They had done their best, all of them. Gilbert had talked at length to Jack on the state of the economy, about which neither Alex nor Charles was concerned. Caitlin and Elizabeth, as though the birthday and the passing of the years had brought it all back, had spoken quietly and sadly, recalling the days when the house had been filled with the wounded from France, then apologised for bringing such a melancholy note to the evening. Teddy had addressed himself to Rose on the state of the elm trees in Old Wood, and the other ladies had discussed the films they had seen lately. *Magnificent Obsession*, starring the flawlessly handsome Robert Taylor with the serenely beautiful Irene Dunne. And what about *Anna Karenina*, in which Greta Garbo had died so dramatically and so movingly in the final reel? The beguiling Cary Grant, the gentlemanly Ronald Colman, oh, and Charles Boyer and the dreamy Leslie Howard. And had Aunt Sophie seen *The Gay Divorcee*, in which the grace, the wit, the charm and the skill of Fred Astaire and Ginger Rogers had rendered everyone in the cinema speechless with admiration?

Brittle social chatter to cover the almost unbearable silence hovering like a menacing cloud over the heads of Alex and Charlie. It seemed they were not even willing to talk to anyone else about the table, let alone one another, and the atmosphere had been so tense Elizabeth had retired to her room with a headache so acute she could barely see. Clare and Teddy had begged to be excused since Clare was driving their ancient Vauxhall, and the unlit lanes between Woodall Park

263

and Beechwood Hall were hazardous at night and she must drive slowly, she said.

'One would think they would put themselves out if only to please mother,' Maris continued to Rose, 'but no. All they did was nod to one another in greeting as Alex came in, and that was only for *her* benefit, and then not another word. Really, it is most embarrassing *and* mysterious, since it has gone on so long, and I can see no reason for it. Oh, I know they have been at one another's throats ever since they were children, but the affection and loyalty were there. They always stood up for one another against all comers. Now they seem to find it hard to remain in the same room as one another. Do you think it's something to do with mother letting Alex have great-grandmother's house? though why that should upset Charles I can't imagine. After all he has Woodall. Or is it because Alex has an income of his own now which he earns as estate manager, instead of what he used to call "hand-outs"? Perhaps Charlie liked to see Alex "playing" at life, riding to hounds because there was nothing else to do, shooting in season and generally larking about with Freddie Winters and the others, or brooding round Woodall until something exciting turned up. It made Charlie feel superior in some way perhaps, and you know how competitive they have always been.'

If Rose had any explanation for it she did not divulge it to Maris.

Meanwhile, the royal family, like the Woodalls, had its share of trouble. At the beginning of the year the King fell ill and on January 20th he died, his last reported words being, 'How is the Empire?'

'Now isn't that just like him?' Ellen remarked tearfully, 'thinking of others even on his deathbed.' Her tears were genuine, as they had been at the death of his father, old King Teddy. Members of the royal family they might be, but to Ellen it was almost as though they belonged to her, so familiar was she with their lives. She had liked King George, she said, Mother of Jesus rest with him, just as if she had been personally acquainted with him. A simple, straightforward sort of a chap whom she would have been happy to have in her own kitchen any day of the week. A man who had been devoted to his parents and his brothers and sisters, just like any ordinary family man might be. Pity he had not got on as well with that eldest lad of his, the future King, or the King as he now was, may the Holy Mother bless and keep him. But that was sometimes the way in families, she added sadly. She could remember the day when the King, the one who had just passed away, crossing herself reverently, had spoken for the first time on the wireless. Christmas Day, it was, and his royal voice had come right into her home, an honour indeed, and this had been repeated every Christmas since, but she would never forget that first time, poor old man. Still, death came to us all and the Prince of Wales was a popular chap and would no doubt make a popular King. A bit wild at times, the newspapers reported, or at least he liked to enjoy himself, but what was wrong with that, Ellen asked? He'd settle down now, and surely, at his age, which was forty-one, he'd get himself a wife fit to be his Queen? Another coronation to look forward to, she went on, cheering up immediately. The second one in her lifetime and – philosophically – bound to be the last.

But in the meanwhile there were other, more pressing matters abroad than the coming coronation, or even the more local feud between the Woodall boys, matters which had a more far-reaching effect than the one existing at Woodall Park.

Michael O'Shaughnessy was discussing it on New Brighton Beach with his brother Callum when he was home at Easter, having just arrived from one of the long sea voyages he seemed to make these days. South Africa, South America, Australia, New Zealand, away for months at a time, leaving his young wife to her own devices, which was not a wise thing to do in Michael's opinion. A young woman, a beautiful young woman, particularly one with no outlet for her youthful high spirits and need for affection, might get herself into mischief as thousands of men, soldiers, had found to their cost during the war.

On the other hand, she was never very far from the keen eyes of his mother, her mother-in-law who, thanks to the deep-scouring, hard-polishing Mrs Flynn, knew every moment of her daughter-in-law's day from the time she got out of her bed – usually about ten-thirty, give or take a half-hour or so – until she got back into it, often after midnight.

'This League of Nations thing seems to be pretty useless, wouldn't you say, Callum?' Michael remarked to his brother on Easter Monday. 'Sure, an' all the idiots did last year when Italy invaded Ethiopia was to impose economic sanctions, God help them, which made no difference to the poor bloody Ethiopians, and now would you look at the way that Hitler chap has just walked into the Rhineland as bold as you please. The Treaty of Versailles completely ignored, and has anyone done a thing? Not a bit of it. Sure, I don't like the look of it, so I don't.'

'Aye, you're right, Michael, and these nationalist movements are springing up all over Europe, and here

266

too. That fellow . . . what's his name? . . . Mosley, Sir Oswald Mosley and his blackshirts are mouthing their anti-communist slogans, but it's only a front for other nastier carryings-on. They say he's to march through the streets of Liverpool later in the year, and there's to be a rally at the Stadium where himself's to speak.'

'Folk round here'll not like it, so they won't. And there's to be trouble in Spain soon, if I'm any judge. General Franco's ready to lead an uprising to unseat the Republican . . .'

'Now that's enough from the pair of you, so it is. See, Michael, have another sandwich, pet. An empty sack won't stand, an' it's little enough you've got inside you the day,' Ellen chided her eldest son, forty-six this year and getting as grey as a badger, as though he was still a growing lad. 'Now will it be ham, or egg and cress? Sure, there's plenty of both, an' see, Maeve . . .' turning to her granddaughter, '. . . run up to Henshaws, darlin', an' fetch another pot of tea, an' take Sinead with you for between them haven't these lads drunk all the lemonade. She can carry another bottle.'

It was the annual ritual outing which the O'Shaughnessys had been taking for over forty years now, though most of the family had expressed the desire to let it go, since, with so many of them, it had become increasingly difficult to arrange; and besides, there were other, far more exciting diversions than had been available forty years ago which they would like to sample, but none of them had the nerve to say so to Ellen. They had been going to New Brighton on Easter Monday since their Gracie was a child, each year adding another member to the outing as Ellen and Mick's family grew. Rain or shine, for even when it rained there was always something to do in New Brighton, they had waited expectantly at the landing stage for the ferry boat, as they had done today, amongst the vast crowds who had the same destination in mind.

They loved New Brighton, did the people of Liverpool. Its sands were not more splendid anywhere in the world, in their opinion, though none of them had been elsewhere to check, except perhaps in Blackpool. The sun was not more gloriously hot – on a good day – than that which poured its golden benison on them all as they jammed themselves cheerfully shoulder to shoulder along the water's edge, their 'cossies', their buckets and spades, their 'sarnies' and 'pop' spread out about them.

Ellen directed operations from the comfort of her deck-chair, which had been placed in the centre of the rugs the children had enthusiastically spread out. There were four of them, and on them sprawled all the grandchildren from Francis, Eammon's youngest and Ellen's youngest grandchild at a year old, right up to Amy's Devlin, at sixteen the oldest of those not yet 'grown-up'. Twenty-seven of them all told, together with Michael and Gracie, Amy and her Tommy, Eileen and Denny, Eammon and Tess – for once not pregnant, though it was hard to tell with the weight on her – Donal and Mary, Rose and Alex, and at the last moment and only because he could find no excuse to avoid it, Callum and Maris. The adults all had deck-chairs spreading out in a circle from the hub of their universe – in her opinion – Ellen O'Shaughnessy.

They had paddled their feet in the waters of the Mersey, even Ellen lifting her skirts to her knees and shrieking with the rest as young Joseph and Lorcan splashed her. They would no doubt go home with the rest of the holidaymakers looking like boiled lobsters, and there would be many a moan that night when the red and painful sunburn was eased between the sheets, but they did not think of that as they lounged in their deck-chairs or sprawled upon their rugs and towels, eating sand-filled sandwiches and drinking lukewarm tea and lukewarm lemonade. There was the fair to visit, when the novelty of making sandcastles and draining the tidal waters of the river into rapidly filling and emptying little pools had worn off, and Ellen sighed contentedly as she surveyed them all, reaching into the bottomless bag at the side of her for another packet of sandwiches.

Aye, they were all there, thank the Holy Mother, except Cliona and Christian, from whom not a word had been heard, nor a sight seen since the day they had vanished. Michael had spent weeks in Ireland, moving from place to place, starting in Dublin, going wherever there was known to be Republican sympathy or where an IRA incident was reported. These included, the shooting of a British soldier in County Cork and two police guards in Tipperary; the rescue of several IRA members from a train as they were being taken to court and thence to gaol; a cinema blown up, raids on sheriffs' offices and Garda stations and army barracks, any of which activities might have included Michael's daughter or his nephew.

He had learned nothing, and it had taken the heart out of him, so it had, but he wouldn't give up hope, he said, that one day his daughter would come to her senses and return to the family who loved her.

'. . . the government are for rearmament, and Labour's for continuing sanctions . . .'

They were still at it, her sons, and this on Easter

269

Monday when surely, being the time of year it was, it should surely bring peace. Would you listen to the spalpeens going on about war of all things!

'Well, a general election should show them what the electors want.'

'Aach, the electors aren't interested in rearmament or even foreign policy. 'Tis housing and unemployment they want to talk about.'

'You're right, God save us, nearly thirty percent of the adult population without work, poor sods . . .'

'Michael, will you hold your wisht now. There's folks here who want something more cheerful to talk about on Easter Monday, aren't there so? Now then, Rosie, tell us your plans for that fine weddin' of yours, darlin'. Has your man here decided on who's to be best man or is that . . . ?'

Those about Ellen suddenly became still, for there was not a person present, barring the younger children, who did not know of the rift between Alex Woodall and his brother Sir Charles, and rumour had it that Sir Charles had even declined to be his brother's best man, that is if he had been asked, which was doubtful. Ellen had been about to ask Alex, innocently enough, if he had found a replacement, and she could have bitten her tongue at her own tactlessness. The expression of distress on Rosie's face told her that there was something badly wrong, and that whatever it was could not be discussed here.

Callum and Michael had both looked away politely, not wishing to appear morbidly interested as one or two of the others were doing. Michael, quite casually, had put out a hand, resting it briefly on Alex's shoulder, a sympathetic gesture, for there was nothing more heart-breaking than dissension in a family. And over what, most of them were asking, and if Rosie and Alex knew they were not about to disclose it.

'Oh look,' Gracie said brightly, doing her best to divert the party from the young couple's embarrassment, and they all turned to stare where she pointed as though they had never seen a boat before. It was the paddle steamer *Jubilee Queen*, a pleasure-boat bound for Blackpool, just leaving Princes Landing Stage on the other side of the river, the sign on it proclaiming that it was 'ALL ABOARD FOR BLACKPOOL'. It was packed from bow to stern on every deck with those who wished to head up the coast for a screaming, laughing, candy-floss filled afternoon on the 'Golden Mile' and the Pleasure Beach, followed by an evening's dancing at the famous 'Tower'.

'Can we go and watch the pierrots, Mammy, can we?' Maeve was shrieking at Mary, and all the children sprang up, terrified of being left behind, scattering sand and sandwiches on the rugs, which were already almost buried. Terence and Lorcan, who had been paddling half-heartedly, longing to swim but forbidden to do so until their sandwiches and cake and biscuits and 'pop' had 'gone down', at once scampered from the water, leaping over supine, par-boiled bodies with scant regard for their comfort or safety.

A wooden platform had been laid on the sand, and already dozens of excited children were jostling with one another to be nearest to the stage. Several of the company, dressed in their distinctive costumes, were strumming on their banjos, and in minutes every child on the beach was converging on the show.

'Well, that's better,' Eammon said thankfully, giving the rug a good shake, causing screams of protest from his sisters and his wife as sand flew in every direction.

271

He lay down on the rug, put a handkerchief over his face and began to doze.

Maris lounged gracefully in a deck-chair as far away as possible from her mother-in-law, unconcerned by the disapproving glances which were cast frequently in her direction. She was the only one of the ladies to wear a bathing costume. It had a top similar to a brassière, cut low at both the front and back, with narrow shoulder straps. The skirt was very short and flared, and was worn over what was supposed to be concealed knickers, brief and high-cut. The outfit was a vivid scarlet, and about her head she had tied a broad scarlet turban. She had caused a mild sensation, and not only because of the bathing suit, though it *was* very revealing. Almost every woman on the beach under thirty wore one just like it, only more modest; but it was the way in which she had carelessly unbuttoned her scarlet cotton dress and stepped out of it. For an appalled moment, her mother- and sisters-in-law had thought she wore nothing but her underwear, though they had *never* seen *scarlet* knickers before, and when they realised that it was a bathing costume they were not much more relieved since it was scarcely any more decent.

Ellen turned a stern look on Callum, for surely he did not approve of his wife parading herself dressed like that, and with so many young and impressionable boys about, but her son seemed unconcerned by the sight of those slim white legs, on view for every man to ogle at, and those perky white breasts, which seemed to Ellen to be about to fall out of the top at any sudden movement. What were things coming to, she marvelled, when a man did not care that his wife was being leered at by every man within a range of a hundred yards?

And she would keep getting up and sauntering to the water's edge to dip in her *scarlet*-painted toes, or worse still, playing ball with Joseph and Devlin and Tomas, which brought every male who had been lying down having a doze, into an instant sitting position.

It was not long before they began to fidget, those who were not concerned with children and ice-creams and buckets and spades. They had come on this outing for one reason only, and she had fallen asleep in her deck-chair, the large, old-fashioned sun-hat she wore tipped rakishly over one eye. Rose and Alex, Callum and Maris, and Michael. They had done their duty. Ellen had commanded and they had obeyed for the sake of peace, but it was becoming increasingly evident as the afternoon wore on that they were eager to be away to other things, though none of them disclosed what they might be.

Michael was the first to stand up and casually begin to brush the sand from his trousers, and at once Ellen woke from her nap.

'Well . . .' her son said.

'Yes, it's time we were away, too,' Callum proclaimed, and almost before he had finished speaking, his wife was on her feet reaching for her dress and moccasin sandals.

'It's been lovely, Mrs O'Shaughnessy,' she smiled, annoying her mother-in-law further by the formal tone of address. 'Call me Mammy,' she had told Maris on the day of the wedding, but Maris had yet to do so.

'You're not off already?' Ellen uttered incredulously. 'Begorra, but the day's not half over.'

'It's almost three o'clock, Mammy.'

'And Rosie and I must be away too, Mrs O'Shaughnessy,' Alex pronounced in that well-bred drawl which

273

was at such variance with the Irish and Liverpool voices all around him. He smiled, a sudden outburst of rare good humour that was irresistible, and also fleetingly familiar, and Ellen fell silent to the amazement of those about her. They had expected at best a harangue, at worst an out-and-out command to sit down and behave themselves on this family day, but it seemed Ellen was about to give them neither.

'The ferry goes at three, Ma, so I think I'll catch that. I've things to do . . .' Michael said vaguely, and into several minds came the memory of what Christian Osborne had said last year about seeing his uncle with a woman. Could it be true, they wondered, and if so why was he so secretive about it? Mammy wouldn't care for it, not unless she was Irish, Catholic, and young enough to bear children, but good luck to him nevertheless, poor devil. He must be lonely all on his own in that detached house he occupied in rural West Derby.

They travelled across the river together, Michael, Callum, Maris, Rose and Alex, smiling and shaking their heads at the absurdity of these family outings that pleased the Mammy so much but which surely must come to an end soon? So many now in the family and all reproducing at a quite phenomenal rate – except, of course, Callum and Maris, though it was not mentioned, naturally – and when the Mammy went, which, the Holy Mother allowing, would not be for a long while yet, would the family drift apart? Again, it was not voiced, but the division amongst families was becoming wider, and accepted, as better education became available and was taken up by more and more of them, drawing brother apart from brother. The sons of Gracie and Amy and Eileen continued to work on the docks as labourers, but Donal, who was manager of the warehouse, Michael, who had his own thriving business, and Callum, who was captain of his own vessel, found it increasingly difficult to hold any kind of conversation with the others, unless it was about football and the possibility of Liverpool or Everton winning the Cup. They had in common only one thing and that was Ellen, and though they would die for one another should the need arise, they found it more and more difficult to spend more than an hour in their company.

They said goodbye at the Pier Head, Maris and Callum climbing into the little MG sports car which Michael had restored to its original perfection, roaring off in the direction of Dale Street, but what their destination was neither had said. Michael, eager to be away, his face as youthful as Alex's for some sudden reason, smiled and kissed Rose, then put a hand on Alex's shoulder in that odd, affectionate way he had with him.

'I'm sorry, lad,' he said simply, his eyes kind and understanding, and Alex did not flinch away but merely shook his head and smiled. 'Sure I'll not ask what the trouble is, but if you need to talk you know where I live.'

'Thanks, Michael, but . . .'

'To be sure. 'Tis proud I am to be giving away my niece here to you. A grand day it'll be.'

He climbed into his elderly Lanchester which was parked next to Alex's bright blue Triumph, waved his hand to them and drove away with a flourish, evidently in a great hurry to get where he was going.

'Let's go home.' Alex put the roadster in gear then turned to smile at Rose. They did not speak again as the car roared off in the direction of the house Alex had lived in now for over six months. Six months since the day he and Charlie had spoken their last words to one another, and next week, in the tiny church at Colton where his ancestors were at rest, he and Rose were to be married.

15

Rose Osborne was, quite simply, magnificent on her wedding day, and the expression on her husband's face told her so, and on those of the assembled congregation, as he led her proudly from the dim, back reaches of the old church towards the luminous sunshine which flooded in at the porch door. She was Rose Woodall now, his to love and cherish, as he had just promised to do, his to have love, honour and obey *him*, as she had just promised to do, for as long as they both should live. The smiling elation, the adoration which glowed in his darkened hazel eyes, the jaunty lift to his step, was quite incredible, those who knew him for a dark-natured, even brooding young man decided; and would he and his brother, who stood stiffly by his mother's side, now become reconciled, they wondered.

The wedding was lovely, though simple by the standards of many of the county's gentry who were invited. Of course the bridegroom was the second son and therefore of less importance than the first-born, who would, no doubt, when it was his turn, have an affair of great splendour with a bride to match. And then there were . . . well, one could only call them the *other* side, and could they have *managed* a society wedding of the sort the son of Sir Harry Woodall would normally have? Rose Osborne, though a lady in a manner of speaking on her father's side, was related to some strange and colourful persons on her mother's, her mother included, if the Paris creation Lady Mara Hamilton had on was anything to go by.

What an assortment they were. There was the spritely old lady who had cried fiercely and loudly from the moment the bride came out of the sunshine and into the dust-dancing timelessness of the ancient church, and continued to do so on and off for the rest of the day.

'Sure an' it's lovely you look, darlin',' she was heard by everyone in the congregation to whisper as the bride passed by her, and with dreadful regularity she sketched a hasty cross on her bosom in the manner of someone arming themselves against the devil himself.

There were women in cheap summer dresses of rayon, in drab colours, with flat hats and high brims, wearing sensible shoes and lisle stockings. Men in dark suits, somewhat ill-fitting, double-breasted, carrying trilby hats in a self-conscious manner. Irish, all of them, glancing about them fearfully as if they thought themselves to be in a den of iniquity instead of the House of God.

There were exceptions, naturally. For instance, the man who gave the bride away, her uncle it was said, bore himself with gentlemanly dignity, but then he *had* been an officer in the war, mixing with others of like rank in the officers' mess, and one presumed their ways and customs had rubbed off on him. Handsome and immaculate in his light grey morning-coat outfit, carrying a grey top hat. In his buttonhole he had a white carnation, and a white handkerchief was folded in his breast pocket. His thick, dark hair was brushed and glossy, the streaks of white at the temple giving him a most commanding and attractive appearance.

They came out into the warm sunshine, the bride and

groom, bending their heads to avoid the low lintel of the porch, for they were both tall, smiling and clinging to one another in that delightful way the newly married have, scarcely able to bear a moment without physical contact. The bride's mother was behind her, Lady Mara Hamilton with her husband Sir Miles, both of them with that faintly bored and supercilious look about them which told the congregation at their back that they were accustomed to far more exciting stuff than this. A lovely woman, the congregation agreed, even after all these years, and smart as paint in her wedding outfit, an ankle-length gown of blue-green silk jersey which exactly matched her eyes, with a pillbox hat of the same shade dipping saucily over one of them. It was swathed in net, like a fan standing out from above her eyebrows, fastened at the back in a knot of satin ribbon. As slender as a girl too, which, of course, it was fashionable to be nowadays, but obsessed with her own upper-class connections since she had remarried, for why else would she have neglected those children of hers all these years?

It was a glorious spring, starting just before Easter, the days lengthening and becoming warmer all the time. Of course Easter had been late this year but day after lovely day dawned, ending with evenings which faded from gold and amber to deep, dusky, magical blue. It will not last, Rose and Maris agonised. It will rain on the day. But it hadn't, and the churchyard was soft with the gentle dreaming air which only an English spring can bring.

Rose was in white. She was a virgin bride, a matter of great pride to Alex, since he had known from that first day in great-grandmother Lacy's house that Rose was willing to spend her love on him in that abundance of generosity which was her nature. There had been many occasions, many opportunities. He had a house of his own now, that little house set at the edge of the formal gardens of Beechwood. A bed, Lacy's bed, in the bedroom which he and Rose had scrubbed and polished together but not altered in any way. At any time he might have laid his love on that bed and she would have allowed – *allowed!* – joyfully given of herself, but something in him had needed to take his bride to the altar still a maid. Old-fashioned perhaps, or even prudish, he knew, but there was a quality in his character, which, though it was obvious that only he and Rose would know of it, needed this lovely girl to come to him before her family and his, before the whole congregation, in a traditional virginal state. Something that valued her innocence and untouched purity, which he himself, as her husband, would change.

He had turned to watch her progress on Michael O'Shaughnessy's arm as the splendid flaunting of the organ music brought her to him, the love in her green eyes misted and mysterious behind her gauzy veil. She had pearls in her ears and at her creamy throat, his wedding gift to her, white lace floating about her like a drift of snow, glorious and glorying in what was to take place. For a moment only, as she turned at the steps of the altar to pass her apricot and white bouquet to one of her sisters, his eyes met those of Sir Charles Woodall. The deep brown depths of them were enigmatic, revealing nothing of his feelings. A cold blank stare which did not look away but waited until Alex had turned back to his bride and the vows they were about to exchange.

They had all left on that night he and Rose had announced their intention to marry a year ago. At least

280

he had announced it whilst Rose stood quietly, steadfastly by him as she had always done, right through his
life. She had left with Aunt Clare and Uncle Teddy to
spend the night at Beechwood, since it had seemed very
evident to her that her Aunt Elizabeth had something
she needed to say to her son, and she needed privacy
to do so.

She had. 'Why are you doing this, Alex?' she asked
him.

Her question mystified him and he began to laugh.

'Why? That's a strange question, mother. You know
why.'

'Do I, darling? Tell me just the same.'

'Mother, what is this? I thought you loved Rose. You
have been . . . her mother almost . . . for as long as I
can remember. You and father treated her as you did
Maris. We all loved her . . .'

'I know that.'

'Then why . . . ?'

'Why am I questioning your determination to marry
her?'

'*Determination?* Good God, what a way to put it. I
want to marry her because I love her and she . . .' His
face became soft and dreaming for a moment, losing
that challenging darkness which was so familiar to her.
'She loves me, mother. We have always been close . . .'

'Yes, I have seen it but perhaps . . .'

'What . . . ?' He was wary, sensing something he
would not care for.

'Perhaps it is . . . because you have been brought up
together, you and she are mistaking your affinity with
one another for something that it is not.'

There was a sense of desperation in his mother's
voice which baffled Alex, for what in this world could

she be desperate about? He and Rose were so . . . so compatible. Surely she could see it? She loved Rosie and must know what a splendid wife she would make. Rosie was *good* for him. She steadied him when the . . . when the . . . he could not really put a name to the moods which sometimes flooded him, but at times he had the feeling he was being pulled in two directions at once, painful and senseless, since he could not understand nor explain how he felt. It was not a state of depression exactly but of *being* someone else. Alex Woodall on the well-bred, correct exterior of himself, but inside a restless, rootless vagabond who wanted nothing but to pack a bag and go blithely off on some road leading God knows where. Rosie brought him back, fortified him, gave him strength, invigorated him, unflagging and tireless in her deep, enduring love.

'Mother, don't do this.' He was steady now, for he knew what he was about to do was right.

'You are so young, both of you.'

'There is something else, isn't there? Nothing to do with our age or our shared upbringing.'

'Where is Charlie, Alex?'

He was startled. 'Charlie? How should I know? You know what he's like, flinging himself off in a temper because . . .'

'Because of what, Alex?'

'He's always the same, wanting what I have, just because I have it.'

It was out then. At last it was out in the open, and his mother sank back in her chair, letting out her breath on a long painful sigh. The fire in the grate crackled cheerfully as though to mock the woman's mood, and the clock ticked momentously. The dogs dozed with their noses on their paws and one yipped as he chased rabbits in his sleep.

'You have always been that way, both of you, ever since you were old enough to face one another. Whatever Charlie had, you wanted it, and he was the same.'

'Good God, mother.' Alex was aghast. 'Do you really believe that I would marry Rose for the sheer enjoyment of putting Charlie's nose out of joint? That I would go to such lengths, ruin my own life and Rosie's, just to spite Charlie? You don't have much of an opinion of me, do you?'

'I love you, Alex, and I love Charlie, but all your life I have seen you fight one another over puppies and kittens, trains and books and cricket bats . . .'

'I love her. Godammit, I *love her* and she loves me.'

'Tell me this, then, if the boot had been on the other foot, would you now be as Charlie is? Would you have now been coveting Charlie's fiancée as he – or so *you* say – covets yours?'

There was another long, appalled silence.

'I cannot believe this, mother. You cannot mean what you are saying. It is not the . . . the conflict between Charlie and me which troubles you, or which you seem to be implying is troubling you, but something else entirely, isn't it?'

'What else could it be? Rose is a lovely girl, and had it been Charlie . . .'

'Yes, mother? Had it been Charlie?' Alex's voice was dangerous, and it was obvious that he was trembling on the edge of some sort of violence, not directed at his mother, since he was a gentleman, but at the pretty ornaments which stood about the fire-glowed room, perhaps. His mother put out a placatory hand, but he refused to take it.

283

'Of course I didn't mean that, darling,' she said hastily. 'Or perhaps I meant Charlie is ready for marriage . . .'

'He is only a year older than I am.'

'But the eldest . . .'

'The heir, you mean. The man to father the next baronet?'

'Something like that. I did not mean . . .'

'Whatever you meant, mother, I shall marry Rose.'

'It will cause . . . ill-feeling between you and Charlie.'

'It already has, and I can do nothing to ease it. Rosie means more to me than my brother, so you surely cannot think that I should give her up just to keep the peace between him and me.'

'No . . . no, of course not.'

'Then we shall be married next spring. We will live in Lacy's house.'

'Lacy's house?'

'That is what we call it, Rose and I. We intend to live there, at least until Christian comes home, if he ever does. I shall continue to help Uncle Teddy . . .'

Elizabeth Woodall sighed, and her face was pale and troubled as her younger son poured out his heart and his love to her. Revealed his enthusiastic hopes for his future, his and Rosie Osborne's. Elizabeth loved them both, and she loved Charlie, and her heart contracted with pain at the dreadful prospect of what lay ahead for them all.

And now, on this soft spring day her niece had become her daughter-in-law and her radiance enveloped Elizabeth's son in an almost visible cape of devotion. There was no doubt that they loved one another, not as the young do, though that was there,

284

the passion and the joy, but with a steadfast emotion, a deep understanding that the years had brought them. There was rapture, need, ecstasy in their exchanged glances, in the way they clung to one another as though to remove one would mean the collapse of them both. Their lips met in a kiss that was almost reverent when the photographer called for it, and there was no need for him to ask them to look into one another's eyes since they did nothing else, ablaze with the fierce joy of, at last, belonging to one another.

They were surrounded by their guests then, family and friends congratulating the groom on his good fortune, kissing the bride and beseeching her to be happy, which of course she would, and it was noticed by not a few that Sir Charles Woodall did neither. He stood apart from the beaming throng, aloof, handsome, decidedly patrician in his detachment from the excited mass of the Irish who, it appeared, must show their pleasure in the most extrovert, one might almost say, *common* way. Like birds in an aviary, they were, darting from perch to perch, twittering endlessly and pecking at one another in affectionate accord.

There was an open carriage to take the bridal pair to Woodall Park, the one in which Rose's grandmother, Serena Osborne, had taken her drives over thirty years ago. Rescued from the old coach-house, cleaned and polished and oiled, the interior lined with white silk and decorated with apricot rosebuds from the Woodall hothouse, and pulled by a matching pair of greys, they drove off in style. Bells rang, sweet and melodious across the fields, and the air was a drift of rose petals and rice. Ellen cried, as did every female on the O'Shaughnessy side. Elizabeth made herself pleasant to each and every one as the general shuffle for the motor cars took place, and in the confusion it went unnoticed that she did not drive the journey home with her son, who had mysteriously disappeared, but with Michael O'Shaughnessy. And if anyone *had* seen them, would they have thought it strange since Mr O'Shaughnessy had given away his niece to her son?

'Well,' Ellen said to Matty as she eased off the new pair of shoes she had bought for the occasion, '. . . 'twas a lovely wedding and Rosie made a lovely bride, so she did. I'm only sad 'twas not in Holy Mother Church, for how can I set me heart at ease knowing the poor wee thing has not been properly blessed? God love 'em but they made a beautiful pair, so they did, but sure an' I'm glad 'tis over. These shoes'll have to be stretched or they'll not go on me feet again. A potato in each toe'd do the trick. Why is it that shoes aren't comfy any more, tell me that? See, pull the fire together, there's a good lass, an' wet the tea. That there champagne is all right but sure an' it does nothing when you've a thirst on you. Elizabeth, God love 'er, had that butler fetch me a pot of tea, but it tasted like nothing you an' I would call tea.'

She sighed deeply, putting her feet up on the stool Matty pushed towards her, kicking the offending shoes beneath the table. 'I'll wear me old pair for the Coronation,' she added, as though she had been invited to the Abbey to watch the ceremony. 'Them things kill me, so they do.'

She and the rest of the nation were badly shocked six months later to learn that the as yet uncrowned King had for some time been conducting what the press discreetly termed an 'affectionate' relationship with a married woman, an American lady by the name of Mrs Wallis Simpson, and that he wanted to marry her as soon as the divorce she had obtained from her husband became absolute. It seemed, the London newspapers reported, breaking their long silence, that Mrs Simpson had left the country and had 'withdrawn from the scene', but Edward was determined to follow her. He would be King and she would be his Queen, he said, or failing that there would be some sort of morganatic marriage with Mrs Simpson as his wife if not his Queen.

The country was in uproar. There were demonstrations outside Buckingham Palace in favour of the King doing as he wished, but Mr Baldwin would have none of it, it was said, and his party stood behind him. There was strong feeling against Edward, particularly in the north of England, probably brought about by the suddenness with which the news had been sprung on the public. Duty, not divorce, was the cry, a sentiment Ellen shared. She was incensed when the inevitable group of children singing Christmas carols at her door chirped:

> Hark the herald angels sing,
> Mrs Simpson's pinched our King,

but it was true, for even as she wept for the witty, handsome and charming man the public had loved and admired for more than twenty years, he was planning his departure to join the woman it seemed he could not live without.

On December 11th Edward abdicated in favour of his brother Albert, Duke of York, who took the title of George VI. Edward left England, was created the Duke of Windsor, and later married his Mrs Simpson, and when Ellen learned of it she wept again.

Meanwhile she wore her new shoes – stretched to a

more comfortable fit – on May 12th, 1937 when George and Elizabeth were crowned as her new King and Queen, though she was not in the Abbey but in her own kitchen listening to the Coronation service on her wireless. She had looked forward to it with great eagerness, and with the usual hordes of her children and grandchildren about her – for any excuse, or none at all, was needed for a party – she shushed the children, nursed the youngest, stuffed the lot of them with her good food, kissed and hugged them, laughed and wept with them at the sound of their new monarch's hesitant voice in his broadcast speech, and declared at the end of it that she hadn't enjoyed such a good coronation since 1911. The Duke and Duchess of York, God love 'em, were enormously popular, and everyone, including herself, thought the world of the two little princesses, Elizabeth and Margaret Rose.

What a day it had been. Liverpool had exploded, there was no other word for it, into a great riot of gaiety and pageantry unequalled anywhere outside London, and it was said that the lavish celebrations surpassed even those which took place on the occasion of the opening of the Mersey Tunnel. Bells rang hour after hour so that Ellen swore she couldn't hear herself think, but mind, she wasn't complaining. There were flights over the city by the 611th Company of the Lancashire Bomber Squadron of the Auxiliary Air Force. The Mercantile Marine Display in the river was something those who saw it said they would never forget. The ships, including Callum's *Alexandrina Rose*, were decorated with flags and lit up at night with strings of what seemed to be millions of diamonds reflected in the water, rippling from bank to bank of the wide estuary. There were processions and bands, and on the recreation grounds at St Martins and at Rupert Lane the public were invited to listen to the relay of the Coronation service from Westminster Abbey in uncomfortable but good-humoured congestion. There was a massed gymnastic display called 'Rhythm and Beauty', and a pageant which was named 'Drums and Bells'. There were fireworks and funfairs, an illuminated tramcar, a searchlight display and illuminations, and an elaborate and beautiful floral cart drawn by four magnificent shire horses.

The non-stop celebrations went on day and night for a week. Liverpool at its brightest and best, and Ellen said she felt quite exhausted though she had in fact not stirred from her house during the whole time. The truth was that Ellen O'Shaughnessy was beginning to feel her age, becoming more and more content to stay in her warm kitchen and let the world come in to her. She still baked her cakes and biscuits and bread, and had a constant pan of 'scouse' simmering on her stove, since who knew when one of her 'lot' might come bursting in through the front door, and how would she feel if she could not provide them with a bite to eat? Great events were beginning to take shape in the world but Ellen's world was intact and safe, moving on as it had always done in the enduring rhythm of family life and family laughter, joys and small sorrows, the joys outweighing the latter.

Eammon's Tess gave birth to her tenth child and third daughter, a day for great rejoicing, for weren't all children a welcome gift from God, Ellen told Tess, though her daughter-in-law was tight-lipped on the subject. The sadness, at least to Ellen, was the apparent inability of Alex Woodall, and her own son, Callum, to get their wives pregnant at all. Twelve months now since Rosie was wed and two years for Callum and Maris, and Ellen could not understand it. Of course, Callum was at sea for long periods of time, but in her experience the wives of sailors 'fell' every time their husbands were in port,

'Sure an' weren't I up the spout before he's took his cap off,' her friend Bridie O'Neill used to wail when her Seamus was on the Manchester liners, coming home, it seemed, only to get her in the family way. That was years ago now, but nothing had changed, surely, so what was stopping her Callum from getting *his* wife in the family way, Ellen worried.

Maris could have told her.

She was a frequent visitor to Lacy's house, dropping in, often at great inconvenience to Rosie, whenever she felt like it, though naturally Rosie never complained. It was usually while Alex was out and about the estate, in which he had become increasingly and actively engrossed, and quite often, a fact which worried Rose, Maris was accompanied by Freddie Winters.

'Should you . . . go about so much with Freddie, darling?' she asked her cousin cautiously. 'You know how people talk. I know it is perfectly innocent because I know how much you love Callum, but those who see you in his company, and that sports car of his is very distinctive, do not know you as we do.'

'Heavens, Rosie, he and I merely keep one another company. Angela practically lives in Richard Temple's pocket now they are engaged, and with you married and living a life of sheer heaven, or so you and Alex would have me believe, I have no one to go about with. No one who is any fun, that is. So can you begrudge me an outing or two with Freddie? He says Charlie's an old grouch and is preoccupied with the estate, so he

290

and I comfort one another in our hour of neglect.'

'Are you neglected, Maris?'

'Well, you know what I mean,' pouting, 'Callum seems to have taken it into his head to stay away for weeks on end, so what else am I to do with myself?'

'But Callum is home, isn't he? I thought he returned on Monday.'

'So he did, Rosie darling, but it appears his ship would sink at its berth if he were not there to check on it every moment of the day, and most of the night too, so am I to sit at home and twiddle my thumbs or am I to accept Freddie's invitations to lunch with him and his friends? They seem to think I am rather splendid which I find quite . . . rewarding.'

'Callum doesn't mind, then?' Rose's voice was careful.

'I couldn't say, darling. He doesn't enquire, and that house is quite detestable and I cannot wait to get out of it, especially as the old battle-axe is on my doorstep with the milk every morning. I swear she only arrives so early to check that I am sleeping alone . . . Well, she certainly makes *my* business *her* business, which she then reports back to the old lady . . . oh, I'm sorry, darling, I know she is your grandmother, but I do get so *bored* with the everlasting questions on my condition, or lack of it. She will go on about how quickly I *fell* – what a ghastly word – the first time, and how strange it is that I have not done so again. Naturally, I don't enlighten her.'

'Enlighten her?' Rose felt the unease settle about her. She had known for a long time now that relations were strained between Callum and Maris, for why else would Maris have that brittle, vulnerable look about her, that quality of fragile, breathless seeking for

291

something which was just out of her grasp? She was quite exquisite now that she had reached maturity. She was always dressed in the height of fashion, since her husband had shown himself to be unconcerned after all about how she spent her own allowance from her family's estate. Her silver pale curly hair was forever tousled about her small head, wisping over her ears and neck so that she looked as though she had just spent an hour in delightful dalliance with a lover, her skin flushed at the cheekbones, her eyes sparkling with feverish wickedness. What did she get up to when she was not at Lacy's house? Rosie despaired, praying that whatever it was, it was not with Freddie Winters.

'What do you mean, darling?' Rose asked Maris now, not awfully sure she wanted to know the answer, and when Maris sprang up, looking at her wrist-watch with an air of someone who has not a moment to spare, she was ashamed of her own relief.

'I must be off, Rosie. Freddie and I are . . . now don't look like that, Rose Woodall. It's a foursome. Angela and Richard, Freddie and I, are off to see *It Happened One Night*. I shall be quite safe, so stop worrying.'

She had gone when Alex came home an hour later, and as he undressed his wife, slowly removing each of her garments with the care and delicacy and delight of the true lover, all thought of Maris and Freddie and the worry which Rose meant to share with him evaporated from her mind. His hands moved slowly, his mouth smiled and his nostrils flared in that way which had become so familiar to her as he drew in the womanly smells of her, his senses, all of them, sharing the experience of loving his wife. Each button on her bodice was sighed over as it was undone. She raised her arms to display the lovely lift of her breast and the long slender line of her waist and hip and leg, not submitting but offering, taking, sharing, proud of what she was and what she had to give, eager to give it, and when they were both naked they drifted to the bed in which Lacy and James had loved one another for forty years.

'Lacy is watching,' Rosie sighed, as her husband's mouth moved at her breast and high-peaking nipple, and his strong hands lifted her at the hips, preparing her body to receive his. She was ready to dissolve, to flow, to erupt into that maelstrom of joy which his hands and lips brought her to.

'She would understand. It is in her eyes,' Alex answered, and so beneath the tolerant and smiling gaze of the woman who had given them both life, a gaze which said she knew well about love, Rose and Alex Woodall loved one another as they did every night beneath her picture, and when it was over, though of course it would never be over, he leaned above her, his elbows one on either side of her head, his smile gone now.

'You are mine. You always will be.' It was a statement of fact.

'Of course,' since there had never been any dispute over it.

'No matter what happens.'

'What could happen?' but to both their minds came suddenly the picture of the day when Charlie and Alex had fought over something which both had denied to themselves had been her. Beside the lake three years ago.

'Nothing, but if it should?'

'Nothing ever will.'

'Well then . . .' smiling and at peace, with her and with himself, '. . . shall we repeat the whole lovely performance?'

The young couple linked arms as they stepped ashore from the ferry boat which had left Dun Laoghaire the night before. They were both simply dressed, as most of the working-class passengers on the crowded decks had been. The girl wore a long woollen coat in a drab shade of grey, absolutely straight, with a high collar which brushed her ears. Her shoes were black and sensible, and on her head, jammed down to the collar of her coat, was a black woollen beret. Though she was a pretty girl and her dark hair did its best to escape the beret, a vagrant wisp curling against her cheek, no man would have given her a second glance.

The young man was the same. He wore a nondescript belted mackintosh over grey flannels and a wide 'snap brim' trilby hat. His heavy workman's boots were well polished and he wore a muffler around his neck. They each carried a small suitcase.

They smiled at one another and exchanged the occasional word as they moved with perfect familiarity across the landing stage and up the tunnel to the Pier Head where they boarded a tramcar, the sign at the front declaring its destination to be Everton.

'Nearly there,' the young man was heard to say as they left the tramcar at the corner of Everton Road and Shaw Street. They walked along Shaw Street for a hundred yards or so, her arm linked through his again, and when they reached an arched doorway above which the sign read 'Catholic Working Men's Club' they climbed the three steps and went inside.

*　　*　　*

Mr and Mrs Callum O'Shaughnessy drew slowly apart, spent and gasping. Their bodies were slicked with the sweat of their love-making. The room was hot despite the curtains drawn against the midsummer sun which poured its rays against the window. The curtains were a deep buttercup yellow, and the light shining through them turned the white walls and the white body of Maris O'Shaughnessy to gold, and darkened the already amber skin of her husband to a rich mahogany.

Their limbs seemed reluctant to part, her legs entwined in his, her curving hip still lying snugly along the length of his, and yet both had turned their faces from one another, she to stare sightlessly at the curtained window, he at the dressing-table which stood on the opposite wall. The floor was strewn with their discarded garments, high-heeled shoes kicked unceremoniously to the corner of the room, a shirt, the sleeves inside out as though testifying to some urgency on the part of the wearer in discarding it, a jacket flung in the direction of a chair which it had missed, and trousers in a puddle on the floor. A wisp of lacy knickers lay beside white underpants, silk stockings tossed willy-nilly in the air just as though two lovers had joyfully, urgently fallen upon one another, unable to wait another moment.

They did not speak. From the open window against which the curtains lay limp and still in the close and sultry heat came the sound of the noisy invasion of a flock of swifts which had made their nests under the eaves of the house. They could hear the drone of a pollen-heavy bee as it bumbled from flower to flower in Maris's rose garden, and further away the clattering intrusion of a neighbour's lawn-mower.

'Well . . .' Callum said at last, as though the polite

interval which should follow love-making was decently over. 'Pleasant as this is, I suppose I had better get up.'

'Of course, you must have a million things to do.'

'I have, as a matter of fact. My duties . . .'

'One of which you have just performed.'

He sighed, easing himself away from her until they were completely separate, then reaching for a cigarette lit it, inhaling deeply.

'Don't, Maris,' was all he said.

'Don't what, Callum? Don't disturb this . . . this well-mannered routine we go through every time you are home? Don't rock the boat, as your seaman's parlance would have it? Don't draw attention to the façade behind which we hide, the hollow pretence we keep up for the sake of . . . well, I don't know *who* we do it for, do you, Callum? Is it your mother perhaps, who, as a Catholic with a Catholic son, must keep up appearances for the Church which, by the way, would not approve of that *thing* you are wearing and which you can remove now . . .'

'Oh for God's sake, can you not let it lie . . . ?'

'Let it lie? You are preventing me from having a child and you want me to let it lie. Ask your sainted mother to let it lie, since she's the one who never, *never* stops pestering me, *me* not you, about the child we don't have, and if I was to tell her that it was *you*, you, you bastard . . .'

She began to weep broken-heartedly.

'Sweetheart . . . don't . . .'

'I *am not your sweetheart* and I never have been. You married me because you were forced to it, and now you make love to me when you can't avoid it, making sure I can't conceive. Well, you're not the only man in the world with the equipment necessary to . . .'

296

'Drop it, Maris. God's teeth, woman, we have this over and over again every time I come home . . .'

'Which is only when you can't escape it.'

'Which is whenever my life as a seaman allows it, which you were aware of when we married. Now I really *do* have things to do, if you will excuse me.'

He was gone when she dragged herself listlessly from the bed, and when he returned later that evening, a strained smile on his face and a dozen red roses in his hand, she was not there.

16

In March 1938 German troops occupied Austria, the event passing with no more than a paper protest from European leaders. Neville Chamberlain raised his voice yet again on the question of rearmament, pointing out that Germany's armed forces, which had been a mere 100,000 in 1932, now stood at 730,000, and that Britain's army, 192,000 in 1932, was still only a pitiable 237,000, which was disturbing but nevertheless not a catastrophe, since Chamberlain was of the opinion that, like himself, Adolf Hitler, and Mussolini as well, were rational statesmen and could be appeased by rational discussion. Great Britain and France could still lay down the law to Europe, whatever some members of the Foreign Office thought. France had the Maginot Line and Great Britain the English Channel, so even if Germany became the predominant power in Eastern Europe and the Balkans, which it seemed was Hitler's goal, Great Britain and France had nothing to fear.

It was a pale spring day, as pale and yellow as the sunshine itself, and as the rather ancient Bullnose Morris chuntered through Colton village, women who lingered on their cottage steps reluctant to leave that lovely hint of the summer to come, waved at its driver.

The pub was not yet open but a few 'ancients' were already seated on the bench which stood to the right of the door, gnarled hands on gnarled walking sticks, patiently waiting for their first pint.

'She looks smart this mornin',' one remarked to another, watching the progress of the motor car as it skirted the green.

'She do that. Where d'you reckon she's off to then?'

'Nay, don't ask me. These young 'uns 're for ever traipsin' off somewhere. Now in my day . . .'

'. . . an' mine . . .'

'. . . a woman knew 'er place *an'* bloody well kept to it.'

'Yer right there.'

There were Easter lilies growing in thick clusters on the green. The badge of Easter, as country folk called the great angel-trumpeted cream, yellow and orange of the spring daffodils. The most glorious symbol of the Resurrection that nature could provide, it was said. The churchyard at Colton glowed with them, and the woman driving the motor car pulled into the side of the road, turned off the engine, got out, and walked over to the drystone wall which surrounded the church. She did not go inside but stood for five minutes or so by the lych-gate, her face pale and dreaming, her eyes serene.

'You will understand, my darling,' she murmured out loud. 'Wherever you are now, and I know you are somewhere, you will understand. Wish me joy.'

A throstle sang, patiently and sweetly from a small cypress tree some yards along the churchyard wall. More wild daffodils nodded their splendid heads in the light breeze. In the protection of the wall primroses grew, and the wood sorrel was already in bloom, its delicate pink and white flowers clustered among its heart-shaped leaves, and to the woman's delight a yellow butterfly alighted briefly on one of them. An omen, a pledge for their future, she thought. Such a

299

pretty thing on such a pretty day must surely mean that at last, at last it was to be *right*. There were storms ahead, terrible storms which made her shiver a little even before they had begun. Things to be got through which would not be easy, but surely the butterfly and the loveliness of the day for which they had both waited so long gave promise of hope, of peace, of joy for the future. For them all.

She turned then, the pale and beautiful woman, and as she did so the sound of another motor car disturbed the tranquil peace of the late morning sunshine. It drew nearer and the woman smiled.

It came round the bend in the lane, and the sun glimmered on all its carefully polished surfaces, and all about it there appeared to be a golden haze as though it had come from some other and quite magnificent world. The woman's smile deepened at her own fond and foolish thought. It was an immaculately kept Lanchester 40.

It stopped, its bonnet almost touching that of the Morris, and she stepped forward as the engine died. The driver got out, holding out his hand to her. She put hers in it.

'Are you ready, my darling?' she said, her eyes quite incredibly beautiful with her love for him.

'I've been ready for twenty-seven years, sweetheart,' he answered.

It was without doubt the most talked-of event to have taken place since James Osborne had been forced to marry Mara O'Shaughnessy over twenty-five years ago, Liverpool's and the county's 'good' families agreed, and the irony of it was it concerned James Osborne's sister and Mara O'Shaughnessy's brother! It was also ironic that the outrageous behaviour of their mother had, if only temporarily, brought the Woodall boys together as nothing else could.

It was, so it was rumoured, almost two years since Alex and Sir Charles Woodall had exchanged more than the barest civilities, and then only in the presence of their mother, who was at her wit's end with the pair of them, and now it was she herself, though in a manner not one person approved of, who had reunited them.

They came straight from the registry office, Mr and Mrs Michael O'Shaughnessy, the bride and groom, and when they walked, hand in hand, it was reported, into the drawing room at Woodall Park, you could have heard a pin drop. Mr and Mrs Alex Woodall, Sir Charles Woodall, and Mrs Callum O'Shaughnessy, who was as usual on her own. Those who were most concerned in the matter and who had been requested by Lady Woodall – now Mrs Michael O'Shaughnessy – to present themselves for lunch.

They all stood up, and for several dazed, incredulous moments they looked as though some terrible joke had been played on them, though they were not at all amused.

'Darlings . . .' their mother said, her smile tremulous with joy and yet very nervous. She was being careful, walking on eggshells, or so it seemed, as she and Michael O'Shaughnessy stood, hands clasped, just inside the door which a poker-faced Wilson had closed behind him as he left the room.

'Mother?' It was Sir Charles who broke the ghastly silence, his voice rising, not asking what had happened but questioning her very identity, for would Lady Elizabeth Woodall, widow of Sir Harry Woodall, hold the hand, in that very intimate way, of Michael

O'Shaughnessy, who was after all no more than a mechanic? The others said nothing.

'We have something to tell you, Michael and I.' Her voice was soft but far from apologetic.

No one spoke. It was as if they knew. They didn't *want* to, at least not the Woodall boys, but they knew just the same.

'Mother.' There was a warning note in the voice of her younger son, and it was to him and, it seemed, his mother's new husband, for how could he be anything else, that she looked as she spoke.

'Michael and I were married an hour ago. We came to tell you at once.' Her smile was very lovely, and Rose Woodall's face softened and her eyes began to brim with tears. She was ready to kiss the bride and congratulate the groom, for their happiness, though mixed with anxiety, was very apparent, but her husband held her arm.

'Rose.' His voice was harsh.

'But Alex . . .'

'No, Rose.'

There was another long and painful silence, and the sweet and lovely smile began to slide away from the bride's face. Her two sons stood like stone, wanting to do something very savage, to say something very offensive; but their training at one of England's best public schools, their upbringing as gentlemen, and the love they had for their mother, kept them silent, and it was not until Maris began to laugh, quietly at first, then growing and growing, becoming louder and more hysterical, that they broke from their awful trance.

'Be quiet, Maris.' Charlie's voice was a snarl, the wild and tortured snarl of a man who can do nothing to ease his own pain.

'Dear God, Charlie, can't you see how funny it is? Every bloody one of us, at some time or another, in some degree or other, seems destined to marry an O'Shaughnessy. First Uncle James, then Uncle Teddy, me, God help me, and now mother. Two Mrs O'Shaughnessys, mother and daughter, both married to brothers. Do you realise we are not only mother and daughter but sisters-in-law? Jesus Christ, are you absolutely sure we are not committing incest somewhere in this . . .'

'Be quiet, Maris.' This time it was her mother who spoke, but still she did not look at her daughter and neither did her husband. It was at Alex that their gaze was directed, and it was Alex who spoke the first awful words.

'How long has this been going on? How long have you and this . . . this man been . . . ? Jesus, my father has been dead no more than . . .'

'Three years, Alex. It's been more than three years.'

Elizabeth O'Shaughnessy's voice was anguished, and she held out her hands to her son in desperate appeal. 'I have been a widow for three years and . . .'

She stopped then, laying her face against her husband's shoulder. He put an arm about her protectively, sighing deeply, sadly.

'Sure an' we thought it might be like this, didn't we, darlin'?' he murmured into her hair, then he turned her to face him just as though they were alone. ' 'Tis a shock to them but they'll accept. They'll have to, begod . . .'

'Will we? We'll see about that . . .'

'. . . as my family will have to accept,' ignoring Charlie's interruption.

'Why didn't you tell us, mother? How could you have done it like this? How could you have done this to us?'

'I suppose she knew you'd object, son, that's why.'

'I am not your son, sir, and I never will be.' Alex's eyes were slits of pure green rage, the brown flecks in them dissolved by his devastating emotion, and he spoke as though he had ashes in his mouth. Michael winced and his wife put a warning, soothing hand on his arm to steady him.

'We thought it best, Alex, your mother and I.'

'Yes, I suppose you would. It would be more convenient without my mother's children to restrain her from making this horrifying mistake, wouldn't it? and I expect it's too much to ask a man such as yourself to have the guts to . . .'

'Alex . . . Alex . . . stop it . . .'

'It's all right, darlin'. I can stand up for myself, so I can, and I'll not have this whippersnapper calling me a coward, not on my wedding day nor on any other day. This is your mother here, Alex Woodall. A gracious lady if ever there was one, and I'll not be having her distressed like this. She and I are married now, and no one distresses my wife, *ever*. Do you hear me, boy? Now will you sit down to lunch with us, your mother and I, before I take her home . . . oh aye, she's to come and live in her husband's house . . . or will she and meself go off on our wedding journey to France without the good wishes of her children? She'd not be happy to do that, and what makes her unhappy, *I* don't like, and neither do you, I'm sure. Now, we'll say no more. There's nothing, *nothing*, to be done about it, by you or anyone, lads, so you can stop that glowering and stamping your feet . . .'

'I'll be damned if . . .'

'Oh, Charlie, for God's sake, stop it. There's no point in arguing and shouting that you don't like it, because it makes not the slightest difference.' Maris moved towards her mother, lifting her arms ready to embrace her. 'I for one wish mother and Michael all the good luck in the world.'

'And so do I, Aunt Elizabeth *and* Uncle Michael.'

'Oh Jesus, we're going to have tears and kisses now. Bloody women, you've only to let them smell the orange blossom . . .'

'Alex, oh Alex darling . . . please, *please* won't you . . . just try . . . I am so happy. Michael and I have waited . . . I knew you and Charlie would be . . . upset. I loved your father and I have mourned him sincerely, but three years is enough. He would not have wanted me to . . .'

'It is always convenient to believe that, isn't it, mother? That the first husband sends his good wishes from the other side, conveying in some mysterious way that he's all for it.'

'I won't have you speaking to your mother in that way, boy . . .'

'Won't you? And how are you to stop me?' Charles Woodall was wild with pain and fury at what he saw as his mother's disloyalty and her lack of refinement in marrying a man so far beneath him. The O'Shaughnessys, despite their connection with the Osbornes and Woodalls, as Maris had said, were of the working class. *His* father had been a baronet with a patrician heritage going back four hundred years. His mother was from a good family with a sprinkling of nobility in its past, since Charles Hemingway, his own great-grandfather, had been married to the niece of an earl. It had been bad enough when his Uncle Teddy had taken up with this man's sister, and his *own* sister with this man's brother; but his *mother*, his lovely, gracious mother, who was every inch a lady, to demean herself and the family in this way was more than he could bear.

'I can't stop you doing anything, Charlie,' his mother's husband was saying. 'You're a man now, so you are, and will please yourself, but surely you owe your mother more than this.' Michael's face was drawn and angry, not for himself, it was very evident, since Charlie Woodall meant nothing to him, but for the woman who had just become his wife. He still had a sheltering arm about her, though she stood erect now, pale and proud and determined. Her clear green eyes, so like those of her niece who was also her daughter-in-law, looked from one son to the other then turned to Maris and smiled luminously.

'I'll have that hug now, darling, and from Rosie too. God bless you both.'

When the moving embraces of her daughter and daughter-in-law were done with, she turned to Alex, her expression sad but filled with her love for him.

'Alex, will you not wish me happiness? We may not always have agreed on . . . certain things . . .' making an oblique reference which only he understood and which took him back to their argument before his wedding day, '. . . but I accepted . . . if we love, we accept and allow . . . oh darling, you must understand now what it means to . . . so please, don't let me go with bad feelings between us.'

He was truculent and agonised, hovering on the brink of what could be a final and permanent separation, for if he let his mother walk away from him, would he ever be able to close the distance between them again? He was badly shaken, still ready to glare and shout and demand to know how she could throw away the memory of the special man his father had been, but

306

she was his mother, just as special as his father, and he loved her. There was nothing that could change what had taken place this morning. There was no going back.

He felt Rosie's hand slip into his, telling him something, reminding him of something, bringing back to him in a great and overwhelming rush *his* love for *her*. Begging for his understanding since *he* knew about love now. Alex Woodall grew up in that moment. Attained a measure of maturity, and though he could not say he would ever *like* it, he knew he must *accept* it. He had, for some reason, always felt an affinity with Michael O'Shaughnessy. A liking and respect, an admiration for what Michael had achieved and what he had overcome. He remembered the day on which Christian had revealed that there was a woman in his uncle's life, and how he himself had felt a certain sympathetic approval. It had been some months after his father's death, so what was he to make of that, and did he really care to make anything of it?

'I . . . am not sure I have it in me to . . . My father was . . .'

'Darling, I know, I know, so there is no need to speak, really there isn't. Give me a hug, that's all I need, and perhaps . . . if you would . . . a hand to Michael.'

It was a touching moment, and Rose, through her smiles, had tears coursing across her cheeks as Alex embraced his mother and somewhat stiltedly took the hand of her new husband. She turned to Charlie, for surely he would follow his brother on that first reluctant step towards conciliation, but Charlie Woodall was half-way across the room, his tall figure snapping with frustrated loathing. His face was like clay, and his brown eyes were flat and empty. He turned at the door.

'Don't expect me to join in this bloody farce,' he snarled through clenched teeth, '. . . and don't expect me to invite this man to sit at my father's table or sleep in his bed. I trust you and your things will be gone by the end of the day, Mrs O'Shaughnessy, and if any of my servants can do anything to expedite your move don't hesitate to ask them.'

It was not much better at Ellen's, so Rose heard later. Even though her grandmother had great affection and admiration for Elizabeth Woodall, that didn't mean to say she wanted her for a daughter-in-law. Her Michael had lost so much in the past few years, still searching for his daughter whenever some rumour seemed to point perhaps in her direction, sailing over to Ireland on the slightest pretext but finding nothing. He grieved silently and alone, his mother knew, and what could be more healing than the love of a good woman and perhaps the chance of more children? He was forty-eight now, no age for a man, and he could breed himself a daughter to replace the one who was, it seemed, irretrievably lost to him; or a son, a son to carry the name of Michael as the eldest boy of the eldest boy had done for a century now.

Elizabeth Woodall was a good woman, one of the best, but not Catholic and no longer young, and when she and Ellen's son walked into her kitchen bringing with them the strong and – Sweet Mother – the unbreakable sweetness of the love they had borne one another for more years than Ellen cared to remember, even before they spoke a word she threw her apron over her head and began to weep.

Her son knelt at her feet, whilst his wife stood quietly waiting beyond the table. Matty, her hand to her bosom, dithered in the doorway of the scullery, not knowing whether to come or go, but after all, she was a member of this family too, if not by blood then by time, sharing its griefs and its joys all these years; and if it was to be the former that was to be revealed and overcome, then here she was to help overcome it.

'Don't cry, Mammy, 'tis a day for happiness, not tears. Won't you kiss Elizabeth?'

'Mother of Jesus . . .' and her sorrow wracked her, '. . . how can I? She's not for you, Michael O'Shaughnessy. Sure an' isn't she the widow of Sir Harry, and not for the likes of you.'

'Mammy, stop it, stop it. It counts for nothing these days, you know that.'

'I know nothing of the sort. God put us all on this earth in a certain place, and bejasus, that's where we were meant to stay.'

'And what about Mara? She's married to a baronet . . .'

'Aach, that one . . .'

'Aye, and now me. Elizabeth's my wife, Mammy. Part of this family now . . .'

'God love her, son, I've nothing against her. A lovely lady, but I wanted . . .'

'She is what I want, Ma.'

'. . . children, Michael . . .'

'I have a child.'

'So you have, pet, so you have, but with a nice young wife you could have . . .'

'Mammy, look at me, look at me . . .'

'Aah, Michael . . . after all these years . . .' Her voice was muffled in her apron but her son heard her. He sat back on his heels, looking towards the woman who still remained by the door as though anxious not

309

to intrude herself in this family drama. He held out his hand, and she came to kneel beside him.

It was almost as though they were in church, kneeling to take their vows, as they waited for Ellen to look at them. Slowly, she lowered the apron. Her face was sad, and yet there was a peaceful resignation written on it. Leaning forward, she took each face in turn between her hands, kissing first her son, then her new daughter-in-law.

'Sure an' it's taken a long time, darlin',' she said to Elizabeth.

'You . . . knew . . . ?'

'Aye, I guessed.'

'But how . . . ?'

'He's my son and a mother knows her own son, doesn't she, pet? All these years I knew there was someone in his heart, so I did. Wisht, don't look like that, child. I knew you wouldn't dishonour your husband when he got back from the war, but my son was a man, a real man, an' I prayed he'd . . . find a woman who would . . . but, the Blessed Virgin didn't hear my prayers, or perhaps she did an' knew better than me. You're a fine an' lovely woman, so you are. So, a kiss for my son and his bride, an' you can stop grizzlin' in that doorway, Matty, an' wet the tea. No, to hell with the tea. See, run up to the parlour an' fetch that sherry Callum brought me at Christmas, an' we'll toast Michael an' Elizabeth in a proper way. My son an' his wife. The bride an' groom.'

'What's Charlie supposed to be doing at Woodall these days, rattling around all by himself with no company but that of the servants? He has asked me and Callum to dine a time or two, but Callum and he can't abide one another so I made some excuse and put him off. I have driven over with Freddie for cocktails, Sunday lunch and things like that, but he seems not to mind being alone. My God, when I think only a few years ago the place was alive with children and dogs and kittens, mother in the drawing room, father in his study, the house bursting at the seams with what appeared to be far too many people for its size, and now only poor old Charlie is left. I say poor old Charlie, but he has only himself to blame. I know mother and Michael drove over several times, but it seems he was "out", so though she didn't like it, Michael insisted she go on her own and she got in. Afternoon tea, he offered her, as though she was a casual caller, so she's not been again. Bloody hell, Rosie, it really is awful the way he is. He's at odds with you and Alex, and now mother and Michael. Does he not care about family anymore? Where the devil does he get that dreadful bitter stubbornness? It used to be Alex who was always out of sorts, but marriage seems to have softened the rough edges with which he used to scrape people. And where does it come from? Neither mother nor father were abrasive, nor so implacable. Have *you* been over, darling? I know of course that Alex won't, but I thought perhaps you might . . . well, no one could be cross with you, Rosie.'

Maris lit another of her endless cigarettes, throwing the spent match into Rosie's empty fireplace, careless of the superb arrangement of spring flowers and grasses which stood on the hearth. She draped one trousered leg over the arm of the settee, and stared moodily at the wedding portrait of Rose and Alex which hung over the fireplace.

Rose and Alex had made 'Lacy's house' into what

Maris recognised, probably because of the lack of it in her own home, as a warm and fragrant haven in which their marriage and their love had grown quietly and steadily from the love of boy for girl into the deep maturing love of man and woman. It could be felt the moment you bent your head to enter the low doorway into the entrance hall. It was heady with pot-pourri, made by Rose herself, and with the beeswax she polished into the old furniture. They had no servants apart from a 'girl' in the kitchen who did the heavy work and Rose herself was often to be seen on her knees polishing the old wooden floor, which was dark with age and glowing with loving care. There were fringed rugs, in the soft and muted colours Lacy had admired, which her grandchildren had cleaned and kept just as she had. Armchairs of honey velvet with foot-stools to match. A log-fire in the winter, and a log bucket of burnished copper with fire-tongs and a poker to match. Lamps in shades of autumn, and a gate-legged table standing in the window alcove; plump velvet cushions, and thick velvet curtains, and on every surface wide bowls and vases filled with flowers.

On the rug a fat tabby lay sleeping, its fat tail curled about it, as sleek and burnished and fitting as was everything in the room.

Upstairs it was the same: pale walls of silk, frayed but still beautiful, deep carpets and old furniture, lace curtains, and a deep warm bed in which Maris's brother and his wife exhausted themselves, bemused themselves in their passion, which had nothing of it at all in Maris and Callum O'Shaughnessy's marriage.

'They say he has a woman there . . . women . . .'

Maris was startled out of her melancholy contemplation of her surroundings and the Woodalls'

312

happiness, and she turned to stare, her mouth falling open.

'Women! Good God. Who says so?'

'Oh, the servants. Those at Woodall tell those at Beechwood. You know how these things are. It gets to Uncle Teddy and then to Alex. I suppose it's *his* business though, and nothing to do with us.'

'I know but . . . *Woodall* . . . I mean . . . does mother know, d'you think?'

'I suppose not. She hasn't said. You know Uncle Michael has given her a car of her own, don't you . . . anyway she gets about to see her . . . well, not her *old* friends since they only cared for Lady Woodall and not Mrs Michael O'Shaughnessy . . .'

'Bitches . . .'

'Yes, I know. She *has* come to you as well, but she says you're never in.' Rose smiled affectionately, taking the sting from the remark. 'Well . . . she calls on me, and grandmother of course, since the pair of them are as thick as thieves now . . .' Rose stopped speaking abruptly and her eyes widened. Maris leaned forward.

'Yes . . . now?'

'Well . . . since Aunt Elizabeth married Uncle Michael,' but that was not what Rose had been about to say and Maris knew it. The gossip about Charlie and his 'women' was quite forgotten as she scented something far more fascinating.

'*Now*, Rosie? What is this conspiracy? Why are mother and Mrs O'Shaughnessy so matey all of a sudden? I thought your grandmother was not best pleased with her new daughter-in-law, wanting some young, childbearing . . .'

'Really Maris, it is nothing to do with me.'

313

'What isn't? What's going on here? What are you and . . . mother keeping from me?'

'I can't tell you, Maris. It must come from your mother. She wouldn't have told me only I'm in the . . .'

Rose's face flushed and Maris looked at her more closely, seeing the starred eyes, like bright emeralds, the lovely blooming, the sleek and well-fed appearance of . . . plumper of late, and even more stately, as though she had slowed down to accommodate the . . .

'You're pregnant.'

'Yes.' A joyful pride, shining and good.

'And . . . and mother?'

'Yes . . .'

'Oh Jesus, wait until Charlie hears about this.'

17

'I want a child, Callum.'

'Because both your mother and Rosie are to have one, is that it?'

'No, I want a child to replace the one I lost three years ago. It has nothing at all to do with mother and Rosie, though I suppose if I'm honest I will admit that it's brought it home to me how much I . . . miss him.'

'Miss him? Who?'

'Our son, Callum, who would have been three years old . . .'

'Oh, of course, I'm sorry. I wasn't . . . thinking.'

'No, I don't suppose you were, unless it's about ships or cargoes or manifestoes, whatever they may be. There's nothing else worth thinking about, is there?'

'Oh, I wouldn't say that, my pet,' grinning in that way she found so irritating and yet so irresistible. 'I was actually thinking you might like to come with me to see the launching of the *Mauretania* this morning. Lady Bates, wife of the chairman of Cunard-White Star, is to do the honours. There will be champagne flowing, and all the right people will be there . . .'

'So how did you get invited?' she interrupted rudely.

'Really, Maris, you'd never think you were brought up to be a lady. Your manners leave a lot to be desired. And to answer your question, I know one or two people with . . . influence, shall we say, and of course, being married to a Woodall who has the blood of Hemingways in her helps somewhat.'

'So I am useful for something.'

He sighed in deep resignation, his efforts to keep the moment light and pleasant, coming to nothing. He had hoped to divert her in the way one would divert an obstinate child, with an outing, a treat, anything in fact to get her off the bloody subject which had become like a bone between them, chewed over again and again, buried, dug up, and the whole process repeated until he could have hit her. She had become more and more insistent about wanting a child, and now the shattering revelation that her own mother, a woman of forty-three and only four months married, was to have one, had fuelled her own desire until it seemed to consume her. And really, why shouldn't he give her one, he thought distractedly, right now in the five minutes it would take to impregnate her, in the five minutes he had to spare before he shaved and dressed for the ceremony at Birkenhead?

He often asked himself why he hung back from this final commitment to his wife, this final bond which would tie them together irrevocably, and that was why, he supposed. The bond, the *bonds*, would be even stronger than they now were, and he would never be able to escape them. Never. A child was for life, but . . . Jesus, he was sick of the charade they were forced to enact whenever he was home, bitterly so, and why, he wondered, had he not just walked away from it? or better yet, *better yet*, why could he not *love* her? She was lovely, bright, with a beguiling whimsical charm sometimes that had him reaching for her in laughter and genuine pleasure. She had courage and humour, so why could he not fall in love with her? She was his equal in bed, a willing and exciting partner in any need or fancy that took him, sighing and languorous, uninhibited and enjoying her own and his fulfilment. She showed no reluctance in allowing him the flights of eroticism which now and again his maleness demanded of her, lying for hours, the whole night, whilst he explored every sweet moist hollow, every satin curve of her delightful body, doing the same to him to their mutual satisfaction.

But still the resentment festered in him. That bitter, corroding rancour that ate away any possibility that he and Maris might live together in any kind of harmony. He had, in sailors' parlance, been 'shanghaied' into marriage by the oldest snare in the world, and he could not seem to rinse the acid of it from his soul. Through his own weakness, for what else could that moment of compassion for a grieving girl be called? he had been caught in the oldest trap woman could set for man, and he could not get over it, nor live with it, or Maris, for much longer. If the child, the reason for this . . . this masquerade they dutifully performed, had lived, perhaps things might have been different. Perhaps with a son or even a delightful little daughter to come home to, to stand as a buffer between his wife and himself, they might have made some sort of fist of it, but each time he sailed into Liverpool Bay he could feel his heart sink in a strange and bewildering despair. It seemed the last place in the world he wanted to get to was Seymour Road, and yet some compulsion kept him going there long after any hope of improvement in the relationship had died. He *had* hoped, for a while, that they might have made something together, but the moment he came in through the front door, and after the initial intoxication of their love-making was over, despite his determination to be otherwise, it seemed they were at each others' throats.

317

Or had been. For the last year, or was it more than that? she had no longer run eagerly to meet him, her arms lifting to cling about his neck, her eyes glowing in the semi-gloom of the hallway, her face flushed with some emotion she could not, and made no attempt to conceal. She had been warm and yielding, wearing some slipping, filmy garment with ribbons, which appeared to come unfastened the moment he put his bag to the floor. Her love had wrapped about him, *smothered* him, his inner self whispered, and yet it had been very . . . pleasant, nonetheless. A candlelit dinner later, kisses and soft laughter, mostly hers, since she was so happy to have him home, she said time and time again, wine and French perfume until he was bemused by it.

But the sweet glow of it had never lasted. When she was asleep it would pound in on him like the huge rollers of the Atlantic, the sheer bloody domesticity of it all, the foolish pretence that they were a happily married couple, which he kept up and which, as she began to understand the true shape of his feelings, *she* kept up.

Lately, when he came home, she was simply not there. She had bought herself a smart little Triumph Roadster coupé with its distinctive 'waterfall' grille. Somewhat like the one her brother Alex had, but the very latest model. A vivid and very noticeable scarlet with a cream hood, and a loud and very impatient horn, which she sounded constantly as she drove. The purchase of the car had created a further tension between them which had never been eased.

'I thought it was understood right from the start that you were not to buy a car.' They had been the first words he had snarled at her as he entered the house,

318

not only incensed that she had bought the thing against his wishes, but that it was parked in front of the bloody garage doors where his own MG was locked up while he was away.

'Well, hello to you too, darling. How lovely to see you,' offering a cool cheek for his kiss, which he had ignored, brushing past her roughly to throw his bag into the back room. He had felt ready to put his hands about her throat and strangle her, really he had, wondering why even as the emotion roared out of control inside him.

'I cannot afford to buy or run that vehicle outside, which I presume is yours since it is parked on our path.'

'Yes, it is mine, and it has not and *will* not cost you a penny, my darling. I bought it from my own allowance as I said I would, and what I do with my money is surely *my* affair?'

'Is that right? Despite the fact that I expressly forbade you to buy one, since you are the wife of a man who . . .'

Christ, would you listen to him, he had thought, even as he was speaking the asinine words, amazed at his own petty, pedantic raving, for really if she wanted a car and could buy one herself, why shouldn't she? He did not own her, nor did he want to, nor did he really *care*, so why was it she aroused this bewildering asperity in him, this dangerous and hot-blooded fury with almost everything she did? Because he did not love her, he supposed, and was forced to live beside her and her foolish, upper-class banality whenever he was home. He was a prisoner held in a cage of his own making, held by the ties of responsibility to this woman, by the ties which bound him to the work he loved and the ship he loved; and only by a gargantuan effort of his will,

319

his mind and his body could he survive the misery which came to him in this bleakest hour of the night.

And now she was asking for a child, a child he could not give her since to do so would burden him with a load he could not carry, or would add to the one he already had. Jesus, sometimes he wondered why he did not give it all up, and her, but something had held him back, something which was getting weaker and weaker and which would really have to snap soon.

'Come on, my pet, put on some stunning outfit and put poor Lady Bates in the shade. Let's go and drink their champagne and eat their Beluga caviar and watch the second dear old *Mauri* get herself under way . . .' for what else were Maris and Callum O'Shaughnessy to do, his manner asked? Certainly not make a baby! '. . . and if she's as good as her predecessor she'll be a great lady. The first *Mauri* made the fastest Atlantic crossing between Bishop Rock in the Scilly Isles and Ambrose Light off New York. She took the Blue Riband from the *Lusitania* and kept it, as well, until 1929, did you know that?' His enthusiasm, as usual, for anything to do with ships and the sea put a deep glow in his eyes, one he had never shown to his wife.

'Is that so?' Her jealousy made her scornful, letting him see she cared nothing for his *Mauri* or his *Lusi* as the two liners were affectionately called by those from Liverpool, or indeed anything he considered worthwhile.

'Yes . . . so will you come?' His tone had cooled considerably.

'I suppose so. I've nothing else on today. Rosie is so bloody boring with her broody amiability, forever fiddling with "little things", and as for mother . . .'

'Go and put your best hat on then . . .' eager to

change the subject and divert her from her contemplation of her own barrenness.

It was a cool day with a threat of rain in it despite the time of the year, but the noise and movement and raw excitement of the scene filled Callum with the intoxicated satisfaction he had known whenever he was about the dockland from being a boy. There were people everywhere, most of them remembering the old *Mauretania* which had been at berth here so often in her twenty-eight years of service with Cunard until she was broken up for scrap only three years ago. Young boys, would-be mariners, jammed the area behind the slipway, almost disappearing amongst the massed crowds who had come over on the ferry or driven under the new Mersey Tunnel to Birkenhead to see the great ship begin her journey into the river. She looked cumbersome, ungainly with her bow rearing up on to the shore, like a beached whale with a fretwork of cranes bobbing and weaving about her.

They stood to the back of the platform on which Lady Bates was to perform the launching, amongst the élite of the shipping world, the invited guests who had come from all the great shipping houses and shipbuilding firms on both sides of the river. There were Hemingways and Osbornes who greeted Maris with surprise since they had not known she was interested in this side of the family business, they said. Her husband? Of course . . . Captain O'Shaughnessy was master of the *Alexandrina Rose*, was he not, and would she care to come and be introduced to . . . ?

There was a great deal of commotion coming from the deep cavern in which the hull of the ship seemed sunk: men's voices, whistling, a great roar of cheering; and when Lady Bates, her voice indiscernible to the men at the ship's keel, spoke the words which gave the ship her name, smashing the bottle of champagne against her side which gave the ship her passage, the vessel began to move. Slowly, so slowly those about her thought she had not begun; then, gathering speed, she went on her way, entering the river stern first in a tremendous spume of water which threatened to sink the small boats around her. Hats were thrown in the air, and the joy brought about by the initiation of any new ship was so great many of the rugged and dour men who had built her were in tears.

She was sipping her fourth, or was it her fifth glass of champagne? bored and ready to leave, her eyes roaming about the room looking for Callum to take her home, when she saw him.

The woman he was with was strikingly beautiful, tall and slim as a wand, but with that svelte femininity that men recognise and immediately want, and women hate though they could not say why. A sensuality which, though she was simply dressed in a neutral shade of pearl grey touched with white, was flaunting in its immediacy. Her dress was of some soft clinging material, very expensive; her shoes, with heels so high she was as tall as Callum, were of grey lizard, and her hat was a tiny nest of pearl-grey feathers on her smooth, dark brown hair. She was laughing, her head thrown back to reveal the snow-white column of her lovely throat. Callum was leaning towards her, whispering something in her ear, her eyes warm, deep blue wells of admiration and something else which any man, or woman for that matter, could not fail to recognise. The woman certainly didn't and she liked what she saw.

The whip of agony flicked at Maris with all the speed and menace of a striking cobra, hurting her so badly

322

she flinched away from it, spilling her drink down the front of her own very expensive dress, and causing mild consternation amongst the small group of men who stood admiringly about her. She looked her best, she knew she did, in a lovely colour of blue so pale it was almost white. A dress so expensive she knew Callum would throw a fit if he heard what it cost. It was of silk jersey, cleverly draped, and as clinging as the woman's who had captured Maris's husband's attention, and each gentleman was very ready to assist in any way he could, a handkerchief perhaps, one ironed most likely by his own loyal wife, whilst Maris O'Shaughnessy thought she would wither away and die – if only she could – like a flower which has been exposed to the searing heat of the desert sun. She needed very badly to lock her arms about her breast to stop herself from running across the room and using them, or the nails at the end of them, to viciously scratch at the woman's flawless face. To flail and strike at her husband's *smiling* face; and if she did not get a grip on herself she knew she would, since, quite simply, she could not stand the pain without doing something, *anything*, to ease it. She knew she must live for ever with her love for Callum O'Shaughnessy battened down in the depths of her severely wounded heart, unreturned, she had known that for at least a year now; but was she to stay and witness what had probably, she agonised, happened more than once since their marriage three years ago? What a fool, what a bloody naïve fool she had been. She had realised, devastatingly, that Callum did not love her, but somehow it had not occurred to her that he might love someone else. Who was this woman? How long had he known her, and how well? Oh God, oh sweet Christ, she hurt so much, so much. What was she to do? She couldn't stand here sipping champagne and exchanging pleasantries with these inane fools just as though nothing had happened, nothing was happening, and if it was, it didn't matter, whilst her husband carried on, or began, an affair with the most beautiful woman in the room.

'Who is that woman over there?' she asked abruptly, too badly injured to care whether Mr Smith or Mr Jones or whoever he was, thought her odd. 'The one talking to my husband.'

Mr Smith or Mr Jones obligingly looked in the direction Mrs O'Shaughnessy was indicating with her slopping champagne glass.

'That's the wife of one of the directors of Hemingways,' he answered, wondering whether Mrs O'Shaughnessy should be taken to her husband since she seemed so . . . ill, perhaps, certainly not herself, which he had heard was very fun-loving.

'Her name?'

'Well, I'm not sure, but her husband is Ernest Duckworth. He and his family have been associated with . . .'

'Thank you,' and putting her glass in his hand she began to weave – that was the only word the gentleman could think of to describe her action – towards her husband.

'I would like to go home now, Callum,' he heard her say, as did two or three dozen other people about them. Her husband turned, visibly startled, and that certain, narrow-eyed, speculative look with which a man regards an attractive woman, slipped dramatically from his face.

'Maris,' he said, courteously enough, 'is there something wrong?' and the demon which was tearing Maris's heart to excruciating shreds turned at once in an attempt to do the same to his.

'I don't know, Callum. Is there?'

'I'm not sure I take your meaning?' but the warning lights in his eyes had turned them from the hot and very evident sensual blue of desire to the ice-cold chips of menace which told her to be careful.

'Oh, I'm sure you do, and I'm sure Mrs Duckworth does, don't you, Mrs Duckworth? My husband here has a fancy to take you to bed, Mrs Duckworth . . .' She was beyond reason, beyond caution, beyond anything which could be called sense, of the mind, that is. The only thing she knew, felt, ached with, was jealousy and the dreadful hollow unreturned love she had carried in her heart for Callum for over three years. It raced her on to her ultimate destruction and to the rending apart of what she had called her marriage and which Callum had called his imprisonment.

'Maris, for God's sake . . .'

'. . . and I'll tell you how I know, shall I? He has that same look in his eyes when he wants *me* to perform for him, you see. He has some . . . quaint fancies, Mrs Duckworth, which I can assure you are very . . . pleasant, if a little wearing, which I am not awfully sure you are up to. You look a cool sort of a person, Mrs Duckworth, in your pale grey and your hair so smooth and neat, whereas I am, as you see, ever ready for some . . . sport . . .'

'Sweet Mother of God, Maris . . .' Callum held her arm now, his fingers sinking so deeply into her tender flesh he could feel the crunch of bone beneath them. He would kill her, of course, when he got her home. Put his hands about her slim white neck and slowly choke the bloody life out of her, and gladly, *gladly* go

325

to the gallows for her. He had never hated as he hated this woman who had done so much damage to the smooth and well-run order of his life. She had taken his peace of mind; the pleasant pace and calm of his life in port; the sometimes cruel but always exciting challenge of his life at sea; the easy and fleeting encounters of a sexual kind; the comradeship which only men enjoy and can understand, but in the meanwhile, before he could attend to the satisfying task of doing away with her, he must get her out of here and away from the cool though amused contempt in Alice Duckworth's deep brown eyes. *The same colour as Maris's!* The thought flashed horrifically through his mind, even as he turned to apologise to Alice and began to move with a pretence that he was not really *dragging* his quite intoxicated wife across the deep carpeting of the function room and out into the hallway.

'You're hurting me, Callum.'

'Really,' and his fingers bit more cruelly into her arm. Down the stairs and across the yard to where the car was parked, and when he had flung her inside he leaned over her, his face no more than an inch from hers.

'If you move a muscle, lady, I swear I'll knock you unconscious.' She began to weep, continuing to do so all the way through the Mersey Tunnel, up London Road and on until he turned into the gateway of their home in Seymour Road. She was still weeping when he hustled her inside, crashing the door to behind him, and as she began to back away from him up the hallway he followed her, his black snarling anger, his white-lipped, blank-eyed anger so terrible she knew she was in the greatest peril.

'Now, would you like to tell me what the hell that was all about, madam?'

'You tell *me*,' for despite her terror she could still feel the arrow-like pain devastating her, killing her. 'It was that bloody woman you were nearly . . .' Here she used a word so graphic and so obscene, he gasped, since no woman he had ever known, high or low, would ever speak it out loud, '. . . in public, and with your wife in the same room.'

'I see, so instead of waiting until an opportune, *private* moment occurred where your paranoid obsession might be discussed . . .'

'Discussed? What is there to discuss? You and she were . . . were carrying on under the noses of *your* wife and *her* husband . . .'

'Really! Is that what I was doing? Jesus and all his angels, give me strength and patience, for I swear I can stand no more of this. That woman is nothing to me. I was being pleasant to her. No more. Jesus Christ, everywhere I turn I see your eyes on me, watching . . . I do my best to be patient, to be what you want me to be . . . I try not to hurt you, but it is you who wanted this marriage . . . your brothers . . . but I'm wearing a strait-jacket, that's how it feels. The consequences of what we did . . . the price we . . . I have had to pay. I do my best to become resigned to it but the feeling of being . . .'

'Trapped. Is that how you feel, Callum?'

'God's holy nightgov'n, but it gets harder and harder to keep up this charade we act out. To keep what has always been weak and handicapped from the start, alive and functioning. Every time I come home . . . Holy Mother, every time I come home I'm faced with . . .'

'With what, Callum?' She was calm now. The tears had streaked on her face, that little-girl face of hers with its frame of tousled silver curls. It had suddenly

327

grown up, that child's face, become drawn, old, fallen in on itself as a face does when the flesh withers away from the bones of a skull. Her eyes, so glowing and clear with the zest of youth, had sunk into deep purple sockets and her lips were colourless. Her girlish beauty had gone, her lively spirit quenched, and she looked as she would on her deathbed.

But he did not see it. He was dying his own death, his back to her, his arm resting on the newel post at the foot of the stairs, his forehead bowed to his arm.

'We cannot go on like this, Maris. It's too much for either of us. Three years . . . I have tried to be what you want, to do what is right to make it work, our marriage, but my heart's not in it. We were . . . well, with the baby and then the irony of losing it . . .'

'Irony! Is that what it was? I thought it was I who killed him when I crashed your car.' Her voice was flat, dead, as lifeless as the child she had borne him.

'Well . . .' He shrugged, his back still turned to her, 'whatever . . . it is gone. The reason for . . .'

'The reason you married me is gone, is that it?'

'I suppose that must be it.'

'Suppose . . . ?'

He turned to face her then, all the menace gone, all the sardonic amusement with which he treated her, treated life, this sad and sorry state their human fumblings had brought them to, gone, leaving only a deep and unutterable sadness. He sighed deeply, his shoulders sagging, and she felt her heart break. He was going. She would never see him again. He was going out of her life, ripping it apart and leaving a jagged hole in the fabric of it. The pain inside her was terrible, and it was going to get worse with every bitter moment of their parting. It was overwhelming her, and soon, if he didn't go she would fall to her knees and beg him . . .

The telephone shrilled into the aching numbness which had invaded the narrow hall, the very house, with its intensity; and they both jumped violently, the everyday sound it made an intrusion in this nightmare they had found themselves in. It was two-thirty in the afternoon, not an unusual or alarming time for the telephone to ring, but they both turned sharply in its direction, apprehension on their faces, as though the horror they were in had induced other and just as fearful consequences which would be brought to their attention by way of the shrilling instrument. It rang for what seemed hours before Callum moved slowly towards it, picking it up with the care of a man about to defuse a bomb.

'Yes?' he said sharply, his face quite grey, Maris thought, in the gloom of the hall, the shafts of mid-summer light from the square window in the front door which should have been amber and gold, colourless, timeless, dead. Everything was muted as though to match the feeling in her dragged-down, hollowed-out being, neutral and drab as her life would be without Callum.

'When did it happen?' she heard him say, and '. . . what did the doctor say . . .' and '. . . I'll be right over . . .' before crashing the instrument down into its cradle. His distress, which he had not shown on *her* behalf, was so alarming she moved towards him, her hands reaching out to him, for surely he was about to fall. He was already turning towards the door, not even concerned with the necessity of telling her who had telephoned or why, and her voice was sharp, but stopping him for no more than a fraction of a second.

329

'Callum, for God's sake, who . . . ?'

'My mother, she's had some sort of stroke . . .'

'Dear God . . .'

'I must go . . .'

'Of course . . . Callum . . . ?'

'What? I haven't time for any . . .'

'May I come with you?'

'Of course, but be quick.'

'I'm ready now.'

It was only a slight stroke, the doctor said, looking about him at what seemed to be a great multitude of Irish faces, surely more than could possibly be crammed into Mrs O'Shaughnessy's kitchen, young and old alike all wearing the same expression of anxious dread. How would they manage, that expression beseeched him to tell them, without the big-hearted, good-humoured woman who had chastised and kissed them at one and the same time, every last one of them, since the day they were born? The woman from whom all bounty had unfailingly, unceasingly flowed. Endearingly hot-headed, consistently exasperating in her own belief that she ruled their lives. Beloved, irreplaceable, unique, the linch-pin of the family without which, surely, they would all fall apart.

'Will she . . . survive, doctor?' Michael asked as the head of the family, his strong face working, and his hand clasped in that of his brand-new wife, herself bearing a child, the doctor had heard.

'Oh yes . . .' and the collective sigh of relief nearly swept him off his feet, '. . . but she'll need good nursing for a while.'

'She'll get it,' her eldest daughter declared fiercely, as though the doctor had thought otherwise. 'Sure an' there's enough of us to nurse a hospital ward . . .' and

330

all about the room there were smiles and the muted whispers which accompany illness.

The doctor left, promising to return later that day unless he was needed, when a telephone call would fetch him immediately.

'Right.' Gracie, as the oldest, took charge of the women, shooing the youngsters out into the garden, organising poor Matty into the task she knew so well and which she had learned in over fifty years alongside Ellen O'Shaughnessy, which was the feeding of Ellen O'Shaughnessy's family.

'We'll need a roster, so we will,' Gracie continued briskly. 'We've all got homes to see to, but between us we can make sure that there's always someone here with Matty . . .' accepting a cup of tea from the stunned but slowly steadying old servant. 'So, there's Amy, who's with the Mammy now, and you, Eileen. Now, Tess, I'd say you had enough to do, begorra, wouldn't you, so that leaves Mary and Elizabeth and . . .'

'No, Gracie, not Elizabeth . . . not at the moment . . .' for didn't everyone know that a woman of Elizabeth's age and in her condition could not be expected to share in anything of a stressful nature.

'Sure an' you're right, Michael,' with a fond and indulgent glance at Michael's wife, for hadn't they all become fond of the sweet-natured and gracious woman who was so amazingly to bear his child. 'So, that leaves Rosie . . . oh no . . .' If Elizabeth was not to be included, then of course Rosie, who was younger certainly, but in the same condition, must be accorded the same treatment. 'Caitlin's too far away and Clare has her hands full, God love her, so if Maureen could spare an hour . . . yes . . . and Teresa . . .' naming her own daughters, 'and you, Maris . . . well we should manage, so we should.'

They drove home in silence, a silence so dense and pitchy black Maris thought they would never pierce it again. The day stretched out behind her in a nightmare kaleidoscope of shapes and colour and words which would never be erased, never be forgotten, no matter how the weeks ahead progressed. But for Ellen's collapse there was no doubt that Callum would have been long gone . . . where, her tired brain asked? but she didn't know the answer to that one, only the absolute certainty that he would have left her. That their marriage would have been over. It *was* over. It was dead. The strands which had tied them together had slowly unravelled, leaving them both free to step away, to turn in any direction they cared to, since their commitment was dead.

But now they had been tightened again, those bonds, and the reason for it lay sleeping peacefully under the influence of the sedative the doctor had given her.

'I'll sleep on the couch,' her husband said politely. 'You will need your rest if you are to help with my mother's nursing.' He paused for a moment in the doorway of the sitting room, not looking at her, though, and she wondered dully if he ever would again.

'I'm immensely grateful, Maris,' he went on, but this makes no difference to you and me, you know that, his stiff back told her as he shut the door behind him.

18

Ellen was out of her bed and sitting beside it when, on
September 15th, Neville Chamberlain flew to Munich
over what was called the 'Czechoslovakia Affair'. She
read the newspapers or had them read to her by one
of her 'nurses', but she did not take a great deal of
interest in the wranglings between the French and the
British, which seemed to have some connection with
it, nor the wilfulness of that Hitler fellow.

She tried out her first faltering steps round the back
garden on the arm of her eldest son later that month,
when the Prime Minister again flew to Germany, but
by now the man in the street had become aware of the
'Czechoslovakia Affair' and was aghast at the idea of
a small democratic state being bullied. He was for
resistance, he said, the man in the street, since his con-
science would not allow him to think otherwise; and
suddenly, from nowhere, it seemed to those who had
previously had no idea that 'things' were so serious,
preparations were being made for *war*, for God's sake!
There was talk of trenches being dug in the London
parks, and anti-aircraft guns were trundled out. Warning sirens were tried over the wireless, to Ellen's
consternation since she had never heard such a cater-
wauling in all her life, but worst of all, 38 million gas-
masks were being distributed to regional centres, she
read.

Holy Blessed Mother, what was the world coming to
all of a sudden, she screeched, seriously alarming her

granddaughter, Maureen, who was 'on duty' that day, and who had just read out the news that 83% of parents in London had applied to have their children evacuated to safer parts of the country. The fleet was immobilised on Chamberlain's orders, and up and down the country apprehension began to affect those who had previously wanted to 'stick up' for poor old Czechoslovakia.

Again Neville Chamberlain flew to Munich, and though the details were not clear to Ellen, who was tired of it all anyway, it seemed it had all been resolved, some agreement or other being accepted between the French and the British and the Germans over Czechoslovakia, thank the Blessed Holy Mother. They were not to go to war with one another after all, which was a vast relief to a mother and a grandmother many times over, as she was.

And when he came home, Mr Chamberlain, God love him, he waved that precious bit of paper at the window of number 10 Downing Street, telling the cheering crowds, who were quite delirious with the relief of it, that he believed that it was to be 'peace for our time'. Well, it was only sensible, Ellen said. Life was precious, as she herself knew only too well, and no one wanted war, did they, not when peace could be achieved so amicably.

It seemed that as soon as one crisis was got out of the way another came to take its place. The bombing campaign began formally on January 12th, 1939, with an ultimatum to the British Prime Minister, the government of Northern Ireland, and anyone else whom the Irish Republican Army thought might be moved by such a document. It demanded the withdrawal of all British armed forces stationed in Ireland and a declaration from the government renouncing all claims to interfere in Ireland's domestic policy. If their demands were not met, the ultimatum said, they would be compelled to intervene actively in the military and commercial life of Britain as the British government was now interfering in theirs.

On the same day and at almost the same hour, Elizabeth O'Shaughnessy and her niece Rose Woodall, gave birth to sons.

'Michael O'Shaughnessy, so it is, an' will you look at him, the spalpeen. The spit of his Daddy at the same age an' with the same pair of lungs on him. I could hear him as I came up the road, so I could, an' it knocked the heart of me sideways. I says to Donal, I says, that's himself, so it is, so get a move on. He can't even wait until his grandmammy gets here, impatient like the rest of 'em. See, let me get a hold of him an' tell that nurse to go an' get herself a cup of tea or something, for the child's grandmother is here now an' we've no need of her.'

'Mammy, Mammy, you shouldn't be exerting yourself like this, and you only just getting about. See, let the nurse have the boy. He needs to be bathed . . .' but it was very evident that Michael O'Shaughnessy was as eager as his mother to get his hands on his son; and on the bed the tired woman who had, no more than ten minutes since, given birth to him, turned her face into the pillow and wept.

Instantly, as though there was no one in the fire-lit bedroom but the two of them, Michael knelt beside her.

'Sweetheart . . . what is it?' His arms reached out to hold her, his hand to smooth back the long damp tangle of her hair, his mouth to shower kisses on her face in an agony of love. 'Are you in pain . . . Oh God, there's

335

nothing wrong, is there . . . See, nurse, run and fetch the doctor from the kitchen. Tell him he's needed back here . . .' for having known for the last ten months the greatest happiness ever given to a man, how could he bear it if it was taken from him? 'Nurse . . . quickly . . . my wife . . .' but Elizabeth turned to him, burrowing her wet face in the curve of his neck.

'No . . . no, my darling, I'm fine, really I am.' Her voice was muffled beneath his chin, and he held her close to him, for her distress could not be borne. 'I'm just . . . happy, that's all. Despite my great age . . .' lifting her face to smile up at him with that radiance which had recently come to her, '. . . I'm a strong woman. Somewhat like your mother here.'

Ellen had the baby in her arms, doing what she had been born to do, which was to nurture, to give solace and love to those she loved; and Michael's boy, the son he had longed for and who had come so late to him, was held gently, strongly, lovingly against the clean white front of her blouse despite the blood and detritus of birth which still clung to him.

'Madam,' the nurse said reprovingly, 'I really must insist on the child being bathed. If you would be so good as to hand him to me,' holding out her starched arms for her charge; but Ellen had sat down in the rocking-chair Michael had bought for his wife, cradling the child, Michael's child and therefore *hers*, who was nothing to do with this intruder, to her breast.

It might have gone on for a long time, the silent battle between Ellen and the nurse whilst Michael and Elizabeth watched smiling, content for the moment to see their child and his grandmother forge that special bond Ellen wove with all the members of her family. He was a beautiful, perfect boy, dark as a gypsy or an

336

Irishman, with rosy rounded cheeks and winging black brows in exact duplication of his father. The curling whorls on his unwashed head were dark and would be thick, and his nose was no more than an unformed blob in the middle of his yawning face. It had not yet been revealed to them what colour his eyes were to be.

There was a sudden commotion coming up the stairs of the old detached house in which Michael and Cliona had lived and where Michael and Elizabeth lived now. A frantic knocking at the door, and before Michael had time to stride across the room to open it, Maris burst in, her face a lovely blooming pink, looking, Elizabeth thought sadly, as it had once looked when . . . well, when she was younger.

'You'll never guess,' she yelled, just as though they were in the next street, the nurse was inclined to think, not awfully sure she could cope with this great Irish ebullience most of these people shared. Not her patient, of course, for she was a lady, a real lady, or had once been, but the rest of them – and there were a great many – roaming about the kitchen and the hall-way of Mrs O'Shaughnessy's home.

'Sweet Mother of Christ, what now?' Ellen was ready to moan, though she could tell it was good news by the glow in her daughter-in-law's eyes.

'It's Rosie . . .'

'What . . . what darlin'? Tell us before I have another stroke.'

'A boy, she's had a boy not half an hour since. Alex has just telephoned, and they're both well, and if it's all right with you, mother . . .' to the woman on the bed beside which she had gone to kneel, '. . . I'll go over right away. It's not every woman who has a new brother and a new . . . now then . . . what will he

337

be . . . a second cousin? . . . all in the space of an hour.'

Elizabeth put a tired hand to her daughter's cheek, noting the thinness of it where once it had been soft, rounded, girlish. Her eyes were bright now, a lovely golden brown in which excitement had lit stars, but Elizabeth had seen them dark and brooding and unutterably sad for the last six months. She and her husband, when he was home from the long sea voyages he took, were perfectly polite, even amiable in one another's company, but it was very evident to her who was so happy and had known such an abundance of love in her life, that her daughter and her daughter's marriage was in desperate straits. This should have been *her* child, she thought sadly, then was attacked by a sudden need to cross herself as Ellen did, to keep away bad spirits which might be lurking about the beloved person of her new son.

'Go darling,' she said, '. . . and give Rose and her son . . . oh Lord, my grandson . . . a kiss and a hug from me. My grandson . . .' she repeated. 'It is not every woman who has a son and a grandson in the space of an hour, Maris. Tell her, and Alex, that I love them and . . . well, Rosie and I will compare our sons soon. Mine will be the most handsome, of course, though I daresay my grandson will not be far behind. Go now, sweetheart . . .' since it was very evident that Michael O'Shaughnessy's wife was ready to weep again.

The first bomb exploded in a street main in Manchester, killing a twenty-seven-year-old fish porter on his way to work. In London there were three explosions, all at electricity plants, for it seemed the Irish Republican Army wished to inconvenience rather than maim or kill.

It went on throughout the spring and summer, in the north and midlands as well as the capital, other power units, gas and electricity mains being the chief targets. In July a young Scotsman, who was unfortunate enough to have been standing in the left-luggage office at King's Cross Station, was killed in a devastating explosion which severely injured his wife and fourteen other people.

But the worst incident was in August, when five people were killed, including a man of eighty-one and a schoolboy of fifteen, in the thoroughfare of Broadgate in Coventry. Twelve more were badly injured and forty less seriously hurt. The man who actually left the bomb in a carrier-bag outside the shop where it went off, had arrived on a bicycle which he had left parked there and where it was to explode amongst the innocent and bewildered victims.

Bombs exploded in most of the major cities. In letter-boxes, lavatories, telephone boxes, railway cloak-rooms, cinemas, post offices and business premises of all kinds. In Liverpool a cinema was emptied by tear-gas, and several porters at Lime Street Station had a lucky escape when a bomb failed to go off in a mail-bag. IRA agents were rounded up in their dozens, it was reported, but still the explosions continued.

It was towards the end of August when Maris and Rose saw Cliona.

'Let's have a day out, Rosie. Let's dump young Harry with mother and go . . .'

'I have no intention of "dumping" my son with any-one, Maris O'Shaughnessy, let alone with your mother, who has enough to do with her own boy.'

'Oh, you know she loves having her grandson, and with that woman Michael insists on employing, though

339

he refuses to call her a Nanny, she manages very well. Do you know, I don't think I have ever seen anyone so beautiful, so supremely happy and so well-loved as mother is, unless it's you, darling Rosie.'

Maris stood up abruptly, lighting one of her innumerable cigarettes before moving slowly to the window of Rose's sitting room to stare out blindly into the sun-drenched garden beyond it. A stylish cream baby-carriage stood on the lawn, a present from Elizabeth to her son and daughter-in-law. She had said it was time the ancient perambulator in which two generations of Osbornes had been trundled about Beechwood Hall was done away with, since it was beyond carrying another, though *his* name was Woodall. The new one was deep and roomy with a foot-extension for when her grandson was older, with a navy-blue lining, and hung on what were known as 'C' springs shackled to the side of the pram. There was a firm foot-brake and a good-sized hood, for it was the fashion to leave one's baby outside in all weathers, since fresh air was known to be good for infants of all ages. Elizabeth had an identical one for young Michael O'Shaughnessy.

Rose watched her cousin, her compassion showing plainly on her serene face. Maris was right. She could not really describe to anyone, should anyone have enquired, the lovely, slow-moving, deep contentment of her days, her life with Alex and their son, Harry Timothy Hugh Woodall, who was named for the three brothers, one of them her husband's father, who had all been killed by the 'great' war. Her days were flawless, so much so she was afraid to face them boldly, openly, in case some hag of fate, sniggering behind her faithless hand, might come and snatch them from her, and so, smiling inwardly at her own superstitious need

340

to 'touch wood', she touched it just the same. She treasured the delicate mingling of trust and humour, of love and passion, of liking and respect which blended together into the element which was her marriage to Alex. The pressing, everyday tasks of waking early to the sounds her son made as he called to her; the sighs of her husband as *he* made known *his* need of her; the mewing of the cats to be let out; and the knocking of Polly, her maid of all work, to be let in. The barking of the puppy who was to be Harry's; fires to be lit when it was cold; and flowers to be gathered when it was fine. Vegetables she herself had grown, to prepare; pot-pourri to be mixed from the rose petals she herself had picked. Herbs and fruit, and lavender for the sachets she made to be put among her underwear. Honey from her own bees; and Harry, growing sweet-tempered and handsome like the grandfather he had never known, like her own father whom *she* had never known.

'Can you talk to me about it, darling?' she said to the back Maris presented to her. 'Only if you want to, of course.'

Maris shrugged, and rummaging in her handbag, found and lit another cigarette from the end of the one she had just smoked.

'There's not a lot to tell, Rosie.'

'Well then, just as you like. I am always here.'

'He goes his way and I go mine, though mine leads nowhere in particular, not even to Freddie Winters, who would like it to.'

'Oh, Maris, I'm so sorry.'

'I know you are, Rosie. It should have ended a year ago when Ellen was ill. We had . . . been cruel to one another and . . . well, Callum told me a few home truths which, gallantly, he had kept hidden from me

341

since our marriage. You know the sort of thing. How he had married me because he was forced to it . . .'

'No, oh no, Maris, he loves you . . .'

'Don't be silly, Rosie. I know you see the best in everyone, but even you must know Callum has no feeling for me, at least above the waist, nor, I do believe, for anyone.'

'Darling, don't torment yourself . . .'

'Oh, I'm used to it now, Rosie. Tormenting myself, I mean. Picturing him with that woman . . .'

'Woman . . . ?'

'Oh, yes, the one whom we argued about at the launching . . .'

'Launching . . . ?'

'Alice Duckworth. Very beautiful, of course, since Callum likes beautiful women.'

'*You* are beautiful, darling.'

'Really?'

'You know you are.'

'Do I?'

She sounded only vaguely interested in her own appearance, as though it had no relevance in her life. She was twenty-three now, stylishly dressed, soignée and sophisticated where once she had had the soft bloom of innocence and immaturity in her face. A rosebud in its first sweet awakening with the dew of the early morning moistening its petals. Gone now, with her girlhood, except for her hair which still burgeoned in riotous curls about her small head somewhat in the fashion of a dandelion 'clock'. She was smart, sharp-etched, fine-drawn and often bitter-tongued.

'Well, it makes no difference, not really, what we do, he and I, since he is to be off to war soon, or so he tells me.'

342

'War!' Rosie was visibly horrified.

'Good God, Rosie, do you and that brother of mine do nothing but make love and . . . and pick flowers in this idyll of yours? Do you never read the newspapers?'

'Well, yes, from time to time, when I have a moment, but I have seen nothing about war, not since last year when Chamberlain came back from Munich after settling the dispute over Czechoslovakia. Of course, I *have* been pretty preoccupied with Harry, and Alex is . . . well, he has become very concerned with the estate, particularly with the game. He shoots in the traditional way, naturally.'

'Naturally. Would Alex do anything else?' Maris's voice was sardonic, but Rose did not appear to notice.

'He says it's wicked to see the method used by so many so-called sportsmen today, with birds being killed in their thousands. He goes out with a pair of gun dogs he borrows from Uncle Teddy, and a gun, and will shoot no more than ten birds a day, which is enough to keep them in check. He says that the essence of the county community has gone now with the . . . well, he calls them the new rich who have come since so many estates have been broken up. Particularly since the war. He says . . .'

'Rosie, have *you* nothing to say? Do you not know which way this country is headed, never mind the bloody county. Even I, empty-headed as I am, know that something is about to take place which will not be pleasant, and I am surprised that you and Alex . . . Do the pair of you take no interest in anything outside this cottage of yours?'

'I have so little time, Maris, what with Harry and Alex and . . . well . . . I suppose I had better tell you, though I am sure you will scold me for making love to

343

my husband. I am to have another child at Christmas.'

'Christmas! My God, that brother of mine wastes no time, does he? Well then, all the more reason for you and me to have a day out before you get too enormous to get into my car. You will need new clothes . . .'

'What for? I'll be as fat as butter soon.'

'Come to think of it, you *have* put on weight, so I will buy the new clothes and you shall admire me in them.'

'I always do. You are so smart and so lovely and slim . . . oh, I'm sorry, darling, really, I didn't mean to . . . I know that you . . . or so it seemed to me. I'm so stupid and thoughtless . . .'

'Yes, you're right, and no, you are the least thoughtless person in the world.' Maris's face became pensive. She had returned to sprawl in Rosie's honey velvet chair in her usual position when she wore what were called 'slacks', one leg over the arm of the chair, the other stretched out to the fireplace. 'I did want a child once, after . . . the other . . . but my husband refused to let me have another, and of course he was right. Look how worthless I have turned out to be. Not a fit person to bear his children at all . . .'

'No, oh no, darling. How can you say such a thing?' Rose was deeply upset, ready to spring up and draw her cousin into her own approving embrace, but Maris laughed and jumped up, reaching for her handbag and her eternal cigarettes.

'Because it's true, Rosie, that's how. I have been married for four years and what do I have to show for it? I have put nothing into my marriage and so I have got nothing from it, and neither has Callum.'

'That's not true.' Rose's voice was passionate and

344

she stood up, not at all sure what to do in her distress. 'You must not belittle yourself . . .'

'Oh sit down, Rosie,' lighting another cigarette. 'There's nothing to get excited about, really there isn't, and you must not upset yourself on my account. But I'll say this, if there is a war I might get a chance to do something interesting. God, I get so bored . . . so bloody bored . . .'

Her voice faded away like the smoke which wreathed around her head, and she sighed as though she was in the deepest despair.

'It won't come to that, darling, not war, will it?' Rose turned to look at the garden where her child slept in peaceful innocence, and beyond to the surrounding estate where her man worked in much the same condition. Alex had found the world he wanted to live in, the life he wanted to live, and the people with whom he wanted to live that life. The only thing, in *his* mind, that could disturb that peace was Christian Osborne, and Alex would be perfectly happy to have his cousin remain in Ireland, playing at soldiers, as he put it, for the rest of his life. He seemed unaware that something else might take it all from him.

'It won't come to that, will it?' she repeated. 'Not after all that happened during the last one. I know it's still as clear as though it was yesterday to people like grandmother and Aunt Elizabeth. And I suppose to mother too, with father being killed at Gallipoli. And if they remember it so vividly, so will others. They won't let it happen again, will they?'

'I don't know, darling, really I don't. I only know what I hear Michael and Callum talking about. I don't read the newspapers much, only the gossip column, being the shallow kind of person I am . . .'

'Stop it, Maris, I won't have it . . .'

'Only teasing, Rosie, but I did hear them say that something called the "Anglo-Polish Treaty" has been signed, which is meant to stop that awful Hitler person from getting his hands on Poland, which he has apparently been trying to do since last March. Don't ask me how it works, just pray that it does. Now then, will you let me ring mother to see if she will have Harry tomorrow?'

They were crossing London Road when they saw her. They were on their way to the Odeon Cinema where Leslie Howard was playing Professor Higgins in *Pygmalion*. The matinée began at two-fifteen, and already at ten to two there was a long queue of fashionably – and not so fashionably – dressed women, many of whom, like themselves, had spent the morning browsing round Lewis's, Bon Marché and Owen Owens, having lunch at Lewis's smart restaurant, and now they were ready to swoon at the feet of the beautifully spoken English gentleman who, with his slightly dreamy, bashful air of charming shyness, was delighting women the length and breadth of the country. At a shilling a seat in the balcony, the best in the house, well worth every penny.

London Road was crowded and bustling as it always was, with the busy to-ing and fro-ing of shop girls and clerks, factory workers and secretaries hurrying back from their dinner hour. There was the clangour of the trams, and the stream of motor cars and bicycles which passed on either side of them. Street musicians, who had been part of the city fabric for as long as it had stood, entertained the crowd waiting to go into the cinema. A trumpet player on one corner, a 'Phil the fluter' on the other, and ambling between the two were the pathetic 'sandwich-board' men exhorting their brothers – and sisters too, one presumed – to REPENT FOR THE END OF THE WORLD IS NIGH. No one, it seemed, was much concerned. There was a pavement artist, colouring a startlingly effective vase of flowers, praying that the rain which threatened would not come, and along the kerb were flower-girls offering bunches of violets from their baskets.

The shabbily dressed girl came round the corner from Stamford Street into London Road and began to hurry in the direction of William Brown Street. She carried a small suitcase and had the queue not suddenly surged as the commissionaire urged half a dozen women forward, causing a temporary blockage on the pavement, they would not have noticed her. The line of women almost swept her into the road, and caught off-balance for a moment, her suitcase hit a stout lady at the back of her knees.

'Mind what you're doin' wi' tha', queen,' she said amiably enough. 'Nearly had us over, yer did.'

'I'm so sorry,' the girl apologised, getting a firmer grip on her suitcase, and turning swiftly, her haste very evident, she came face to face with her own cousin.

They all three turned the colour of tallow. The queue of women continued to surge and jostle against them, and not a few were heard to expostulate that if *they* didn't want to get inside some of them did, and to stop blocking the pavement.

They stood as though, like Lot's wife, they had been turned to pillars of salt, three young women who had not been in one another's company for over four years, and in that time, for all two of them knew, one of them might have been dead. Maris and Rosie were arm in arm, and Maris was to remark later that if she had not had her cousin's support she would have crumpled to the ground since her legs had turned to jelly.

No one spoke. It was as though each one thought she was looking at a ghost, a ghost which would vanish as mysteriously as it had appeared. None of them moved, waiting, or so it would seem, for one of the others to do something: speak, put out a faltering hand, smile, burst into tears, make some greeting, fall to the ground in a faint, *anything* to break the awful stillness and silence which had frozen their limbs, their minds, their tongues.

It was Rosie who did it. Strong, steadier than the other two, and perhaps because of it, more resilient. The shock had eased, and her joy was beginning to snap. The white clay of her face had become flushed with some lovely emotion, and her eyes began to glow. She let go of Maris's flaccid arm, and taking a step forward, leaving her cousin to support herself, she put her arms about Cliona and held her in a wordless embrace.

'Will you get out of the way, please,' an irritable voice ordered. 'We are trying to get into the cinema,' but it was several minutes before the three women, tears brimming, smiles ready to break out, could get themselves into some kind of order and out of the flow of pedestrians. There was a doorway of a shop which was closed, it being Wednesday afternoon, and they huddled together in there, still not able to speak, merely making sounds in their throats, the kind women make when they are soothing a hurt child, hugging one another, until at last Rosie stood back and looked directly into Cliona's face.

'Darling . . . ?' A question in her eyes and in her voice, though she really had no coherent idea of what it was she wanted to know, or even if she really wanted to know *anything*. It was enough for the moment that Cliona was alive, well, here in Liverpool, which surely indicated that she was to come home to her family. Why else would she be hurrying along London Road with a suitcase in her hand?

'Rosie . . . please . . . don't ask me . . .'

'What? Ask you what?'

'I can see the questions in your face and I can . . . please . . . don't ask.'

'You are coming home . . . Cliona?'

'Don't ask me that.'

'But Cliona, your father is . . .' Maris put out her hand to the girl whom she had always thought of as a cousin, though they were not, strictly speaking, related. The girl who had been lost to them and to Michael for so long, and the tears welled in her eyes and fell to the cool white linen of her dress.

'I know . . . I'm sorry . . . there's nothing I can do for him.'

'But what . . . where have you . . . ?'

'Don't ask me, I said *don't ask me!*'

She was dressed in the grey drab of the poor: a woollen overcoat, though it was warm midsummer; a beret pulled down to her eyebrows; sensible shoes and black stockings; very neat and clean, but had they passed her on the street they would not have recognised her for the beautiful girl they once had known. There were deep smudges beneath her blue-green O'Shaughnessy eyes, and the girlish roundness of her cheeks was hollowed-out. She looked sad, care-worn, years older than either of the other two. But there was something about her which made them edge away from her now, despite their longing to have her back with them in the love and protection of her family. Something, though the word sounded foolish, *frightening*, a look of disciplined exaltation, cold and yet fervent, as though she were a worshipper serving at the altar of some mystical cult from which those outside were totally excluded.

'Tell us what you are doing here, at least.'

'You know better than that, Rose.' Scornfully.

'Do I? Why? What is it you are hiding?'

'I am not at liberty to tell you.'

'*Not at liberty* . . . Dear God, Cliona . . . how can you talk like that? Surely . . . you will go and see your father?'

'No . . . I cannot, in fact I must go now or I will miss my . . .'

'Cliona, please.' Rose's voice was appalled, while Maris simply stood beside her, speechless, her mind concerned with the pain this would cause the man who was this girl's father and her own brother-in-law. A good man who, though he had recently found great happiness, did not deserve what his daughter was doing to him.

'I must get back to my . . .'

It came to them then, both at the same time. The recollection of the spate of explosions which had taken place in the city over the last few months, and an awful, horrified dread washed over them like the beginning of some murky, nightmare fog. It was said to be the work of Irish patriots, as they called themselves, who were, as they had done for so long now, fighting for a united and free Ireland; but surely this once sweet and lovely girl could not . . . surely not . . .

'What must you get back to? What are you doing here? Where are you going?' Maris had both hands on Cliona's shoulders, ready to shake the answer from her, and for a fraction of a second the brilliant blue-green of Cliona's eyes seemed to narrow to slits of pale, glittering granite, and her free hand moved to hover at her pocket.

'Take your hands off me, Maris.'

'*Cliona!*'

'I'm sorry but . . . I am . . . I cannot stay . . . I have things to do before I . . .'

'What sort of things? How long have you been in Liverpool?'

'*Sweet Jesus. I must go.* Leave me alone, for God's sake . . .' and for a moment *their* Cliona was back, the lovely warm-hearted, laughing girl with whom they had both grown up. Then her face became quite anguished, her teeth bared, her eyes narrowing again like those of a soldier who has the enemy in his sights as she stepped back from their clutching, pleading, loving arms. She turned, looking up and down the busy thoroughfare, her eyes everywhere at once, ready to dart out and be off to wherever it was women like her went. She looked haunted, hunted, watching for that knife in the back, or at least that sudden hand on her shoulder.

'Wait.' Rose put out her hand, and Cliona turned impatiently.

'My brother . . . where is Christian?'

'In prison.'

'Oh, dear God . . .'

'Goodbye . . .' She relented at the last moment and smiled, the sweet Irish smile belonging to all the O'Shaughnessys.

'Don't tell the Daddy you've seen me. Sure there's nothing he can do and it would only hurt him.'

'We saw Cliona today.' The bald statement halted Alex Woodall in his tracks and he turned to stare in amazement at his wife and sister. They had just entered the house, coming into the low-ceilinged, dimly lit hallway from the brilliance of the sunshine. He had heard Maris's car, and, waving cheerfully to them from the window, was on his way to the kitchen to tell Polly to put the kettle on.

Rosie had the baby in her arms, and above his smiling, golden-brown face her own was the colour of clay. Maris huddled against her, bewildered and tearful and not at all sure she wanted to be the bearer of this appalling news, for what were they to do with it now they had it? The trauma, not only of seeing Cliona, but of picking Harry up from her mother's house without disclosing what had occurred that afternoon, still showed in her anguished eyes and the clenching of her small jaw which ached with the effort of smiling and smiling, in her mother's presence. She could not tell her mother's husband that his only daughter was skulking about Liverpool. That she looked shabby and furtive and . . . fanatical, and, having seen her, could they be blamed for believing she had been involved with the bombing campaign which had killed old and young alike in England this year? Dear God, it would crucify him, and surely, *surely* it would be kinder to let him believe that, if she was not dead, then she was carrying out some hopefully innocent role in Ireland, a passive role, if such a thing existed, in the support of the IRA?

They both waited for Alex to speak, and when he did his voice was harsh and at the same time sorrowful. He knew at once what his wife's face told him, and what was in her mind, and though she had said no more than those four bare words, he answered as though she had asked him a question.

'We can do nothing, Rosie. It is *her* business and it

would serve no purpose to . . . distress Michael,' and through him Alex's mother, his jerking voice said.

'Darling . . . is it right . . . should it be *our* decision? Michael is her father.'

'I know, but I can see no other option. She must have been one of those who . . . the bombs . . .'

'Yes.'

'Jesus Christ, Michael would never get over it.'

'Why would they . . . the people she . . . why would they send her to Liverpool where she is known?'

'Don't ask me. Perhaps because she knows the place.'

'Perhaps.'

Maris, who had stood silently just within the doorway, stepped forward and took her brother's arm, like a small child trying to catch the attention of an adult.

'She has not told you . . .'

'What, Maris?'

'Christian . . .'

'Christian? . . . yes . . . ?' and did she see a gleam of what she could only describe as *hope* in his eyes? Christian . . . perhaps *dead*?

'He's in prison.'

The gleam died. 'Let him rot there.'

'*Alex!*'

'If it hadn't been for him, Cliona would be safe at home with her family. I hope they bloody hang him.'

'But we will never know. Alex, he *is* my brother and I *must know*.'

Immediately he went to his wife and gathered her and his son into his arms, burying his face in her neck. The baby began to wail, trapped in his parents' anguish, and Maris wept, not for Christian who might die but for Cliona who was, surely, already dead to them all.

353

'I'll find out, my darling . . . hush . . . hush, I'll find out. I'm sorry, forgive me . . . I should not have said that . . . don't cry, I cannot bear to see you cry . . .' and who cared if Maris O'Shaughnessy cried, she thought as she drove wildly in the direction of her empty, loveless home.

19

'But it can't be. It can't. Not again. Sure an' I can't
stand the thought of it, not again. My Sean and
Dermot, and Gracie's Rory and Terry, and only the
Blessed Mother knows how many more. Twenty-one
years, an' now they're to be at it again. Mother of Jesus
look down on us . . .'

Ellen was beside herself, flinging her clean white
apron over her head and sketching hasty crosses on her
breast, and the child on her knee, one of Tess's, began
to wail. Even that did not halt the flood of Ellen's
despair, which she could not contain. She didn't care,
she wept, about those people in Poland. Let them
defend their own country. She didn't want her boys
sent to those dreadful trenches again. Oh no, not again.
There was Joseph, Donal's eldest at eighteen, with
Lorcan not far behind. There was Flynn and Francis,
Gracie's lads, and Devlin, Amy's youngest and only
just twenty. There was Finbar, and Guy, Caitlin's only
son, and Mara's Christian, wherever he was. And what
about Callum, and Eammon who was only thirty-five,
God love him, and Donal, thirty-seven, and James
and Paul, the Conroy brothers, and her grandsons?
All her boys, her lovely boys, sons and grandsons
who would soon be glad enough to fight. But surely
they wouldn't take the older ones, not with children
to rear and homes to see to? She could not bear it.
All her sons and grandsons in the greatest peril
again. Sweet Mother, she didn't think she would ever

have lived to see the day when it would all happen again.

'It said men between the age of eighteen and forty-one, grandma,' Joseph, excited beyond measure at the anticipation of being a soldier, or even an airman, since he was old enough, was rewarded by a clip round the ear from his father, but Ellen only wailed the louder.

'Mammy, will you hold your wisht now, for isn't himself about to speak.'

'Himself, is it? an' has himself any sons to send to the front an' if he had would he be flinging this blessed country into war again? I'll not have it, so I won't, an' there'll be women up an' down the land saying the same.'

They gathered round their wireless sets, those same women Ellen was convinced felt the same way she did, their families about them, solemn-faced and heavy-hearted, and when Mr Chamberlain's words had died away, telling them that 'this country is at war with Germany', many of them ran into their gardens to scan the skies as though they fully expected to see German bombers overhead and German soldiers dropping from them.

They couldn't believe it, they said, just as Ellen had. It had crept up on them without them noticing, they complained, and what was to happen now? and minutes later, when the first air-raid warnings sounded, though they were seriously put out, not being ready for it, they all trooped obediently to the air-raid shelters. The fate of Poland was upon *them*, they told one another as they huddled together in the shelter, and within minutes of war being announced as well; but it turned out it was a false alarm. No bombs fell on English soil, and Ellen voiced the thoughts of many of them when she declared that that Hitler fellow wouldn't *dare* bomb England. Poland, yes. They were foreigners, but not England!

Well, she said, a month later, if this was all that was to happen, then perhaps it wouldn't be too bad after all. She had her gas-mask, of course, silly damn thing, and if they imagined that she was going to stuff her face in it at her age, then they had another think coming, so they did. Mind you, she was glad she was not one for going out at night, and how anyone could find their way about in the cavernous dark of the streets now that all the street lights were extinguished, she simply couldn't imagine.

But it was the children who distressed her the most, for how were the poor wee mites to manage without their Mammies and Daddies in this dreadful mass evacuation which was taking place, the idea of whole families being broken up and parted absolutely appalling her. Yes, she was perfectly well aware that the children were under the careful supervision of their teachers on the special trains which were to take them to places of safety somewhere in the country, but it wasn't the same as having their Mammies with them, was it? And did you ever see the likes of those luggage labels they had tied to them just like so many parcels?

Tess agreed with her, saying that despite the chaos which perpetually reigned in her house there was no power on earth which could separate her from her ten, even if the schools *were* closed. Anyway, nothing was happening. There were no air raids and no invasion, and she wouldn't mind betting that all those who had gone would all be back home by Christmas. In fact, neither she nor Ellen would be surprised if this phoney *war* was not over by Christmas.

They both sang another tune when the Ministry of

Labour began operating the registration for compulsory military service and nine male members of the family all went off to register at what was to be called 'The Ministry of National Service'. They were somewhat more excited about it than their womenfolk would have liked since they only wanted men up to the age of twenty-seven as yet. That let out Donal and Eammon at least.

But after all that, none of them was to be called up immediately. Donal had overheard one sergeant say to another that the army was not yet equipped to receive them. The British Expeditionary Force which had been conveyed across the Channel to France on September 11th was, of course, made up of regular soldiers, and they had landed without losing a single man. Infantrymen and army nurses, confident and well-equipped, the best in the world; so Mammy and Mary and Tess and all the other women who were so afraid on this day, must dry their tears and not worry in the least.

'To be sure, isn't that what they said in the last one, and look what happened to them,' wept Ellen, refusing to be comforted.

So, the war was running quite satisfactorily. There were no air raids, though enemy aircraft were sighted as far north as the Shetlands – dropping no bombs – and as far east as the Northumbrian coast. The Royal Air Force made a sortie or two on the German Fleet, and Alex and Charlie Woodall both volunteered in the same week, thought not at the same recruitment centre, to become fighter pilots.

Rose was bathing her son when her husband looked through the deep mullioned window into the sitting room. He had parked his car some way from Lacy's house, coming in to Beechwood from Liverpool along

Childwall Valley Lane, cutting up Whiteleaf Lane and stopping at the Hare and Hounds on the corner of Whiteleaf Lane End for a quick tot of brandy. It had put a warmer in his stomach, which quivered painfully at the thought of the confrontation with Rosie, but perhaps, knowing her forgiving nature, she might understand what he was about to strike her with.

The bath-tub was placed, as it always was, on a large bath-towel in front of the fireplace. The room was aglow with the flames of the fire, painting a patina of gold and amber on the satin skin of the baby and the absorbed, Madonna-like face of his wife. She was six months pregnant with their second child, bearing herself with that placid and patient identity of the breeding female, her pulsebeat and heartbeat slowed to the growing pace of the child within her. She smiled as the boy splashed the flat of his hands on the surface of the water, for nine-month-old Harry Woodall was strong and sturdy, with a bloom on his cheek, and a rapturous capacity for joy which came from his mother.

The scene tore at Alex's heart, and it contracted with love for her. Rosie was his life, and without her constant presence, her day-by-day, hour-by-hour loving support which he had known all his life, how was he to manage? He could not remember a day when she had not been there, and now he was to leave her. *She* would manage, for it was in her nature to be strong, to carry any burden put on her back, to smile and grit her teeth and get on with living, but could *he*?

It was two days since they had heard about Charlie, and it was Michael who had come over to tell them. Charlie had sent a brief letter to his mother with nothing in it but the terse report that he was somewhere in England, though the postmark had been Norfolk. He had volunteered for the Royal Air Force, he had said, and was to train as a fighter pilot, though of course he could already fly. He would make arrangements for a manager, probably a man too old to fight, to look after Woodall Park, as soon as he could get a bit of leave, and in the meanwhile he would be grateful if his mother would see to the servants for him. What exactly she was to *do* with them, he didn't say.

'Your mother wondered . . . sure an' she knows how you and he were . . . but Woodall . . . could you go over and see what needs doing outside? She'll drive over and have a word with Wilson and Mrs Preston, probably tomorrow . . .'

'So he expects me to take over his responsibility while he buggers off playing the bloody hero, does he?'

'No, *he* doesn't, but your mother is worried about it. I'd do it myself, but what I know about the land could be written on a postage stamp. And it won't be for long, lad. The government will be taking over the agricultural side of things. You know they've already made an appeal to farmers and gardeners to grow more food, and big estates like Woodall and Beechwood will certainly be turned over to the production of . . . well, it'll not be for long, Alex, and it would ease your mother's mind.'

But what he had done today would not ease his mother's mind, nor his wife's, but it was what he knew he *must* do. He was not awfully sure he would have done it quite so soon had it not been for Charlie; and again, as it had always done since they were boys, the bitter need to be the *best*, the *first*, the *strongest* had returned to plague him. He *knew* he would have answered the call to defend his country sooner or later as any right-minded, decent-thinking man would, but it was Charlie's decisive action in being the first to do so that had spun him into the wild and hasty race to Liverpool and the nearest RAF recruiting office. He couldn't let Charlie put one over on him, could he? It was as though anything Charlie did triggered some response in himself which he could do nothing to staunch. He could not ignore the challenge, and though he and Charlie had barely exchanged a word in three years, he knew this was Charlie's way of challenging him and of saying he was best.

They had learned to fly together. Back in the old days when they had still been brothers. Oh, they had argued and fought and scrambled to outshine one another, but they were still brothers then. It had been in 1933 when Speke Airport had just been opened. Sir Alan Cobham had persuaded the City Fathers that commercial flying had a brilliant future and that Liverpool must not miss out on the coming prosperity it would bring. There had been flying exhibitions over the Speke farmland, and when Sir Alan brought his famous Flying Circus to Liverpool, giving displays of stunt flying and offering joy-rides to those with the money to pay for them, Alex and Charlie were at the head of the queue, squabbling, naturally, on who should go up first. July 1933, and all the latest and most up-to-date aircraft had been there when the airport opened. The 'Percival Gull', the 'Spartan Clipper', the 'De Havilland Moth', the aeroplane in which he and Charlie first took to the controls. Jim Mollison had been one of those who had come on that special day, and with him was his record-breaking wife, Amy Johnson, 'Wonderful Amy', the darling of the British public.

It was then that he and Charlie had made up their minds that they wanted to fly, and when a flying school was set up to cater to the sons of the wealthy who decided they would like to do the same, the two boys, eighteen and nineteen respectively, had spent every penny of their allowance on the new sport. They had been neck and neck in the hours they put in and in their achievements, and had gone 'solo' on the same day.

Now he and Charlie were to be in competition once again.

His wife and son both turned smiling faces to him as he entered the room, and the boy clapped his hands.

'Darling, there you are,' his wife said, 'we wondered where you had got to, didn't we, my lamb?'

The child crowed and beat the water with his plump hands, delighted with the effect it had on his mother and father, who evidently thought he was exceedingly clever, so he repeated the action.

'There, you finish him, sweetheart, while I go and give the stew a stir.'

'Stew?'

'Well, shall we call it casserole, then? It sounds better but it's still plain old stew.'

'I don't mind what we call it, Rosie, because whatever its name I'm sure it will be delicious,' but the false bonhomie in his voice drew his wife back to the bathtub and the splashing boy who was now squirming to get out of it and on to his father's grey-flanneled knee, as he knelt beside him.

'Alex . . . ?' she said.

'Yes, my love?' not looking at her, his whole attention taken up with the boy who, failing to get out with his father, was doing his best to get his father *in* with him.

'Is everything all right?'

362

'Not really, my darling, but let's get this imp to bed before we talk.'

'Alex, you're frightening me.'

'Not you, my dearest heart. You have the bravest spirit I know, and where Harry and I would be without you, I shudder to think. No, it's myself I'm frightening, but I had to do it.'

She sat down abruptly in the chair beside the fire, putting her hand defensively to her belly, as though, no matter what, the child it contained would be protected. The lovely glow had gone from her face, leaving it drawn and apprehensive, and knowing as well, for really, what was it that every woman feared in these worrying times?

'What have you done, Alex?'

'I've joined up, Rosie. Forgive me but it seems I had to do it.'

'Charlie . . .'

'I don't know, sweetheart.' She could always read his thoughts. He sighed deeply, and the baby stared with interest into his father's face as though he too was affected by the poignancy of this moment. 'I suppose that had something to do with it. You know me and Charlie, damn him, but I don't think I could sit here and let others do the fighting for me. I'm twenty-four, Rose. A man, and I can't just . . . I have to help, darling. You do understand, don't you?'

'Yes, but I don't like it.'

'I know, sweetheart, and perhaps it won't last long. Perhaps the Germans, now they've rattled their sabres, will be satisfied and withdraw, but in the meanwhile someone has to make a stand.'

'You and Charlie?'

'I can't let him grab all the glory, can I?' grinning

363

now when it seemed his lovely wife was not to berate him, or weep and scream, but then had he really expected her to? No, she would allow him to make his own decisions, whether they be good or bad, whether she agreed with them or not; and if they should turn out to be wrong she would be here to stand beside him, to comfort his wounds should he be injured, to offer her love and her body and anything else he found he might need, whatever it was. Rose, Rosie, his love, his life.

'When do you go?' Her voice was steady, but her eyes were harrowed.

'I don't know, darling. They'll . . . call me.'

'Let's go to bed. Put Harry in his cot, will you?'

The casserole was forgotten, as Alex Woodall and his wife loved one another in the deep, lavender-scented comfort of their bed, Lacy's bed, and Lacy watched over them from her portrait above the fireplace, as she was to watch over the agonised weeping of Rose in her long, empty, lonely nights which were to follow.

Callum O'Shaughnessy's ship, the *Alexandrina Rose*, sailed into port three weeks after war was declared. She had managed, unescorted, as most merchant ships were in the first months of the war, to cross the North Atlantic ocean without mishap. Some made it, some did not. The *Alexandrina Rose* was one of the lucky ones. The war had been no more than twelve hours old when the passenger liner *Athenia* was torpedoed without warning 250 miles west of the Irish coast. One hundred and twenty-eight passengers lost their lives, and there were many casualties, but though the *Alexandrina Rose* had passed the very same spot where the *Athenia* went down she was not spotted by German submarines. Of course, the submarine which had sunk the *Athenia* had happened on her by sheer chance, it was thought, and was so placed that the liner had presented an easy and opportune target.

Maris was dressing to go out when she heard his key in the door, and for one rapturous moment her heart leaped in her breast. It was always the same, whenever he came home, in that fraction of time it took her brain to register that it made not the slightest difference how *she* felt, it was nothing to Callum. Just another stay in port, but nevertheless, for an instant, her heart overflowed with joy to have him home. To hear the familiar thud of the front door closing, his bag dropping to the floor, his footsteps up the hall as he moved towards the kitchen.

'Anyone at home?' he always called, casually, as one might to a servant, or someone of no importance whose presence or absence was all the same to him.

'Only me,' she would answer lightly, not even coming downstairs, since it was nothing to Callum whether she did or not.

Ever since Ellen's illness they had lived like this, the surface of their life unruffled and calm, neither one enquiring too closely into the other's whereabouts, thoughts, companions, hurts or joys, though she was well aware that should she bring any sort of scandal or shame to the name he had given her, it would be a different matter entirely. She lived her own life, going about with the friends she had known before her marriage, to parties and dances, the theatre, cinema and even, when Callum was at sea, to weekend 'Friday to Mondays' with the 'crowd'. She had ample opportunity to be unfaithful, but if the day came when Callum no longer made love to her she was sure she would. But they still shared a bed and his body 'loved' hers, and while she had that she would not betray him. She was, of course, aware that he had not the same scruples, though he was very discreet.

'Very smart,' he remarked as she entered the small 'back' room, though it could not be said he really *looked* at her. 'Going somewhere nice?'

'Not really, just to dine with Angela and Richard. Why don't you come with me?'

'No thanks, you know I can't stand that idiot.'

'That idiot, as you call him, is off to join his regiment at the end of the week. Somewhere in England as they say, so Angela is having a farewell dinner party.'

'Grand.' He was still in his officer's uniform, smart and looking undeniably attractive, and Maris felt the familiar ache begin in the middle of her chest, longing to have this man who was her husband look at her, just once, with something other than polite indifference. Jesus, since they last met a war had begun. He had, she presumed, come across seas which were now hazardous with submarines, mines and all the perils of the German navy, and yet he might have just come in from a day at the office. He had a glass of whiskey in his hand, one arm resting on the mantelpiece, and he was studying the *Liverpool Echo*, scarcely bothering to even pretend an interest in his wife.

'So how was the trip?' she asked, pouring herself nearly half a glass of the same drink. What the hell! Did it bloody matter? Was it any different to any other homecoming, and really, was she surprised? After all these years, did she care? and the answer, of course, was yes. But things were different now. For four years she had roamed about this city and this county looking for something to occupy her time, something to fill the sheer, unadulterated boredom of her days. Dashing here and dashing there in search of some elusive something to take her mind off her loveless marriage, her faithless husband, her never-ending, unbreakable, *miserable* love for him, which, no matter what she did, what *he* did, would not die.

But a war had begun. She didn't know why, not really, though they had talked a great deal about Poland, and she didn't know for how long, or what shape it would take but surely, *surely* there was something *she* could do? Something worthwhile. Something to make *her* feel worthwhile again. To give her the feeling that she was a valuable human being, if not to her husband, then to her country.

'Oh, uneventful,' he answered absently.

'No submarines attack you?'

He smiled, still not looking at her. 'No.'

'And what are you to do now?'

He looked up, surprised.

'What d'you mean?'

'Now that we are at war. What is *your* part in it?'

'Well, the country still has to eat and will need all the other commodities a country at war needs. War supplies, that sort of thing. I imagine I shall carry on as usual.'

'Of course,' and he would be in danger. This beloved man who acted as though she was some slight acquaintance to whom he must be polite but to whom he owed no explanations, would be in constant danger, as the *Athenia* had been, and his ship might even share her fate. The thought devastated her, churning her insides until she felt physically sick, but she continued to sip her drink, her face quite expressionless in the way she had taught herself in the past four years. She must not let him know how she still felt about him, since it would only serve to embarrass him, embarrass them both. Calm, pleasant, courteous, the fire inside her tamped well down, except in their bed when their bodies took over from their careful minds and they shared a satisfaction which often surprised them both.

'Well, I must be off,' she said briskly. 'It's a devil getting about in this black-out and with the nights drawing in . . .'

He looked up sharply, and she was quite bewildered by the expression in his eyes.

'You're not driving to Rainhill in that car of yours, are you?'

'Yes, why not?'

'Damn it, Maris, will you never learn discretion? You'll have a bloody accident driving with no lights, particularly the way *you* drive. Can you not take a taxi?'

'A taxi? Have you tried getting a taxi these days?'

'I've just come up in one. I could have asked him to wait if I'd known.'

'Well, you didn't, so I shall just have to hazard myself to the unlit streets of the city. I've done it before, and I find it quite a challenge seeing how many pedestrians one can frighten to death. And my driving is as good as yours any day of the week.'

'Don't talk rubbish. Look, I'll drive you over.'

'Callum, what chivalry, but you have no need to worry about me. I promise to be very careful, and besides, I shall have to get used to greater perils than the streets in and around Liverpool.'

'Oh, and why is that?' His voice was dangerous with something she did not recognise, though she supposed it to be the usual male attitude to the 'little woman' who might be about to get out of hand.

'There has been an appeal on the wireless for recruits for the ATS . . .'

'ATS . . . ?'

'Auxiliary Territorial Service, so I've joined.'

He smiled then. How very amusing, the smile said, but he drew slowly away from the mantelpiece, putting his glass on it before turning to her, giving her his full attention for the first time.

'I beg your pardon?'

'You heard me, Callum. I can't sit around here for the rest of my life, though it seems that would have been my fate had the war not come along, so . . . I joined up.'

'Joined up! I see, and what are you to do then? Man canteens, hand out cigarettes to the boys as they come from the railway stations as I believe women did in the last war?'

He was clearly not at all pleased at the thought of his wife doing such things, and when she had had her say, he would have his, his attitude said, and it would not be polite.

'Apparently there are five trades at the moment. Cooks, drivers, equipment assistants, clerks and orderlies. I've put in for driver.'

'I see, and where in Liverpool are you to drive?'

She put her glass carefully on the tray, studying it for a moment before she turned back to him. She had on a simple black dress, a plain sheath of velvet which emphasised every curve and line of her fine and slender body, the high tilt of her breasts. It skimmed her waist and hips, and at the back was inclined to caress her buttocks and the division between them rather more than he liked, though he could not have said why. The low front plunged, showing the valley between her breasts, and the back plunged to show off the fine white satin of her back to just below the waist. She wore nothing with it, no jewellery except her wedding ring, and nothing beneath it that he could see. Her eyes were deep and brown, great golden pools of light, her face slightly flushed, from the drink perhaps, and her hair tumbled in its usual silver mass of curls, falling over her forehead to her eyebrows, wisping in fine silver tendrils about her white neck and delicate ears.

She squared her shoulders before she spoke, and his eyes were drawn involuntarily to the lift and bounce of her half-exposed breasts.

'I don't think I will be posted in Liverpool, Callum.' Her voice was casual, but her eyes watched him carefully.

'Posted! You sound like a letter.' What a bloody stupid thing to say, he thought, wishing he could drag his eyes from his wife's breasts, since she evidently did not care to have him look at them in that way, indeed in any way.

'Yes, silly isn't it? but that's the term.'

'Well, whatever it is, you had better go and tell them that your husband does not care to have his wife *posted* anywhere.'

'Why, Callum? What difference does it make to you? You are scarcely here yourself.'

'True, but that is me, and it is you we are talking about.'

'Callum.' Her voice was very calm. 'Married women without a family will be expected to do something. Work on the land, in factories, or in the Armed Forces. I have chosen the latter.'

'Perhaps I might change my mind about that child, then.' He was, for some reason she could not under-

370

stand, quite incensed, and she had been ready to laugh, to smooth him down, to win him over, but his words and the implication behind them brought a blood-red madness to her brain, a dazed, incredulous rage she could really not contain. She felt the need to pick up her glass and fling it at him, to pick up the poker and hit him with it, to hurt him with the same devastating agony with which he had struck at her.

'You mean, to stop me from doing what you consider unfit for me to do, you would impregnate me, despite refusing to do so when I wanted it?'

'Well, if you put it like that . . .'

'I do, and you can go to hell, Callum O'Shaughnessy.'

Turning on her heel, she flung herself like some small but very vicious tornado from the room, striking sparks from the surface of the carpet as she went. The door slammed behind her, and he winced as the furious sound of her sports car roared off up the road into the pitchy darkness of the blacked-out streets. He did not move until the sound had died completely away, and when it had he sank slowly into the fireside chair and put his head in his hands.

20

'I'll be seeing . . . dah de dah . . . de dah, de dah, de . . . dah . . .'

Matty sat at the sewing machine, and her old piping voice rose with the dust motes which danced in the shaft of sunlight streaming through the parlour window. She loved all the popular songs, did Matty, those sung with tear-filled eyes and tear-choked voices in the super-abundance of emotion the war had created. All the lovely, sentimental songs couples were singing and whistling, with a faraway look in their eyes, as they polished floors, or rifles, washed baby linen or army smalls, scrubbed kitchen floors, or barrack-room floors; and all over the country, in army camps, on airfields, even further away in the middle of the high seas, the volume on wirelesses and gramophones was turned up as the words, for a moment or two, brought a loved one closer. Matty knew them all and sang them constantly, to Ellen's pretended annoyance, though she was the first to admit, if only to herself, that the sound of Vera Lynn singing brought a lump to her own throat.

They had been down to St John's Market that morning, the two old ladies, making their slow but steady way, arm in arm since Ellen was not the woman she had been before her stroke, across the road to the tram depot, and then on the tramcar down Brownlow Hill to Lime Street.

The market had been busy, for there were many women like themselves who had come to town not only

372

to buy black-out material at fourpence a yard, but anything at all which might come in useful in this crazy, mixed-up world in which they found themselves.

'If you spot any soft fruits worth buyin', Matty, sure an' we'll be havin' ourselves a pound or two. I'll make some jam. Blackberries would be nice, so they would. I can get the lads to pick us some apples from the trees, an' put up some blackberry an' apple. You know how our Callum likes that an' himself to be home soon. Wisht, he'll be in need of a bit of feedin' up, an' sure he'll get none at his place. Did you ever hear of such a thing when a man comes home from war to an empty house? A fine one *she* turned out to be, so she did, the devil take her. Not a child in the house in all these years, an' now, when a man needs a bit of comfort, where is she, tell me that? Off in her grand uniform and only the Blessed Mother knows where.'

It was a sore and festering wound to Ellen, the sorry state of her son's marriage, and the even sorrier state of her son's wife, and how he allowed himself to be talked into letting her go was a mystery to her, so it was, she said a dozen times a day to anyone who would listen, mostly the patient Matty. The Auxiliary Territorial Service, whatever that might be, though it certainly had a grand name to it, so it had. Thundering off in that murderous little car of hers two months ago, and never a sight of her, nor a word from her, since.

And what was she up to, Ellen begged Matty to tell her, far from home and the protection of her family and her husband's family, mixing with men from all over the country, and Lord only knew what kind *they* were; and if she'd had her way she'd have tied her daughter-in-law to the bedpost or the kitchen sink where she belonged.

There had been some sad times, sad, sad, times and no mistake since Mr Chamberlain had told them they were to go to war again. Poland had fallen to those wicked Germans, though it was said some small sections of the Polish Army were fighting on. The Germans had bombed Warsaw until the city was a sea of flames with thousands killed and wounded. And then if they hadn't gone and sunk the battleship *Royal Oak* in Scapa Flow. Torpedoed her they had, and upwards of eight hundred officers and men went down with her. Ellen had cried sharply, being the mother of a seaman, knowing exactly how those who had sons and husbands aboard felt as they waited for news. A grand ship like that and all those grand lads, and sometimes it was more than she could bear to read about it.

She hated it! Hated it, and she hated that damned Anderson shelter she had been forced to have put up in her lovely back garden. She didn't want it, she told the men who came to erect it for her. No, not if they paid her, and if the German bombers came over then she'd get under her bed, so she would, she and Matty both. And as for those damned barrage balloons in the park at the back of the house, well, she felt like writing to Mr Chamberlain about it, she told their Michael. Fancy putting a balloon site right where she could see it from the back bedroom window. It frightened the life out of you, so it did, having one of those monsters hanging almost over your own back garden. It kept the light out and was for ever getting loose, and if a German bomber bumped into one, where would it fall? Into Ellen's back garden, that's where, begorra! She couldn't think why they *had* the blessed things in the first place. There was no danger, scanning the empty skies disparagingly, and if there was any necessity for

374

her to use the shelter in the garden, she failed to see it. At her age, could you imagine her running down the stairs and sitting in a hole in the ground, especially with that damned *balloon* hanging over her head, guiding the German bombers right to her! No, give it to someone else, she said, because she didn't want it.

The black-out curtain was another thorn in her side. Matty had dragged out the old sewing machine, the one old Mick had bought Ellen over fifty years ago. Handsome it was, with lovely motifs on its casing. You turned the handle with your right hand and guided the material with your left, and it still worked as good as new even today. She had sown hundreds of little garments on it for her growing family, and had even made Michael's shirts for him, buying the material, as she had the black-out material, at St John's Market.

Matty and herself had taken turns sewing the coarse black fabric into large squares as they had been shown by Mrs Donavan's daughter, who was to be an Air Raid Precaution Warden and had been specially trained for it, or so Mrs Donavan said. You put a dozen curtain rings across the top, which were then supposed to be hung on hooks set in the window frame, or so they had been instructed.

'Slide a thin piece of wood into the hem at the bottom to hold it taut,' Mrs Donavan's daughter had continued in that superior way she seemed to have developed in her new-found and important glory, '. . . and then with the rings over the hooks not a chink of light should be seen.'

'An' tell me this, Sally Donavan,' for though Sally was married to Ernie Kelly no one had ever called her by anything but her maiden name, '. . . who's to get up an' put the thing to the window, that's what I'd like to know, so I would, for it'll not be me nor this old woman here,' indicating Matty.

It was Michael who put it up for her, coming each day towards dark and fixing it a treat, and then each morning to take it down again; and grand it was to see him twice a day, for he often pushed his son round in his baby-carriage, which was a joy, so the war was not a complete waste after all. His 'war effort', Michael called it, since there was nothing else they'd let him do at his age, he said furiously, in that way her sons had when they were thwarted. Thank the sweet Mother of Christ, Ellen added silently. Hadn't he done enough in the first one with a grand medal to show for it? Elizabeth needed him at home with her, Ellen told him soothingly, dangling young Michael on her knee, the little pet, for neither of them was young any more, and where she, in her youth, had been able to cope single-handedly with child after child, it took the pair of them all their time, or so she liked to think, to manage this one. No, she'd sent enough of her family marching off to war, twice now, and she had no compunction in emphasising to Michael that there was absolutely no way Elizabeth, and herself, could do without him.

She was heart-broken again in November when the Dutch passenger liner *Simon Bolivar* was mined in the North Sea with heavy loss of life: children, babes in arms, women; and it seemed to Ellen that the wicked enemy did not care who they killed. Those mines they were laying sank seven ships on the same day in what the government called 'Germany's new campaign of frightfulness', indiscriminately sinking merchant vessels, and it was slowly borne home to her that her son, her clever son the sea captain, was in the gravest of danger. There had not been a great deal happening up to then. Life had gone on much as usual with only Maris, so far, going off with herself on some escapade; but now, suddenly, with the growing number of merchant vessels sunk, some only just out of Liverpool Bay, war struck at Ellen O'Shaughnessy.

Her grandsons were the next to go, and when they came to say goodbye to her – Devlin, Joseph, Lorcan who was eighteen now, and then Guy, Caitlin's nineteen-year-old son from Yorkshire, all excited and longing to be away – she was inconsolable. The others would be next, swallowed up by the war machine which was slowly swinging into action. Finbar and Flynn and the rest of her handsome boys, for they would always be 'boys' to her, and even Eammon and Donal, despite their age, would have to go some time.

'All the young men,' she moaned into Matty's comforting shoulder, 'all the lovely young men . . . the sons I sent last time an' now it's me grandsons they're takin' from me. Will I ever see them again?'

Rosie brought Harry Woodall and the brand new Ellen Woodall to see her several days later, and when the baby, named for her great-grandmother, was put in her arms, it was as though Ellen found a renewal of peace.

'Sure an' isn't there always the children, Rosie dear. Always the little ones coming along, and that's a fact. Life renewed every year, at least it was with me an' you're to be the same, it seems.' It gave her the greatest satisfaction to see her grandchildren carrying on the function of procreation. Claudine, Mara's eldest, had three little ones, as did Amy's Paul, and now little Rosie, not so little any more but with two small Woodalls; and if that there Charlie, who was her brother-in-law and as irresponsible as a toddling child, got himself killed in that aeroplane he flew, Ellen was holding the next but one baronet on her knee.

'What's the word on Alex, darlin'? Have you heard?'

'There's nothing much doing, he says.'

'Sure, an' the whole war seems to be the same, in my opinion,' jiggling young Harry Woodall on her comfortable lap. 'See,' she said to him, 'sit you still then on grandmammy's lap an' she'll do the "Lady's horse" for you. Now then, off we go . . .

The lady's horse goes trot, trot, trot,
And the gentleman's horse goes trot, trot, trot,
But the farmer's horse goes gallopy, gallopy,
    gallopy . . .'

setting the child to squealing delight as she bumped him on her knee, which brought laughter to the homely kitchen, which was, after all, what it was used to. The flames from the fire flickered on the white walls and bright copper pans, touching, as they had done for almost eighty years, the faces of the family, generations of them now, who had dwelled and prospered within its walls. Ellen, who was of the second generation, her daughter Gracie in the opposite chair who was of the third, her granddaughter Rosie, the fourth, and now the two babies who would be the fifth. How could anything destroy this, the continuity, the unbroken and blessed immortality of the O'Shaughnessys?

'So what's he up to then, that lad of yours? Sure an' if I know him he'll not be sitting on his behind staring into space.'

'No, when he's not training he helps to fill sandbags, he says.'

378

'Sandbags? Holy Mother, an' what would they be for?'

'It's for blast protection, he says.'

'Whatever next?'

'And he says he has developed a great taste for beer, since he and his fellow cadets spend a great deal of time in the local pub.'

'The divil he does.'

'But they're longing for action, all of them.'

The women fell silent, not at all sure they understood the male preoccupation with battles and the paraphernalia of war. Longing for action. Where had Ellen heard that before? and of course it had been twenty-five years ago when the young and impatient had been 'dying to get in on it', prophetic words, for that's just what they did! *Die!*

'Oh, and I had a letter from Maris, grandmother.'

'Did you indeed?' Instantly Ellen's face became stiff with disapproval, and Matty glided away to the scullery.

'I'm off now, Mammy,' Gracie shrilled, reaching for her coat, and with a kiss and a promise to call tomorrow was off up the hall before the full blast of her mother's scathing displeasure could fall about *her* ears.

'She's doing a good job, grandmother.'

'She had a good job, didn't she so. Wife to my son, she was, an' if that's not a fit job for any woman then tell me what is, so?'

'Callum is away so much, and, as a woman without children she would have certainly had to . . .'

'Aye, an' there's another thing, so it is. Why were there no children? I hate to say this . . .' She lowered her voice and glanced about the kitchen, taking to heart, it seemed, the propaganda slogan which told them that 'walls have ears'. 'I hate to say it, child, but

I have me suspicions that Maris, God forgive her, was using something. You know, them things that godless women use to stop babies,' crossing herself hastily. 'Not that I know anything about them, and don't want to, God help me, but I have heard tell that such things are available at . . . well, clinics an' . . .' She crossed herself again for good measure.

'Well, I don't know about that, grandmother,' remembering the anguished face of her cousin, who had begged her husband to let her have a child, 'but she's helping to defend her country now with what she's doing.'

'Sure an' what's that, pray?' Ellen sniffed.

'She's going to drive an ambulance.'

'Holy Mother, so tell me how *that's* going to win the war?'

But Rose had no answer for her grandmother. Rose was in a state of what she called 'suspension'. A feeling of being suspended in time, in space, in the hollow vacuum the absence of Alex Woodall had left her drifting in. She had the most dreadful feeling that she would never see him again, that he had somehow fallen out of her life, taking with him the deep and peaceful content they had known together, not only since the day they had married but all of their lives. They had been friends since they were children. Their friendship had grown and matured with them, and had gained adult love and passion. They had been happy together, loving one another in tranquillity, easily; a love which had, when he was born, encompassed their son. She knew she would get through each day, each week, perhaps even moving on to each year if the war should last so long; conduct her life and those of her children at a basic level of need; but how was her heart, her soul, her mind, the core of Rose Woodall to survive? The need she had for her husband was so deep she was like the frayed end of an electric cord without him, connected to nothing, bare and in peril, perilous even, until he came home to her?

Elizabeth, in Charlie's absence, had engaged a man who would, had the war not begun when it did, have been retired. A man who had worked at the Shipping Office but who, because he had a great deal of experience in management, was to take over the running of Woodall for the time being. His name was Alfred Rogers, and he and Mrs Rogers were to move into the Lodge, and it was already rumoured that the land, the whole estate, was to be put to the plough. To grow food to feed the country. The Women's Land Army, girls, young women who had volunteered for the job, were to work the land, and the new Ministry of Agriculture and Fisheries was to tell them what was required of them. The same was to happen at Beechwood, and Uncle Teddy was certainly not able to supervise the setting up of all the necessary organisation which would be required. So who was to do it if not Teddy Osborne? and, of course, the answer was Rose Woodall. Perhaps if she should have some task apart from the rearing of her children, she would be able to concentrate the energies which Alex had taken from her, into other channels; give her mind, which went on and on endlessly despairing for him, something on which to focus. Wear her down to exhaustion so that her restless body and darting, grieving mind could rest. He was safe at the moment, at least she thought he was, though there were rumours that already British patrol aircraft had been shot down, and an RAF fighter patrol had attacked five German seaplanes which were employed

381

in mine-laying. The attack was made at low altitude with machine guns, the newspapers reported, and all the British aircraft had returned safely. *This time*. She had no idea if, by now, Alex had been in one of those aircraft, since his letters said nothing at all except how much he loved and missed her. He talked of the days they had shared in the sunshine and shade of Old Wood, the boat on the lake, the wild gallops they had thrilled to across the fields to the east of Woodall, their child in whom he had found such fulfilment, and the day on which they would take up that shining life again.

He had discovered, through a man in the government who had known his father, that Christian Osborne had indeed been arrested in London and had served a short sentence in prison, but he had been released and had, presumably, returned to Ireland. But his name was known now and he would find it difficult to return to the land of his birth. Should he ever want to. The Offences against the State Act which allowed for imprisonment and detention without trial had become law in June 1939, and the Irish Republican Army was declared an unlawful organisation. In December there had been a big swoop in Belfast made by the Royal Ulster Constabulary, putting thirty-four IRA men behind bars, and who was to say Christian Osborne was not one of them? Rose had no way of knowing. There was only one thing that was certain, and that was the estate of Beechwood, and indeed all the inheritance which belonged to Christian and which was now in total disorder since Alex had left, was unsupervised and neglected by the man who should one day have it in his care, and only *she* could keep it together, for his heir. She was not even sure who that would be, and could only assume that Charlie, as Christian's cousin and

Elizabeth O'Shaughnessy's son, was as good a guess as any. Or would it be Claudine, his eldest sister? Claudine had three girls, and Mairin and Ailis were not yet married, and it seemed from their strange and what one could only call unconventional way of life, never would be. Which left only Harry. Her own son. The great-great-grandson of an Irish immigrant and working man.

Food rationing began in January. Everyone had a ration book, which Ellen could make neither head nor tail of, she said, and she and Matty would be exceedingly grateful if Rosie would sort it all out for them. Gracie and Amy and Eileen had taken on the job of 'minding' their various young grandchildren whilst their daughters and daughters-in-law had found what they called 'war work' in a newly constructed munition factory in Everton, but which was, in Ellen's opinion, no more than an excuse to go out and earn themselves some extra money.

The land war in France was bogged down well short of the Siegfried Line on which the most popular song of the winter told the people it would 'hang out the washing'. It appeared the RAF was mainly occupied in dropping leaflets and not bombs, and Eammon was fined for lighting a cigarette in the blackout!

'Keep calm and carry on,' the posters on the hoardings told the British people. 'Your courage and your cheerfulness will bring us victory.' Leaflets poured through Ellen's letter-box telling her 'What to do about your gas-mask.' 'Make your home safe,' 'Mask your window edges with black paint,' and 'Don't dig a trench unless you know how to make one properly.'

Ellen said she felt as though she was back at school with a teacher wagging a finger at her, a teacher who does not want trouble and will be obeyed at whatever the cost. Dig trenches indeed, and at her age. 'The struggle ahead' was another, emphasising the grit and determination expected of the public, showing representatives of the three services and called 'The Empire's Strength'; plus, under the heading 'Britain's War Effort' a shipbuilder, a coal miner, a munitions worker and a land girl were depicted hard at work, which, so Maureen and Teresa, Bridie and Ginny, Marion, Martha and all the other O'Shaughnessy women had said, had prompted them to leave their children to their grandmother's care.

They came by the droves, those pamphlets, treating the public as though they were children, Ellen grumbled. Even she, at her age, knew how to put on her gas-mask, and she was fed up to the teeth with being told to 'Put out that light' and that 'Careless talk costs lives,' for who was she to tell the country's secrets to, had she any to tell! And as for hiding in her shelter during an air raid and drinking the coffee which as the advertisement declared was supposed to make it *all right*, she'd never heard anything so daft in her life. She'd never drunk coffee in her life, either, and had no intention of starting now.

Alex came home in January on a seventy-two-hour leave, roaring up the drive in his little blue Triumph roadster, smart and dashingly handsome in his air-force blue officer's uniform and peaked cap, scattering gravel as he turned towards Lacy's house, which didn't matter in the least since no one had raked it in months. The old gardener still pottered about amongst the flower beds, those which were left, tidying and weeding and doing a bit of pruning ready for the spring, since no one had told him not to. He had seen them 'land girls' striding about the place in their tight trousers, and had even been given a bit of 'lip' by one of them, but they were nowt to do with him, and neither was the gravel on the drive. *They* were tearing up the lawns he had cut so carefully for over a quarter of a century, putting to the plough acres of parkland, and filling the lovely old house with their silly women's chatter and shrieking laughter, and was it any wonder Mr Eaton, butler at Beechwood for longer than anyone could remember, had removed himself to one of the estate cottages, declaring he would end his days there in peace? Mrs Pritchard was still in the kitchen, though, cooking for Mr Teddy and Mrs Osborne and *them*; and what old Mrs Osborne, Mrs *Serena* Osborne that was, would have made of it, the old man couldn't bear to think.

They stood for perhaps five minutes in a wordless embrace, straining against one another, their senses reeling in need, and for three days the sorrow and loneliness, the sheer and desperate agony they both knew when they were apart, was dissolved. Apart from a brief visit to his mother, the door was shut on the outside world as they poured out the banked-up fire of their love, and when it was spent, they began the process of stoking it up again in preparation for the day he would leave and they must survive until the next time. She wept as he smoothed kisses on her eyes, her cheeks, her lips, the curve of her jaw and the strong arched column of her throat. Her fingers gripped the dark hair at the back of his head, pulling his face closer to hers, and her tears wet them both.

'Where have you been?' she gasped in that first moment of meeting, as though he was late for a meal, but he knew what she meant.

'The children . . .'

'. . . are at your mother's for a few hours. She wanted us to have some time to ourselves . . .'

'God bless her . . . a bath I think, first . . .'

Rose turned on the taps and began to fill the deep, old-fashioned tub with water, putting in a stream of lavender-scented salts, and as the water inched up the sides of the bath they undressed one another. Like two starving travellers come in from the wilderness, they fell hungrily upon one another, and as his hands moved on her white breasts, the nipples proud and rosy, she reached for his erect penis. They took one another then and there. Before the bath had filled, his body entered hers as she leaned back to accommodate him.

'Now we will bathe . . .'

'The children . . .'

'Later . . .'

He carried her into the bedroom, still wet and smooth as satin from the bath water, and laid her before the fire she had lit in their bedroom, and beneath the understanding gaze of Lacy Osborne, they loved and loved again. Their bodies dried in the heat of the fire and became slicked again with sweat. He could not seem to get as much as his urgently starving body needed of her, her splendid woman's body gilded by the flames of the fire to delicate gold, to amber shades and rose-tipped peaks, licking the rim of her ear with his warm tongue, her arched eyebrows, the lovely line of her throat down to her breasts, which he drew, one at a time into his mouth. Down her rounded stomach, that which had so recently carried their daughter, to between her legs and the sweet and secret moistness of her womanhood, which she offered to him, generously and wantonly as wife and lover.

She caressed the hard muscles of his shoulder, sliding down his body, kissing each rib, teasing his nipples with her tongue, the hollow of his navel, the inside of his thigh, the lean strong length of his legs, the arch of his foot, the fine bones of his ankle, then up again until her mouth took the waiting, straining magnificence of his erect penis.

They were spent, at last, all the pent-up lonely need they had of each other drained away in a great wave of rapturous orgasms, and as she lay on his chest, her hair spread in a dark shimmering cloak across them both, he felt the need to shed tears, as she had done, for how could he stand it if all this was lost to him?

'My dearest heart . . . I love you . . . there is nothing in this world which will ever be to me as you are.'

'I know . . . I know . . .'

'I loved you as a boy and now I love you as a man. It is . . . hard to get through . . . without you, Rosie.'

'I am the same.'

'We are like the two sides of one coin, you and I.' He ran his hands down her body, then cupped the soft weight of her breasts as she sat up.

'Is . . . are you . . . ?'

'I am . . . going away, my darling.'

'So this is . . .'

'For a while.'

'To France . . . ?'

'Darling, I *will* come home.'

'You must . . . really you must, Alex. I am nothing without you.'

'Kiss me . . .'

'The children . . . ?'

'Later . . .'

21

The order came for the convoy to scatter just as the grey sea and the grey sky had begun to merge into one another, so that it was difficult to see where one ended and the other began, and at once the *Alexandrina Rose* and the rest of the thirty-five merchantmen changed course and began to disappear into the coming night.

He had been thinking about Maris. He was not at the wheel but standing just to the left and behind the man who was, and for some reason her face had appeared on the darkening window of the wheelhouse. Laughing she had been, radiant and vivid in that way she had when she was happy, which was not often, he supposed, with a bastard like himself for a husband.

Where was she now, he wondered, that defiant, stubborn woman with a spirit to match his own, who had grown, phoenix-like, from the shell of the naïve child he had married. Smart as paint and as slick as spilled oil, and yet for all that, vulnerable as a child. But how exquisite she had been with her body turned to gold in the fire's flames in their bedroom. Ivory and gold and silver, fine as spun silk, firm coral-tipped breasts, making him light-headed, reeling with her sensuality. God, what a fire-brand. All those years they had been married and all the women he had known, and there had been no one like her. What a bloody waste. They had been out of step from the moment they met, she too late for him, he too early for her, and so they had never come together at exactly that right moment.

He had heard from Rose the last time he was in port that his wife was stationed down south somewhere, marching up and down a parade ground, Rose said laughing, living in a Nissen hut with thirty other girls, and so far had been nowhere near an ambulance except to put her head under the bonnet or to crawl beneath the wheels. The biggest problem she had found, she had written to Rose, was the nits from which a great many of the young women with whom she was billeted seemed to suffer, passing them on carelessly to all those with whom they came in contact. She was not awfully sure which was worse, she said, the nits or the treatment to cure them.

She had often made him laugh, quite against his will at times, and he had done so then as he drove back to the cold and cheerless home in which they had lived for so long and so uneasily.

Jesus, was he mad? letting his thoughts wander as they were doing, when every tingling sense, every warning bell, every instinct for self-preservation that the human body possesses was needed in these perilous storm-tossed seas, in which for the past five months the German U-boats had lain in wait for British shipping. The Battle of the Atlantic had begun from the moment war was declared, for it was across that ocean that the vital lines of support stretched to the United States of America and to Canada. From there supplies of food and fuel had to be carried back to Liverpool in order to maintain the struggle against Nazi Germany and without which starvation and disaster would face the whole British nation.

Callum O'Shaughnessy had crossed these seas several times now in the convoy system which had hurriedly been put into operation in September, leaving

Liverpool on the first one a few weeks after the war had begun. Bloodless skirmishes they had been, with reported sightings which had turned out to be everything from seagulls to floating planks of wood. But that had not lasted long, as the great fleet of German U-boats had grown. Poorly armed and inadequately converted to war, the 'cruiser' which was supposed to escort thirty to forty merchant ships across the Atlantic was an easy target, along with those it was meant to protect. He had seen ships all around him go down, struck by magnetic mines, torpedoed and bombed, ships of the merchant navy, the 'Red Duster' with no defence against the enemy; their crews spilling into the icy waters like dolls broken and discarded by careless children; clinging to any bit of flotsam that came to hand; waiting in seas which were as cold and cruel as war itself to be dragged under, or, if they were lucky, to be picked up by other vessels in the vicinity. They were all aware, of course, that orders had been given to the effect that no ship should stop to pick up survivors, but in some cases an escorting destroyer might try a rescue if the convoy was no longer under attack.

But on this convoy they had two brand-new corvettes and an older destroyer, all fully armed and with experienced men of the Royal Navy to protect them. They had left Liverpool, thirty-eight ships of all shapes and sizes, freighters, tankers, even coasters, willing to brave the hazards of the Atlantic. Deep-laden, most of them, others in ballast and sitting high in the water, in single file and out into Liverpool Bay from the narrow Mersey channel to where the corvette was to meet them, their pennants flying bravely in the raw February sunshine. There had been an early mist drifting across the estuary, but it had dissipated as the sun rose, and the men had been cheerful, their goodbyes over and forgotten, and they waved to the Navy men on the corvette as they began to crack on speed, spreading out as they were checked by the captain of one of the navy vessels, the stragglers rounded up and kept in formation.

There had been one or two ships, a tanker in particular, ploughing on regardless of the irritable voice on the loudhailer, determined, or so it seemed, to get to the front of the convoy; or simply because of the sheer pigheadedness of the master since many of them did not care for taking orders. Finally they had attained some sort of discipline.

There were two 'action stations' during the first night. The first was caused by an aircraft flying low over the convoy, which proved to be 'one of ours', and the second when U-boats were reported in the area immediately ahead of them; but by then the full fury of the Atlantic weather was upon them and the convoy found itself dispersed over more than fifty square miles, and the U-boats never materialised.

It was the third night, black as pitch but calm for once, and because of it Callum distinctly heard the torpedo come through the water, and though he had given an order to zig-zag, somehow he knew quite positively that it would catch his ship; and when it did, the force of the explosion failed to surprise him.

At once the *Alexandrina Rose* keeled over at an impossible angle, and he felt himself begin to hurtle from one side of the wheelhouse to the other. He could see the black water rushing past his stricken ship, hear the cries of his men, their voices hoarse with fear; and there was a thick smell of oil which did its best to choke him.

For a moment he felt a blinding surge of panic. The alarm bell was clanging, and even at the angle at which the ship lay there was the sound of a furious rush of feet as those who were able to ran for their lives.

'Get a move on, lad,' he said calmly to his second officer, though his own insides were churning and the nausea of fear rose in his throat. 'We've not got all day.'

He could hear the awful sound of seawater flooding into his vessel under enormous pressure, and as he and his second officer . . . Good God, he couldn't remember the man's name . . . fell out of the wheelhouse a blast of heat from the smashed engine room rose to meet him. The ugly angle of the deck appalled him for a moment and he was disorientated. He had been on decks at a worse slant than this in bad weather, but then it had been a natural thing, an element to which he was used; but this, this man-made thing was something he could scarcely comprehend, and was the worst moment of his life. There was noise coming from below him, the terrified howling of men in the engine room, men cut off from escape by the damage done by the torpedo and by the rising water which was about to engulf them. Oh, Jesus, Joseph and Mary . . . His mother's prayers, which she had taught him at her knee, circled like whipping tops in his brain, and he saw her face as it had been then, calm and infinitely comforting to a small boy, and he was calmed and comforted, ready to calm and perhaps comfort others.

'This way, lads,' he said to the men at his back, and they reached the open space between the lifeboats at the same time as the rest of the crew, or those who were still capable of it. Men blundered to and fro, bumping into each other, cursing; and the young ones,

392

taken on in the catering department, were yelling for their mothers since some of them were only boys of sixteen.

'One of the boats is jammed, sir,' somebody gasped. 'It's no bloody good . . . it's jammed . . .'

'Get the rafts . . . clear the rafts . . .'

'Aye, sir . . .'

The confusion was appalling. They all wore life-jackets, but not one wanted to be flung into the sea with nothing else to keep him afloat until he was picked up. They would be picked up, of course, since there were a dozen ships in the immediate vicinity which could come to their rescue, or so they told themselves, for to consider anything else did not bear thinking about. It was no more than five minutes since the order had come to scatter, and most of the vessels had scarce had time to turn aside.

The stern had begun to tower over the rest of the ship, steadily lifting higher and higher, the bows going straight down into the sea, down into the deep of the water. It would be gone soon, the *Alexandrina Rose*, the ship he had commanded for nearly ten years, and he was reluctant to let her go, to leave her, to see her die, but quietly he gave the order to pipe 'abandon ship'.

The mass of men milling about him had become silent now, edging up the sloping deck towards the higher stern, afraid of losing their balance, afraid of sliding into that black and gaping pit into which their ship was being sucked. The two life-rafts had been launched, and though they still struggled with the lifeboat it was securely jammed.

'Leave it now,' he said. 'Jump lads, and head for the rafts.'

'Sir . . .' A boy was weeping, his face a mask of fear, his eyes pitiful in the streaked oil which coated him.

'Time to go, lad. Come on, be brave, we'll all be with you. Good luck.'

Most of them went, jumping into water which was so cold it took their breath away. The boy was beside him, and he put out a hand, grasping his life-jacket and pulling him towards him.

'All right now, son. Good boy. Your Mam'd be proud of you.'

'Thank you, sir.'

'Good lad, keep with me.'

'I will, sir.'

But those who had hesitated had left it too late, and when, finally, they got up their nerve to go, they slid slowly, agonisingly down the barnacle-encrusted hull, which tore the clothes from their bodies, the flesh from their bones; losing their faces, their testicles; screaming and bleeding until, mercifully, the sea which gathered them in numbed their minds and their pain.

'She's going . . . dear sweet Christ, she's going . . .' and so she was. With his arm about the boy, who appeared to have gone to sleep, so deep in shock was he, Callum trod water as his ship ploughed madly, swiftly, down into the tumult. Another explosion deep in the vessel flipped the sea about them into hundreds of dipping waves, then, with the obscene smell of oil incarcerating them in its disgusting stench, the sea flattened and she was gone.

But this was not the time for mourning. He himself seemed to be in a state of calm, a blessed state which allowed him to speak to those who huddled about him in the water, like sheep about a shepherd, giving orders to those who had remained steady and were capable of carrying them out.

'Now then, my lad,' to the boy, 'let's get you on to the raft.' There would not be room for them all, but it would not be long, surely, before they were picked up. No other ship appeared to have been hit. The attack was over, it seemed, so with a bit of luck and a prayer or two, since he could hear one being murmured quietly close by, the destroyer would come back for them. The red safety lamps were on, and in the meanwhile they could cling to the rat-lines, turn and turn about, those who must remain in the water, until their rescuers came.

They were quiet, calmed by his calm, doing as they were ordered, but it was bloody cold, a cold which probed deep within them, biting not only into their flesh and muscle and bone, but numbing their minds as well; and when those who could no longer hold on, slipped away, drifting off into the appalling blackness, nobody noticed. It was exactly seven minutes since the torpedo struck.

Private Maris O'Shaughnessy was polishing the windscreen of the ambulance which she had come to think of as hers when she was told that her Commanding Officer wanted to see her at once.

'*Now?* What for?' she asked foolishly. She could think of nothing she had done wrong recently.

'How the hell should I know?' Private Betty Thompson answered logically. 'She doesn't take me into her confidence. Perhaps she's heard about the party at the "Dog and Bottle". The one where you and Ginger Mills did that . . .'

'Don't be daft. She was there.'

'She wasn't! I never saw her.'

'She was just going into the private dining room with another officer, but she turned a blind eye. She's not a bad old stick, and we were only singing.'

'Yes, but the *song*! "Roll me over, in the clover, roll me over, lay me down and do it again. Now this is number five," I think you were up to, "and he's tickling my thighs, roll me over, lay me down and . . ."'

'Oh, for God's sake, Betty, shut up and let me think.'

'Think, what d'you have to think about, except to get over to the CO's office as quick as you can.'

'Have I to get dressed up?'

'No, I shouldn't say so, but wash your face though. You've a streak of oil on it a mile wide.'

Maris had been a trainee ATS driver for three months now. She had learned not only to drive her ambulance but to service it as well. There was a growing demand for drivers, but a driver was of not much use unless she could keep the bloody vehicle on the road, was she, the Sergeant asked her?

She slept on a pallet on an iron bed, and ate the worst food she had ever eaten in her life, and she doubted if she would ever, to the end of her days, forget the medical examination she had been forced to undergo. Made to strip to her knickers and brassière, she, and the rest of the intake, stood in a row whilst a medical officer peered, first down the front of her knickers and then down the back and then, without so much as a by-your-leave or do-you-mind, took out each of her breasts and studied them in turn.

'D'you think the sheikh will pick us for his harem?' the girl next to her hissed when he had moved on. 'Makes you wonder what the hell he was looking for.'

Betty Thompson, that was, and from that slightly hysterical moment they had been friends.

Though Maris had been away to school and had slept in a 'dorm' with half a dozen other girls, it had been nothing like this. For a start they had all been of the same class, *hers*; and the young women with whom she was now billeted were from every class and walk of life in the country. Betty's father drove a tram and Betty had worked as a waitress at the 'Kardomah' in Bolton. But class distinction had been thrown out of the window as the girl who had never worked in her life found herself with others from very different circumstances than her own, for did not their muscles ache in exactly the same way, did they not grouse in the same way, and lose their frayed and homesick tempers in the same way?

They talked of everything under the sun, from their boyfriends and the state of their sex lives; the possibility of leave; the bloody-mindedness of the Sergeant; the foul food and the foul beds; the chances of catching VD, now that they had the whole British Army, or so it seemed, waiting to get their knickers off; and the advisability of carrying a rubber sheath, or a French letter, as it was rudely called, and the possibility of making their partner actually *wear* it. Maris could have told the girls in her billet all about *them*. She was the only married woman in the hut, and at first the girls had been wary of her since that made her a different species from them, and besides, they could barely understand what she said with that cut-glass accent of hers. But when it became apparent to them that she was as keen on a 'good laugh' as the rest of them; that she had no intention of putting on airs and that she was often the ringleader in some wild escapade; that she had no interest in any man since she had one of her own, leaving the field clear for them, she was completely accepted. She had become, in fact, a kind of mother confessor to many of them, listening sympathetically to their tales of unrequited love – who knew better than she – and love which had *been* requited and the awful possibility that the one making the confession might have to bear the appalling consequence and shame.

Maris, who was herself only just twenty-four and not the youngest girl in the hut, found it all highly amusing, but at the same time she was proud that these young women liked and trusted her. She had come through so much: the training, the medical, the 'square bashing', the loneliness and heartache, the dreadful longing for Callum which she knew now would never leave her. She had become, entirely by her own efforts, a person of worth, a valuable and *valued* member of the *female* human race. Not Maris Woodall, daughter of a baronet and bright young thing. Not Maris O'Shaughnessy, failed wife and mother, but Private O'Shaughnessy who did her job efficiently, who was a friend, a true friend to the girls with whom she served, and she carried herself straight and tall despite her lack of inches.

She saluted smartly the ATS officer who was in command of her, and after an order to stand at ease was surprised when she was told, gently, that she might sit down on the straight-backed chair which was placed before the desk.

The officer stared down at her own hands for a long moment, and Maris supposed it was then that she knew. For a start, a lowly private was not invited to seat herself in the presence of an officer, and it seemed to her that that officer was at a loss for words. So what could that mean, she asked herself, whilst her heart lurched uncomfortably in her chest and her mouth dried up. She held her own hands tightly clasped together in her overalled lap, whilst her mind shied away from the dreadful pictures her devilish imagination had conjured up a thousand times in the last five months. In fact, ever since war had been declared and the *Athenia* was torpedoed off the coast of Ireland, in the very stretch of water the *Alexandrina Rose* had steamed over half a dozen times in the twelve months prior to the start of hostilities.

'This is the first time I have had to perform this sad task, Private, and you must forgive me if I am not as skilled as perhaps I should be. I can think of no way of telling you except truthfully and at once. Your husband's ship has been torpedoed and . . . I am sorry, but Captain O'Shaughnessy is . . . missing. It seems there were no survivors, or at least none have been picked up.'

Maris could think of nothing to say. The CO was evidently much distressed by the news she had to impart, and that she had to impart it, and Maris was sorry for her. It must be an awful job to tell someone, another woman, that the man she has loved for almost six years, the man who has been the centre of her world, *is* her world, no longer exists. That he has fallen off the edge of that world into whatever eternity men such as he go, and that she would never see him again.

That was what it meant. No survivors. *No survivors*. She remembered once, on one of the occasions when she and Callum had been – momentarily – in accord. They had walked the length of the Marine Parade, and over their heads was a sky full of screaming seagulls, floating on the wind before diving for the refuse which washed against the dock wall.

'Did you know they carry the souls of drowned seamen?' he had said abruptly, afraid she would laugh, ready to join in if she did, but liking the idea nevertheless.

'No, I didn't, and I think that's lovely, Callum,' she had answered, and he had squeezed her arm gratefully.

So was he carried, as the gulls were carried, drifting on the sea breeze above the dockland and the ships he loved, handsome and graceful, free and unconcerned with eternity, or was he buried in the black and heaving waters of the ocean which had killed him?

She felt no pain, though evidently the CO did and was expecting Maris to be the same, but all she felt was a great hollow nothing, a void, an empty distancing of herself from the sympathetic woman on the other side of the desk, from this room, from this camp and everyone in it, from this world and everyone in it, since none of them was Callum.

'I am going to give you compassionate leave, Private. You may go home to . . .' she looked hastily at the sheet of paper before her, '. . . to Liverpool. There may be news there . . . the shipping line . . . er . . . Hemingways, it says here. Perhaps you know someone there who may . . . will have something more to tell you . . .'

Yes, she did. She knew someone at Hemingways, after all she was one herself, though she did not say so.

'Will you be all right, Private?'

'Yes, ma'am, thank you.'

'Good girl, and I hope you . . . well . . . good luck.'

'Thank you, ma'am.'

Betty began to cry when she told her, clasping Maris

in a tight embrace, embarrassed by her own emotion, surprised at the lack of it in Maris.

'I'll drive you to the station.'

'What about . . . ?' those in authority, she had been about to say, since Betty had no pass to get out of the camp, but her friend bundled her out of the hut and into a small staff car she had just serviced. The pass the CO had given Maris got them through the gate and even a rough 'good luck, gal' from the sentry who looked at it. It seemed the news of Private O'Shaughnessy's loss had reached even his ears.

It took her seventeen hours to reach Liverpool, in trains which were packed to overflowing with soldiers and sailors and airmen moving from one part of the country to another. They stood in corridors or lolled on their own kitbags, trying to sleep, to play cards; some singing, one playing a mouth-organ. She got a seat and slept fitfully, waking to pictures of steam-filled stations, dimly lit; porters shouting; women sobbing into handkerchiefs as trains steamed out; women sobbing into khaki or blue shoulders as men poured from open train doorways; women laughing in joy, kissing, being kissed in the constant flow of meetings and partings.

She telephoned Rose from Lime Street Station and when Rose came, three-quarters of an hour later, in the old Morris which had once belonged to Elizabeth Woodall and which was hardly ever taken out of the garage since petrol rationing, she was still standing just outside the telephone box, dazed, filthy, not awfully sure who she was or where she was, willing to be put wherever Rosie chose to put her.

'Darling . . . oh darling . . .' Rose's wet cheek was pressed to hers and Rose's strong arms lifted her up and held her tight, almost carrying her across the fore-court of the station, past the jostling, cheerful, milling crowds on the pavement and into the car. She talked all the way back to Lacy's house.

'You must not believe he is dead, Maris. *You must not!* I have spoken to Albert Johnson at Hemingways, you know, and he has spoken on the telephone to the captain of the corvette who was in charge of the convoy. He's in New York with . . . with the rest and will be back in this country . . . well, he is not allowed to tell us his movements, naturally, but when he comes home he will be able to give us more details of what happened. He saw Callum's ship go down, he told Mr Johnson, but he also saw two life-rafts with men clinging to them, and possibly another ship picked them up. He had not spoken to every ship's captain, he said, not yet, but . . .'

'They are not allowed to turn back for survivors.'

They were the first words she had spoken since she had told Betty that Callum was missing. Had she drunk anything? She wondered, idly, a cup of railway tea, perhaps, or had anything to eat? She didn't know, she didn't remember, but her voice came out of her mouth like the sound of rusty, unoiled hinges on a gate, which grated on her own nerves, and out of the corner of her eye she saw Rosie's hand clench tightly on the wheel.

'Callum told me that,' she continued. 'If the action was over they *might* go back to search but . . .'

There it was again. The need to feel sorry for Rosie who was so visibly upset, as she had for the CO. Just as though she felt guilty at giving them cause for concern.

'Perhaps the attack *was* over. The captain didn't say, or at least Mr Johnson didn't say he had mentioned it.'

'Perhaps.' She was silent again, falling into the great

booming hollowness of her own devastation which, in Rosie's anguished presence, was beginning to come to life, to hurt badly, just as hands or feet which have been frozen, numb, painless will hurt as warmth reaches them. Rosie was warm. She loved Rosie and she knew Rosie loved her, but really, it had been better when she had been alone, for despite the thousands on the trains she *had* been alone. It had been easier to bear when it was not spoken about. Words made it real and she didn't want it to be real. A nightmare, perhaps, from which she would soon awaken. She had made a mistake, running at once to what she had thought would be comfort, support, shelter from the gnawing uncertainty, the dread and horror, the tearing agony which she knew would come.

'You mustn't stop believing he will come back to you, Maris. Don't give up hope. None of us must give up hope. Alex is . . . going out on patrol now . . . like all the others, like Callum. He is in . . . well . . . I worry about him and . . . but I can only bear it if I tell myself *he will come back to me*. You must do the same.'

She was to wonder later why the thought of death coming to the man who did not in the least care for her, who had never cared about her, had not even loved her on their wedding day, should lay waste her heart in such a pitiless manner. It was an enigma so complex it would never be answered. It just *was*. She loved Callum O'Shaughnessy. He did not love her.

So what? her heart demanded to know of her logical mind. That did not mean that Maris O'Shaughnessy should not hurt, grieve, be destroyed by the death of the man she loved. The heart cannot reason. It feels, it mourns. Should she never see him again, the essence of her love for him would overwhelm her for the rest of her days. She would see for ever, wherever she went, the whimsical blue-green eyes of Callum O'Shaughnessy smiling at her, or at something only he seemed to know about. See the tanned smoothness of his face, the arrogant curl of his strong mouth which had explored every curve and hollow of her own body, memories which would render her lonely and empty for all the days to come. He had brought something into her life, delight as well as pain, a lovely rapture as well as desolation, a heart which ached, excitement in an equal measure to despair. A complex man, a strong man, a man of reality and sensitivity, and her life would be hollow without him.

She had thought it could not be worse. She was wrong. Ellen O'Shaughnessy, surrounded as always by the loving support of her family, was simply fading away before their eyes. Gone was the effervescent humour and good will, the volubility with which she had filled her own and her children's lives, inexhaustible and endearing. Gone was her endless belief that they could not manage their lives, their children, their very existence, without her behind them, and what was left was silent, gagged, dry.

'Mother,' Maris said for the first time, laying her head in the old lady's lap, and also for the first time, beginning to weep.

'Maris . . . child . . . what . . . ?' Ellen put a hesitant, confused hand on the tumbled mass of pale silver hair of the woman her son had married, and suddenly it was as though her daughter-in-law's grief had brought back to life something which had died in her when they told her she had lost another son. Three out of six living sons, and how could any mother be expected to bear that, but here was the silly, giddy little thing he had married, weeping and flinging herself about when she, Ellen, was so calm.

'Wisht darlin', sure an' you mustn't take on so. You'll have the poor lad consigned to the deep and him only gone these four days. Now aren't my lads the strongest in Liverpool, isn't that so . . . ?' looking about her for confirmation, and the company began to brighten and nod their heads, '. . . and not only that, the spalpeens, but the most stubborn, most self-willed Irishmen this side of the Channel.' She began to warm to the theme, her daughter-in-law's hopelessness kindling hope in her. 'Holy Mother of God, would that boy of mine give up if he had the smallest spark of life in him, would he? Our Lady forgive me.' She crossed herself humbly and the others did the same. 'Sure an' wasn't I committing the gravest sin of them all? The sin of despair, an' didn't it take this child's tears to show me how wicked I was? Get up, darlin', an' give me a kiss an' dry your eyes, for I'll not have it. Jesus, we've given him up an' wrong it was of us, but I'll tell you this. I'll weep for no more of my sons, nor grandsons, for surely the Holy Mother and her Son will bless and keep them safe. Now then, come to the fire, pet. Matty, wet the tea, for Maris here'll be wantin' a warm drink, so she will. An' will you look at her in her grand uniform? Isn't she the fine one . . . ?'

Private Maris O'Shaughnessy had been back in camp for two days when she was again summoned to the CO's office. The CO was smiling this time, the same woman who had a week ago told her that her husband was missing. He had been picked up, she told Maris, by the last ship in the convoy, a coastal tramp which surely should not even have made the perilous Atlantic crossing, and which, through engine trouble, had lagged far behind the others.

She was sure Private O'Shaughnessy would be delighted, as she was, though of course it was tragic that only two out of the ship's company had survived. Captain O'Shaughnessy and a galley-boy. They were not yet back in Liverpool, but when the Captain returned to port she was sure she could arrange for Private O'Shaughnessy to have a couple of days' leave.

'Thank you, ma'am, but that won't be necessary.'

'Not necessary, Private? I don't understand.'

'Thank you, ma'am, for your kindness, but that . . . I don't need leave.'

A cold fish, the Commanding Officer thought when Private O'Shaughnessy had smartly saluted and left her office, though she could have sworn when the private had been told that her husband was missing last week, she had been totally devastated. Now it appeared his return from the dead, so to speak, had left her completely unmoved.

Well, as they said up north where she came from, 'there's nowt' so queer as folk.'

No one heard Private O'Shaughnessy weep that night, only Private Thompson.

22

The black-out was, without a doubt, the worst thing about the war so far, those who suffered it agreed. The impertinence of the air-raid wardens and policemen if you left the faintest chink of light showing was absolutely unbelievable, and the accidents which occurred in the dark were appalling. Everyone knew someone who had fallen into the canal, tumbled headlong down steps, plunged off the pavement or fallen under a bicycle with no lights, and if the bloody black-out didn't end soon they would all go mad with it.

Hand torches were allowed, dimmed to such an extent one could hardly see with them, and most people who had no need to go outside their own homes after dark, didn't. Social motoring had finished when petrol rationing began three weeks after the war started, and Michael said he might as well close his garage for the duration since nobody would be buying a motor car, even if petrol was available to run it, which it wasn't.

He had been offered a post at a local engineering works which, it was rumoured, was about to begin the manufacture of war weapons. Tanks, he had heard, but then it could be anything to do with the fight they were about to have on their hands. With his engineering skills and experience, he was a man worth having, the chap who had come to see him had said, and it was also a way of doing his bit for the war effort. The factory was on the outskirts of Liverpool and, laughing as he said it, was within a bicycle ride of his home. Him on a bicycle again, could you believe it, after all these years, remembering the mad dash he had made every other Monday morning from his home in Edge Lane to his job in the stables at Woodall Park. A bit of a lad he had been then, and now he was a grey-haired old man he said, the look he bestowed on his serene wife belying the words.

So, they all stayed at home, those whom the black-out defeated, and listened to Lord Haw-Haw, whose broadcasts were meant to undermine the British people but who made them laugh instead, saying he was as comical as Tommy Handley and ITMA. *It's that man again* was one of the most popular programmes on the wireless, with his 'Minister of Aggravation' and his assistant 'twerps', and it did you the world of good to listen to him.

The winter had been fierce, January and February proving the coldest for forty-five years. The Thames froze hard for eight miles of its length, and main line express trains were over a day late. Huge falls of snow cut off villages and towns, but when spring came it was as though the fickle gods had decided to give those it toyed with a treat. There was a particular brilliance about it: the exquisite beauty of warm blue skies and warm golden sunshine, and postmen whistled as they delivered letters from the 'boys'. 'We'll meet again' was by far and away the favourite.

Easter came at the end of March. Trippers flocked, as usual, to the seaside, and had it not been for the empty chairs at the tables no one would have known there was a war on.

The weather continued glorious, and as Private O'Shaughnessy remarked to Private Thompson as they leaned on the rail of the ship that was taking them across the Channel to France, they might have been setting off for a weekend in Paris, their mood was so cheerfully optimistic.

On Easter Monday, as she worked in her vegetable garden admiring the splendid growth of her early potatoes, the 'new' potatoes so eagerly awaited by those who had eaten nothing but the *old* ones all winter, Rosie Woodall was surprised when a bright red sports car drew up with a snarling roar outside her garden gate.

She lived a quiet life with her babies. The shortage of petrol made it difficult to get to her grandmother's, or to visit her Aunt Elizabeth. Besides, most of her time was spent working with the girls from the Women's Land Army, who had arrived at Beechwood Hall in February to turn the grassland of the park into one huge allotment where the crops to feed the nation would be cultivated; to put to the plough land which had, for centuries, known nothing but the quiet and delicate presence of the deer. Livestock on the home farm was to be drastically reduced since the Ministry of Food pointed out that one acre of arable crops fed more human beings than one acre of grassland, and one acre of wheat saved as much shipping space as seven acres of the best grass in England. DIG FOR VICTORY was plastered over every spare bit of wall, meaning not only on the farms but in gardens and allotments. The Ministry of Agriculture was profligate with information to farmers, amongst whom Rosie was beginning to count herself, on the best methods of stock breeding and tillage, exhorting her to 'manure well', plant early and look after her machines. Her land – though it was of course Christian's land – was rich with stored-up fertility and would provide record yields of wheat and oats to put food on the nation's table.

She had two land girls to help her, and over at Woodall where Mr Rogers was still in charge with a farm labourer brought out of retirement to advise him, there were five. The two at Beechwood 'lived in' with Clare and Teddy Osborne, overawed with the splendour of their 'billet', and they and Rose worked from dawn to dusk, seven days a week, ploughing and planting, hoeing and weeding, working with machinery she at least had never even known existed. She mended hedges and chopped wood and milked cows. Wherever there was a need, she provided it, and also found time somehow to do all the accounts, fill in the forms and make telephone calls, which must be done to accommodate the Ministry of Agriculture.

She would take the babies with her, one at each end of the smart pram Elizabeth had bought her when Harry was born – and a sorry sight it was becoming in the often mucky conditions in which she laboured – or strapped into the small dog cart which Teddy Osborne had once used to get about the estate, tethering the pony and putting the trap beneath one of the huge oak trees which grew in their hundreds and which seriously inconvenienced the progress of the tractor. She thanked the fates which had sent it to them for the glorious weather, wondering how she would have managed if she had been unable to take her children about with her.

'Heavens, Rosie, you have only to say the word and Michael will get the car out and bring me over to Lacy's house to keep an eye on Harry and Ellie for you. He has a can or two of petrol,' when she mentioned her anxiety to her Aunt Elizabeth. 'You'll be weaning Ellie soon, won't you? Well then, when that happens I shall be only too glad to do it for you. Call it my bit to help win the war.'

So, if the weather should turn against her in the vital months to come when she must get out into the fields with Muriel and Lou, the land girls, her mind could rest easy knowing that the calm and loving presence of Elizabeth O'Shaughnessy, whose own boy was the same age as hers, would guard her son and daughter.

Potatoes, carrots, cabbages, onions, were but a few of the vegetables which filled the broad acreage of Beechwood Hall where once there had been flower beds and rose gardens and parkland, and later there would be oceans of golden rippling wheat and corn and hay. A small dairy herd was kept at what used to be the home farm, with help from the government, and a dairyman was employed, a man in his late forties who was too old to fight. All over England, golf courses and bowling greens, swamps and marshland, bracken land and even the land among scrub willow and reeds, were ploughed and cleared in order to grow more food.

Rosie did not recognise the smartly uniformed RAF officer who got slowly out of the sports car. For an excruciating moment of delight her heart had turned over at the sight of him, though Alex's car was blue, then it dropped sickeningly. Were they sending young men such as this to break the news that one of their own had 'bought it', as the rich idiom of the RAF would have it? No pilot ever crashed a plane, he 'pranged' it. If things did not go as they should, they had 'gone for a Burton', in which case the pilot was never put out or fed up, he was 'browned off' or 'cheesed off'; and if his performance of his duties was not quick enough to suit, he was told to 'take his finger out'. All very amusing, or so Alex thought, though Rosie was not awfully sure she would care to tell his mother that her son had 'bought it'.

The officer removed his cap and the sun burnished his pale blond hair to newly minted gold. He grinned in a familiar and amiable way which suddenly, since she had never noticed it before, reminded her of Alex, and again her heart was moved. She was glad of the hoe on which she had been leaning, for it served to support her as Pilot Officer Sir Charles Woodall walked towards the gate which led into the side garden.

'Rosie,' he said softly, his brown eyes lighting to a tawny gold, just like Maris's she had time to think; then he was inside the gate, letting it bang to behind him, holding out his arms, still grinning, his teeth incredibly white against the sun-bronzed smoothness of his face.

'Have you no welcome for your brother-in-law then?' he asked wryly. 'After all this time can you not spare him a hug?'

She felt her body relax, the muscles in it dissolving in pleasure and relief. She had not seen him since last summer when he had called briefly on Teddy Osborne. There were certain documents which, as a director on the board of the Hemingway and Osborne business concerns, he must discuss with his uncle, who was also involved, and which needed signatures from them both.

It had been an awkward moment for Rose was very well aware what it was that had caused the final rift between Alex and Charlie, as did Alex and Charlie, though she was not prepared to take all the blame. Alex loved her. Charlie had *wanted* her, and the two emotions were very different. The brothers had fallen out over it, if such a childish expression could be used, and circumstances, so many of them happening together, had made a reconciliation impossible. The death of Sir Harry, which gave Woodall to Charlie. The disappearance of her own brother, which had allowed Alex to take over the running of Beechwood. Their mother's marriage to Michael, for which Charlie could neither forgive Elizabeth for *doing* it, nor Alex for *accepting* it. Charlie had led his own life, infringing not even in the most casual way on theirs since their marriage. There had been talk of wild parties at Woodall and the presence of females who were not *ladies* and then, when the humour took him, Charlie had left the management of the estate to his mother, or his uncle, or indeed anyone who cared to have a shot at it whilst he roared off in his scarlet sports car to the next diversion, which happened to be a war. He was a fighter pilot, as Alex was, and was that a coincidence or was it once again the Woodall boys' everlasting compulsion to get one over on the other?

He put his arms about her, enfolding her rather more warmly than she would have liked against the smooth blue cloth of his jacket, pressing himself against her in an enormous embrace. She was almost as tall as he and when she turned her head to smile into his face since he *was* her brother-in-law, he pressed his lips swiftly against hers, a butterfly kiss which he would have her believe was light and meaningless but which, nevertheless, was not.

She stepped back abruptly, almost tripping over the hoe which she had dropped, and he took her hand to steady her, keeping a tight hold on it whilst he studied her from head to toe.

'Well Rosie, my sweet, you look absolutely glorious, but then you always did, and *very* fetching in those overalls.' He winked and she was suddenly conscious of how tight they were. They had been meant for a slimmer Rosie, but somehow, after the birth of Ellie, she had not returned to the weight she had once been. Her breasts were fuller and so were her hips, and though her waist was quite neat, due no doubt to the bending and stretching she did in her work about the estate, she looked the very personification of womanhood, of motherhood. Her dark slipping hair was bundled carelessly into a loose knot at the nape of her neck, tied with bright red ribbons, and shining strands fell about her sun-browned forehead and neck. The shirt she wore was open at the throat, and the deep and inviting valley between her breasts was very evident and she wished with all her heart that she had time to button it up. She didn't know why, really. This was Charlie, her husband's brother who offered no threat to her, and yet she felt uncomfortable as though a stranger had invaded the peaceful stretch of her sunlit garden.

The baby crowed in the pram, and from the play-pen which Michael had made for her, as he had for his own son, and which was so useful when she worked in the garden, Harry Woodall shouted his displeasure at being ignored by his mother and the person who had joined her. He rattled the wooden side of the pen vigorously, gratified by the noise it made to add to the sound of his own voice, then laughed engagingly, showing off the splendour of his new teeth. He was fourteen months old, and when he was let out of the pen, stumbled about on sturdy brown legs, destroying everything in his path; his father's pride and joy, his mother's darling, as dark as she was and as rebellious as Alex, but sweet-natured and merry. His eyes were the same colour as Rose's, a lovely deep and transparent green.

'Well, what have we here, then?' Charlie murmured,

turning in the direction of the boy, but though he took a step or two towards the pen, peering in at the child in that rather reluctant way young bachelors have with infants, he made no attempt to touch his brother's son.

'This is Harry . . .' Rose began, ready to lift her son out of the pen, but Charlie had turned away, his face set in lines of grim and tight disapproval.

'Yes, I had heard you called him after my father.'

'Alex's father, too,' she added quickly.

'Really?'

'*Really!* What does that mean? Surely Alex can name his son for his father?'

'Indeed he can, but I had hoped to call *my* boy Harry.'

'And have you a son, Charlie?'

'You know I have not.'

'I know nothing of the sort. I have not seen you for . . .'

He began to laugh then, disconcerting her all over again, lounging away from her in that arrogant way she remembered, towards the old cane garden seat which was placed in the shade of the trees and where he sat down.

'Rosie, my darling, don't let's quarrel in our first five minutes. Of course you may call your son whatever you fancy. Now come and sit over here with me and tell me all the news of the county. I have been . . . well, as they say, somewhere in England . . . away from home at any rate, for six months, and surely something exciting has happened in that time. What about Freddie? Freddie Winters? Have you heard from him, or about him? Where has he got to . . . ?'

Bewilderment fell about her like an invisible cloak, but she sat down hesitantly beside him. Freddie

Winters? Why should *she* know anything about Freddie Winters? He had been Charlie and Maris's friend, not hers nor Alex's.

'I don't know . . .'

'Well, what about Angela and Richard? Has he marched off to defend his king and country yet, or more to the point, has Angela *allowed* it? And Maris? Is she still tied to that sailor she took up with . . . ?'

'Look, Charlie, I know nothing of those people you mentioned, and as for Maris, surely you know she is in the ATS? Her husband was torpedoed and . . .'

'Really, but d'you mean to tell me you have no gossip . . . no scandal . . .'

'Charlie, I'm far too busy with my children and the land to have . . .'

'The land?'

'Yes, didn't you know that Beechwood has virtually been turned into a farm, the park ploughed under and planted? Surely you have heard from Mr Rogers about Woodall, where they have done the same?'

'Aah yes . . .' languidly lighting a cigarette and blowing smoke rings into the air above his head, '. . . there was something I had to sign. What a devil of a mess it all is, and how we shall get it back to what it was before the war I cannot imagine. Still, one can only try. Now tell me about . . .'

'Charlie, don't ask me any more questions about the local "gentry" since the answers would only bore you. I lead a very dull life . . .'

'Do you indeed, then we shall have to see if we can't change that, little Rosie.'

'. . . and I have no time to socialise . . .' just as though he had not spoken. 'I see your mother and Michael and my grandmother, and of course, Clare and

Teddy, but no one else.' She smiled, her face sweet and soft, her eyes luminous. 'Isn't your mother marvellous with that lovely child? At her age to be so . . .'

'I have not seen her, or her child, and I have no intention of doing so.' His face was closed, his jaw set in a line of cold authority, as though he was a man speaking to a servant who had questioned an order.

'Charlie, you can't mean . . . ?'

'Oh, indeed I can, Rose. She is nothing to me since she dishonoured my father's memory by marrying that bog Irish boyo from the stews of Liverpool. To choose to . . . ally herself with a man who would not have been fit to clean my father's boots is reprehensible, and it makes me sick to think of her . . . well, I *don't* think of her, nor will I see her. I am aware that you are related to him . . . and if I have offended you I apologise, but if you don't mind that is the end of it and we shall not speak of it again. Now, Rosie . . .' He grinned good-humouredly as though the last vituperative words had been nothing more than a comment on the weather, '. . . suppose you and I put on our glad rags and go and see what the city can provide in the way of entertainment. You must have some garment other than that *thing* you are wearing, so go and put it on and . . .'

'Charlie, it may have escaped your notice but I have two children now and . . .'

'*Two!* Really!' He looked about him in amazement.

'Yes, Charlie. I have a daughter in that pram and . . .'

'You don't say.' His brown eyes glowed with good humour and his mouth curved into a mischievous, beguiling smile, looking so like Alex's she could not help but smile back.

417

'I *do* say, and I cannot just take off . . .'

'Can you not leave them with Nanny?'

'No Nanny.'

'*No Nanny?* Then you must have some female lurking in the scullery who can look after them whilst you and I go and dance the night away to the tune of "Only make believe", or how about "Cheek to cheek"? Quite appropriate, Rosie dear, you and I cheek to cheek at the Adelphi. The dear old Adelphi. It seems years since I took a turn about the dance floor there. Come on, Rosie, put on your best frock and I'll ring up and see if I can reserve a table. I'm sure if I tell them who I am they will find a corner for us.'

He sprang up, boyish and charming, the old Charlie she remembered from years ago, laughing and persuasive, holding out his hands to her, ready for a bit of 'fun' if she was.

'No, Charlie, really. I couldn't leave them with Polly, the girl who works for me. She goes home at six. The only person I would trust them with is your . . .' she had been about to say 'your mother' but she changed it quickly, '. . . well, there is no one, really. They are far too young.'

He changed at once to another tack.

'Never mind, my pet . . .' when had she become his *pet*? '. . . we shall dine at home. We will be *domesticated*. I'm not much of a cook but while you put the children to bed, or whatever it is one does with them at night, I will cook us a meal. I have a couple of decent bottles of wine in the car . . . oh, and Rosie, it would be no trouble to you if I stayed with you for a couple of nights, would it? Only those damned land girls are living in at Woodall . . . no, I haven't been, but old whatsisname told me about them in one of the tedious

418

reports he will insist on sending to me and . . . well, to be honest, I don't think I could stand the dear old place with strangers in it. Wilson has been pensioned off, and can you imagine Woodall without Wilson in it because I can't, so I would be eternally grateful if you could manage a bed, or even the drawing-room sofa for a night or two.'

How could she refuse, and *why* should she? He was her husband's brother, cordial and well-mannered, agreeable even, offering her no threat; and though she deplored the way he had treated his mother she supposed it was understandable that it should hurt him to see some other man take the place of the father he had loved and deeply admired. She had not cared awfully for the casual, almost contemptuous way in which he had regarded her baby son and daughter, Alex's children, which was perhaps the reason for her unease, but how could she refuse him her hospitality? What excuse could she give? That she felt . . . uneasy, wary in his company? That she disliked his brittle chatter, his flippant manner, the impudent way in which he had thrust himself into her garden, her life, when he had made it quite plain that he wanted nothing to do with the people she loved? How could he expect her to be exactly as once they had been, in their childhood and young adulthood, after what had gone between him and his brother, her husband? And yet apparently he did. Despite the fact that they had barely exchanged a word in three years, he was treating this encounter as though it was nothing out of the ordinary. And could she turn her back on the chance to bring together, as perhaps it might, her husband and her brother-in-law? This might be a turning point, an opportunity to mend the breach, to bring back together the shattered pieces of what had

419

once been a close and affectionate family relationship. A healing, not only between brother and brother, but mother and son. She knew her Aunt Elizabeth grieved deeply the disunity which existed between herself and her son and between Alex and Charlie. If she, Rose, could talk to Charlie, make him see, in a diplomatic way, of course, what pain he was causing his mother, might he not make the effort, if not to be a part of her life, at least to mend the awful rift with a kind word, a letter now and again. In these days of uncertainty and danger, could he refuse to . . . ?

'What d'you say, Rosie?' He interrupted her thoughts boyishly. 'Surely you can put me up for a night or two, old girl? I shan't be in the way, honestly. I might even give you a hand with this farming you seem to have taken to so splendidly. Is there a hack at Beechwood? A canter through Old Wood or across the grouse moor would be most welcome. We could take a picnic.'

'Charlie, Charlie . . .' She had begun to laugh now, for his charming and absolute certainty that he was welcome, that a couple of nights' bed and board was not too much to ask for, and that the pair of them could relive some of the pastimes of their youth, was quite disarming. '. . . You keep forgetting that I have two children to care for, a job to do which I cannot drop just like that, and besides, there are no horses at Beechwood or Woodall. We had to let them go. There was no one to look after them . . .'

'Not Ruby?'

'Yes, even Ruby. We have a couple of farm horses but that's all.'

'Well, it can't be helped. We can find something else just as congenial to occupy our time. Now then, show

420

me to my quarters and I'll get out of this uniform, and a bath would be lovely.'

'Well, I'm not awfully sure there will be enough hot water after I've bathed the children and done their nappies and . . .'

'Please, Rosie, spare me the details, and I'm sure I can manage on whatever water there is.'

She was swept along on the enthusiastic tide of his belief that what he asked was not at all unreasonable; and the tiny, prickling seeds of warning, the insidious shiver of doubt which invaded her female senses were pushed firmly to the back of her mind. She had not really named them as doubts, or fears, since to bring whatever it was out into the open, to examine them in any detail, was absurd, giving credence to them, making them *real*.

'I'll show you where to sleep then, Charlie, and then I must see to the children. You won't mind if I leave you for an hour or so, will you?' She had Ellie to feed, which now must be done in the privacy of her bedroom instead of the small sitting room-cum-nursery where she normally attended to her children. The pen would have to be carried upstairs, since she could not leave Harry on his own whilst she nursed the baby. And then there was the tub in which she bathed them both . . . Lord, it was going to be very awkward since Charlie was strolling up the stairs ahead of her, his bag still in the car, she presumed, from where he was anticipating some servant would bring it up to him. Was he expecting to be waited on whilst he was her guest? His bag unpacked, perhaps, his bath drawn, his uniform pressed, his bed turned down? She tried to imagine his reaction to the rather bovine presence of Polly, a willing and conscientious worker when told exactly what she was to do, but, as they said in Liverpool, only elevenpence-halfpenny in the shilling, and therefore not suitable for the armed services or even factory work.

God help her, she wished he'd chosen someone else to impose on, since she really did not have the time nor the inclination to entertain him, her mind whispered, as he so obviously intended, for the next couple of days.

He did nothing to alarm her. In fact, he was the perfect house guest, helping with the domestic chores – apart from those which involved the children – laying the table for their evening meal, preparing the vegetables as she instructed him, peeling the potatoes and stretching out her tiny meat ration to go into the beef casserole they were to have; even helping her with the dishes, over which there was great hilarity since he insisted on wearing Polly's apron and rubber gloves whilst drinking a great deal of wine at the same time. He picked fruit which, she apologised, was all she had for dessert, with some cheese; poured the wine; even lit candles on the dinner table, seating her at it with all the courtesy, the gallantry, even, of the English, public-school educated gentleman that he was.

He made her laugh with his witty and amusing stories of what they got up to in the mess, awed her with the splendour of the aircraft he flew, a 'Supermarine Spitfire' with a speed of 362 miles per hour and a Browning machine gun mounted in the guns, and the simply splendid chaps he flew with, reassuring her on how safe it was and how short the war would be. He was wickedly funny, and gravely attentive as long as she didn't talk about her children, when he became restive. He was quite fascinating in his grasp of international affairs; a charming companion in fact.

She knew she looked her best. She had put on a long loose dress she had worn in both her pregnancies. It floated about her in a cloud of the palest green, with satin ribbons tied beneath her breast and edging the low neckline. She had brushed her dark hair until it gleamed, twisting it into an enormous knot at the back of her head and tying pale green satin ribbons in it, and on her bare feet she wore silver sandals, the whole effect somewhat grecian in style. The wine, and yes, she admitted it, the excitement of male company after nothing but women and children for weeks on end, had touched flags of rose to her golden skin at the cheekbones, and her great sea-green eyes were brilliant. She knew she was sparkling, a scintillating companion, pleasing; and she was enjoying it. Enjoying the effect it had on Charlie. She had been wife and mother for so long now. That was who she was. That was her identity. Rose, Rosie, was buried beneath the enormous weight of the domesticity her life consisted of, the work she did, day in and day out with such mundane things as manure and seeds, tractors and hedge-cutters, invoices, reports, forms, and all the trivia with which her life was bogged down. She wouldn't change it, not one bit of it, not for anything in the world, but it really was lovely to be someone else for a short time. It quite took her out of herself, made her forget fertilisers and seed catalogues and the endless red tape she was forced to deal with each week. Charlie really made her feel . . . giddy, feminine, female!

When he took her in his arms in the kitchen it was as though it was Alex. Why was it the way they smiled had suddenly become so . . . so alike? The way their mouths were, like their mother's, well-shaped and . . . and when he kissed her . . . no butterfly thing this time

423

. . . when he kissed her it was firm, warm, his lips parting hers . . . harder, more assertive, and his hands were at the ribbons of her dress, so delicate . . . not rushing . . . Oh Alex . . . Alex, I love you so much and my body needs yours . . . aches with need.

His hands were inside the bodice of her dress, one to each breast, smoothing the roundness, pinching the hardness of her nipples . . . Dear God . . . Alex . . . please . . .

She wrenched herself away, stepped back and slapped his face with every ounce of her strength, outraged, affronted, deeply shocked, with him and with herself, and at the same time she wanted to laugh. So that was how it felt, her giddy mind kept repeating. She had seen it happen so often at the cinema. Offended heroine hits offensive hero, who falls to his knees in remorse, begging for forgiveness, but Charlie did no such thing, in fact he was smiling.

'God, Rosie, you're a fine woman, and beautiful too, and your husband is a damn lucky chap. So, no hard feelings, old girl. I got a bit carried away. It was . . . fun, though. Now then, if we've finished here, I'll toddle off to bed. I must go over to the Winters place in the morning, and then I might call on Angela and see where Dickie has got to. Oh, and thanks for a wonderful evening. That was a jolly good casserole, if I say it myself. I might even go in for catering after the war.'

Well, that took the wind out of my sails all right, she thought dazedly, as he ran whistling up the stairs to his room, and the next morning when he thanked her again profusely, saying he thought he might 'push off' today, she was speechless.

'It's been wizard, Rosie, really it has. Remember me

to Uncle Teddy, won't you, and . . .' winking, '. . . we must do it again on my next leave. Who knows, it might be even . . . more delightful.'

Charlie smiled round the cigarette he held clenched between his strong white teeth and which he had just lit, as he stopped for a moment at the gates of Beechwood. What a marvellous idea it had been. What a bloody marvellous idea, and by God, he'd nearly pulled it off. She'd been willing. He had felt it in the yielding of her body, in the suppleness of her bones which had begun to melt in that certain way women had when they were ready, when they *wanted* what it was he was telling them they could get from him. Her breasts had positively *jumped* into his hands, pushing against his palms, and if he hadn't gone a tiny bit too fast for her he would have had her on the floor, across the kitchen table, or indeed in any place he could have laid her. Of course she had drawn back, which he had expected the first time, a decent girl like Rosie, but she was *starving* for it, you could tell that just by looking into her eyes, and given a bit of patience – and leave – he, and she, would get what they both wanted.

His brother's wife. Jesus, what a way to make that bastard pay . . . *his brother's wife*. Play your cards right, Charlie, old man . . .

He threw the cigarette end out of the car and began to whistle as he roared off in the direction of Liverpool.

23

Maris and Betty had been in France no more than five weeks when, on May 10th, the German Luftwaffe raided airfields and towns in Holland, Belgium and Northern France. Within five days the Netherlands was beaten and Belgium was crumbling.

The two girls and the rest of their unit had been posted to the British Expeditionary Headquarters at Lille, and were to drive their ambulances whenever and wherever they were needed and wherever they were told to go.

'It's pretty bloody boring,' they were told by those who had been there since January. 'In fact, only the Lord and of course those mighty ones who are so far above us they must be floating with the barrage balloons, know why you've been sent over, since there's nothing to do. It probably means that something is going to happen, or they think there is, and about time too. All we do is wash up and clean the hut and help with the sewing. Honestly, we could have stayed at home with our mothers and done that. Mind you, if you want some fun there's plenty to be had in Lille. Officers, NCOs, take your pick. You could dine out every night of the week, if you'd a mind to. And then there's Paris. Some lucky so-and-so's, drivers just like you and me, have been sent there. Don't ask me why. Living the life of Riley, so they say, and not in a bloody hut like this one, either.'

It turned out to be true. There was no driving to do,

and Maris boasted that she could do the best 'darns' in the whole British Army, so neat and even were they, and she challenged anyone who was lucky enough to wear the socks she had darned to find the darn! She swept floors and scrubbed latrines and even cleaned windows, things she had never done when she had been a housewife. She played cards and wrote letters, to her mother, to her mother-in-law and to Rosie. She went to parties in the mess and learned to sing more soldiers' songs.

'First there came the General's wife . . .' she would warble, as she cleaned and serviced the ambulance she had not yet driven, at least in the function which was its purpose.

'I touched her on the knee and she said you're rather free,' she piped, whilst she showered in the somewhat primitive ablution block, progressing quite casually to parts of the female anatomy, ending up with,

> And when the baby came
> the bastard had no name.

But it all changed dramatically at daybreak on May 10th. They were out on what Betty facetiously called 'manoeuvres', a small convoy of ambulances following a gun battery of the Royal Artillery which was on the move, as it seemed most of the men of the British Expeditionary Force were. The weather was absolutely glorious. Day after day of warm sunshine, and the cab of the ambulance was stifling. Maris would have liked to discard her battle-blouse and drive in her shirt-sleeves, but she knew she'd be for it if she was caught 'out of uniform'.

The convoy slowed down and then stopped

altogether, and Maris sighed. It looked as though it was going to be another long and boring day, bouncing along in the hot sun. Still, what else had she to do? She sometimes felt that she was in limbo, in transition from one life to the next, the life Maris O'Shaughnessy had known, and possibly might know again; and in between Private O'Shaughnessy passed the time fiddling about with her head under the bonnet of this vehicle and that, waiting . . . waiting, and for what? For the war to end, and then what would she do when she returned to Liverpool?

She had heard from Ellen that Callum was safe and well, if a bit thinner, after his ordeal on the life-raft. Of course, to his mother, one of the worst things about the whole tragedy, all those poor boys dying in the waters of the Atlantic, was her son's lack of sustenance for two whole days. Nothing to eat, God love him, him and the boy whose life he had saved and for which he was to receive some sort of medal. Frost-bite they both had, and they had thought Callum might lose two toes, but he was off again on another merchantman of the Hemingway Line, one of those which were built to replace those lost, and were being turned out as fast as the biscuits Ellen herself made in the oven. The ship-yards of Liverpool and Birkenhead were working full steam ahead, and Callum's new ship was to be called by one of the names which were part of the tradition of the Hemingway Shipping Line. The SS *Bridget O'Malley*, though God alone knew where *that* name came from, though there was a rumour that Lacy Hemingway, or Lacy Osborne as she had become, had been connected with a woman of that name in the middle of the last century.

Much of Ellen's letter had been censored since she

cared nought for 'keeping mum', but Maris read between the lines, getting the gist of what the writer had to tell her.

Callum. She had lost him once, not that he had ever been hers to actually lose, but now he was again riding those dangerous lanes of shipping, backwards and forwards, in peril every hour of the night and day for weeks on end. At least those who flew the Spitfires and Hurricanes, like Alex and Charlie, though in the same appalling danger, had a respite from it when they returned to their airfields. Alex was in France now, in one of the Hurricane squadrons, attacking bridges and light ack-ack guns, sleeping in barns, he had told her when they met briefly, shaving in any handy stream, living a life of total confusion. He had been fired on by Heinkel IIIs, which were bombing shipping in the harbour at Le Havre, and was heavily shelled on many of the patrols he flew on, seeing men with whom he had forged a strong bond, going down in flames. He had changed, her brother Alex, as she knew she had changed, even in the short space of six months, and had Callum?

Again, as she did at so many moments in the dark of the night or even on a bright sunny morning such as this, she pictured him as she had seen him so many times. His wryly smiling face when she had said or done something which had unwillingly amused him, the sensuality of his mouth which she had recognised since she was familiar with sensuality herself in their moments of shared pleasure. The deep clefts at either side of it; the blue-green light of his narrowed eyes. Arrogant, strong, humorous. Callum. Did he ever think of her as she thought of him, or was he concerned only with his men, his ship, and his women?

At midday the convoy was still jammed on the country road, and she and Betty and several of the other drivers decided there was time for a 'brew' and a cigarette. It was quite pleasant sitting on the running-board of the ambulance in the sunshine. There were fields on both sides of the road, ploughed and ready for planting, their deep brown furrows running away from the ditch in pleasing symmetrical lines. Wild flowers grew, and she and Betty might have been on a picnic. The tea was hot, sweet and milky, just as she liked it, and the thick slab of the cheese sandwich Betty had produced was quite delicious. Sometimes Maris wondered what her mother would make of it if she could see her daughter, once a lover of foie gras, quail and caviar, eating 'doorsteps' made of French cheese, but somehow she didn't think Mrs Michael O'Shaughnessy would be greatly put out.

It was the soldier up ahead who brought the first stab of unease to the two girls. He was shouting something, and they got to their feet, straining to hear what he said. He was standing beside a truck, his hand shading his eyes as he stared up into the deep blue heaven of the skies. His attitude was one of tension, and others about him followed his gaze.

'What is it?' Betty asked nervously. She had been about to light another cigarette and it hung from her lower lip like a long tooth.

They heard it then, they both did. Everyone on the road did. The high-pitched intermittent sound of an engine, and over it the soldier's voice could be heard, hoarse with urgency. He was a sergeant, and those about him listened as he barked his orders; but the ambulance drivers, young women who had never known fear, real fear, never known what the seasoned

430

soldier knows, just stood there, mouths agape, frozen, faces uncomprehending.

'Get down . . . get off the bloody road . . . take cover . . .'

Above them, in the innocence of the French sky, the nine dots he had seen had begun to take shape, packed tightly together in the perfect arrow-head formation of attacking dive-bombers, growing bigger and bigger as they came towards the road. The first plane banked sharply, and then, in a straight and menacing line, dived at the column of trucks and ambulances, at the foot soldiers and the ambulance drivers, at women and children and old men, refugees who were the cause of the hold-up and who were fleeing the terror of what they had been told the German Army would do to them. At the handcarts and wheelbarrows and prams and bicycles, at the human column which became, as devastation struck, a seething mass of people and machines, all doing their best to get out of the way of the lethal gunfire. The first plane brought a deafening, high-pitched shriek with it as the wind tore through its structures, the scream of the engine, and then, with a noise which filled the universe to its vast extremities, all they could hear was the close and annihilating explosions of its mighty bombs.

She was in the ditch, and Betty was beside her, though God knows how they got there. Flashes turned the field about her into an illuminated nightmare, and showers of earth and grass, the pretty wild flowers she had admired only minutes before, and other, more dreadful things she did not care to examine, rained down on her. The next plane dived, and the next and the next. Women screamed, children sobbed or retreated into shocked and terrified silence, men

431

moaned in pain. The air was filled with the sound of death and human suffering. The dust rose in reeking heat, a pall of horror drifting up to the suddenly empty sky, the field of battle left to those who had been unlucky enough to be in the path of the enemy. There were broken toys and broken bodies and broken push-carts, and for several dreadful moments Maris lay with her face in the dirt, struggling to get up and look at it, to do her job, the one she had been trained for; but every instinct urged her to stay where she was, to lie still and quiet and safe until the 'bogeyman' had gone away.

She got up and so did Betty. They moved towards their ambulances and began, in the way they had been taught in the camp in England, to prepare for the wounded. The gunners helped them, lifting the bloody, the motionless, the screaming, the silent wounded in gentle arms and packing them swiftly into the ambulances. Old women and children, mothers, soldiers, those who had provided easy targets for the dive-bombing German aircraft.

A dead child, her face sweet and unmarked, in her mother's rocking arms. 'Don't wake her. Let her sleep,' the mother begged Maris, when Betty, who did not speak French, would have taken her from her mother's arms. An old man, still in his wheelchair, but dead. A young soldier, his left leg not only gone but vanished, spirited away it seemed, in a smoke-filled mystery.

'I must find my leg, Private,' he said firmly to Maris. 'I refuse to move without my leg.'

They could scarcely move for the litter, the smashed handcarts and bicycles and several burning trucks, though thankfully none of the ambulances had been hit, and all the while she could hear someone crying

432

over and over again, 'Oh, God . . . oh, sweet Jesus . . . Oh, God . . . Oh, God . . .'

It was herself, but she did not falter. When they finally got under way her hands were so wet with blood they slipped on the steering wheel – where were her gauntlets? – and the bottom of her shoes skidded off the accelerator, sticky with something she did not stop to investigate. Her senses were ready to slip away from her, but she held on to them tightly, for who else would drive her ambulance if not her?

A soldier with a piece of shrapnel in his arm was in the back with the rest of the wounded, doing his best to staunch the blood, his and theirs, and calm their pain and terror, and behind her Betty's vehicle was packed with men – and women – doing the same. Maris's mind dwelled on the horror of those they had left behind on the dusty, bloodsoaked road, those pathetic dead and wounded with their bewildered eyes turned up to the serene and empty skies; but nothing could be done for them now, not even a hole dug to put the dead in.

The road ahead was clogged with refugees heading towards Lille, as they were. There was a casualty clearing station there, and as they inched their way towards it, the British Army with their French counterparts moved on into the Low Countries to counter the German attack, and through those next days – and nights – Maris was at the wheel of her ambulance, sometimes for eighteen hours at a stretch, evacuating the wounded from the forward areas.

The Dutch Army had capitulated. The Germans had broken the French front near the ancient Fort of Sedan, pouring their troops, their armoured cars and tanks through the break, moving at a pace never before known in the history of warfare. The British Army was in full retreat before them.

Brussels fell, and the order came that they were to make their way to the coastal town of Dunkirk.

Maris had a dozen badly injured men in the ambulance, as did each vehicle in the company. Betty was directly behind her as they struggled to get through the thousands of refugees and the British soldiers who had been told to get to the seaport as best they could, all making for the ships which would get them across the Channel, and all the while above their heads were the constant air battles as their young airmen, themselves being decimated at a rate which was incalculable, were sent to cover the evacuation. Spitfires and Hurricanes encountering German bombers and Messerschmitts, doing their best not only to down the foe but to boost the morale of the retreating troops.

'Will we be long now, Miss?' a polite voice from behind her asked.

'Not long, soldier, but there are an awful lot of people going in the same direction as us.'

'Yes, Miss, but . . .'

'What is it? Are you in pain?'

'No, Miss, only . . . there's a lot of blood.'

She was so tired she could barely think. For the past two weeks now she had shuttled wounded men here and there, sleeping like a fallen log when she was allowed, sometimes in the uniform she had worn for forty-eight hours, snatching a bite to eat and a cigarette with Betty, not speaking much, for what was there to say? They were each going through the same hell, as they all were: nurses, doctors, soldiers, civilians; holding on, waiting, retreating, knowing they were defeated but carrying on just the same. They were defeated but they wouldn't be beaten, not in the long run, they told one another, so they smiled and cracked a joke or two, she and Betty, leaning against one another in exhaustion before going out again to pick up their 'boys'.

The one who was in the back of the ambulance, no more than eighteen, she would have thought, had a dreadful stomach wound. His liver was ripped to pieces, the sister had told her quietly, and she was amazed he was so lucid. His face had been yellow and sweated, his agony almost more than Maris could bear as he was lifted into the ambulance, and yet he was so polite, calling her 'miss' as though he was a child in a classroom.

'It won't be long, soldier. Can you hang on a bit longer?' she called to him brightly. It could take hours, days, before they even reached the comparative safety of Dunkirk, and he would bleed to death by then, if he was not shelled, or bombed, and her with him. The Germans had reached the coast, a laconic sergeant had told her only that morning, as shattered remnants of the BEF fought their way along it to reach Dunkirk. Isolated detachments had been left behind to fight delaying actions, and it was said that nowhere had the Germans succeeded in actually breaking through, in dividing the British Army or destroying the major part of it. But the perimeter of Dunkirk must be held so that the rest might withdraw, step by slow step, to escape and safety.

It was May 27th when Maris and the rest of the company reached Dunkirk. Again they were forced to stop, held up by the slow-moving, massed confusion of the refugees. The soldiers on foot simply skirted round them, stepping off the road into the fields or the ditches. With nothing more than a haversack and a rifle

435

it was easier for them to get on, their landmark the column of black smoke which was Dunkirk. Others, so weary or so badly wounded they could not walk, travelled on garbage trucks, on tractors and even astride dairy cattle, on anything that would carry them towards their goal. The road was completely blocked by abandoned vehicles now, and soldiers were doing their best to remove them to let the ambulances through.

'Soon 'ave you 'ome, sweet'eart,' one called out to her cheerfully, and overhead another wave of grey-green bombers with their distinctive German crosses under the wings, flew towards their already devastated target. The soldier raised two fingers at them in defiant obscenity. The explosion made by the bombs they dropped rocked the ambulance, and dust and debris flew high in the air, enveloping them in a cloud in which it was difficult to breathe, let alone speak.

'Where are the ships?' she managed to gasp. 'Can you direct us to the harbour?'

'Nay, love, there's not a lot left of the 'arbour, but you just keep goin' towards that smoke. They're burnin' the oilfields, yer see, an' mind them bloody 'orses.'

''Orses?'

'Aye, chuck, gallopin' up an' down the bloody streets in a right funk, poor beasts, an' where they've come from is anybody's guess. Poor buggers.'

'What did he say?' Betty was standing on the running-board of her vehicle, her face black with dust and oil and exhaustion. Her cap had gone and her dark hair was coated with the dust of the roads, giving her the appearance of a grey-haired old lady.

'Just keep going.'

'What else have we been doing for weeks now?'

A crippled aircraft spiralled down from the sky – one

of theirs, one of ours? – crashing in a roar of flames and exploding ammunition into an already badly bombed house further up the road, but they drove precariously on, skirting the rubble and the flames and the heat, creeping forward through the chaos; and as they approached the old harbour it was like going into one of those pictures Maris had seen depicting the descent into Hades under a ceaseless hail of shells and bombs.

The hospitals were being evacuated and all about them were flames, the crashing of bombs and the crack of the anti-aircraft guns. Buildings were collapsing, but guided by instinct since her mind was in a state of numbed narcosis, Maris steered her ambulance, followed by the others, towards the north end of Dunkirk harbour, where she had been instructed to go by an officer. There was a stone causeway and from its seaward end a strong pier thrusting out into the sea, and moored there was a white painted hospital ship. The huge red cross stood out on its side and Maris breathed a sigh of relief. At last they were safe. They had arrived, and within the hour the poor maimed and mutilated young men she carried would be in comfortable beds. They had not only been wounded in battle but bombed and shelled and strafed, thrown about on the agonising journey, every hole in the road a jarring, grinding addition to what they had already suffered.

It was to be five days before Private Maris O'Shaughnessy left the beaches of Dunkirk. She had seen the wounded aboard the hospital ship and watched it move away. The young soldier was dead, as she had expected, and for a while she had felt quite devastated as though he had been one of her own family. She and Betty had stood side by side watching as their ambulances, those they had sweated over and wept over and had been chained to for so long, went up in smoke; for the order was to destroy anything which might be of value to the enemy, and the British soldiers were doing just that, savaging anything they could get their hands on, taking out their frustrated anger on the inanimate machinery.

'I should get on board, Private,' a burly sergeant told her, but somehow, as though to leave these desperate men beside whom she and Betty had fought would be an act of betrayal, she could not take his advice. They both shook their heads, she and Private Thompson, and began to make their way back to the East Pier where the column of battle-weary troops was queuing . . . queuing . . . but what for?

It was then, now that their duty was done and they had time to look about them, that they could really *see* the destruction which was Dunkirk and the scene in the harbour unfolded in its true havoc before their eyes, exploding on their numbed and bewildered senses.

Boats . . . hundreds and hundreds of boats. Boats of all shapes and sizes, vessels which were surely not meant to sail or steam through the perils of the English Channel, for many of them would not have looked out of place on a boating lake in a park. Paddle-boats and pleasure-boats, rowing-boats, dinghies and tiny yachts mixed in with, and in danger of being swamped by, destroyers, corvettes, trawlers, barges, naval craft, merchantmen and private craft. Into them were being hauled the soldiers who waded out to them, swam out to them, were carried on their mates' backs to them. There were fishing boats, shrimpers and crabbers, whilst behind them, and across which they had sailed, were the minefields of the Channel. Mines waiting to blow them out of the water on their return, and above them were the German Stukas waiting to finish off

438

those who got through, through the wreckage of vessels which had come to bring the 'boys' home and which had not made it. There were Channel steamers and ferry boats, one Maris recognised from the River Mersey, brave and battered and bloody, but here nevertheless, and eager to get their lads aboard and safe home where they belonged. And when they got them home, they'd come back for another load, see if they didn't. And bugger the Germans!

'Bloody hell . . . bloody hell . . . !' The two girls began to laugh then, Private O'Shaughnessy and Private Thompson, capering about on the sandy beach just as children will in an ecstasy of joy.

'Now then, ladies, there's work to be done. This is not a Sunday school outing, you know. You'll be getting your buckets and spades out next. Who are you, anyway?'

'Ambulance drivers, sarge, but our lot have just gone on the hospital ship.'

'Right then, Private, there's some wounded over by that truck. Go and see what you can do for 'em, there's good lasses, but I suggest you get on one of them ships out there as soon as you can. No place for ladies, this.'

The feeling of exhilaration died in them then. This was no time for hysteria. Beneath the constant strafing by the German Luftwaffe they spent the next hour doing their best to get back up the beach to the truck. There was a doctor who had set up a small and ill-equipped medical station just beyond it in the dunes, and for the rest of the day and night, working under a tarpaulin, they helped to bandage and stitch and even hold limbs whilst they were amputated, until they were both bloody from neck to toe and mindless with exhaustion, moving like mechanical dolls which have been wound up and will keep going until the mechanism runs down.

'I thought I told you two to get on a ship,' the sergeant who had first spoken to them, said the next day. 'Now do as you're told or I'll put you on a charge,' but his smile was warm with admiration and respect. They would go soon, they told one another but somehow there was always just one more lad to see to, to comfort, or who needed his cigarette lighting.

She was sitting with her back to the wheel of the truck when she heard her name called. She was nursing the head of a young soldier in her lap, and his hand was in hers as he babbled on about some cricket match in which he had scored a hundred not out, and a girl called Nancy. She had bandaged the stump of his leg, which had been removed by a mortar shell, but he was dying, and in between his longing for Nancy and his jubilation about his cricket score, he screamed out his agony.

The doctor, an almost senseless automaton who was kept on his feet, as they all were, by the simple reality that if he fell down they all would, and by some power, some enduring quality none of them could explain, had they the strength, had given him a massive injection, heroin, he had murmured in Maris's ear, since he would not last above an hour. Now, the young soldier lay completely relaxed in a dream world where pain and loss could no longer hurt him, and she stroked his smooth young face whilst he died.

'Come on, Maris, we've *got* to go, the sergeant says. It's the last of the boats out there and if we don't get a move on we'll be the guests of Adolf.'

She looked up, uncomprehending, her face unrecognisable beneath the layers of dirt and blood, of tears

440

and sweat and agony, and there was Betty whom she had lost sight of recently and who really did look bloody awful.

'What?' she said.

'We've got to go now, love. The sergeant says we've to go.'

'But what about all these . . . ?' indicating the hundreds and thousands of men who still lay or sat about the chaos of the beach.

'I know, lovey.' Betty's face was compassionate, sad; but she was a realist, and would it do any good if she and Maris were to stay? and she knew the answer was no. They had done more already than was expected of them. They were not nurses or soldiers, and besides, the bloody sergeant was standing over them with a bayonet and would not be slow to use it if they should turn awkward, or so he said.

'Come on, Private, five days is long enough. I reckon we've done our bit.'

'*Five days!*'

'That's how long it's been, chuck.'

'But . . .'

'No buts, Private, get into that water and no arguments.'

The doctor who had spoken smiled at her and gave her a hand to help her up.

'The boy . . . the soldier.'

'I'll look after him, Private. You and your friend can go home now.'

Home? Where was that?

The sea around her was littered with wreckage and the heaving, rolling bodies of men who had not made it to the flotilla of small boats which had come in as close as they could. Bombs were still dropping among

441

the tens of thousands of men who still waited for a place in the boats, huddled amongst the sand dunes for shelter. A paddle-steamer further out was hit, and immediately she turned turtle and sank. A merchant-man surged through the debris she left, through the mass of small craft and the fountains thrown up by the bombs in the bright morning sunshine.

'Betty . . . oh God, Betty . . . where are you?'

'Right here, love, so get a bloody move on.'

There were several other ATS drivers who had stayed on, and they were being shoved forward by the soldiers, who stood up to their armpits in the watery queue.

'Ladies first, if you don't mind,' a soldier was saying. 'Pass further down the tram an' make way for the ladies,' for even amongst the carnage which was taking place the morale – and humour – of the British Tommy would not be broken.

There were ropes and rope ladders hanging over the side of the barnacle-encrusted hull looming above her, and khaki-clad exhausted arms pushed her towards one.

'Up you go, ducks, hang on . . . go on, one foot in front of the other,' and senselessly she obeyed. Up and up, her fingers bleeding, her arms almost torn from their sockets, and for a moment she would dearly have loved to drop back into the sea and simply slip away. She was so bloody tired, so bloody *filthy*, so bloody drained of every emotion which she had known as a woman, as a female. She was nothing more than a being, senseless, mindless, in a khaki uniform, and really, was it worth the bother? Let somebody else go instead of her, for there was nothing waiting at the other end of the journey she was about to embark on.

Hands grasped hers and lifted her bodily over the ship's rail where she wobbled dangerously on the deck, small, pathetic, bearing no resemblance to anything other than an old rag doll which some child had thrown away. There were dozens of others coming up behind her, pushing and jostling, for this was reported to be the last transport. They could take no more, this gallant armada, and this was to be the last of it.

She could feel the unreal drifting of her mind and her weary body, and in a moment she would fall to the deck and lie there, uncaring, among the noise and the chaos; but his voice came to her from somewhere, and even in the sorry state of her since she *knew* what a sorry state she was in, she felt it put a spark of life in her.

'Maris . . . oh Jesus . . . oh Jesus . . .'

Yes, it was definitely his voice, and then his arms, *his arms* about her, as though she was the most precious thing in the world, holding her, pouring new life into her.

'Darling . . . I've got you, I've got you, my darling . . .' he was saying. *My darling*, he had called her, and his mouth was at her temples and her blood-caked cheeks and finally on hers, and she heard the soldiers about her begin to clap and whistle with delight as the captain of the merchantman come to save them from the enemy, passionately embraced the small drowned rat of an ATS private they had just fished out of the sea.

24

She had been dreaming about Callum, and when she awoke her face was wet with tears. She turned on her side and burrowed her head deeper into the pillow, or tried to, but it was an exceedingly thin and hard pillow. Just like army issue, she told herself so, why was she surprised, her exhausted mind asked. It was one of the hardships she had found almost impossible to get used to when she joined the ATS, but she had done so, and to the hard mattress she and the other girls in the billet had to sleep on.

She opened her eyes, finding the lids immensely heavy to lift; in fact they were so heavy she let them close again, but not before she had caught a fleeting glimpse of a bare and completely unfamiliar room. One she had certainly never seen before. The bedroom of a . . . well, what before the war she would have, somewhat disparagingly, called a working man's home. Plain brown woodwork, nondescript mushroom-coloured wallpaper, a dark wardrobe and dressing-table, with a chair beside the bed. Lying next to her in the bed was Betty.

She turned her head cautiously, the movement stiff and clumsy just as though her body had not been used for a long time and had seized up. She looked up at the ceiling from which a bare light bulb hung on a flex, then towards the narrow window, the curtains of which were drawn. Daylight scraped through round the edges. She could hear sounds from outside: the cry of seagulls and what sounded like a ship's hooter, footsteps hurrying by, and someone whistling 'Roll out the barrel'.

Where in hell was she and how had she got here? What had happened to her, and to Betty? Thank God for Betty, for if her friend had not been beside her she would have been seriously concerned. To wake up in a strange room and – peering quickly beneath the coarse cotton sheets – in a strange nightie, was most unnerving, but if Betty was here then nothing particularly awful could have happened to her, could it?

She sighed and turned over, stiffly again, so that she and Betty were back to back, snuggling down in the hard bed and pulling the equally hard sheets closely about her neck. What did it matter? She was going to have another five minutes, at *least* another five minutes. She was warm and comfortable and after all she had gone through in the past few . . .

The world stopped for a moment, leaving her feeling slightly giddy, unbalanced, and her breath stopped with it. Slowly her head emerged from the warm cocoon of the blankets and she turned again to lie on her back.

Callum. The beach. The ship . . . the ships . . . *Callum* . . . the dying boy . . . blood . . . screams . . . confusion . . . *Callum*. He had been there, hadn't he? Callum *had* been there, oh please God, let Callum have been there. The rocking explosions as the bombs fell, the soldiers clapping and whistling, the smells, the filth . . . and the contours of his mouth on hers. Had he . . . had it really been him?

Flooding now, the instant recall of that rapturous, confused, but rapturous moment when Callum's arms had lifted her against him, when Callum's lips had fitted against hers, and Callum's voice had called her his 'darling'. It was real, wasn't it? or was it a dream, a dream in which nightmare had overlaid sweetness, deceiving her, laughing at her as it had so often? How many times had she woken with his name on her lips? the feel of him so real she had wanted to weep, and often did, when she found he was not there at all. But surely this had been real? It must be. Why were she and Betty in this strange bed together? Where were they? How long had they been here *and where was Callum? Where was Callum?* Where was the man who yesterday, or was it the day before, had called her his darling, *his darling*, and clasped her to him in joy and gladness and what had seemed to be anguish at what had been done to her, perhaps at what *he* had done to her.

Betty grumbled in her sleep and flung an arm out of the covers, then with a mighty heave turned on to her back and opened her eyes. They were unfocused, blurred with the sleep of deep exhaustion which has not really been satisfied. There were black pits about her eyes and her hair was still matted with the filthy dust of France. God, she looks awful, Maris thought, as she studied the girl with whom she had shared and suffered so much. Her skin was sallow and she was not awfully clean. I must look just the same, she decided, and as she continued to look at Betty, her friend turned her head and looked at her. Her expression was of the utmost bewilderment.

'Where the hell are we?' she said, or rather croaked. 'I can't remember a damn thing. God, I feel awful . . .'

'You look it.'

'Thanks, pal, so do you.'

There was silence for several minutes and Maris thought Betty had gone to sleep again, and who could blame her? She had no idea how long they had been

446

here or how long they had slept since they were brought here, but she still felt that however long it was she could stay here for another week at least; but she must rouse herself, get herself up somehow because she must find out where Callum was. *If* he was, or if he had been a figment of her poor wearied brain, her imagination, her longing for him which never abated.

'Can you remember anything at all, Betty?' she asked carefully. 'I mean, after we got on the ship?'

'Oh aye.'

'What?'

'You being kissed by some sailor who called you "his darling" and didn't half kick up a fuss over the state of you.'

A blaze of joy flared up inside her, racing through her whole body until she was consumed in it, engulfed in the loveliness of the knowledge that it *had* happened, that she had *not* dreamed it. Jesus . . . oh sweet God . . . Callum had actually kissed her and . . . said what she thought he had said and . . . oh glory, what did it mean? How had he come to *be* there, just when she most needed him, and where in hell's name was he now? Downstairs perhaps, in this funny little house, in this town, the name of which she didn't even know.

'What happened then?' she asked, trying to be calm.

'Don't you remember?'

'I wouldn't be asking you if I did. I have a vague recollection of being put in a truck and then some woman . . . several women . . .'

'Never mind that, Private O'Shaughnessy. Who the devil was that bloke? and if it was who I think it was, what was he doing there? I thought he was on the Atlantic run . . .'

'So did I, and I would like to know as much as you

447

. . . Oh, Betty, there's nothing in this world I want more than . . .'

'All right, chuck. You've never said much about him so I put two and two together and came up with the . . . well, that you and him weren't exactly Mr and Mrs Lovey-dovey, but by the looks of him the other day, or whenever it was . . . God . . .' she moaned feebly, '. . . it seems like a year, anyway; from the state of him when he saw you I'd say I was wrong, and so were you. He was, to put it mildly, a bit peeved to find you in such a bloody mess and could hardly bear to part with you until some officer reminded him he had to sail the damned ship. And that's *all* I remember. Now don't start again because all I want is a cup of tea and a fag, so kindly ring the bell for the maid.'

The last word had scarcely left her lips when the bedroom door opened an inch or two, and a pair of eyes squinted through the crack. Eyes enormous with excited interest which widened even further when they discovered that Betty and Maris were awake. The door opened a bit more, not much, but enough to reveal a small girl in a voluminous apron with two long plaits across her shoulders, which were neatly tied at the ends with blue ribbon. She let out a piping squeak, then her mouth split as she yelled to someone who was evidently downstairs.

'They're awake, Mum. Our ladies is awake.' She beamed then, sliding into the room to survey them with the possessive pride of someone who has acquired two rare and exotic specimens from a species different from her own.

'Mum won't be long,' she told them confidentially. 'She's just seeing to the other one.'

'The . . . other one?'

448

'Oh aye, we got three.' Her pride was enormous.

'Three what, love?'

'Three soldier ladies.'

'Really, and . . . where did we come from?'

'Don't you know then?' She found this hard to believe.

'We were on a boat . . .'

'Course you were. Hundreds and hundreds o' soldiers an' me mum said she couldn't do anything else but take some in, like. Me dad's a soldier an' me brother Billy, an' when the lady came to see if we 'ad a spare bed . . . well, me mum said there was our Billy's goin' beggin'.'

The door was flung wide open and a smiling, good-natured face beamed in at them. A round, rosy face that said there was not much that could get its owner down, not the perfidy of her Albert who had volunteered when he had no need to, not yet at any rate; nor the wilfulness of their Billy who had followed his dad; nor the rationing; nor the black-out; nor the arrival in Dover of thousands upon thousands of poor lost souls who had come straight from the beaches of Dunkirk. And certainly these two scratty little ATS girls and the Army nurse she had taken in, as hundreds of households along the south-east coast were doing, weren't a scrap of trouble. She'd stripped them off, the three of them, with the help of her next-door neighbour, Mrs Formby, and their Pauline who, though she was only seven, had her head screwed on the right way and could fetch an' carry like the little good 'un she was. Blood an' oil an' muck all over them, sand in their hair and other unmentionable places, and they could hardly stand they were so exhausted, the poor beggars, but she'd done her best, put them in her own and Mrs

Formby's spare nighties and packed them off to bed. And that had been thirty-six hours ago.

'Well then, there you are,' she chirruped brightly in her cheerful southern accent, drawing back the curtains and letting in the brilliant sunshine which had shone, non-stop, during the whole of the evacuation from Dunkirk. Both girls blinked, peeping over the top of the fat pink eiderdown like two little birds in a nest, she said later to Mrs Formby, poor things, an' them no more than kids, the pair of 'em.

'And how d'you feel this morning? Better? I thought you were never goin' to come to again, so I said to our Pauline pop up an' see if them two would like a cup of tea, but she's been dyin' for you to wake up so she was none too quiet about it. No use askin' how you slept, is there? That one downstairs is still dead to the world and her only on the settee. A nurse she is but she come in with you, on the same boat like, so they brought her here. Everybody's got somebody, that's if they'd a bed to spare.'

Her face crumpled suddenly, her eyes as sad as a spaniel's, her expression changing so completely Maris felt as though she wanted to leap out of bed and comfort her. 'Course, there's all them left behind. What's to become of them? The WVS lady told me that the chap what brought you in said he'd seen some terrible things since the war started, but nothing had troubled him like them poor buggers left behind on the beach.'

Again her expression changed, brightening like the dawn sky as the sun comes up. 'Still, it was a great victory, Mr Churchill said so on the wireless this morning. He's a great chap, that. He don't half cheer you up.' She put her hand to her mouth as though somehow she must put a stop to the unceasing flow of words

450

which poured from her. 'Eeh, will you listen to me . . .' which they had been doing for the last five minutes, '. . . jabbering on an' you've not even had a cup of tea. Now then, I've a bit of sugar left from this week's ration, so who takes it?' Nothing was too good for these heroines who had slept under her honoured roof.

She and Pauline beamed, proud as punch the pair of them to be part of this great national endeavour, this great British exploit the news of which was winging round the world, and Maris spoke the words she had been longing to speak ever since she woke up.

'Who was the chap who brought us here, Mrs . . .'

'Baker, duck. Edie Baker. Call me Edie.'

'Thank you, Mrs . . . er Edie. But did a . . . merchant seaman bring us here?'

'A merchant seaman? Eeh no, love. It was the lady from the WVS. A truck . . . well, there were dozens of them but it was them ladies from the WVS who were organising . . . why, lovey, what's up?'

'I just wondered if . . . ?'

Betty sat up in the bed, Edie Baker's tent-like nightdress slipping off her narrow shoulders. She looked gaunt in the bright light of the morning sunshine, and Edie rushed to the wardrobe and lifted a worn plaid dressing-gown from a hook on the back of the wardrobe door and wrapped it solicitously about her shoulders.

'Don't catch cold, love,' for Betty looked so frail, as did the other one who had sunk back on her pillow as though someone had clouted her one.

'My friend here . . . it was her husband who brought us from Dunkirk.'

Edie put the flat of her hands to her cheeks. Her eyes widened and her ample bosom heaved with her ready emotion.

451

'Eeh, get away.'

'Yes, and she was wondering where he might have gone. Do you know?'

They were talking about her as if she was not there; and turning her head on the pillow, half closing her eyes, it seemed to Maris that she had indeed slipped a little sideways, retreated into herself, turned off the part of herself which had so joyfully been reunited with Callum and then torn so agonisingly away from him again. She was still weary, tired to the very marrow of her bones and the aching fibre of her heart with the burden of *not knowing*, and somehow she must find a way to carry that burden. To go on, if not towards Callum, then hopefully no further away from him. She had braced herself, *taught* herself in the past few years to accept his indifference, and she would have carried on doing so had this not happened; but now, after the rapturous moment on the deck of his ship, it would be hard.

'I don't, love,' she heard the woman called Edie say, 'but our Pauline could slip down to the WVS office and speak to Mrs Alexander. She's in charge and she'd know if . . . well . . . if anything's been . . . perhaps a message or something. Course, he wouldn't be able to leave his ship, would he, love? Not with all that's been going on. He was one of the last to come out, so I heard.'

'What's the date, Mrs . . . Edie?'

'It's the 4th of June, duck.'

They travelled from London together, she and Betty. They had been given a first-class railway warrant by a smart sergeant who had a green-blancoed belt and a knife-edge crease in his battledress trousers, and told to go home and await posting orders. They parted at

452

Bolton Station where Betty left the crowded train to catch a bus to her home.

'Will you be all right, love?'

'Of course.'

'Would you like me to come home with you? I could catch a train tomorrow to me mam's.' Her face was anxious. She didn't like the look of Maris at all, to tell the truth, and would have felt better if she could have handed her over to some . . . to some responsible person like Maris's mother or this Rosie Maris talked about. She'd hardly had a word for the cat ever since Mrs Baker's Pauline had come running back from the WVS office, full of importance at this critical stage of her own involvement with the war effort. She'd had nothing to report, though Mrs Alexander, the lady in charge at the WVS, had promised to see if she could find out what had happened to the ship and its captain which had brought the two ATS privates into Dover. But in these days of 'keeping mum' and 'walls have ears' it was very difficult to ascertain the whereabouts of the tramcar into town, let alone one of His Majesty's merchant vessels.

It was as though Captain Callum O'Shaughnessy and his ship had never existed, which really, could you wonder at? In all the confusion and chaos, the hundreds of ships, big and little, which had taken part in the evacuation, it would have been impossible not only to find him but to confirm that he had actually been there. Maris, of course, said he was, and Betty had seen with her own eyes the passionate nature of the embrace in which Maris had been clasped. The soldiers had seen it, those who had whistled and clapped, but what had happened to that weary, gaunt-faced man who had held Maris to him in such an agony of love?

'There's no need, Betty, honestly,' Maris was saying. 'Your family will be waiting for you and you can't disappoint them. Besides, Rosie will meet me. You saw the telegram I sent her.'

'I know, love, but I hate to see you so . . .'

'I'm fine, Bet, really I am. Go on, the train's about to leave. I'll phone you tonight to let you know I've arrived.'

'We've no phone.' The train had begun to move, and for a moment the hands of the two girls clung together, unable to let go, to break that link which was between them, which had been forged on the bloodstained beach at Dunkirk. No one, only those who had been there with them, knew how it had been; and when, later, they were back with their families, how could they speak of it, share it, transfuse the pain into something which could be borne so that they might go on, as they *must* go on? Only with one another could they manage it, and yet they must part for now.

'I'll come over in the car if I can get some petrol,' Maris shouted through the open window, and instantly felt better as Betty's face grinned in pleasure.

'Will you, love? That'd be grand. You know my address.'

'Yes . . .' and their hands parted just before Betty's running feet came to the sloping end of the platform.

There was no word at her mother-in-law's, no letter at Seymour Road, and Michael had not seen his brother since he had returned to sea after being torpedoed in February. He had been back in port in April, Ellen said, after holding the thin little wisp of her daughter-in-law in her comforting arms for several long minutes, appalled by the lost look of her, but he'd said nothing about going to Dunkirk. Not that any of them were

454

allowed to tell anyone, even their own Mammies, where they were off to.

They couldn't get over it, none of them could. Their Maris, for she belonged to the O'Shaughnessys now, body and soul, being at Dunkirk, and what was it like? And Callum as well, and for him to be the one to bring her home an' all. You could knock the lot of them down with a feather, really you could, and had she seen young Joseph, who had been sent to France and as far as they knew was still there, and did she think the Germans had got him? If only Callum had known he could have picked Joseph up with her . . .

Their voices buzzed and twittered round the kitchen, fading and then becoming louder before fading again as, in their simplicity and absolute ignorance of what it had been like on those beaches, they speculated on the whereabouts of one of their own.

She could see it now and always would: the bodies lying on the beach or floating in little groups in the churned-up water and along the tide-line. The rows of wrecked and abandoned vehicles and guns, like a vast and noisy graveyard. The queues of soldiers up to their armpits, still waiting patiently to get on a ship, the film of oil through which she herself had waded and swum and, ironically, the ferry boat *Royal Daffodil*, out of Liverpool, the last ship she had recognised and which had finally been put out of action by a bomb which had passed through three of her decks. Had the *Daffodil* got back to England, that gallant little boat on which she herself with her brothers and cousins had sailed so often across the Mersey?

Ellen sent them home, all except Michael, who had driven Maris over in his beloved Lanchester which he had got off the blocks and out of the garage just for her. He saved his petrol coupons, he said – a monthly allowance getting him about 120 miles – for important occasions, and this, surely, was one of those, and when she was ready he would take her wherever she wanted to go, even to Bolton to see that friend of hers if she wanted to. They were all very kind to her, treating her as if she was recovering from some serious illness or a dreadful injury, and she longed with all her heart for Betty, who knew how she felt, who felt the same way.

Where was Callum? Dear God, where was Callum?

Ellen held her hand and asked her the same question whilst Michael cleared his throat and looked out of the kitchen window at the vivid, sunlit garden and the hated air-raid shelter. He and Donal had planted marigolds about it in brilliant golden splashes, with soft lavender in between, and the shelter was almost hidden beneath their splendour. It had not yet been used.

'Sure an' I don't know what to tell you, pet,' he heard his mother say gently, but Maris's answer was subdued, so quiet he could not hear it. It was a bloody mystery, this marriage between his brother and his own wife's daughter. For years they had lived a sort of casual, come-day, go-day existence, surviving uneasily beside one another when Callum was home, going their own ways, indifferent, and not at all concerned with the usual commitments of marriage. Callum went to sea and Maris went dancing; but now, with the suddenness of a summer storm, they had, or so it seemed from reading between the lines of Maris's disjointed and brief description of their last meeting, discovered their true feelings for one another. But had they? If it was so, where was Callum? Even if he had been forced to leave for sea immediately, which was more than likely, could he not have left a note? and if he had not known

456

her whereabouts in the confusion of disembarking at Dover, could he not have sent a message, a letter to his mother, to *her* mother, to Rosie, even to his own home, for his wife? Would they ever know?

Dear God, what a tarradiddle, he thought as he yearned towards the peace and love which existed with his wife and small son in his own home . . . Thank God . . . thank the good God . . .

Callum O'Shaughnessy looked at the letter which lay on the tiny desk in his cabin. He read the words again, crossing one out here and there, crossing out a whole sentence, putting in an extra word; then with a stifled oath he tore it up and threw it in the waste-paper basket at his feet. In it were the remains of several others.

He put his head in his hands and sighed deeply, painfully, the image of that senseless, staggering, bloodstained girl who was his wife, and which he could not obliterate, crowding out the words he was trying to put on paper. He would never, no matter what happened in the future and no matter how long he lived – which might not be long if the German U-boats had their way – he would never forget the state of her, the appalled shock of seeing her there, and even now behind the closed darkness of his eyelids he could visualise her as she was hauled over the side of his ship, falling to her knees the moment her wet feet touched the deck. The blow to his heart had been so fierce he thought he might choke, and the great and overwhelming need to get to her, to pick her up and cradle her to him, had him pushing aside roughly even the poor sods who had come up the ladder with her.

He had just steamed into Liverpool and his cargo had been unloaded when the call had come for ships of any sort to sail for Dover, where they would be refuelled, and then proceed to France to fetch back as much as they could of the beleaguered British Army. He had obtained permission to go and had spent three days, hardly off his feet, ferrying thousands of soldiers, French and British, back to Dover. His ship had been raked by bombs and machine-gun fire which had scythed through her crowded decks, killing and wounding many of the men who had been brought from the beach. The thirty-mile route from Dover to Dunkirk had to be abandoned during daylight hours due to the enormous loss of shipping, and so other routes had been worked out, but it had doubled the sailing time, even though Fighter Command of the RAF had patrolled the area, holding off the Luftwaffe.

It had been on what he knew would be his ship's last journey that he saw her. He had not even known she was in there, or even *where* she was. Somewhere in England, he had supposed, since he had not been told otherwise by his mother or Rosie, and the shock had turned him white and trembling as not even the three days of constant dragging danger and exhaustion had done.

She had been like a little whipped child, wet and shivering and paralysed, her mind deadened by what she had seen, what she had experienced, and by the shambles, the seething mass of scrambling men who were in the same stupefied state as herself; and in that moment, when he saw her, stunned himself by her sudden appearance, an apparition from the past, he had felt it well up in him like a great river which has been dammed but which an explosion has just released. He was not awfully sure at that moment what it was he felt, he only knew that something started to thump and

458

shake inside him; and the longing, the absolute need, the yearning – not a romantic, but a fiercely masculine yearning – to have her *here*, in his arms where he could protect her, took him over, so that he was no longer, for the space of several minutes, Captain O'Shaughnessy in whose hands the lives of all these men lay, but Callum, husband to the bedraggled and noisome creature on his deck and about whom his arms longed to be.

She had hardly been sensible, only half-aware that it was him, hanging like a limp doll against him, her arms at her sides, her lifeless hair plastered to her skull, her eyes blank and scarcely focused; but for an exquisite moment her mouth had responded to his before she was taken from him, and he had been reminded of his duty by an officer who had been in the same filthy state as herself.

He had not seen her again, not even when they arrived in Dover and his exhausted, stupefied passengers had been taken ashore and put into the compassionate and welcoming hands of the ladies of the WVS, and now, in the middle of the Atlantic Ocean, ten days later, he was writing her a letter.

But what to say? How to tell his wife of five years, the wife he had been forced to marry and whom he had never loved, that now he did?

'Action Stations' brought him instantly to his feet, and the notepad fell to the floor of the cabin as Captain O'Shaughnessy flung himself up the companionway and along the deck to the wheelhouse of his vessel.

25

On the morning of June 17th, HMT *Lancastria* was anchored some miles off St Nazaire, a port on the French Atlantic coast. Along with a number of other ships she had been ordered to assist in the repatriation of many British servicemen and civilians who had been left in France after the evacuation of Dunkirk.

By mid-afternoon of that day almost 6,000 people were packed aboard the ship when she was hit four times by enemy bombs. Within thirty minutes she had sunk, suffering a loss of life at least equal to the combined losses of the *Lusitania* and the *Titanic*. One of those aboard her was Sapper Joseph O'Shaughnessy, who had been directed to one of the top decks, where his pal was left to look after their kit whilst Jóseph went in search of the ship's galley and some food, which had been in short supply during the last few weeks. He was just about to pick up a thick cheese sandwich one of the stewards had made him when the ship seemed to heave up beneath him and an enormous piece of timber fell right across his 'butty', narrowly missing his hand.

When he was asked afterwards, Ellen's grandson, the one who had – or so it seemed to her – only recently played boyish pranks on New Brighton sands, could not give an accurate, or even anything like a lucid account of what had happened to him in those next few minutes. He must have got on deck as the ship keeled over, and when he was told to jump he did so, joining others struggling to keep afloat in the water on anything that came to hand.

Men were shouting to be helped, and being a strong lad and a good swimmer, he obliged, pulling many to a raft nearby, managing to keep himself and six others afloat until they were all picked up by a French trawler. He was considerably embarrassed later, when they had all been transferred to HMS *Havelock*, to be thanked by a man who told Joseph he had saved his life.

He got a three-day pass when he was landed at Plymouth. Of those who had boarded the *Lancastria*, half went down with her, and when he arrived at Edge Lane with his burstingly proud father, Ellen's son Donal, and his tearfully thankful mother Mary, he was further embarrassed by the tumultuous welcome his jubilant family gave him, since it appeared he was to be recommended for an award.

A week later, on June 25th, shortly after midnight, the first night alert sounded in Liverpool, and for a full five minutes Ellen could make neither head nor tail of the eerie wail which had wakened her. She thought it was Matty having some dreadful nightmare, she told Michael, and Matty had thought the same about her, and for several minutes there had been total confusion on the landing as the two old ladies rushed to one another's assistance.

It had all come to nothing, though, and why the dratted thing had gone off was a mystery to her. They ought to be ashamed, frightening the life out of them like that. The shelter? Don't be daft. She'd said from the start she'd not use the thing and she meant it. Anyway, if all the air raids were to be as piddling as last night's then there was no need to stumble out into the black of night and crouch in the thing, was there? They'd be just as safe and a ruddy sight warmer in their beds.

By the beginning of July the three armed services had absorbed more than half the British males aged between twenty and twenty-five and more than one fifth of the entire male population between sixteen and forty.

Ellen mourned the fact deeply. Joseph had come home from France unhurt, thank the Holy Mother, but when you think what could have happened to him, shot or bombed or drowned, so he could, an' him no more than a lad, and Lorcan already over in Africa, though of course they weren't supposed to know that. He had devised a cunning method of letting his Daddy know where he was by putting a dot beneath certain letters in his censored air mails, spelling out the name of the nearest town. A chip off the old block, was Lorcan, with a clever brain just like his Daddy, her son Donal. What in the name of the Blessed Virgin they were doing fighting in Africa, for goodness sake, when the war was between us and the Germans, she couldn't imagine, but that was where he was, God love him, and the balaclava she had been knitting for him would be no earthly good to him *there*, she complained. And Amy's Devlin, him that was born nine months after the end of the *last* war was learning to be a navigator in a bomber, of all things, which she supposed would drop bombs on innocent people like herself and her grandchildren, which didn't bear thinking about, but she thought about it just the same. Guy, Caitlin's boy, was a pilot officer, like the Woodall boys, and next they would be calling up James and Paul, Amy's older boys, Eileen's Finbar who was twenty-nine, and Flynn McGowan, Gracie's lad, whose father had gone and not come back from the last lot.

And those dratted gas-masks didn't help. She'd gone

down to the end of Edge Lane with Matty to test the thing in a gas van which had parked there, and had been asked by the nice Civil Defence chappie if she'd mind wearing it for a quarter of an hour each week, at home of course.

'Just ter get used to it like, queen. Practise puttin' it on an' tekkin' it off, then, if that old Adolf drops gas on us yer can gerrin yer mask quicker'n Dixie Dean can score a bloody goal.'

There had been a few air raids, nothing much to speak of. One in Clacton and another in Middlesbrough, the Midlands and East Anglia, but no more near *her*, but still, better safe than sorry, so she and Matty had obliged, sitting in the front parlour where the masks were kept, with the things on their faces, giving their Michael the fright of his life when he walked in on them unexpectedly.

The Home Guard was formed, giving the 'old sweats' a new lease of life since the upper age limit was sixty-five, and that not very energetically enforced, though Jesus and all His angels help them if they had to depend on old Mr Sanderson along the lane to keep them 'nasties' from raping and pillaging! They came from all over Liverpool, volunteering in their thousands, civil servants and teachers and shopkeepers, holding meetings and marching about with bits of wood over their shoulders whilst they waited for their rifles to be issued, but they meant well, Ellen was sure of it.

It was on July 10th that the Luftwaffe began their attacks on convoys passing through the Straits of Dover, but they found that they were losing twice as many aircraft as the RAF and not a great deal of shipping was sunk. But the dog fights which took place over the tip of Kent around Dover, nicknamed 'Hellfire

Corner', developed into what was to be called 'The Battle of Britain'. Those who lived beneath the blue skies in which the aerial fights took place would stand in fields or in their own back gardens, hands shading their eyes from the sun which had poured its benison down on them day after brilliant day during that summer, watching as a Junkers 87 came plummeting down in flames; as a man drifted in his parachute on the wind; as long and flaunting vapour trails criss-crossed the skies, sunlight picking out the planes in the high blue dome; watching the twisting and turning of the aircraft; listening to the machine guns rattling.

From those same blue skies came thousands upon thousands of leaflets, purported to be from Herr Hitler himself appealing to the British people to be reasonable and to give up the fight. The British believed they *were* being reasonable and had no intention of giving up, laughing in the face of his impertinence; and on the next day, Goering, a henchman of Hitler's, or so Ellen read in the papers, had ordered the Luftwaffe to completely destroy the RAF. If Britain was to be invaded these cocky RAF pilots must be knocked out of the skies first, he said, or words to that effect, which was a damned cheek when you thought about it since it was *him* and them over there who had started the whole damn thing in the first place.

But the RAF pilots, amongst them the Woodall boys, one flying a Spitfire, the other a Hurricane, and Ellen's grandson Pilot Officer Guy Templeton, refused to be knocked out of the skies, and everywhere the bombers of the Luftflötte and the ME 109s flew, in nearly 1,800 sorties a day, they were ignominiously routed. From the northern counties to the southern suburbs of London, huge attacks were successfully combated. The whole of the country south of a line from Hull to Liverpool was under 'red' warnings, their sirens sounding from morning till night and from night until morning.

All that month and the next, the people of Britain looked up at the blue sky, sometimes whilst they were picnicking on a beautiful afternoon. The sensation of being spectators at a sporting event persisted since not one of them could conceive of the terrors of the pilots overhead. The German raiders were concentrating their attacks on the Channel convoys and the coastal defences now, but the RAF boys who had so far kept the enemy from their territory had lost nearly a quarter of their thousand pilots.

There was a rumour of invasion barges gathering across the Channel, and people were asking one another anxiously, 'when will he come?', 'why doesn't he come?' but Mr Churchill kept them calm, at the same time gathering his own flotilla of barges and small boats in the Channel ports ready to defend them, and his bombers massed on Channel airfields.

On a September afternoon, wave after wave of German bombers crossed the south-east coast, heading in the direction of London, and though at the time they did not know it the *blitzkrieg*, meaning 'lightning attack', was to be the first of seventy-six nights of intensive bombing those in London were to suffer.

The sirens wailed at five p.m., but by then Pilot Officer Sir Charles Woodall was in the air, having taken off from Hornchurch with the rest of his Hurricane Squadron. They flew directly into the setting sun.

The bang surprised him, and for a moment he wondered what it was. He couldn't have been hit or he would have felt it more keenly, but it came again, then again, that strange bang, and as if by magic, just as though some giant hand had reached out and prodded his aircraft with a giant finger, a gaping hole appeared in his starboard wing.

A hole! In his wing! Where the hell had that come from? For a moment he felt a desire to laugh in sheer disbelief since he had not even seen the enemy aircraft which now, from God knows where, had come to brush him from the skies to which he precariously clung.

His open-mouthed and, he realised, stupid surprise changed instantly to fear, and at once the instinct for self-preservation which is bred in all animals be they two- or four-legged, began to take over. Screaming at the top of his voice he threw his head back from the flames which had appeared from his ruptured engine, his right hand groped for the release pin which secured the restraining Sutton harness, and when it found it the cool relieving fresh air flowed across him as he tumbled from his burning aircraft. Sky, sea, sky poured over and over him until his hand . . . God, oh God . . . it hurt . . . reached for the ripcord, pulling the chromium ring.

It acted immediately, and with a jerk the silken canopy above him billowed out into the clear summer sky. It was icy cold when he hit the water of the Channel, even though the autumn day was warm, but somehow, despite his badly shocked body and mind, he kicked himself to the surface and, knowing that if he did not discard it the waterlogged parachute would drag him down, he struggled with the vital release mechanism which would set him free. His hand, the one that hurt so much and which he did not care to study too closely, was almost useless, but at last the disc surrendered, and kicking away blindly he fought free of the parachute and swam wildly away from it.

When he tried to blow up his life-jacket he found

466

that the flames had burned a hole in it, and knowing his life depended only on himself he began to swim towards the hazy outline which he knew to be the south coast of England.

He was at the gate waiting for her when she came up the drive pushing the pram. The children were babbling, young Harry, his feet in the 'well' of the baby-carriage showing off his infant vocabulary which, at twenty-one months, was becoming quite extensive. She tried hard to answer his endless questions, to listen to them, but she was very tired after almost fourteen hours harvesting with Muriel and Lou and the casual labour, old men and under-age boys who could be found to help.

'Bird, Mamma . . . bird in tree . . .'
'Yes, darling.'
'Is going to fly away, Mamma?'
'Yes it is, darling.'
'Where Mamma?'
'Oh, another tree, I suppose.'
'Which tree, Mamma?'
'I don't know, sweetheart.'
'That one there?'
'Probably, darling.'
'Why?'
'Well, perhaps its nest is there.'
'Why?'
'It's a good tree for a nest.'
'Why?'
'Well, it has lots of leaves so that its nest is hidden.'
'Play hide seek?'
'No, darling, birds don't play hide and seek like little boys.'

'Why?' and on and on until she really thought she would scream. It was so hard on her own. There was no one to give her a hand with the children, though Elizabeth, whom she no longer called Aunt since they were now friends, had offered to have them. If she had still had her Nanny, the woman Michael had employed to help his wife when young Michael was born, Rose wouldn't have hesitated, but the girl had been called up, and the elderly, who were all that were available these days, did not want to be bothered with young children and babies. Three of them were too much for Elizabeth with Michael at the factory, sometimes far into the night as the demand for greater production grew, and so Rose had refused Elizabeth's offer to have her two, gently, of course, saying that between them she and Muriel and Lou would manage them. But it was difficult keeping Harry close to the pram where his sister slept and woke to chirrup good-naturedly at the canopy of the trees above her head, firmly strapped in, naturally, but one could hardly tether a boy of almost two years to the pram. He was active and sturdy, wanting to 'help', shouting to get on the tractor or the horse or the haystack with the rest of them. What she would do when winter came was a worry which nagged at her constantly.

And Uncle Teddy wasn't well. He had had a bad bout of what had almost been pneumonia just after Easter, and being so immobile, he had not seemed to throw it off. She knew Clare was worried about him and so she, Rosie, took as much off Clare's shoulders, and therefore off Uncle Teddy's shoulders, as she could.

Sometimes she felt like a machine, mindless, no thought nor sense, a pair of eyes and arms and legs and

468

a strong back which laboured constantly from morning until night, doing automatically the tasks for which it was designed and only running down when dark fell and it stopped dead to lie uselessly in its corner until it was switched on again for the next day's labour. She hardly had time to think of Alex and yet at a deep and basic level of her consciousness she was constantly aware of him, the desperate worry and dread as the news came through of the RAF's ordeal over Kent, niggling like an abscess which can never be lanced.

The sports car was a scarlet Alvis, and at once her spirits lifted. It was Charlie, dear Charlie, who, two weeks ago, had been shot out of the skies above the English Channel and had been miraculously picked up by a British merchant vessel. His left hand had been badly burnt, and his wrist, but by some twist of fate that was all the injury he had sustained and, so his letter had said, he was to return to duty as soon as the burns had healed sufficiently for him to fly his Hurricane.

He had been writing to her since last Easter, short, witty, innocent little notes in which there had been nothing to alarm her. He had begged her to write back, saying he was short of news of dear old Woodall, and she had seen no harm in it. He had been home on a forty-eight-hour pass in June and had 'popped in' to say hello, again doing nothing at which she might take offence, staying for no more than an hour, kissing her lightly on the cheek as he left to go up to see Uncle Teddy; and now here he was on a short convalescent leave, as he had said he would be, before returning for duty at the camp in the south of England where he was stationed.

'Charlie, hello. I wasn't expecting you until Wednesday.'

'I know, pet, but the MO gave me a clean bill of health yesterday afternoon so I thought I might as well come today. I hope that's OK with you. I was brassed off hanging about that bloody hospital so I grabbed a lift as far as Crewe, jumped a train and came up here full bore, picking up the old Alvis from Woodall. My new "Hurri" won't be ready until next week, so I thought I'd grab me a piece of nice . . .'

'Charlie, I don't know what the dickens you're talking about with all that RAF slang you fliers have made up, but it's good to see you all the same. Where are you staying?' Best get that clear right away.

'Oh, Uncle Teddy's putting me up for as long as I like, then I thought I'd do a recce to see what else was up for offer. Not at Woodall, I hasten to add. Not with that chattering crowd of twerps who are staying there.'

'Twerps . . . ?'

'Those land girls. The old place doesn't look at all the same, so I beetled over to Beechwood for a look-see and scrounged a bed there. Uncle Teddy looked a bit ropey, poor old sod . . .'

'Ropey . . . ?'

'Sorry, my pet. I mean he doesn't look too good.'

'No, he's not at all well, but let me get these two fed and up to bed and then I'll do us a meal.'

'Wizard! I've got a bottle of the old soaking wet stuff . . .'

'*Soaking wet stuff?*' lifting Ellie from the pram and putting her on her hip.

'Sorry, old girl, gin.'

'Good God, a gin! I haven't had a "gin and it" for

470

years. Pour me a stiff one, will you? I need it after the day I've just put in.'

He leaped out of the car without bothering to open the door, looking incredibly attractive in his blue uniform. He wore no shirt and tie but had on a blue, high-necked sweater beneath his jacket, casual and sporty. His hair had blown across his forehead in thick pale feathers, and his brown eyes were deep and dark and laughing. He was at his most charming best, light-hearted and gallant as he opened the gate for her, his experience appearing not to have daunted him in the least. He was just as he had always been in his youth, and she pushed the incident which had occurred at Easter to the back of her mind. She could not be so churlish as to deny him her hospitality. He was one of the 'few', those about whom Mr Churchill had said, 'never in the field of human conflict was so much owed by so many to so few'. He was her husband's brother, likeable and engaging, though as yet she had not told Alex that she was in touch with Charlie, that she had seen him and was writing to him now and again, not even when Alex had been home on a short leave last month. She meant to when the time was right. Alex had been taut and jumpy, wanting nothing more than to lie in her arms at night, drawing on her strength to renew his; to play with his children, particularly the pretty little girl who met his overtures with an ecstatic gurgling. He simply liked to be with his daughter, watching her, talking to her, feeling her small fingers curl about his own, her warm body, the soft petal touch of her skin, her simple, tender innocence so far from the bloodbath of the skies he fought in. He loved his son but his son played at war games which Alex wanted to forget, and the connection he had established with his girl child was very dear to him.

But despite this, Rosie sensed that it was not a good moment to talk of Charlie. She meant to convince Alex that Charlie had changed, that the war, as it had so many, had made him aware of the value of life, of the importance of friends, of family, in these perilous times, of the sadness of quarrelling with them. That Charlie wanted to heal the rift, as he had hinted, between himself and his brother, himself and his mother, and surely it was worth incurring Alex's anger at what he might think of as her deceit if she could bring it about. She wanted nothing more than to reunite the two brothers and their mother, and Charlie must have something in his mind on the same lines, else why should he bother to keep in touch with *her*? And the answer to that was that only she could play mediator. They were fond of each other, she and Charlie, and she enjoyed his witty company. It made a break in her own overworked, lonely and drab existence. He made her laugh again, made her young again, female again, so what was the harm in it? She would ask him when the time was right and she was sure she would know when it came, if he would let her speak to Alex about a reconciliation, a family reunion, perhaps at Christmas, which, being a time of peace, was surely appropriate.

She laughed a great deal that evening as he played the fool for her entertainment, parodying many of the men he flew with, exaggerating in a kindly way their idiosyncrasies and superstitions, prattling on about 'getting blotto', 'the Bosche', the moment when he had 'hit the silk' over the English Channel, making light of his moment of terror. He talked of 'bogeys' and 'bandits' and a 'streamlined piece', a WAAF corporal he had met at 'The Shovels', the local pub where he and the

472

other 'fighter boys' got 'pickled' every night. Of 'tail-end Charlies', winking as he did so, of the 'Goldfish Club' of which he was now a member since he had been 'downed' in the sea and been saved from it.

At the end of the evening he kissed her lightly, laughingly, on the cheek, called her 'old girl' and thanked her for the splendid meal, promising, if his bandaged hand and arm would allow it, to 'buster' over to Far Paddock in the morning and give a hand, only one at the moment, smiling endearingly, with the harvesting.

In that month of September it was said you could read a newspaper in Shaftesbury Avenue by the light of the fires in the London dockland five miles away, as mile after mile of dock warehouses went up in flames. The Surrey shore was ablaze, Rose heard on the wireless, warehouses, wharves, piers, barges, with a wall of smoke and sparks spreading across the River Thames. It was only the beginning of London's ordeal, though, and in one night alone 430 civilians were killed and 1,600 were badly injured. Hundreds were made homeless, thousands, as night after night the German bombers came over. The streets were chaotic. There was no gas, no electricity, no telephone. The nation was numbed with shock, for nothing in the war, *any* war, had prepared them for this.

Mr Churchill went amongst them, and putting his hat on the end of his stick, he twirled it round and roared, 'Are we down-hearted?' and they roared back 'No' with amazing gusto. 'Hit 'em back, Winston,' the Eastenders cried. 'Hit 'em hard,' but just the same the fear and the sorrow and the pain could hardly be borne.

They bore it, though, even if, as many ordinary housewives wept, they couldn't stand it any more, but when, five days later, the authorities opened up the gates to the London Underground tube stations so that people might shelter in their deep safety, the people of London began to adjust to what, after all, could not be changed. It was warm and safe down there. You were not alone, and, most important of all, you could not hear the bombs, and though they hated the sound of the sirens they became used to them.

And during this time, knowing that Alex would be one of those intrepid 'few' who were facing the might of the German Luftwaffe, who was each night and day facing that seething sky of aircraft, swooping and swerving in and out of the vapour trails and tracer smoke, Rose lay awake staring into the shadowed but understanding eyes of her great-grandmother, wondering if he was still alive, wondering if, as she tried to forge a shield of protective love about her husband with her agonised thoughts, he was already dead. She did not pray but concentrated every fibre of her anguished heart on the man without whom, if he should die, she could not live. She had no confirmation, of course, that Alex would be playing that grim game of hide and seek above the roof-tops in London, in that crowded, terror-filled sky, but in her heart which cringed in a terror of its own, she knew.

She saw Charlie every day. The sun continued to shine on the harvesters. In the midge-filled shade of the hawthorn trees Rosie's babies slept, undisturbed by the roar of the harvesters which moved from farm to farm, from estate to estate, gathering in the fruits of the labour she and Muriel and Lou and the thousands of other land girls up and down the country had broken their backs, if not their spirits over during the past six months.

Muriel and Lou fell instantly and completely in love

with Charlie, who turned up when the mood took him, resplendent and dashing in the fine cream shirt, the sleeves rolled up to the elbows, and the immaculately tailored jodhpurs he had picked up from Woodall, his bandaged hand and arm a badge of the daring courage they worshipped. A hero of their very own to brag about. Sir Charles Woodall, who winked at them and looked them up and down in a way which caused their female hearts to miss a beat and their female loins to throb with longing. He shared their packed lunch, even on one occasion bringing a bottle of 'bubbly' on which the pair of them got – in his words – 'pickled', and giggled all afternoon, in danger of not only scything off their own feet but anyone else's who got in their way.

It was a great time for butterflies that month. It was as though nature was doing her best to make up for the destruction of one of her species by the multiplying of another. Towards noon, at the warmest part of the day, hundreds of the lovely creatures danced over the shorn pasture and alighted in the hawthorn hedge which bordered Far Paddock. Brimstone butterflies, golden-yellow and exquisite, moving in elfin abandonment, their rich colouring vying with the buttercups which flowered wherever there was an inch of soil. Tortoiseshells came to rest on the bright blue of the field scabious, and beneath the enormous horse-chestnut tree in the corner of the paddock Rose and Charles, Muriel and Lou, Harry and Ellie, dozed to the sounds of the tiny blue-tit and its shivering little song.

And each night he turned up at Lacy's house, so immaculate in his uniform which he had charmed some willing female into pressing for him, she felt duty-bound to dress up herself.

He had been home a week. They had dined that night on game, handed in at her back door by the quiet and elderly man who had taken it upon himself to become 'gamekeeper' to many of the estates which were now without one. She had puréed apples from her own trees, scrounged a jug of cream from what had once been Home Farm, made a rich plum cake, the fruit again from her own trees, and with the bottle of wine Charles always seemed able to produce from some-where – probably Beechwood cellars – they had dined well and easily. The children were asleep in their beds, and though it had not gone unnoticed by her that not once had he touched his brother's son and daughter, she was relaxed with him now. He was like an engaging schoolboy home from boarding-school, playing pranks and making her laugh, not pressing her for anything she was not prepared to freely give him, so that when he took her in his arms and laid his mouth on hers, softly, so softly and gently, she felt it would be uncivil to refuse him, and she allowed it. It meant nothing. Not to him and not to her. It was not unpleasant. Not at all like the kisses she and Alex shared, of course, and when he lifted his head and smiled down at her, she smiled back, refusing to acknowledge the deep longing in the pit of her belly and along the length of her limbs for the feel of Charlie's . . . Alex's . . . hands and mouth upon them.

'Rosie . . .' His voice was a husky murmur, and his eyes were deep and unfathomable.

'Charlie . . . ?'

'You know, don't you?'

'What, Charlie?'

'That I love you.' God, it was so easy to say and nearly true, for had he not wanted her ever since he had become aware that his brother was in love with her?

'Don't, Charlie . . .' but she did not move away.

'I can't stop myself, lovely girl, so, before any damage is done I had better go . . .' and neither did he.

'Yes . . .'

'Do you want me to?'

'No . . . yes . . . of course . . .'

'Rosie . . .' His mouth came down on hers, not softly now, not gently, but with a hot urgency she answered with a need of her own. She understood urgency, the urgency of love, the fierce heights of emotion which will not be refused, the mingling of heart and mind and orgasm, and when hers came and Charlie groaned, his body pinning hers to her own kitchen floor, she cried out sharply before she began to weep.

26

Callum's ship was at the tail end of the convoy as it made its way upstream. They were passing the Crosby Light Vessel when he became aware of the sudden unease on deck where none should have been, for the danger was over now, the perils of the Atlantic put behind them for the time being. The men who were standing on the fo'c'sle, getting out the mooring wires, were shading their eyes against the strong May sunshine, staring across the waters of the river towards the city, and others were clustered on the upper deck, doing the same. There was a curious stillness about them, a silence which had a jagged edge of tension in it, and he turned his head, narrowing his eyes to squint across the sun-dazzled Mersey to the Liverpool skyline.

Liverpool was a seaman's town now, the largest of the Western Approaches bases, and the merchant ships of all the allied nations lined the quays and docks. The port was crowded, for it was from here that the convoys which criss-crossed the Atlantic began and ended. Callum often marvelled that the harbour master could co-ordinate the docking and sailing of the hundreds of ships which used the harbour daily. There was a thirty-foot tidal rise and fall, and it was only possible for larger vessels to use the river entrances for about two and a half hours before and after high water. Ships were packed like sardines in a tin in the Sandon Basin, brought from other berths and waiting to be undocked at the earliest possible moment, so that as many of those waiting in the incoming convoy as possible could be brought in on the same tide.

Since the south coast ports had been closed to military traffic after Dunkirk, Liverpool had become the main outlet for military expeditions, and vast amounts of war supplies and men were sent from here to Libya and North Africa. After the pasting London had received with the devastation to the dockland during the September Blitz and the many other air attacks, Liverpool had become the most important port in the country.

Callum picked up his binoculars and trained them on the familiar skyline of his city, his home, looking up the river towards the Liver Building, and what he saw brought a cold sweat of fear down the length of his back and in his armpits. His heart jerked painfully, even before his stunned brain could assimilate the message his eyes were sending to it, and he drew in his breath on an appalled gasp.

'What is it, sir?' the man beside him asked hesitantly.

'It seems "Jerry" has paid our city a visit, lad.'

There was a pall of smoke hanging from just above the roof-tops to hundreds of feet into the air, and as he ran his glasses from one end of the dockland to the other, from Hornby Dock in the north to the Herclaneum in the south, there were great gaping holes where none should have been. The *Bridget O'Malley* had steamed past the graves of many marine casualties in the area of the Bar Lightship as she came into the mouth of the river, the *Lady Mostyn*, the *Sharpsburg*, the *Westmorland*, and many others who had not made the safety of the estuary, and now he was looking at land casualties.

There had been air raids in the city last August and

479

in each month since until Christmas, some of them small and mostly ineffective, though in November there had been a full-scale attack upon the port, which had increased the number of lives lost.

But nothing like this, surely, nothing like this?

The acrid tang of the smoke blew down the river, stinging the eyes of the watching, fearful men, many of whom, like himself, had families here. It was home to more than a few of the seamen in the convoy since some had married Liverpool girls and others had brought their families to live here, since this was where escorts and the convoys they protected were based.

A big warehouse just above Gladstone Dock was split from its roof to its cellar, a gigantic mass of rubble, part of it blackened and still smouldering. Canada Dock no longer seemed to exist. The Bramley Moore Coaling berth was no more than a crumbled, yawning, leaning tower of bricks with cranes hanging at impossible angles over the water. The Stanley Tobacco Warehouse had gone, so had Alexandra Dock, but surely the worst of all these appalling sights was what had once been the south-west side of Huskisson Dock. Where was it? Where were the ships which were usually crammed there? The warehouses and wharves, the cranes and all the paraphernalia which were needed for the unloading of vessels in the great dock? The dock which had been a beehive of bustling activity when last he had steamed past?

He hardly dared look any further. He could see the ruins of row upon row of what had once been homes, small houses in which a dozen people might be crammed, for the Liverpool seaman was very often Irish and Catholic like himself, prone to large families. Whole streets gone or lying ruined in the centre of a great scorched circle. Fires were still burning, and what buildings were left were blackened with smoke.

The smoke and the filthy stink of devastation blew thick and strong towards him, and he dropped his glasses, shocked and desperately afraid of the destruction, at the naked ruin of his city which, when he had left it only a few weeks ago, had been whole and proud and thriving.

Maris had just arrived home on leave when the siren sounded on May 2nd, and she groaned, burrowing deeper beneath the bedcovers.

'Bugger off, the lot of you,' she muttered. 'If you think I'm getting out of my bed when I've only just got in it then you can think again.'

She had come up from her unit only that day on a week's leave, the first in four months, travelling for more than eighteen hours on a train packed with servicemen and women, and going straight to Seymour Road in a taxi which had miraculously stopped for her in Lime Street.

The house had been in darkness, the black-out securely tight against the windows, for the hard-polishing, hard-scrubbing Mrs Flynn who still came round to 'do' – if not for Maris then for the sake of the home which belonged to Ellen O'Shaughnessy's son – once a week and to report to Ellen that all was as it should be, did not trust the flighty Mrs O'Shaughnessy to perform the job as the air-raid warden liked. Not *Mrs* O'Shaughnessy now, of course, nor even Private O'Shaughnessy, but *Corporal*, and still driving ambulances.

Mrs Flynn, warned by Mrs O'Shaughnessy, the *real* Mrs O'Shaughnessy, that her daughter-in-law was to

481

be home, had left her some milk and marge, a quarter of tea and a loaf of bread, a jar of Ellen's pickled onions and a lump of cheese of some unknown origin, and Maris had eaten ravenously before falling into bed just after eleven-thirty.

There had been a raid the night before. Though the inhabitants of Liverpool did not know it at the time, the raid was described as a comparatively light one, involving forty-three bombers which dropped forty-eight tons of high explosives and 112 canisters of incendiaries.

Tonight the siren sounded just before twelve o'clock and finished just before three, but in that time 110 people were killed. The sky was cloudless and the destruction was widespread. The Dock Board and White Star Buildings were badly damaged and the Corn Exchange was destroyed, but Corporal Maris O'Shaughnessy slept through it all.

She was quite amazed the next day, a Saturday, when she set off to walk up to her mother's house, no more than half an hour, to find evidence of incendiaries as she crossed the Cheshire Lines railway bridge along Thomas Road. There were blackened patches all along the railway embankment, still smouldering, and several members of the Civil Defence were inviting inquisitive children to 'bugger off out of it' as they tried to climb over the fence and on to the railway line to look for souvenirs.

'Must've bin tryin' fer the goods yard,' she heard someone remark.

'Nearly bloody gorrit an' all.'

She was further bewildered when she came to Prescot Road to find a long line of buses all heading away from the city, each one crammed with women and children, and along each pavement, going the same way, groups of harassed women, and some men, dragging their protesting, wailing offspring with them. They carried suitcases, haversacks, shopping baskets; they trundled prams or wheelbarrows on which mattresses were piled, small pushcarts, and – what was obviously some small lad's pride and joy – a couple of short planks fixed to the four wheels of a discarded baby-carriage. They all had an urgency about them, a white-faced need to hurry, which brought back a memory she could not at first place, but when she did her heart began to plunge frantically in her chest.

Dunkirk. Refugees. That appalling flight from Lille to the coast which she and Betty had endured. But this was England. Liverpool. Where were these frightened people going? Had the Germans landed at the Pier Head? Why were they in such a panic? Where were they off to, and why?

She asked them.

'It's them bloody bombs, queen. We've 'ad enough so we're gettin' out. Campin' up near Croxteth 'All. Some're goin' ter Huyton Woods . . .'

'Camping? But why?'

'Where was you last night, chuck?' though it was evident her 'posh' accent inclined them to think that wherever it was the likes of *her* would be in no danger.

She reached her mother's house in Craven Road just as Rosie did. The old Morris Rosie drove when her petrol coupons allowed it, seemed to be filled with babbling, excited children. Harry, at two and a half assertive and wilful, was demanding to see Michael 'at once', and Ellie, just eleven months younger, was doing the same. Maris noted wryly that Rosie was pregnant again.

'Rosie, I see that brother of mine has been busy

again. You're a dark horse. You might have told me, but my God, don't you look blooming,' and was surprised when Rosie blushed a deep and riveting scarlet.

'Hell's bells, Rosie, there's no need to look so guilty. Husbands *are* allowed to get their wives pregnant, you know, especially in wartime,' but not *hers*, of course, and how could he, since, apart from that brief encounter on the deck of the *Bridget O'Malley* at Dunkirk she had neither seen nor heard from him since the war began over eighteen months ago.

'Darling, we didn't know you were home.' Rosie was busy with Ellie all of a sudden, whilst Harry was determined to run across the road to look at what he swore was a genuine 'Jerry bomb'.

'A Jerry bomb! Ye Gods, where did he hear that?'

'Oh, there are evacuees in some of the cottages at Beechwood and they get into the garden. I can't keep them out. You should hear the language, and of course Harry picks it up and passes it on to Ellie. It's like a soldiers' barracks at times.'

'Dear Lord!'

'Exactly.'

After the raid of the night before, Rose explained, she had come over to see if Elizabeth and the two Michaels were all right, but it was not until Harry and Ellie, with young Michael O'Shaughnessy, were secure in Elizabeth's safe back garden where they could come to no harm, that the three women had a chance to look properly at one another.

'Well, mother . . .'

'Well, darling . . .'

'You look marvellous.'

'. . . and so do you.'

'And Rosie . . .'

'. . . of course . . .'

It was true of all three women. Elizabeth O'Shaugh-nessy was in her forty-seventh year, and though she constantly worried about her husband who worked for too long each day, she said, eighteen hours sometimes, at his hush-hush job in the factory, and about her two sons who risked their lives in the skies above the south of England and who, it was said, after eighteen months of it were living on 'borrowed time', she glowed with an inner serenity which her love for her husband and new son gave her. She had not seen Charlie for more than two years and grieved silently for him, but her daughter-in-law, who was in touch with him and was doing her best, she had told Elizabeth, unsuccessfully so far, to effect a reconciliation, gave her news of him. It was not much to a mother who longed with all her heart to be reunited with the son she loved, but it was better than nothing.

They drank tea, weak and sugarless, and talked and laughed about old times, since was that not what every-one did these days? About Maris's job as an ambulance driver and about Rosie's duties as a farmer, which were to be severely curtailed by the imminent expected arrival of her third child. Alex had been home last August and again at Christmas, which had been lovely, but she had been unable to persuade Charlie to join them.

'You see him?' Maris asked incredulously.

'Now and again. He stayed with Uncle Teddy after he was shot down, so I could hardly avoid it.'

'How's his hand?'

'Back to normal now.'

'That's good . . .' and Maris's lack of interest in her brother's health was very evident as she lit a cigarette and turned her head to watch the children in the garden, '. . . but what about those women who are dragging their families into the country,' she continued, '. . . hundreds of them going up Prescot Road.'

'They are badly frightened, darling. Night after night of bombing, and last night was particularly awful.'

'But surely you're safe out here . . . and Rosie.'

'Oh, of course. The Germans are aiming for the docks.' It was well known that one-third of the nation's pre-war maritime trade came via the River Mersey, and the port of Liverpool.

They were still laughing when they parted outside Elizabeth's smart front door. Rosie had offered to give Maris a lift to her mother-in-law's house in Edge Lane, but she refused, saying the walk would do her good.

'I'll be over as soon as I can get my car from Michael's place *and* if he can let me have a gallon of petrol.'

'You promise,' and for the first time Maris noticed the look of strain about her cousin's eyes, and a pinched expression of what she could only call desperation in the set of her soft mouth.

'Try not to worry about him, darling.' She put a hand on Rosie's arm, a gentle touch of understanding, for as well tell the sun to try not to shine than a woman not to worry about the man she loves.

'I will,' but the almost haunted look did not leave Rosie's eyes and Maris felt a pin of unease prick her. Rosie really did look . . . despairing . . . that was the word, and in all the months since the war had begun and Alex had marched off, as men will, to join it, she had never seen her cousin take it as badly as she was doing now.

'I'll be over tomorrow, darling,' she promised. 'We'll talk.'

It would be many months before that promise was kept.

The siren wailed at eleven p.m. just as Maris was going into 'Chips' night-club with Freddie Winters and several other army officers of his acquaintance.

Freddie had telephoned just as she had arrived back home from Ellen's, where she had spent the whole afternoon listening to her mother-in-law repetitively savage the whole German nation and in particular the German Luftwaffe on its appalling and indiscriminate bombing of innocent people.

'Tired of it all, so I am, an' I said so to that ARP chap who comes snooping round to see if I'm showin' a light. When's it all goin' to end, I asked him . . .' just as though it was all his fault and consequently up to him to put a stop to it, '. . . 'tis bad enough seeing me sons and grandsons being took to only the Holy Mother knows where, but now aren't we plagued night an' day with bombs in our own homes. Poor old Matty's terrified, aren't you, pet, but I say if I'm to go, then I'm to go and there's no use hidin' in that blasted thing out there in the garden. An owd woman like me to be gettin' out of me bed the minute I've got in it, well, 'tis bound to shorten me life, so it is, an' me with not much of it left an' certainly none to spare. Old Mr Sanderson's home got a direct hit, poor soul, an' we can only thank the Blessed Mother that he wasn't in it at the time. In the Home Guard, God save us, an' away off somewhere that night, an' when he brings himself home there was nothing left but a heap of rubble. I offered him a bed an' glad of it he was for a couple of nights, an' then off to his sister's in Tuebrook, an' then last night 110 souls all took at once. Did you not hear of it? Sheltering in the crypt of St Brigid's Church, may they all rest in peace. If you can't be safe in God's holy Church then what hope is there for us all? An' that poor baby, did you not hear of that, pet?' looking at her daughter-in-law as if to ask had she come from another planet. 'No? Well, 'twas over Wallesey way. The rescue workers heard what they thought to be a kitten mewing, so they dug into the rubble an' found a baby girl, only a few months old, an' her Mammy an' Daddy dead beside her. She'd been buried for over three days, they say. Jesus, Mary and Joseph, what's the world coming to when innocent babes are torn from their Mammies' arms like that? It doesn't bear thinking about.'

It was a long time, eighteen months in fact, since Maris had dressed up, *really* dressed up, and she decided to do so when Freddie telephoned. He'd heard she was home on a spot of leave and so was he, he told her, and a couple of chaps he knew had asked him to go for a drink at 'Chips', so would she like to come along? Cheer them all up no end if she would.

She wore a long sheath dress of silver satin, backless and cut low at the front with ribbon straps which went over her shoulders and crossed at the back. She had elbow-length silver satin gloves to match, and a scatter of diamanté stars in her short cap of silver curls, and every man in the company declared he was in love with her. They vied with one another to dance with her in the basement night-club where the well-to-do of Liverpool were as safe from the bombing as those in their shelters. Despite the growing shortages she ate pâté and caviare, and drank champagne cocktails, along with the hundreds of others who could afford to pay for such luxuries. The dance-floor was packed and the noise, made by the jazz band and the shrieking laughter of those determined to have a good time no matter what, drowned out the siren, the menacing drone of enemy bombers overhead, the bombs they dropped and the answering roar of the heavy anti-aircraft barrage. It was Saturday, a day, or rather evening, which was tradition-ally a sacred institution of the British way of life. Work is done with, the football match is over, so why not take the wife to a show and perhaps a 'bevvy' afterwards.

They were not to know, those who, damning the enemy, had gone out on their Saturday night spree, that this was to be like no other Saturday night they had ever known. It was to be known as the night 'Lewis's went up'!

They came out of 'Chips' at two o'clock in the morn-ing. They had felt a bump or two when they had been dancing but they had been told that the 'all clear' had sounded, so they were still laughing, still joking, still larking about, quite 'pickled' as Charlie and his RAF chums would have put it, those at the back shouting to those who had gone out first to get a move on. But those at the front, those who had gone up the stairs and through the door of the club before the others, could not bring themselves to 'get a move on' since it meant they would have to leave the protection of the club, and who wants to be the first to step out into hell? That is what it was like. A scene from hell, a conflagration so intense, so mind-numbing, so appalling and unbelievable, they simply stood there, their mouths open, the flames which were all around them reflected in the stunned depths of their eyes. The flames leapt, even as they watched, from building to building, gener-ating a heat so enormous Maris could feel the hairs on her bare arms prickle and singe. The whole city was alight, and stark against the sky above the roof tops, the tower of the cathedral was floodlit by a vicious red glare. A great wind blew, fanning the flames to an even more menacing ferocity, and blazing fragments blew through bomb-blasted windows, whirling and dancing like will o' the wisps.

The wind roared and the greedy flames licked across the road towards the group of paralysed revellers, and one of the women began to scream. The sound broke their trance, and immediately Maris turned on her, slapping her fiercely across her open mouth.

'Shut up, you silly cow. Screaming your head off will do no good. We've got to find a way out of this and we won't do it by panicking.'

'Jesus Christ, Maris . . . which way to turn, old girl. Right or left, d'you think?' Freddie, as cool as herself, showing the spirit of those Winters who had fought at Waterloo, Balaclava and the Somme, held her arm in a vice-like grip, and the other officers, now that the first stunned shock had worn off somewhat, had taken charge of the women who were becoming hysterical in their terror, rearing and bucking like nervous colts, doing their best to get back into the club from where the sound of pandemonium could be heard.

'Perhaps it might be best to stay where we are,' one suggested, but those at the back were pushing at those at the front and they had no choice but to go.

Freddie and Maris began to run along Morrow Street in the direction of Ranelagh Place, but it seemed it had been even more badly hit than where they had come from. Lewis's department store was a holocaust, seven storeys of roaring hell, the flames from it spreading to the nearby store of Blacklers.

'Where in hell's name are the fire brigade?' Freddie shouted, shielding his face with his forearm.

490

'They'll be spread a bit thin in this lot.'

Explosion after explosion tore great holes in the air around them, sucking them along Ranelagh Place towards Lime Street, and as they looked towards the station, searching from habit for a taxi, it was possible to see the night sky about the William Brown Library, the Museum and the Walker Art Gallery, a vivid orange and red canvas against which the lovely old buildings were being ravaged.

The smell was appalling, acrid and burning the throats of those who gulped the air in order to get breath. There was a harsh smell of burning overlaid with the stink of the high explosives contained in the bombs which had been dropped. A smell of gas, seeping, Maris presumed wildly, from fractured pipes, and another smell, rank, raw, the stench of death itself, for there were bodies contained in these broken buildings.

There were people about now, shocked and unrecognisable, running this way and that, their clothing torn away from them, shouting the names, some of them, of those with whom they had set out to 'make a night of it'. A man, his face a black and red mask of blood and burned flesh, blundered into them, beseeching Freddie to tell him where 'their Mary' was, and though she tried to keep hold of him for surely he should not be allowed to go on as he was, he slipped through Maris's fingers, running away from them into what appeared to be the heart of the flames, the name of Mary still on his lips.

The whole geography of the once familiar streets seemed somehow to have altered as entire buildings collapsed in flames of burning rubble. Hot debris had spilled into the road, an inferno of molten rubbish which looked to Maris exactly like the lava which

491

poured from an erupting volcano. The very road seemed to be melting, and as though to emphasise it the tram tracks had twisted and risen up, curving like a gigantic roller-coaster in the middle of the road. There was an enormous round chasm just beyond the corner where Ranelagh Street ran into Ranelagh Place, and in it, its rear end pointing up to the livid scarlet and orange sky, was a tramcar. There were one or two slumped figures in it, those who had been trapped by the slatted seats which had stopped them from tumbling down into the pit where the front of the tram rested. There was someone screaming.

'Oh Jesus . . . oh sweet Jesus . . .' Freddie whispered, and through the roar of the flames, the shouts of men, policemen and civil defence workers, Maris heard his words. Poor Freddie, he had seen nothing like this, as she had at Dunkirk, since he had not as yet 'been to war', and as she had in the past for those who were suffering, even though only at second hand, Maris felt great compassion for him.

First aid posts had been set up in the city as early as 1938, one to every 15,000 inhabitants, since even then it was believed that Hitler would stop at nothing to get his hands on what he considered to be German territory, to defeat those who stood in his way, and what better way to do it than to destroy their innocent civilians? Of course, the people of Liverpool, of London and Hull, Birmingham and Coventry and others were not the primary targets. In Liverpool it was the docks and the same in Hull, or wherever the industry of war was situated.

The first aid posts were manned by doctors, nurses and nursing auxiliaries. There were mobile first aid units which could be despatched to a particularly bad

492

'incident', as these disasters were clinically called, and one was at this moment standing half-way up London Road.

Maris had made up her mind that she would try to get up to Edge Lane to her mother-in-law's house, the nearest place of shelter from this bottomless pit of hell, this lake of fire and torment which lapped around her and Freddie in savage waves. Ellen would be terrified. Her house was somewhat closer to the factories and important buildings which were involved in war work than others of her family, and not for a moment did Maris think that the old lady would consider going into her shelter. Her own mother and Rosie were too far out of the city to be in any great danger, so she was not worried about them. Her own home was not within walking distance and she and Freddie must go somewhere. She needed to get out of these clothes, have a bath, a cup of tea, or something stronger to calm her trembling nerves and those of the two old ladies.

Daylight was breaking, a soft spring morning which, when it came, would reveal such devastation it could not be comprehended. All along London Road, even so far away from the dockland where the enemy bombers had aimed their death and terror, whole streets had been destroyed, flattened, great piles of smouldering debris amongst which, as the sun rose, could be seen a complete wall of a house, floors attached to it, jutting out into nothing, a bed neatly made, a wardrobe tottering in mid-air, skeletons of brick and mortar with smoke and a great pall of dust eddying around. Interior walls were exposed for all to see – though no one looked, not having the time nor inclination – revealing their owners' taste in wallpaper

493

and fireplaces. A pathetic display of violated privacy, and everywhere were the harrowing remains of what had once been some family's life. Dented saucepans, demented dogs, shoes, some still in a pair, chamber-pots, a bowl containing a couple of apples, smashed cups and, by some freak of accident, complete and unharmed dishes perched on a pile of shattered timber. Pictures, books, clocks, broken furniture, all flung about or compressed into an impenetrable sludge of debris as fire hoses were played over them.

There was a sense of frantic urgency now as the men and women of the Civil Defence clambered over the remains of what had once been a public air-raid shelter and which appeared to have taken a direct hit. The mains water had failed, and the fire brigade were taking water from emergency tanks, old baths, pails – anything they could lay their hands on and which could hold the life-saving precious liquid, and which had been brought by willing helpers some of whom had already lost their own homes. Small squads of firemen fought desperately with stirrup pumps as blazing pieces of wood from buildings which were still burning whirled past in the wind.

'Don't stand there gawpin', yer silly buggers,' a warden snarled as Maris and Freddie watched, appalled and terrified. A man in overalls, filthy and black-faced and wearing a tin helmet, held a child in his arms. The little girl's hair was matted with the filth from which they had just clawed her, and her eyes were open and staring in the absolute paralysis of shock. The man was smiling down at her, crooning some comforting tuneless song, his bony, dirt-encrusted, bloody hands gentle about her small body. The warden who had spoken gestured to Maris and Freddie to give him a hand with

494

a piece of charred timber which was too heavy for him to lift alone.

They both sprang to help him, and when they had removed the timber, doing as the warden instructed, they began to delicately scratch with their hands through the rubble of the air-raid shelter. Every minute or so at a sharp word from the local warden, they stopped, listening intently for a sound, a voice, knocking, anything which might reveal the existence or whereabouts of the people inside, seventy-six in all, the warden who had counted them in said, his voice calm and steadying.

It was Maris who found the first. No more than a bit of blackened, filth-encrusted cloth but which seemed to her, having worn one herself when she was under the bonnet of her ambulance, to be the intricate folds of a 'turban'. There was no sound from it, and when she shouted to the nurse who was working beside her, the woman sighed.

'A serious one,' she murmured, 'or she'd be screaming.'

As they moved bits of wood, mortar, broken bricks, a handbag, a child's book, the turban became a head, a face, eyes which were closed, the eyelashes almost hidden beneath the weight of dust on them.

'Move back now, chuck. Don't want to disturb her too much. Not until we've seen what's what, like. See, go up there an' 'elp that chap what's wanderin' around. Take 'im up to't mobile canteen an' gerrim a cuppa. 'Is wife's under this lot so it'd be best if 'e weren't around when we fetch 'er out.'

Some time later there was an explosion of such appalling proportions everyone had instinctively dropped flat in terror, losing several vital minutes, for had the

495

German bombers come back? It was so violent, surely some dreadful catastrophe had occurred, but wherever it was it must not stop the work they did here.

Her mind had become mercifully numb as she moved slowly up London Road in the direction of her mother-in-law's house in Edge Lane. She was choked with the dust and fumes. Sewage spilled out from broken pipes, and excrement lay thick and foul across broken pavements along which lay the shattered, blessedly covered remains of men, women and children, bits and pieces of bodies which somehow must be put together to make, and identify, a whole. Freddie had been lost somewhere in what had been his once immaculately tailored khaki officer's uniform. She herself was almost naked. She had ripped off the bottom half of the skirt of her satin evening dress, which had hampered her clamber over mountain after mountain of debris, and her dainty dancing shoes had long gone. Her bare feet were black and bleeding and her continuous tears, which she had not even known she shed, had left pale runnels down her soot-blackened face. Her hair was caked with grit and dust, and her finger-nails were torn and bloody.

She passed shifting piles of rubbish, where husbands, just come off night-shifts at the factories in which they worked, dug frantically with bare hands in the ruins of the homes they had left at dusk the night before, calling in broken voices for the families they had left in them. Rows of stunned survivors sat on the kerb, their hands hanging limply, their heads lowered, whilst women of the Civil Defence pityingly pressed cups of tea on them, doing their best to lead them away to one of the rest centres in the area, set up in schools and church halls. Ambulances and mobile canteens, the latter gifts from

496

the Dominions or the United States, wobbled dangerously along roads thick with rubble and craters, bringing tea, sandwiches, or even 'scouse' to those who were
not too deep in shock to eat it.

It was ten o'clock in the morning when Maris turned
into Edge Lane, almost nine hours since she and
Freddie – where was he, her mind wondered dully? –
had left 'Chips' night-club. There was smoke hanging
over the Botanic Gardens and Wavertree Park, and a
thin film of white ash lay over the road, the pavements,
the roof-tops, the gardens. Incendiaries had fallen, and
a man hanging over his garden wall asked her if she
was all right, but she did not answer him. The row of
houses in which number eleven stood was thankfully
untouched.

She put her hand on the gate and pushed it open.
The garden, bright and pretty with the plants Donal
and Michael had put in for their mother, was flooded
with the morning sunshine, showing up more clearly
that same thin film of ash which, though she was not
at the time aware of it, came from the millions of books
in the William Brown Library which had gone up in
flames. The door to the house stood open. She moved
inside and as she did so she felt it: the pain, the devastation, the harrowing agony of loss, and the skin of her
arms and the back of her neck prickled warningly.

She heard it then, coming at her in waves, a terrible
sound which rose to an agonising howl, the howl of a
soul in torment or of a man who is in the depths of
such grief it cannot be borne.

It was the voice of Michael O'Shaughnessy.

27

The queue of men waiting outside the single dockside telephone box was long and patient. Nobody spoke because nobody knew what to say. One could hardly remark to an anxious seaman, 'don't worry, mate, they'll be all right,' when it was patently obvious that 'they' might be beneath the flattened rubble which was scattered about the dockland perimeter.

There was an air of thankful relief on some faces as they came away from the kiosk, those who had got through and spoken to wives or mothers, frightened, distraught some of them, but alive, begging Jack or Fred or Alfie to get home quick. But others who had heard only the high-pitched continuous tone which meant the line was out of order, were white-faced and trembling, and it was these who were given special leave to get on home and find out if home was still there.

Callum rang Michael's number since his mother still had no telephone. The line was 'out of order'. He telephoned Rosie and got no reply. Clare answered at Beechwood and said as far as she knew everyone was fine, but Teddy was not at all well and though she hoped to see her brother soon she'd best get back to her husband, if Callum didn't mind.

There was no way up Dale Street and on to London Road except by foot, clambering over the rubble and glass and smashed woodwork, the detritus of the bombardment which had come to ravage the city of Liverpool. Wrecked houses, the smell of newly extinguished fires, fractured gas pipes and sewers, past schools and shops and cinemas and churches which were blasted and in ruins. Everywhere he looked were scenes of tragedy and pain. Women, and men too, weeping and distraught as they surveyed the craters of the homes that had once been theirs. Wrecks of little houses with staircases climbing up walls open to the skies, curtains flapping, wallpaper frayed, broken glass. Men in dusty blue overalls picked over what was left, some in controlled desperation since it was known a living survivor was beneath, others more slowly, or erecting the flags which said there was no hope.

'Give us a hand, mate,' one shouted as he struggled with a piece of brickwork the size of himself. 'Come on, lad, never knew a merchant seaman who wasn't willin' ter lend a birra muscle,' but Callum pretended not to hear and hurried on. *Michael's phone was 'out of order'*.

He turned into Pembroke Place and then again into West Derby Street, going by the shortest possible route, cutting through back streets in which, as a lad, he had often played with his mates, some untouched, others a heaving hive of wardens and nurses, ambulances and fire engines, until he came to Botanic Road.

There was smoke drifting over the Botanic Gardens, and for a moment his heart surged into his throat in terror, for the gardens were bordered on one side by Edge Lane. He was running now, over the sooty grass which had a thin film of white ash across it just like paper which has been burnt in a grate. There was the tram depot, undamaged, thank the Blessed Virgin, and opposite was his mother's house, and in her garden were a dozen children, drooping about in a most

499

unchildlike manner which was so unlike them he knew at once that something was wrong.

He heard the howling as he opened the front gate. Mrs Donavan was at her front window, her face screwed up in bewildered sorrow, but when she saw him she hastily dropped her white net curtains as though she had been caught spying on some private thing which she truly mourned.

It had been the only house to be hit in Craven Road, a direct hit, probably caused by an enemy bomber, the warden had explained sadly, jettisoning its load before it headed back to its base in France. Elizabeth and her son, Michael, when they were found, were quite dead, and had it not been for the timely intervention of the same warden, who had seen her husband pick up the shard of glass and begin to hack at his own wrists, Michael would have been dead, too.

The kitchen at Ellen's was in utter chaos, a madhouse of lamenting and oppression, and in the corner of the chimney Maris sat quietly, waiting to be told what she should do next in this world which seemed, slowly but surely, to be stripping her of all the people she held most dear. No one took a great deal of notice of her. Their concern was with those who could not help themselves, and her quiet acceptance, her trance-like stillness which they did not recognise as the deepest state of shock, did not seem to need attention. The cries of her mother's husband were like those of a severely injured animal, and Maris wished she could do something to put him out of his pain, as one does with a wounded beast which is certainly not going to survive, at least with any quality of life. He was flinging himself about, ricocheting off walls, hurting himself badly, fighting with his two brothers who were doing their best to restrain him whilst they waited for the doctor to give him a 'knock-out' of something or other to put him to sleep. Grace and Amy were crying in a broken-hearted way, milling about in an effort to give aid to Donal and Eammon, whilst Eileen herded wailing children out of the kitchen and into the hallway since it was no place for them at a time like this. Not now. Not in the face of the bitter and savage grief of her brother, who threatened the minds and the fragile flesh and bone of them all. Michael was likely to hurt not only himself but anyone who stood in his way towards the death he longed for, for what had life to offer him now?

Ellen sat in her rocking-chair and rocked backwards and forwards, silent, dry-eyed, old and withered, her expression, her posture which was slumped and brooding, saying she could really no longer be a part of this eternal suffering. Her son was insane, gone quite mad with grief, and she herself could not pull them together, her badly shattered family, as once she had done. The kettle sat idle on the fire-back, empty and lifeless, the fire almost out, and on the opposite side of the grate was Matty, her hands frail and trembling, waiting for an order that did not come.

It was this which met Callum as he hesitated in the kitchen doorway. No one saw him. He had kissed the distraught Eileen at the front door, unable to ask her and she unable to tell him who it was who had been taken from them, but it was obvious who it was the moment he entered the kitchen.

It was Matty who first noticed him. Her sad old eyes brightened, and she put out a compassionate hand to Ellen, drawing her attention to her son. Ellen turned, and for a moment or two it seemed she did not recognise him. He was just a quiet figure in a uniform.

A policeman, perhaps, like the one who had gone to get Donal and Eammon, since someone must hold on to her poor demented son until the doctor came. Not more bad news, her weary face pleaded, but as he moved forward, dropping his seabag to the floor, she saw who it was and lifted her old arms to him. Sinking to his knees, he held her to him, rocking her sudden outpouring of grief, her poor, time-worn body, until her tears wet the navy-blue serge of his jacket, the tears of the old which are so painful but which are the first step towards healing.

'Callum, oh Callum, darlin'. When's it to end, pet? Poor Elizabeth . . . and the child . . . an' will you look at himself . . . will he ever get over it . . . ?' Not content with taking his first wife and his lovely young daughter, the gods who, it seemed, could bear no one to be happy for long, had deprived him of his lovely Elizabeth, and the little son who had come to bless him and replenish the aching hollow the desertion of Cliona had left. How was he to withstand this last savage blow? How would he ever pick up his life again and go on? Did he want to? and the answer, of course, was no, not by the sounds of the tormented cries which were being contained in the strong and compassionate arms of his brothers. Michael's world was shattered and swept away. His, and all the others who had had theirs stolen from them in the last horrific months. Wives and children lost. Not just soldiers, men who went away to fight, but families in their homes, exterminated, or wounded so badly they would never be the same again. God, it was not to be borne and yet it must be. Men must go away not only uncertain of their own return but of the expectation that their loved ones would be waiting for them if they did.

'. . . go to him, pet . . . I'm all right . . . go to him an' see if . . . I can't bear to see him suffer . . . May the Holy Mother ease his pain for I can't . . . Oh son . . . what are we to do, that lovely woman and the boy . . . so fine and strong . . . the apple of his Daddy's eye, so he was . . . an' her . . . his wife . . . always, all these years he's waited . . . waited, an' now she's gone . . .'

Callum was bewildered by what his mother was saying, babbling on about her son and his wife and waiting, but would you blame her for being confused? Her mind was deep in shock. She was an old woman who had been struck many blows in her long life. She had survived them, but perhaps each one had weakened her, making her more defenceless, less able to manage the next. Strong she had been in her early years, nurturing, supportive; with comforting arms, a shrewd and practical mind which could tackle problems head-on, *and* find the answers. Never uncertain or doubting, and now *he* and those of the family who were capable of it must do the same for her.

The doctor came, dishevelled and bloodstained, evidently straight from some other family's tragedy, and, held down by his brothers, Michael was given an injection and helped up the stairs where he was put in the bed which had been his as a boy.

'He'll sleep, or should do, for twenty-four hours, Callum,' Doctor Fraser, who had treated the O'Shaughnessys ever since the old Doctor had retired, told the older brother. 'He'll need watching. Someone to sit beside him until he wakes, and then only the Blessed Mother herself knows what's to become of him, poor chap.' He shook his head, bewildered and sorrowful, the pain and grief he had seen, not only in this home but in many others in the past eight months since the air raids had begun, something he found hard to accept and never would, not if he lived to be as old as Doctor Fogarty who still pottered about at the surgery.

'There's plenty of us to do it, Doctor,' but they had been sadly decimated by the war, the O'Shaughnessy male adults, not dead, but gone off to wherever they were sent, and it would need someone strong and determined to control the savagery brought on by the devastating grief suffered by his brother Michael. Callum himself must try to get back to his ship before the day was out, but he had been told that the *Bridget O'Malley* was to have a refit, which would mean long leave. The men badly needed it. Life in the Atlantic convoys was a matter of mounting strain, taking a toll of men's nerves and patience, leading to quarrelling in the wardroom, outbreaks of fighting in the mess decks, and its only cure was a proper rest with relaxation from fear, danger, discipline. A replenishment so that they, and he, could take up their burden again. For eighteen months they had known nothing else, and the six weeks' course of rejuvenation would give them all a chance to wind down from the constant state of tension in which they lived whilst at sea. He, of course, would have to be on board for a good deal of the time they were in port, but he was sure, on compassionate grounds, he would be allowed to spend time ashore with his brother, who would need him, and with . . . with Maris . . . Maris, who was his wife and who sat so quietly in her corner, placidly staring at nothing, and who seemed to have been overlooked in the trauma of Michael's breakdown. It was not only Michael's wife and son who had been killed but Maris's mother and half-brother.

'Maris,' he said gently, standing before her, and

when she looked up at him he was shocked at the expression in her eyes. No, not her expression, but the *lack* of any expression at all. Like two windows where no light shows, the blinds drawn, the shutters pulled to. He had scarcely looked at her in the confusion which had orbited the kitchen, but now that some order was being restored, he had the time to study her more closely. Gracie had replenished the fire and filled the kettle. Amy was holding her mother's hand, patting it, talking to her quietly, tears still falling, but now that some cohesion had been effected, calmer, stronger, both of them ready to take up what had bludgeoned them and deal with it as best they could. Matty and Eileen were lifting dishes from the dresser and laying the table, scratching their heads over what could be put in the mouths of those who would surely need some sustenance after what had happened. The children had gone, taken away by their mothers who had come from the munitions factory where they worked, to be put in the care of Tess who didn't, or a handy neighbour who would 'see' to them until the crisis was over.

Maris was still wearing the scrap of silver satin she had put on almost twenty-four hours ago. Her legs were bare, and so were her feet, bare and filthy and blood-stained, scraped at the knee and with deep purple bruises where she had come into contact with the vicious tumble of bomb-blasted homes. Her hands were in the same condition, and her finger-nails were torn and brown with dried blood. She looked just like one of the victims she herself had helped to dig out from the treacherous rubble under which they had been buried, the illusion added to by her air of having slipped away from the world of reality, the feeling that she was not really there, or at least, only in the flesh. Not unlike the last time he had seen her on the slippery deck of his own ship, almost a year ago.

He had never sent the letter he had tried to write to her. He had acknowledged to himself, quietly and with no great surprise, that his wife meant more to him than he could have believed possible and – more to the point – than he could honestly manage. That he was not at all prepared to begin the long and what might be unsuccessful courting of the woman who in all probability no longer wanted him. The whole world was spinning out of control as this war, this second *world* war as it was sure to be, gathered momentum. He might be dead within the week, the month, so what could possibly be the purpose in renewing, or trying to, a relationship which might come to nothing anyway? If she still cared about him, as he was well aware she had done, long ago, there would only be fresh sorrow for her if he did not return from the dangerous Atlantic run, and if, as seemed most likely, she had found someone else – the pang at this thought slicing him to the bone – then it would serve no purpose, to him or her, if he should throw the bombshell of his love which, unknowingly, he had probably always carried inside him, at her feet. She had her life, the one she had built with her own guts and tenacity, when war began. A worthwhile life as she played her part in the defence of her country. She had become somebody and no longer needed Callum O'Shaughnessy to give her an identity. They both had undertakings which must be finished before their own personal relationship could be considered. What was involved? To go on with what they had, to build on it and make it strong, or to divorce, must be left until later. They must wait, he had told himself sorrowfully, he and Maris, until another time, and if that time did not come then they must go on, apart, perhaps one of them no longer of this world, without dwelling on what might have been.

So he had told himself until his wife, this beloved woman who did not know of his feelings, looked up with blank eyes into his face. He lifted her up into his arms and held her gently against him with a great compassionate love. He looked over her head at his mother and met her understanding eyes, and they told him what he should do. They could manage without him until Michael woke up, they said. Go, they said. Take her. Love her, for that is what she needs. What you both need. It will give you both the strength for what is to come when the numbing, merciful shock wears off her. As it surely will.

She fought against the arms that held her, screaming and struggling in terror. They held her down, dragging her further beneath the mountain of broken masonry which had fallen on her, and the dust filled her mouth and blinded her eyes. The sweat of panic slicked her body, and the arms held her tighter, and the voice roared in her wounded mind that it was all right, that she had nothing to fear, which she knew to be untrue for her mother was dead. The beautiful gracious mother who had never been anything but unfailingly kind and loving and patient towards her for all of her life, and without whom she really did not think she could manage.

'Mother . . .' she called, screamed, and the arms loosened and let her go and she slid back thankfully into the black pit of emptiness where she stayed, though she was not aware of the passage of time, for over twenty-four hours, and when she awoke Mrs Flynn was sitting by her bed, her fingers busy with the khaki sock on which she was about to turn the heel.

She glanced up and what Maris had always thought of as her 'sour puss' face was lit with a pitying kindliness.

'Sure an' didn't you sleep the clock round, alannah? Himself had to go over to Edge Lane to see to that poor brother of his, but didn't he ask me to bide a while until you woke up. He'll be back directly, says he . . .'

Of course, and where else would he be but beside that old woman at Edge Lane, beside his brothers and sisters and the growing multitude of children who, despite there being so many of them, all supporting one another whenever there was trouble, had to have her husband in their midst, sucking at his life to nourish theirs, taking from *her* what was rightfully hers, demanding as a right, claiming without thought, the comfort, the support, the arms which should be about *her*. But what did it matter? Had she expected it to be any different? Had she expected anything different from Callum after all these years? She had lost her mother in the most devastating way. Her mother, who had been torn from her family where she had been dearly loved and would be sorely missed, and Maris must grit her teeth and overcome her sorrow and the pain which would come, but sometimes, just once, could she have been blamed for expecting her own husband to show a certain . . . sympathy? He had brought her home and put her to bed – whilst Michael slept, she supposed, for though she had been senseless and shocked in Ellen's kitchen she had been aware in a drifting kind of way what had been happening. She had seen Callum with her blind eyes and felt him lift her from her corner by the chimney, but from then until now there was nothing but a void in which no memory stirred.

She still felt numb. She could not really believe that she would never see her mother again, that was the trouble. She fully expected her to put her head round the door and ask her how she was and could she do anything for her? There was a great emptiness inside her. Not hurting, not ready to weep with it, just a refusal to believe that it had happened. That Elizabeth, that her precious son, the boy Michael were . . . were as the poor, pitiful broken bodies she had seen brought from the wreckage . . . that her lovely mother was . . . her face smashed . . . the child . . . a limp and lifeless doll . . . The pictures in her mind were too awful to contemplate after what she had so recently seen . . . she must not think of it . . . if only Callum had been here to . . . Christ . . . oh Jesus Christ . . . please . . .

'Will I fetch you a cup of tea, Mrs O'Shaughnessy?' Mrs Flynn was saying, folding her knitting into the large bag she always carried round with her. Maris had never known what it contained. Knitting apparently, and who could the sock be for? she wondered indifferently. She had never thought of Mrs Flynn as a *real* person, with a husband, children perhaps, one of whom might be a soldier who needed warm woollen socks. She had always been the 'spy', the one Ellen had wheedled into Maris's house, Callum's house, for the sole purpose of keeping her eye on Maris's 'comings and goings'.

'She was a foine lady,' Mrs Flynn said abruptly.

'I beg your pardon?'

'Your Mammy. A lovely lady. Sure an' I'm not meanin' to upset you, pet, but I can't leave without sayin' it . . .'

'I didn't know you knew her.'

'Oh indeed. Wasn't she one of me ladies?'

'Your . . . ?'

'I "did" for her, so, an' a finer one I've never met. Kind an' . . . thoughtful. Now then, shall I be fetchin' that cup of tea? An' you'll be wantin' a bath, so you will, an' that man of yours says I'm to stay with you until he gets home . . .'

'No, that won't be necessary, Mrs Flynn . . .'

'I know it won't, pet, but don't let her out of your sight, says he, an' I'll telephone soon, says he, an' anything she wants she's to have, says he . . .'

'I want my mother, Mrs Flynn.'

Instantly she was snatched up from her pillows and smothered in an embrace which was as soft and warm and comforting as it was amazing, and when she began to weep with an abandonment which was terrifying, it was not Callum O'Shaughnessy who comforted his wife as he had wanted to, as he had tried to in their bed during the night, but his wife's cleaning woman whose well-hidden heart was as big as the bucket she used to scrub Maris's kitchen floor.

They learned later that the explosion which had occurred after the 'all clear' on that unreal Sunday morning had been that of the merchant vessel *Marakand* which at the time had been laden with 1,000 tons of bombs. Incendiaries had dropped on her. They had been extinguished by the crew, but a barrage balloon, one of those hated by Ellen since they hung over her back garden wall, had broken loose and by a stroke of chance had fouled the rigging of the ship. The hydrogen gas had ignited, setting the hatch covers on the deck alight. Even whilst bombs fell about them, the crew and firemen tried to fight the fire, but eventually the ship had had to be abandoned and it had exploded like an earthquake. The damage done was devastating.

510

Sheds about the ship simply vanished. A four-ton anchor was thrown 100 yards, sinking a dock board hopper and several other vessels which were near by. Steel plates landed two and a half miles away, one of them falling on and instantly killing Roddy O'Shaughnessy, the eleven-year-old son of Eammon and Tess O'Shaughnessy, and his brother Patrick, who was a year younger and who had been searching along Dock Road for the souvenirs beloved of small boys.

At 11.55 that night the sirens sounded again. The Luftwaffe had returned with their deadly cargo, and the fires from the previous night's raid, which were still blazing in many places, guided in the crews to their targets.

The following night, which was a Monday, they came again. People had done their best to get to work on that morning but roads were blocked, bridges destroyed, and railway and tramlines were twisted and unusable. Exchange Station was still ablaze after three days, and troops had been brought in to help with restoration. The bombers, it was thought, were aiming not only for the dock area but for the huge complex of the Edge Hill railway sidings, not a skip or a jump from Ellen's house in Edge Lane, and though bombs and incendiaries fell again in Wavertree Park and the Botanic Gardens, Ellen's house was undamaged. Not that she, nor any other member of her stunned and silent family would have noticed, Doctor Fraser was inclined to think, as they struggled to cope with the mad grieving of Michael and Eammon and Tess.

Again the bombers came over, the sixth night in succession, and the people of Liverpool shuddered beneath the terrible blows which fell on them. On the seventh they returned, and again on Thursday, May

8th, and 70 out of 144 berths at the docks were put out of action. 80,000 tons of shipping had been sunk or destroyed, access to and from the docks to the river was blocked, and the railways could neither deliver nor collect the cargos which remained undamaged. 10,840 houses had been destroyed and 184,000 damaged. 1,453 persons had been killed and 1,056 injured in Liverpool alone, and that was not counting the towns of Bootle, Birkenhead and Wallesey.

And as suddenly as it had begun, it ended.

On Friday, May 9th, the funerals took place of Elizabeth and young Michael O'Shaughnessy, who were buried together, not in the Catholic cemetery of her husband's family but at Colton parish church with the Osbornes and the Woodalls and the Hemingways who were a part of her heritage.

'She would have wanted it,' her husband said, the first words he had spoken in a week. 'She'll be . . . with her own there. I don't want her to be lonely until I follow . . .' and it did not go unnoticed that beside her was her first husband, which her second did not seem to mind, and nobody, not even his own mother, cared to argue with him. He did not weep, nor bow his head, but stared with unfocused eyes across the grave into which his own reason for life was being lowered, across the fields, bright with the sunshine and flowers of spring, across the woods to where Woodall Park lay. He appeared to be listening, not to the parson's words but to some sound only he could hear, perhaps from long ago when a young girl of fifteen had been kissed by a young man in Old Wood.

Elizabeth's sons were there, standing side by side in the immaculate officer's uniform of the Royal Air Force, not speaking, exchanging not even a glance, and

512

it was not missed by those present that the moment the last word of the committal was spoken, Sir Charles Woodall turned on his heel and left.

Pilot Officer Alex Woodall held the hand of his wife, who wept with the abandonment of a child, clinging to him as if she could scarcely stand, which was not surprising really since she had given birth to their third child, a son, on the night her Aunt Elizabeth had been killed. All by herself, it was said, with no one to help with the delivery beyond the simple girl who scrubbed her kitchen floor.

Captain Callum O'Shaughnessy's wife, the daughter of the dead woman, was like stone, unmoved and unmoving, no one but her own cleaning woman having seen her tears, and when her husband would have taken her arm as they made their way towards the motor cars which were to take them on to the funeral of Captain O'Shaughnessy's two young nephews, it was noticed by several of Elizabeth O'Shaughnessy's – or as they still called her, Elizabeth Woodall – old friends, that Maris pulled it out of his grasp quite fiercely.

There was a young woman standing by the arched gateway of the Catholic cemetery of St Xavier's. She was all in black, and when the party, including the stiff figure of Maris O'Shaughnessy moved behind the two small coffins, behind the strangely silent mourners who were still stunned by what had happened to them in one short week, the woman followed. She stood slightly apart from the others, as though she did not want to intrude herself on this grieving family which had buried four of its own on this day.

The kitchen at Edge Lane, the parlour, the hallway and the gardens were crowded as they had been so many times in the past. Crowded with people and with the emotions the house had always known. Many joyful, but now with the sorrow which was vital and loud and outpouring. There was a slight lessening of the strain which had gripped them for a week. They had buried their dead and the ritual of committing to God's care their loved ones had comforted them. The laying to rest of those they loved had brought a small measure of peace to the ones left behind. A decent burial with family and friends, with the sad hymns and the tears, the sympathy and the flowers, the relief when it was all over, when life would resume, with holes in it, naturally, but got through, until the grief lessened and acceptance came.

Tess wept quietly still for her two handsome boys, her youngest on her knee to comfort her, her grieving husband's hand on her shoulder, ready, should he be needed, to comfort her too.

Ellen was still stunned by what she could only describe as the worst week of her life, even the death of her old Mick not as sorely felt as this. Mick had been at the end of his life, and her three grandsons only at the beginning, and as for Elizabeth, had any woman had such a dear friend or daughter-in-law? She remembered the day her Bridget had died, thirty years ago now, when the young Elizabeth, herself no more than seventeen and almost a stranger, had come to offer her condolences to Bridget's grieving mother. God rest her sweet soul and the Holy Mother give her eternal peace. Ellen's son, the widower – for the second time, God love him – sat frozen and ashen-faced, facing a future he could not bear to contemplate, an untouched cup of tea he had been holding for the past hour, in his hand. He spoke not a word, which Ellen didn't know whether to be glad about or to worry over. His cries on the day of his wife's death had been agonising, but was this lethal silence any better, she asked herself?

The young woman came through the open front door, up the hallway and into the kitchen. She passed by the suddenly silenced multitude of people and paused in the doorway, her eyes going at once to the man by the fire. They knew her, of course they did, and yet they didn't, since she had changed beyond recognition.

It was six long years, but Cliona O'Shaughnessy had come home.

28

'Christian is dead.'

The flat, almost detached tone of Cliona O'Shaughnessy's voice made the statement even more compelling, and in her chair by the fire Ellen crossed herself sadly, unable as yet to absorb the death of another of her grandsons. It was too much for any woman to bear, and so she switched off that part of her mind which needed to grieve, and gloated instead over the faint colour in her eldest son's face, the pale light of . . . yes, *hope* in her son's eyes as he held his daughter's hand and gazed into her care-worn face. He had come alive again, only barely, but his daughter's return from the dead, as it were, had raised him too.

'I've come home, Daddy,' she had said in that first moment, her voice falling into the absolute silence of Ellen's kitchen, where even the youngest was in thrall to the emotion which thickened the very air they breathed. 'I could stay away no longer when I heard . . . will you not greet me, Daddy?' for Michael O'Shaughnessy sat in his chair, an old man, frozen there like some granite statue which has been carved from living stone but is now dead. His gaunt face, stripped of its firm flesh during the past week, and already, or so it seemed, bearing the waxy pallor of death, took on the hue and texture of the ash which spilled in the fireplace, and his breath rattled in his throat as though he was about to choke. The cup and saucer fell from his hand with a clatter that shifted the old tabby indignantly from her time-honoured position by the fire. The crockery broke, and as Michael stood up, cautiously, for it appeared he was afraid he might shatter as the cup and saucer had done if he made any sudden movement, his foot crunched on the broken pieces.

The company waited, its breath held, and in the scullery doorway Matty wept helplessly, her breath coming in short, hiccuping gasps. Tears were flowing freely down more than one face, and as Gracie said later to her sisters, it was a wonder any of them had any moisture left in them, the tears which had been shed lately. Fill a bucket they would, or even two.

'Child . . .'

'Daddy . . . ?'

'Is it you . . . really you . . . ?'

'It is, Daddy . . . if you'll have me . . .' and as her father lifted his arms, and his voice in a great roar of rejoicing, she flew into them. They closed about her hungrily, and father and daughter rocked together, their tears meeting and mingling. No one spoke nor scarcely breathed for five long minutes, watching and waiting, giving blessed thanks to the Holy Mother who had sent one of their own back to them to help replace those who had gone this week.

But where had she been? What had she done? Why had she gone? Why had she done it? And why had she come back? How had she known of her father's desperate need of her? The questions were at first put to her anxiously in the spirit of loving, caring kinship, for was she not theirs and had she not gone away without warning? But she had left her Daddy wild with worry, they began to remember, so they became truculent, for how could she have done it to him? To her

517

Daddy, who had gone out of his mind with fear and desperate dread for her safety. They had thought better of her, really they had. Not a minute's trouble had she given to her Daddy before this and him so good to her, so loving, and then to leave him like that. How could she have done it? How could she? Christian was well known to be . . . thoughtless and wilful . . . but *Cliona*? And where was he, the spalpeen? 'Twas down to him, this tragedy which . . .

'Christian is dead.'

'Holy Mother of God.'

'May his soul rest in peace.'

'Mother of Jesus rest with him,' for despite his wild and even wicked ways, if one was to believe the stories of what the IRA got up to, he was an O'Shaughnessy and the son of a Catholic family who believed in forgiveness and redemption for one's sins.

'He's been dead these two years . . .'

'*Two years!* Jesus, Mary and Joseph, and his family not knowing.' Gracie leaned from the circle of accusing faces, then covered her own with a shaking hand. She, like the rest of them, had not been overly fond of Christian Osborne but he was family and should have been properly mourned.

'There seemed no purpose in telling you. He was dead to you all the moment he set foot on the soil of Ireland. He loved it. It became his family. It took the place of you all, and when he died he made me promise not to get in touch with you. He was an Irish patriot. He believed in a free and united Ireland and you did not.'

'And what about you, Cliona O'Shaughnessy?' Amy's voice was accusing, unforgiving, that first jubilant delight which the sight of her niece had stirred in her swept away as the pain and hurt and cold disapproval was remembered. 'Are you still involved in . . . ?'

'*That's enough!*' It was Michael's voice which thundered through the kitchen and crowded hallway, rising up the stairs to the very attics. 'That's enough. She's come home. My daughter has come home an' for now that's enough. Sure an' she's only just over the doorstep and explanations can come later, but darlin' . . . oh my darlin'' – turning to pull her into his arms again, '. . . welcome home.'

'No . . . Daddy, they have a right to know.'

'They can wait at least until you've a cup of tea took.'

'Please let me tell them; then, if it's no bother, I'd like to rest. I'm very tired.'

She had taken off her hat, an old shapeless beret which Maris remembered she had worn on the day she and Rosie had seen her in London Road. She shook her head and her thick curling hair fell about her shoulders, and they all gasped with shock. It was no longer dark and glossy but grey, a drab grey with no white in it, no silver or indeed anything to lift it from the neutral shade of old age. Her skin was much the same colour, only her eyes remaining of the girl they had once known, the clear blue-green brilliance of her O'Shaughnessy inheritance. She was no more than twenty-three but she might have been twenty years older. Her sadness, the weariness of her soul as well as her body was unmistakable, and those about her became quiet, falling back from her patient, submissive humility, waiting for her to begin.

It was a short tale. She wasted no words and certainly no emotion in the telling of it. It had already taken six years of her young life, the cause in which she had

519

believed, and still did; but the execution of it, the tactics employed by its soldiers, the bloodshed and slaughtering of those not involved in it had turned the resolve which had been hers at the beginning into a belief that if this was the only way to achieve their purpose, which was a free and self-governing united Ireland, then she wanted no part of it. There must be another way, a peaceful way, and if it could be found she would lend herself to its cause again.

'And Christian?' her father prompted.

'He was shot just before the war began in 1939. We had . . . he was here, as I was . . .' turning for a moment to Maris, '. . . there had been a declaration by the army . . . the Irish Republican Army that we . . . they were to intervene in the military and commercial life of Britain as the British had intervened in . . . ours. There was . . . there were deaths . . . in Coventry . . .'

She stopped and slowly her head bowed. She put her face in her hands and her shoulders shook, and in an instant, despite the horror they had all felt at the time of the bombings and which they could clearly remember, they reached for her, patting her shoulder, ready to comfort, for was that not their nature? Big-hearted, forgiving, loving. Michael took her in his arms, and drew her closely to him. She was sitting at his knee on the stool on which Ellen usually rested her feet, and she leaned into him in what seemed to be to them, thankful relief, as though some great load was being lifted from shoulders which had never really been strong enough nor determined enough to carry it. A young girl whose head and heart had been turned by an idealism, an *idea* that had not really been hers in the first place.

Her voice was muffled against her father's chest and they strained forward to hear it.

'It was August. We knew there was to be war. Christian had been imprisoned . . .' her voice was stronger now, '. . . for a short time. When he was released we were called back to . . . We went. A week later, the last week in August, he and some others were sent to release a man who was being taken for trial. There was shooting and Christian was hit.'

'Holy Mother bless him . . .' Ellen reached out to Gracie, who took her hand.

'He lost a lot of blood before they got him back to me . . . to where . . . it was a safe place but there was no doctor. He died in my arms.'

'God rest his eternal soul.' They all crossed themselves piously, all except Maris, and Michael O'Shaughnessy, whose faith in a living, loving God had been severely shaken on the day Michael's wife and son were killed.

'Did he have a decent burial, pet?' Ellen begged to know tearfully, meaning was he buried, shriven in the Faith and by the offices of the Catholic Church.

'He had a soldier's burial, grandmother, for that was what he was.'

'And you, darlin'? What about you?'

'I am to come home to be with Daddy, if he will have me.'

'Why did you not come when Christian died?'

'I . . . could not. I still felt there might be . . . something I could do. That I might . . . take Christian's place, but it was not in me to fight as some of our women did, so . . . I nursed those who were wounded in the cause . . . for a while . . . then I went to the nuns and they let me work with them . . . in a hospital for the poor . . .' Her voice trailed away and there was silence for a moment.

'An' how did you know about . . . your Daddy's loss?'

'We . . . they . . . the movement have ties here, links in Liverpool. They told me, and I knew it was time to come home.'

'Thank God . . . thank the good God . . .' and father and daughter wept together, the tears which are the beginning of healing.

They rode back in silence to Seymour Road as they had done so many, many times. Michael had managed to get some petrol for the MG, and Callum drove it carefully through the blacked-out streets, navigating the debris and craters, taking diversions where streets were still blocked.

The house was in darkness, the black-out carefully fixed by the vigilant Mrs Flynn. She had left a loaf of bread and some cheese, a few slices of bacon and a couple of eggs on the kitchen table, all carefully covered by a snowy white cloth, and thankfully, a small fire still glowed in the fireplace of the front room.

'Would you like me to cook you some bacon and eggs, Maris? You ate nothing at the Mammy's. In fact, I've seen you eat nothing all day.'

'No thanks, I'm not hungry.'

'How about a bacon "butty" then?' smiling wryly at her, hoping for some response, perhaps a flicker of a smile. 'I'm quite a dab hand with bacon butties. Guaranteed to be delicious and thick as a doorstep, as they should be.'

'Thank you, Callum, but no. I think I'll turn in.'

'A cup of tea, at least.'

'I seem to have done nothing but drink tea,' reaching into her handbag and lighting a cigarette from the packet she took from it.

'And smoke cigarettes.'

'Aah . . . yes.'

'You smoke too much, you know that?'

'Really,' clearly unconcerned, about that, or about anything and certainly about *him*, and Callum felt his gut twist in pain. She had been like this for the past week. Not caring, it appeared to him, whether he came or went, spoke or was silent, herself like a pale, drifting copy of the spirited woman he had once known. Not that he had seen much of her in the past eighteen months, so how could he judge what her feelings were? but her grieving for her mother and her small brother was not done in his presence. She was quiet, withdrawn, polite, cycling up to Beechwood and Lacy's house on a bicycle she had borrowed from one of the land girls, being with Rose and her new son, who was called James after his maternal grandfather. Never at home when Callum came back from the ship and not speaking in his company unless he spoke to her. She went to the bed they had shared before the war and he to the one they had bought to accommodate Rose when he and Maris were first married. He was nothing to her now, he could see that, and the irony of the situation, had it not been so wretched, might have made him smile ruefully. All these years when he might have had her love he had ignored it, been embarrassed by it, irritated by it, scorning it and her, because it and she had been forced on him.

Now, as though to punish him for his indifference, it was all turned about and *he* was the one who loved, who suffered, who was rejected. And yet, on the two occasions they had met and he had pulled her hungrily into his arms she had – he was sure of it, or had been then – she had responded. She had clung to him. Her lips had clung to his, and for a perfect moment they had been equal in love.

Well, she was certainly not responding to him now, staring blindly at the glowing end of her cigarette, hardly aware that he was there. A small and pathetic figure all in black, her face a pale ivory oval of sadness, no make-up, not even lipstick, which somehow added to her fragile beauty. Only her hair was as it had always been, a halo of silver pale curls which nothing could subdue. Her hands and the fingers between which her cigarette drooped were still marked by the grazes and cuts she had suffered after the air raid last week.

'Let me . . . help you, Maris.' The words surprised them both and she looked up, her eyebrows raising in a question.

'Help me? How could *you* help *me*?'

He winced at the coldness of the question. 'I don't know. I only know I would like to.'

'Why?'

'I'm not an ogre, my love. You have . . . suffered this week. Your mother was very dear to you . . . and the boy. I just thought . . .'

'What?'

'That if you needed . . . anything, I would be only too glad to . . . to . . .' to put my arms about you and hold you close. Tuck your stubborn head beneath my equally stubborn chin and hold you close, console your grief, share it, take it from you. Kiss you and love you and ease your sorrowing mind until it is emptied of sadness. Fill it with my love until there is no room for hurt, only joy . . . dear God . . . dear sweet God, to do this to them, to play this appalling trick on them. Just when she needed what he would give his right arm to have her take, it no longer interested her. She no longer cared. Chance, fate, the laughing, scornful gods had taken Callum and Maris and twisted what might have been good between them, precious, dear to them both, and made a mockery of it. The silent, indifferent woman who lounged by the fire smoking one cigarette after another, the carefully polite man who watched her, might, this night, have found consolation, some respite from the fear and horror of the war they fought, the sorrow it had brought them, in one another's arms.

'I'm perfectly all right, really I am, Callum. Just tired, though it is very kind of you.' The words she had been taught by her Nanny to say, polite, as a well-bred little girl was polite.

'I wish you would . . .'

'What?'

What indeed? What could he offer her? Once he had held her in his arms and comforted her, and look what had come of that. The day her father was buried . . . Holy Mother . . . that had been the start of it . . .

'How different you are.' His voice was bemused.

'Different?' She raised her head and stared at him.

'On the day of your father's funeral. You wept then.'

'And I have not wept today. Is that what you mean?'

'Yes, but I'm sorry. I should not have said it. You are still shocked . . . to lose your mother . . . for her to die so young and so suddenly . . . Christ, I'm sorry . . .'

'No, you're right. She was too young to die. She had so much to live for. Michael loved her so . . .'

'I know. She was . . . everything to him . . .'

'And their child. Such a handsome little boy . . . so bright and . . . promising . . .' Her voice died away and she bowed her head again and his whole body leaned towards her in a great male yearning to protect her from harm, from grief, from hurt, this woman who had become so beloved, so dear to him. Brave she was, and spirited, and to see her brave spirit quenched tore the heart from him.

'I scarcely knew your mother but she was always . . . kind to me.'

'She was a kind woman. She loved people. She was kind to them, seeing . . . the best in them and letting them know she admired them for it. She gave . . . herself, I suppose you would say . . . to my father when he would have let go. He was so ill sometimes. To me and my brothers . . . both of them . . . she tried . . . but they were wilful. If only she could have seen them united, but even at her grave they didn't speak. Not even at her grave, and I cannot forgive them for it.'

'Maris, don't . . .'

'After what she had done for them, for us all . . .'

'I know . . . I know, darlin' . . .'

Somehow they had drawn nearer to one another as the ice about her began to melt, to show the first hairline crack. Her spectacular tears, those which flowed like great crystal raindrops from her enormous eyes and down her drawn cheeks, had begun to form on her bottom lashes, to fill and overflow, and he reached into his pocket and silently handed her his handkerchief. She took it but just held it in her hand as her face became awash, the moisture running from the very pores of her skin, or so it seemed to Callum.

'Oh Jesus . . . Callum . . .'

'Maris . . .'

'Oh Jesus . . . she didn't deserve it . . . not her . . . not that innocent baby . . .'

'None of them deserve it, Maris . . . none of them . . .'

'And Michael . . . what will he do . . . ?' She had begun to howl in her anger, her angry, frustrated sorrow, flinging her head from side to side in an explosion of grief. He put out his hand to her but she knocked it aside, losing her balance and falling heavily against the fireplace.

'Christ . . . Maris . . .'

'It's not fair . . .'

'I know, I know . . .' He took her by the shoulders, ready to steady her, or shake her, for her savage pain was turning to hysteria, violent and damaging.

'Callum . . .' Her weeping would become uncontrollable if he did not stop it, so he did the only thing he could, what he had longed to do since they had entered the house, since the day her mother was killed, since the day he had dragged her over the side of his ship at Dunkirk.

He wrapped her in his strong arms until she could no longer thrash about. 'Hold on to me, for God's sake, hold on to me. I've got you . . . Don't let go . . . I'm here . . .'

She awoke the next morning to an enormous purring contentment, her body rosy and rumpled, drugged with love. Her eyes had the narrowed unfocused stare of a woman who has been completely and utterly fulfilled. Not just a fulfilment of the flesh but of the heart and mind. Something brought about when Callum's body had entered hers, entered it repeatedly throughout the night. It had been a wonder, a marvel, a loving they had never known, with something in it, on her part and his, which she could swear had never been there before. Ask her to say what it was and she could not, but

527

perhaps when she turned to Callum and looked into his eyes – if he was awake – the answer might be there. An expression which . . . dear God . . . an expression she had looked for since . . . would it be there, would she see it at last . . . would she *know* when she did? She hardly dared turn to him. She hardly dared open her eyes wide and turn to him, but she felt so . . . alive . . . refreshed . . . renewed . . . she could not wait . . . she would waken him . . . Callum . . .

He was not there, and when she went downstairs he was not there either, and no, Mrs Flynn, who was, said she had not seen him, and would Mrs O'Shaughnessy like a cup of tea, or perhaps a plate of bacon and eggs since it would be a shame to waste them? Not that they would be wasted, since her old man would see to that, but Mrs O'Shaughnessy was already half-way up the stairs, and when Mrs Flynn ventured up them after her to see what all the banging and crashing was about, Mrs O'Shaughnessy had gone and *Corporal* O'Shaughnessy was packing her bag.

'I've come to say goodbye, darling,' Maris said to her cousin an hour later. 'I've cycled over to return Muriel's bike, and then I'll get a taxi if such a thing can be managed these days.'

'Where are you going?'

'Back to camp.'

'But you have extended compassionate leave.'

'I know that, Rosie, but I'm fine now.'

'No, you're not. You're not ready . . .'

'Don't lecture me, darling. Just give me a kiss and say thank you to Muriel for the loan of the bike. Oh, and my niece and nephews, let me have one last look at them and then I'll be off.'

'Maris, don't go. I don't like the look of you.'

'I don't like the look of myself either, Rosie, but there, I'm all we've got.'

'Maris, darling, please . . . stay with me if you don't want to be . . . at Seymour Road. If it's awkward . . .'

'Rosie, it's not awkward, it's bloody impossible, and I'm not taking any more of it.'

For a moment, a riveting moment when she thought she might scream with the pain of it, Callum's face smiled in wry amusement on the back of her closed and anguished eyelids. He'd done it again to her when she'd sworn she would never, never allow him to get near her one more time. He'd seemed so . . . so understanding. So . . . warm, wanting to help her in her grief, she had been sure of it. There had been . . . *something* . . . a difference in him which had persuaded her to let down her guard, which was already badly dented by her mother's and young Michael's death. She had wept in his arms, which had soothed and comforted her, allowed him to undress her and put her into bed, and when he had climbed in with her he had held her close, making some sound in the back of his throat which she could only compare to the one Rosie made as she cuddled her little son when he had fallen and scraped his knee. She had clung gratefully to him since he seemed to her a rock, a solid reliable rock in the shifting quagmire of her pain.

When he began to make love to her it was the natural conclusion or continuation of what she could only describe as their sudden . . . equality . . . harmony . . . a pairing of their hearts and souls and bodies which had, at last, come together at exactly the right moment.

But it had ended as it had always done. Satisfied, his

masculine body fulfilled, his male needs served, he had gone when it suited him to wherever it suited him to be, off to the ships and the docks and the world of the sea which was his *real* life, his *true* love.

Rose put her arms about her and hugged her for a full minute then, briskly, put her from her and wiped away the tears which slipped down her cheeks. As she did with those she truly loved she allowed her cousin to know what was best for her, without argument.

'Take care then. Write to me. You know you are always welcome here if you should find it . . . difficult at Seymour Road.'

'I know, Rosie, thank you.'

She had been gone no more than an hour when the green MG came up the drive, scattering gravel six feet into the air, so great was its speed, and scarcely before it had stopped its driver leaped out, ignoring the door since the opening of it might have held him up for a second or two. Leaving the engine running, he ran down the steps and across the forecourt to Rose Woodall's front door.

'Callum . . . !' She had the baby in her arms and young Harry Woodall at her feet. At almost two and a half the boy knew he was the most important person in the world, and of course, so must everyone else, in his opinion, so it was several hazardous minutes before Rose could give her full attention to the frantic man who crowded her hallway. The baby wailed, since his lunch had been interrupted, and so did Harry Woodall. He did not care to be ignored nor shoved ignominiously into the arms of Polly in the kitchen. Ellie Woodall, eighteen months old and as beautiful as her mother, rattled the bars of the playpen for *her* share of attention.

'Is she here . . . Rosie . . . for God's sake, is she here . . . ?'

'Ellie, will you be quiet while Mamma speaks to . . .'

'For Christ's sake, Rosie, have you seen her . . . ?'

'I'm sorry, Callum, let me get these two into the kitchen as well. I can't hear what you're saying . . . *Polly* . . .'

But in the kitchen Polly and Harry were now informing those who might be concerned that they would 'Hang out the washing on the Siegfried Line', both warbling off-key and at two different tempos.

'Rosie . . . *is my wife here or not*? Jesus, can't you shut these brats up . . . ?'

It was not until all three were flung into the accommodating arms of Polly, who wafted them away on promises of 'gingerbread men' which she had just made, that the flustered Rose could answer Callum's frantic questions.

'She *was* here, Callum, but she . . .'

'Where's she gone?' He took her by the forearms and began to shake her so savagely her head shook wildly from side to side.

'Callum . . . please . . . you're hurting me.'

At once he let her go, the strange – Rose thought it might be *frightened* – expression leaving his face. He was pale, she noticed, beneath the smooth brown which was his customary colour, and his mouth was clamped in a line of ferocious self-control, as though should he let it go, he might smash something, or someone.

'She went back to her unit, Callum.'

'Jesus . . .' He passed a hand over his face and bowed his head. His broad shoulders sagged. 'I thought . . . I thought we . . . that this time . . .'

'What is it, Callum?' She put a compassionate hand on his arm and he covered it with his own, which was trembling. He managed a smile, then shrugged.

'Nothing, Rosie. Nothing you would understand. Only me and Maris . . . you know how we are. Everyone knows how we are . . . but I did think . . .'

'What, Callum?'

He sighed deeply and turned away towards the front door, which still stood open and through which the sound of his car's engine could still be heard.

'Oh, that . . . well, never mind. Thank you, Rose, and . . . your children are not brats.'

'I know. Will you not stop for a cup of tea?' but he had gone, and a moment later the full-throated roar of his sports car's engine shattered the peaceful midday sunshine into a million shards which mended slowly as the sound died away.

29

On June 22nd, 1941, Hitler attacked the Soviet Union, and the concentrated bombing of the 'Blitz' ended. Just as it was becoming intolerable to those who suffered it, it ended. It was expected that the Russian Forces would hold out no longer than three months, and that ahead of them all was a long, miserable and hard slog.

The people's morale began to sag. They were tired of hearing that Britain could 'take it', and when were *they* going to 'dish it out'? They would win the war in the end, of course, there was no doubt in their minds about that, if not this year, or the next, then eventually, but in the meanwhile prospects were gloomy and depressing. German troops had occupied Athens, taking just three weeks to do it. British and Empire soldiers withdrew, demolishing bridges as they went, and then it was the turn of Crete as the war in the Mediterranean gathered momentum. British and Empire troops had fought side by side, but evacuation from the small but vital island was inevitable.

The Russians continued to withstand the Germans, fighting hand to hand on their own doorsteps, it was rumoured, and the British Press reported that the growing strength of the RAF was beginning to find expression in destructive night raids on enemy territory in north-west Germany, Tripolitania, and in daring sweeps across France. In one day our 'boys' brought down thirty enemy planes over France for the loss of two of ours.

They were beginning to 'dish it out' at last.

The 'V' sign, a symbol of the unconquerable will of the territories occupied by Nazi tyranny, began to emerge as Mr Churchill announced in July that the mobilisation of the 'V' army had begun. Men and women all over occupied Europe were dedicating themselves to the continuation of war against Nazi Germany, and in unconquered Britain the 'V' signs were chalked on walls, on planes and tanks, and all manner of machines in factories as they came off the assembly lines, and in fact wherever there was space to allow it.

The Syrian campaign was brought to a successful conclusion when units of the Empire's army marched into Beirut; and in Tobruk British and Empire troops lived in sand, and in bomb-shattered buildings, among fleas and flies, as they defended the vital garrison on the sea coast of North Africa, and amongst them was Ellen O'Shaughnessy's nineteen-year-old grandson Corporal Lorcan O'Shaughnessy. She'd had a snap of him in his shorts and tin helmet with his feet in the sea, looking for all the world as though he was paddling off the sands at New Brighton. Giving her the 'thumbs up' sign, he had been, the cheeky young spalpeen, and would he be home to see his grandmother before she died of old age and exasperation, she wailed, for sure wouldn't this old war drive anyone into an early grave?

The food rationing for a start. How could a body make a decent biscuit or a bit of cake with four ounces of sugar, which was what she and Matty were allowed for a week? One egg a fortnight, was it, or two if the hens were laying well, and sure wasn't she thinking of doing what Tess and Mary, and even Mrs Donavan next door was doing, and that was to let Donal put up a hen-run in her back garden and keep a few chickens,

534

though that cockerel of Mrs Donavan's was a divil, waking everyone in the street at the crack of dawn each day. But it'd be worth it to have an egg when she fancied it and, she said to Matty, she'd have a cow too, if it had been allowed, since this dried milk which was brought all the way from America wasn't worth the packet it came in. Omelettes and Yorkshire pudding like rubber, and even her puddings, she mourned, looked like linoleum tiles, remembering the deliciously light concoctions she had created before the war.

She'd tried her hand at 'Woolton's pie', named after the Minister of Food, Lord Woolton, the ingredients being potatoes, swedes and carrots and made with, of all things, potato pastry, and really, she'd been ashamed to put it on the table in front of Michael and Cliona when they sat down to their dinner. Fatless pastry, eggless cakes – *cakes without eggs!* – sugarless puddings and meatless soups, of all things. Wholemeal flour which made *brown* bread when everyone knew bread was *white*, and how they survived only the Holy Mother knew. It was more than a body could bear, so it was, especially one like Ellen O'Shaughnessy, who functioned for one purpose only and that was to nourish her family, spiritually, emotionally and through their stomachs.

Mind, the babies and children had never looked bonnier, those you saw in the street with their working-class mothers, no doubt due to the special cheap milk they were allowed, the cod liver oil and orange juice which was poured regularly down every infant throat.

And had she tried that there spam, she asked her granddaughter on one of the rare occasions Rose came over with the children, petrol being so scarce. Spam fritters, she and Matty had eaten for tea last night, and if anyone had told her two years ago that she'd be eating something with a name like *spam*, she'd have laughed in their faces.

Rosie looked better than she had for a long time, Ellen was inclined to think, as her latest great-grandchild suckled at his mother's breast in the chair opposite to hers. She'd been right peaky during the whole of her last pregnancy, inclined to be jumpy and nervous, which was not uncommon when a woman was in the family way, but it was not as though it was her first, and with the others she'd been as placid as the tabby who was forever under Ellen's feet.

Ellen had Ellie, her namesake, on her own lap, drowsing peacefully, but the boy, young Harry, was a live wire if ever there was one, hurtling round the kitchen table and up the hall, clattering up the stairs and down again, making that awful noise all children seemed to make these days as they pretended to shoot one another with a machine gun. Jesus, Mary and Joseph, what a world it was when a boy not yet three spent his days 'killing' the enemy, his young mind filled with 'Jerries' and 'dive-bombers' and 'sprogs', a word he had learned from his father and which, Ellen supposed, was something to do with the RAF.

'Have you heard from Maris, darlin'?' she asked her granddaughter. 'Sure an' isn't it over a month now since she wrote, an' then 'twas only a line or two. They're to get two lots of leave a year, she said, of a fortnight apiece, so that's better, though I doubt I'll see much of her when she does come home. Here, there an' everywhere, so she is . . .' She spoke with something of her old sharpness towards her daughter-in-law, which had lessened during the war years.

'An' sure wouldn't you know it, in the very same

post, didn't I hear from your Mammy, God love her. She's persuaded Claudine to go and join her in America for the duration, taking the children with her, of course, so when I'll see those great-grandchildren of mine again only the Holy Mother herself knows. And what's the word on Mairin and Ailis? Have you heard? There's another two who never put pen to paper an' me worryin' meself into an early grave over them, as I do you all.'

'I know, grandmother. They've managed to stay together, working for the Ministry of Defence in London. Very hush-hush, they told me in the last letter I received, which was ages ago. But you know what they are like. Absolutely inseparable and needing no one but each other.'

'Aye.' Ellen studied the sleeping face of her latest great-grandchild, the nature of the twins evidently completely mystifying, since it was in *her* and in the rest of those with her blood in their veins to be open and sharing.

'Ah well,' shrugging off the oddness of her twin granddaughters.

'What about Alex? When's he to see that boy of his? Five months old and him not even met his own Daddy.'

'Soon, grandmother, so he said in his last letter.'

'An' about time too,' just as though Alex Woodall stayed away on purpose to irritate Ellen O'Shaughnessy.

Rose sighed and Ellen looked at her sharply. She'd have no despondency in her house, not if she could help to allay it and if the child – for what else would her children and grandchildren ever be to her – was in trouble, or was sad, then she'd best let it out and give Ellen the chance to put it right.

'Pull the fire together, Matty,' she instructed the old maid, who crept about the kitchen and scullery like some elderly tortoise, ''an wet the tea, that's if there's any left. Mind, the tram drivers fetch me a quarter now and then. D'you know, they've brought a lot of retired chaps back into service, so they have, to let the young ones go to fight, an' one of them told me he remembered dancing in the street with our Cliona on the night the Mersey Tunnel opened. Can you imagine?'

Her old face became gently sad as she looked back to those happier times and, as happened so often lately, she completely forgot what she had been about to say to Rose.

'I'd best get back, grandmother. I don't want to be caught out in the black-out. It's dark by five.' Rose stood up, putting the baby on her hip.

At once Ellen was all bustle and purpose, since to be caught on the streets in the horror of the black-out, particularly if you were a young mother driving a motor car with three children in it, was the worst catastrophe Ellen could imagine. Bags and bottles and nappies were collected, all the paraphernalia Rose took with her and her children wherever she went. She needed a pantechnicon, she laughed, instead of the old Morris which had served the Woodalls so well. One with handcuffs and chains to keep Harry from taking over the driving as he demanded to do. His Daddy 'drove' a plane, he told great-grandmother Ellen, and there seemed no reason that he could see why he should not drive his Mamma's motor car.

They were at the front door laughing, Ellen and Rose, watching the strutting man-child with the indulgence of the female for the posturing of the male, and the shouted greeting at the front gate startled them.

'Who's that, God love us?' Ellen called, peering down the garden path, for her eyesight was not what it was.

'It's me, mother-in-law, and I'd be glad of a cup of tea if you've not drunk all your ration. I've had nothing to drink since I left camp nearly twenty-four hours ago except that putrid stuff they serve on the station.'

'Holy Mother, 'tis Maris an' us just talkin' about you, weren't we, darlin'?' Ellen said to Rose. They both moved eagerly down the garden path, the lively boy before them. Ellen had put the little girl in Matty's arms, and her own reached out for her son's wife, for despite her disapproval of almost everything Maris did, from joining the ATS and all that led up to it, which included her refusal – or so Ellen believed – to bear a child, she had grown fond of this wilful child, this girl who had married her son and then done nothing but make him, and herself, miserable. But Ellen admired *grit*, and Maris had grit, which she'd proved at Dunkirk, though of course she shouldn't have been there in the first place, and in the way she kept going no matter what adversity she met.

Maris was still and awkward in her mother-in-law's embrace, and her face was strained, though wasn't that to be expected after such a journey?

'God, those trains,' she groaned when the greetings were done with, when they had moved back into the kitchen and the babies had been examined and exclaimed over, for 'hadn't they *grown*'; when Harry had proved his prowess as a fighter pilot like his Daddy, arms extended, voice like that of a droning plane; and they were all seated with a good hot cup of Matty's tea, courtesy of the tram drivers opposite. 'They stop at every lamp-post and touch every town between here and London, and here and Hull. There were seven air-raid warnings, which of course meant we had to stop, and honestly, we were like sardines. I stood, or squatted on my kitbag for twelve hours and even when we got to Crewe I couldn't get a seat. Some chap let me sit on his knee . . .'

'*On his knee!* Mother of God, what next?'

'Believe me, mother-in-law, I was glad of it, I can tell you. I finally got a seat, but I was afraid to leave it even to get a cuppa, so this is very welcome . . .' nodding at Matty who nursed Rosie's sleeping daughter.

'Were you bombed, Aunty Maris?' Harry interrupted.

'No, pet, I wasn't, thank God.'

'Did you see any Germans . . . ?' since anyone in the khaki uniform of a soldier was *bound* to have seen Germans.

'No, sweetheart.'

Harry turned away, bored with this aunt of his who obviously had done or seen nothing which might interest him.

'And how long have you got?' The inevitable question, usually the first one to be asked as the returned soldier, sailor or airman came through the door. Maris's face clamped tight shut, and her brown eyes deadened to the colour of wet soil. Her expression was suddenly bitter, introspective, as though she looked deep within herself and was not at all pleased with what she saw. She seemed dragged down, sullen even, Rosie would have said, and her own brave heart dropped since she knew that look of Maris's and it spelled trouble.

'Is it one of those fortnights you were telling me about, darlin'?' Ellen asked, '. . . because it's about time. Five months since you were last home and then it was so sad . . .' She wiped a tear from the corner of her eye, for no matter what came to give her joy as Rosie's children gave her joy, the sorrow for Elizabeth and the boy would never really lessen. Time, they said, but no matter how much time went by, did you ever lose that great hole in the heart of you that their going had left?

'No, mother-in-law, it isn't,' and Maris's voice was as hard as granite.

'Sure an' it's not one of them seventy-two-hour passes, is it? Katy Murphy's lad came up from Devonport only last week on one of them things, and he was no sooner through the door when he was out of it again, wasn't he? Not that she was complaining, for a mother is glad of the sight of her son even for an hour, isn't that so?'

'No, it's not seventy-two hours, mother-in-law.'

'Then . . . ?'

'It's for good. I'm not to go back.'

'They've not discharged you . . . ?' Dishonourably, Ellen meant, since that was what happened . . . but not in wartime, surely, when every man and woman was so sorely needed to fight the foe which threatened this land of theirs? And it would have to be something drastic to make them do it. Holy Mother . . .

'They have, mother-in-law.'

'Maris . . . what . . . ?'

'It seems I am to have a child and pregnant women are of no use to anyone.' The words dropped like a rock into the silence, and her face twisted into what she meant to be a smile but which was in reality a grimace at the bitter irony of fate, which had given her *now* what she no longer wanted. But was it fate? or

541

was it the twisted mind of Callum O'Shaughnessy, who had decided whilst his wife was frail and defenceless with grief that the time had come to plant his seed within her and keep her at home firmly attached to the stove and the bedroom, where the women of his family had always been happy to be? After all these years, for some purpose of his own, he had deliberately left off the 'French letter' he had always used and got her 'up the spout', given her a 'bun in the oven' as it was coarsely termed in the billet, and she would never forgive him, never.

Rosie had written to her last May, telling her that her husband had been looking for her on the day she left, but she had attached no importance to it since who knew what devilment Callum was up to? He had wanted something of her, no doubt to do with his precious family, chasing after her to Rosie's, but she had, thank God, been gone by then. She had left behind the confines and commitment to family which existed in Liverpool, and was glad to be returning to her unit, to Betty and the other girls and a certain sergeant-major from a nearby army camp who was mad for her and to whom she herself was strongly attracted. Not love, of course. She would never feel love again, but a thing of the flesh which is still very much alive even if the heart has died. Most of the girls, freed from all family ties for the first time in their lives, were out for a damn good time when they were off the camp and she meant to be the same.

She didn't notice at first. She had been attached to an army hospital unit, and she and Betty were flat out driving their ambulances with the wounded and ill who had been shipped back from all the theatres of war. She felt well, very well, better than she had for years and when, for the second time she missed her 'monthlies', or *noticed* that she had missed twice, she had scarcely given it a thought; and when she did, when she found she could not comfortably fasten the bottom button of her khaki jacket, the knowledge hit her a blow so low and so deadly she began to vomit all over her newly made and meticulously neat bed.

'Bloody 'ell, Corp! What did *you* eat last night?' the girl who had the next bed to hers shrieked, and from then on it had been a constant problem to keep it not only from Betty and the others but from those in authority whilst she decided what to do. An abortion seemed the only possible solution, but the simple fact was that she had not the faintest idea of how to go about it, nor indeed was sure she could go through with it if she had. And what other option was open to her? and the answer, of course, was none. She must leave the service she loved, that was plain, the life she had found so satisfying and which she had meant to make a career of when the war was over. Even the sergeant-major whose ardour for her she, for some reason, continued to parry, must be forgotten. She must go home, wherever that was, to bear the child, Callum's child, not hers, no, not hers. *His!*

She had hated him relentlessly for a long time, and all the while she hated she made her plans, and here she was in Ellen's kitchen ready to carry them out.

Ellen began to cry, her joy so explosive she could not express it in any other way, and for a moment, a sad moment, Maris was sorry for her, for she was as fond, in a constrained way, of her mother-in-law as Ellen was of her. They had been friends as well as enemies, and it was not Ellen's fault that she and Callum were so totally and irrevocably lost to one another.

543

It would be hard on her. It was obvious that she was under the impression that 'things' were, at last, all right between her son and his wife and that, after all these years, Maris was to settle down to the task God put women on this earth to perform. Callum would come home to a warm house, hot food, darned socks and a docile wife in his bed. A child in the pram in the garden and, God willing, another in his wife's womb by this time next year. The natural, *right* way of things, *at last*.

'I'd like to come and stay with you, Rosie, if I may, until I get settled,' Maris said coolly, putting the first part of her plan into action, waiting for the 'balloon to go up', as they said in the latest 'slang', which it did.

'At Rosie's?' Ellen's mouth dropped open and her face became truculent. 'And what for would you do that, when you've a perfectly good home of your own? Sure an' if you don't like to be alone just now, and who can blame you, Mrs Flynn would move in with you. Her old man wouldn't mind for a month or two, or better yet . . .' brightening even further, '. . . you could stay here with me an' Matty.' A young and pregnant daughter-in-law would put new life in both of them.

'No, I'm sorry, mother-in-law, that wouldn't suit me. If Rosie can put me up for a week or two . . .'

'Darling, you can stay with me for as long as you like, you know that, but when Callum comes home . . .'

'We can discuss all that later, Rosie, if you don't mind. Just now I'd like to get back to your place, have a bath and then go to bed. I'm absolutely wacked.'

'It's only for a few weeks, Rosie, perhaps not even that, and then I'll be out of your hair, *and* Alex's, for the last thing he wants is me hanging about when he comes on leave. At the end of next week, you think? Well, I'll be long gone by then, darling, so don't worry.'

It was the next day. Maris had fallen into the spare bed at Lacy's house after her bath and slept the clock almost round. It was mid-afternoon, and outside Rosie's window the rain pelted down, falling in absolutely vertical lines from a leaden sky. Autumn had gone, it seemed, and the long grey days of winter were here. The trees were bare, stark, ugly against the low sky, and underfoot, across paths and lawn and flower beds, was a carpet of dank, sodden, rotting leaves. A dismal scene and one that appeared to match Maris's sombre mood. A child wailed from somewhere in the house, and Rosie sighed, for in this weather it was hard to keep the children amused, at least the two older ones who were accustomed to be out of doors. She could, of course, no longer work on the land, not with three babies and with winter coming on, and the paperwork she had undertaken was piling up in the office at Beechwood awaiting her attention. Worry after worry, and now here was Maris with another.

'I'm not worried about *that*, Maris, and well you know it. I love you. You are . . . my friend as well as my sister-in-law, and I want to know what you're up to. It's something, isn't it? Why aren't you at Seymour Road . . . ?'

Maris stood up, moving away towards the window of Rosie's back parlour, reaching for her handbag, which was on the low table beside it. She undid the clasp, then tutted irritably and swung about, resting her buttocks on the window-sill and clenching her hands deep in the pockets of her extremely tight slacks.

'I keep forgetting I don't smoke any more. God, it's

545

murder after all these years. Sheer bloody habit, of course, but hard to break.'

'But better for you, and the baby.'

'Aah . . . the baby.'

'Look, Maris, there's something on your mind and I would be extremely grateful if you'd let me in on it. What are you up to? Why aren't you at Seymour Road? What's this air of . . . secrecy you seem to have about you? And the baby? You don't seem particularly over-joyed and yet for years now all you've done is bemoan the fact that you haven't a child. And what about Callum? Is he not to . . . ?'

'We'll leave Callum out of it, if you please, at least for now.'

'That will be difficult, since the child is his. At least . . .' she frowned and her eyes searched Maris's face fearfully, '. . . it *is* Callum's . . . ?'

'Oh yes, it's his all right. All his.'

'Maris, oh darling, what are you planning? I know you so well and I know you are going to do something which no one is going to like. You've already upset grandmother, *and* worried her, which is really not right at her age . . .'

'Don't *you* start, Rosie. All I've ever done since I married Callum is consider his damn family, put them first in every situation, as *he* does. I've tried . . . tried so bloody hard to be what he wants, to please him and them, at least until I joined the ATS. Since then I've been free, myself, my own person and not Mrs Callum O'Shaughnessy who must conform to *their* idea of what a good wife should be. It was *me*, not Callum, who got the blame when there were no more children and, to spare Ellen, I let her go on believing it. Can you imagine what it would have done to her if she had learned that her precious son used a French letter? Well, five months ago, to suit his own purpose, I'm sure, he didn't, and now I'm pregnant . . .'

'But surely, if . . . if you and he were . . . well . . . if you . . . if he . . .'

'Claimed his conjugal rights, is that what you're trying to say in that delicate and diplomatic way of yours, Rosie darling? We have a much more colourful way of describing it in the service. But yes, we shared the same bed for one night. We made love and I thought . . .'

Her eyes became, for a split second, soft and dreaming, a deep golden brown in which an expression of wonderment glowed; then they hardened, darkened, and her voice was cold as she continued.

'He caught me at a . . . vulnerable moment and . . . and when I woke the next morning he was gone. To his bloody ship, I suppose, or round to his Mammy's for his breakfast . . .'

'So that's why you came here . . . that morning when . . . ?'

'Yes. I ran away from it again. This time for good, or so I thought but . . . he put one over on me . . . the bastard . . .'

'He was looking for you. I told you so in my letter.'

'I know you did, but you don't know him like I do, Rosie. He doesn't love me, you see, not at all . . .'

'He does, Maris, I'm sure he does.'

'No, darling.'

'But he married you, so he must . . .'

'No . . . *no* . . . Rosie. I was pregnant. He was sorry for me and . . . well . . . I do believe my brothers had something to do with it as well. He *does* work for Hemingways, you know.'

'Callum wouldn't . . .'

'Wouldn't what? He took advantage . . . no, that's not true. I was going to say he took advantage of me when my father died, but I was very willing. I . . . God, I loved him . . . now, he's done it again and . . . I was . . . he did not force me, Rosie. But he forced this child on me and I'll never forgive him. He didn't want me to go into the ATS. He even offered . . . Dear God . . .' She threw back her head and the pain in her was unendurable, '. . . he offered . . . *offered* to make me pregnant . . . to give me the child I wanted . . . bait . . . a prize if I would give up the idea of going into the service. Oh Lord, Rosie . . . sweet Christ . . . I cannot forgive him . . . ever . . .'

'Maris . . . oh darling, I am so sorry . . . what can I do . . . ?'

'Help me.'

'How?'

'I can't live with him again and I don't want his child.'

The stark words were spoken with no expression. Flat, undramatic and all the more horrendous because of it. They seemed to go on for ever, hanging in the air like smoke before it disperses, echoing in Rosie's appalled ears until she wanted to put her hands up to cover them. To shut them out. Her face had lost all its colour and her mouth trembled, but she did not speak.

'Oh, don't look like that, Rosie.' Maris reached for her handbag again, rummaged in it, then threw it to the settee in exasperation. 'Damn it,' she muttered. 'Why do you have to give up smoking just when you need it the most?' She turned back to her cousin. 'It's all right, darling. I'm not going to do anything silly. I did consider an abortion . . . no, you've no need to cover your face. I'm not going to. I shall give birth to Callum's child and then I shall get back to my own life,

Rosie, if they'll let me. Do you realise how important it is to me, what I've done for the past eighteen months? Do you realise how I feel? I'm *doing* something at last, something that is *significant*, and I'm doing it well. I am valued . . .'

'Is there no value in motherhood, Maris?'

'*Of course* there is, Rosie.' Maris's voice was passionate. 'You are the most . . . treasured and valuable woman. To Alex who loves you more than anyone in the world. To your children, who would not survive without you, to *all* of us who hold you so dear, to *me*, who would not know what to do without your . . . presence in my life. But I am . . . not the same. I have not been given what you have . . . or have not earned it, perhaps, and so I must find my . . . well . . . fulfilment sounds pretentious but you know what I mean . . . in other ways . . .'

'How? Dear God, what are you to do?'

'I am going to take that cottage, you know the one I mean, near Home Farm where the dairyman used to live. He's gone in the army, and his wife and family have left to stay with her mother, or so Uncle Teddy told me when I wrote to him. It's been empty for twelve months, and when I asked him if I could have it, without even asking why I wanted it, he said yes . . .'

'But *why*? Why can't you . . . ?'

'I have just told you, Rosie. I cannot live with Callum, or even in his house again. I don't even want to see him, but I suppose I'll have to if only to make arrangements for the . . . well, I suppose you would call it . . . handover.'

'Handover . . . ?'

'Yes, darling.'

'What handover? Handover of what?'

'His child.'

'Maris . . .' Rosie's voice was dangerous and she stood up slowly, threateningly. 'If you mean what I think you mean and I really can't believe you do, then you may consider yourself no friend of mine.'

'*Rosie* . . . don't . . .' Maris's voice was appalled.

'I mean it, Maris. A woman who can speak so calmly of giving away her child is . . . inhuman.'

'No . . . *no* . . . don't judge me . . . you have never had to . . . suffer . . . how can you condemn what you know nothing about? Your life has been . . . smooth and . . .'

'Has it really?'

'You know it has so you cannot . . .'

'I must do as I see fit, Maris. I will help you now in whatever way I can. You may stay here until your cottage is ready, and during your pregnancy . . . if you need me I am here.'

She softened suddenly and then she smiled, a lovely glowing smile in which all her own warmth and the tender care she gave her children and to all those who had need of her shone bright as a star on a frosted winter night.

'But you won't do it, Maris, when the time comes. You see you have no conception of how it is. Being a mother, I mean. Just wait . . .'

'Nonsense.'

'Wait and see.'

Her letter was waiting for him when he got back to Seymour Road just before Christmas, and he was alarmed by the way his hand trembled as he opened it.

The word jumped out at him, separating itself from all the others, and the notepaper on which it was writ-

550

ten shook so badly he had to look away, hold it to his thudding chest, draw in a deep shuddering breath before he could look at it again.

Child! There it was, the word he had read – disbelievingly, ecstatically – in the very first sentence, as though Maris herself was in a fervour of excitement to tell him and must do so at once.

'I am to have a child,' it said. Again he had to stop, as for some reason his vision blurred and the words ran together in a dancing blaze of joy. Christ . . . oh sweet Jesus Christ . . . thank you, Jesus, in your mercy . . . Maris was to have a child . . . *his* child, she said, conceived on the day her mother was buried . . . just like the last when her father . . . dear Mother of heaven . . . it must be . . . *it must be* . . . a good omen . . . surely . . . ?

Throwing his seabag to the floor, he shut the front door, which was still open, as carefully as though he must make no commotion, no sudden movement to shatter and disperse this . . . joy, this . . . this hope . . . this . . . what? How could he describe it for surely, *surely* this meant that he and Maris had been given another chance. That they were *meant* to have another chance. This would make a difference to their present relationship, which was really no relationship at all. It must. If they were to be parents, to have a son or a daughter, then there would be common ground on which they would . . . could . . . meet. A bond, a link, something to get them together. To talk. It would be hard, wellnigh impossible, but . . . well, he had felt it twice in the past two years. A . . . a . . . softness in her, a willingness, and though it had escaped him before he could get a firm grip on it, it *had* been there, so surely, if they were careful there might be a chance to . . .

He threw back his head in a convulsion of gladness, then, his sight and reason somewhat restored, he took the letter to the kitchen window and read it through from beginning to end.

It took him over two hours to get to the cottage where she now lived. He had to walk to Michael's to beg a couple of gallons of petrol, then back again to Seymour Road – he should have known really, his numbed mind kept repeating, since she would have been here, in their home, wouldn't she? – to get the MG, which was temperamental after two months off the road, started and then to find his way to Home Farm Cottage.

When he left an hour later, grey-faced and blind-eyed, he knew, finally, that what had existed, frail little thing that it had been, between himself and Maris, was finally dead.

30

Rosie was right, of course she was, and as she leaned over Maris O'Shaughnessy and her son of ten minutes she smiled at the stunned expression on her cousin's face.

'May I hold him, Maris?'

'No, you may not, not yet anyway.'

'I thought you might say that.'

'Well . . . he's . . . he's . . .'

'He won't break, darling.'

'Oh God, he might . . . he's so . . . fragile . . .'

'No, he's not. He's strong like his mother, but won't you let me give him to the midwife to be bathed?'

'Lord, Rosie, isn't he the most beautiful thing you ever saw?'

'Indeed he is, but darling, let Nurse Atkinson have him now. You're tired and need to sleep.'

'Just another minute, Rosie, please. Oh look . . . look, he's yawning. He knows how to yawn already and him not half an hour old,' just as though the infant had performed a couple of handstands, '. . . and will you look at his expression. So cross about something. He looks just like . . . like . . .'

Like Callum, she had been about to say. She slowly lifted her head and her eyes met Rose's, finding compassion and concern there and a question which she knew must be answered. But she wasn't ready to answer it yet, or indeed to consider anything but the incredible beauty of her new son and the equally incredible emotion he had already lit in her heart, which had been cold and dead but which was now alive, warm, and beating to the rhythm of her love for him. She could feel the pull of the invisible cord which already tied them together, a cord which was loose, slack, relaxed as he lay close to her breast, but which, she was perfectly aware, would tighten most painfully the moment the midwife took him from her. It would become so taut and stretched it would draw her to him wherever he was *for the rest of her life*.

So this was motherhood. It had caught her off-guard.

'May I take him, Mrs O'Shaughnessy?' the woman asked kindly, having seen the same doting expression on more faces than she'd had hot dinners. 'He needs a good wash and you need rest, lass.'

'She's right, Maris, but just for a moment . . . let me hold him.'

'Lord, Rosie, don't you have enough with your own?'

'Never.'

'Very well, but . . . carefully . . .' and for the full five minutes Rosie held him, crooning into his angry face, soothing his male fury at being dragged into a world he was not awfully sure he was ready for, Maris hovered, if such a word could be used to describe someone who was in bed, ready to leap up from it, her manner anxious, her face creased with worry until the nurse whisked him away. Even then her gaze followed her son and remained on the door through which he and the nurse had gone.

'I'm not sure I care for that woman, Rosie,' she fretted. 'Her eyes are too small and close together. She has a shifty look about her. I've a good mind to follow her . . .'

'You'll do no such thing. She's a perfectly capable

and kind woman who has delivered and cared for hundreds of babies, including two of mine, and I'm sure when . . . what is to be his name . . . ?'

'I have no idea.'

'Well, whatever you are to call him . . .'

'I hadn't thought . . . I had no way of knowing that . . .'

'That you were to love him as you do?'

'Yes.' Maris's voice was awed.

'I hate to say I told you so.'

'But you will anyway.'

'Naturally, and as I was saying, when he is bathed and you have had a good sleep . . .'

'*Sleep!* I can't sleep knowing he is in the hands of a woman who I'm sure will drop him on his head or stick a pin in him when she puts on his nappy . . .'

'Maris, stop being so absurd . . .'

'It is *not* absurd.'

'It is, but if you are so worried would you feel better if I went to oversee . . . ?'

'Oh, would you, darling? I think I could sleep if I knew you were with him. And when you leave to go home will you promise to bring him here? I'll have his crib next to my bed.'

'Very well, I promise, now go to sleep. I have left Harry and Ellie with Mrs Flynn, who is an absolute Godsend, by the way, and she says to remind you that she will be over tomorrow to see to you, which sounds ominous, but you know what she means. Jamie's asleep, the lamb, in his pram in the garden so I'll stay until you wake up. Sleep, darling . . .' and Maris did but with that light, one-ear-attuned kind of sleep which mothers adopt from the moment they give birth.

She had lived at Home Farm Cottage right through

555

the winter, and on her own, determined to prove, not only to her new self which had come into being during her eighteen months in the ATS, but to her mother-in-law, to Rosie who had been so sceptical, to her O'Shaughnessy relatives who thought of her as a flighty and spoiled child, despite her married state, to Alex and Charlie who thought her to be mad and told her so when they visited her – separately, of course – but most of all to her husband, that she could manage her own affairs and her own life.

The encounter with Callum had been hard. He had to know, naturally, and she had to see him, if only to tell him that the moment the child was born, he, or someone of his choice must come and take it away since she had no use for it, and just before Christmas he had driven over in his racing green MG, causing her heart to thud so painfully in her chest when she heard it outside her door she was furious with herself.

Home Farm was set at the back of Beechwood Hall. It could be reached by walking through the stand of beech trees which surrounded the main house, across the park, through what was known as the back gate; and from there, beyond the fields, could be seen the slate roof of the old farmhouse. The cottages, all set in their own bit of garden with a drystone wall about each one over which wild flowers grew in the summer, were to the left of the farmhouse and could also be reached by the lane which edged Beechwood Hall estate.

Her cottage, which was not hers at all but Uncle Teddy's, was the last one beyond the farm, standing slightly apart from the others and looking out over undulating fields towards Bride Wood. It had been empty for twelve months when she took it over, for the dairyman's wife, who was a city girl from Bradford and glad of the excuse to get back there, had moved lock, stock and the bedroom furniture given to her as a wedding present, back to her mother's house in Yorkshire.

Despite the fact that she meant to live in it no longer than was absolutely necessary after the birth of the child, when she meant to rejoin the ATS, Maris had a fancy to 'do it up', make it into a cosy winter nest. After all, she'd nothing else to do with her time, had she, she asked Rosie.

The kitchen was mellow with pine, functional and simple. A dresser, loaded with blue willow-pattern crockery in true cottage style, and a Toby jug from which she meant to drink the stout which the midwife had said would do her good – and the baby! There were brass candlesticks on the window-sills, though electricity had been installed between the wars, and alongside them were terracotta jars filled with dried flowers from the hedgerows. A fire glowed in the kitchen range in front of which two kittens boxed one another or dozed, a present from Uncle Teddy to keep her company in the winter nights ahead, he said. Beside the fire was a basket of logs, applewood to lend a fragrant aroma to her temporary home, and in the centre of the room was a scrubbed deal table on which she had placed a shallow copper bowl planted with winter hyacinths, and round it were four, rush-seated ladder-back chairs common to Lancashire farms and cottages.

She had a 'front' parlour, small but uncluttered, with one or two fragile-legged rosewood tables, a deep velvet sofa, lamps, and bowls of potted winter plants: snowdrops and crocus. Rich red velvet at the windows and a carpet to match, and all culled from the attics of Beechwood where Uncle Teddy said she must take whatever she needed.

Her bedroom, the bigger of two, was low and slope ceilinged. Pine again, with plain whitewashed walls, pretty chintz curtains and an enormous pine bed over which she had thrown a white, handmade lace bed-spread. There were great bunches of sweet-smelling dried flowers hanging from the beams in every room, and bowls of pot-pourri which Rose had made for her, and in each fireplace a fire burned night and day.

The house she had shared with Callum – she could never, now, bring herself to call it a *home* – had been no more than a child's toy, and she the child who delighted in the idea of playing in it. So young she had been, with stars in her eyes which had blinded her. She was to live in what amounted to a fairy story, she had believed, one which she would create for herself and the handsome prince she had won. But the make-believe had become reality and the reality was too sharp and hurting, and the life she was to build had become a chimera on which nothing was steady. She had had no substantial ground on which to build a home even though she had been pregnant *then*, and so, when she had lost the baby she had given up. Become bored. Disillusioned. Let it go as she had let Callum go.

But now, the subconscious instinct of the breeding female had taken her over again, the instinct strong in any animal to make a home for its young. She meant to have this child and leave, the new Maris O'Shaughnessy told herself, but in the meanwhile, though she did not reason why, she had made this temporary haven a rest-ing place of peace and comfort and in it she settled herself placidly, as pregnant women do, to wait.

Her front door was never locked and Callum had merely crashed through it, putting his shoulder to the sturdy wood which had stood for well over a hundred years, almost taking it from its hinges.

'What the bloody hell's this?' he snarled, backing her up against her own kitchen dresser as he waved her letter under her nose. It had scarcely left his hand since he had opened it, and it bore the marks of the oil and grease he had picked up as he tried to get the engine of his MG to start. There was a streak of it on his cheek and his hair was wildly disordered. He still wore his uniform.

'Exactly what it looks like. A letter from me to you which I presume you've read?' Her heart was banging so hard it hurt the inside of her chest, but her head was high and defiant and her eyes were the same flat brown they had been when she had told Ellen that she was pregnant. Grim, determined, like the rock which is hewn from the hard cold earth.

'I have, madam, and I would like an explanation.'

'You have it in my letter.'

'It tells me nothing but that you are . . . to have a child which presumably, because it is *mine*, you do not care to keep.'

'What else is there to say? It's the truth.'

'*Jesus . . .*' He faltered for a moment, then his face twisted into a grimace of pain, but a pain which was ready to terrorise the cause of it. The muscles of his throat were taut and his flesh was pared down to the bone. His face was thin, and working with his deep, almost unmanageable emotion. His mouth was stretched in a rictus of rage which told her she must step very carefully, for he seemed ready to strike her, her and the child inside her, which all her instincts cried out for her to defend.

'Listen to me,' he jerked, his jaw tight and menacing,

559

his hand suddenly vice-like on her arm. '*This* is what you're going to do. You're going to come home with me and have your child, *our* child, in your own home . . .'

'This is my home.'

'*No, it is not.* My child is to be born in . . .'

'Yes, *your* child which you gave me when I no longer wanted it, or *you*. I am not disputing it, Callum. This is *your* child, not mine . . . no, not mine, and when it comes you are to take it away, *and yourself*, and never let me see either of you again . . .'

'Sweet God! . . . you're not human . . .'

'Let's get it over with, Callum.'

'*Godammit, you're not human!*'

'I don't wish to continue this . . .'

'For pity's sake . . .' He tried to say her name but he could not, so great was the damage to what he had felt for her. He wanted to clench his fist and smash it into her face, for she was crucifying him. He wanted to see her bleed as he was bleeding deep within himself, from a wound she had inflicted on him and which he longed with all his agonised might to return.

She spoke harshly. 'There really is no point in going on . . .'

'Shut your mouth . . . shut your mouth, you bitch . . .' and for a moment she was terrified of him, of the violence in him which was a bare few inches from her. She wanted to back away, but she was cornered in the angle of the cupboards, afraid not only for herself and the child, but for him, wanting to save him from . . . from what? She didn't know and it confused her until he spoke again.

'If you loathe the idea of having my child why didn't

you get an abortion?' He had closed his eyes in a spasm of what she knew to be self-protection against the images his words had conjured up, his face grey and drawn and sweating with it.

'I . . . couldn't . . .'

'Why not?'

'The child . . . had done me no harm. Only you.'

'So . . . you will hand it over to me. Give it away as one does an unwanted puppy?'

'You will provide all it needs, I'm sure. You and . . . your family. I want *nothing* of yours in my life.'

'Very well.'

'You agree?'

'I have no choice,' and he was gripped now with an overwhelming need to get it over with, to get away from this cold-faced, hard-voiced creature whose body was soft and lovely, rounded and womanly with the child it held.

'Someone will let you know,' she said brutally.

'Take care of my child,' he answered, just as brutally, *her* well-being of no concern to him now.

'I have done so up to now. You had better go.'

'Aye, you're right. 'Tis no place for me here.'

The menace in him was visible and ready to be lethal, and he knew it. If he didn't leave, and at once, he would kill her, and with her the child, *his* child. *Leave*, the voice of reason whispered within him, barely heard, but there just the same.

'Then go.'

'When is the . . . ?' his mouth so stiff he could barely form the words.

'February.'

'I'll be on my way then.'

The tumult inside her chest and stomach caused her

561

to gasp and double up as though in pain, as he flung himself from her front door and into his car, but slowly, as the sound of the engine died away she unwound herself and straightened up, lifting her head to stare sightlessly through the open door to the spot in the lane where the MG had stood. She felt bruised and exhausted, but it was over. *At last* it was over. She and Callum O'Shaughnessy need never see one another again. The pain, the anguish, the unendurable anguish was all over and done with, at last, and she could get on with her life as though he had never been a part of it. Ah . . . Callum . . .

'What are you to do, darling?' Rosie asked two days after the birth of Thomas Sean O'Shaughnessy. 'Would you like me to . . . well, I don't know. Is there anything I *can* do for you?'

There was no need to ask what she meant, and Maris sighed as she looked down into the sleeping face of her son. She loved him passionately. The dark curling fluff on his head. The shape and blue-green O'Shaughnessy colour of his eyes and the gold tint to his silken flesh. His rosy pouting mouth when it reached for her nipple, his starfish hand which rested peacefully, amicably on her white breast whilst he took his fill. She smiled down at him, marvelling at her own naïvety in thinking that when he was born she would have needed time to learn to love him, and therefore before she did, all that was required was for him to be snatched from between her legs the moment he was born and transferred into the welcoming – she was sure of it – bosom of the O'Shaughnessy family where another child, or even two, would be fondly received.

What a bloody fool she had been. What an absurd,

ignorant, smug fool who had believed she knew her own self, her own mind, her own needs so well. So well, in fact, that she could order her life and that of her child, to her own pretentious shaping. And yet she had never known motherhood. She had seen it in Rosie but had believed it was something you learned, like playing the piano or dancing the foxtrot. She knew better now, of course, so what was she to do? How was she to go about what must be done? Her heart quailed at the thought of another encounter with Callum, but it must be done. She could not part with this tiny scrap of humanity, this joy, this warm, needing human being who was hers, her son; the only person who had ever needed her, depended on her, totally accepting her just as she was, his mother.

'They know? The family?'

'Yes. Grandmother is coming over . . . I'm afraid . . . this afternoon. Michael is bringing her. I couldn't put her off, after all she *is* his grandmother. She has been confused enough by your refusal to live at Seymour Road before Thomas was born . . .'

'Tom. Thomas is too . . . daunting just yet.'

'Why Thomas Sean, Maris?'

'I like the name Thomas, and we *do* have a Thomas Hemingway among our ancestors, Rosie.'

'So we do, and Sean for our grandfather Osborne, of course.'

They both smiled down at Tom, absorbed in the miracle and beauty of Maris's son, then Rose sighed and leaned back in her chair.

'She doesn't know, you see.'

'Know what? Who?'

'Grandmother. That you had intended letting Callum have Tom. That you were giving him up.'

Maris raised her head from her bemused contemplation of the child and her eyes widened in astonishment.

'Callum hadn't told her?'

'Apparently not, and can you blame him? It would distress her immeasurably. I suppose, if it had happened, he would have had to tell her when the time came. He couldn't have avoided it, obviously but . . . well, it seems he's told no one since no one's mentioned it. They all believe that you and he will . . . be together again.'

'They are mistaken.'

'Maris, could you not . . .'

'No, never. Callum and I . . . both of us . . . know that it could never work. Not now. There will be a divorce when the war is over, I suppose, but until then there is the question of Tom. I can't give him up. You knew that before he was born but I didn't, and now I have made such a . . . such confusion, in my life and Callum's and somehow it must be put right. I suppose I shall have to see him and explain.'

'He won't keep you to what you said. You know that.'

'He'd better not try.'

'But Tom is his son and he will want to see him.'

'I . . . I don't like the idea.'

'Maris, you can't . . .'

'I can if I have to. He is *my* son . . .'

'But only last week, two days ago even, you were swearing you couldn't wait to get rid of him.'

'I hadn't met him then. I didn't love him then.'

Rose relented, and leaning forward put a finger in the curled hand of her cousin's child.

'I know, darling, but it will be hard.'

564

'Dear God, do you think I don't realise that?'

It seemed to the nation that when Japan attacked the United States Naval Base at Pearl Harbor in the Hawaiian Islands in December 1941 and declared war on the United States of America that things were at last, in the latest vernacular, 'looking up', since it surely meant, with the Yanks in it, the end of the war would come that much sooner. When the tally of the death toll on that day was counted up they were not quite so sanguine, and two days later when the Japanese navy sank two of their own great battleships, the *Prince of Wales* and *Repulse*, off Malaya, the shock was even greater. On Christmas Day Hong Kong had fallen to the Japanese, and in February 1942, just a week after Tom O'Shaughnessy lustily bawled his way into the world and his mother's heart, the British Army surrendered in Singapore. 130,000 British soldiers were taken prisoner in the greatest single defeat in British history. Among those captured was Private Flynn McGowan, Gracie's son.

The year had begun with a run of disasters, or so it seemed to the war-weary people of Britain. First the fall of Singapore, and then the escape down-Channel – after steaming *up*-Channel undetected – of the German battleships *Scharnhorst* and *Gneisenau*. It was the most mortifying episode in naval history, the newspapers said, since the Dutch got into the Thames in the seventeenth century. How, the public wanted to know, had the Germans managed to outwit our own superior British commanders? A disgrace it was, and would we ever live it down?

Rationing had taken an even firmer grip in November, covering canned foods, meat, fish and vegetables, which was only right, as Ellen pointed out, since there had been an unfair distribution of unrationed foodstuffs, mainly to those who were 'well-to-do' and could afford black market prices. She hadn't had a tin of best salmon for months, she lamented. In January it was the turn of dried fruit, rice and sago; and in February, tinned fruit, tomatoes and peas; and in the same month the ration of soap was reduced to sixteen ounces every four weeks, and how any decent woman could keep herself clean on that she couldn't imagine, let alone one with children.

But when the basic civilian petrol ration was abolished in March, that was the last straw, for how was she to get about to visit her family, she asked, without even the gallon or two Michael was allowed and which she at least considered was at her disposal. There was Maris stuck out at that blessed cottage with Ellen's latest grandson, not able to get into Liverpool, and Ellen not able to get *out*, and if anyone needed a bit of advice and personal experience in the rearing of a child it was her daughter-in-law; and when Callum came home, by the Blessed Mother, she'd make sure he brought his silly, wayward wife to the home where she belonged and where Ellen could get at her on the tram!

But the war at sea was going badly. The U-boats had complete ascendancy by now and they used it with savage ruthlessness, keeping a hundred of their vessels at a time in the Atlantic. They spread themselves out in a long line across the convoy routes, intercepting and then collecting into a pack to home in on the shipping which crossed their path. In March, a month after Thomas Sean O'Shaughnessy was born, ninety-four ships were sunk, one of them the *Bridget O'Malley*. A

566

week later, after being picked up by a frigate which steamed into Liverpool, Tom O'Shaughnessy's father came home. He was in hospital for three days suffering from frost-bite and exposure, but longing to see his new son, his mother reported to Cliona when her grand-daughter walked up to see her after her shift at the hospital where she now worked. Why the divil his wife couldn't have made some effort to visit him there was beyond her. Surely a drop of petrol could have been found for such an emergency? Even Michael said he had none, which Ellen found hard to believe, him being such an important chap in the factory and having the supplementary allowance which was given to those who needed a car for their work. After all, Callum was his brother, a hero, and though not exactly wounded, sadly debilitated by his second experience of being tor-pedoed.

Maris was never to know how he got the petrol, but five days after he came into port Callum's MG drew up outside her cottage. Quietly this time, as though the fire which had consumed him three months ago had burned itself out.

He got out slowly, stiffly she thought, as she watched him from her parlour window. He closed the car door carefully and turned to face the cottage.

She was shocked by his appearance. He looked . . . *old*. He was almost forty-two now, but in the eight years she had known him he had never looked his age, growing no older, handsome and dashing and vital. Even at their last meeting, perhaps because of his fury, he had been alive and filled with the vigour of it. Now he looked . . . beaten . . . no, not exactly beaten, but self-controlled, calm, tempered by something which had taken the arrogance and vitality from him. Grim, with the purpose of the warrior who had defeated death, not just the twice he had been torpedoed but in the many times he had crossed the Atlantic. Grim with the times he had seen ships and men go down, or blown out of the water; the dead faces he had looked into; the burned and mutilated bodies he had been shocked by; the cries he had tried to shut his ears to; the lifeboats he had looked out for on watches that seemed to go on for ever.

'Maris,' he said as she opened the door to him, polite, a stranger, no warmer expression in his eyes than the courtesy a stranger shows another.

And why not? she asked herself as she took his greatcoat from him, since they were nothing to one another, and yet she felt her shoulders slump a little as she directed him into the parlour where their son lay in his crib.

She watched as he came slowly to life. As the good colour flowed beneath his skin and his eyes grew brilliant with wonder. Even his step was lighter as he moved closer to the sleeping child.

For some reason she felt the need to go out of the room. To leave this man to meet and greet his son in private, since he did not need her to hover about him as he did so. He was no threat, not to her or the boy. She knew that at once, and the awful dread that he might snatch Tom up and drive away with him, as she had told him he was to do, died at once within her, for good.

She moved to the fire and made a great play with the poker and the fire-tongs, letting him know he was not being watched, putting a small log of applewood on the fire, watching the sparks fly up the chimney and the smoke curl up after them, taking several minutes with the hearth-brush while Callum studied his son.

'He's . . . a handsome lad,' he said at last. He was bending over the crib, his back to her when she turned to him, and she could not see his face.

'Yes. I think so. A true O'Shaughnessy.'

'I'm sorry about that . . . for your sake.'

'No . . . please, I can find no fault with it.'

'You are very generous.' Was he being sarcastic, this polite stranger who was so totally unconcerned with *her*?

'Not at all . . . but . . . pick him up if you would like to.' She had not meant to say that. She had meant to stand between her son and his father, a lioness defending her cub, giving Callum no more than a glance at the boy who was *hers*, whilst she told him so, but it appeared she had no need and the realisation made her generous.

'No, thank you. If I did I would . . . it would be . . . no, but thank you.'

'Then . . . ?'

'I knew, really, that you would not give him up, Maris. Even in our . . . darkest moments when . . . we said . . . fought . . . I knew you would not do that to your child. You are not . . . cruel, only . . . well . . .' He shivered slightly, as though throwing off something which had suddenly touched him in a way he did not care for, then, 'I only came to . . . look at him.' For the first and last time, she knew he was telling her, and her foolish, wilful heart contracted in pain since he could only mean . . . he had been torpedoed twice now and when she had been told of it the second time she had schooled herself not to . . . to be unduly . . . to care only as one would for any man . . . any stranger . . . but he was implying . . . surely . . . that he might

569

not survive the next and . . . this was his son whom he wanted to see at least once before . . .

'Callum . . .' She put out her hand to him but his eyes were only for the boy.

'You have been very kind,' he said, *kind*! '. . . but I must go now.'

'Will you . . . perhaps a cup of tea?' Why was she trying to keep him here?

'No, thank you.'

He left as quietly as he had come, but as she stood in the doorway, the strong March wind lifting her hair in a swirl of silver pale curls about her head, he turned and smiled at her, polite again, cool, no emotion for her, concerned only with his son.

'You do know I would never try to take him from you, don't you? No matter what happens in the future.' When we are divorced and no longer husband and wife, he was saying, the unspoken words creating a coldness and a stillness in her which was physically painful. 'He is meant to be with you, his mother.' And I can have others, with another woman, he was telling her, wasn't he?

'Callum . . . will you . . .'

'Goodbye, Maris. Good luck.' He started the engine, put the car in gear and without looking at her again, drove away.

31

In June the long siege at Tobruk ended with the passage into captivity of 33,000 survivors of its garrison, as the seaport fell to the German army, one of them Corporal Lorcan O'Shaughnessy. Libya, where we were supposed to be strong and invincible, the nation mourned, and they couldn't understand it since they had worked so hard and so long in the production of armaments which had now been handed as booty to the enemy. It was a hard blow, but in August a new Commander was put at the head of the Eighth Army. Lieutenant-General Montgomery, he was called, so perhaps 'things' would take a turn for the better now, the man in the street told his neighbour.

The fighting went on in Russia where the Germans had now reached the city of Stalingrad on the River Don, and the Russians were conducting a street-by-street defence of the ruins; and the British public didn't know where to concentrate its interest, its eyes turning first to Russia and then back to North Africa.

In the same month, troops, mostly Canadian, landed on the French coast at Dieppe: an experiment really, it was later said, in the organisation of large-scale landings, and the nation was wildly enthusiastic; but when it was learned that the whole thing had been a dismal failure and that six thousand men had been killed, it caused great disquiet. 'Things' were not going so well after all.

Tom was three months old when Maris decided that

the time had come to do what she had been planning ever since he was born.

Her determination to rejoin the ATS had, of course, been abandoned. Her devotion to her son had put paid to that and she had given up the idea willingly, but she could be useful to the war effort in other ways, she told herself, using the skill and initiative she had acquired during her time in the service.

She had been helping Rose, Muriel and Lou on the land right through the early summer, she and Rose taking turn and turn about in looking after the four children. The two babies were put end to end in Rosie's big pram, and Harry and Ellie, carefully supervised by whoever was in charge that day, were allowed to 'help' in the fields. They were both still napping for part of the day and whilst they did, on a rug beneath a tree or in the back of the trap, the four women worked side by side.

They grew as dark and wild as gypsies, roses in their cheeks and the good solid flesh of healthy young animals on their bones. They laughed a great deal, she and Rose, as though both had shed great burdens of some sort in the winter months, and the two land girls were heard to say what 'good sorts' the gentry were, and after all they had heard about them being 'stuck up'. They grew crops of shallots, leeks, cabbages, and potatoes from the seedlings the government provided, which must be planted, hoed, weeded, manured, as well as the other arable crops the Ministry of Agriculture, or WAR AG, as it was nicknamed, demanded. They kept bees and hens and goats, and even several cows which Maris learned to milk. It was a good time. She worked hard, long hours, and was as lean and fit and sunburned as a Red Indian, her mother-in-law told her tartly, and when was she going to start her *real* job of looking after her mother-in-law's son's home? a question Maris neatly side-stepped.

But it was not enough. The sense of purpose and fulfilment she had known for nearly two years and which was hard to abandon, a need to find work where she could use the training she had received in the ATS, was uppermost in her mind when she applied to become a member of the Civil Defence.

Anyone can dig, she told Rosie. Anyone could plant seeds and weed the crops and even learn to drive the tractor, but she had been trained in the care and running of an ambulance, the care of the wounded. She had a knowledge and an ability which could be used, which should not be wasted, and between them, surely they could each do the work which would be the most help to the country.

'And what is that?' Rose asked somewhat coolly, since she did not care to be told that anyone, inferring that it took no intelligence to do it, could dig.

'You have talents in the running of this estate, the land, in producing food which is sorely needed. A talent which is being forced to lie fallow – no pun intended, Rosie darling – because of your children.'

'Are you saying I should not have had them?'

'No, of course not, but with someone to look after them you can give yourself full-time to the production of . . . well, whatever the government needs. You were marvellous at it, right at the beginning when you only had Harry, but the actual *management* has fallen into decline since the other two were born. No fault of yours, let me hasten to add, but you simply can't do it with *three* children. Oh, you've worked alongside Muriel and Lou and done wonders, the three of you, but with another land girl to take your place and your-self in charge you could expand. The government will give you anything to help you produce more food, you know that. The National Farmers' Union will send someone to advise you, tell you how to get the best out of the land, where to plough, what to plant, you know how badly they need to increase production. You could grow wheat, oats, barley, sugar beet . . .'

'You *have* studied it, haven't you, Maris?'

'. . . all the things we've been unable to do before. Really get your teeth into it, and then when Alex comes home you and he could keep the whole thing going as a regular farm. The government will even provide machinery . . .'

'Apart from the fact that Beechwood will not belong to Alex when the war is over, a matter you seem to have overlooked in your enthusiasm, what will *you* be doing whilst I'm taking all this on? You've something in mind, I know that, and I also know I'm not going to like it by the way you are trying to persuade me how marvellous it will be.'

'I shall look after your three during the day and . . .'

'Yes?'

'You will have Tom for me at night.'

'Oh yes, whilst you're doing what?'

'Doing whatever is needed of me in the Civil Defence. I was trained to be resourceful, Rosie. To be . . . well . . . a soldier, if you like, and I want to fight . . .'

Her voice trailed away and was followed by a deep and painful silence. Maris watched her cousin's face anxiously, for the whole plan depended on Rosie's will-ingness to be a part of it. She knew her cousin mourned the fact that with the arrival of her babies her manage-

574

ment of the estate and her plans to turn it into a pro-
ductive farm and not just a rather large allotment, had
been badly curtailed. They did what they could with
what they had, but it needed someone to *run* it, and
here was Rosie's chance. It would be hard work for a
period of time, the length of which no one could even
guess at, perhaps years, but if it helped to win the war
and bring home the men, Alex and . . . well . . . all
the others – disconcerted for a moment as Callum's
face flashed before her eyes – then surely Rose would
think it was worth *trying*, at least.

She said so, and all the while Rose stared blindly out
of Maris's kitchen window into the small square of
sunny back garden where the children, or at least
Harry, was doing his best to climb the apple tree in its
far corner. He was three and a half now, her elder son,
as wilful and stubborn as his father, a real 'handful' as
Ellen called him, and needed a man's firm hand to
guide him. His father's hand, which at the moment was
totally concerned with guiding his escort fighter Spitfire
through the black skies over Germany and France as
he protected the bombers which went over there almost
nightly. The 'Lancaster' and 'Stirling' bombers, and,
with the arrival in Britain – often through the port of
Liverpool which had been known to send a trainload
of American troops on their way every hour for thirty
hours at a stretch – of the US 8th Air Force, the 'Flying
Fortress' and the 'Liberator'. Anywhere in Germany
where there was oil, electric power, aviation industry,
transportation, chemicals and machinery, anywhere in
fact where the destruction of such commodities would
be likely to put 'Jerry' out of action.

In May a '1,000 bomber raid' had been launched
against Cologne, and Alex had been part of it, lending

575

protection to the aircraft which dropped the bombs; and though he did not speak of it except in terms of the sorrow he had felt at the death which rained down on innocent people, she knew the strain on him, and the rest of the aircrews, was appalling. He, and they, should be at home. Alex needed her and his children to heal him and *they* needed him. She needed him so badly she honestly did not know how she got through the days and nights, each one worse than the last. How was she to get through what could be years of being without him, or even worse, a lifetime of being without him? Only the ending of the war, as soon as it could be managed, would bring him home, and though what she and Maris did was no more than a tiny droplet in the great ocean of the battle, it was all they could do. And if everyone did *all* they could do, surely, *surely*, her husband might be got home safely, and sooner rather than later.

There had been no air raids over Liverpool since January, when fifteen people had been killed, but that did not mean there would be no more. The docks were a primary target for the enemy bombers, and there had been astonishment that the bombing had stopped, and it was believed it would begin again. Maris would be needed then.

'Tell me about it,' Rose said to her.

Maris offered her services to the Civil Defence the following week and was accepted as a part-time warden. She cycled each evening the four miles from Rosie's house where she left her precious son, on the bicycle Michael had found and restored for her, into Liverpool. The first thing she did was to attend a first aid class where lectures were given and first aid was practised, not only on supposed victims with many and varied injuries but on 'mothers' who had just given birth, for it was quite common, she was told, for expectant mothers to begin premature labour during an incident. She learned 'gas' cleaning exercises, though it was readily agreed that the dropping of 'gas' seemed to be now no longer a possibility. She learned fire-fighting, and how to run in her brand-new dungarees and rubber boots, since it was not known in any emergency what skills might be needed.

She was already well versed in car maintenance and running repairs on most vehicles. Now she had to practise driving in the dark in a gas-mask, without lights of any kind; avoiding palliasses stuffed with straw, scattered on the road to represent casualties; avoiding anything which might loom up in front of her, including trees, buildings, other vehicles – all without lights, which they would be during a raid – and on one occasion avoiding them so well she found herself out in the countryside beyond Knotty Ash! She was a member of the Civil Defence, though the public still preferred the familiar initials of the ARP Warden. She was, officially, an ambulance driver but must be ready, she was told, to do anything which was needed of her during an air raid. She was paid nothing as a volunteer 'part-timer'.

It worked very well, the arrangement between herself and Rosie, though, instead of becoming easier with habit, it became harder each night to part with her son. Though there were no raids at the present time, and if there were they would hardly present a problem out near Colton, she was haunted by the prospect of Rosie and the children buried alive under the debris of Lacy's house. Could she ever forget the harrowing scenes she herself had witnessed during that night of the May

Blitz, and to imagine . . . well . . . she did her best not to, putting it to the back of her mind as so many were doing with their own pictures of horror they would prefer to forget.

All day, apart from when the children slept, as did she, her mind was consumed with the need to grasp as much of her child's life as she could. She was tired, exhausted sometimes beyond sleep, needing it nevertheless; but instead she sat in an old deck-chair, her son in her arms, studying his infant face from which Callum O'Shaughnessy's eyes looked out at her. Rosie's garden was in full summer bloom. The drone of the bees and the muted sound of the tractor engine in the distance lulled her to peace and, she told herself, to acceptance.

Though she had, so far, been called upon to do no more than patrol the streets, she was to be always on the alert, reporting periodically to the 'control room'. She was supposed to know where everyone in her sector slept at night so that, should an incident occur, she could direct the rescue team to the appropriate quarter of the debris. When a bomb fell she must report its position quickly and concisely to Control, calming the public whilst she was about it. She must make it her business to 'pop in' to air-raid shelters and tell its occupants how the raid was proceeding, but was in no way to alarm them. If an incident was 'minor' then her fire-fighting training was to be put into action and she was to rescue any inhabitants, administer first aid and direct the homeless to the rest centre, but all this seemed to her to be completely irrelevant since during a raid she would, she was positive, be driving her ambulance.

There were no raids. She continued her duties as a warden, not of course wishing an air raid would hap-

pen, but not at all pleased with the work she had not
really volunteered to do. She met a variety of people,
mostly men who, like herself, were part-timers. Railway workers, post office sorters, lawyers, newspaper-
men, garage hands, all anonymous in their blue overalls
and steel helmets, coming straight from their daytime
work, many of them, to their duties with the Civil
Defence. But still there were no air raids, and she
began to feel that she was wasting her time in this job
where she did nothing but amble about the dark streets
shouting to some careless householder, 'Put out that
bloody light.'

Rose, on the other hand, was shaping the estate of
Beechwood into a production line from which, at har-
vest time, a vast amount of 'food for the nation' would
pour. Three and a half million acres of permanent
grassland across the country had gone under the plough
since the war began, amongst them those of Beechwood. With the government's help she improved the
drainage, ploughing land which had known only the
steady munching of cattle and the dainty feet of
the deer which had browsed there. A new tractor was
provided and something called a 'disc harrow', along
with the two new land girls Rose had asked for, and
the tons of fertilizer, also provided by the WAR AG.

The summer of 1942 was glorious, following a foul
winter, and record crops were expected, which meant
that harvesting might drag on well into the autumn,
perhaps even to Christmas. Rose was told what to
grow, how to sell it and at what price, and her sense
of achievement, unlike Maris's, was enormous.

She had gone over to Beechwood Hall that day to
deal with the increasing and unwieldy pile of forms
which had to be completed each week. She had told

Maris she would be home for lunch, that is if she could make it. Uncle Teddy was still not well, keeping more and more to his room, his wife Clare with him, both knowing perhaps that time was not on their side. A fragile man with the mental strength of two, if only his health had allowed it. There was no one in the house now but Mrs Pritchard the cook, an old woman with nowhere else to go, had she even wanted to, and the elderly housemaid called Betty who had been with the family since before the First World War. Between them they kept such rooms as were used, clean and tidy; and in the evening Mrs Pritchard cooked the land girls a satisfying and tasty meal since, as she said, if those living on a 'farm', which the estate of Beechwood now was, couldn't have a bit extra in the way of meat, milk and eggs, then who could? Nothing like the meals she had cooked once upon a time when old Mrs Osborne had been alive, of course, since who among *that* lot would appreciate quails' eggs, a fillet of pheasant done in her special sauce, mock turtle soup, wild duck and champagne jelly? Her apricot torte would be wasted on them, if she could have got the fresh apricots, which she couldn't. She sent them out each day with a 'door-step' apiece filled with cheese or jam, perhaps a flask of her home-made soup if the day was cold, but at lunchtime all Mr Teddy and Mrs Clare wanted was a slice of chicken or fish, or a mouthful of soup. If she could manage it, Rose strode across the park to her own home for lunch and for Maris's company. Besides which, she missed her children, and to have half an hour with them at midday was a joy to her.

They had just sat down to a 'treat' of kippers which Maris had queued for at the market before coming home and which Harry was viewing with great suspicion, when the roar of a car's engine coming up the drive, growing louder as it approached the house, lifted the heads of both women to a listening attitude.

'I don't want one of those things, Mamma,' Harry said loftily. 'I want treacle pudding and custard.'

'They're good for you, darling.' Rose's answer was automatic and was spoken in the way she did when she was not listening to him, Harry knew.

'No, they're not,' guessing he was on safe ground arguing with her.

'Eat up, sweetheart.'

'They make me sick.' He pretended to vomit. Overcome with admiration at their brother's audacity and seeing there were to be no repercussions, his brother and sister did the same. Tom, sitting on his mother's knee and at five months quite accustomed to being entertained by his cousins, smiled with delight and began to clap his hands.

'Who is it?'

'Who is it?' Harry echoed boldly, quite beside himself at his own daring.

'I . . . don't know.' Was it a green MG, or a blue Triumph Roadster? though why the former should jump into Maris's mind was a bewilderment to her.

It was neither, and when Charlie climbed out of the scarlet Alvis, Maris was astonished by the sudden onset of trembling which shook her cousin's frame, and by the draining of every vestige of colour from her face. Of course, Rose *had* thought it might be Alex, and if so was it any wonder she should look so sick and shaken?

'Oh God,' Maris groaned. 'Hide the damned kippers. There aren't enough to go round.'

'He can have mine, Aunty Maris. I hate the damned

581

things,' Harry shouted, already half-way to the front door. He meant to be the first to greet this stranger in the same uniform his own Daddy wore, and who had come just in time to prevent Harry eating the horrid thing on the plate Aunty Maris had put before him.

Strangely, when he got out into the garden the boy did not, as he was inclined to do with male callers, climb all over the faintly familiar figure of the RAF officer who was brushing an imaginary fleck of dust from his immaculately pressed trousers, but hesitated several feet away from him, moving in what seemed a wary manner from one foot to the other as he studied him.

'Hello, sprog,' the man said.

'My Daddy calls me that.'

'Does he indeed? Wizard for him.'

'Who are you?'

'Never you mind, you cheeky little beggar. Go and tell your mother Charlie is here to see her.'

'I can see that, Charlie,' Rose said from the doorway. For some reason she had picked up her daughter, settling her on her hip, leaving Jamie, who was just a year old, in his high chair, yelling in fury at being left behind and banging with his spoon as he made a determined effort to stand up in it and climb over the side.

'Rosie, there you are, and looking absolutely marvellous, if I may say so. Those breeches suit you so well.' Charlie's eyes had run down from her white face to her flat belly, neat waist and slim hips, to the shapely curve of her calf, then back up again to the swell of her breasts and the deep and shadowed valley between them. She had worked hard, physically, since the birth of her son last year, and the rather matronly fullness she had retained after the birth of her first two children had fined down to a lithe but very comely slenderness, only her breasts still as deep and lovely. His eyes told her he liked what he saw.

'Working in the open air certainly seems to agree with you, my love,' he went on. 'You are even more . . . attractive than the last time we met.'

In the dim hallway behind Rose, from where she had been about to call out to Charlie and carry forth her new son to meet his uncle for the first time, Maris hesitated. She didn't know why. There was just a feeling, a whisper in the warm air of something strange, something not quite right, something she hesitated to call menacing but which was certainly frightening Rosie. But why? What was there to be afraid of? It was only Charlie, who could be a bit of a sod at times, but who, perhaps because of the way he lived – and saw men die – which affected servicemen in different ways, had become somewhat changed from the correct English gentleman he had been before the war. Nevertheless, he was still harmless. She had seen very little of him in the past three years, and when she had it was only on the light and airy level of two people who had once known one another but who had lost touch. She had always been closer to Alex who, though volatile and quick-tempered, had a warm side to his nature which allowed for closeness and which was lacking in Charlie.

Still, there was nothing in Charlie to alarm Rose, was there? And if there was, what was it? She knew Rose had seen a bit of him a while ago and had even written to him, she seemed to remember, but when she thought about it Rose had never mentioned him in months. She had hoped to reunite the brothers, Maris recalled, and heal the breach between Charlie and their mother, but perhaps, with their mother dead, Rose had given up the idea.

'What d'you want?' Rose asked abruptly, her manner so hostile Maris was amazed. Rose the peacemaker, Rose the gentle mother, the caring wife, the loving friend. She spoke as though Charlie was her enemy, and her manner seemed to indicate a defence, an appearance of protecting her home and her family against an intruder.

'Now then, Rosie, is that any way to speak to an old . . . friend?'

'What d'you want, Charlie? I'm very busy and have to get back to work. In fact, I'm late now and . . .'

'Come, don't be like that, sweetheart.'

'Stop it, Charlie, stop it . . . go away . . .'

'Go away? You didn't say that last time we met, and so I thought, as I was in the neighbourhood, I would buster over and renew our . . .'

'That's enough, *that's enough*. Go away and leave me alone. I won't have you here . . . never again.' A high note of hysteria had entered Rose's voice, and though her back was turned it seemed to Maris that in every line of it, in the set of her cousin's strong shoulders and the very stance she took up, was her loathing of Charlie Woodall, and not only of him but of herself.

The child on her hip began to wail and strain away from this unfamiliar mother who had never, in her short life, been anything but calm and loving. Young Harry had moved away, step by slow step, from Charlie Woodall, and reaching his mother put his arms about one of her legs in a way he had not done for two years.

It was then that Maris stepped out into the sunlight,

her own son beginning to grizzle, and had it not been so highly charged, the very air about them crackling with some lethal tension, the look of ludicrous surprise on Charlie's face might have made her laugh. There was another expression there, as well as astonishment, one that was quickly submerged but not before she had recognised it as malevolence and that it was directed at Rose.

'Good God, Maris, I had no idea . . .'

'That I was here?'

'Well, you must admit that you kept pretty quiet.' His expression changed and he began to smile. 'Hoping to hear some hot chat, were you? Something which is nothing to do with you but is between myself and Rose?'

'What does that mean, for God's sake?'

'Ask Rose, she'll tell you.'

'Look, Charlie Woodall, I don't know what you mean and I don't think I want to, but whatever it is it's upsetting not only Rose but the children,' which was true, with three of them shrieking at the tops of their lungs and Harry, wide-eyed and sucking his thumb, clinging to his mother like a limpet.

'For Christ's sake, Maris, what a bloody flap. I only called on my sister-in-law, which seems to me to be a perfectly natural thing to do . . .' which it did to her, but there was more to it than that, and when she got Rose back inside and the children settled she intended to find out what it was.

Rose, whose arm she held protectively, was shaking like an aspen tree in a storm, beginning to weep most alarmingly, and if something wasn't done soon there would be full-scale pandemonium.

'Go away, Charlie, there's a good chap. You've done

585

something to upset Rose, and standing there grinning like an idiot and denying it isn't going to help. Where are you staying?'

'Well, I was rather hoping Rose might give me a bed for a night or two,' and with the most appalling expression on his face, one Maris could hardly believe it was so incredible, he winked lewdly.

'Charlie . . . what . . . ?' The implication was so foul, so absolutely gross she could scarcely absorb it, and didn't want to. She didn't want anything to do with it, any of it. *Any of what?* her bewildered mind was asking, but her senses knew, her female senses which were not unfamiliar with male sexuality. Rose . . . Rose and Charlie . . . sweet Christ . . .

Rose had collapsed against her, the child in her arms frantic with fear, and about her legs her son clung, beginning to hiccup softly as he returned in his terror to babyhood.

'Darling, don't . . . please Rosie . . . come inside. Oh sweetheart, what is it? . . . come, lean on me . . . Harry, let go of Mamma, she can't walk . . . come inside . . . there, there . . .' uttering the motherly sounds one used when soothing a child, which Rose appeared to be; and when they were in the hall, a stumbling, fumbling group of women and crying children and the cats which had come to see what all the fuss was about twining round their legs, she shut the door in Charlie's terrible smiling face.

It took her half an hour to calm the children, putting them all together in one bedroom in the hope that they would feel more secure in one another's company. She petted them to sleep, Harry included, closing the curtains against the bright sunlight, noticing as she did so that Charlie and his car had gone, before going down

586

the stairs and into the tiny parlour where Rose sat like a woman carved in granite.

In the kitchen, incredibly, she could hear Polly, Rose's maid of all work, letting the world know that 'fools rush in, where angels fear to tread', her voice high and off-key, and had time to thank God that Mrs Flynn was not here today but away up at Home Farm Cottage giving Maris's place 'a good bottoming', which she had been promising herself for weeks.

She moved slowly into the room, then, pulling up a chair until she and Rose were knee to knee she took her hand, looking compassionately into the tragic face of her cousin.

'Tell me, darling,' she said, but Rose did not answer, only stared off over Maris's shoulder at some dreadful thing only she could see.

'What has Charlie done to you, Rosie?' she asked, though of course she knew.

'It is what Charlie and I have done to Alex.' The words sighed up from Rose's rigid throat, so softly Maris barely heard them.

'Do you want to talk of it, Rose? I'm here if you do.'

'What is there to say? It is such a . . . common thing, or at least they say it is, these days. With men away for years and women . . . lonely . . . but with . . . dear God, with one's own brother-in-law. My husband's brother. Once . . . only once, I swear it and now . . . I thought I would be all right . . . but it will never be all right. You see . . . I don't know whether James is Alex's child or Charlie's.'

Maris kept a tight hold on her definite need to fling Rose's hand away from her in horror. To stand up and shout her abhorrence; to stamp about the room and smash something, preferably Rose's face. Rosie who had, in her eyes, always been perfect. A woman with no flaws. A woman worthy of anyone's love and respect: Alex's, her own, her family; and now, in one bright, sun-filled half-hour, her cousin, her friend had become . . . had become . . . ?

She sighed then, tiredly, resignedly, and she felt some emotion move quite tangibly within her. A maturity, she supposed it to be, a completeness, an adult acceptance of not only Rosie's human weakness, frailty, but her own. How could she judge in her cousin what was in them all? In her, in Callum, in Alex and Charlie? The war had done this to them, for in war defences which seem impregnable, crumble and allow in all manner of weakening emotions. And should Rose be immune from loneliness and fear and the despair which came in the night to haunt a woman alone? Maris loved Rose and must, because of that love, tolerate her fall from . . . from grace, if that was what it was, as she had never, not once tolerated Callum's.

How different life would have been, she thought sadly, if they had been kinder to one another, holding out her hands for Rosie to cling to as she wept.

32

It was a month later when the two brothers came face
to face. It was in a pub called 'The Running Fox' which
was situated almost mid-way between Kenley, where
Alex was stationed, and Biggin Hill, where Charles had
been transferred only two weeks previously.

Flight-Lieutenant Sir Charles Woodall, DFC, and
Pilot Officer Alex Woodall, DFM and bar, both pilots
of Fighter Command, had not clapped eyes on one
another since they had stood side by side at their
mother's grave well over a year ago, and before that
since the beginning of the war. Once in three years,
and for a split second both of them were ready to smile,
to greet one another with the cheerful warmth they
had known as boys. Even their quarrels then had had
warmth in them but not now, and as quickly as the
instinct to greet one another had come, it was rapidly
frozen over with the bitter enmity which had grown
between them since Rose Osborne had become a
woman.

They were both well known in their respective squadrons and even beyond. They were both 'Aces', having
been credited with shooting down at least five enemy
aircraft. Top performers then, and though it had never
been spoken of by either of them, to anyone, it was
understood that there was a rivalry between them, in
the air, and that for reasons known only to themselves
they were not on the best of terms, in the air or on the
ground.

'The Running Fox' was full that night. A full comple-
ment of RAF officers and men, standing at the bar or
lounging at the tables which were placed close together.
It had been rumoured that the landlord had obtained
a supply of gin, and lads from Kenley had 'bustered
over' for a 'soaking glass of wet' and also to see, as
was their wont, if there was any spare 'skirt' available.
'Shooting a line with a popsie' was a very favourite
pastime with them, and a uniform, particularly an
officer's uniform, was definitely an advantage in getting
into the 'twilights' or 'wrist breakers', as the knickers
of an obliging female were aptly named in the RAF's
peculiar vernacular.

The noise was so appalling it was impossible to hear
what was being said unless it was howled at the top of
one's voice, though the landlord and barmaid, well used
to it, seemed to have no trouble in taking orders. It
appeared to be a question of keeping one's eyes on the
speaker's lips, and it was perhaps this and the positive
'pea-souper' of cigarette smoke thickening the atmosphere which allowed Charlie and Alex Woodall to stand
almost back to back at the bar for the best part of half
an hour before either realised the other was there.

After the initial shock when their eyes met they both
looked away, turning their backs on one another again,
not awfully sure at that moment what to do, both continuing to talk with the chaps they had come in with,
or at least to listen to the roared conversations which
went on about them. Conversations concerned with
'scrambles', 'recce's', 'briefings', 'DROs' and all the
other 'small talk' which was their very own and which
was so completely incomprehensible to anyone not of
their élite circle. Spoken not just by the officers but by
every other rank in the Royal Air Force.

The landlord called 'time' but no one took a great deal of notice since it was the custom to 'get one in', or even two or three, ready to be drunk after the last order. These men were risking their lives, many of them every day or night, in the dangerous skies across the Channel, Battle of Britain heroes, some of them, and who would begrudge them a bit of fun; but gradually the crowd began to thin out and the continuous uproar died to a murmured level, interspersed with bursts of laughter, where it was possible to hear the conversations of men several feet away.

'Will you have the other half, Willy?' Flight-Lieutenant Sir Charles Woodall was heard to say in his cultured voice to the man who stood next to him.

'Righto, Charlie, and then I must be off.'

'Oh, come on, old boy, don't be like that. The night's young yet, and I'm sure mine host could find us a bottle of some sort to see us through it. How about it, landlord? What's under that bar counter of yours? Scotch? A bottle of gin, perhaps . . . ?'

'Now, Charlie, behave yourself.'

'I *am* behaving myself, Willy, aren't I, chaps . . . ?' grinning round at the officers who were loosely grouped about him. 'More's the pity . . .' and it was at that precise moment that his eyes, such a deep and golden brown, innocent of all but the desire for a bit of a lark, which was what they all got up to, became something else. Something, if one was charitable, which could be called malicious but which was really much more than that. A look of merciless cruelty which might have been recognised by those German pilots of the Luftwaffe who had come up against him and were now in oblivion.

'Not that I'm always a good boy, you understand, Willy,' he went on, winking wickedly.

591

'Don't I know it, Charlie. I remember that time you and I went to London. We had dinner at "Quags" and then went on to that little . . .'

'I was referring to a bit of naughtiness I got up to further north than that, Willy.'

'Really? Well, I can't say I remember being there with you, old chum. I've never been further north than Leicestershire and that was before the war when I did a bit of hunting with the Quorn.'

'The Quorn, by jove!' There were many men in the squadron who were not of the 'toffee nose' type, as those from the upper classes were good-naturedly called. Men who came from working-class backgrounds but who had nevertheless qualified as pilots, navigators, gunners, officers like Charlie Woodall, some of them, and who did the same terror-striking job as that performed by those who had been known before 1939 as their 'betters', and it was they who were making fun of Willy Andrews and of Sir Charles Woodall. It was perhaps this – or perhaps not – that set him on the path which was to lead to such destruction.

Alex Woodall could feel his brother at the back of him. Actually *feel* the flesh and muscle and bone of his brother which was a part of himself, as though he and Charlie were touching. It was taking all his control to stop himself from turning round and smashing his fist in his brother's face. He really didn't know why. He and Charlie were nothing to one another now. They had no quarrel, not really, since they had no . . . no link any more. They were two strangers who shared nothing; but still the rancour was there, that hidden antipathy which warned him he really should walk out of the pub and away from the man who had once been his brother. But he was tired. Exhausted to the marrow of his bones, as they all were to one degree or another. He had flown only the night before, escorting bombers to the German town of Essen, and, if he had been wise, should now have been in his bed back in the officers' mess; but he had felt taut, as tense as stretched wire, and so he had joined Dickie Parker and Pip Harrison, both Canadians attached to his squadron, hoping the company and the booze would help him to 'wind down' and perhaps get some sleep. Thank God he was going home the day after tomorrow. Home to Rosie and the children he scarcely knew. Harry, a smashing little kid of almost four. All he seemed to remember of him, though, was an eager male rush and tumble of sturdy legs, vivid bold green eyes just like those of his mother, and the constant demand on his father's attention, probably because of the child's contact with only female company. His daughter, Ellie, who would soon be three, dainty and eternally feminine, shy with him and inclined to hide behind her mother's skirts, ready to burst into tears over nothing, or so it seemed to him who was not used to children's ways, and the new boy, Jamie, handsome and noisy and almost, though he would not dream of saying it to Rosie, a changeling to his father.

And Rosie, ah Rosie, his dearest heart. It was to her that he was returning, not his children who, though he held them dear, really had not taken a good grip on him yet since he and they were almost strangers to one another. Two weeks he was to have. Two weeks of Rosie's healing presence. Her arms protectively about him each night. Her body, her heart, her mind, her soul completely his to work their magic, their miracle, the wondrous renewal of his own depleted self. Three years now. Three long years since he had raced off to compete – once again – with the man at his back who was even now, in that loud and truculent way of those who are drunk, boasting of some conquest he had made.

'Now then, Charlie, you are well and truly pissed, my lad,' his companion was saying, 'so Jock and I will take you home and put you to bed . . .'

'I haven't finished giving you the "gen" about the popsie in Liverpool yet, Willy, so just shut up, there's a good chap.'

'Liverpool? Do they have popsies in Liverpool, Charlie?'

'Would I shoot you a line, Willy, now would I? This one was some streamlined piece, I can tell you, at least she was the last time I saw her a month ago. Lost a bit of weight, she had, but the first time I had her she was a corker, a real armful, and what a party we had that night, Rosie and I, I can tell you, if you get my drift.'

'I do indeed, Charlie, but come on, old lad, chocks away . . .'

'No, Willy. I'm not that smashed. I can walk without your bloody help, or anybody's.'

'OK, old chum, just as you like.' Willy stepped away from him, for Charlie Woodall had been known to turn nasty if he was crossed, and as he moved backwards he bumped into a pilot officer who stood behind him.

'Sorry, chum,' he said, smilingly apologetic, for he was sure the man would see the state of *his* chum and would not be offended; but the officer was staring at Charlie with the most appalling expression Willy had ever seen on any man's face, and he'd seen a few in his time in Fighter Command. Men who had done things, seen things, heard things they would rather forget but never would.

'I say . . .' he began, confused, since the man had turned the colour of unbaked bread and his eyes had sunk deep into the taut flesh about them, but the officer was not looking at him but at old Charlie, who was smiling. A strange smile, Willy would have said, just as though something had happened which gave him a great deal of satisfaction.

'Why, hello Alex.' His smile broadened. 'This *is* a surprise. Fancy seeing you after all this time.' He turned smoothly to Willy and Jock and all the other 'bods' who were lounging about him.

'Can you believe it, this is my brother, Pilot Officer Alex Woodall. He and I haven't met for ages, have we, brother?'

His eyes were quite deadly, just as they were when he had his enemy in his sights, and he licked his lips as he got ready to shoot Alex Woodall down in flames.

'And how are the children, Alex? Fine specimens, aren't they? all three of them, particularly that last one. A handsome chappie just like his father, I would say. And Rosie . . .'

Rosie . . . oh Christ . . . *Rosie* . . . Willy Andrews just had time to register . . .

'. . . is she well and as . . . streamlined as she . . .' before Alex Woodall sprang, as silently as a panther for his brother's throat, cutting off the words and Charlie's air supply with hands which were so strong, so tenacious it took five men a long time to prise them loose, and when they did Charlie Woodall was almost unconscious.

'Get them out of here,' the landlord was bawling, ready to send for the MPs who patrolled the area of his pub. In all the thrashing about, chairs had been

595

smashed and tables knocked for six, and though it had not been the usual kind of fisticuffs which occurred when a man who was under strain took offence at another – who was in the same condition – it had been even more destructive. The pilot officer who had attacked the flight-lieutenant was still violently struggling in the grasp of his companions, his face a frightful mask of loathing – over what, for God's sake, the landlord was asking himself? – but in his eyes was, well, it was a kind of death. He had seen it when men came into his bar to drink to a mate who had 'gone for a burton', and perhaps that was what was wrong with this chap, but it did not explain why he had gone for the other officer.

'Get them out of here, lads,' he ordered. 'If they want to scrap then let them do it outside,' though the flight-lieutenant looked to be in no shape to 'scrap' anywhere, holding his throat on which livid bruises were already beginning to form, and sucking in great gulps of air.

He still managed to speak, though.

'She was a bloody good fuck, Alex,' he said.

She was in the garden. He had been nineteen hours on the train from London, without sleep or any relief from the foul and tortured pictures which ravaged his mind. Without sleep for three days now, but despite this he walked from Lime Street Station along Wavertree Road, through Childwall to Childwall Valley Road, stumbling along the lovely autumnal lanes which were so achingly familiar, through the past when he and Rosie had been young and free from the weary cares of today.

She was picking apples. The boy, *his* boy, was throw-

ing them into a basket, and he heard her voice tell him
to be more gentle with them.

'They bruise so easily, darling, and then if they bruise
they can go rotten. You understand?'

'Of course, Mamma,' scornfully, since he was nearly
four.

'Of course you do.'

Ellie was placing the ones she picked up from the
grass very carefully into *her* basket. None of *hers* would
be bruised, her manner said; and playing with a tumble
of puppies, two in fact though there seemed to be more,
was the boy. The boy Jamie.

Rose was absorbed in her task. Maris would be over
soon to drop Tom off before she cycled up to the ARP
post in Picton Road, and she wanted to have all the
apples safely stored by the time her cousin arrived. She
would make some apple and blackberry jam, she had
decided, for the brambles in the hedges bordering the
lanes beyond the estate were loaded with luscious, sun-
ripened fruit which she and Maris meant to pick on
Sunday. That is if Alex hadn't arrived by then.
Strangely, she had received no word from him about
the exact day and time of his arrival as she usually did,
but it was to be before the end of September he had
said in his last letter.

She fell to dreaming then, standing in her old dungarees on the step ladder, a ripe, smooth apple in her
hand, her breath sighing in smooth-textured anticipation, her eyes soft and unfocused. Six months it had
been since Alex had had a '295', the leave pass issued
to men of the RAF. Six long months in the arid desert
which was her life without him, but soon, *soon*, he
would be here to nourish her starving mind and body,
to unlock the hopes and joys which lay dormant when

he was away, to free the warm love which she would pour over him and which was his alone. They would make love, as friends do, as lovers do, in that delicate, easy and natural way, as they had done hundreds of times before, and she would be restored, refreshed, able to go on again until he should return.

She smiled, a radiant, joyful smile, and tossing back her head she allowed her cape of dark hair which, unlike her contemporaries, she had never cut, to ripple down her straight back; and beyond the wall the man who watched her felt the pain, the harrowing, crucifying agony slash at him, and his first words were cruel.

'Did you do that for Charlie, Rose?'

Either she did not hear exactly what he said, or she mistook his meaning for, in one lovely graceful movement she turned, her face alight with her love, leaped from the ladder and began to run like a child, her arms spread wide to receive him.

'Don't touch me, Rose,' he said flatly, 'or I think I might just kill you.'

She faltered then, her smile of gladness welling away, not really believing what she had heard, ready to smile again if it had been meant as a joke – *a joke!* – ready to throw her arms about this beloved person but not quite daring to, for his face was a mask of . . . a mask so horrific she stopped completely.

Harry, who was right behind her – for this was *his* Daddy, the marvellous Daddy who flew a Spitfire, who called him Sprog and played the most marvellous *rough* games with him, the sort *men* played – ran into the back of her legs, nearly taking her from her feet. Ellie clutched her basket and hung back shyly. She knew who he was, of course, since Mamma showed her his picture every single day and allowed her to kiss it each night, and the last time he had been home he had taken them all down to see the boats, and even *on* one. Nevertheless, she thought she'd wait and see what he did before she ventured any nearer to him.

Jamie stood up, disentangling himself from the new puppies given to him for his birthday in May, or at least one for him and one for Harry, brought to them when the pups were eight weeks old by Uncle Michael. Pipsqueak and Wilfred, they were called, his Uncle Michael had told them, of no particular breed, rough and ready for any game he and Harry cared to invent. His eighteen-month-old enthusiasm for anything Harry did had him hurtling towards the tall stranger who stood outside the garden gate.

'Alex.' Rose no longer made any move towards her husband, even his name no more than a whisper on her ashen lips, for she knew that it had happened. That what she had lain awake in the night agonising over had somehow – *how?* – come to his ears, and he was here, not to kill her as he seemed intent on doing, at least not her physical body, but to end her life just the same. To do whatever a husband did when he learned his wife had been unfaithful to him. She had heard of it from her grandmother who had it from Gracie. Brutal fights when a serviceman, warned by neighbours of his wife's misconduct, would return unexpectedly to sort out her fancy man.

But she had no fancy man and it seemed Alex was more likely to sort *her* out than the man who had . . . what was the word . . . she didn't really know, nor even care now, for the perfect, unshakeable, complete love she and Alex had shared all their lives was very obviously irrevocably shattered, and what did *words* matter? What did anything matter in this wide world, what did even her children matter if she was to lose this man, as it seemed she was?

'May I put the children in the kitchen with . . .' she quavered, for surely Alex, even the strange and awful Alex who stood just beyond her gate, would not . . . do whatever he intended to do before the innocent and startled gaze of his children.

'Please do.'

'Thank you.'

He was in exactly the same spot when she returned, the children, Harry protesting bitterly since it was his *Daddy* out there, as though his mother had not recognised him, placed in the bewildered protection of Polly and Mrs Flynn, who had come to 'do' for her that day. To scrub and polish and deep scour the house in her own inimitable way, and who had been having a cup of tea and what passed for a 'chat' with the simple Polly.

'Aren't you . . . coming in, Alex?' She did her best to keep her voice steady.

'Why?'

'It is your home . . .'

'Not any more. Nothing I thought was mine . . . is mine any more . . .'

'Alex . . .' Her voice cracked in agony.

'I really don't know why I came, except perhaps to hear it from you. He was . . . boasting of it . . . in the local pub. The men . . . *my* men . . .' He swallowed most painfully. 'So I know it's true, for not even Charlie would . . . Oh Jesus, Rosie . . . tell me it's not true . . . for Christ's sake, tell me it's not true . . .' and he began to weep as he had not wept since he was a boy. He was bowed and defeated, and in a moment she was at the gate ready to fling it open, ready to fling her strong, protecting arms about him, but he reared back from her, his wet face a mask of horror.

'Don't touch me. For Christ's sake, I cannot bear you near me after what you have done. *He is my brother, my brother*, you whore. I might . . . *might*, I don't know, might have been able to . . . any other man . . . but not Charlie Woodall . . . never . . . not my own brother . . .'

'Alex.' She began to cry broken-heartedly.

'Why . . . oh God . . . *why* . . . ?'

'I don't know . . . it was only once . . .'

'Please . . . I cannot bear . . .'

'Alex . . . I love you . . .'

'I believe you do, Rosie, which makes it worse, but you see I can't live with the thought of you and him . . .'

Her eyes widened in terror at the implication of his words and she took a step nearer to him, throwing out her arms in anguished appeal.

'You wouldn't . . . oh please, Alex . . . tell me you wouldn't . . . I simply couldn't bear it if you . . .'

'I shan't need to, Rosie. Jerry will . . .'

'Alex . . . don't . . .' Her voice rose in a scream, and inside the house Polly and Mrs Flynn cowered against one another, each holding a child, the third burrowing his face in Mrs Flynn's apron.

'Don't what? Don't fly into danger? Is that what you were about to say? Well, I have no choice, have I? I'm a "fighter boy" as your lover is . . .'

'Alex, he is not my lover . . . never . . . it was not . . . *love* . . .'

He went on as if she had not spoken, '. . . so there's a chance, more than an even chance after all this time, I would say, that neither of us will come back.'

601

'Please . . .' Her voice was hoarse, no more than a guttural whisper, '. . . come into the house. Let me . . .'

'What? What would you have us do? Drink tea and discuss this rationally like two grown-up people who are well aware that this sort of thing happens in wartime . . .'

'Not to us, Alex, not to you and me.'

'It *has* happened. You have *lain* with your husband's brother, which I'm sure is not only immoral but could be illegal, and that child of his . . .'

'*No! No!* He's yours . . . yours . . .'

'Is he? How can you know that . . . ?'

And suddenly she did. Deep within her where the dread of it had hidden truth, the truth that she had allowed to turn sour in her own shame, was the calm and certain knowledge that the child she had borne, the boy Jamie, was this man's son. How many times had she seen it in him, the infant and now the child? How many times had she seen Alex Woodall's impish charm, his truculent anger, his warmth and goodness shine from Jamie Woodall's eyes, which though they were the colour of her own were the exact depth and length of those of his father? Alex Woodall. There was nothing of Charlie Woodall in him. Nothing.

She said so.

'His eyes . . .'

'Are the same colour as yours.'

'They are yours nevertheless.'

His strength, which had been held together by his madness, suddenly left him, and he began to tremble; and at once, as it was in her nature to do, she leaned towards him, defending him from hurt, longing to comfort and cherish, her tear-stained face compassionate,

602

filled with sorrow, not for herself who deserved this torment but for him who did not.

'I cannot let this happen, Alex.' Her voice was stronger now, a cry from the heart, his pain overwhelming her; and yet she was ready, if his pain demanded it, to suffer violence at his hands if he wished to unleash it. Physical violence, which would be easier to bear than his contained and bitter hatred.

'Alex . . .'

'You can do nothing to stop it, so . . . for Christ's sake, let's get it over and done with.'

'In what way . . . ?' And yet she too wanted it ended, for she could see she was crucifying him.

'I'm going . . .'

'No, Alex . . . no . . .'

'I can't forgive it . . . and never forget . . .'

'Please . . . please . . .' She was pleading for her life.

They did not see Maris as she trundled the once elegant pram which had been Elizabeth O'Shaughnessy's gift to Rose when Harry was born. She had come across the shaggy grass and along the edge of the drive which led to Rosie's gate, and for a long moment she stood, her mouth agape, watching as her brother lifted his hand and struck his wife so brutally across the face she fell to the ground.

'Alex!' Maris's horrified scream lifted a flock of rooks from the tall trees at the back of the house, and by the time they had settled again Alex Woodall had gone.

'Thank God for Mrs Flynn,' she was to say again and again during that long and unendurable day, remembering sadly the times she had called the good-hearted woman every name she could lay her tongue to when she had first come to Seymour Road. 'An interfering old biddy' had been the kindest.

With a sharp word to Polly to 'stay in the kitchen and keep her eye on them bairns', the 'interfering old biddy' had helped Maris to lift the prostrate figure of Rose Woodall from the garden path and place her tenderly on the settee in the back parlour.

'I'll take them young limbs off your hands for a while, pet,' she said to Maris, plonking young Jamie unceremoniously in the pram with his cousin Tom. 'Get hold of that pram handle, Master Harry, if you please. *Yes*, you *do* have to go for a walk with Mrs Flynn an' see, take your sister's hand. *No*, you can't take them dratted dogs, they can go in the shed. Your Mammy's tired an' she's to have a rest. No, your Daddy's had to go . . . on an errand an' if you don't get hold of that pram handle an' walk like a little gentleman I'll land you a fourpenny one you won't forget in a hurry.'

Not awfully sure what a 'fourpenny one' was, Harry complied.

Rose drank the neat brandy Maris poured for her, and allowed the eye which was rapidly swelling and closing and had already turned the colour of a plum to be bathed. She no longer wept. She simply sat, her hands folded, and waited, for her husband to come back, for death, or madness to overtake her if he didn't, since it was obvious, at least to her, that she could not stay in this world without him.

Maris wanted to soothe her but Rose was not violent, not weeping nor hysterical nor displaying any of the emotions which needed to be calmed; and when her children returned with Mrs Flynn she simply ignored them, and when Harry became peevish in his need for her attention and Ellie wept since she wanted to sit on Mamma's knee, Rose stood up and left the room, going up to her bedroom and closing the door.

Maris hovered on the landing, listened at the door, went in a time or two, speaking to her cousin who sat in a chair by the window, watching for her husband, Maris presumed. She held her flaccid hands and begged her to have a cup of tea, a sip of broth Mrs Flynn had brought up from Mrs Pritchard's kitchen; and through that long night, when her husband did not come, Rose Woodall waited and grieved for her deeply wounded marriage.

Michael O'Shaughnessy was turning over the rich black soil in the garden at the side of his house, absorbed as men are when they work with the earth. His broad shoulders rippled beneath his checked shirt and his back bent rhythmically as his foot lifted to the spade. He was to plant potatoes and perhaps carrots and some onions, and when he was finished he would go over to the Mammy's and do the same in her garden. There was this great cry across the country to the 'little' man to 'Dig for Victory', and he had found that besides this effort for the war and the abundance of vegetables which made their way into his own cooking pot and those of his older neighbours unable to dig for themselves, he gained a measure of peace to fill the jagged hole the death of his wife and son had left. Pain such as no man should suffer and which never, never let up, not in the year since they had been savagely taken from him; but hard work and the blind blackness of the hole he fell into each night because of it, got him through it, that and the benevolence of his returned daughter's presence.

He did not hear the approach of the uniformed serviceman, and it was not until a shadow fell across the patch of soil his spade cut into that he was aware that someone was there. He turned sharply and was surprised to see Alex Woodall at his back, or at least he *thought* it was Alex Woodall, this caricature of the man who looked as though he was dead and had been for several days, refusing, it appeared, to lie down decently as corpses do.

Michael wiped both hands carefully down the legs of his cord trousers, his heart beginning to thud, for surely Alex brought news so horrendous it had already killed him.

'Alex?' he asked sharply. 'What is it, lad?'

Alex said nothing, his mouth tightly clenched as though he was having a great deal of trouble in keeping it from opening in a scream of pain, or was it terror? Michael had known both in the last year. 'Lad . . . what is it . . . ?' and in his voice was something more than the concern one man has for another.

Alex began to shake then, so uncontrollably all the paraphernalia servicemen carry about with them, steel helmets, kitbags and the like, shook with him; and when Michael lifted his arms in a gesture of enormous compassion, Alex Woodall stepped into them.

He was at the gate of Lacy's house the next morning. No one knew how long he had been there, perhaps all night, lurking in the trees or tramping across the park in his wild grief and pain. His bag was still over his shoulder, his cap still on his head, his helmet on his chest. His face was grey and his chin was dark with stubble, but he was calm now.

They watched, Maris and Mrs Flynn and Polly, none of them breathing much, as Rose, her own face like death except where the lively bruise lay, moved slowly down the path towards him in the manner of someone who is faced with a timid woodland creature which she does not wish to startle into flight.

She reached the gate and opened it, and through the half-opened window Maris heard her speak her husband's name.

'Alex.'

'It is too important to throw away, Rose, what we have. Too precious to lose. So many have been . . . have had what they cherish taken away . . . by force . . .' Alex Woodall saw for a moment the anguished face of Michael O'Shaughnessy as he repeated the words Michael had said to him.

'You are my wife, Rose. You give me . . . love . . . life, and I cannot allow it to . . . waste. *We* must not let it waste . . .'

'Come back to me, my darling. Come home.'

'Yes . . .'

Gently she took him in her arms, and the three women at the window began to smile through their tears.

33

The city centre was always crowded with servicemen, Ellen grumbled after one of her rare visits down to the shops, at least those that remained, for would any of them ever get over the loss of Lewis's. Yes, she went on, you might just as well be in a foreign country for all you could understand what the lot of them were saying.

There were the Yanks, of course, but then they spoke English, so that was all right, and weren't they the friendly ones, to be sure, and generous to a fault with children, giving away bars of chocolate in the street as though their lives depended on it. Thousands of them, there were, most of them longing to trace the route followed by their emigrant grandparents or great-grandparents, stopping to talk to complete strangers, particularly the young girls, asking if they knew the Malones, or the Johnsons, or the Prices, handsome in their smart uniforms and ready to hand out such lux-uries as nylon stockings to anyone who was nice to them. She had invited a couple of them back for Sunday dinner, Hank and Elmer, they were called; she and Matty scratching their heads over how to make them something special out of their ration, when didn't the spalpeens turn up with tins of ham and fruit, real coffee, boxes of chocolates and enough nylon stockings to cover the legs of every female in the O'Shaughnessy family.

There were men from France, Belgium, Holland,

Norway, Czechoslovakia and Poland, strolling up and down Dale Street and Bold Street, a chattering, ever-flowing river of peaked caps, forage caps, berets, kepis, Polish mortar boards, French pom-poms, naval cap ribbons, uniforms of khaki, dark or light blue, polished Sam Browne belts, gleaming brass buttons and medal ribbons.

In October the army mounted a major invasion exercise in the city which was to involve street fighting, and the population were invited to stay indoors; but the Liverpool character, though good-humoured, was perverse. Besides which, they wanted to see their soldiers in action and it was a free country, wasn't it?

The soldiers were met by the genial crowds of men, women and children, who looked on the thing as a good day out put on specially for their entertainment. They were ready with advice and helpful street directions, wanting to be told how the machine gun worked and what the mortar team were up to, and would Fred or Alf or Jack like to come in and have a cup of tea? Sugarless, of course.

And day after day telegram boys cycled all over the city with their grim news of men killed, wounded or missing in action, and day after day women wept and children were bewildered by it all, going out into the streets where 'things' were normal, to play marbles, or hopscotch, or whipping tops.

Alex came home for three days at Christmas, though he was quiet, withdrawn to some inner recess of himself which no one could reach, not even Rose. It was obvious that he and Rose were doing their best to appear normal, even cheerful for the sake of those about them. The children were too young to know what a traditional Christmas could be like, but Alex had found a small fir tree in the beech wood at the back of the house and brought it home, decorating it with lights and tinsel and silver balls raided from the attics at the big house, hanging it with the somewhat battered 'angels' and 'fairy dolls' with which the Osborne children had, long ago, decorated their own Christmas tree. Rose had saved up their sweet coupons and had queued for chocolates and pear drops which she had wrapped in silver foil and hung on the tree.

Ellen's 'Yanks', to whom she had taken a real 'shine', she said fondly, had been splendid, bringing her a whole ham, oranges, which Jamie had never seen, and the other two so rarely they were not quite sure what to do with them. The American soldiers had produced dried fruit and butter and marzipan, and the Christmas cake Ellen made was so wonderful, so incredible to those who had not seen one for three years, she hardly had the heart to cut into it. She did, of course, giving every one of them, including Hank and Elmer, a sliver of the richness with a mouthful of marzipan and icing.

From somewhere, a source he would not reveal, Uncle Teddy had produced a turkey which he insisted Rose took to her grandmother, and with that and the Christmas pudding made to one of Lord Woolton's wartime recipes, they all shared the memories of what Christmas had been 'before the war'. Ellen shed a tear for Lorcan and Flynn, who were so cruelly locked up by the enemy; said a prayer for James and Paul and Devlin, who were with 'them bombers' as she put it, James and Devlin as navigators, Paul a gunner; for Finbar and Joseph who were fighting only the Holy Mother knew where; and for Callum who was in such dire peril on the sea. Her eyes followed her son, Michael, who abruptly left the room, the swiftness of his exit causing all her Christmas cards to fall off the mantelpiece, and could you blame him for being upset when his wife and baby son, who should have been here with him, were buried in the cold ground of Colton parish church?

And amongst all the joviality which followed Christmas dinner, the sing-song round the piano with Cliona playing as once she had done, 'Good King Wenceslas' and 'Hark the herald angels sing', her granddaughter's husband sat quietly in a corner, his little daughter on his lap, his eyes never leaving the thin face of his wife; and not once did he pay any attention to his youngest son, Ellen noticed, though she could not imagine why. A lovely boy he was, dark and handsome, and so like Michael's dead son, young Michael, it was uncanny. He had not the blue-green loveliness of the true O'Shaughnessy eyes, but they were the vivid green of his own Mammy's. And would you look at him, eighteen months old and doing his best to take the peel off the orange which had just been given to him, stubbornly refusing anybody's help and willing to fight the first person who tried. As determined and wilful as his Daddy had been ever since Ellen had known him, which was a long time.

There was something not quite right with Alex Woodall *and* with his wife, and Ellen meant to find out what it was, and in the meanwhile she'd keep a sharp watch on the pair of them. This dreadful war was doing such tragic things to people's lives, as the last one had, and when would it all end? There was the sorrow of the outright refusal of Callum and Maris, despite their boy, to live together at Seymour Road, or even to communicate in any way, and though Ellen knew her son yearned to see his own son, he never went near the lad. She had tried to blame Maris, as she had always done in the past, but Callum had told her bluntly that it was not Maris's fault. That Maris had told him he might see his son whenever he wanted to but that it seemed best to him, in the circumstances, to stay away.

What circumstances? she wanted to know tearfully, for really, how could it be best for a boy not to know his own Daddy; but her son had told her, told *her*, to mind her own business and that she was not to worry her head over it. *Not worry!* What kind of a mother would she be if she were not to worry over her own children, and *their* children, but there, when this sad war was over perhaps the Blessed Mother would put it all right for them, for Callum and Maris and for all the other husbands and wives and sweethearts who had been torn apart by it.

Tom O'Shaughnessy had his first birthday. Harry Woodall had learned a new song which he sang to his great-grandmother and the admiring company at a party Maris and Rose held at Lacy's house.

'She's the girl that makes the thing that drills the hole that holds the spring that drives the rod that turns the knob that works the thingamybob . . .'

Tom's father was not present. The boy was walking now, staggering from knee to knee and smiling up into every indulgent adult face, enchanted with his own cleverness; and Ellen had to slip into Rosie's kitchen to hide her distress, something she was not accustomed to doing, that her son was not here to see him, consoling herself with the thought that there were thousands upon thousands of children who had never seen their own Daddies, which was a sadness in itself. Four and a half million men were in the forces and a large proportion had fathered children before being sent overseas.

612

But the war news was good at last. The Allies were on the move, the headlines said. The Russians were rolling back the Germans, and in March Rommel was 'kicked out' of North Africa. The wily old 'Desert Fox' had been outwitted at last. The Axis forces which were left behind surrendered on May 13th, the Allies taking 130,000 prisoners of war. The Tunisian campaign was over, and when would Lorcan be home, Ellen wanted to know, imagining that her grandson who had languished in a prisoner-of-war camp all this time would now be set free and put on the first ship for home.

But what a victory it was. Those 'Desert Rats', as the Eighth Army were called, had not only got Jerry on the run but chased hell out of them. Of course the visit of dear King George to North Africa must have been a decisive factor in helping them to keep their spirits high, Ellen confided to Matty. He was so popular, not only here at home amongst his own people but with the British soldiers as well, God love him. If anybody could raise morale – not that it was needed since morale was already high – then it was himself.

So what next, the nation wanted to know, and the answer was Sicily, which would be a jumping-off place for Italy; and on July 10th the invasion of the island by Allied troops began, and by the middle of August Sicily had fallen to the Allies. On September 8th the invasion of the Italian mainland was to have begun some thirty miles south of Naples, but even before a shot was fired news came that Italy had surrendered. That Mussolini had gone and Italy had surrendered! They couldn't believe it at first, the cautiously jubilant nation, as the newspapers reported that the Allies had landed at Salerno the next day. Unopposed, it was mistakenly said, for instead there was fierce fighting as the Germans

613

brought up six divisions of their own army. But when the Eighth Army, straight from North Africa, arrived they soon had Jerry on the run, as Ellen had known they would, beside herself with glee. They were on the move at last. They were 'dishing it out' at last!

But on the other side of the world in another – almost forgotten – theatre of war the Allied forces were fighting a battle which was just as fierce as those closer to home. Perhaps because of its remoteness it did not capture the attention of the British public as those in Europe did. In New Guinea 'our boys' were fighting the Japanese in an endless war of 'pocket' and 'foxhole', sniper and ambush, which sounded mysterious and frightful to Ellen. And the Australians and New Zealand lads who were giving a hand would be mentioned in Ellen's prayers, so they would. Had anybody ever heard of . . . where was it, Matty? . . . oh yes . . . Guadalcanal, because *she* hadn't, but it seemed there had been total victory for the American Marines, may the Holy Mother bless them one and all. It really was a puzzle to her, she said over and over again, what *our* lads were doing in these unknown and God-forsaken places, but if Mr Churchill and Mr Roosevelt said it was needed then that was good enough for her.

But best of all – apart from Ellen's belief that Lorcan would be home before the month's end – was the news that in May, forty-one U-boats had been sunk in the Atlantic, and continued to be destroyed right through the summer of 1943. It was due to the organisational, tactical and technical superiority of convoy escorts over the U-boats, she heard Callum tell Michael, and though she hadn't the faintest idea what he meant she didn't care. All she cared about was that the danger her son was in had lessened. The Allied air power had become increasingly effective and there was better intelligence concerning U-boat movements, whatever that might mean, but whatever it was it was all right with her.

She was still worried about Rosie. The girl was barely a shadow of the one who had borne three children in as many years, worked for most of those three years in the hard, often filthy conditions of what amounted to a farm labourer's job, run a home and the estate office, and at the same time waited in good heart and staunch spirit for her husband's return.

She was so thin where once she had been almost Junoesque, though that was not the word Ellen used. Good hips on her and a deep bosom, broad-shouldered and long-legged, with a flawless skin which could only be likened to the cream off the top of the milk. Though she had always been somewhat reserved, perhaps in contrast to her irrepressible Irish cousins, her sense of humour and smiling green eyes had warmed the heart of you and drawn you to her like a bee to a flower.

She was still generous, kind, understanding, but deeply withdrawn into herself and so quiet. Still steadfast and hard-working but with a constant, harrowed look about her which seemed to say she was approaching, or had arrived at, some crisis with which she was not awfully sure she could cope. Mrs Flynn spent most of her time over at her house these days, giving her and Maris more leeway when it came to what Ellen scornfully called their 'war work', especially since her daughter-in-law had started that new job of hers. She was of the opinion that the only work women should do was in their own homes with their families. It didn't matter to her that a woman under the age of forty could not avoid war work unless she had heavy family responsibilities, which let Rose off, if not Maris. They had no choice. They would be conscripted, as the men had been, either to one of the services, a munitions factory, into some sort of nursing, on the land, in Civil Defence, or domestic service in a hospital. Ellen did not like it at all and said so to everyone who would listen.

Maris had applied for and had been taken on at the Royal Ordnance Factory near Chorley, where recruits travelled from as far away as Blackpool, Manchester and Liverpool. Her daily travelling time was often two, three or even four hours, due to the distance and the unreliability of the trains. When she reached the factory, which was so enormous it was scattered over more than a thousand acres, employing, it was rumoured, over 35,000 people, she had a half-hour's walk before she arrived at her shop, and when she got back to Lime Street at the end of her shift there was the half-hour's bike ride from there to Rosie's.

There were three shifts, and because of her child she was allowed to pick the one most convenient to her, an eight-hour shift filling shells, from eight in the morning until four in the afternoon. She had moved in with Rosie now so as to cut out that extra journey across Beechwood Park to her own cottage at the beginning and end of each day. Besides which, it was easier and more convenient to put Tom to bed with Rose's children and leave him there, since she had to be away by five-thirty in the morning; and they were saving fuel by living in one house.

The work was tedious and dangerous though she wouldn't admit it to Ellen. New recruits were all too prone to employ a hammer on components filled with explosives, or to use a stick of TNT as chalk, but there were surprisingly few accidents, at least since she had been there. She was doing something important again, but that did not mean that Ellen had to like it, she said, nor did she like the idea of her 'fiddling about' with those dratted shells. What if she was blown up or turned yellow as she had heard had happened in the First World War, due to the effects of the TNT? What was the world coming to, she and Matty asked one another, when a woman would rather fill shells than look after her own child?

Another Christmas came and went, and in February Rose and Maris and the children, giving in to the incessant demands of the determined Harry, who had begged to be allowed to see it, had motored down to the docks on the gallon of petrol Michael had scrounged from somewhere to watch the victorious return of the convoy led by Captain Frederick John Walker, who was Commander of the 2nd Support Group of escorts operating out of the port of Liverpool.

The sun had no warmth in it that February day, but its brightness danced on the waters of the river, making golden ripples which lapped against the craft which crowded it. Ships of every shape and kind, most of them painted uniform grey. Aircraft carriers, cruisers, destroyers, frigates, corvettes, armed trawlers and mine-sweepers. Famous names were there on what had once been ocean-going passenger liners but which were now serving as troopships, their decks crowded with soldiers who hung over the rail waving to anyone who would wave back.

Maris held her son by the hand, her other hand in Ellie's, while Rose did her best to keep hold of her two roving sons. Harry was in earnest conversation with a heavily kitted soldier who was about to embark. He wanted to know everything, did Harry. Where the

617

soldier was going, and why? How his rifle worked? What was that for, and this, and that thing there? and did the soldier know anything about 'Spits' because Harry did and would be glad to enlighten him since his own Daddy flew one.

A white painted hospital ship clearly marked with red crosses was edging towards its berth where a long line of ambulances waited. There was a mobile canteen manned by the women of the WVS. There were nurses and doctors and orderlies all ready to take 'their boys' who had come home to them, thank God, alive at least.

And there were merchant vessels, hundreds of them being loaded or unloaded, scenes of frantic activity which, at the same time, had a sense of order about them, a vast armada of ships which were the veins and arteries of the nation, bringing foodstuffs, fuel oil and petroleum, iron and steel, metals and timber, cotton, chemicals, machinery, tanks and aircraft, which were now plainly on view as they waited to be sent to their destination. Cranes swung out over the ships, and men in crumpled caps groaned and heaved as they man-handled enormous crates.

Plainly visible in the water were the masts and upperworks of sunken ships, and large, green-painted wreck buoys which marked the graves of vanished vessels. And plying through and around the shipping were the ferry boats, always on time and always reliable no matter what.

Above the city a barrage of balloons floated, close hauled now, and a training aircraft of the RAF flew overhead and above them. There was a sudden burst of distant machine-gun fire from the estuary, and Harry and Jamie were beside themselves with excitement, not really believing that it was only the pilot of the plane practising his strafing technique.

'I bet it's a Jerry U-boat come to torpedo the convoy. I bet it is, Mamma. I bet the pilot's sunk it by now. I wish the ferry would take us out there to see it,' he went on wistfully, gazing without much hope in the direction from which the firing had come.

The westward-bound convoy which had left Liverpool in January had come up against twenty-two U-boats which had congregated to attack Allied shipping, and the battle which had ensued had lasted for twenty days and had ended in a complete rout of the U-boats: eleven sunk and one being forced to the surface where the crew was captured. Only one merchant-man was sunk.

It was the greatest naval occasion in the Mersey's history. A huge crowd had gathered around the river entrance to Gladstone Dock. There were crews of every escort vessel in port, including the entire ship's company of the battleship HMS *King George V*. There was a band of the Royal Marines, ships' officers, wives and families of the incoming crews, merchant seamen and dock workers, cheering and waving in proprietorial rapture, for these were *their* boys and *their* ships. There were flags and music as Liverpool went mad with jubilation, and suddenly, there were the ships, pushing through the morning mist and up the channel in line ahead, signal lamps flashing a greeting, and every vessel in port sounding its welcome, the deep-throated bellow of merchant fog horns competing with the 'whoop-whoop-whoop' of warships' sirens.

The old sea shanty 'Down among the dead men' floated across the water, and as the crews of merchant seamen who were lining the rails of their ships threw their caps in the air, Maris found, to her surprise, that she was weeping.

On the other side of the entrance to Gladstone Dock a man watched her, his eyes only leaving her face briefly to study the small boy who held her hand. He was dressed in the smart uniform of a captain of the merchant navy, and on his chest were several ribbons. His cap was set almost straight on his dark head as that of an officer should be, since he must set an example to his men, but there was the slightest suggestion of a tilt to it, to the left and over his eye, as though, despite his rank and the responsibility which went with it, he had a certain dash, a wry and humorous twist in his character.

The boy was pulling on Maris's hand, pointing to something which had caught his attention, and both she and the man turned their heads to see what it was; but the child's excited gaze was captured by something else, the cap of a sailor which fell into the water, or was it the seagull which dived to investigate? He jigged about, his highly polished shoes scarcely touching the ground, his vivid blue-green eyes smiling at everybody about him in the perfect knowledge that they would smile back, which they did. The man's heart swelled painfully in his chest, and something caught like barbed wire in his throat, and for several minutes he was under some difficulty as he did his best not to weep for the small excited boy who was his son and whom he did not know.

The three leading ships of the convoy, *Starling*, *Wild Goose* and *Magpie* – *Starling* commanded by Captain Walker – were entering the dock, and for several minutes the man lost sight of Maris and his son, and he was seen by those about him to become agitated, craning his neck painfully, even walking impatiently up and down the dock at the back of his companions, and it was not until he caught sight of her again that he became still. There was an expression on his face which none of his men would have recognised. A soft yearning, and yet a hard clenching of his jaw, a tightening of his cheek muscles and a pulse which beat rapidly in his temple before he turned away.

Another convoy had arrived on the last tide, a big one, and ships were crammed ten deep in many of the docks. The areas around the Pier Head and stretching north and south were alive with sailors of every nationality. Beyond, where the trams turned round, seamen of the Royal Navy vied with men of the 'Red Duster' as the merchant navy was called, to get aboard them. They were all exhausted to the point where any little thing could spark off a fight. For weeks on end they had not taken their clothes off, and when they slept at all it was with one hand on their life-belts. They had seen nothing but a forest of moving masts, funnels, samson posts and cargo booms, as cargo ships, tankers and passenger ships had rolled, pitched and heaved their way towards British shores. A constant hum from auxiliary machinery, dynamos and ventilating fans had assailed their ears, and their nostrils were clogged with the stench of stale cooking, oil, and the acrid blend of steam and electricity. All they wanted was to get home to Lil, or Glad, or Mam, to get in some 'shut-eye', and then get down to their local for a 'bevvy'.

He was about to climb into a gleaming, dove-grey Rover motor car, one of those made just before the war, when she saw him, and with him was an elegantly beautiful, dark-haired woman of the sort men dream about. For a dreadful moment as she reeled from the shock of it, she thought that Tom, tired after all the excitement and whom she had picked up in the crush, would slip through her arms and fall to the ground; and Callum, who had seen her at exactly the same moment, evidently thought so too, for he made a sharp movement towards her. The woman, surprised, turned to stare at her, and it was perhaps this which gave Maris the strength to keep upright, to return the stare coldly as though she, and the man with her, meant nothing, why should they, to her. The pain had caught her unprepared for it, but not by the slightest tremor would she allow either of them to see it.

The woman took Callum's uniformed arm possessively and smiled up into his strained and weary face, knowing, of course, who Maris was, since had they not met, years ago, at the launching of the *Mauretania*. Alice Duckworth. Alice Duckworth, smart as paint then and glisteningly beautiful, and still the same in an outfit which had not been obtained with the meagre clothing coupons they were allowed. She wore furs, dark and glossy, a saucy little hat over one eye, nylon stockings and high-heeled shoes, her expression letting Callum, *and his wife*, know exactly what she had to offer a returned and weary officer in the way of reward for his bravery.

'It was just a surprise,' Maris said later, casually, or so she would have Rosie believe, '. . . seeing him there, though why I should be surprised I can't imagine . . .' laughing gaily, '. . . after all he is a seaman and seamen do come home on leave.'

'You're upset.' It was a statement, not a question.

'Don't be ridiculous. Why on earth should I be upset?'

'I don't know. You no longer love him, or so you keep telling me.'

'*I am not upset.*'

'Very well then, shut up about it.'

'*Rosie!*' For of all the people Maris knew, Rosie was the one from whom she expected understanding . . . and compassion. But Rosie had become sharp lately, and could you blame her with Alex still walking about like a zombie, and after all this time.

'Look Maris, either you and Callum are to get a divorce, which you say you are, and are therefore of no further interest to one another, in which case there is no need to discuss him, or, as seems more likely seeing the pair of you as you were today, you love one another still, and if that's so, for God's sake, go and get him.'

'He was with someone else, Rose, or didn't you notice?'

'She is a married woman who is enjoying this war immensely and if she hadn't got your husband in her bed she would have someone else's. Is that not so?'

'Yes . . . it's true.' Maris's voice was flat, then she sighed. 'Yes, you're right, it has upset me and I'm bloody furious with myself. I don't know why I expected anything else. He wasn't faithful to me when we were together. I knew he would have . . . someone. He's not a man to be celibate and why should he? We are separated and yet . . .' She threw back her head and fixed her gaze on the ceiling and the muscles of her throat worked as she fought to contain her tears. 'Jesus, Rosie . . . when . . . *when* am I going to cut him out of my heart? When? How long does it take? I've seen him no more than three or four times in three and a half years and yet he's still here . . .' banging painfully on her chest. 'I have a son . . . *his* son . . . and yes . . . I will admit that I thought . . . hoped . . .

that . . . Tom might . . . well, bring us closer, but he doesn't give a fig for him, or me. I am less than nothing in his life and yet he still has the power to hurt me. God, I hate him . . . I hate him . . .'

'And love him.' Rose's voice was gentle now.

'Yes.'

What was to be called 'The Battle of Berlin' began at twenty-four minutes to eight in the evening of August 23rd, 1943, when a Lancaster bomber took off from an airfield near Lincoln. A further 718 followed from other airfields carrying 1,800 tons of bombs. Their target was Berlin.

Seven months later, in the early hours of March 25th, 1944, 739 bombers returned from another raid over Berlin, on this night leaving 72 aircraft lost over German-occupied territory or having crashed into the sea.

One of them was flown by Flight-Lieutenant Sir Charles Woodall who, as a 'fighter boy', had been shot out of the sky protecting the bombers against the German fighter patrols.

Another was that of his brother, Pilot Officer Alex Woodall, who, though no one had actually seen him go down, did not return; and he was posted 'missing, believed killed'.

34

'He is not dead. *He is not dead*, Rosie. He is reported missing. No one saw his aircraft go down as they did Charlie's. There are many aircrews who can't get back and who parachute to safety and he is bound to be one of them . . .'

'*Why?* There are many aircraft that nobody sees go down but that *go down* nevertheless, and they are never heard from again. So why should Alex be any different?'

'*Why not?*' Maris pushed her hand through her hair in desperation, then, turning sharply on her heel, strode across the room to stare out into the wild garden where the day was more like March than May, Mrs Flynn had declared as she arrived on the push-bike she had acquired. Most people had them these days. A 'sit up and beg' hers was called, but once you'd mastered the control and balance they were as safe as any of the newer models, and better than walking when you had four miles to cover.

Maris and Rose often debated how old Mrs Flynn might be, since she seemed likely to go on for ever, but whatever age she was she certainly kept it to herself. Her 'old man' was retired and she had sons and grandsons in the services, but that was about all they knew of her except that she was unswervingly reliable and ever-lastingly kind.

The children were playing in the garden. The wind had lifted what remained of last winter's leaves, blowing them in a dancing reel across the garden. Pip-squeak and Wilfred chased them in frantic excitement, and after the dogs came the three boys, yelling and brandishing stout sticks which were, of course, really 'machine guns' and which they levelled at the dogs which were 'enemy aircraft'. Jamie tripped and fell so heavily the breath was momentarily knocked out of him, but he jumped to his feet, his face screwed up in an effort not to cry, and looking so incredibly like Alex, Maris was tempted to call Rosie to the window to point it out to her. He was almost three years old, a sturdy, tumble-legged child who gave his affection and loyalty with an endurance which was unusual in one so young. He was brave and merry, but as stubborn as a mule and without a mean bone in his body, so obviously Alex's child Maris could not understand why Alex had any doubt about it. Dark-haired and green-eyed, a true Osborne as his grandmother had been, as his own father was, and yet there was something in him as there was in Alex which seemed to be neither Osborne, nor Woodall, nor O'Shaughnessy. Some mysterious characteristic which was entirely separate from any the rest of the family shared.

It was almost two months since that tragic night when the two aircraft, one a Spitfire, the other a Hurricane, had vanished from the skies above Germany. Two months since the young telegraph boy, defensively carrying the yellow telegrams, one to Maris as Charlie's next of kin and the other to Rose, had cycled out to Lacy's house on the Beechwood Hall estate. Rose's moan of agony would remain for ever in Maris's ears, a sound made more harrowing by Rose's brave attempt to contain it, since to let it out as she wanted to, as she needed to, would frighten the children.

But Mrs Flynn was there, staunch as a rock, showing no obvious signs of pity or time-wasting tears as Maris was doing, just taking the children and the bewildered Polly from the scene of the grieving. That Charlie Woodall had been a bit of a bugger, by all accounts, but he was Mrs O'Shaughnessy's brother after all, and was entitled to *somebody's* sorrow. And as for Mrs Woodall's husband, that *was* a tragedy, especially with them little 'uns, but still, where there was life there was hope, and the two young women, one a wife, the other a sister, must not give it up lightly, which she told them both later. There were many fliers in the German prisoner-of-war camps, her own nephew amongst them, and they were safe there for the duration, weren't they, and Mrs Woodall must take comfort from that.

So they had gone on, the two young women. Picked themselves up as women were doing all over the country, taking their anger and grief and locking them away somewhere, and though they didn't show they were there all the time, as wounds that are deep and unhealed are, hurting and ready to bleed beneath their concealing bandage.

Harry had started school now. The village school at Colton, and each morning at half past eight Mrs Flynn arrived on her bicycle, storing it at the back of Lacy's house before setting off, the four of them in tow since Polly was not quite reliable enough to be left alone with the three youngest. Tom and Jamie, and often Ellie on the way back, were dumped unceremoniously in the battered pram, for Mrs Flynn stood no nonsense from any of them. No, she didn't care if Jamie *was* three years old and too big for a pram, she told him, ignoring his furious face, in the pram he went since she'd not the time to dawdle about the lanes between Beechwood and Colton. She'd her pantry to scrub out this morning and Polly to supervise in the spring cleaning of the bedrooms, and then after dinner she meant to nip across to Home Farm Cottage on her bike while the three of them were safely tucked up having a nap, and do a bit to Mrs O'Shaughnessy's place before the walk to Colton to pick young Harry up from school.

In her kitchen at Edge Lane Ellen continued to knit an endless stream of scarves, gloves, socks and balaclava helmets in the three colours of the services, listening to the news bulletins, interspersed with 'flashes' for important items whilst she did so. She liked 'The Kitchen Front', which was broadcast at eight-fifteen every morning, trying out the recipes, and absorbed by the good sense and humour of the 'Radio Doctor', who was so helpful in the matter of minor ailments of which Ellen had a few. Tommy Handley and 'ITMA' were, of course, a must, as was 'Sandy's Half Hour'. 'Saturday Night Theatre' with its wonderful plays to which she and Matty listened without fail, and 'Workers' Playtime', broadcast three times a week in the dinner-hour from a factory 'somewhere in England'.

'You know that static water tank just down the road,' was one of the jokes she heard, 'well go and put your head in it three times and only take it out twice', and when she repeated it to her great-grandson Harry she was convinced he was about to have a seizure, he thought it was so hilarious.

'Why does Hitler sleep with a net over his head?' was another. 'Because he's afraid of our "mosquitoes".' Mrs Flynn declared she had never got the lad to school as easily as she had the next day, all because he couldn't wait to tell Archie, who, it seemed, was his own special pal. Harry had repeated it to his brother Jamie, but the

628

'sprog', he had told Mrs Flynn loftily, was too young to understand it.

In the evening when Maris came home, sitting in the parlour window with her boy in her arms, watching the sky turn as the sun went down, Rose would slip out of the house and go up through the quiet woods, moving silently past the badger sets where the bracken, the leaves and moss which the badgers had discarded for newer bedding, lay in the mouth of the hole. They would be about soon, after dark, the badgers, or perhaps before in this secluded beech wood, but she did not stop to watch them nor the foxes which would be peeping from their own warrens shortly, probably with their cubs. Rose had seen them years ago when she and Alex had come here to watch for them, and the thought brought a fresh pang of desolation to her already anguished heart. Alex, Alex . . . dear God . . . Alex . . .

She had barely slept since the telegram had been put in her trembling hand, staring with eyes as dry and bleak as rock into the darkness of the room she had once shared with Alex. Her grieving was deep, deep inside her, cutting away at her flesh and paring it down to the bone, so that she had become even thinner, hollow-eyed, her once vibrant hair hanging straight and lifeless down her back. She wore it scraped back from her triangular face, from which her high cheekbones almost pierced her skin. The sweater she wore was barely lifted by the smallness of her breasts, that once had been proud and full and were now almost flat. Her breeches hung on her so that she was forced to wear a belt to keep them about her waist. She lived in a daze of pain and grief from which she had no relief, not even through her children, for though she loved them and would give her life to save them a moment's pain, Alex Woodall was the focal point of her existence, the centre around which she revolved, and without him in it she whirled in space with nothing to stabilise her terrified spirit.

The path through the wood was still well lit by the early evening light which had a pale, translucent quality about it. There was a small stream cutting across a glade in which the clear water burbled and sang as it moved on its musical way. She and Alex had often lounged here, in this clearing, Alex with his back against the trunk of the fine old hornbeam, hers against his chest, his hands gently cupping her breasts; day-dreaming, whispering, laughing, kissing, planning their future and how many children they would have. Three, he had said, two boys and a girl. Four, she had said, two of each, and now . . . now he was right. She would have no more daughters. No more sons.

She placed her hands on the rough bark of the tree and bowed her head in despair, the spirit of Alex Woodall all about her as she brought him to her. His hair so dark and thick and springing, between her fingers. In her mind she pushed it back from his brow and reached to kiss him, then with a deep groan for was she not torturing herself, she turned and began to run violently, away from the ghosts of the two young lovers who drifted there.

The glade was ringed by beeches, holly and hornbeam and deciduous trees which had been bare all winter but were now bright green with new leaf. A dense field layer of wood sorrel had grown through the carpet of old leaves deposited there in November, and everywhere she looked there was new life, a new beginning, a new hope for the coming year.

But not for her. Not for Rose Woodall, who was as empty as the old chestnut husks which lay about where the squirrels had discarded them. What was she to do without him? Dear God, what? She thought she'd go mad, *had* gone mad at times when she found herself in some place she had not meant to go, wondering how she'd got there, how her poor mindless body had wound up in the rose garden, or the stable when she had meant to be in . . . where? . . . where had she been going in the first place? she agonised, falling in a moaning heap on the old horse blanket someone had left to rot there. As *she* was rotting without Alex.

She blundered out of the wood and across what had once been the deer park but which now lay in neat furrows of planted vegetables, their young green beginning to show and thicken. Right down to the lake they ran, and she followed them until her booted feet were almost in the clear, unrippled water.

The colours in the western sky were glorious. She watched them change as the sun sank, from yellow and then to green as it disappeared. Slowly the colours changed again just above the tops of the darkening trees, from brown and then to orange, and minutes later an arch of rose-pink formed and spread.

For half an hour she stood completely still and silent, speaking without words into the clear and perfect sky above her, willing Alex to answer her, but when the sky had gone from violet to a rich plum purple and her heart was still empty and hopeless, she turned and moved through the darkness to the house where her children were. They were all she had now.

A month later, on the sixth of June, the Allies landed in Normandy. Mrs Flynn was not a bit surprised. Her old man, who was in the Home Guard, had heard rumours of a great tide of vehicles, convoys of lorries and tanks and bulldozers, all going southwards, she said. And an old army pal of her old man, from the last 'do', that is, and who lived down south somewhere and with whom her old man still corresponded, had told him that there were enough landing craft and such, in the harbour nearby where he lived, to start another navy. Tanks and trucks and God knows what else, so they knew *something* was up.

It was a Tuesday, that sixth of June, and the night before, those who lived in the south of England had been kept awake hour after hour by an apparently endless stream of aircraft making for the coast, some of them with gliders swooping behind them like great silent birds. Silence on the roads, deep and menacing, like the very graveyards they were, but in the sky above a noise like thunder the whole night through with no one beneath getting a wink of sleep.

They heard it on the eight o'clock news, Ellen and Matty, though there was no official confirmation until nine-thirty, when the calm voice of John Snagge announced that 'D-Day has come. Early this morning the Allies began the assault on the north-western face of Hitler's European fortress.'

For the first time Ellen wished she had a telephone. She must tell *someone*, she said to Matty, half delirious with joy, and without further ado she rushed out of her house and down the garden path to share the glad news with any passer-by, spry as a girl, grabbing first the postman, telling him proudly as though it was all her doing, that 'hadn't our boys landed in France, begorra'. It was the turn of a perfect stranger next, astonished and inclined to think she had gone mad, she said later to Gracie, but beginning nevertheless, as she was, to do a little jig right there on the pavement. 'D-Day at last' they told one another jubilantly. 'Invasion, God bless King George,' and then, right there in her own garden among the early roses and petunias, with the sunshine filtering through gently moving leaves on the branches above her head, she sank to her knees and began a devout and thankful prayer to Our Lady, for this must surely be the end of it.

That evening the whole nation listened to the King's broadcast.

'Four years ago,' he began, 'our nation and Empire stood alone against an over-whelming enemy . . .'

'. . . 'tis true, so it is,' Ellen murmured, crossing herself reverently, and Matty echoed it.

'. . . tested as never before . . .' His Majesty went on.

'. . . Holy Mother of God. He never spoke a truer word . . .'

'. . . at this historic moment . . .'

'. . . historic, so it is . . .'

'. . . a nationwide vigil of prayer as the great crusade sets forth.'

The two old ladies gathered their rosaries and began at once.

In the small house in the grounds of Beechwood, the two young women sat quietly by the open window of the parlour as the King's speech faded away and the strains of the national anthem filled the room.

Maris sighed as it ended, then leaned forward and switched off the wireless. There was silence for several minutes, for both of them realised that this was the turning-point of the war, and not only of the war but in their lives. For nearly five years they, and the rest of the nation, had had one goal, one objective, one great endeavour to share, and that was to end this war and get on with what were their normal lives. But what *was* normal now? What were they to get back *to*, and with whom? The men they had loved, many of the *people* they had loved, were gone. Their lives were turned about and were so completely different it was unbelievable, but more than anything else *they* had changed. Rosie Osborne and Maris Woodall were as dead as though they had never existed, and yet dimly they could both remember the flighty, pleasure-seeking, naïve young Maris, and the tranquil, unruffled innocence of her cousin Rose. They were gone, those inexperienced girls, and in their place were mature women, enduring and undiminished by what they had suffered. Fragile at times and ready to break, brittle with pain, frail as women are frail, but with the stubborn will-power to climb from their knees where life had knocked them, to straighten their backs and have a damned good try at getting on with it. With whatever came next.

But what *was* to come next? When it was finally over. The land would still be there, Beechwood Hall and Woodall Park, but could they go back to the lives their mothers had known, the lives which would have been theirs had the war not intervened? Maris would certainly not continue to fill shells, so what *would* she do? and Rose, Rosie who was the mother of the boy upstairs in his small bed and who would be the next baronet. Sir Harry Woodall, as Maris's father had been.

'Let's have a cup of tea.' Maris's manner told Rose, since she knew the same thoughts had been in her head, that there was no point in dwelling on it. Not yet. There was so much to be done. Battles to fight and wars to be won . . . and decisions to be made, the voice in her head reminded her. She could not forever keep putting them off, particularly the one that must be . . . she sighed again, leaving Rose still gazing across the darkening garden as she moved towards the kitchen to put the kettle on.

She was coming out of the station the following evening when she heard her name called. The crowds were dense, as they always were about railway stations these days. Men and women of the armed services moving from one posting to another, or going on leave. Workers such as herself coming off duty, or going on, and all in a tearing hurry, pushing their way through harassed factory workers and elderly shop assistants and clerks who, having been brought out of retirement to take the place of those who had gone to war, could not wait to get home and put their feet up.

She did not at first recognise the smart young woman who was pushing her way through the masses towards her, waving and 'cooee-ing' and brandishing an umbrella to the intense irritation of those about her. It must have been four, or was it five years, the woman was babbling, even before she got to where Maris waited, and when she did it took several moments for Maris to realise that it was Angela Knowles, or, as she had become when she married Dickie, Angela Temple.

'Maris, darling . . . where *have* you been all these years? I can't imagine how we managed to lose touch . . .'

'Angela, how good to see you . . .' but was it? Was it really? she asked herself after the first surprise and delight had worn off five minutes later, which was all the time it took to realise that what she had been musing over the night before was true. She *was* different and so, probably, was Angela, though she did not appear to be. Frivolous, shallow, smart, bored, inquisitive Angela, and apparently doing exactly what she had done before the war but with different people. Different *men*, it seemed. Dickie had been killed at Tobruk, hadn't Maris heard, oh yes, and no, Maris was not to be sad since it was quite a long time ago now, and though she didn't exactly say so, Angela was enjoying being a young widow . . . oh no, no children, which was perhaps as well . . . in a city full of handsome officers. Had Maris heard about Freddie? Oh indeed . . . so very sad to lose his sight like that . . . a stray bullet at . . . now where was it . . . ? Yes, she had a little job in an office which Daddy had found for her since she did want to help in the war effort, even if her rather delicate constitution would not allow her to go into one of the services. And Maris was . . . ? In munitions . . . at where? Chorley, how . . . unusual, and she had . . . *a son* . . . how perfectly splendid. Two years old . . . yes, before she and that gorgeous husband of hers had . . . parted. What a shame, so handsome and *gruff*, by which Maris knew she meant not of their class, but exciting because of it.

And had Maris heard about Alice? Maris *did* know Alice, didn't she? Alice Duckworth? Oh yes, older than they were, of course, but a dear friend of Angela's sister. Oh indeed, quite a scandal. Hadn't Maris heard? Her husband was divorcing her for adultery, the last word whispered as though it had been murder. Citing some officer, Angela had heard, though she didn't know his name since there were so many of them, it seemed. Naval, she had heard, waiting for Maris's response.

She got home somehow. She had retrieved her bike from the bicycle rank which had been erected to accommodate the hundreds which were now in use instead of the motor car, and cycled, by instinct, she supposed, rather than any sense of where she was actually going, back to Lacy's house.

They both wept that night, their arms about one another, giving in as they seldom did, to the breaking of their hearts by the men they loved. Intentionally, or unintentionally, they were broken just the same.

D-Day was not followed by immediate victory as many of those in Britain had hoped, especially Ellen, since she couldn't wait to get her sailor son home and back in the arms of his wife, where he belonged. And her grandsons, whom she'd missed sorely. James and Paul and Finbar, Joseph, Lorcan and Devlin who were, so it was rumoured, fighting in Normandy now. Flynn, from the prisoner-of-war camp in Singapore, and Guy, her Caitlin's son, who was a flier like the Woodall boys. When, sweet Mother in heaven, would they be home, she begged to know, since she hadn't all that much time left.

The first 'flying bomb' clattered across the Channel in the early hours of June 13th, just a week after D-Day, and when the first V1s, flames spurting from their tails, crashed to earth, those who saw them fall were jubilant, thinking raiders had been shot down.

They were soon to be disillusioned.

'When the engine of the pilotless aircraft stops,' Herbert Morrison warned them, 'and the light at the end of the machine goes out, an explosion will follow in within five to fifteen seconds.'

When the devilish things went overhead it was said that people cowered in their beds, praying 'For God's sake keep going', concerned, not with the poor souls on whom they would finally fall, but that it should not be them. A new terror, just when they thought it to be almost ended, had been unleashed on the people of the south of England, and right through June, July and August, more than seventy flying bombs a day rained down on the capital city. The casualty rate was high, for the bombs came down at all hours of the day while people were going about their everyday lives, congregated together in offices and shops, in churches and hospitals. It was worse than the Blitz, they said, for then you had some warning and could get into a shelter.

Hopes faded in the autumn that the war would end this year when an airborne landing at Arnhem in September was a hopeless failure, and in December there was another serious setback with the German breakthrough in the Ardennes. The BBC's Christmas Day feature that year was called 'Journey Home' but as Maris said grimly to Rose, it seemed a bloody slow journey.

The following week, on the first day of January, 1945, after a severe heart-attack which he could not endure in his weakened condition, Teddy Osborne died in the arms of his devastated wife, Clare. He was not quite forty-eight years old. Since the age of nineteen, when both his legs had been amputated after the Battle of the Somme almost thirty years ago, he had existed in his wheelchair. At his funeral, tributes were paid not only to his own bravery but to that of his devoted wife who, they told one another, had given him life, love, peace and content, and what would she do now, poor woman, without him to care for?

'I'm to go into a convent, Mammy,' she told her mother, Ellen O'Shaughnessy, who didn't know whether to be jubilant – since she had not had the joy of giving any of her children to the Church – or to be sad, for it seemed to her that after a lifetime's service to her crippled husband who, poor soul, could give her no children, Clare might marry again and still have time to bear a couple. After all, she was only thirty-eight.

'A convent where I shall be trained in nursing, Mammy,' she went on kindly, for didn't she know exactly what was in her Mammy's mind, and when the will was read it was clear, at least Ellen thought so, why her daughter wanted to get out of Beechwood Hall which had been her home for twenty years. Teddy had left a generous bequest to his wife which would keep her in comfort for the rest of her life, but the estate, the house and everything it contained had belonged to Christian, James's heir, and then since he had died in Ireland, to his sister Claudine who was next in line to inherit.

Rose wept sharply when the lawyers had gone, not because she begrudged the house to her older sister but because the irony of it tore her already damaged heart to shreds. The house she and Alex – who was dead, she was sure of it – had loved so much going to a woman who cared nothing for it.

'Don't say that, Rose Woodall. Don't you *dare* say that. Until I have the proof of it in my hand, my brother is not dead. I may be wearing black but it's for Uncle Teddy, not Alex, and I'm surprised at you, Rosie, really I am, giving in the way you have done. I haven't liked to say it because you were so . . . unhappy, but you have got my brother dead and buried when all the time he is probably in a prisoner-of-war camp . . .'

'Then why haven't we been notified, Maris? Tell me that. The Germans report the names of all men who are taken prisoner. When Lorcan was captured at Tobruk it was no more than a month before Donal was notified,

639

and the same with Flynn McGowan. It has been a year, Maris, a whole year and even you must agree that . . . Alex is . . . he cannot possibly be alive. He . . .' She turned away, putting her hands over her ears as though to shut out the sounds of the dreadful words she herself was speaking. 'He must be dead, Maris . . . and I don't know how to go on without him. The pain inside me is terrible and it seems to get worse with every bitter moment . . .'

'I know, darling, I know . . .' and so she did, for though Callum O'Shaughnessy was not dead he was as lost to Maris as though he were.

A month later Rose was astonished and sombrely elated to receive a letter from her sister Claudine saying that if Rose wished to purchase Beechwood Hall, the home of the Osbornes for so many years, Claudine was willing to sell it to her for a nominal sum. She herself, being the wife of a wealthy man and not wishing to live in it nor have the trouble of finding someone to manage the estate, did not want the problem of it now that Uncle Teddy had gone.

And so Beechwood passed, without fuss and as was right, into the hands of the Woodalls: Rose and, if he survived, her husband Sir Alex Woodall.

In February more than 1,200 Allied bombers struck at Dresden. On the first night it was the RAF Bomber Command and on the second it was the turn of the American Air Force, and it was said that eleven square miles of the city were still on fire from the previous night's raid. Yet again on the following morning, American bombers went in, and for seven days and nights the city burned.

Those in the blitzed areas of Britain who had lived through their own nightmare could not help but feel pity for the residents of Dresden, where it was reported the destruction was awesome.

And in April the nation, indeed the whole of the Allied world, was shocked and saddened by the death of President Roosevelt. Ellen was quite devastated, for not only was it sudden but the dear soul was only sixty-three, which was no age at all. It was Friday the 13th though, which was not a day she cared for at all, being of a superstitious turn of mind, and really, if he was to go, was it any wonder the poor gentleman had been taken on that day? His bravery and courage in over-coming the infantile paralysis which had struck him at the age of thirty-three was an example to them all, and you'd only to look at that lovely smile of his to know what a merry and good heart he had. She and Matty would go down to St Xavier's at once and light a candle for him, so they would, the Mother of Jesus rest with him.

They could smell victory now, the war-sickened peoples of the world, for Ellen believed even the Germans and the Japanese people were heartily sick of it all. The Ninth Army tanks were across the Elbe on their last lap to Berlin. In Italy the Eighth Army offensive went well with the Santerno river crossed in strength, and the Russian troops, involved in the battle for Vienna, declared it to be almost over.

In the same month the Allies had overrun a Nazi concentration camp at Buchenwald, and a few days later, another at Belsen. What was found there could not be described, not in any detail, since it could only undermine all faith in human nature, the journalists who were there said. The *Daily Mirror* described the British soldiers as being 'sick with disgust', and the photographs which appeared later in the newspapers could scarcely be looked at. Holy Mary, Mother of God, Ellen wept, and Matty with her, two bewildered old ladies who had never imagined in their wildest nightmares that they would live to see the things men could do to one another, going down on their knees to ask for pity and forgiveness, not for those who had committed the atrocities, for even Ellen's Christianity could not stretch that far, but for mankind itself.

With the arrival of the Allied armies, which were sweeping so gloriously towards victory, at the launch site of the V1 bombs in France, the 'doodlebug' attacks, as they had been christened, had come virtually to an end, although an isolated long-range version of the weapon continued to be launched towards Britain from Holland. V2s they were now, and two of them which fell on Croydon damaged two thousand houses between them. You could not hear these monstrous things coming, it was reported, since they travelled so fast before they exploded, sometimes in mid-air in a huge flower of smoke. Most of those which got through landed in London, though there were others which got further north than that. Seven had actually fallen in Yorkshire, six in Cheshire, three in Derbyshire and eight in Lancashire.

It was a Sunday and Rosie had gone up to the big house to say goodbye to Clare, who was to leave the next day for the convent in Northamptonshire where she was to begin her training as a nursing sister.

'I'll take the children if you like, Maris. Let them run off some of their energy through the wood. Why don't you come with us?'

'No, I've some washing to sort out. I'll go over later this evening, tell Aunt Clare. I want to talk to her about grandmother's jewellery. She's entitled to it, you know, as Uncle Teddy's widow but she won't taken even one small piece as a keepsake.'

'Well, I suppose she has no need of it where she's going.'

'I suppose not.'

'Come on then, kids, get your sweaters on and we'll take the dogs up to the big house. No, you don't have to sit and talk to Aunty Clare, Harry. You can go and play in the old stables if you promise not to get into mischief,' which was like asking a bee not to buzz!

The V2 exploded in Coppice Wood just outside and across the road from the Beechwood estate, not a stone's throw from the two tiny hamlets of Tarbock and Tarbock Green. Both of them were almost flattened by the blast. The stout wall which had stood for generations about the estate disintegrated like a glass jar dropped from a great height, hundreds and thousands of pieces flying into the air in a towering pall of smoke and dust, before falling like so many filthy snowflakes back to earth, where they settled across the blasted ground.

Trees which had stood for centuries were uprooted and tossed a hundred yards or more, or were reduced to the size and shape of matchsticks in a storm of splinters which were lethal. The blast from the bomb instantly killed Muriel and Lou as they bent down to study what they thought might be 'blight' in their early potatoes. When they were found there was not a mark on their bodies except for a trickle of blood from their mouths, which came from their lungs which had been torn apart by the blast.

Cottages and farms hundreds of yards away pitched like ships in a stormy sea, and every window in every building within a two-mile radius shattered with a noise like a thousand machine guns.

When it all finally settled the house which had been christened 'Lacy's house' by Rose and Alex Woodall was no more than a heap of slowly settling rubble.

35

The *Sweet Jane*, which had been in Captain Callum O'Shaughnessy's command since the sinking of the *Bridget O'Malley* three years ago, was at berth in St Johns, Newfoundland, when the news reached him that she was to have a refit on her return to Liverpool.

Crossing the Atlantic Ocean had, for some months now, been like moving along the streets of a dead town where the inhabitants had gone off for some purpose only they knew about. A victorious ocean in which a U-boat was rarely to be seen, and convoys, most of them enormous, made the journey unmolested through the grey waters, bringing the vital supplies which the expanding battlefields of Europe must have.

But now he and his ship were to be at home for several weeks, and the idea depressed him. It was easier whilst he was at sea, and as the thought crossed his mind he wondered exactly what it was he meant. *What* was easier? What did he mean by *it*? and the answer was, as he had known all along, his wife Maris and his son Tom, whom he had seen only twice in the three years since he was born. He had snapshots of him even now, tucked carefully away in his wallet which he took out from time to time when he felt he could manage it without tearing himself into shreds. One of the boy with his mother, both turning to smile at the camera held by Uncle Michael, who had taken it and then offered it compassionately, diffidently to his brother. There was one taken of the boy on a tricycle, grinning from ear to ear, his feet barely touching the pedals, his look of enchantment so like that of Maris's when she was pleased about something it was all Callum could do not to groan out loud in his agony of spirit.

The force of the gale, so late in the year, which the convoy met, took them all by surprise, and for several days he scarcely had time to fling himself into his bunk for an hour, let alone dwell on what he was to do with the rest of his life after the war ended, which would not be long now, they were all aware.

The weather took a turn for the better. Though the sea was still jumbled and violent, though the wind still sang on a high note and the ship still rolled and staggered, some of the teeth of the storm had been drawn. A hot meal could be cooked and the green seas no longer rose in front of them like a wall, but it took the escort forty-eight hours to round up the rest of the convoy, which had been scattered by the tumult.

It was known that the enemy still had about seventy U-boats at sea, but when, just inside the Irish Sea, one of the merchantmen to starboard of them was suddenly hit by a torpedo close to the bows, they were all badly shocked.

'The bloody war's still on, Jenkins,' he said testily to the man at the wheel, who was watching the vessel slowly sinking as though he couldn't believe his eyes.

'But it's nearly the end, sir, and no U-boats are operating in home waters.'

'Is that so? Well, tell that to the poor bastards in the water.'

It appeared to the men that the enemy was making a last vicious effort to avoid defeat, but the U-boat was neatly despatched by a destroyer, and *Sweet Jane* was one of those ordered to rescue the merchant seamen from the water.

The men were edgy, all of them, rescuers and rescued alike, for with the end of the war almost in sight they did not want to be picked off at this late stage. And what was a bloody U-boat doing in the Irish Sea, anyway? They must be stark, staring crazy, they told one another, standing in groups which dispersed as Callum approached. Perhaps 'Jerry' didn't care now they were so close to being beaten. Just the same, none of the ships wanted to stop a torpedo when they were nearly home and dry. Our lads were over the Rhine in Germany, weren't they? and Hitler might be dead for all they knew, so what did the men in the U-boat hope to gain by it? and the answer was they didn't know.

They had passed the Crosby Light Vessel when the message came that Captain O'Shaughnessy was to report to the harbour master's office with all possible speed the moment his ship was berthed. It was Sunday.

She and her mother were playing hide-and-seek with Alex and Charlie as they had done ever since she could remember. Father sometimes joined in too, when it was one of his good days, but he was always a 'seeker', never a 'hider', because of when he was a soldier in the trenches, her mother had explained to her. He didn't like to be shut in anywhere. His breathing would become painful and his chest was not quite as strong as it should be, so it was often herself and her mother who went off to quiver excitedly in some far-off cupboard, or in one of the many attics which crowded under Woodall's roof, whilst Alex and Charlie, like great overgrown puppies, thundered about in search of them while father followed more slowly.

She took a deep breath, for it was dreadfully cramped and airless in the cupboard, reaching out for her mother's hand. She was not awfully sure she liked to be so enclosed, but if mother was there and she could hold her hand then it would be all right.

'Mother,' she whispered, since she didn't want Alex or Charlie to hear her. Somewhere, a long way off, she heard Charlie laughing, and the sound of him and Alex pushing one another in the horseplay in which they always indulged when they were competing to be the first 'finder'. It was very quiet in here, though, with mother. Apart from that one burst of laughter from Charlie, which had faded away, there wasn't another sound, and it was dark. A deep, impenetrable dark which frightened her because she couldn't even see mother's face, nor was her hand where she expected it to be.

'Mother?'

Yes, darling, I am here, mother said in that lovely tranquil voice of hers, which told you that there was absolutely nothing to be afraid of and which immediately calmed your fear.

'I can't feel your hand, Mother.'

It's all right, darling, I can feel yours; and so that was a comfort to her though she didn't quite understand it.

She tried to take a deep breath because she really did feel winded and restricted by the smallness of the space in which she and mother crouched, but the air was filled with a thick dust of some sort which clung to her face and closed about her nostrils.

'Mother,' she panted. 'Mother, let's get out, I can't breathe.'

I've got you, darling. Just keep still and hold on to me.

648

'I can't feel you, Mother . . .'

Don't worry.

'I'll try, Mother. When are the boys coming?'

Soon . . . soon . . .

Michael was there, in the harbour master's office, look-ing exactly as he had done four years ago, when Callum had come to Edge Lane after Elizabeth and young Michael had been killed. Frightful was the word Callum would have used. Eyes set deep and haunted in the bony sockets of his face, his skin quite grey, silvery stubble on his chin, and his clothes thrown on any old way just as though Michael had put them on in a tearing hurry.

Sweet Jesus, what . . . surely not another tragedy come to crucify his poor brother, who, for Christ's sake, had had enough . . . more than his share . . . Cliona, was it? and that movement perhaps . . . but then, if that was so why had they? . . . why were they here in the harbour master's office? . . . why had *he* been brought? . . . Jesus, Mary and Joseph . . . no . . . not . . .

He stood quite still, not even blinking as he waited for the blow to fall, the terrible blow, since he knew it *would* be terrible if Michael's face was anything to go by. It was Maris . . . or Tom . . . but then why *here*? . . . what? . . . could they not have waited until he was in his own home, or his mother's? . . . it would have been kinder to be told . . . whatever it was they were to tell him without the sympathetic and urgent face of the harbour master hovering . . . *urgent*? Why did the harbour master look so urgent? Why that look of frantic haste . . . ?

'What . . . ?' Was that himself who spoke? Was that

649

cracked voice his own? It was, and he wanted to hide from it and from whatever his brother was going to tell him. Michael seemed unable to speak, so great was his emotion, and the harbour master made a sound of impatience, kind but definitely impatient.

Michael found his voice. ''Tis Maris, lad,' and Callum felt the cruel knife turn and scrape away the last vestige of life and hope that he had, he realised it now, clung to tenaciously all these long years. Everything that had any meaning was draining away in a killing surge, leaving a great emptiness which could never be filled, never.

'Dead?' His voice sounded hollow as he fell deep into shock.

'We . . . don't know.'

Hope flared up again, a bright shining hope which caused Callum to feel bewildered and slightly irritated, but hope nevertheless, for they *did not know* if she was dead so there was a chance that she was *alive*. He didn't understand it at all, but if there was a chance . . .

'What . . . ?'

'They're at Beechwood now. We've to be quick, lad.'

'*Why* . . . for God's sake, Michael . . . ?'

''Twas one of those flying bombs . . .'

'A . . . ?'

'Aye . . . they say they're launched from aircraft . . . Heinkels . . . forty miles off the east coast. They fell near Manchester . . . another at Preston . . .'

'Oh sweet Jesus Christ . . . and the boy . . . ?'

'Safe. She was alone except for the . . . the girl who cleans for Rose. The house . . . was destroyed. The rescue squads have gone . . . it's been three hours . . . she's beneath it . . . and they can't find her.'

'What the bloody hell are we hanging about here for?'

The 'heavy rescue' team were men who had been, in peacetime, skilled bricklayers, plumbers, carpenters and labourers, men with an understanding of buildings, who could apply their building techniques in reverse, so to speak. They were specialists at their jobs, skilled in the art of burrowing into rubble and debris. They knew how to get safely through shifting walls and fallen timber. How to shore up shaky ceilings and deal with burst pipes of one kind and another.

They were, for a moment only, flabbergasted when the madman in the dishevelled uniform of a merchant naval officer flung himself from a motor car and began, without a word to anyone, to dig frantically into whatever he could get his hands on and heave it behind him.

'Hey, you, what the bloody 'ell d'yer think you're up to?' one bellowed, not moving from his precarious perch on the hideous pile of debris which had once been Lacy's house. There must have been a dozen of them in dark blue overalls and steel helmets, with policemen, firemen at the alert by the fire engine, several ambulances and an ARP team.

'Grab that chap, for God's sake,' the man thundered, and two policemen leaped forward, one on each of Callum's arms, as he would have continued his frantic digging in the mountains of rubble which once had been a home, a home as peaceful and lovely as a sleeping woman but which, in the space of thirty seconds, had become nothing but a great, uneven mass of tortured rubbish. Splinters of glass and broken window frames, shreds of material and shards of crockery, tatters of carpet and flakes of plaster, doors and clocks and scraps of what had once been books, fractured pipes and exposed electrical wiring; and all held together like some huge plum pudding with chunks of old, unsound masonry and enormous beams of timber from which the house had been constructed early in the last century. A pall of dust still hung several feet above it. It had not taken a direct hit but the blast had reduced it to a pile of debris two storeys high, over which the rescue team were now carefully picking their way just as though what they crept over was as fragile as eggshells.

'*My wife* . . .' he screamed, and behind him someone moaned, and he knew deep inside himself, at a level which still could feel compassion for others, that it was his brother Michael whose own wife had . . . But not Maris, not *his* wife, not that pig-headed, defiant, *beloved* woman who was Maris O'Shaughnessy.

'Rightio, mate, we'll see to this . . .' the policeman began soothingly, ready to lead him away towards the mobile canteen of the WVS and perhaps a cup of tea. This was not the only 'incident' in the area, for the bomb had devastated two small hamlets and severely damaged several outlying cottages, and comfort such as was given by the ladies of the WVS would be needed by those suffering from shock or distress.

But Callum had no intention of being led away, or even of standing idly by and watching others go about the business of bringing out from this . . . this monstrosity the woman he had loved so passionately and so hopelessly for nearly five long years. When he had got her out, and he *would* get her out, there was no doubt about that, single-handedly, if necessary, and if . . . oh Jesus Christ, let her live . . . let her be alive and unharmed . . . well, if when she was out she wanted to stay as they were then she must do as she thought best and he would walk away from her, and his son

. . . *no, you will not* . . . and let her get on with her
. . . *no* . . . whatever she wanted to do . . . *no, oh no,
not again.* He *would not* . . . *no, never* . . . *he would not
leave her again. He would fight her, fight for her* . . .
Oh Mary, Mother of God . . . please, *please* . . .

'Come on, lad, come an' have a cuppa . . .'

'No . . . *no* . . . take your bloody hands off me, damn
you . . .'

'Look, mate . . .'

'My wife is in there, and if you won't let me dig with
the rest then let me . . . hand down bricks . . . or . . .
whatever . . . I promise I won't interfere . . .' since he
knew at the layer of his mind that was trained to deal
with emergencies that each man has his own trade, his
own skill, and that each man must apply that skill where
it was needed. These men did not require an amateur,
however well-meaning, or involved, to interfere in what
they were experts at, but it was Maris . . . *Maris* . . .

'Yes?' she said, opening her eyes and turning her head
as her name was called, but she was suddenly blinded,
no, not blinded since she could already not see, but
hurt by something which fell into her eyes and made
them smart. She closed them at once and kept her head
motionless, but they still prickled with something sharp
and irritating, making her want to rub them, but when
she tried to lift her hand she found she could not do
so. It just would not . . . function. She tried with the
other one and that was the same, tied down by something to . . . to what . . . where was it? . . . where was
her hand? her *hands*, her right hand and her left hand
which, only a moment or two ago, had been sorting
out the washing in the cellar ready for Mrs Flynn to
assault it the next morning. Monday was wash-day and

today was Sunday and Rose had gone with the children up to Beechwood. She and Polly were in the kitchen . . . *no*, Polly was in the kitchen, and she had gone down into what she and Rose laughingly called the 'laundry' where Mrs Flynn 'steeped' her whites in the old sink and . . .

What on earth was she doing lying here in the dark? Had she fallen and hurt herself? She was not in pain. She hadn't put the light on, that was certain, because it was so dark, so perhaps she had slipped on the old worn steps and . . . But she *had* put the light on. She had. She distinctly remembered having to shift the bundle of bedding from her right arm to her left because the switch was on the right-hand wall . . .

There was silence and a suspension of movement all about her, a feeling of being so completely *inactive, dormant, alone*, she felt her heart surge in terror inside her chest, filling it, ready to suffocate her it was so enormous. Quite simply, she had no idea where she was or how she had got to wherever she was, and the thought *appalled* her. The last thing she could recall was . . . was what? The bedding, yes and . . . Polly singing one of her everlasting songs . . .

'Is that the lot, Polly . . . ?' Her own voice, yes, and the light-switch, the steps going down into . . . and then someone had . . . *pushed her*. An enormous hand at her back throwing her down the steps and then . . . *nothing*.

So, having been pushed down the steps she was in the bloody cellar, but why couldn't she move? . . . had she broken something? . . . and why couldn't she *see*? . . . and who had pushed her . . . ?

Oh Christ . . . where the hell was that gormless girl? Why hadn't she come to find out why Mrs O'Shaughnessy had not returned to the kitchen? Here she was lying in the cellar in the dark with no one but a simple girl to remember where she was, and there was . . . *something holding her down* . . . and the lights were fused . . . was that it? Had she had an electric shock? Polly was probably babbling on about 'How deep is the ocean' or some such nonsense whilst she lay here waiting for her to notice that Mrs O'Shaughnessy was mysteriously missing.

'Polly' she quavered, lifting her hands to rub at her grainy eyes, but again they would not move and she was aware of a drifting layer of something light and gritty which she distinctly felt settle on her face.

'Polly . . . for God's sake, Polly, where are you?' she moaned, but like her eyes, her ears seemed to have lost their power and she could not even hear her own voice. What was wrong with her? . . . Oh God . . . what had happened to her?

'Polly!' She screamed the maid's name now, beginning to panic, beginning to struggle against whatever it was that held her, heaving and bucking, and at once whatever it was moved, shifting and tumbling, edging this way and that as though it was eager to see her pressed even further into the nightmare in which she had diabolically been thrust. She screamed again and again until she fell, suddenly and mercifully, into a deep black pit of peace.

'Quiet . . . quiet the lot of you.' The man turned, a hand frantically signalling to the rest and at once all movement and sound stopped. The silence was absolute except for what seemed to be a tap dripping somewhere.

Callum felt himself whimper in the back of his throat,

655

and the hand which was on his arm gripped it soothingly. It was his niece, Rose. She had been there for
the last hour, her face a mask of grey putty, her eyes
hot and dry, her teeth chattering, and yet she was
steady, ready to comfort him should he show signs of
needing it, to calm his terror, to speak, or not, as he
wanted; there, with the promise in her expression that
she would not leave him until he had his wife in his
arms.

'I must get her out, Rosie. You see I have to tell her
how much I love her.'

'You will, Callum.'

He made a desperate choking sound in his throat,
and though she did not look at him she knew he was
weeping. She had seen her own husband cry, and her
female intuition told her how difficult it was for the
male to admit that he could, and did; but she knew
how to comfort, and before the compassionate but
embarrassed gaze of everybody there she took him in
her arms, holding his head to her shoulder, bearing his
frantic clasp that hurt her.

'She'll be all right, Callum, she will. She's strong and
brave.'

At her words he began to babble, his voice hoarse,
speaking the truth which he had never spoken before,
pouring out from his soul the depth and strength of his
love for Maris, baring himself mercilessly to his niece
whose own heart understood such things. He talked
brokenly of babies and his own intolerance, of unfaith-
fulness and pride and blindness, burrowing his head in
her shoulder, and she patted his back and murmured
soft words and held him as close as she did her own
children when they were hurt.

He raised his head, his eyes bloodshot and wild.

'I'm a . . . I've been a bastard . . . but I swear if she comes out of this I'll make it up to her . . . she'll . . . I won't let her go again, Rosie . . .'

'I know, and she doesn't want to go, Callum.'

'If they'd only let me dig . . .'

'They know what they're doing.'

'Do they?'

He turned to watch the men. It seemed to him that there was very little activity as they moved quietly, lightly and yet swiftly about their business, each one appearing to know what was in the other's mind. There were other such men working across the area where the bomb had fallen to earth, with stretcher bearers waiting, standing by until casualties were brought out, or the shattered building was safe to enter.

Again and again the clatter of activity stopped, and the man who appeared to be the leader of the rescue team would call for silence, whilst his men listened for some sound which might lead them to the two women who were known to be somewhere beneath the debris. A doctor had raced up in a motor car an hour ago with a couple of nurses, and he lit a cigarette, waiting. Sightseers stood about vacantly, not from the cottages on the estate, for the Woodalls and Osbornes were well known about this area, well liked, and no one would dream of intruding on their tragedy, or indeed on any of the others who had been devastated that day. Help they would, if asked, but not stand and stare, as the morbidly curious from miles around were doing, on what they saw as a Sunday afternoon's outing, craning their necks in order not to miss anything.

'I can't just stand here like some bloody stuffed dummy.' Callum wrenched his arm from Rose's restraining hand, and pushing aside the policemen and wardens who were, at least it seemed to him, doing nothing but stand in groups watching, he began to clamber up the dangerous, shifting mass of broken masonry and splintered lathes of wood which had, so far, been delicately removed and passed down to others. Dust rose like smoke, terrifying him even further, and in his face horror worked as, for a merciless moment, he thought there was a fire. A long length of heavy beam was thrust in his direction, and as if knowing that unless they tied him up and forcibly removed him he would just keep on coming back, they allowed him to take it.

'I'll work under your supervision,' he said savagely, 'but don't ask me to stand here and do nothing.'

'Put yer 'elmet on fer a start, then.'

They worked steadily and far too slowly for Callum's liking, and when, at the end of another hour, several men moved down to the mobile canteen for a 'cuppa an' a fag', he became abusive, calling to his brother . . . his brothers . . . Good God, when had they arrived? . . . Michael, Donal and Eammon . . . to give him a hand.

'Another word from you, matie,' the leader said through gritted teeth, '' 'an I'll get the bobbies to put you in handcuffs.'

'You can go to hell.' Callum's voice was menacing. 'That's my wife in there, and if you think I'm going to stand here and watch you lot drink *tea* while she . . . dear Christ almighty . . .'

'These men 'ave been diggin' for the best part of five hours, lad. They need a rest, an' if I say they're 'avin' one, then that's what they'll do. Now why don't you bugger off and let us do our job.'

'Callum, come down, son, they're doing all they can . . .'

658

'Leave go of me, Michael, or I swear I'll knock you down.'

'Let *them* do it. Sure an' you're only wasting precious time that Maris might need . . .'

'Jesus . . . *Jesus* . . .'

'Aye, lad, come down for a minute . . .'

'No . . . no . . .' He held up his hands which were bloody and blackened since he was not as skilful as the men with whom he worked. 'No . . . I promise not to get in their way . . . please let me . . . I must . . . I *must* . . . it's Maris . . .'

There it was again, her name, and this time she recognised the voice. She didn't try to move again. Her back was pressed ferociously to the hard flagged floor, and to her left she thought she recognised the wall which was directly beneath the old stone sink. She could see nothing and feel nothing except an enormous pressure bearing down on her, but she could just move her head a fraction, and when she did her cheek came to rest against something metallic, like a pipe. A waste pipe? She was lying *under the sink*, in the cellar, *in the dark*, and from somewhere – in her mind perhaps, which was undoubtedly going mad – Callum was calling her name. There was a deathly quiet, a hush so deep she felt ripples of terror run all over her like . . . like spiders . . . Oh Jesus, save me . . . 'Callum . . . Callum . . .' She screamed and screamed, though again there was no sound. From somewhere . . . *all about her* . . . there came a rustling, crackling sound, as though someone was methodically tearing paper, and though the silence had been terrible this was even worse since she didn't know what it was. Then, very gently but gaining momentum, things began to fall . . . *things?*

. . . what were they? some small and light and feathery, others heavier, striking her in the face, dusty, choking and evil-smelling . . . Jesus God, she was being buried alive . . . she was in her grave and she was not dead . . . 'Callum' . . . he was near her . . . he had called her name . . . how? . . . Callum . . . she could smell lavender . . . Mother, so there you are, and where am I, mother? Her mother . . .

The deep black hole welcomed her again.

The line of men methodically passed bits and pieces of what had once been Lacy's house from one to the next, the last dumping the rubble into a container, which was carried away and replaced by another. The biggest of the enormously heavy old beams were being lifted by a mobile crane, one after the other, each carefully moved so as not to disturb further the sludge of debris which was systematically being removed. The mass of rubble had been dramatically reduced, but still neither of the two women had been found nor even heard from, though the leader of the team called their names every few minutes.

'Maris . . . Polly . . . Maris . . .' he shouted, and each time he did Rosie shivered. It was like a game. You hide and I'll count to a hundred and then come and search for you. But after a while you got tired of looking, so, impatiently, you began to call the name of the one who is hiding. After all, there is a limit to how long you can keep going, that is if you are a child and you are playing a game. But these were no children and this was not a game. She held Michael's hand, doing her best to let him know she understood exactly how he felt, since he was reliving in sick horror the day his own wife and son had been killed, and how, just as

Callum was doing at this moment, he had scrabbled on all fours like some demented dog searching for a bone, in the ruins of his own home. He was sharing every moment of Callum's agony.

The sun was about to set, sinking at their backs into the great River Mersey, lighting the scene of ugly devastation with tints of rose and amber and the palest orange, with long, dusty shadows amongst which the men moved. The garden was gone and the lovely old redbrick wall which had surrounded it. For at least a hundred yards in every direction the ground was pulverised, and into it had been trodden all the smaller pieces of debris which had been flung there when the blast hit. And yet, by a curious freak of nature, the apple tree still stood and on it, perfect and undamaged except for a coating of dust, were several sprays of apple blossom. Just beneath it, as though someone had thrown it against the trunk of the tree, was a box. She let go of Michael's hand for a moment and moved across to the tree, absent-mindedly picking up the box, not recognising it as any she knew, then went back to Michael and, slipping her hand once more in his, waited.

Something touched her face. Not the dust, nor the fragments of debris which . . . had she been asleep? . . . fell now and again, but something quite heavy and warm and . . . sticky. She could feel . . . oh God . . . God . . . if she could just move some part of her, free her hands to investigate what it was . . . against her face. It felt like . . . like flesh . . . human flesh . . . she couldn't stand it . . . please . . . please mother . . . help me . . . Darling, don't be frightened. Be a brave girl for mother . . . Mother, don't leave me . . . I feel so tired now and . . . Mother, I'm sorry but I've wet my knickers . . . Never mind, darling . . .

'Hold it . . . hold it, lads . . . there's something . . .'

'What is it, Arthur?'

'I can see part of a . . . it's a leg, I think. Hard to tell. Hello, down there, can you hear me . . . ?'

It was too much for Callum, and in one enormous bound he was up past the startled and extremely annoyed rescue men, even savagely pushing aside the leader, peering down into the carefully excavated hole beside which the man stood. In the absence of calls from the buried women, and the squad's lack of knowledge as to where in the house they had been when the blast hit it, the rescue men had been forced to burrow in several places.

'Maris . . . where are you? Maris . . . answer me, darling . . . it's Callum . . . Maris . . .'

'Sir, if you don't stand back I swear I'll have you locked up. I know it's your wife down there . . .' The man's face was compassionate. He had seen this so often. Men maddened and frantic as they looked at the obscene pile of debris which was their home and beneath which their families lay. Women screaming the names of children from whom they had become separated. Whole families lost, except one member who could barely be restrained from burrowing like a mole to find loved ones. But just the same they could not be hampered by them, by this man who was doing his best to fling himself headlong into the hole where, amongst the glass and brick, the masonry and timber and all that remained of the old house, a filth-encrusted leg could just be seen. They were below ground level now, everything that had been above having been searched with no results. They were working by the light of torches since the rules of the black-out still applied, and his own swung violently as the missing woman's husband tried to push him to one side.

'Grab him, lads . . . bloody hell, mate, you'll have the whole damned lot caving in again . . . that's it, take him down there . . .'

They brought Polly out half an hour later, her body so badly crushed and blood-soaked it was barely recognisable as a woman. Her right arm was missing.

When she awoke, the deep and appalling blackness about her appeared to have changed to a shadowy grey. A swirling, dipping misted grey where shapes moved and made faint, barely discernible sounds. She felt as though she was floating, light and airy as a dandelion clock in summer, or a feather from a bird's wing, perhaps. The weight had gone. In fact, she felt nothing at all about her. The fear had gone and the feeling of slipping into a great goosedown bed was very pleasant. She held Callum's hand and smiled into his dirty face . . . why was he so dirty? . . . and told him not to weep . . . why was Callum weeping? . . . and said goodbye to her mother, who thought she might stay here.

You go, darling, she said. You go with Callum, and of course she did, for was that not what she had wanted since that first day on the ferry?

36

Rose stood at the window of the bedroom at Beechwood Hall, which had been hers when she was a child
called Rose Osborne. A pretty room, a little girl's
room, with light curtains and a pale carpet, white furniture, dolls sitting in a row on the window-sill, and a
bed with a bright quilted bedspread.

In the bedroom next door, which had been her
brother Christian's, her two sons, Harry and Jamie,
had twin beds; and on the other side of her room was
Ellie's. Years ago a child called Claudine, who had
been Rose's sister, had slept and day-dreamed in it,
wanting to be a princess and being treated like one,
since she had been the first child to be born to Rose's
parents.

They had been here at Beechwood, her childhood
home, for two months now, and Rose knew she must
soon make some decision about a future for herself and
her children, but really it was just too much for her at
present and so she had drifted on from one day to the
next, putting off the moment when she must begin her
plans.

There was just such a *lot* of it. Beechwood belonged
to the Woodalls now, and the land. But there were
also the combined Hemingway, Osborne and Woodall
estates, Woodall itself, shares in shipping and other
investments which must be supervised. The title, held
by generations of Woodall men, and which, without
Alex, must go to the next male heir, who was their son,

Harry. Such a muddle. Hours spent with lawyers and men who knew about such things, whilst they waded through legal papers and precedents, all the rights of due process, statutes and constitutions – words which they used and which were like a foreign language to her – correspondence with the War Office, since Alex must be presumed dead, and all the time holding in to herself her agony of spirit which must suffer this. Alex was dead and all she wanted to do was to be left alone, to find some quiet and secluded place where she could get on with her grieving until it dropped to a bearable level, where she might pay attention, *real* attention, to her children again.

The war in Europe was over. On April 30th, Adolf Hitler had committed suicide in the ruins of Berlin, which had by then been encircled by Russian soldiers. On May 4th the German forces in north-western Europe had surrendered at Montgomery's head-quarters on Luneberg Heath, and three days later the German Supreme Command had given up at Rheims.

Unbelievably, the war was over.

It was VE Day, Victory in Europe Day, May 9th, just after midnight, and on the River Mersey right down to the Crosby Light Vessel, starting with the largest destroyer, the joy began to sound as she let out a deep-throated Victory V-sign bellow, and one by one the other vessels, large and small, joined in until every ship in port was roaring or piping its jubilation; and to the crowd's astonishment and wonder, the searchlights flashed out across the sky the sign of V for Victory in morse code. Men and women wept unashamedly.

When dawn broke, it came as the loveliest May morning, on which even the sun shone more brightly in celebration. Everyone who could converged on the city, and Ellen and Matty put on their best hats, and, accompanied by Ellen's three daughters, by her son Donal and his wife Mary, by Eammon and his Tess and all the smaller children, caught the tram at the depot opposite the house, crowding on the top deck so that they could see the fun, the O'Shaughnessys together again as they had not been for a long time; but when the tram got down to Lime Street the crowds were so dense it was stuck there for over an hour. Nobody minded, though, for spread out as far as the eye could see was a moving ocean of flag-waving people, singing, dancing, hugging one another, all overcome with the joy of it; girls wearing the caps of servicemen and being soundly kissed in return. Nobody minded that, either!

In towns and cities and villages all over Britain, church bells were pealing the joyful sounds of freedom. Great crowds gathered that afternoon wherever there was a space to hear Mr Churchill's broadcast over the loudspeakers. Lord mayors had a word or two to say from their town hall balconies, bands played and people sang, *roared* their jubilation, and as night fell, far and wide could be seen the still unlawful glow of the bonfires which lit up the dark skies.

Children stared in round-eyed amazement, looking apprehensively over their shoulders for the ARP warden as their mothers opened wide the curtains and allowed the light to pour out into the forbidden street where none should be, and where their neighbours had formed long weaving lines and wobbled their noisy way from one end to the other, shaking first their right foot, then their left, whilst they 'did the Hokey-Cokey'. The children were somewhat alarmed by this adult hysteria, since for years they had never been anything but disciplined and orderly in all things, from queueing for 'spam' to quietly going to the air-raid shelters when the siren sounded.

The 'boys' would be coming home, Ellen had exulted as she and Matty, just as they had done on Armistice night twenty-seven years ago, turned the oven on and baked jam tarts and fairy cakes, the ingredients supplied by the successors to Hank and Elmer from Warrington where the American army base was situated, her first two 'Yanks' having gone to Normandy a year ago. The party in Edge Lane lasted until well after midnight, and though there were many tears shed, for Elizabeth and young Michael, for Roddy and Patrick, for Mrs Donavan's grandson George, killed at El Alamein, and for many others who would never clasp their Mammies, their wives or sweethearts in their arms again, Ellen said a small prayer of thanks to Our Lady that none of her 'boys' would be among them. James and Paul, who had come through so much in the raids they had been in over Germany; Devlin, Joseph, Lorcan, Finbar, Callum, young Guy Templeton in his Spitfire; only Flynn, Gracie's boy, who was a prisoner with the Japanese and would surely soon be home since they were almost beaten, not yet accounted for. There was Rosie's Alex, of course, and Alex's brother Charlie, but they were not *her* blood, and though she grieved for Rosie and lit a candle for Alex every time she went to Mass, it was not quite the same.

At sea, U-boats were surfacing to surrender to the nearest Allied warships, and a week later one was brought into Gladstone Dock, and Eammon's lads went down to see it, reporting to Ellen that the German sailors looked no different from any other, as though

667

they had fully expected the dreaded 'Jerry' to have at least two heads, or a forked tail. They were very pale though, Duald told her earnestly, due to being under the water for days on end, and their hair was long and brushed back from their foreheads.

'Sure an' isn't that because they've no Mammy at sea to make them go for a haircut,' she answered serenely, to which Duald said he thought he might like to be a submariner when he grew up.

But now it was done with, and the next task was the enormous one of demobilising the millions of men who were in the services; and the first to come home would be craftsmen in the building trade, it was reported, since they were urgently required for reconstruction work. The rest were to be formed into an orderly queue in which age and length of service would determine who should be first. Ellen couldn't wait, she said to Gracie, and what should they do about a party, just as though the lot of them would be pushing their way through her front door before she had time to turn round, as they had once done six years ago. She bit her lip and wrung her hands, for where were they to get all the things she needed – by which she meant food to fill their bellies which had not known a bit of proper cooking, *hers*, in fact, for so long. But even if she had to resort to the 'black market' then by Our Lady, she would she declared, just this once, for surely it would be a very special occasion?

'Sure an' it'll be a wee while yet, Mammy. The war's only been over a week, an' even if they were all to be demobbed tomorrow 'tis a long way from Germany and further from Singapore . . .'

'Oh, to be sure, an' d'you think I don't know that, girl, but these things have to be planned, so they do, an' 'tis to be the best party this house has known for a long time. I only wish . . .'

'What is it, Mammy?'

'That those two young 'uns of Eammon's, the wee spalpeens, God love 'em and bless their sweet souls . . .'

'I know, Mammy.'

'And Elizabeth and the boy . . .'

'Aye . . .' sadly.

'Himself's glad the thing's finished with, but isn't he feeling badly all over again, realising what would have been his now if they'd lived, God rest their eternal souls. Still . . .' cheering up at once, for wasn't she 'made up with it'? '. . . Maris and Callum will be there an' together, thank the Holy Mother. Come to their senses at last, an' about time too. Now then, how long d'you think it'll be, Gracie . . . ?'

They were not home, any of them, by the end of June, and Rose leaned forward, putting her forehead against the cold glass of the window as she watched the small procession which wound its slow way up the drive towards the house. It was Maris, and pushing her wheelchair was Callum, and about them flowed the changing ripples of the children and the dogs. Harry, as usual, led the way, holding forth over his shoulder to his Uncle Callum who, though until recently unknown to him, was now, in Harry's mind, *his* property, *his* own special hero, *his* mentor and playmate and *best* friend. He knew, of course, that Uncle Callum was, surprisingly, Tom's Daddy, a fact which Tom didn't seem to know much about either, but nevertheless reminded Harry of, menacingly, at least half a dozen times a day, surprised to find himself in possession of such a splendid father. Just the same, Harry *was* six and a half, and Tom was only just over three, and therefore, logically, Harry and Uncle Callum had much more in common.

Tom, the top of his head only just reaching the handle of the wheelchair – which had been Uncle Teddy's and in which mother went for a 'walk' – 'helped' his father steadfastly to push, not *quite* sure that he liked the way the man he had been told to call Daddy kept kissing *his* mother, but Mother didn't seem to mind so it must be all right.

Ellie was picking daisies, from which she meant to weave a chain each for Pipsqueak and Wilfred. She kept getting left behind as she stooped to reach for the 'best' ones, gathering a few frantically, calling all the while for the others to wait for her, her small fist carefully wrapped around those she had already picked. Her darting figure made a feverish pattern on the spread of green lawn which had been saved from the plough, as she pounced first on one side of the drive and then the other, her pointed face scowling in concentration.

Jamie was 'training' the dogs, which he meant to use as gun dogs when he was old enough to go shooting, which would probably be pretty soon in his opinion. After all, he was four now, and in the gun room at Woodall were the most marvellous guns in a locked case. His Daddy had used them when he was a boy, his mother had told him, and his Uncle Charlie who was a dead hero, and his grandfather, who had been a hero in the last war, named Harry like his brother. He was going to be a gamekeeper when he grew up and have lots of dogs, and in the meanwhile Pipsqueak and Wilfred would have to do.

'Heel,' he bellowed now to the wildly excited animals, and when they came, for a second only, his boyish treble grew shrill as he endeavoured to make them 'sit'.

How lovely they all were, these children, her children and Alex's, who would never know the joy young Tom was experiencing as he became acquainted with the patient man who offered his love and protection so diffidently. They would never know the blessed peace of their father's lap when they were tired, as Tom did. The serious, man-to-man conversations about matters which are dear to the heart of a boy, the glorious romping in careful hands, the sweet and steady security a father can bring, as Tom was learning. The three boys all gravitated towards Callum, bewitched by the novelty of having a man to listen to their masculine – and therefore not really understood by their mothers – opinions and ideas, to take them on *men only* jaunts, which were the best sort, in the woods. It was what they needed. The loving existence of those that were gone, not just these three but all the small boys who, for the past six years had known little but women's company or that of elderly men, most of whom had forgotten what it was like to be a child.

She bent her head in sorrow, then, turning away from the window, leaned on the small chest of drawers which stood beside it. Though she did her best not to be envious of her cousin's happiness and her nephew's enchantment with his new father, it was very hard to see it, to live with it, to have it constantly about her and not be affected by it. Callum, Maris and Tom were staying at Beechwood for the time being, that is if she didn't mind, Maris had said to her, since there was so much room and it was so convenient with Maris as she was. Home Farm Cottage was far too small; and as for Seymour Road, there seemed to be some unspoken agreement between her and Callum that it had too many wounding memories for them to go back there. Callum was down at the docks for part of each day. His ship was having a refit, but he was still a merchant seaman and would, presumably, be going back to sea in the near future.

So, if Callum and Maris and their son were to make their home here, for a while at least, perhaps the time had come for Rose to move to Woodall, which was really what she should do since it was her children's birthright. They were Woodalls and should live at Woodall Park where their ancestors had lived for hundreds of years. There was so much to do, now that hostilities were ended, returning the old house which had been neglected for so long, into a home again. The land girls had lived there, of course, but no member of the family since Charlie had left to join the RAF in September 1939. The grounds would have to be restored to their former beauty, when the WAR AG allowed it, naturally, since food would still be in short supply for a while and farming land would still be needed. There would be a lot of work involved in the keeping together of her sons' patrimony, and really, had not the time come for her to get on with it? To let go of the past and take hold of the rest of her life, and that of her children? It was *her* responsibility, and it would give her something to cling to, something tangible and *necessary* to fill her days – and what of the nights, her mind agonised? – until the painful memories of Alex should become blurred with time.

She opened the top drawer of the chest and reached for a clean handkerchief to wipe away her tears. There were two dozen or so, all with her initials on them. RO they said, for they had been there since she was a child, and as she took the top one from the pile her hand touched the box.

The box. The box which had been propelled from some hidden place in Lacy's house and flung out into the garden against the apple tree, from where Rose had picked it up. She had carried it away with her, she supposed, she couldn't remember, when Maris was brought out of the rubble and the nightmare was over, bringing it up here after Maris and Callum had been driven off in the ambulance, and shoving it in the first place her confused mind had come across. And there it had lain forgotten for over two months.

She picked it up reverently, blowing away the dust – surely *old* dust – which coated it, then placed it on top of the chest of drawers. It was exquisite and very old. It was made from some soft, glowing wood with an inlaid design of flowers in its lid, beautifully crafted and lovingly polished. It was as smooth as silk, and felt warm, as though the wood from which it was carved was still living. It had paw feet and delicately wrought handles at each side, made of some metal which had rusted slightly. It still had soil adhering to it from where it had come to rest when the blast from the flying bomb had done with it, and there were several deep dents in the soft wood. There was a lock for a key which was missing, but when Rose tried the lid it opened at once. Inside it were some ear-rings, pearl by the look of them, drops threaded with tarnished silver, a jewelled comb, a small jet pin and a few odds and ends of trinkets that did not look to be of any value.

For some strange reason Rose felt a tremendous sense of disappointment. Why she should have imagined that the lovely box would contain something out of the ordinary, she didn't know, unless it was the out of the ordinary occasion of its finding. It must have been hidden somewhere . . . why? . . . and lain there for years undisturbed until the devastation of the V2 had revealed it, but why had great-grandmother Lacy, whose box it must be, have hidden it away, since nothing inside it was of any worth?

It was then that she noticed that the box did not look . . . well . . . she could not say what it was, but it was not quite right. Its proportions were not quite symmetrical. The depth of the box did not match the depth of the inside where the trinkets lay. Set in the lid was a small mirror, and when she closed it then opened it again, something seemed to . . . to click! Something that had nothing to do with the clasp. She pressed the keyhole and the hinges, and turned the box this way and that. She took out the few pieces of jewellery, and then shook it, and . . . yes . . . something still inside definitely *moved*.

She had no idea what she did, what she pressed or touched, and afterwards, when she tried, she could never open it again; but with a soft hiss which released the aroma of some delicate perfume, the front of the box fell open like a small drawbridge, and from it, from the bottom beneath the layer where the trinkets had lain, some papers fell out.

Oh Lord . . . oh dear God . . . she breathed reverently, scarcely daring to put out a hand to them, they looked so fragile. They lay on the white lace runner which covered the chest of drawers, one yellowed and smooth and traced with a lovely copperplate handwriting which surely . . . surely must be that of her great-grandmother, Lacy Osborne. The second was wrinkled and torn and had what appeared to be water stains on it.

Well, she would never know what they contained by staring at them in this bewitched state, she told herself firmly, but she was still reluctant to touch them. It seemed like prying. Like reading another person's letters; and even if that person was dead it just did not seem right to examine something which was obviously private, or it would not have been hidden away.

The first paper she tentatively picked up was no more than a scrap, torn, it seemed to Rose, from a larger piece, the writing on it scrawled and barely legible. Taking it to the window, she began to read what was written.

'Lacy,' it said, 'if you loved me, please come. I am to have the child . . . James's child . . . soon. There is only Maggie here and . . . dear friend, I need you . . . love you . . .'

It was signed 'Rose'.

Rose? . . . James? . . . Lacy? What did it mean? Who was Rose and what child? . . . whose child? . . . Her head was whirling, and then, suddenly, into her mind's eye came the image of that little miniature she and Alex had found, years ago, before they were married. Standing on a dressing-table in the bedroom that had been Lacy's and which had become theirs. A woman with dark hair and a broad, serene brow, deep green eyes and a white skin. Green eyes like . . . like Johnny Osborne's, her grandfather, like Elizabeth Woodall's, who had been his daughter, and like *her own*, who was his granddaughter . . . and like Jamie's. Sweet Lord . . . what? . . . did this mean? Surely not . . . not . . . what it *seemed* to mean.

Her hand trembled as she reached for the second piece of paper. It was dated January 3rd, 1869. It was very simple. It said:

'I have a son today. I did not bear him. My dearest friend died giving him to me and to my husband, James, who is his father. Her name is Rose O'Malley, and I do not wish it ever to be forgotten. I loved her.'

It was signed 'Alexandrina Osborne'.

Lacy! Rose continued to stare at the yellowed paper for several blank moments, then, very slowly and carefully she smoothed it and folded it, doing the same to the first, placing them both on the dresser. She caressed them briefly with her fingertips, then moved back to the window.

They were still there, the dogs, the children, Maris and Callum. The children and the animals were swirling about the wheelchair in some everlasting game which only children can devise and understand. 'Let's pretend' it is called, and their imaginative minds turned them into anything they wanted to be. *Anything they wanted to be, but who were they?* She, Maris, the four children had, moments ago, been the great-grandchildren, the great-great-grandchildren of Lacy Osborne, who had once been Lacy Hemingway, but somehow these letters . . . what were they saying? They seemed to imply . . . *no* . . . they *said* that Rose's grandfather and Maris's grandfather was not Lacy's son but was this other woman's. Rose O'Malley.

A tiny bell rang in her mind. A distant memory of sitting one day in the library with Uncle Teddy. She must have been no more than fifteen or so. He had been married to Clare by then, Uncle Teddy, rescued by her from the prison in which his dreadful war experiences had locked him, and he had found an interest in the old records of the shipping lines which had been part of his family for generations. The records had gone back to the first Hemingway, Robert, who had bought shares in a trading ship in the 18th century, and a great business concern had been born. Lacy, Robert's great-granddaughter, whose life had been somewhat shrouded in mystery, had begun her own shipping business and called it 'Hemingway and O'Malley'. Uncle Teddy had mused on the strange events which had taken place in the 1850s or 60s. Rose couldn't quite remember what he had said. What she *did* remember was the name of O'Malley. Grandmother Lacy had had a partner, another woman, a woman called O'Malley, and was this the one? Was *she* the wellhead from which all these green-eyed Osbornes had sprung? Was it *her* blood which ran in the veins of herself and her sisters, in Maris and Charlie and Alex, in Harry, Jamie, Ellie and Tom? Was the beautiful green-eyed woman in the miniature her great-grandmother and not, as she had always thought, Lacy Osborne?

She stood completely still for a long time, then, very carefully but very surely, she returned the letters to their hiding place, laid the trinkets on their velvet tray, closed the box and put it in the top drawer amongst her clean handkerchiefs. The unhurried and strangely dreamlike action had a finality about it which said that Lacy Osborne's secret would go no further, at least while Rose Woodall lived.

She returned to the window and sighed, her gaze on the couple in the garden, who were absorbed in one another to the exclusion, at that particular moment, of everyone in the whole wide world. Callum knelt before the wheelchair, his face looking up into that of his wife, and in it, shining and clear and uncomplicated by the past, was his love for her. He put his arms about her and drew her head down to his and they remained, their foreheads touching, for several long moments in the posture of two supplicants in prayer, giving thanks for the great gift of their love which had been returned to them.

From the moment Maris had been lifted from the wreckage of Lacy's house he had wrapped her about in his passionate love, refusing to leave her for a moment even whilst she had her wounds dressed at the hospital, giving great offence to the doctors and nurses, who were not used to being snarled at by a madman, they told him. He had nursed her, day and night, never leaving her side, sleeping on the floor of her room, waking the moment she stirred, haggard and wracked with his own guilt over what he had done to her in the past. When her appetite had been fickle he had fed her with a spoon from a bowl of Ellen's good beef broth which Ellen brought over, allowing no one, not even Rose, to attend to the slightest, and most intimate, of her needs; and Maris let him, smiling at him from her nest of bandages, lifting her hand weakly to smooth his straining face and brush away his unashamed tears. A woman at last who understood the meaning of love. How to give it and how to receive it.

She had been badly cut by the glass in which she had lain, splinters which had pierced her skin in many places; and she would always carry the scars, particularly the one at the corner of her mouth where several stitches had left a small indentation. Her face had been a mask of blood, and Callum's voice had been hoarse with terror as he called her name, but most of it had been from poor Polly whose body had protected Maris's and had saved her life. She had taken the full force of the enormous main beam which had crushed the life out of her. Maris had suffered, apart from the cuts and bruises, no more than a broken leg.

There was a scuffle breaking out on the edge of the lawn as Harry and Jamie fought over something Jamie had picked up; and for a moment Rose saw two men, white-faced and trembling, bristling up to one another in exactly the same way, swearing to beat one another to pulp, each demanding savagely that the other back down. Charlie . . . and Alex. Brothers, as these two were, and her heart shivered, for were *her* sons to be the same? Then Jamie laughed and Harry put his arms about his neck, wrestling him to the ground, and in a moment they were like two puppies who nip and snarl but mean one another no harm, doing no more than having a game. Callum moved across the lawn to them and picked them up, one under each arm. Tom raced across, grabbing the legs of his father, who dropped to the grass, and the squeals of delight as the three boys clambered all over him rose on the soft summer air to her window. Alex . . . oh Alex . . . and at her back she felt the presence of Alex Woodall's ghost, ready to put his arms about her, to place his warm lips in the curve of her neck, just below her ear, to cup her breasts then slip his hands inside her blouse until they held the naked flesh of her. His fingers would roll her nipples, and inside her the female core of her began to melt from the ice in which it had lain for so long now . . . so long. The physical pain of her own need slashed at her, and she began to moan, twisting her head from side to side, and the tears she shed again flew in a crystal arc about her as she sobbed helplessly, desolately, for a man who would never come back.

'He was my whole life,' she mumbled. 'What am I to do without him?' but there was no one to hear, no one to answer.

The telephone rang somewhere in the far reaches of

679

the house, and the sound startled her. There was no one to heed it now. Mrs Pritchard took so long to get to it the caller would hang up thinking there was nobody at home, and Betty was hopeless with what she called 'the fiendish contraption', still, after all these years, inclined to speak into the receiver instead of the mouthpiece. Rose had told her kindly that she must ignore it when it rang.

Scrubbing at her face with her already sodden handkerchief, Rose moved slowly down the stairs, hoping whoever it was would ring off. She knew she would scarcely be able to speak, but she must answer it. Even though the war was over you could not simply ignore the thing when it rang, just in case it was news of . . . well, there were still members of the family in Europe, and there was Grandmother Ellen, who was not as young as once she had been. Besides which, if it *was* her grandmother ringing from her home where Michael, who lived with her now, had installed a telephone, she would want to know every last detail of why Rose hadn't answered her call, since she expected that when she made one, which was not often, whoever she wished to speak to was honour-bound to be there.

The telephone was situated in the small passage which ran from the main hallway to the side entrance of the house, where Serena Osborne had thought it suitable to put it. In those days it had not been considered the essential item of communication it was to become, since one had servants to deliver messages to one's friends, and so it was placed discreetly and inconveniently away from the mainstream of the house.

Rose picked it up, her mind still misted and unfocused in grief, still numbed by the pain which became no easier to bear.

'Hello,' she said, her voice still muffled and thick with tears. 'Rose Woodall speaking.'

The silence which followed was punctuated by squeaks and flutters and sighs, the sort of noises one hears on a telephone, flickering along the wires and across the miles.

'Hello.' Her voice began to tremble, a quiver in it like that in her son's when he was afraid, and it was then, she realised afterwards, that she began to know. Still there was no answer, and her heart began to pound until it frightened her. She put out a hand to the back of the chair which stood there, and when she had finally found it she lowered herself carefully to the seat.

'Who . . . is it . . . who . . . ?'

The silence, hollow and disembodied, eddied about her, and she felt her senses begin to spin away. She clutched at the edge of the table to steady herself. She must not faint now, not now . . . dear God . . .

Still the caller did not speak, and she began to weep helplessly. 'Dear God,' she said out loud. 'Oh dear God, Alex . . . I just cannot bear it if it isn't you. Please . . . please . . . answer me . . .'

'Rosie . . .'

'*Alex* . . .' His name came from her in a scream.

'Rosie . . . Rosie . . . I'm coming home to you.'

He had been in France, he said, since his aircraft had been shot down fifteen months ago. He had parachuted to safety and had hidden for a time in a wood, burrowed deep in a blackberry thicket where he had remained until daylight. The wood was on the edge of some fields, and in the one nearest had been a cart loaded with straw beside which two men had been gossiping as though they hadn't a care or worry in the world.

He smiled at the memory, his thin, calm face crinkling into deep furrows about his mouth and eyes, his hand gripping Rosie's as though he would never leave go of the lifeline she offered him and which he had loosened so carelessly in his despair and jealousy.

'They jumped a foot into the air when I called out to them, asking me where I had been as they had been looking for me since they saw my "Spit" come down. Anyway, I was thrust into the cart and hidden among the straw, and when we reached the farm I was put in one of the farm buildings. I was fed and then questioned by the two men, who told me I was to stay there, and when it was safe I would be taken to a safe house where the Resistance would arrange my return to England; and it was then I knew that I couldn't do it any more.'

'Do what, darling?' Rose held his hand, looking intently into his face, knowing the answer before he spoke it.

'Come home. I couldn't face it any more. For months I had lived with it, tried to accept it . . . you and . . .'

'Don't, sweetheart . . . I understand.'

'No, you don't, Rosie. It was slowly killing me. Eating away at my guts until I could . . . I didn't care whether I lived or died. I *knew* at one level of my mind that you loved me, but at the same time I kept on scraping away at the wound, picking and picking at it with pictures of . . . never allowing it to get on with healing. I *knew* that the thing . . . with Charlie had been . . . nothing, but it was corroding my . . . whatever part of me which tried to believe in you.'

'Alex, don't . . . I cannot bear . . .'

'So . . . I stayed. With them. They agreed not to let the War Office know that I was alive. They couldn't understand it and I didn't tell them why, but they let me stay. I helped them. I speak good French, as you know, and the boys, fliers like myself who were rescued by them and were got away, thought because of my fluency and the way I dressed that I was your ordinary, run-of-the-mill Frenchman. Then the Allies came. I was near Dunkirk, which you know held out until the end of the war. I knew by then . . . that I had done you a great harm . . . caused you more grief than you deserved so . . . I gave myself up to them and . . . I was sent home.'

'Why didn't they let me know?'

'Well, there was a little matter of what might be considered desertion, but I think my friends in France managed to convince them that I had still been fighting the enemy . . . so . . . here I am, my darling.'

They were seated on the settee. He leaned his weary body against her, the tension, the strain, the despair, the pain draining away as she took him in her arms, cradling his head to her breast.

'Yes . . . here you are . . . home . . .' was all she said, but the light in her green eyes was incredibly beautiful, welcoming him into her heart, which had always been his. Rippling shudders moved through them both now as they wept, this time with joy. Rose could feel Alex's breath against her throat and his hand cupping her cheek, warm, warming her so that her heart which had been still and lifeless though it continued to beat, was filled with a pain which was unenduringly exquisite as life returned to it. They did not speak any more. There was no need, they just sat and rocked and wept and whispered one another's name.

The children, awed and silent, stood cautiously before them, waiting to see what was expected of them from this new father they had met a time or two but scarcely knew. His tears, and their mother's, alarmed them, and they were inclined to cry themselves, their safe and protected environment tottering somewhat in this unsteady world where mothers and fathers wept tears like children.

Alex sat up slowly and so did Rose, both of them suddenly aware that they were frightening their children with their fierce and joyous emotion, with the power of their love which was to create for them, as a family, a firm and loving stability in which they could all grow.

'Come to me,' he said gently, and they did, hesitantly, standing before him in a subdued line, waiting to see what he did, since they had little knowledge of Daddies. Tom's was all right. They liked him. He was fun, but this one cried and kissed their mother, so what were they to make of that?

He put out a hand to Ellie, and drawing her to him, he held her in the crook of his arm.

'Will you give me a kiss?' he asked her. 'I love pretty girls to kiss me, that's why I kiss your mother.' The child instantly giggled, pleased to be called pretty like Mamma, since was she not female, too? She moved closer to him trustingly, pursing her child's mouth for his kiss.

'Would you like to see my daisy chains?' she enquired of him. 'I made them for Pipsqueak and Wilfred.' Her eyes were no more than six inches from his, and in them was trust.

'Indeed I would,' letting her go, and when she scampered from the room he turned to Harry.

'And what about you, son? Have you a hug for me? I can remember when you and I used to wrestle on the parlour rug. You had some muscles on you then. Are you still the same? Let me feel your arm.'

At once the boy proudly held it out, flexing his muscles, grinning with delight. He was not awfully sure he remembered the wrestling, but if there was to be some more of it then that would be splendid. He put his arms about his father's neck, hugging him with all his young boy's strength.

Jamie watched Alex with the searching, steady look of a young child, not quite ready to give *his* heart as the others had done. He could not remember this man at all, and it was in his nature to be prudent with his affections. He was not afraid, just careful.

'Are you really my father?' he asked, hopefully.

'I really am, Jamie.'

'How do you know?'

'I *know*, son,' and the boy, convinced, ran into his father's arms.

Post·A·Book

A Royal Mail service in association with the Book Marketing Council & The Booksellers Association.

Post-A-Book is a Post Office trademark.

AUDREY HOWARD

THE MALLOW YEARS

Kit Chapman is the beautiful daughter of a rich Lanca-shire mill-owner; a man ruthless in his exploitation of his workpeople. She is to inherit the business – but only if she can prove herself as hard and determined as he.

Joss Greenwood is a weaver. A radical who has seen his own father cut down by the cavalry at the great Reform rally in Manchester. He and his family have been driven into abject poverty by the new machinery. Now his life is dedicated to the struggle against the factory owners.

Kit and Joss, two people from very different, hostile worlds, meet by chance up on the moors they both love. It is the start of a friendship that turns into wild love that has to struggle for fulfilment through times of terrible distress, of violence and passion.

HODDER AND STOUGHTON PAPERBACKS

AUDREY HOWARD

SHINING THREADS

The sequel to *The Mallow Years*

When beautiful Tessa Harrison and her twin cousins
take over the lucrative Lancashire mill from their
parents, they are plunged into responsibilities for
which their luxurious upbringing has ill-prepared
them.

For Tessa, there is an added but forbidden attraction
at the mill. The foreman, Will Broadbent, with his
genuine understanding of the business and its workers
could not be more different from the dashing cousins.
Yet, like the twins, he is hopelessly in love with this
untameable girl. Their love for Tessa will lead one to
death, one to the arms of another woman, a third too
faint-hearted to take up his rightful inheritance.

And Tessa, the girl who could choose any man she
wanted, is forced into more commitments than she
could have imagined, before she can be united with
the one man she truly needs.

HODDER AND STOUGHTON PAPERBACKS

AUDREY HOWARD

A DAY WILL COME

When Miles Thornley rides into her life, everything begins to change for Daisy Brindle. For the first time she catches a glimpse of a very different life to the one she has always known.

Daisy is a field girl, tramping the roads of Lancashire in a gang of women and children, hired out by a brutal master for stone picking, harvesting, winter work down the pits.

But Miles, heir to a great estate, arrogant and spoilt, who teaches her to love, seduces her and casually casts her aside. He teaches her to hate.

Driven onto the streets of Liverpool, Daisy is rescued by a man of honesty and restless energy, sea captain Sam Lassiter.

First as his mistress and then as his wife and business partner, Daisy comes to enjoy the better things in life. But her unrelenting drive for revenge on the dissolute Miles begins to threaten the destruction of everything she has worked for and achieved. Begins finally to threaten her relationship with Sam Lassiter himself . . .

HODDER AND STOUGHTON PAPERBACKS

AUDREY HOWARD

ALL THE DEAR FACES

Edwardian Liverpool – the greatest port in the Empire, a sprawling, brawling city of poverty and wealth, slum tenements and civic pride, vice and hard-won respectability.

Mara O'Shaughnessy, eighth of thirteen children, longs to escape from the crowded tumult of her family, while her sister Caitlin, quiet but determined, is already, to her mother's horror, involved with the Suffragettes.

Woodall Park, 2,000 acre estate home of Elizabeth and her parents, Sir Charles and Lady Woodall, could have been a million miles away. With their neighbours, the Osbornes of Beechwood Hall, life is lived in servanted ease, country pursuits and suitable marriages.

Yet in the golden years before World War I, Liverpool Irish and English gentry are to become fatefully, passionately entangled . . .

HODDER AND STOUGHTON PAPERBACKS